HARRY POTTER

AND THE HALF-BLOOD PRINCE

BY

J. K. ROWLING

ILLUSTRATIONS BY MARY GRANDPRÉ

SCHOLASTIC INC.

NEW YORK • TORONTO • LONDON • AUCKLAND • SYDNEY
MEXICO CITY • NEW DELHI • HONG KONG • BUENOS AIRES

Arthur A. Levine Books hardcover edition
art directed by David Saylor,
published by Arthur A. Levine Books,
an imprint of Scholastic Inc.,
July 2005.

ISBN 0-439-78596-0

Library of Congress Control Number: 2005921149

12 11 10 9 8 7 6 5 4 3 2 1   6 7 8 9 10 11/0

Printed in the U.S.A.   40

First Scholastic trade paperback printing, September 2006

This book is printed on paper containing a minimum of 20% post-consumer recycled fiber.

To Mackenzie,
my beautiful daughter,
I dedicate
her ink-and-paper twin.

CONTENTS

HARRY POTTER

AND THE HALF-BLOOD PRINCE

THE OTHER MINISTER

It was nearing midnight and the Prime Minister was sitting alone in his office, reading a long memo that was slipping through his brain without leaving the slightest trace of meaning behind. He was waiting for a call from the President of a far distant country, and between wondering when the wretched man would telephone, and trying to suppress unpleasant memories of what had been a very long, tiring, and difficult week, there was not much space in his head for anything else. The more he attempted to focus on the print on the page before him, the more clearly the Prime Minister could see the gloating face of one of his political opponents. This particular opponent had appeared on the news that very day, not only to enumerate all the terrible things that had happened in the last week (as though anyone needed reminding) but also to explain why each and every one of them was the government's fault.

The Prime Minister's pulse quickened at the very thought of these accusations, for they were neither fair nor true. How on earth was his government supposed to have stopped that bridge collapsing? It was outrageous for anybody to suggest that they were not spending enough on bridges. The bridge was fewer than ten years old, and the best experts were at a loss to explain why it had snapped cleanly in two, sending a dozen cars into the watery depths of the river below. And how dare anyone suggest that it was lack of policemen that had resulted in those two very nasty and well-publicized murders? Or that the government should have somehow foreseen the freak hurricane in the West Country that had caused so much damage to both people and property? And was it *his* fault that one of his Junior Ministers, Herbert Chorley, had chosen this week to act so peculiarly that he was now going to be spending a lot more time with his family?

"A grim mood has gripped the country," the opponent had concluded, barely concealing his own broad grin.

And unfortunately, this was perfectly true. The Prime Minister felt it himself; people really did seem more miserable than usual. Even the weather was dismal; all this chilly mist in the middle of July. . . . It wasn't right, it wasn't normal. . . .

He turned over the second page of the memo, saw how much longer it went on, and gave it up as a bad job. Stretching his arms above his head he looked around his office mournfully. It was a handsome room, with a fine marble fireplace facing the long sash windows, firmly closed against the unseasonable chill. With a slight shiver, the Prime Minister got up and moved over to the window, looking out at the thin mist that was pressing itself against the glass. It was then, as he stood with his back to the room, that he heard a soft cough behind him.

He froze, nose to nose with his own scared-looking reflection in the dark glass. He knew that cough. He had heard it before. He turned very slowly to face the empty room.

"Hello?" he said, trying to sound braver than he felt.

For a brief moment he allowed himself the impossible hope that nobody would answer him. However, a voice responded at once, a crisp, decisive voice that sounded as though it were reading a prepared statement. It was coming — as the Prime Minister had known at the first cough — from the froglike little man wearing a long silver wig who was depicted in a small, dirty oil painting in the far corner of the room.

"To the Prime Minister of Muggles. Urgent we meet. Kindly respond immediately. Sincerely, Fudge."

The man in the painting looked inquiringly at the Prime Minister.

"Er," said the Prime Minister, "listen. . . . It's not a very good time for me. . . . I'm waiting for a telephone call, you see . . . from the President of —"

"That can be rearranged," said the portrait at once. The Prime Minister's heart sank. He had been afraid of that.

"But I really was rather hoping to speak —"

"We shall arrange for the President to forget to call. He will telephone tomorrow night instead," said the little man. "Kindly respond immediately to Mr. Fudge."

"I . . . oh . . . very well," said the Prime Minister weakly. "Yes, I'll see Fudge."

He hurried back to his desk, straightening his tie as he went. He had barely resumed his seat, and arranged his face into what he hoped was a relaxed and unfazed expression, when bright green flames burst into life in the empty grate beneath his marble mantelpiece. He watched, trying not to betray a flicker of surprise or alarm, as a portly man appeared within the flames, spinning as fast as a top. Seconds later, he had climbed out onto a rather fine antique rug, brushing ash from the sleeves of his long pin-striped cloak, a lime-green bowler hat in his hand.

"Ah . . . Prime Minister," said Cornelius Fudge, striding forward with his hand outstretched. "Good to see you again."

The Prime Minister could not honestly return this compliment, so said nothing at all. He was not remotely pleased to see Fudge, whose occasional appearances, apart from being downright alarming in themselves, generally meant that he was about to hear some very bad news. Furthermore, Fudge was looking distinctly careworn. He was thinner, balder, and grayer, and his face had a crumpled look. The Prime Minister had seen that kind of look in politicians before, and it never boded well.

"How can I help you?" he said, shaking Fudge's hand very briefly and gesturing toward the hardest of the chairs in front of the desk.

"Difficult to know where to begin," muttered Fudge, pulling up the chair, sitting down, and placing his green bowler upon his knees. "What a week, what a week . . ."

"Had a bad one too, have you?" asked the Prime Minister stiffly, hoping to convey by this that he had quite enough on his plate already without any extra helpings from Fudge.

"Yes, of course," said Fudge, rubbing his eyes wearily and looking morosely at the Prime Minister. "I've been having the same week you have, Prime Minister. The Brockdale Bridge . . . the Bones and Vance murders . . . not to mention the ruckus in the West Country . . ."

"You — er — your — I mean to say, some of your people were — were involved in those — those things, were they?"

Fudge fixed the Prime Minister with a rather stern look. "Of course they were," he said. "Surely you've realized what's going on?"

"I . . ." hesitated the Prime Minister.

It was precisely this sort of behavior that made him dislike Fudge's visits so much. He was, after all, the Prime Minister and did not appreciate being made to feel like an ignorant schoolboy. But of course, it had been like this from his very first meeting with Fudge on his very first evening as Prime Minister. He remembered it as though it were yesterday and knew it would haunt him until his dying day.

He had been standing alone in this very office, savoring the triumph that was his after so many years of dreaming and scheming, when he had heard a cough behind him, just like tonight, and turned to find that ugly little portrait talking to him, announcing that the Minister of Magic was about to arrive and introduce himself.

Naturally, he had thought that the long campaign and the strain of the election had caused him to go mad. He had been utterly terrified to find a portrait talking to him, though this had been nothing to how he felt when a self-proclaimed wizard had bounced out of the fireplace and shaken his hand. He had remained speechless throughout Fudge's kindly explanation that there were witches and wizards still living in secret all over the world and his reassurances that he was not to bother his head about them as the Ministry of Magic took responsibility for the whole Wizarding community and prevented the non-magical population from getting wind of them. It was, said Fudge, a difficult job that encompassed everything from regulations on responsible use of broomsticks to keeping the dragon population under control (the Prime Minister remembered clutching the desk for support at this point). Fudge had then patted the shoulder of the still-dumbstruck Prime Minister in a fatherly sort of way.

"Not to worry," he had said, "it's odds-on you'll never see me again. I'll only bother you if there's something really serious going on our end, something that's likely to affect the Muggles — the non-magical population, I should say. Otherwise, it's live and let live. And I must say, you're taking it a lot better than your predecessor. *He* tried to throw me out the window, thought I was a hoax planned by the opposition."

At this, the Prime Minister had found his voice at last. "You're — you're *not* a hoax, then?"

It had been his last, desperate hope.

"No," said Fudge gently. "No, I'm afraid I'm not. Look."

And he had turned the Prime Minister's teacup into a gerbil.

"But," said the Prime Minister breathlessly, watching his teacup chewing on the corner of his next speech, "but why — why has nobody told me — ?"

"The Minister of Magic only reveals him- or herself to the Muggle Prime Minister of the day," said Fudge, poking his wand back inside his jacket. "We find it the best way to maintain secrecy."

"But then," bleated the Prime Minister, "why hasn't a former Prime Minister warned me — ?"

At this, Fudge had actually laughed.

"My dear Prime Minister, are *you* ever going to tell anybody?"

Still chortling, Fudge had thrown some powder into the fireplace, stepped into the emerald flames, and vanished with a whooshing sound. The Prime Minister had stood there, quite motionless, and realized that he would never, as long as he lived, dare mention this encounter to a living soul, for who in the wide world would believe him?

The shock had taken a little while to wear off. For a time, he had tried to convince himself that Fudge had indeed been a hallucination brought on by lack of sleep during his grueling election campaign. In a vain attempt to rid himself of all reminders of this uncomfortable encounter, he had given the gerbil to his delighted niece and instructed his private secretary to take down the portrait of the ugly little man who had announced Fudge's arrival. To the Prime Minister's dismay, however, the portrait had proved impossible to remove. When several carpenters, a builder or two, an art historian, and the Chancellor of the Exchequer had all tried unsuccessfully to prise it from the wall, the Prime Minister had abandoned the attempt and simply resolved to hope that the thing remained motionless and silent for the rest of his term in office. Occasionally he could have sworn he saw out of the corner of his eye the occupant of the painting yawning, or else scratching his nose; even, once or twice, simply walking out of his frame and leaving nothing but a stretch of muddy-brown canvas behind. However, he had trained himself not to look at the picture very much, and always to tell himself firmly that his eyes were playing tricks on him when anything like this happened.

Then, three years ago, on a night very like tonight, the Prime Minister had been alone in his office when the portrait had once again announced the imminent arrival of Fudge, who had burst out of the fireplace, sopping wet and in a state of considerable panic. Before the Prime Minister could ask why he was dripping all over the Axminster, Fudge had started ranting about a prison the Prime Minister had never heard of, a man named "Serious" Black, something that sounded like "Hogwarts," and a boy called Harry Potter, none of which made the remotest sense to the Prime Minister.

". . . I've just come from Azkaban," Fudge had panted, tipping a large amount of water out of the rim of his bowler hat into his pocket. "Middle of the North Sea, you know, nasty flight . . . the dementors are in uproar" — he shuddered — "they've never had a breakout before. Anyway, I had to come to you, Prime Minister. Black's a known Muggle killer and may be planning to rejoin You-Know-Who. . . . But of course, you don't even know who You-Know-Who is!" He had gazed hopelessly at the Prime Minister for a moment, then said, "Well, sit down, sit down, I'd better fill you in. . . . Have a whiskey . . ."

The Prime Minister rather resented being told to sit down in his own office, let alone offered his own whiskey, but he sat neverthe-less. Fudge pulled out his wand, conjured two large glasses full of amber liquid out of thin air, pushed one of them into the Prime Minister's hand, and drew up a chair.

Fudge had talked for more than an hour. At one point, he had refused to say a certain name aloud and wrote it instead on a piece of parchment, which he had thrust into the Prime Minister's whiskey-free hand. When at last Fudge had stood up to leave, the Prime Minister had stood up too.

"So you think that . . ." He had squinted down at the name in his left hand. "Lord Vol —"

"He-Who-Must-Not-Be-Named!" snarled Fudge.

"I'm sorry. . . . You think that He-Who-Must-Not-Be-Named is still alive, then?"

"Well, Dumbledore says he is," said Fudge, as he had fastened his pin-striped cloak under his chin, "but we've never found him. If you ask me, he's not dangerous unless he's got support, so it's Black we ought to be worrying about. You'll put out that warning, then? Excellent. Well, I hope we don't see each other again, Prime Minister! Good night."

But they had seen each other again. Less than a year later a harassed-looking Fudge had appeared out of thin air in the cabinet room to inform the Prime Minister that there had been a spot of bother at the Kwidditch (or that was what it had sounded like) World Cup and that several Muggles had been "involved," but that the Prime Minister was not to worry, the fact that You-Know-Who's Mark had been seen again meant nothing; Fudge was sure it was an isolated incident, and the Muggle Liaison Office was dealing with all memory modifications as they spoke.

"Oh, and I almost forgot," Fudge had added. "We're importing three foreign dragons and a sphinx for the Triwizard Tournament, quite routine, but the Department for the Regulation and Control of Magical Creatures tells me that it's down in the rule book that we have to notify you if we're bringing highly dangerous creatures into the country."

"I — what — *dragons*?" spluttered the Prime Minister.

"Yes, three," said Fudge. "And a sphinx. Well, good day to you."

The Prime Minister had hoped beyond hope that dragons and sphinxes would be the worst of it, but no. Less than two years later, Fudge had erupted out of the fire yet again, this time with the news that there had been a mass breakout from Azkaban.

"A *mass* breakout?" repeated the Prime Minister hoarsely.

"No need to worry, no need to worry!" shouted Fudge, already with one foot in the flames. "We'll have them rounded up in no time — just thought you ought to know!"

And before the Prime Minister could shout, "Now, wait just one moment!" Fudge had vanished in a shower of green sparks.

Whatever the press and the opposition might say, the Prime Minister was not a foolish man. It had not escaped his notice that, despite Fudge's assurances at their first meeting, they were now seeing rather a lot of each other, nor that Fudge was becoming more flustered with each visit. Little though he liked to think about the Minister of Magic (or, as he always called Fudge in his head, the *Other* Minister), the Prime Minister could not help but fear that the next time Fudge appeared it would be with graver news still. The sight, therefore, of Fudge stepping out of the fire once more, looking disheveled and fretful and sternly surprised that the Prime Minister did not know exactly why he was there, was about the worst thing that had happened in the course of this extremely gloomy week.

"How should I know what's going on in the — er — Wizarding community?" snapped the Prime Minister now. "I have a country to run and quite enough concerns at the moment without —"

"We have the same concerns," Fudge interrupted. "The Brockdale Bridge didn't wear out. That wasn't really a hurricane. Those murders were not the work of Muggles. And Herbert Chorley's family would be safer without him. We are currently making arrangements to have him transferred to St. Mungo's Hospital for Magical Maladies and Injuries. The move should be effected tonight."

"What do you . . . I'm afraid I . . . *What?*" blustered the Prime Minister.

Fudge took a great, deep breath and said, "Prime Minister, I am very sorry to have to tell you that he's back. He-Who-Must-Not-Be-Named is back."

"Back? When you say 'back' . . . he's alive? I mean —"

The Prime Minister groped in his memory for the details of that horrible conversation of three years previously, when Fudge had told him about the wizard who was feared above all others, the wizard who had committed a thousand terrible crimes before his mysterious disappearance fifteen years earlier.

"Yes, alive," said Fudge. "That is — I don't know — is a man alive if he can't be killed? I don't really understand it, and Dumbledore won't explain properly — but anyway, he's certainly got a body and is walking and talking and killing, so I suppose, for the purposes of our discussion, yes, he's alive."

The Prime Minister did not know what to say to this, but a persistent habit of wishing to appear well-informed on any subject that came up made him cast around for any details he could remember of their previous conversations.

"Is Serious Black with — er — He-Who-Must-Not-Be-Named?"

"Black? Black?" said Fudge distractedly, turning his bowler rapidly in his fingers. "Sirius Black, you mean? Merlin's beard, no. Black's dead. Turns out we were — er — mistaken about Black. He was innocent after all. And he wasn't in league with He-Who-Must-Not-Be-Named either. I mean," he added defensively, spinning the bowler hat still faster, "all the evidence pointed — we had more than fifty eyewitnesses — but anyway, as I say, he's dead. Murdered, as a matter of fact. On Ministry of Magic premises. There's going to be an inquiry, actually. . . ."

To his great surprise, the Prime Minister felt a fleeting stab of pity for Fudge at this point. It was, however, eclipsed almost immediately by a glow of smugness at the thought that, deficient though he himself might be in the area of materializing out of fireplaces, there had never been a murder in any of the government departments under *his* charge. . . . Not yet, anyway . . .

While the Prime Minister surreptitiously touched the wood of his desk, Fudge continued, "But Black's by-the-by now. The point is, we're at war, Prime Minister, and steps must be taken."

"At war?" repeated the Prime Minister nervously. "Surely that's a little bit of an overstatement?"

"He-Who-Must-Not-Be-Named has now been joined by those of his followers who broke out of Azkaban in January," said Fudge, speaking more and more rapidly and twirling his bowler so fast that it was a lime-green blur. "Since they have moved into the open, they have been wreaking havoc. The Brockdale Bridge — he did it, Prime Minister, he threatened a mass Muggle killing unless I stood aside for him and —"

"Good grief, so it's *your* fault those people were killed and I'm having to answer questions about rusted rigging and corroded expansion joints and I don't know what else!" said the Prime Minister furiously.

"*My* fault!" said Fudge, coloring up. "Are you saying you would have caved in to blackmail like that?"

"Maybe not," said the Prime Minister, standing up and striding about the room, "but I would have put all my efforts into catching the blackmailer before he committed any such atrocity!"

"Do you really think I wasn't already making every effort?" demanded Fudge heatedly. "Every Auror in the Ministry was — and is — trying to find him and round up his followers, but we happen to be talking about one of the most powerful wizards of all time, a wizard who has eluded capture for almost three decades!"

"So I suppose you're going to tell me he caused the hurricane in the West Country too?" said the Prime Minister, his temper rising with every pace he took. It was infuriating to discover the reason for all these terrible disasters and not to be able to tell the public, almost worse than it being the government's fault after all.

"That was no hurricane," said Fudge miserably.

"Excuse me!" barked the Prime Minister, now positively stamping up and down. "Trees uprooted, roofs ripped off, lampposts bent, horrible injuries —"

"It was the Death Eaters," said Fudge. "He-Who-Must-Not-Be-Named's followers. And . . . and we suspect giant involvement."

The Prime Minister stopped in his tracks as though he had hit an invisible wall. "*What* involvement?"

Fudge grimaced. "He used giants last time, when he wanted to go for the grand effect," he said. "The Office of Misinformation has been working around the clock, we've had teams of Obliviators out trying to modify the memories of all the Muggles who saw what really happened, we've got most of the Department for the Regulation and Control of Magical Creatures running around Somerset, but we can't find the giant — it's been a disaster."

"You don't say!" said the Prime Minister furiously.

"I won't deny that morale is pretty low at the Ministry," said Fudge. "What with all that, and then losing Amelia Bones."

"Losing who?"

"Amelia Bones. Head of the Department of Magical Law Enforcement. We think He-Who-Must-Not-Be-Named may have murdered her in person, because she was a very gifted witch and — and all the evidence was that she put up a real fight."

Fudge cleared his throat and, with an effort, it seemed, stopped spinning his bowler hat.

"But that murder was in the newspapers," said the Prime Minister, momentarily diverted from his anger. "*Our* newspapers. Amelia

Bones . . . it just said she was a middle-aged woman who lived alone. It was a — a nasty killing, wasn't it? It's had rather a lot of publicity. The police are baffled, you see."

Fudge sighed. "Well, of course they are," he said. "Killed in a room that was locked from the inside, wasn't she? We, on the other hand, know exactly who did it, not that that gets us any further toward catching him. And then there was Emmeline Vance, maybe you didn't hear about that one —"

"Oh yes I did!" said the Prime Minister. "It happened just around the corner from here, as a matter of fact. The papers had a field day with it, 'breakdown of law and order in the Prime Minister's backyard —'"

"And as if all that wasn't enough," said Fudge, barely listening to the Prime Minister, "we've got dementors swarming all over the place, attacking people left, right, and center. . . ."

Once upon a happier time this sentence would have been unintelligible to the Prime Minister, but he was wiser now.

"I thought dementors guard the prisoners in Azkaban," he said cautiously.

"They did," said Fudge wearily. "But not anymore. They've deserted the prison and joined He-Who-Must-Not-Be-Named. I won't pretend that wasn't a blow."

"But," said the Prime Minister, with a sense of dawning horror, "didn't you tell me they're the creatures that drain hope and happiness out of people?"

"That's right. And they're breeding. That's what's causing all this mist."

The Prime Minister sank, weak-kneed, into the nearest chair. The idea of invisible creatures swooping through the towns and countryside, spreading despair and hopelessness in his voters, made him feel quite faint.

"Now see here, Fudge — you've got to do something! It's your responsibility as Minister of Magic!"

"My dear Prime Minister, you can't honestly think I'm still Minister of Magic after all this? I was sacked three days ago! The whole Wizarding community has been screaming for my resignation for a fortnight. I've never known them so united in my whole term of office!" said Fudge, with a brave attempt at a smile.

The Prime Minister was momentarily lost for words. Despite his indignation at the position into which he had been placed, he still rather felt for the shrunken-looking man sitting opposite him.

"I'm very sorry," he said finally. "If there's anything I can do?"

"It's very kind of you, Prime Minister, but there is nothing. I was sent here tonight to bring you up to date on recent events and to introduce you to my successor. I rather thought he'd be here by now, but of course, he's very busy at the moment, with so much going on."

Fudge looked around at the portrait of the ugly little man wearing the long curly silver wig, who was digging in his ear with the point of a quill. Catching Fudge's eye, the portrait said, "He'll be here in a moment, he's just finishing a letter to Dumbledore."

"I wish him luck," said Fudge, sounding bitter for the first time. "I've been writing to Dumbledore twice a day for the past fortnight, but he won't budge. If he'd just been prepared to persuade the boy, I might still be . . . Well, maybe Scrimgeour will have more success."

Fudge subsided into what was clearly an aggrieved silence, but it was broken almost immediately by the portrait, which suddenly spoke in its crisp, official voice.

"To the Prime Minister of Muggles. Requesting a meeting.

Urgent. Kindly respond immediately. Rufus Scrimgeour, Minister of Magic."

"Yes, yes, fine," said the Prime Minister distractedly, and he barely flinched as the flames in the grate turned emerald green again, rose up, and revealed a second spinning wizard in their heart, disgorging him moments later onto the antique rug.

Fudge got to his feet and, after a moment's hesitation, the Prime Minister did the same, watching the new arrival straighten up, dust down his long black robes, and look around.

The Prime Minister's first, foolish thought was that Rufus Scrimgeour looked rather like an old lion. There were streaks of gray in his mane of tawny hair and his bushy eyebrows; he had keen yellowish eyes behind a pair of wire-rimmed spectacles and a certain rangy, loping grace even though he walked with a slight limp. There was an immediate impression of shrewdness and toughness; the Prime Minister thought he understood why the Wizarding community preferred Scrimgeour to Fudge as a leader in these dangerous times.

"How do you do?" said the Prime Minister politely, holding out his hand.

Scrimgeour grasped it briefly, his eyes scanning the room, then pulled out a wand from under his robes.

"Fudge told you everything?" he asked, striding over to the door and tapping the keyhole with his wand. The Prime Minister heard the lock click.

"Er — yes," said the Prime Minister. "And if you don't mind, I'd rather that door remained unlocked."

"I'd rather not be interrupted," said Scrimgeour shortly, "or watched," he added, pointing his wand at the windows, so that the curtains swept across them. "Right, well, I'm a busy man, so let's get down to business. First of all, we need to discuss your security."

The Prime Minister drew himself up to his fullest height and replied, "I am perfectly happy with the security I've already got, thank you very —"

"Well, we're not," Scrimgeour cut in. "It'll be a poor lookout for the Muggles if their Prime Minister gets put under the Imperius Curse. The new secretary in your outer office —"

"I'm not getting rid of Kingsley Shacklebolt, if that's what you're suggesting!" said the Prime Minister hotly. "He's highly efficient, gets through twice the work the rest of them —"

"That's because he's a wizard," said Scrimgeour, without a flicker of a smile. "A highly trained Auror, who has been assigned to you for your protection."

"Now, wait a moment!" declared the Prime Minister. "You can't just put your people into my office, I decide who works for me —"

"I thought you were happy with Shacklebolt?" said Scrimgeour coldly.

"I am — that's to say, I was —"

"Then there's no problem, is there?" said Scrimgeour.

"I . . . well, as long as Shacklebolt's work continues to be . . . er . . . excellent," said the Prime Minister lamely, but Scrimgeour barely seemed to hear him.

"Now, about Herbert Chorley, your Junior Minister," he continued. "The one who has been entertaining the public by impersonating a duck."

"What about him?" asked the Prime Minister.

"He has clearly reacted to a poorly performed Imperius Curse," said Scrimgeour. "It's addled his brains, but he could still be dangerous."

"He's only quacking!" said the Prime Minister weakly. "Surely a bit of a rest . . . Maybe go easy on the drink . . ."

"A team of Healers from St. Mungo's Hospital for Magical Maladies and Injuries are examining him as we speak. So far he has attempted to strangle three of them," said Scrimgeour. "I think it best that we remove him from Muggle society for a while."

"I . . . well . . . He'll be all right, won't he?" said the Prime Minister anxiously.

Scrimgeour merely shrugged, already moving back toward the fireplace.

"Well, that's really all I had to say. I will keep you posted of developments, Prime Minister — or, at least, I shall probably be too busy to come personally, in which case I shall send Fudge here. He has consented to stay on in an advisory capacity."

Fudge attempted to smile, but was unsuccessful; he merely looked as though he had a toothache. Scrimgeour was already rummaging in his pocket for the mysterious powder that turned the fire green. The Prime Minister gazed hopelessly at the pair of them for a moment, then the words he had fought to suppress all evening burst from him at last.

"But for heaven's sake — you're *wizards*! You can do *magic*! Surely you can sort out — well — *anything*!"

Scrimgeour turned slowly on the spot and exchanged an incredulous look with Fudge, who really did manage a smile this time as he said kindly, "The trouble is, the other side can do magic too, Prime Minister."

And with that, the two wizards stepped one after the other into the bright green fire and vanished.

CHAPTER TWO

SPINNER'S END

Many miles away the chilly mist that had pressed against the Prime Minister's windows drifted over a dirty river that wound between overgrown, rubbish-strewn banks. An immense chimney, relic of a disused mill, reared up, shadowy and ominous. There was no sound apart from the whisper of the black water and no sign of life apart from a scrawny fox that had slunk down the bank to nose hopefully at some old fish-and-chip wrappings in the tall grass.

But then, with a very faint *pop,* a slim, hooded figure appeared out of thin air on the edge of the river. The fox froze, wary eyes fixed upon this strange new phenomenon. The figure seemed to take its bearings for a few moments, then set off with light, quick strides, its long cloak rustling over the grass.

With a second and louder *pop,* another hooded figure materialized.

"Wait!"

The harsh cry startled the fox, now crouching almost flat in the undergrowth. It leapt from its hiding place and up the bank. There was a flash of green light, a yelp, and the fox fell back to the ground, dead.

The second figure turned over the animal with its toe.

"Just a fox," said a woman's voice dismissively from under the hood. "I thought perhaps an Auror — Cissy, wait!"

But her quarry, who had paused and looked back at the flash of light, was already scrambling up the bank the fox had just fallen down.

"Cissy — Narcissa — listen to me —"

The second woman caught the first and seized her arm, but the other wrenched it away.

"Go back, Bella!"

"You must listen to me!"

"I've listened already. I've made my decision. Leave me alone!"

The woman named Narcissa gained the top of the bank, where a line of old railings separated the river from a narrow, cobbled street. The other woman, Bella, followed at once. Side by side they stood looking across the road at the rows and rows of dilapidated brick houses, their windows dull and blind in the darkness.

"He lives here?" asked Bella in a voice of contempt. "*Here?* In this Muggle dunghill? We must be the first of our kind ever to set foot —"

But Narcissa was not listening; she had slipped through a gap in the rusty railings and was already hurrying across the road.

"Cissy, *wait*!"

Bella followed, her cloak streaming behind, and saw Narcissa darting through an alley between the houses into a second, almost identical street. Some of the streetlamps were broken; the two women were running between patches of light and deep darkness. The pursuer caught up with her prey just as she turned another corner, this time succeeding in catching hold of her arm and swinging her around so that they faced each other.

"Cissy, you must not do this, you can't trust him —"

"The Dark Lord trusts him, doesn't he?"

"The Dark Lord is . . . I believe . . . mistaken," Bella panted, and her eyes gleamed momentarily under her hood as she looked around to check that they were indeed alone. "In any case, we were told not to speak of the plan to anyone. This is a betrayal of the Dark Lord's —"

"Let go, Bella!" snarled Narcissa, and she drew a wand from beneath her cloak, holding it threateningly in the other's face. Bella merely laughed.

"Cissy, your own sister? You wouldn't —"

"There is nothing I wouldn't do anymore!" Narcissa breathed, a note of hysteria in her voice, and as she brought down the wand like a knife, there was another flash of light. Bella let go of her sister's arm as though burned.

"Narcissa!"

But Narcissa had rushed ahead. Rubbing her hand, her pursuer followed again, keeping her distance now, as they moved deeper into the deserted labyrinth of brick houses. At last, Narcissa hurried up a street named Spinner's End, over which the towering mill chimney seemed to hover like a giant admonitory finger. Her footsteps echoed on the cobbles as she passed boarded and broken windows, until she reached the very last house, where a dim light glimmered through the curtains in a downstairs room.

She had knocked on the door before Bella, cursing under her breath, had caught up. Together they stood waiting, panting slightly, breathing in the smell of the dirty river that was carried to them on the night breeze. After a few seconds, they heard movement behind the door and it opened a crack. A sliver of a man could be seen looking out at them, a man with long black hair parted in curtains around a sallow face and black eyes.

Narcissa threw back her hood. She was so pale that she seemed to shine in the darkness; the long blonde hair streaming down her back gave her the look of a drowned person.

"Narcissa!" said the man, opening the door a little wider, so that the light fell upon her and her sister too. "What a pleasant surprise!"

"Severus," she said in a strained whisper. "May I speak to you? It's urgent."

"But of course."

He stood back to allow her to pass him into the house. Her still-hooded sister followed without invitation.

"Snape," she said curtly as she passed him.

"Bellatrix," he replied, his thin mouth curling into a slightly mocking smile as he closed the door with a snap behind them.

They had stepped directly into a tiny sitting room, which had the feeling of a dark, padded cell. The walls were completely covered in books, most of them bound in old black or brown leather; a threadbare sofa, an old armchair, and a rickety table stood grouped together in a pool of dim light cast by a candle-filled lamp hung from the ceiling. The place had an air of neglect, as though it was not usually inhabited.

Snape gestured Narcissa to the sofa. She threw off her cloak, cast it aside, and sat down, staring at her white and trembling hands clasped in her lap. Bellatrix lowered her hood more slowly. Dark as her sister was fair, with heavily lidded eyes and a strong jaw, she did not take her gaze from Snape as she moved to stand behind Narcissa.

"So, what can I do for you?" Snape asked, settling himself in the armchair opposite the two sisters.

"We . . . we are alone, aren't we?" Narcissa asked quietly.

"Yes, of course. Well, Wormtail's here, but we're not counting vermin, are we?"

He pointed his wand at the wall of books behind him and with a bang, a hidden door flew open, revealing a narrow staircase upon which a small man stood frozen.

"As you have clearly realized, Wormtail, we have guests," said Snape lazily.

The man crept, hunchbacked, down the last few steps and moved into the room. He had small, watery eyes, a pointed nose, and wore an unpleasant simper. His left hand was caressing his right, which looked as though it was encased in a bright silver glove.

"Narcissa!" he said, in a squeaky voice. "And Bellatrix! How charming —"

"Wormtail will get us drinks, if you'd like them," said Snape. "And then he will return to his bedroom."

Wormtail winced as though Snape had thrown something at him.

"I am not your servant!" he squeaked, avoiding Snape's eye.

"Really? I was under the impression that the Dark Lord placed you here to assist me."

"To assist, yes — but not to make you drinks and — and clean your house!"

"I had no idea, Wormtail, that you were craving more dangerous assignments," said Snape silkily. "This can be easily arranged: I shall speak to the Dark Lord —"

"I can speak to him myself if I want to!"

"Of course you can," said Snape, sneering. "But in the meantime, bring us drinks. Some of the elf-made wine will do."

Wormtail hesitated for a moment, looking as though he might argue, but then turned and headed through a second hidden door. They heard banging and a clinking of glasses. Within seconds he was back, bearing a dusty bottle and three glasses upon a tray. He dropped these on the rickety table and scurried from their presence, slamming the book-covered door behind him.

Snape poured out three glasses of bloodred wine and handed two of them to the sisters. Narcissa murmured a word of thanks, whilst Bellatrix said nothing, but continued to glower at Snape. This did not seem to discompose him; on the contrary, he looked rather amused.

"The Dark Lord," he said, raising his glass and draining it.

The sisters copied him. Snape refilled their glasses. As Narcissa took her second drink she said in a rush, "Severus, I'm sorry to come here like this, but I had to see you. I think you are the only one who can help me —"

Snape held up a hand to stop her, then pointed his wand again at the concealed staircase door. There was a loud bang and a squeal, followed by the sound of Wormtail scurrying back up the stairs.

"My apologies," said Snape. "He has lately taken to listening at doors, I don't know what he means by it. . . . You were saying, Narcissa?"

She took a great, shuddering breath and started again.

"Severus, I know I ought not to be here, I have been told to say nothing to anyone, but —"

"Then you ought to hold your tongue!" snarled Bellatrix. "Particularly in present company!"

"'Present company'?" repeated Snape sardonically. "And what am I to understand by that, Bellatrix?"

"That I don't trust you, Snape, as you very well know!"

Narcissa let out a noise that might have been a dry sob and covered her face with her hands. Snape set his glass down upon the table and sat back again, his hands upon the arms of his chair, smiling into Bellatrix's glowering face.

"Narcissa, I think we ought to hear what Bellatrix is bursting to say; it will save tedious interruptions. Well, continue, Bellatrix," said Snape. "Why is it that you do not trust me?"

"A hundred reasons!" she said loudly, striding out from behind the sofa to slam her glass upon the table. "Where to start! Where were you when the Dark Lord fell? Why did you never make any attempt to find him when he vanished? What have you been doing all these years that you've lived in Dumbledore's pocket? Why did you stop the Dark Lord procuring the Sorcerer's Stone? Why did you not return at once when the Dark Lord was reborn? Where were you a few weeks ago when we battled to retrieve the prophecy for the Dark Lord? And why, Snape, is Harry Potter still alive, when you have had him at your mercy for five years?"

She paused, her chest rising and falling rapidly, the color high in her cheeks. Behind her, Narcissa sat motionless, her face still hidden in her hands.

Snape smiled.

"Before I answer you — oh yes, Bellatrix, I am going to answer! You can carry my words back to the others who whisper behind my back, and carry false tales of my treachery to the Dark Lord! Before I answer you, I say, let me ask a question in turn. Do you really think that the Dark Lord has not asked me each and every one of those questions? And do you really think that, had I not been able to give satisfactory answers, I would be sitting here talking to you?"

She hesitated.

"I know he believes you, but . . ."

"You think he is mistaken? Or that I have somehow hoodwinked him? Fooled the Dark Lord, the greatest wizard, the most accomplished Legilimens the world has ever seen?"

Bellatrix said nothing, but looked, for the first time, a little discomfited. Snape did not press the point. He picked up his drink again, sipped it, and continued, "You ask where I was when the Dark Lord fell. I was where he had ordered me to be, at Hogwarts School of Witchcraft and Wizardry, because he wished me to spy upon Albus Dumbledore. You know, I presume, that it was on the Dark Lord's orders that I took up the post?"

She nodded almost imperceptibly and then opened her mouth, but Snape forestalled her.

"You ask why I did not attempt to find him when he vanished. For the same reason that Avery, Yaxley, the Carrows, Greyback, Lucius" — he inclined his head slightly to Narcissa — "and many others did not attempt to find him. I believed him finished. I am not proud of it, I was wrong, but there it is. . . . If he had not forgiven we who lost faith at that time, he would have very few followers left."

"He'd have me!" said Bellatrix passionately. "I, who spent many years in Azkaban for him!"

"Yes, indeed, most admirable," said Snape in a bored voice. "Of course, you weren't a lot of use to him in prison, but the gesture was undoubtedly fine —"

"Gesture!" she shrieked; in her fury she looked slightly mad. "While I endured the dementors, you remained at Hogwarts, comfortably playing Dumbledore's pet!"

"Not quite," said Snape calmly. "He wouldn't give me the Defense Against the Dark Arts job, you know. Seemed to think it might, ah, bring about a relapse . . . tempt me into my old ways."

"This was your sacrifice for the Dark Lord, not to teach your favorite subject?" she jeered. "Why did you stay there all that time, Snape? Still spying on Dumbledore for a master you believed dead?"

"Hardly," said Snape, "although the Dark Lord is pleased that I never deserted my post: I had sixteen years of information on Dumbledore to give him when he returned, a rather more useful welcome-back present than endless reminiscences of how unpleasant Azkaban is. . . ."

"But you stayed —"

"Yes, Bellatrix, I stayed," said Snape, betraying a hint of impatience for the first time. "I had a comfortable job that I preferred to a stint in Azkaban. They were rounding up the Death Eaters, you know. Dumbledore's protection kept me out of jail; it was most convenient and I used it. I repeat: The Dark Lord does not complain that I stayed, so I do not see why you do.

"I think you next wanted to know," he pressed on, a little more loudly, for Bellatrix showed every sign of interrupting, "why I stood between the Dark Lord and the Sorcerer's Stone. That is easily answered. He did not know whether he could trust me. He thought, like you, that I had turned from faithful Death Eater to Dumbledore's stooge. He was in a pitiable condition, very weak, sharing the body of a mediocre wizard. He did not dare reveal himself to a former ally if that ally might turn him over to Dumbledore or the Ministry. I deeply regret that he did not trust me. He would have returned to power three years sooner. As it was, I saw only greedy and unworthy Quirrell attempting to steal the stone and, I admit, I did all I could to thwart him."

Bellatrix's mouth twisted as though she had taken an unpleasant dose of medicine.

"But you didn't return when he came back, you didn't fly back to him at once when you felt the Dark Mark burn —"

"Correct. I returned two hours later. I returned on Dumbledore's orders."

"On Dumbledore's — ?" she began, in tones of outrage.

"Think!" said Snape, impatient again. "Think! By waiting two hours, just two hours, I ensured that I could remain at Hogwarts as a spy! By allowing Dumbledore to think that I was only returning to the Dark Lord's side because I was ordered to, I have been able to pass information on Dumbledore and the Order of the Phoenix ever since! Consider, Bellatrix: The Dark Mark had been growing stronger for months. I knew he must be about to return, all the Death Eaters knew! I had plenty of time to think about what I wanted to do, to plan my next move, to escape like Karkaroff, didn't I?

"The Dark Lord's initial displeasure at my lateness vanished entirely, I assure you, when I explained that I remained faithful, although Dumbledore thought I was his man. Yes, the Dark Lord thought that I had left him forever, but he was wrong."

"But what use have you been?" sneered Bellatrix. "What useful information have we had from you?"

"My information has been conveyed directly to the Dark Lord," said Snape. "If he chooses not to share it with you —"

"He shares everything with me!" said Bellatrix, firing up at once. "He calls me his most loyal, his most faithful —"

"Does he?" said Snape, his voice delicately inflected to suggest his disbelief. "Does he *still*, after the fiasco at the Ministry?"

"That was not my fault!" said Bellatrix, flushing. "The Dark Lord has, in the past, entrusted me with his most precious — if Lucius hadn't —"

"Don't you dare — don't you *dare* blame my husband!" said Narcissa, in a low and deadly voice, looking up at her sister.

"There is no point apportioning blame," said Snape smoothly. "What is done, is done."

"But not by you!" said Bellatrix furiously. "No, you were once again absent while the rest of us ran dangers, were you not, Snape?"

"My orders were to remain behind," said Snape. "Perhaps you disagree with the Dark Lord, perhaps you think that Dumbledore would not have noticed if I had joined forces with the Death Eaters to fight the Order of the Phoenix? And — forgive me — you speak of dangers . . . you were facing six teenagers, were you not?"

"They were joined, as you very well know, by half of the Order before long!" snarled Bellatrix. "And, while we are on the subject of the Order, you still claim you cannot reveal the whereabouts of their headquarters, don't you?"

"I am not the Secret-Keeper; I cannot speak the name of the place. You understand how the enchantment works, I think? The Dark Lord is satisfied with the information I have passed him on the Order. It led, as perhaps you have guessed, to the recent capture and murder of Emmeline Vance, and it certainly helped dispose of Sirius Black, though I give you full credit for finishing him off."

He inclined his head and toasted her. Her expression did not soften.

"You are avoiding my last question, Snape. Harry Potter. You could have killed him at any point in the past five years. You have not done it. Why?"

"Have you discussed this matter with the Dark Lord?" asked Snape.

"He . . . lately, we . . . I am asking you, Snape!"

"If I had murdered Harry Potter, the Dark Lord could not have used his blood to regenerate, making him invincible —"

"You claim you foresaw his use of the boy!" she jeered.

"I do not claim it; I had no idea of his plans; I have already confessed that I thought the Dark Lord dead. I am merely trying to explain why the Dark Lord is not sorry that Potter survived, at least until a year ago. . . ."

"But why did you keep him alive?"

"Have you not understood me? It was only Dumbledore's protection that was keeping me out of Azkaban! Do you disagree that murdering his favorite student might have turned him against me? But there was more to it than that. I should remind you that when Potter first arrived at Hogwarts there were still many stories circulating about him, rumors that he himself was a great Dark wizard, which was how he had survived the Dark Lord's attack. Indeed, many of the Dark Lord's old followers thought Potter might be a standard around which we could all rally once more. I was curious, I admit it, and not at all inclined to murder him the moment he set foot in the castle.

"Of course, it became apparent to me very quickly that he had no extraordinary talent at all. He has fought his way out of a number of tight corners by a simple combination of sheer luck and more talented friends. He is mediocre to the last degree, though as obnoxious and self-satisfied as was his father before him. I have done my utmost to have him thrown out of Hogwarts, where I believe he scarcely belongs, but kill him, or allow him to be killed in front of me? I would have been a fool to risk it with Dumbledore close at hand."

"And through all this we are supposed to believe Dumbledore has never suspected you?" asked Bellatrix. "He has no idea of your true allegiance, he trusts you implicitly still?"

"I have played my part well," said Snape. "And you overlook Dumbledore's greatest weakness: He has to believe the best of people. I spun him a tale of deepest remorse when I joined his staff, fresh from my Death Eater days, and he embraced me with open arms — though, as I say, never allowing me nearer the Dark Arts than he could help. Dumbledore has been a great wizard — oh yes, he has," (for Bellatrix had made a scathing noise), "the Dark Lord acknowledges it. I am pleased to say, however, that Dumbledore is growing old. The duel with the Dark Lord last month shook him. He has since sustained a serious injury because his reactions are slower than they once were. But through all these years, he has never stopped trusting Severus Snape, and therein lies my great value to the Dark Lord."

Bellatrix still looked unhappy, though she appeared unsure how best to attack Snape next. Taking advantage of her silence, Snape turned to her sister.

"Now . . . you came to ask me for help, Narcissa?"

Narcissa looked up at him, her face eloquent with despair.

"Yes, Severus. I — I think you are the only one who can help me, I have nowhere else to turn. Lucius is in jail and . . ."

She closed her eyes and two large tears seeped from beneath her eyelids.

"The Dark Lord has forbidden me to speak of it," Narcissa continued, her eyes still closed. "He wishes none to know of the plan. It is . . . very secret. But —"

"If he has forbidden it, you ought not to speak," said Snape at once. "The Dark Lord's word is law."

Narcissa gasped as though he had doused her with cold water. Bellatrix looked satisfied for the first time since she had entered the house.

"There!" she said triumphantly to her sister. "Even Snape says so: You were told not to talk, so hold your silence!"

But Snape had gotten to his feet and strode to the small window, peered through the curtains at the deserted street, then closed them again with a jerk. He turned around to face Narcissa, frowning.

"It so happens that I know of the plan," he said in a low voice. "I am one of the few the Dark Lord has told. Nevertheless, had I not been in on the secret, Narcissa, you would have been guilty of great treachery to the Dark Lord."

"I thought you must know about it!" said Narcissa, breathing more freely. "He trusts you so, Severus. . . ."

"You know about the plan?" said Bellatrix, her fleeting expression of satisfaction replaced by a look of outrage. "*You* know?"

"Certainly," said Snape. "But what help do you require, Narcissa? If you are imagining I can persuade the Dark Lord to change his mind, I am afraid there is no hope, none at all."

"Severus," she whispered, tears sliding down her pale cheeks. "My son . . . my only son . . ."

"Draco should be proud," said Bellatrix indifferently. "The Dark Lord is granting him a great honor. And I will say this for Draco: He isn't shrinking away from his duty, he seems glad of a chance to prove himself, excited at the prospect —"

Narcissa began to cry in earnest, gazing beseechingly all the while at Snape.

"That's because he is sixteen and has no idea what lies in store! Why, Severus? Why my son? It is too dangerous! This is vengeance for Lucius's mistake, I know it!"

Snape said nothing. He looked away from the sight of her tears as though they were indecent, but he could not pretend not to hear her.

"That's why he's chosen Draco, isn't it?" she persisted. "To punish Lucius?"

"If Draco succeeds," said Snape, still looking away from her, "he will be honored above all others."

"But he won't succeed!" sobbed Narcissa. "How can he, when the Dark Lord himself — ?"

Bellatrix gasped; Narcissa seemed to lose her nerve.

"I only meant . . . that nobody has yet succeeded. . . . Severus . . . please . . . You are, you have always been, Draco's favorite teacher. . . . You are Lucius's old friend. . . . I beg you. . . . You are the Dark Lord's favorite, his most trusted advisor. . . . Will you speak to him, persuade him — ?"

"The Dark Lord will not be persuaded, and I am not stupid enough to attempt it," said Snape flatly. "I cannot pretend that the Dark Lord is not angry with Lucius. Lucius was supposed to be in charge. He got himself captured, along with how many others, and failed to retrieve the prophecy into the bargain. Yes, the Dark Lord is angry, Narcissa, very angry indeed."

"Then I am right, he has chosen Draco in revenge!" choked Narcissa. "He does not mean him to succeed, he wants him to be killed trying!"

When Snape said nothing, Narcissa seemed to lose what little self-restraint she still possessed. Standing up, she staggered to Snape and seized the front of his robes. Her face close to his, her tears falling onto his chest, she gasped, "You could do it. *You* could do it instead of Draco, Severus. You would succeed, of course you would, and he would reward you beyond all of us —"

Snape caught hold of her wrists and removed her clutching hands. Looking down into her tearstained face, he said slowly, "He intends me to do it in the end, I think. But he is determined that Draco should try first. You see, in the unlikely event that Draco succeeds, I shall be able to remain at Hogwarts a little longer, fulfilling my useful role as spy."

"In other words, it doesn't matter to him if Draco is killed!"

"The Dark Lord is very angry," repeated Snape quietly. "He failed to hear the prophecy. You know as well as I do, Narcissa, that he does not forgive easily."

She crumpled, falling at his feet, sobbing and moaning on the floor.

"My only son . . . my only son . . ."

"You should be proud!" said Bellatrix ruthlessly. "If I had sons, I would be glad to give them up to the service of the Dark Lord!"

Narcissa gave a little scream of despair and clutched at her long blonde hair. Snape stooped, seized her by the arms, lifted her up, and steered her back onto the sofa. He then poured her more wine and forced the glass into her hand.

"Narcissa, that's enough. Drink this. Listen to me."

She quieted a little; slopping wine down herself, she took a shaky sip.

"It might be possible . . . for me to help Draco."

She sat up, her face paper-white, her eyes huge.

"Severus — oh, Severus — you would help him? Would you look after him, see he comes to no harm?"

"I can try."

She flung away her glass; it skidded across the table as she slid off the sofa into a kneeling position at Snape's feet, seized his hand in both of hers, and pressed her lips to it.

"If you are there to protect him . . . Severus, will you swear it? Will you make the Unbreakable Vow?"

"The Unbreakable Vow?"

Snape's expression was blank, unreadable. Bellatrix, however, let out a cackle of triumphant laughter.

"Aren't you listening, Narcissa? Oh, he'll *try*, I'm sure. . . . The usual empty words, the usual slithering out of action . . . oh, on the Dark Lord's orders, of course!"

Snape did not look at Bellatrix. His black eyes were fixed upon Narcissa's tear-filled blue ones as she continued to clutch his hand.

"Certainly, Narcissa, I shall make the Unbreakable Vow," he said quietly. "Perhaps your sister will consent to be our Bonder."

Bellatrix's mouth fell open. Snape lowered himself so that he was kneeling opposite Narcissa. Beneath Bellatrix's astonished gaze, they grasped right hands.

"You will need your wand, Bellatrix," said Snape coldly.

She drew it, still looking astonished.

"And you will need to move a little closer," he said.

She stepped forward so that she stood over them, and placed the tip of her wand on their linked hands.

Narcissa spoke.

"Will you, Severus, watch over my son, Draco, as he attempts to fulfill the Dark Lord's wishes?"

"I will," said Snape.

A thin tongue of brilliant flame issued from the wand and wound its way around their hands like a red-hot wire.

"And will you, to the best of your ability, protect him from harm?"

"I will," said Snape.

A second tongue of flame shot from the wand and interlinked with the first, making a fine, glowing chain.

"And, should it prove necessary . . . if it seems Draco will fail . . ." whispered Narcissa (Snape's hand twitched within hers, but he did not draw away), "will you carry out the deed that the Dark Lord has ordered Draco to perform?"

There was a moment's silence. Bellatrix watched, her wand upon their clasped hands, her eyes wide.

"I will," said Snape.

Bellatrix's astounded face glowed red in the blaze of a third tongue of flame, which shot from the wand, twisted with the others, and bound itself thickly around their clasped hands, like a rope, like a fiery snake.

WILL AND WON'T

Harry Potter was snoring loudly. He had been sitting in a chair beside his bedroom window for the best part of four hours, staring out at the darkening street, and had finally fallen asleep with one side of his face pressed against the cold windowpane, his glasses askew and his mouth wide open. The misty fug his breath had left on the window sparkled in the orange glare of the streetlamp outside, and the artificial light drained his face of all color, so that he looked ghostly beneath his shock of untidy black hair.

The room was strewn with various possessions and a good smattering of rubbish. Owl feathers, apple cores, and sweet wrappers littered the floor, a number of spellbooks lay higgledy-piggledy among the tangled robes on his bed, and a mess of newspapers sat in a puddle of light on his desk. The headline of one blared:

HARRY POTTER: THE CHOSEN ONE?

Rumors continue to fly about the mysterious recent disturbance at the Ministry of Magic, during which He-Who-Must-Not-Be-Named was sighted once more.

"We're not allowed to talk about it, don't ask me anything," said one agitated Obliviator, who refused to give his name as he left the Ministry last night.

Nevertheless, highly placed sources within the Ministry have confirmed that the disturbance centered on the fabled Hall of Prophecy.

Though Ministry spokeswizards have hitherto refused even to confirm the existence of such a place, a growing number of the Wizarding community believe that the Death Eaters now serving sentences in Azkaban for trespass and attempted theft were attempting to steal a prophecy. The nature of that prophecy is unknown, although speculation is rife that it concerns Harry Potter, the only person ever known to have survived the Killing Curse, and who is also known to have been at the Ministry on the night in question. Some are going so far as to call Potter "the Chosen One," believing that the prophecy names him as the only one who will be able to rid us of He-Who-Must-Not-Be-Named.

The current whereabouts of the prophecy, if it exists, are unknown, although (*ctd. page 2, column 5*)

A second newspaper lay beside the first. This one bore the headline:

SCRIMGEOUR SUCCEEDS FUDGE

Most of this front page was taken up with a large black-and-white picture of a man with a lionlike mane of thick hair and a rather ravaged face. The picture was moving — the man was waving at the ceiling.

> Rufus Scrimgeour, previously Head of the Auror office in the Department of Magical Law Enforcement, has succeeded Cornelius Fudge as Minister of Magic. The appointment has largely been greeted with enthusiasm by the Wizarding community, though rumors of a rift between the new Minister and Albus Dumbledore, newly reinstated Chief Warlock of the Wizengamot, surfaced within hours of Scrimgeour taking office.
>
> Scrimgeour's representatives admitted that he had met with Dumbledore at once upon taking possession of the top job, but refused to comment on the topics under discussion. Albus Dumbledore is known to (*ctd. page 3, column 2*)

To the left of this paper sat another, which had been folded so that a story bearing the title MINISTRY GUARANTEES STUDENTS' SAFETY was visible.

Newly appointed Minister of Magic, Rufus Scrimgeour, spoke today of the tough new measures taken by his Ministry to ensure the safety of students returning to Hogwarts School of Witchcraft and Wizardry this autumn.

"For obvious reasons, the Ministry will not be going into detail about its stringent new security plans," said the Minister, although an insider confirmed that measures include defensive spells and charms, a complex array of countercurses, and a small task force of Aurors dedicated solely to the protection of Hogwarts School.

Most seem reassured by the new Minister's tough stand on student safety. Said Mrs. Augusta Longbottom, "My grandson, Neville — a good friend of Harry Potter's, incidentally, who fought the Death Eaters alongside him at the Ministry in June and —

But the rest of this story was obscured by the large birdcage standing on top of it. Inside it was a magnificent snowy owl. Her amber eyes surveyed the room imperiously, her head swiveling occasionally to gaze at her snoring master. Once or twice she clicked her beak impatiently, but Harry was too deeply asleep to hear her.

A large trunk stood in the very middle of the room. Its lid was open; it looked expectant; yet it was almost empty but for a residue of old underwear, sweets, empty ink bottles, and broken quills that coated the very bottom. Nearby, on the floor, lay a purple leaflet emblazoned with the words:

——— ISSUED ON BEHALF OF ———

The Ministry of Magic

PROTECTING YOUR HOME AND FAMILY
AGAINST DARK FORCES

The Wizarding community is currently under threat from an organization calling itself the Death Eaters. Observing the following simple security guidelines will help protect you, your family, and your home from attack.

1. You are advised not to leave the house alone.
2. Particular care should be taken during the hours of darkness. Wherever possible, arrange to complete journeys before night has fallen.
3. Review the security arrangements around your house, making sure that all family members are aware of emergency measures such as Shield and Disillusionment Charms, and, in the case of underage family members, Side-Along-Apparition.
4. Agree on security questions with close friends and family so as to detect Death Eaters masquerading as others by use of the Polyjuice Potion (see page 2).
5. Should you feel that a family member, colleague, friend, or neighbor is acting in a strange manner, contact the Magical Law Enforcement Squad at once. They may have been put under the Imperius Curse (see page 4).

6. Should the Dark Mark appear over any dwelling place or other building, DO NOT ENTER, but contact the Auror office immediately.
7. Unconfirmed sightings suggest that the Death Eaters *may* now be using Inferi (see page 10). Any sighting of an Inferius, or encounter with same, should be reported to the Ministry IMMEDIATELY.

Harry grunted in his sleep and his face slid down the window an inch or so, making his glasses still more lopsided, but he did not wake up. An alarm clock, repaired by Harry several years ago, ticked loudly on the sill, showing one minute to eleven. Beside it, held in place by Harry's relaxed hand, was a piece of parchment covered in thin, slanting writing. Harry had read this letter so often since its arrival three days ago that although it had been delivered in a tightly furled scroll, it now lay quite flat.

Dear Harry,

If it is convenient to you, I shall call at number four, Privet Drive this coming Friday at eleven P.M. to escort you to the Burrow, where you have been invited to spend the remainder of your school holidays.

If you are agreeable, I should also be glad of your assistance in a matter to which I hope to attend on the way to the Burrow. I shall explain this more fully when I see you.

Kindly send your answer by return of this owl. Hoping to see you this Friday,

I am, yours most sincerely,

Albus Dumbledore

Though he already knew it by heart, Harry had been stealing glances at this missive every few minutes since seven o'clock that evening, when he had first taken up his position beside his bedroom window, which had a reasonable view of both ends of Privet Drive. He knew it was pointless to keep rereading Dumbledore's words; Harry had sent back his "yes" with the delivering owl, as requested, and all he could do now was wait: Either Dumbledore was going to come, or he was not.

But Harry had not packed. It just seemed too good to be true that he was going to be rescued from the Dursleys after a mere fortnight of their company. He could not shrug off the feeling that something was going to go wrong — his reply to Dumbledore's letter might have gone astray; Dumbledore could be prevented from collecting him; the letter might turn out not to be from Dumbledore at all, but a trick or joke or trap. Harry had not been able to face packing and then being let down and having to unpack again. The only gesture he had made to the possibility of a journey was to shut his snowy owl, Hedwig, safely in her cage.

The minute hand on the alarm clock reached the number twelve and, at that precise moment, the streetlamp outside the window went out.

Harry awoke as though the sudden darkness were an alarm. Hastily straightening his glasses and unsticking his cheek from the glass, he pressed his nose against the window instead and squinted down at the pavement. A tall figure in a long, billowing cloak was walking up the garden path.

Harry jumped up as though he had received an electric shock, knocked over his chair, and started snatching anything and everything within reach from the floor and throwing it into the trunk. Even as he lobbed a set of robes, two spellbooks, and a packet of crisps across the room, the doorbell rang. Downstairs in the living room his Uncle Vernon shouted, "Who the blazes is calling at this time of night?"

Harry froze with a brass telescope in one hand and a pair of trainers in the other. He had completely forgotten to warn the Dursleys that Dumbledore might be coming. Feeling both panicky and close to laughter, he clambered over the trunk and wrenched open his bedroom door in time to hear a deep voice say, "Good evening. You must be Mr. Dursley. I daresay Harry has told you I would be coming for him?"

Harry ran down the stairs two at a time, coming to an abrupt halt several steps from the bottom, as long experience had taught him to remain out of arm's reach of his uncle whenever possible. There in the doorway stood a tall, thin man with waist-length silver hair and beard. Half-moon spectacles were perched on his crooked nose, and he was wearing a long black traveling cloak and a pointed hat. Vernon Dursley, whose mustache was quite as bushy as Dumbledore's, though black, and who was wearing a puce dressing gown, was staring at the visitor as though he could not believe his tiny eyes.

"Judging by your look of stunned disbelief, Harry did *not* warn you that I was coming," said Dumbledore pleasantly. "However, let us assume that you have invited me warmly into your house. It is unwise to linger overlong on doorsteps in these troubled times."

He stepped smartly over the threshold and closed the front door behind him.

"It is a long time since my last visit," said Dumbledore, peering down his crooked nose at Uncle Vernon. "I must say, your agapanthus are flourishing."

Vernon Dursley said nothing at all. Harry did not doubt that speech would return to him, and soon — the vein pulsing in his uncle's temple was reaching danger point — but something about Dumbledore seemed to have robbed him temporarily of breath. It might have been the blatant wizardishness of his appearance, but it might, too, have been that even Uncle Vernon could sense that here was a man whom it would be very difficult to bully.

"Ah, good evening Harry," said Dumbledore, looking up at him through his half-moon glasses with a most satisfied expression. "Excellent, excellent."

These words seemed to rouse Uncle Vernon. It was clear that as far as he was concerned, any man who could look at Harry and say "excellent" was a man with whom he could never see eye to eye.

"I don't mean to be rude —" he began, in a tone that threatened rudeness in every syllable.

"— yet, sadly, accidental rudeness occurs alarmingly often," Dumbledore finished the sentence gravely. "Best to say nothing at all, my dear man. Ah, and this must be Petunia."

The kitchen door had opened, and there stood Harry's aunt, wearing rubber gloves and a housecoat over her nightdress, clearly halfway through her usual pre-bedtime wipe-down of all the kitchen surfaces. Her rather horsey face registered nothing but shock.

"Albus Dumbledore," said Dumbledore, when Uncle Vernon failed to effect an introduction. "We have corresponded, of course." Harry thought this an odd way of reminding Aunt Petunia that he had once sent her an exploding letter, but Aunt Petunia did not challenge the term. "And this must be your son, Dudley?"

Dudley had that moment peered round the living room door. His large, blond head rising out of the stripy collar of his pajamas looked oddly disembodied, his mouth gaping in astonishment and fear. Dumbledore waited a moment or two, apparently to see whether any of the Dursleys were going to say anything, but as the silence stretched on he smiled.

"Shall we assume that you have invited me into your sitting room?"

Dudley scrambled out of the way as Dumbledore passed him. Harry, still clutching the telescope and trainers, jumped the last few stairs and followed Dumbledore, who had settled himself in the armchair nearest the fire and was taking in the surroundings with an expression of benign interest. He looked quite extraordinarily out of place.

"Aren't — aren't we leaving, sir?" Harry asked anxiously.

"Yes, indeed we are, but there are a few matters we need to discuss first," said Dumbledore. "And I would prefer not to do so in the open. We shall trespass upon your aunt and uncle's hospitality only a little longer."

"You will, will you?"

Vernon Dursley had entered the room, Petunia at his shoulder, and Dudley skulking behind them both.

"Yes," said Dumbledore simply, "I shall."

He drew his wand so rapidly that Harry barely saw it; with a casual flick, the sofa zoomed forward and knocked the knees out from under all three of the Dursleys so that they collapsed upon it in a heap. Another flick of the wand and the sofa zoomed back to its original position.

"We may as well be comfortable," said Dumbledore pleasantly.

As he replaced his wand in his pocket, Harry saw that his hand was blackened and shriveled; it looked as though his flesh had been burned away.

"Sir — what happened to your — ?"

"Later, Harry," said Dumbledore. "Please sit down."

Harry took the remaining armchair, choosing not to look at the Dursleys, who seemed stunned into silence.

"I would assume that you were going to offer me refreshment," Dumbledore said to Uncle Vernon, "but the evidence so far suggests that that would be optimistic to the point of foolishness."

A third twitch of the wand, and a dusty bottle and five glasses appeared in midair. The bottle tipped and poured a generous measure of honey-colored liquid into each of the glasses, which then floated to each person in the room.

"Madam Rosmerta's finest oak-matured mead," said Dumbledore, raising his glass to Harry, who caught hold of his own and sipped. He had never tasted anything like it before, but enjoyed it immensely. The Dursleys, after quick, scared looks at one another, tried to ignore their glasses completely, a difficult feat, as they were nudging them gently on the sides of their heads. Harry could not suppress a suspicion that Dumbledore was rather enjoying himself.

"Well, Harry," said Dumbledore, turning toward him, "a difficulty has arisen which I hope you will be able to solve for us. By *us*, I mean the Order of the Phoenix. But first of all I must tell you that

Sirius's will was discovered a week ago and that he left you everything he owned."

Over on the sofa, Uncle Vernon's head turned, but Harry did not look at him, nor could he think of anything to say except, "Oh. Right."

"This is, in the main, fairly straightforward," Dumbledore went on. "You add a reasonable amount of gold to your account at Gringotts, and you inherit all of Sirius's personal possessions. The slightly problematic part of the legacy —"

"His godfather's dead?" said Uncle Vernon loudly from the sofa. Dumbledore and Harry both turned to look at him. The glass of mead was now knocking quite insistently on the side of Vernon's head; he attempted to beat it away. "He's dead? His godfather?"

"Yes," said Dumbledore. He did not ask Harry why he had not confided in the Dursleys. "Our problem," he continued to Harry, as if there had been no interruption, "is that Sirius also left you number twelve, Grimmauld Place."

"He's been left a house?" said Uncle Vernon greedily, his small eyes narrowing, but nobody answered him.

"You can keep using it as headquarters," said Harry. "I don't care. You can have it, I don't really want it." Harry never wanted to set foot in number twelve, Grimmauld Place again if he could help it. He thought he would be haunted forever by the memory of Sirius prowling its dark musty rooms alone, imprisoned within the place he had wanted so desperately to leave.

"That is generous," said Dumbledore. "We have, however, vacated the building temporarily."

"Why?"

"Well," said Dumbledore, ignoring the mutterings of Uncle Vernon, who was now being rapped smartly over the head by the persistent glass of mead, "Black family tradition decreed that the house was handed down the direct line, to the next male with the name of 'Black.' Sirius was the very last of the line as his younger brother, Regulus, predeceased him and both were childless. While his will makes it perfectly plain that he wants you to have the house, it is nevertheless possible that some spell or enchantment has been set upon the place to ensure that it cannot be owned by anyone other than a pureblood."

A vivid image of the shrieking, spitting portrait of Sirius's mother that hung in the hall of number twelve, Grimmauld Place flashed into Harry's mind. "I bet there has," he said.

"Quite," said Dumbledore. "And if such an enchantment exists, then the ownership of the house is most likely to pass to the eldest of Sirius's living relatives, which would mean his cousin, Bellatrix Lestrange."

Without realizing what he was doing, Harry sprang to his feet; the telescope and trainers in his lap rolled across the floor. Bellatrix Lestrange, Sirius's killer, inherit his house?

"No," he said.

"Well, obviously we would prefer that she didn't get it either," said Dumbledore calmly. "The situation is fraught with complications. We do not know whether the enchantments we ourselves have placed upon it, for example, making it Unplottable, will hold now that ownership has passed from Sirius's hands. It might be that Bellatrix will arrive on the doorstep at any moment. Naturally we had to move out until such time as we have clarified the position."

"But how are you going to find out if I'm allowed to own it?"

"Fortunately," said Dumbledore, "there is a simple test."

He placed his empty glass on a small table beside his chair, but before he could do anything else, Uncle Vernon shouted, *"Will you get these ruddy things off us?"*

Harry looked around; all three of the Dursleys were cowering with their arms over their heads as their glasses bounced up and down on their skulls, their contents flying everywhere.

"Oh, I'm so sorry," said Dumbledore politely, and he raised his wand again. All three glasses vanished. "But it would have been better manners to drink it, you know."

It looked as though Uncle Vernon was bursting with any number of unpleasant retorts, but he merely shrank back into the cushions with Aunt Petunia and Dudley and said nothing, keeping his small piggy eyes on Dumbledore's wand.

"You see," Dumbledore said, turning back to Harry and again speaking as though Uncle Vernon had not uttered, "if you have indeed inherited the house, you have also inherited —"

He flicked his wand for a fifth time. There was a loud crack, and a house-elf appeared, with a snout for a nose, giant bat's ears, and enormous bloodshot eyes, crouching on the Dursleys' shag carpet and covered in grimy rags. Aunt Petunia let out a hair-raising shriek; nothing this filthy had entered her house in living memory. Dudley drew his large, bare, pink feet off the floor and sat with them raised almost above his head, as though he thought the creature might run up his pajama trousers, and Uncle Vernon bellowed, "What the *hell* is that?"

"Kreacher," finished Dumbledore.

"Kreacher won't, Kreacher won't, Kreacher won't!" croaked the house-elf, quite as loudly as Uncle Vernon, stamping his long, gnarled feet and pulling his ears. "Kreacher belongs to Miss Bellatrix, oh yes, Kreacher belongs to the Blacks, Kreacher wants his new mistress, Kreacher won't go to the Potter brat, Kreacher won't, won't, won't —"

"As you can see, Harry," said Dumbledore loudly, over Kreacher's continued croaks of "won't, won't, won't," "Kreacher is showing a certain reluctance to pass into your ownership."

"I don't care," said Harry again, looking with disgust at the writhing, stamping house-elf. "I don't want him."

"Won't, won't, won't, won't —"

"You would prefer him to pass into the ownership of Bellatrix Lestrange? Bearing in mind that he has lived at the headquarters of the Order of the Phoenix for the past year?"

"Won't, won't, won't, won't —"

Harry stared at Dumbledore. He knew that Kreacher could not be permitted to go and live with Bellatrix Lestrange, but the idea of owning him, of having responsibility for the creature that had betrayed Sirius, was repugnant.

"Give him an order," said Dumbledore. "If he has passed into your ownership, he will have to obey. If not, then we shall have to think of some other means of keeping him from his rightful mistress."

"Won't, won't, won't, WON'T!"

Kreacher's voice had risen to a scream. Harry could think of nothing to say, except, "Kreacher, shut up!"

It looked for a moment as though Kreacher was going to choke. He grabbed his throat, his mouth still working furiously, his eyes bulging. After a few seconds of frantic gulping, he threw himself face forward onto the carpet (Aunt Petunia whimpered) and beat the floor with his hands and feet, giving himself over to a violent, but entirely silent, tantrum.

"Well, that simplifies matters," said Dumbledore cheerfully. "It seems that Sirius knew what he was doing. You are the rightful owner of number twelve, Grimmauld Place and of Kreacher."

"Do I — do I have to keep him with me?" Harry asked, aghast, as Kreacher thrashed around at his feet.

"Not if you don't want to," said Dumbledore. "If I might make a suggestion, you could send him to Hogwarts to work in the kitchen there. In that way, the other house-elves could keep an eye on him."

"Yeah," said Harry in relief, "yeah, I'll do that. Er — Kreacher — I want you to go to Hogwarts and work in the kitchens there with the other house-elves."

Kreacher, who was now lying flat on his back with his arms and legs in the air, gave Harry one upside-down look of deepest loathing and, with another loud crack, vanished.

"Good," said Dumbledore. "There is also the matter of the hippogriff, Buckbeak. Hagrid has been looking after him since Sirius died, but Buckbeak is yours now, so if you would prefer to make different arrangements —"

"No," said Harry at once, "he can stay with Hagrid. I think Buckbeak would prefer that."

"Hagrid will be delighted," said Dumbledore, smiling. "He was thrilled to see Buckbeak again. Incidentally, we have decided, in the interests of Buckbeak's safety, to rechristen him 'Witherwings' for the time being, though I doubt that the Ministry would ever guess he is the hippogriff they once sentenced to death. Now, Harry, is your trunk packed?"

"Erm . . ."

"Doubtful that I would turn up?" Dumbledore suggested shrewdly.

"I'll just go and — er — finish off," said Harry hastily, hurrying to pick up his fallen telescope and trainers.

It took him a little over ten minutes to track down everything he needed; at last he had managed to extract his Invisibility Cloak from under the bed, screwed the top back on his jar of color-change ink, and forced the lid of his trunk shut on his cauldron. Then, heaving his trunk in one hand and holding Hedwig's cage in the other, he made his way back downstairs.

He was disappointed to discover that Dumbledore was not waiting in the hall, which meant that he had to return to the living room.

Nobody was talking. Dumbledore was humming quietly, apparently quite at his ease, but the atmosphere was thicker than cold custard, and Harry did not dare look at the Dursleys as he said, "Professor — I'm ready now."

"Good," said Dumbledore. "Just one last thing, then." And he turned to speak to the Dursleys once more.

"As you will no doubt be aware, Harry comes of age in a year's time —"

"No," said Aunt Petunia, speaking for the first time since Dumbledore's arrival.

"I'm sorry?" said Dumbledore politely.

"No, he doesn't. He's a month younger than Dudley, and Dudders doesn't turn eighteen until the year after next."

"Ah," said Dumbledore pleasantly, "but in the Wizarding world, we come of age at seventeen."

Uncle Vernon muttered, "Preposterous," but Dumbledore ignored him.

"Now, as you already know, the wizard called Lord Voldemort has returned to this country. The Wizarding community is currently in a state of open warfare. Harry, whom Lord Voldemort has already attempted to kill on a number of occasions, is in even greater danger now than the day when I left him upon your doorstep fifteen years ago, with a letter explaining about his parents' murder and expressing the hope that you would care for him as though he were your own."

Dumbledore paused, and although his voice remained light and calm, and he gave no obvious sign of anger, Harry felt a kind of chill emanating from him and noticed that the Dursleys drew very slightly closer together.

"You did not do as I asked. You have never treated Harry as a son. He has known nothing but neglect and often cruelty at your hands. The best that can be said is that he has at least escaped the appalling damage you have inflicted upon the unfortunate boy sitting between you."

Both Aunt Petunia and Uncle Vernon looked around instinctively, as though expecting to see someone other than Dudley squeezed between them.

"Us — mistreat Dudders? What d'you — ?" began Uncle Vernon furiously, but Dumbledore raised his finger for silence, a silence which fell as though he had struck Uncle Vernon dumb.

"The magic I evoked fifteen years ago means that Harry has powerful protection while he can still call this house 'home.' However miserable he has been here, however unwelcome, however badly treated, you have at least, grudgingly, allowed him houseroom. This magic will cease to operate the moment that Harry turns seventeen; in other words, at the moment he becomes a man. I ask only this: that you allow Harry to return, once more, to this house, before his seventeenth birthday, which will ensure that the protection continues until that time."

None of the Dursleys said anything. Dudley was frowning slightly, as though he was still trying to work out when he had ever been mistreated. Uncle Vernon looked as though he had something stuck in his throat; Aunt Petunia, however, was oddly flushed.

"Well, Harry . . . time for us to be off," said Dumbledore at last, standing up and straightening his long black cloak. "Until we meet again," he said to the Dursleys, who looked as though that moment could wait forever as far as they were concerned, and after doffing his hat, he swept from the room.

"Bye," said Harry hastily to the Dursleys, and followed Dumbledore, who paused beside Harry's trunk, upon which Hedwig's cage was perched.

"We do not want to be encumbered by these just now," he said, pulling out his wand again. "I shall send them to the Burrow to await us there. However, I would like you to bring your Invisibility Cloak . . . just in case."

Harry extracted his cloak from his trunk with some difficulty, trying not to show Dumbledore the mess within. When he had stuffed it into an inside pocket of his jacket, Dumbledore waved his wand and the trunk, cage, and Hedwig vanished. Dumbledore then waved his wand again, and the front door opened onto cool, misty darkness.

"And now, Harry, let us step out into the night and pursue that flighty temptress, adventure."

CHAPTER FOUR

HORACE SLUGHORN

Despite the fact that he had spent every waking moment of the past few days hoping desperately that Dumbledore would indeed come to fetch him, Harry felt distinctly awkward as they set off down Privet Drive together. He had never had a proper conversation with the headmaster outside of Hogwarts before; there was usually a desk between them. The memory of their last face-to-face encounter kept intruding too, and it rather heightened Harry's sense of embarrassment; he had shouted a lot on that occasion, not to mention done his best to smash several of Dumbledore's most prized possessions.

Dumbledore, however, seemed completely relaxed.

"Keep your wand at the ready, Harry," he said brightly.

"But I thought I'm not allowed to use magic outside school, sir?"

"If there is an attack," said Dumbledore, "I give you permission to use any counterjinx or curse that might occur to you. However, I do not think you need worry about being attacked tonight."

"Why not, sir?"

"You are with me," said Dumbledore simply. "This will do, Harry."

He came to an abrupt halt at the end of Privet Drive.

"You have not, of course, passed your Apparition Test," he said.

"No," said Harry. "I thought you had to be seventeen?"

"You do," said Dumbledore. "So you will need to hold on to my arm very tightly. My left, if you don't mind — as you have noticed, my wand arm is a little fragile at the moment."

Harry gripped Dumbledore's proffered forearm.

"Very good," said Dumbledore. "Well, here we go."

Harry felt Dumbledore's arm twist away from him and redoubled his grip; the next thing he knew, everything went black; he was being pressed very hard from all directions; he could not breathe, there were iron bands tightening around his chest; his eyeballs were being forced back into his head; his eardrums were being pushed deeper into his skull and then —

He gulped great lungfuls of cold night air and opened his streaming eyes. He felt as though he had just been forced through a very tight rubber tube. It was a few seconds before he realized that Privet Drive had vanished. He and Dumbledore were now standing in what appeared to be a deserted village square, in the center of which stood an old war memorial and a few benches. His comprehension catching up with his senses, Harry realized that he had just Apparated for the first time in his life.

"Are you all right?" asked Dumbledore, looking down at him solicitously. "The sensation does take some getting used to."

"I'm fine," said Harry, rubbing his ears, which felt as though they had left Privet Drive rather reluctantly. "But I think I might prefer brooms. . . ."

Dumbledore smiled, drew his traveling cloak a little more tightly around his neck, and said, "This way."

He set off at a brisk pace, past an empty inn and a few houses. According to a clock on a nearby church, it was almost midnight.

"So tell me, Harry," said Dumbledore. "Your scar . . . has it been hurting at all?"

Harry raised a hand unconsciously to his forehead and rubbed the lightning-shaped mark.

"No," he said, "and I've been wondering about that. I thought it would be burning all the time now Voldemort's getting so powerful again."

He glanced up at Dumbledore and saw that he was wearing a satisfied expression.

"I, on the other hand, thought otherwise," said Dumbledore. "Lord Voldemort has finally realized the dangerous access to his thoughts and feelings you have been enjoying. It appears that he is now employing Occlumency against you."

"Well, I'm not complaining," said Harry, who missed neither the disturbing dreams nor the startling flashes of insight into Voldemort's mind.

They turned a corner, passing a telephone box and a bus shelter. Harry looked sideways at Dumbledore again. "Professor?"

"Harry?"

"Er — where exactly are we?"

"This, Harry, is the charming village of Budleigh Babberton."

"And what are we doing here?"

"Ah yes, of course, I haven't told you," said Dumbledore. "Well, I have lost count of the number of times I have said this in recent years, but we are, once again, one member of staff short. We are here to persuade an old colleague of mine to come out of retirement and return to Hogwarts."

"How can I help with that, sir?"

"Oh, I think we'll find a use for you," said Dumbledore vaguely. "Left here, Harry."

They proceeded up a steep, narrow street lined with houses. All the windows were dark. The odd chill that had lain over Privet Drive for two weeks persisted here too. Thinking of dementors, Harry cast a look over his shoulder and grasped his wand reassuringly in his pocket.

"Professor, why couldn't we just Apparate directly into your old colleague's house?"

"Because it would be quite as rude as kicking down the front door," said Dumbledore. "Courtesy dictates that we offer fellow wizards the opportunity of denying us entry. In any case, most Wizarding dwellings are magically protected from unwanted Apparators. At Hogwarts, for instance —"

"— you can't Apparate anywhere inside the buildings or grounds," said Harry quickly. "Hermione Granger told me."

"And she is quite right. We turn left again."

The church clock chimed midnight behind them. Harry wondered why Dumbledore did not consider it rude to call on his old colleague so late, but now that conversation had been established, he had more pressing questions to ask.

"Sir, I saw in the *Daily Prophet* that Fudge has been sacked. . . ."

"Correct," said Dumbledore, now turning up a steep side street.

"He has been replaced, as I am sure you also saw, by Rufus Scrimgeour, who used to be Head of the Auror office."

"Is he . . . Do you think he's good?" asked Harry.

"An interesting question," said Dumbledore. "He is able, certainly. A more decisive and forceful personality than Cornelius."

"Yes, but I meant —"

"I know what you meant. Rufus is a man of action and, having fought Dark wizards for most of his working life, does not underestimate Lord Voldemort."

Harry waited, but Dumbledore did not say anything about the disagreement with Scrimgeour that the *Daily Prophet* had reported, and he did not have the nerve to pursue the subject, so he changed it. "And . . . sir . . . I saw about Madam Bones."

"Yes," said Dumbledore quietly. "A terrible loss. She was a great witch. Just up here, I think — ouch."

He had pointed with his injured hand.

"Professor, what happened to your — ?"

"I have no time to explain now," said Dumbledore. "It is a thrilling tale, I wish to do it justice."

He smiled at Harry, who understood that he was not being snubbed, and that he had permission to keep asking questions.

"Sir — I got a Ministry of Magic leaflet by owl, about security measures we should all take against the Death Eaters. . . ."

"Yes, I received one myself," said Dumbledore, still smiling. "Did you find it useful?"

"Not really."

"No, I thought not. You have not asked me, for instance, what is my favorite flavor of jam, to check that I am indeed Professor Dumbledore and not an impostor."

"I didn't . . ." Harry began, not entirely sure whether he was being reprimanded or not.

"For future reference, Harry, it is raspberry . . . although of course, if I were a Death Eater, I would have been sure to research my own jam preferences before impersonating myself."

"Er . . . right," said Harry. "Well, on that leaflet, it said something about Inferi. What exactly are they? The leaflet wasn't very clear."

"They are corpses," said Dumbledore calmly. "Dead bodies that have been bewitched to do a Dark wizard's bidding. Inferi have not been seen for a long time, however, not since Voldemort was last powerful. . . . He killed enough people to make an army of them, of course. This is the place, Harry, just here. . . ."

They were nearing a small, neat stone house set in its own garden. Harry was too busy digesting the horrible idea of Inferi to have much attention left for anything else, but as they reached the front gate, Dumbledore stopped dead and Harry walked into him.

"Oh dear. Oh dear, dear, dear."

Harry followed his gaze up the carefully tended front path and felt his heart sink. The front door was hanging off its hinges.

Dumbledore glanced up and down the street. It seemed quite deserted.

"Wand out and follow me, Harry," he said quietly.

He opened the gate and walked swiftly and silently up the garden path, Harry at his heels, then pushed the front door very slowly, his wand raised and at the ready.

"*Lumos.*"

Dumbledore's wand tip ignited, casting its light up a narrow hallway. To the left, another door stood open. Holding his illuminated wand aloft, Dumbledore walked into the sitting room with Harry right behind him.

A scene of total devastation met their eyes. A grandfather clock lay splintered at their feet, its face cracked, its pendulum lying a little farther away like a dropped sword. A piano was on its side, its keys strewn across the floor. The wreckage of a fallen chandelier glittered nearby. Cushions lay deflated, feathers oozing from slashes in their sides; fragments of glass and china lay like powder over everything. Dumbledore raised his wand even higher, so that its light was thrown upon the walls, where something darkly red and glutinous was spattered over the wallpaper. Harry's small intake of breath made Dumbledore look around.

"Not pretty, is it?" he said heavily. "Yes, something horrible has happened here."

Dumbledore moved carefully into the middle of the room, scrutinizing the wreckage at his feet. Harry followed, gazing around, half-scared of what he might see hidden behind the wreck of the piano or the overturned sofa, but there was no sign of a body.

"Maybe there was a fight and — and they dragged him off, Professor?" Harry suggested, trying not to imagine how badly wounded a man would have to be to leave those stains spattered halfway up the walls.

"I don't think so," said Dumbledore quietly, peering behind an overstuffed armchair lying on its side.

"You mean he's — ?"

"Still here somewhere? Yes."

And without warning, Dumbledore swooped, plunging the tip of his wand into the seat of the overstuffed armchair, which yelled, "Ouch!"

"Good evening, Horace," said Dumbledore, straightening up again.

Harry's jaw dropped. Where a split second before there had been an armchair, there now crouched an enormously fat, bald, old man who was massaging his lower belly and squinting up at Dumbledore with an aggrieved and watery eye.

"There was no need to stick the wand in that hard," he said gruffly, clambering to his feet. "It hurt."

The wandlight sparkled on his shiny pate, his prominent eyes, his enormous, silver, walruslike mustache, and the highly polished buttons on the maroon velvet jacket he was wearing over a pair of lilac silk pajamas. The top of his head barely reached Dumbledore's chin.

"What gave it away?" he grunted as he staggered to his feet, still rubbing his lower belly. He seemed remarkably unabashed for a man who had just been discovered pretending to be an armchair.

"My dear Horace," said Dumbledore, looking amused, "if the Death Eaters really had come to call, the Dark Mark would have been set over the house."

The wizard clapped a pudgy hand to his vast forehead.

"The Dark Mark," he muttered. "Knew there was something . . . ah well. Wouldn't have had time anyway, I'd only just put the finishing touches to my upholstery when you entered the room."

He heaved a great sigh that made the ends of his mustache flutter.

"Would you like my assistance clearing up?" asked Dumbledore politely.

"Please," said the other.

They stood back to back, the tall thin wizard and the short round one, and waved their wands in one identical sweeping motion.

The furniture flew back to its original places; ornaments reformed in midair, feathers zoomed into their cushions; torn books repaired themselves as they landed upon their shelves; oil lanterns soared onto side tables and reignited; a vast collection of splintered silver picture frames flew glittering across the room and alighted, whole and untarnished, upon a desk; rips, cracks, and holes healed everywhere, and the walls wiped themselves clean.

"What kind of blood was that, incidentally?" asked Dumbledore loudly over the chiming of the newly unsmashed grandfather clock.

"On the walls? Dragon," shouted the wizard called Horace, as, with a deafening grinding and tinkling, the chandelier screwed itself back into the ceiling.

There was a final *plunk* from the piano, and silence.

"Yes, dragon," repeated the wizard conversationally. "My last bottle, and prices are sky-high at the moment. Still, it might be reusable."

He stumped over to a small crystal bottle standing on top of a sideboard and held it up to the light, examining the thick liquid within.

"Hmm. Bit dusty."

He set the bottle back on the sideboard and sighed. It was then that his gaze fell upon Harry.

"Oho," he said, his large round eyes flying to Harry's forehead and the lightning-shaped scar it bore. *"Oho!"*

"This," said Dumbledore, moving forward to make the intro-duction, "is Harry Potter. Harry, this is an old friend and colleague of mine, Horace Slughorn."

Slughorn turned on Dumbledore, his expression shrewd. "So that's how you thought you'd persuade me, is it? Well, the answer's no, Albus."

He pushed past Harry, his face turned resolutely away with the air of a man trying to resist temptation.

"I suppose we can have a drink, at least?" asked Dumbledore. "For old time's sake?"

Slughorn hesitated.

"All right then, one drink," he said ungraciously.

Dumbledore smiled at Harry and directed him toward a chair not unlike the one that Slughorn had so recently impersonated, which stood right beside the newly burning fire and a brightly glowing oil lamp. Harry took the seat with the distinct impression that Dumbledore, for some reason, wanted to keep him as visible as possible. Certainly when Slughorn, who had been busy with de-canters and glasses, turned to face the room again, his eyes fell im-mediately upon Harry.

"Hmpf," he said, looking away quickly as though frightened of hurting his eyes. "Here —" He gave a drink to Dumbledore, who had sat down without invitation, thrust the tray at Harry, and then sank into the cushions of the repaired sofa and a disgruntled si-lence. His legs were so short they did not touch the floor.

"Well, how have you been keeping, Horace?" Dumbledore asked.

"Not so well," said Slughorn at once. "Weak chest. Wheezy.

Rheumatism too. Can't move like I used to. Well, that's to be expected. Old age. Fatigue."

"And yet you must have moved fairly quickly to prepare such a welcome for us at such short notice," said Dumbledore. "You can't have had more than three minutes' warning?"

Slughorn said, half irritably, half proudly, "Two. Didn't hear my Intruder Charm go off, I was taking a bath. Still," he added sternly, seeming to pull himself back together again, "the fact remains that I'm an old man, Albus. A tired old man who's earned the right to a quiet life and a few creature comforts."

He certainly had those, thought Harry, looking around the room. It was stuffy and cluttered, yet nobody could say it was uncomfortable; there were soft chairs and footstools, drinks and books, boxes of chocolates and plump cushions. If Harry had not known who lived there, he would have guessed at a rich, fussy old lady.

"You're not yet as old as I am, Horace," said Dumbledore.

"Well, maybe you ought to think about retirement yourself," said Slughorn bluntly. His pale gooseberry eyes had found Dumbledore's injured hand. "Reactions not what they were, I see."

"You're quite right," said Dumbledore serenely, shaking back his sleeve to reveal the tips of those burned and blackened fingers; the sight of them made the back of Harry's neck prickle unpleasantly. "I am undoubtedly slower than I was. But on the other hand . . ."

He shrugged and spread his hands wide, as though to say that age had its compensations, and Harry noticed a ring on his uninjured hand that he had never seen Dumbledore wear before: It was large, rather clumsily made of what looked like gold, and was set with a heavy black stone that had cracked down the middle. Slughorn's eyes lingered for a moment on the ring too, and Harry saw a tiny frown momentarily crease his wide forehead.

"So, all these precautions against intruders, Horace . . . are they for the Death Eaters' benefit, or mine?" asked Dumbledore.

"What would the Death Eaters want with a poor broken-down old buffer like me?" demanded Slughorn.

"I imagine that they would want you to turn your considerable talents to coercion, torture, and murder," said Dumbledore. "Are you really telling me that they haven't come recruiting yet?"

Slughorn eyed Dumbledore balefully for a moment, then muttered, "I haven't given them the chance. I've been on the move for a year. Never stay in one place more than a week. Move from Muggle house to Muggle house — the owners of this place are on holiday in the Canary Islands — it's been very pleasant, I'll be sorry to leave. It's quite easy once you know how, one simple Freezing Charm on these absurd burglar alarms they use instead of Sneakoscopes and make sure the neighbors don't spot you bringing in the piano."

"Ingenious," said Dumbledore. "But it sounds a rather tiring existence for a broken-down old buffer in search of a quiet life. Now, if you were to return to Hogwarts —"

"If you're going to tell me my life would be more peaceful at that pestilential school, you can save your breath, Albus! I might have been in hiding, but some funny rumors have reached me since Dolores Umbridge left! If that's how you treat teachers these days —"

"Professor Umbridge ran afoul of our centaur herd," said Dumbledore. "I think you, Horace, would have known better than to stride into the forest and call a horde of angry centaurs 'filthy half-breeds.'"

"That's what she did, did she?" said Slughorn. "Idiotic woman. Never liked her."

Harry chuckled and both Dumbledore and Slughorn looked round at him.

"Sorry," Harry said hastily. "It's just — I didn't like her either."

Dumbledore stood up rather suddenly.

"Are you leaving?" asked Slughorn at once, looking hopeful.

"No, I was wondering whether I might use your bathroom," said Dumbledore.

"Oh," said Slughorn, clearly disappointed. "Second on the left down the hall."

Dumbledore strode from the room. Once the door had closed behind him, there was silence. After a few moments, Slughorn got to his feet but seemed uncertain what to do with himself. He shot a furtive look at Harry, then crossed to the fire and turned his back on it, warming his wide behind.

"Don't think I don't know why he's brought you," he said abruptly.

Harry merely looked at Slughorn. Slughorn's watery eyes slid over Harry's scar, this time taking in the rest of his face.

"You look very like your father."

"Yeah, I've been told," said Harry.

"Except for your eyes. You've got —"

"My mother's eyes, yeah." Harry had heard it so often he found it a bit wearing.

"Hmpf. Yes, well. You shouldn't have favorites as a teacher, of course, but she was one of mine. Your mother," Slughorn added, in answer to Harry's questioning look. "Lily Evans. One of the brightest I ever taught. Vivacious, you know. Charming girl. I used to tell her she ought to have been in my House. Very cheeky answers I used to get back too."

"Which was your House?"

"I was Head of Slytherin," said Slughorn. "Oh, now," he went on quickly, seeing the expression on Harry's face and wagging a stubby finger at him, "don't go holding that against me! You'll be Gryffindor like her, I suppose? Yes, it usually goes in families. Not always, though. Ever heard of Sirius Black? You must have done — been in the papers for the last couple of years — died a few weeks ago —"

It was as though an invisible hand had twisted Harry's intestines and held them tight.

"Well, anyway, he was a big pal of your father's at school. The whole Black family had been in my House, but Sirius ended up in Gryffindor! Shame — he was a talented boy. I got his brother, Regulus, when he came along, but I'd have liked the set."

He sounded like an enthusiastic collector who had been outbid at auction. Apparently lost in memories, he gazed at the opposite wall, turning idly on the spot to ensure an even heat on his backside.

"Your mother was Muggle-born, of course. Couldn't believe it when I found out. Thought she must have been pure-blood, she was so good."

"One of my best friends is Muggle-born," said Harry, "and she's the best in our year."

"Funny how that sometimes happens, isn't it?" said Slughorn.

"Not really," said Harry coldly.

Slughorn looked down at him in surprise. "You mustn't think I'm prejudiced!" he said. "No, no, no! Haven't I just said your mother was one of my all-time favorite students? And there was Dirk Cresswell in the year after her too — now Head of the Goblin Liaison Office, of course — another Muggle-born, a very gifted student, and still gives me excellent inside information on the goings-on at Gringotts!"

He bounced up and down a little, smiling in a self-satisfied way, and pointed at the many glittering photograph frames on the dresser, each peopled with tiny moving occupants.

"All ex-students, all signed. You'll notice Barnabas Cuffe, editor of the *Daily Prophet,* he's always interested to hear my take on the day's news. And Ambrosius Flume, of Honeydukes — a hamper every birthday, and all because I was able to give him an introduction to Ciceron Harkiss, who gave him his first job! And at the back — you'll see her if you just crane your neck — that's Gwenog Jones, who of course captains the Holyhead Harpies. . . . People are always astonished to hear I'm on first-name terms with the Harpies, and free tickets whenever I want them!"

This thought seemed to cheer him up enormously.

"And all these people know where to find you, to send you stuff?" asked Harry, who could not help wondering why the Death Eaters had not yet tracked down Slughorn if hampers of sweets, Quidditch tickets, and visitors craving his advice and opinions could find him.

The smile slid from Slughorn's face as quickly as the blood from his walls.

"Of course not," he said, looking down at Harry. "I have been out of touch with everybody for a year."

Harry had the impression that the words shocked Slughorn himself; he looked quite unsettled for a moment. Then he shrugged.

"Still . . . the prudent wizard keeps his head down in such times. All very well for Dumbledore to talk, but taking up a post at Hogwarts just now would be tantamount to declaring my public allegiance to the Order of the Phoenix! And while I'm sure they're very admirable and brave and all the rest of it, I don't personally fancy the mortality rate —"

"You don't have to join the Order to teach at Hogwarts," said Harry, who could not quite keep a note of derision out of his voice: It was hard to sympathize with Slughorn's cosseted existence when he remembered Sirius, crouching in a cave and living on rats. "Most of the teachers aren't in it, and none of them has ever been killed — well, unless you count Quirrell, and he got what he deserved seeing as he was working with Voldemort."

Harry had been sure Slughorn would be one of those wizards who could not bear to hear Voldemort's name spoken aloud, and was not disappointed: Slughorn gave a shudder and a squawk of protest, which Harry ignored.

"I reckon the staff are safer than most people while Dumbledore's headmaster; he's supposed to be the only one Voldemort ever feared, isn't he?" Harry went on.

Slughorn gazed into space for a moment or two: He seemed to be thinking over Harry's words.

"Well, yes, it is true that He-Who-Must-Not-Be-Named has never sought a fight with Dumbledore," he muttered grudgingly.

"And I suppose one could argue that as I have not joined the Death Eaters, He-Who-Must-Not-Be-Named can hardly count me a friend . . . in which case, I might well be safer a little closer to Albus. . . . I cannot pretend that Amelia Bones's death did not shake me. . . . If she, with all her Ministry contacts and protection . . ."

Dumbledore reentered the room and Slughorn jumped as though he had forgotten he was in the house.

"Oh, there you are, Albus," he said. "You've been a very long time. Upset stomach?"

"No, I was merely reading the Muggle magazines," said Dumbledore. "I do love knitting patterns. Well, Harry, we have trespassed upon Horace's hospitality quite long enough; I think it is time for us to leave."

Not at all reluctant to obey, Harry jumped to his feet. Slughorn seemed taken aback.

"You're leaving?"

"Yes, indeed. I think I know a lost cause when I see one."

"Lost . . . ?"

Slughorn seemed agitated. He twiddled his fat thumbs and fidgeted as he watched Dumbledore fasten his traveling cloak, and Harry zip up his jacket.

"Well, I'm sorry you don't want the job, Horace," said Dumbledore, raising his uninjured hand in a farewell salute. "Hogwarts would have been glad to see you back again. Our greatly increased security notwithstanding, you will always be welcome to visit, should you wish to."

"Yes . . . well . . . very gracious . . . as I say . . ."

"Good-bye, then."

"Bye," said Harry.

They were at the front door when there was a shout from behind them.

"All right, all right, I'll do it!"

Dumbledore turned to see Slughorn standing breathless in the doorway to the sitting room.

"You will come out of retirement?"

"Yes, yes," said Slughorn impatiently. "I must be mad, but yes."

"Wonderful," said Dumbledore, beaming. "Then, Horace, we shall see you on the first of September."

"Yes, I daresay you will," grunted Slughorn.

As they set off down the garden path, Slughorn's voice floated after them, "I'll want a pay rise, Dumbledore!"

Dumbledore chuckled. The garden gate swung shut behind them, and they set off back down the hill through the dark and the swirling mist.

"Well done, Harry," said Dumbledore.

"I didn't do anything," said Harry in surprise.

"Oh yes you did. You showed Horace exactly how much he stands to gain by returning to Hogwarts. Did you like him?"

"Er . . ."

Harry wasn't sure whether he liked Slughorn or not. He supposed he had been pleasant in his way, but he had also seemed vain and, whatever he said to the contrary, much too surprised that a Muggle-born should make a good witch.

"Horace," said Dumbledore, relieving Harry of the responsibility to say any of this, "likes his comfort. He also likes the company of the famous, the successful, and the powerful. He enjoys the feeling that he influences these people. He has never wanted to occupy the throne himself; he prefers the backseat — more room to spread out, you see. He used to handpick favorites at Hogwarts, sometimes for their ambition or their brains, sometimes for their charm or their talent, and he had an uncanny knack for choosing those who would go on to become outstanding in their various fields. Horace formed a kind of club of his favorites with himself at the center, making introductions, forging useful contacts between members, and always reaping some kind of benefit in return, whether a free box of his favorite crystalized pineapple or the chance to recommend the next junior member of the Goblin Liaison Office."

Harry had a sudden and vivid mental image of a great swollen spider, spinning a web around it, twitching a thread here and there to bring its large and juicy flies a little closer.

"I tell you all this," Dumbledore continued, "not to turn you against Horace — or, as we must now call him, Professor Slughorn — but to put you on your guard. He will undoubtedly try to collect you, Harry. You would be the jewel of his collection; 'the Boy Who Lived' . . . or, as they call you these days, 'the Chosen One.'"

At these words, a chill that had nothing to do with the surrounding mist stole over Harry. He was reminded of words he had heard a few weeks ago, words that had a horrible and particular meaning to him: *Neither can live while the other survives . . .*

Dumbledore had stopped walking, level with the church they had passed earlier.

"This will do, Harry. If you will grasp my arm."

Braced this time, Harry was ready for the Apparition, but still found it unpleasant. When the pressure disappeared and he found himself able to breathe again, he was standing in a country lane beside Dumbledore and looking ahead to the crooked silhouette of his second favorite building in the world: the Burrow. In spite of the feeling of dread that had just swept through him, his spirits could not help but lift at the sight of it. Ron was in there . . . and so was Mrs. Weasley, who could cook better than anyone he knew. . . .

"If you don't mind, Harry," said Dumbledore, as they passed through the gate, "I'd like a few words with you before we part. In private. Perhaps in here?"

Dumbledore pointed toward a run-down stone outhouse where the Weasleys kept their broomsticks. A little puzzled, Harry followed Dumbledore through the creaking door into a space a little smaller than the average cupboard. Dumbledore illuminated the tip of his wand, so that it glowed like a torch, and smiled down at Harry.

"I hope you will forgive me for mentioning it, Harry, but I am pleased and a little proud at how well you seem to be coping after everything that happened at the Ministry. Permit me to say that I think Sirius would have been proud of you."

Harry swallowed; his voice seemed to have deserted him. He did not think he could stand to discuss Sirius; it had been painful enough to hear Uncle Vernon say "His godfather's dead?" and even worse to hear Sirius's name thrown out casually by Slughorn.

"It was cruel," said Dumbledore softly, "that you and Sirius had such a short time together. A brutal ending to what should have been a long and happy relationship."

Harry nodded, his eyes fixed resolutely on the spider now climbing Dumbledore's hat. He could tell that Dumbledore understood, that he might even suspect that until his letter arrived, Harry had spent nearly all his time at the Dursleys' lying on his bed, refusing meals, and staring at the misted window, full of the chill emptiness that he had come to associate with dementors.

"It's just hard," Harry said finally, in a low voice, "to realize he won't write to me again."

His eyes burned suddenly and he blinked. He felt stupid for admitting it, but the fact that he had had someone outside Hogwarts who cared what happened to him, almost like a parent, had been one of the best things about discovering his godfather . . . and now the post owls would never bring him that comfort again. . . .

"Sirius represented much to you that you had never known before," said Dumbledore gently. "Naturally, the loss is devastating. . . ."

"But while I was at the Dursleys' . . ." interrupted Harry, his voice growing stronger, "I realized I can't shut myself away or — or crack up. Sirius wouldn't have wanted that, would he? And anyway, life's too short. . . . Look at Madam Bones, look at Emmeline Vance. . . . It could be me next, couldn't it? But if it is," he said fiercely, now looking straight into Dumbledore's blue eyes gleaming in the wandlight, "I'll make sure I take as many Death Eaters with me as I can, and Voldemort too if I can manage it."

"Spoken both like your mother and father's son and Sirius's true godson!" said Dumbledore, with an approving pat on Harry's back. "I take my hat off to you — or I would, if I were not afraid of showering you in spiders.

"And now, Harry, on a closely related subject . . . I gather that you have been taking the *Daily Prophet* over the last two weeks?"

"Yes," said Harry, and his heart beat a little faster.

"Then you will have seen that there have been not so much leaks as floods concerning your adventure in the Hall of Prophecy?"

"Yes," said Harry again. "And now everyone knows that I'm the one —"

"No, they do not," interrupted Dumbledore. "There are only two people in the whole world who know the full contents of the prophecy made about you and Lord Voldemort, and they are both standing in this smelly, spidery broom shed. It is true, however, that many have guessed, correctly, that Voldemort sent his Death Eaters to steal a prophecy, and that the prophecy concerned you.

"Now, I think I am correct in saying that you have not told anybody that you know what the prophecy said?"

"No," said Harry.

"A wise decision, on the whole," said Dumbledore. "Although I think you ought to relax it in favor of your friends, Mr. Ronald Weasley and Miss Hermione Granger. Yes," he continued, when Harry looked startled, "I think they ought to know. You do them a disservice by not confiding something this important to them."

"I didn't want —"

"— to worry or frighten them?" said Dumbledore, surveying Harry over the top of his half-moon spectacles. "Or perhaps, to confess that you yourself are worried and frightened? You need your friends, Harry. As you so rightly said, Sirius would not have wanted you to shut yourself away."

Harry said nothing, but Dumbledore did not seem to require an answer. He continued, "On a different, though related, subject, it is my wish that you take private lessons with me this year."

"Private — with you?" said Harry, surprised out of his preoccupied silence.

"Yes. I think it is time that I took a greater hand in your education."

"What will you be teaching me, sir?"

"Oh, a little of this, a little of that," said Dumbledore airily.

Harry waited hopefully, but Dumbledore did not elaborate, so he asked something else that had been bothering him slightly.

"If I'm having lessons with you, I won't have to do Occlumency lessons with Snape, will I?"

"*Professor* Snape, Harry — and no, you will not."

"Good," said Harry in relief, "because they were a —"

He stopped, careful not to say what he really thought.

"I think the word 'fiasco' would be a good one here," said Dumbledore, nodding.

Harry laughed.

"Well, that means I won't see much of Professor Snape from now on," he said, "because he won't let me carry on Potions unless I get 'Outstanding' in my O.W.L., which I know I haven't."

"Don't count your owls before they are delivered," said Dumbledore gravely. "Which, now I think of it, ought to be some time later today. Now, two more things, Harry, before we part.

"Firstly, I wish you to keep your Invisibility Cloak with you at all times from this moment onward. Even within Hogwarts itself. Just in case, you understand me?"

Harry nodded.

"And lastly, while you stay here, the Burrow has been given the highest security the Ministry of Magic can provide. These measures have caused a certain amount of inconvenience to Arthur and Molly — all their post, for instance, is being searched at the Ministry before being sent on. They do not mind in the slightest, for their only concern is your safety. However, it would be poor repayment if you risked your neck while staying with them."

"I understand," said Harry quickly.

"Very well, then," said Dumbledore, pushing open the broom shed door and stepping out into the yard. "I see a light in the kitchen. Let us not deprive Molly any longer of the chance to deplore how thin you are."

CHAPTER FIVE

AN EXCESS OF PHLEGM

arry and Dumbledore approached the back door of the Burrow, which was surrounded by the familiar litter of old Wellington boots and rusty cauldrons; Harry could hear the soft clucking of sleepy chickens coming from a distant shed. Dumbledore knocked three times and Harry saw sudden movement behind the kitchen window.

"Who's there?" said a nervous voice he recognized as Mrs. Weasley's. "Declare yourself!"

"It is I, Dumbledore, bringing Harry."

The door opened at once. There stood Mrs. Weasley, short, plump, and wearing an old green dressing gown.

"Harry, dear! Gracious, Albus, you gave me a fright, you said not to expect you before morning!"

"We were lucky," said Dumbledore, ushering Harry over the threshold. "Slughorn proved much more persuadable than I had expected. Harry's doing, of course. Ah, hello, Nymphadora!"

Harry looked around and saw that Mrs. Weasley was not alone, despite the lateness of the hour. A young witch with a pale, heart-shaped face and mousy brown hair was sitting at the table clutching a large mug between her hands.

"Hello, Professor," she said. "Wotcher, Harry."

"Hi, Tonks."

Harry thought she looked drawn, even ill, and there was something forced in her smile. Certainly her appearance was less colorful than usual without her customary shade of bubble-gum-pink hair.

"I'd better be off," she said quickly, standing up and pulling her cloak around her shoulders. "Thanks for the tea and sympathy, Molly."

"Please don't leave on my account," said Dumbledore courteously, "I cannot stay, I have urgent matters to discuss with Rufus Scrimgeour."

"No, no, I need to get going," said Tonks, not meeting Dumbledore's eyes. "'Night —"

"Dear, why not come to dinner at the weekend, Remus and Mad-Eye are coming — ?"

"No, really, Molly . . . thanks anyway . . . Good night, everyone."

Tonks hurried past Dumbledore and Harry into the yard; a few paces beyond the doorstep, she turned on the spot and vanished into thin air. Harry noticed that Mrs. Weasley looked troubled.

"Well, I shall see you at Hogwarts, Harry," said Dumbledore. "Take care of yourself. Molly, your servant."

He made Mrs. Weasley a bow and followed Tonks, vanishing at precisely the same spot. Mrs. Weasley closed the door on the empty yard and then steered Harry by the shoulders into the full glow of the lantern on the table to examine his appearance.

"You're like Ron," she sighed, looking him up and down. "Both of you look as though you've had Stretching Jinxes put on you. I swear Ron's grown four inches since I last bought him school robes. Are you hungry, Harry?"

"Yeah, I am," said Harry, suddenly realizing just how hungry he was.

"Sit down, dear, I'll knock something up."

As Harry sat down, a furry ginger cat with a squashed face jumped onto his knees and settled there, purring.

"So Hermione's here?" he asked happily as he tickled Crookshanks behind the ears.

"Oh yes, she arrived the day before yesterday," said Mrs. Weasley, rapping a large iron pot with her wand. It bounced onto the stove with a loud clang and began to bubble at once. "Everyone's in bed, of course, we didn't expect you for hours. Here you are —"

She tapped the pot again; it rose into the air, flew toward Harry, and tipped over; Mrs. Weasley slid a bowl neatly beneath it just in time to catch the stream of thick, steaming onion soup.

"Bread, dear?"

"Thanks, Mrs. Weasley."

She waved her wand over her shoulder; a loaf of bread and a knife soared gracefully onto the table; as the loaf sliced itself and the soup pot dropped back onto the stove, Mrs. Weasley sat down opposite him.

"So you persuaded Horace Slughorn to take the job?"

Harry nodded, his mouth so full of hot soup that he could not speak.

"He taught Arthur and me," said Mrs. Weasley. "He was at Hogwarts for ages, started around the same time as Dumbledore, I think. Did you like him?"

His mouth now full of bread, Harry shrugged and gave a noncommittal jerk of the head.

"I know what you mean," said Mrs. Weasley, nodding wisely. "Of course he can be charming when he wants to be, but Arthur's never liked him much. The Ministry's littered with Slughorn's old favorites, he was always good at giving leg ups, but he never had much time for Arthur — didn't seem to think he was enough of a highflier. Well, that just shows you, even Slughorn makes mistakes. I don't know whether Ron's told you in any of his letters — it's only just happened — but Arthur's been promoted!"

It could not have been clearer that Mrs. Weasley had been bursting to say this.

Harry swallowed a large amount of very hot soup and thought he could feel his throat blistering. "That's great!" he gasped.

"You are sweet," beamed Mrs. Weasley, possibly taking his watering eyes for emotion at the news. "Yes, Rufus Scrimgeour has set up several new offices in response to the present situation, and Arthur's heading the Office for the Detection and Confiscation of Counterfeit Defensive Spells and Protective Objects. It's a big job, he's got ten people reporting to him now!"

"What exactly — ?"

"Well, you see, in all the panic about You-Know-Who, odd things have been cropping up for sale everywhere, things that are supposed to guard against You-Know-Who and the Death Eaters. You can imagine the kind of thing — so-called protective potions that are really gravy with a bit of bubotuber pus added, or instructions for defensive jinxes that actually make your ears fall off. . . . Well, in the main the perpetrators are just people like Mundungus Fletcher, who've never done an honest day's work in their lives and are taking advantage of how frightened everybody is, but every now and then something really nasty turns up. The other day Arthur confiscated a box of cursed Sneakoscopes that were almost certainly planted by a Death Eater. So you see, it's a very important job, and I tell him it's just silly to miss dealing with spark plugs and toasters and all the rest of that Muggle rubbish." Mrs. Weasley ended her speech with a stern look, as if it had been Harry suggesting that it was natural to miss spark plugs.

"Is Mr. Weasley still at work?" Harry asked.

"Yes, he is. As a matter of fact, he's a tiny bit late. . . . He said he'd be back around midnight. . . ."

She turned to look at a large clock that was perched awkwardly on top of a pile of sheets in the washing basket at the end of the table. Harry recognized it at once: It had nine hands, each inscribed with the name of a family member, and usually hung on the Weasleys' sitting room wall, though its current position suggested that Mrs. Weasley had taken to carrying it around the house with her. Every single one of its nine hands was now pointing at "mortal peril."

"It's been like that for a while now," said Mrs. Weasley, in an unconvincingly casual voice, "ever since You-Know-Who came back into the open. I suppose everybody's in mortal danger now. . . . I don't think it can be just our family . . . but I don't know anyone else who's got a clock like this, so I can't check. Oh!"

With a sudden exclamation she pointed at the clock's face. Mr. Weasley's hand had switched to "traveling."

"He's coming!"

And sure enough, a moment later there was a knock on the back door. Mrs. Weasley jumped up and hurried to it; with one hand on the doorknob and her face pressed against the wood she called softly, "Arthur, is that you?"

"Yes," came Mr. Weasley's weary voice. "But I would say that even if I were a Death Eater, dear. Ask the question!"

"Oh, honestly . . ."

"Molly!"

"All right, all right . . . What is your dearest ambition?"

"To find out how airplanes stay up."

Mrs. Weasley nodded and turned the doorknob, but apparently Mr. Weasley was holding tight to it on the other side, because the door remained firmly shut.

"Molly! I've got to ask you your question first!"

"Arthur, really, this is just silly. . . ."

"What do you like me to call you when we're alone together?"

Even by the dim light of the lantern Harry could tell that Mrs. Weasley had turned bright red; he himself felt suddenly warm around the ears and neck, and hastily gulped soup, clattering his spoon as loudly as he could against the bowl.

"Mollywobbles," whispered a mortified Mrs. Weasley into the crack at the edge of the door.

"Correct," said Mr. Weasley. "Now you can let me in."

Mrs. Weasley opened the door to reveal her husband, a thin, balding, red-haired wizard wearing horn-rimmed spectacles and a long and dusty traveling cloak.

"I still don't see why we have to go through that every time you come home," said Mrs. Weasley, still pink in the face as she helped her husband out of his cloak. "I mean, a Death Eater might have forced the answer out of you before impersonating you!"

"I know, dear, but it's Ministry procedure, and I have to set an example. Something smells good — onion soup?"

Mr. Weasley turned hopefully in the direction of the table.

"Harry! We didn't expect you until morning!"

They shook hands, and Mr. Weasley dropped into the chair beside Harry as Mrs. Weasley set a bowl of soup in front of him too.

"Thanks, Molly. It's been a tough night. Some idiot's started selling Metamorph-Medals. Just sling them around your neck and you'll be able to change your appearance at will. A hundred thousand disguises, all for ten Galleons!"

"And what really happens when you put them on?"

"Mostly you just turn a fairly unpleasant orange color, but a couple of people have also sprouted tentaclelike warts all over their bodies. As if St. Mungo's didn't have enough to do already!"

"It sounds like the sort of thing Fred and George would find funny," said Mrs. Weasley hesitantly. "Are you sure — ?"

"Of course I am!" said Mr. Weasley. "The boys wouldn't do anything like that now, not when people are desperate for protection!"

"So is that why you're late, Metamorph-Medals?"

"No, we got wind of a nasty backfiring jinx down in Elephant and Castle, but luckily the Magical Law Enforcement Squad had sorted it out by the time we got there. . . ."

Harry stifled a yawn behind his hand.

"Bed," said an undeceived Mrs. Weasley at once. "I've got Fred and George's room all ready for you, you'll have it to yourself."

"Why, where are they?"

"Oh, they're in Diagon Alley, sleeping in the little flat over their joke shop as they're so busy," said Mrs. Weasley. "I must say, I didn't approve at first, but they do seem to have a bit of a flair for business! Come on, dear, your trunk's already up there."

" 'Night, Mr. Weasley," said Harry, pushing back his chair. Crookshanks leapt lightly from his lap and slunk out of the room.

"G'night, Harry," said Mr. Weasley.

Harry saw Mrs. Weasley glance at the clock in the washing basket as they left the kitchen. All the hands were once again at "mortal peril."

Fred and George's bedroom was on the second floor. Mrs. Weasley pointed her wand at a lamp on the bedside table and it ignited at once, bathing the room in a pleasant golden glow. Though a large vase of flowers had been placed on a desk in front of the small window, their perfume could not disguise the lingering smell of what Harry thought was gunpowder. A considerable amount of floor space was devoted to a vast number of unmarked, sealed cardboard boxes, amongst which stood Harry's school trunk. The room looked as though it was being used as a temporary warehouse.

Hedwig hooted happily at Harry from her perch on top of a large wardrobe, then took off through the window; Harry knew she had been waiting to see him before going hunting. Harry bade Mrs. Weasley good night, put on pajamas, and got into one of the beds. There was something hard inside the pillowcase. He groped inside it and pulled out a sticky purple-and-orange sweet, which he recognized as a Puking Pastille. Smiling to himself, he rolled over and was instantly asleep.

Seconds later, or so it seemed to Harry, he was awakened by what sounded like cannon fire as the door burst open. Sitting bolt upright, he heard the rasp of the curtains being pulled back: The dazzling sunlight seemed to poke him hard in both eyes. Shielding them with one hand, he groped hopelessly for his glasses with the other.

"Wuzzgoinon?"

"We didn't know you were here already!" said a loud and excited voice, and he received a sharp blow to the top of the head.

"Ron, don't hit him!" said a girl's voice reproachfully.

Harry's hand found his glasses and he shoved them on, though the light was so bright he could hardly see anyway. A long, looming shadow quivered in front of him for a moment; he blinked and Ron Weasley came into focus, grinning down at him.

"All right?"

"Never been better," said Harry, rubbing the top of his head and slumping back onto his pillows. "You?"

"Not bad," said Ron, pulling over a cardboard box and sitting on it. "When did you get here? Mum's only just told us!"

"About one o'clock this morning."

"Were the Muggles all right? Did they treat you okay?"

"Same as usual," said Harry, as Hermione perched herself on the edge of his bed, "they didn't talk to me much, but I like it better that way. How're you, Hermione?"

"Oh, I'm fine," said Hermione, who was scrutinizing Harry as though he was sickening for something. He thought he knew what was behind this, and as he had no wish to discuss Sirius's death or any other miserable subject at the moment, he said, "What's the time? Have I missed breakfast?"

"Don't worry about that, Mum's bringing you up a tray; she reckons you look underfed," said Ron, rolling his eyes. "So, what's been going on?"

"Nothing much, I've just been stuck at my aunt and uncle's, haven't I?"

"Come off it!" said Ron. "You've been off with Dumbledore!"

"It wasn't that exciting. He just wanted me to help him persuade this old teacher to come out of retirement. His name's Horace Slughorn."

"Oh," said Ron, looking disappointed. "We thought —"

Hermione flashed a warning look at Ron, and Ron changed tack at top speed.

"— we thought it'd be something like that."

"You did?" said Harry, amused.

"Yeah . . . yeah, now Umbridge has left, obviously we need a new Defense Against the Dark Arts teacher, don't we? So, er, what's he like?"

"He looks a bit like a walrus, and he used to be Head of Slytherin," said Harry. "Something wrong, Hermione?"

She was watching him as though expecting strange symptoms to manifest themselves at any moment. She rearranged her features hastily in an unconvincing smile.

"No, of course not! So, um, did Slughorn seem like he'll be a good teacher?"

"Dunno," said Harry. "He can't be worse than Umbridge, can he?"

"I know someone who's worse than Umbridge," said a voice from the doorway. Ron's younger sister slouched into the room, looking irritable. "Hi, Harry."

"What's up with you?" Ron asked.

"It's *her*," said Ginny, plonking herself down on Harry's bed. "She's driving me mad."

"What's she done now?" asked Hermione sympathetically.

"It's the way she talks to me — you'd think I was about three!"

"I know," said Hermione, dropping her voice. "She's so full of herself."

Harry was astonished to hear Hermione talking about Mrs. Weasley like this and could not blame Ron for saying angrily, "Can't you two lay off her for five seconds?"

"Oh, that's right, defend her," snapped Ginny. "We all know you can't get enough of her."

This seemed an odd comment to make about Ron's mother. Starting to feel that he was missing something, Harry said, "Who are you — ?"

But his question was answered before he could finish it. The bedroom door flew open again, and Harry instinctively yanked the bedcovers up to his chin so hard that Hermione and Ginny slid off the bed onto the floor.

A young woman was standing in the doorway, a woman of such breathtaking beauty that the room seemed to have become strangely airless. She was tall and willowy with long blonde hair and appeared to emanate a faint, silvery glow. To complete this vision of perfection, she was carrying a heavily laden breakfast tray.

"'Arry," she said in a throaty voice. "Eet 'as been too long!"

As she swept over the threshold toward him, Mrs. Weasley was revealed, bobbing along in her wake, looking rather cross.

"There was no need to bring up the tray, I was just about to do it myself!"

"Eet was no trouble," said Fleur Delacour, setting the tray across Harry's knees and then swooping to kiss him on each cheek: He felt the places where her mouth had touched him burn. "I 'ave been longing to see 'im. You remember my seester, Gabrielle? She never stops talking about 'Arry Potter. She will be delighted to see you again."

"Oh . . . is she here too?" Harry croaked.

"No, no, silly boy," said Fleur with a tinkling laugh, "I mean next summer, when we — but do you not know?"

Her great blue eyes widened and she looked reproachfully at Mrs. Weasley, who said, "We hadn't got around to telling him yet."

Fleur turned back to Harry, swinging her silvery sheet of hair so that it whipped Mrs. Weasley across the face.

"Bill and I are going to be married!"

"Oh," said Harry blankly. He could not help noticing how Mrs. Weasley, Hermione, and Ginny were all determinedly avoiding one another's gaze. "Wow. Er — congratulations!"

She swooped down upon him and kissed him again.

"Bill is very busy at ze moment, working very 'ard, and I only work part-time at Gringotts for my Eenglish, so he brought me 'ere for a few days to get to know 'is family properly. I was so pleased to 'ear you would be coming — zere isn't much to do 'ere, unless you like cooking and chickens! Well — enjoy your breakfast, 'Arry!"

With these words she turned gracefully and seemed to float out of the room, closing the door quietly behind her.

Mrs. Weasley made a noise that sounded like "tchah!"

"Mum hates her," said Ginny quietly.

"I do not hate her!" said Mrs. Weasley in a cross whisper. "I just think they've hurried into this engagement, that's all!"

"They've known each other a year," said Ron, who looked oddly groggy and was staring at the closed door.

"Well, that's not very long! I know why it's happened, of course.

It's all this uncertainty with You-Know-Who coming back, people think they might be dead tomorrow, so they're rushing all sorts of decisions they'd normally take time over. It was the same last time he was powerful, people eloping left, right, and center —"

"Including you and Dad," said Ginny slyly.

"Yes, well, your father and I were made for each other, what was the point in waiting?" said Mrs. Weasley. "Whereas Bill and Fleur . . . well . . . what have they really got in common? He's a hard-working, down-to-earth sort of person, whereas she's —"

"A cow," said Ginny, nodding. "But Bill's not that down-to-earth. He's a Curse-Breaker, isn't he, he likes a bit of adventure, a bit of glamour. . . . I expect that's why he's gone for Phlegm."

"Stop calling her that, Ginny," said Mrs. Weasley sharply, as Harry and Hermione laughed. "Well, I'd better get on. . . . Eat your eggs while they're warm, Harry."

Looking careworn, she left the room. Ron still seemed slightly punch-drunk; he was shaking his head experimentally like a dog trying to rid its ears of water.

"Don't you get used to her if she's staying in the same house?" Harry asked.

"Well, you do," said Ron, "but if she jumps out at you unexpectedly, like then . . ."

"It's pathetic," said Hermione furiously, striding away from Ron as far as she could go and turning to face him with her arms folded once she had reached the wall.

"You don't really want her around forever?" Ginny asked Ron incredulously. When he merely shrugged, she said, "Well, Mum's going to put a stop to it if she can, I bet you anything."

"How's she going to manage that?" asked Harry.

"She keeps trying to get Tonks round for dinner. I think she's hoping Bill will fall for Tonks instead. I hope he does, I'd much rather have her in the family."

"Yeah, that'll work," said Ron sarcastically. "Listen, no bloke in his right mind's going to fancy Tonks when Fleur's around. I mean, Tonks is okay-looking when she isn't doing stupid things to her hair and her nose, but —"

"She's a damn sight nicer than *Phlegm*," said Ginny.

"And she's more intelligent, she's an Auror!" said Hermione from the corner.

"Fleur's not stupid, she was good enough to enter the Triwizard Tournament," said Harry.

"Not you as well!" said Hermione bitterly.

"I suppose you like the way Phlegm says ''Arry,' do you?" asked Ginny scornfully.

"No," said Harry, wishing he hadn't spoken, "I was just saying, Phlegm — I mean, Fleur —"

"I'd much rather have Tonks in the family," said Ginny. "At least she's a laugh."

"She hasn't been much of a laugh lately," said Ron. "Every time I've seen her she's looked more like Moaning Myrtle."

"That's not fair," snapped Hermione. "She still hasn't got over what happened . . . you know . . . I mean, he was her cousin!"

Harry's heart sank. They had arrived at Sirius. He picked up a fork and began shoveling scrambled eggs into his mouth, hoping to deflect any invitation to join in this part of the conversation.

"Tonks and Sirius barely knew each other!" said Ron. "Sirius was in Azkaban half her life and before that their families never met —"

"That's not the point," said Hermione. "She thinks it was her fault he died!"

"How does she work that one out?" asked Harry, in spite of himself.

"Well, she was fighting Bellatrix Lestrange, wasn't she? I think she feels that if only she had finished her off, Bellatrix couldn't have killed Sirius."

"That's stupid," said Ron.

"It's survivor's guilt," said Hermione. "I know Lupin's tried to talk her round, but she's still really down. She's actually having trouble with her Metamorphosing!"

"With her — ?"

"She can't change her appearance like she used to," explained Hermione. "I think her powers must have been affected by shock, or something."

"I didn't know that could happen," said Harry.

"Nor did I," said Hermione, "but I suppose if you're really depressed . . ."

The door opened again and Mrs. Weasley popped her head in. "Ginny," she whispered, "come downstairs and help me with the lunch."

"I'm talking to this lot!" said Ginny, outraged.

"Now!" said Mrs. Weasley, and withdrew.

"She only wants me there so she doesn't have to be alone with Phlegm!" said Ginny crossly. She swung her long red hair around in a very good imitation of Fleur and pranced across the room with her arms held aloft like a ballerina.

"You lot had better come down quickly too," she said as she left.

Harry took advantage of the temporary silence to eat more breakfast. Hermione was peering into Fred and George's boxes, though every now and then she cast sideways looks at Harry. Ron, who was now helping himself to Harry's toast, was still gazing dreamily at the door.

"What's this?" Hermione asked eventually, holding up what looked like a small telescope.

"Dunno," said Ron, "but if Fred and George've left it here, it's probably not ready for the joke shop yet, so be careful."

"Your mum said the shop's going well," said Harry. "Said Fred and George have got a real flair for business."

"That's an understatement," said Ron. "They're raking in the Galleons! I can't wait to see the place, we haven't been to Diagon Alley yet, because Mum says Dad's got to be there for extra security and he's been really busy at work, but it sounds excellent."

"And what about Percy?" asked Harry; the third-eldest Weasley brother had fallen out with the rest of the family. "Is he talking to your mum and dad again?"

"Nope," said Ron.

"But he knows your dad was right all along now about Voldemort being back —"

"Dumbledore says people find it far easier to forgive others for being wrong than being right," said Hermione. "I heard him telling your mum, Ron."

"Sounds like the sort of mental thing Dumbledore would say," said Ron.

"He's going to be giving me private lessons this year," said Harry conversationally.

Ron choked on his bit of toast, and Hermione gasped.

"You kept that quiet!" said Ron.

"I only just remembered," said Harry honestly. "He told me last night in your broom shed."

"Blimey . . . private lessons with Dumbledore!" said Ron, looking impressed. "I wonder why he's . . . ?"

His voice tailed away. Harry saw him and Hermione exchange looks. Harry laid down his knife and fork, his heart beating rather fast considering that all he was doing was sitting in bed. Dumbledore had said to do it. . . . Why not now? He fixed his eyes on his fork, which was gleaming in the sunlight streaming into his lap, and said, "I don't know exactly why he's going to be giving me lessons, but I think it must be because of the prophecy."

Neither Ron nor Hermione spoke. Harry had the impression that both had frozen. He continued, still speaking to his fork, "You know, the one they were trying to steal at the Ministry."

"Nobody knows what it said, though," said Hermione quickly. "It got smashed."

"Although the *Prophet* says —" began Ron, but Hermione said, "Shh!"

"The *Prophet's* got it right," said Harry, looking up at them both with a great effort: Hermione seemed frightened and Ron amazed. "That glass ball that smashed wasn't the only record of the prophecy. I heard the whole thing in Dumbledore's office, he was the one the prophecy was made to, so he could tell me. From what it said," Harry took a deep breath, "it looks like I'm the one who's got to finish off Voldemort. . . . At least, it said neither of us could live while the other survives."

The three of them gazed at one another in silence for a moment. Then there was a loud bang and Hermione vanished behind a puff of black smoke.

"Hermione!" shouted Harry and Ron; the breakfast tray slid to the floor with a crash.

Hermione emerged, coughing, out of the smoke, clutching the telescope and sporting a brilliantly purple black eye.

"I squeezed it and it — it punched me!" she gasped.

And sure enough, they now saw a tiny fist on a long spring protruding from the end of the telescope.

"Don't worry," said Ron, who was plainly trying not to laugh, "Mum'll fix that, she's good at healing minor injuries —"

"Oh well, never mind that now!" said Hermione hastily. "Harry, oh, Harry . . ."

She sat down on the edge of his bed again.

"We wondered, after we got back from the Ministry . . . Obviously, we didn't want to say anything to you, but from what Lucius Malfoy said about the prophecy, how it was about you and Voldemort, well, we thought it might be something like this. . . . Oh, Harry . . ." She stared at him, then whispered, "Are you scared?"

"Not as much as I was," said Harry. "When I first heard it, I was . . . but now, it seems as though I always knew I'd have to face him in the end. . . ."

"When we heard Dumbledore was collecting you in person, we thought he might be telling you something or showing you something to do with the prophecy," said Ron eagerly. "And we were kind of right, weren't we? He wouldn't be giving you lessons if he thought you were a goner, wouldn't waste his time — he must think you've got a chance!"

"That's true," said Hermione. "I wonder what he'll teach you, Harry? Really advanced defensive magic, probably . . . powerful countercurses . . . anti-jinxes . . ."

Harry did not really listen. A warmth was spreading through him that had nothing to do with the sunlight; a tight obstruction in his chest seemed to be dissolving. He knew that Ron and Hermione were more shocked than they were letting on, but the mere fact that they were still there on either side of him, speaking bracing words of comfort, not shrinking from him as though he were contaminated or dangerous, was worth more than he could ever tell them.

". . . and evasive enchantments generally," concluded Hermione. "Well, at least you know one lesson you'll be having this year, that's one more than Ron and me. I wonder when our O.W.L. results will come?"

"Can't be long now, it's been a month," said Ron.

"Hang on," said Harry, as another part of last night's conversation came back to him. "I think Dumbledore said our O.W.L. results would be arriving today!"

"Today?" shrieked Hermione. "*Today?* But why didn't you — oh my God — you should have said —"

She leapt to her feet.

"I'm going to see whether any owls have come. . . ."

But when Harry arrived downstairs ten minutes later, fully dressed and carrying his empty breakfast tray, it was to find Hermione sitting at the kitchen table in great agitation, while Mrs. Weasley tried to lessen her resemblance to half a panda.

"It just won't budge," Mrs. Weasley was saying anxiously, standing over Hermione with her wand in her hand and a copy of *The*

Healer's Helpmate open at "Bruises, Cuts, and Abrasions." "This has always worked before, I just can't understand it."

"It'll be Fred and George's idea of a funny joke, making sure it can't come off," said Ginny.

"But it's got to come off!" squeaked Hermione. "I can't go around looking like this forever!"

"You won't, dear, we'll find an antidote, don't worry," said Mrs. Weasley soothingly.

"Bill told me 'ow Fred and George are very amusing!" said Fleur, smiling serenely.

"Yes, I can hardly breathe for laughing," snapped Hermione.

She jumped up and started walking round and round the kitchen, twisting her fingers together.

"Mrs. Weasley, you're quite, quite sure no owls have arrived this morning?"

"Yes, dear, I'd have noticed," said Mrs. Weasley patiently. "But it's barely nine, there's still plenty of time. . . ."

"I know I messed up Ancient Runes," muttered Hermione feverishly, "I definitely made at least one serious mistranslation. And the Defense Against the Dark Arts practical was no good at all. I thought Transfiguration went all right at the time, but looking back —"

"Hermione, will you shut up, you're not the only one who's nervous!" barked Ron. "And when you've got your ten 'Outstanding' O.W.L.s . . ."

"Don't, don't, don't!" said Hermione, flapping her hands hysterically. "I know I've failed everything!"

"What happens if we fail?" Harry asked the room at large, but it was again Hermione who answered.

"We discuss our options with our Head of House, I asked Professor McGonagall at the end of last term."

Harry's stomach squirmed. He wished he had eaten less breakfast.

"At Beauxbatons," said Fleur complacently, "we 'ad a different way of doing things. I think eet was better. We sat our examinations after six years of study, not five, and then —"

Fleur's words were drowned in a scream. Hermione was pointing through the kitchen window. Three black specks were clearly visible in the sky, growing larger all the time.

"They're definitely owls," said Ron hoarsely, jumping up to join Hermione at the window.

"And there are three of them," said Harry, hastening to her other side.

"One for each of us," said Hermione in a terrified whisper. "Oh no . . . oh no . . . oh no . . ."

She gripped both Harry and Ron tightly around the elbows.

The owls were flying directly at the Burrow, three handsome tawnies, each of which, it became clear as they flew lower over the path leading up to the house, was carrying a large square envelope.

"Oh *no*!" squealed Hermione.

Mrs. Weasley squeezed past them and opened the kitchen window. One, two, three, the owls soared through it and landed on the table in a neat line. All three of them lifted their right legs.

Harry moved forward. The letter addressed to him was tied to the leg of the owl in the middle. He untied it with fumbling fingers. To his left, Ron was trying to detach his own results; to his right, Hermione's hands were shaking so much she was making her whole owl tremble.

Nobody in the kitchen spoke. At last, Harry managed to detach the envelope. He slit it open quickly and unfolded the parchment inside.

ORDINARY WIZARDING LEVEL RESULTS

Pass Grades
OUTSTANDING (O)
EXCEEDS EXPECTATIONS (E)
ACCEPTABLE (A)

Fail Grades
POOR (P)
DREADFUL (D)
TROLL (T)

Harry James Potter has achieved:

Astronomy	A
Care of Magical Creatures	E
Charms	E
Defense Against the Dark Arts	O
Divination	P
Herbology	E
History of Magic	D
Potions	E
Transfiguration	E

Harry read the parchment through several times, his breathing becoming easier with each reading. It was all right: He had always known that he would fail Divination, and he had had no chance of passing History of Magic, given that he had collapsed halfway through the examination, but he had passed everything else! He ran his finger down the grades . . . he had passed well in Transfiguration and Herbology, he had even exceeded expectations at Potions! And best of all, he had achieved "Outstanding" at Defense Against the Dark Arts!

He looked around. Hermione had her back to him and her head bent, but Ron was looking delighted.

"Only failed Divination and History of Magic, and who cares about them?" he said happily to Harry. "Here — swap —"

Harry glanced down Ron's grades: There were no "Outstandings" there. . . .

"Knew you'd be top at Defense Against the Dark Arts," said Ron, punching Harry on the shoulder. "We've done all right, haven't we?"

"Well done!" said Mrs. Weasley proudly, ruffling Ron's hair. "Seven O.W.L.s, that's more than Fred and George got together!"

"Hermione?" said Ginny tentatively, for Hermione still hadn't turned around. "How did you do?"

"I — not bad," said Hermione in a small voice.

"Oh, come off it," said Ron, striding over to her and whipping her results out of her hand. "Yep — nine 'Outstandings' and one 'Exceeds Expectations' at Defense Against the Dark Arts." He looked down at her, half-amused, half-exasperated. "You're actually disappointed, aren't you?"

Hermione shook her head, but Harry laughed.

"Well, we're N.E.W.T. students now!" grinned Ron. "Mum, are there any more sausages?"

Harry looked back down at his results. They were as good as he could have hoped for. He felt just one tiny twinge of regret. . . . This was the end of his ambition to become an Auror. He had not secured the required Potions grade. He had known all along that he wouldn't, but he still felt a sinking in his stomach as he looked again at that small black E.

It was odd, really, seeing that it had been a Death Eater in disguise who had first told Harry he would make a good Auror, but somehow the idea had taken hold of him, and he couldn't really think of anything else he would like to be. Moreover, it had seemed the right destiny for him since he had heard the prophecy a few weeks ago. . . . *Neither can live while the other survives.* . . . Wouldn't he be living up to the prophecy, and giving himself the best chance of survival, if he joined those highly trained wizards whose job it was to find and kill Voldemort?

CHAPTER SIX

DRACO'S DETOUR

Harry remained within the confines of the Burrow's garden over the next few weeks. He spent most of his days playing two-a-side Quidditch in the Weasleys' orchard (he and Hermione against Ron and Ginny; Hermione was dreadful and Ginny good, so they were reasonably well matched) and his evenings eating triple helpings of everything Mrs. Weasley put in front of him.

It would have been a happy, peaceful holiday had it not been for the stories of disappearances, odd accidents, even of deaths now appearing almost daily in the *Prophet.* Sometimes Bill and Mr. Weasley brought home news before it even reached the paper. To Mrs. Weasley's displeasure, Harry's sixteenth birthday celebrations were marred by grisly tidings brought to the party by Remus Lupin, who was looking gaunt and grim, his brown hair streaked liberally with gray, his clothes more ragged and patched than ever.

"There have been another couple of dementor attacks," he

announced, as Mrs. Weasley passed him a large slice of birthday cake. "And they've found Igor Karkaroff's body in a shack up north. The Dark Mark had been set over it — well, frankly, I'm surprised he stayed alive for even a year after deserting the Death Eaters; Sirius's brother, Regulus, only managed a few days as far as I can remember."

"Yes, well," said Mrs. Weasley, frowning, "perhaps we should talk about something diff —"

"Did you hear about Florean Fortescue, Remus?" asked Bill, who was being plied with wine by Fleur. "The man who ran —"

"— the ice-cream place in Diagon Alley?" Harry interrupted, with an unpleasant, hollow sensation in the pit of his stomach. "He used to give me free ice creams. What's happened to him?"

"Dragged off, by the look of his place."

"Why?" asked Ron, while Mrs. Weasley pointedly glared at Bill.

"Who knows? He must've upset them somehow. He was a good man, Florean."

"Talking of Diagon Alley," said Mr. Weasley, "looks like Ollivander's gone too."

"The wandmaker?" said Ginny, looking startled.

"That's the one. Shop's empty. No sign of a struggle. No one knows whether he left voluntarily or was kidnapped."

"But wands — what'll people do for wands?"

"They'll make do with other makers," said Lupin. "But Ollivander was the best, and if the other side have got him it's not so good for us."

The day after this rather gloomy birthday tea, their letters and booklists arrived from Hogwarts. Harry's included a surprise: He had been made Quidditch Captain.

"That gives you equal status with prefects!" cried Hermione happily. "You can use our special bathroom now and everything!"

"Wow, I remember when Charlie wore one of these," said Ron, examining the badge with glee. "Harry, this is so cool, you're my Captain — if you let me back on the team, I suppose, ha ha. . . ."

"Well, I don't suppose we can put off a trip to Diagon Alley much longer now you've got these," sighed Mrs. Weasley, looking down Ron's booklist. "We'll go on Saturday as long as your father doesn't have to go into work again. I'm not going there without him."

"Mum, d'you honestly think You-Know-Who's going to be hiding behind a bookshelf in Flourish and Blotts?" sniggered Ron.

"Fortescue and Ollivander went on holiday, did they?" said Mrs. Weasley, firing up at once. "If you think security's a laughing matter you can stay behind and I'll get your things myself —"

"No, I wanna come, I want to see Fred and George's shop!" said Ron hastily.

"Then you just buck up your ideas, young man, before I decide you're too immature to come with us!" said Mrs. Weasley angrily, snatching up her clock, all nine hands of which were still pointing at "mortal peril," and balancing it on top of a pile of just-laundered towels. "And that goes for returning to Hogwarts as well!"

Ron turned to stare incredulously at Harry as his mother hoisted the laundry basket and the teetering clock into her arms and stormed out of the room.

"Blimey . . . you can't even make a joke round here anymore. . . ."

But Ron was careful not to be flippant about Voldemort over the next few days. Saturday dawned without any more outbursts from Mrs. Weasley, though she seemed very tense at breakfast. Bill, who would be staying at home with Fleur (much to Hermione and Ginny's pleasure), passed a full money bag across the table to Harry.

"Where's mine?" demanded Ron at once, his eyes wide.

"That's already Harry's, idiot," said Bill. "I got it out of your vault for you, Harry, because it's taking about five hours for the public to get to their gold at the moment, the goblins have tightened security so much. Two days ago Arkie Philpott had a Probity Probe stuck up his . . . Well, trust me, this way's easier."

"Thanks, Bill," said Harry, pocketing his gold.

"'E is always so thoughtful," purred Fleur adoringly, stroking Bill's nose. Ginny mimed vomiting into her cereal behind Fleur. Harry choked over his cornflakes, and Ron thumped him on the back.

It was an overcast, murky day. One of the special Ministry of Magic cars, in which Harry had ridden once before, was awaiting them in the front yard when they emerged from the house, pulling on their cloaks.

"It's good Dad can get us these again," said Ron appreciatively, stretching luxuriously as the car moved smoothly away from the Burrow, Bill and Fleur waving from the kitchen window. He, Harry, Hermione, and Ginny were all sitting in roomy comfort in the wide backseat.

"Don't get used to it, it's only because of Harry," said Mr. Weasley over his shoulder. He and Mrs. Weasley were in front with the Ministry driver; the front passenger seat had obligingly stretched into what resembled a two-seater sofa. "He's been given top-grade security status. And we'll be joining up with additional security at the Leaky Cauldron too."

Harry said nothing; he did not much fancy doing his shopping while surrounded by a battalion of Aurors. He had stowed his Invisibility Cloak in his backpack and felt that, if that was good enough for Dumbledore, it ought to be good enough for the Ministry, though now he came to think of it, he was not sure the Ministry knew about his cloak.

"Here you are, then," said the driver, a surprisingly short while later, speaking for the first time as he slowed in Charing Cross Road and stopped outside the Leaky Cauldron. "I'm to wait for you, any idea how long you'll be?"

"A couple of hours, I expect," said Mr. Weasley. "Ah, good, he's here!"

Harry imitated Mr. Weasley and peered through the window; his heart leapt. There were no Aurors waiting outside the inn, but instead the gigantic, black-bearded form of Rubeus Hagrid, the Hogwarts gamekeeper, wearing a long beaverskin coat, beaming at the sight of Harry's face and oblivious to the startled stares of passing Muggles.

"Harry!" he boomed, sweeping Harry into a bone-crushing hug the moment Harry had stepped out of the car. "Buckbeak — Witherwings, I mean — yeh should see him, Harry, he's so happy ter be back in the open air —"

"Glad he's pleased," said Harry, grinning as he massaged his ribs. "We didn't know 'security' meant you!"

"I know, jus' like old times, innit? See, the Ministry wanted ter send a bunch o' Aurors, but Dumbledore said I'd do," said Hagrid proudly, throwing out his chest and tucking his thumbs into his pockets. "Let's get goin' then — after yeh, Molly, Arthur —"

The Leaky Cauldron was, for the first time in Harry's memory, completely empty. Only Tom the landlord, wizened and toothless, remained of the old crowd. He looked up hopefully as they entered, but before he could speak, Hagrid said importantly, "Jus' passin' through today, Tom, sure yeh understand, Hogwarts business, yeh know."

Tom nodded gloomily and returned to wiping glasses; Harry, Hermione, Hagrid, and the Weasleys walked through the bar and out into the chilly little courtyard at the back where the dustbins stood. Hagrid raised his pink umbrella and rapped a certain brick in the wall, which opened at once to form an archway onto a winding cobbled street. They stepped through the entrance and paused, looking around.

Diagon Alley had changed. The colorful, glittering window displays of spellbooks, potion ingredients, and cauldrons were lost to view, hidden behind the large Ministry of Magic posters that had been pasted over them. Most of these somber purple posters carried blown-up versions of the security advice on the Ministry pamphlets that had been sent out over the summer, but others bore moving black-and-white photographs of Death Eaters known to be on the loose. Bellatrix Lestrange was sneering from the front of the nearest apothecary. A few windows were boarded up, including those of Florean Fortescue's Ice Cream Parlor. On the other hand, a number of shabby-looking stalls had sprung up along the street. The nearest one, which had been erected outside Flourish and Blotts, under a striped, stained awning, had a cardboard sign pinned to its front:

AMULETS
Effective Against Werewolves, Dementors, and Inferi

A seedy-looking little wizard was rattling armfuls of silver symbols on chains at passersby.

"One for your little girl, madam?" he called at Mrs. Weasley as they passed, leering at Ginny. "Protect her pretty neck?"

"If I were on duty . . ." said Mr. Weasley, glaring angrily at the amulet seller.

"Yes, but don't go arresting anyone now, dear, we're in a hurry," said Mrs. Weasley, nervously consulting a list. "I think we'd better do Madam Malkin's first, Hermione wants new dress robes, and Ron's showing much too much ankle in his school robes, and you must need new ones too, Harry, you've grown so much — come on, everyone —"

"Molly, it doesn't make sense for all of us to go to Madam Malkin's," said Mr. Weasley. "Why don't those three go with Hagrid, and we can go to Flourish and Blotts and get everyone's schoolbooks?"

"I don't know," said Mrs. Weasley anxiously, clearly torn between a desire to finish the shopping quickly and the wish to stick together in a pack. "Hagrid, do you think — ?"

"Don' fret, they'll be fine with me, Molly," said Hagrid soothingly, waving an airy hand the size of a dustbin lid. Mrs. Weasley did not look entirely convinced, but allowed the separation, scurrying off toward Flourish and Blotts with her husband and Ginny while Harry, Ron, Hermione, and Hagrid set off for Madam Malkin's.

Harry noticed that many of the people who passed them had the same harried, anxious look as Mrs. Weasley, and that nobody was stopping to talk anymore; the shoppers stayed together in their own tightly knit groups, moving intently about their business. No-body seemed to be shopping alone.

"Migh' be a bit of a squeeze in there with all of us," said Hagrid, stopping outside Madam Malkin's and bending down to peer through the window. "I'll stand guard outside, all right?"

So Harry, Ron, and Hermione entered the little shop together. It appeared, at first glance, to be empty, but no sooner had the door swung shut behind them than they heard a familiar voice issuing from behind a rack of dress robes in spangled green and blue.

". . . not a child, in case you haven't noticed, Mother. I am per-fectly capable of doing my shopping *alone*."

There was a clucking noise and a voice Harry recognized as that of Madam Malkin, the owner, said, "Now, dear, your mother's quite right, none of us is supposed to go wandering around on our own anymore, it's nothing to do with being a child —"

"Watch where you're sticking that pin, will you!"

A teenage boy with a pale, pointed face and white-blond hair ap-peared from behind the rack, wearing a handsome set of dark green robes that glittered with pins around the hem and the edges of the sleeves. He strode to the mirror and examined himself; it was a few moments before he noticed Harry, Ron, and Hermione reflected over his shoulder. His light gray eyes narrowed.

"If you're wondering what the smell is, Mother, a Mudblood just walked in," said Draco Malfoy.

"I don't think there's any need for language like that!" said Madam Malkin, scurrying out from behind the clothes rack hold-ing a tape measure and a wand. "And I don't want wands drawn in my shop either!" she added hastily, for a glance toward the door had shown her Harry and Ron both standing there with their wands out and pointing at Malfoy. Hermione, who was standing slightly behind them, whispered, "No, don't, honestly, it's not worth it. . . ."

"Yeah, like you'd dare do magic out of school," sneered Malfoy. "Who blacked your eye, Granger? I want to send them flowers."

"That's quite enough!" said Madam Malkin sharply, looking over her shoulder for support. "Madam — please —"

Narcissa Malfoy strolled out from behind the clothes rack.

"Put those away," she said coldly to Harry and Ron. "If you attack my son again, I shall ensure that it is the last thing you ever do."

"Really?" said Harry, taking a step forward and gazing into the smoothly arrogant face that, for all its pallor, still resembled her sister's. He was as tall as she was now. "Going to get a few Death Eater pals to do us in, are you?"

Madam Malkin squealed and clutched at her heart.

"Really, you shouldn't accuse — dangerous thing to say — wands away, please!"

But Harry did not lower his wand. Narcissa Malfoy smiled unpleasantly.

"I see that being Dumbledore's favorite has given you a false sense of security, Harry Potter. But Dumbledore won't always be there to protect you."

Harry looked mockingly all around the shop. "Wow . . . look at that . . . he's not here now! So why not have a go? They might be able to find you a double cell in Azkaban with your loser of a husband!"

Malfoy made an angry movement toward Harry, but stumbled over his overlong robe. Ron laughed loudly.

"Don't you dare talk to my mother like that, Potter!" Malfoy snarled.

"It's all right, Draco," said Narcissa, restraining him with her thin white fingers upon his shoulder. "I expect Potter will be reunited with dear Sirius before I am reunited with Lucius."

Harry raised his wand higher.

"Harry, no!" moaned Hermione, grabbing his arm and attempting to push it down by his side. "Think. . . . You mustn't. . . . You'll be in such trouble. . . ."

Madam Malkin dithered for a moment on the spot, then seemed to decide to act as though nothing was happening in the hope that it wouldn't. She bent toward Malfoy, who was still glaring at Harry.

"I think this left sleeve could come up a little bit more, dear, let me just —"

"Ouch!" bellowed Malfoy, slapping her hand away. "Watch where you're putting your pins, woman! Mother — I don't think I want these anymore —"

He pulled the robes over his head and threw them onto the floor at Madam Malkin's feet.

"You're right, Draco," said Narcissa, with a contemptuous glance at Hermione, "now I know the kind of scum that shops here. . . . We'll do better at Twilfitt and Tatting's."

And with that, the pair of them strode out of the shop, Malfoy taking care to bang as hard as he could into Ron on the way out.

"Well, *really!*" said Madam Malkin, snatching up the fallen robes and moving the tip of her wand over them like a vacuum cleaner, so that it removed all the dust.

She was distracted all through the fitting of Ron's and Harry's new robes, tried to sell Hermione wizard's dress robes instead of witch's, and when she finally bowed them out of the shop it was with an air of being glad to see the back of them.

"Got ev'rything?" asked Hagrid brightly when they reappeared at his side.

"Just about," said Harry. "Did you see the Malfoys?"

"Yeah," said Hagrid, unconcerned. "Bu' they wouldn' dare make trouble in the middle o' Diagon Alley, Harry. Don' worry abou' them."

Harry, Ron, and Hermione exchanged looks, but before they could disabuse Hagrid of this comfortable notion, Mr. and Mrs. Weasley and Ginny appeared, all clutching heavy packages of books.

"Everyone all right?" said Mrs. Weasley. "Got your robes? Right then, we can pop in at the Apothecary and Eeylops on the way to Fred and George's — stick close, now. . . ."

Neither Harry nor Ron bought any ingredients at the Apothecary, seeing that they were no longer studying Potions, but both bought large boxes of owl nuts for Hedwig and Pigwidgeon at Eeylops Owl Emporium. Then, with Mrs. Weasley checking her watch every minute or so, they headed farther along the street in search of Weasleys' Wizard Wheezes, the joke shop run by Fred and George.

"We really haven't got too long," Mrs. Weasley said. "So we'll just have a quick look around and then back to the car. We must be close, that's number ninety-two . . . ninety-four . . ."

"*Whoa,*" said Ron, stopping in his tracks.

Set against the dull, poster-muffled shop fronts around them, Fred and George's windows hit the eye like a firework display. Casual passersby were looking back over their shoulders at the windows, and a few rather stunned-looking people had actually come to a halt, transfixed. The left-hand window was dazzlingly full of an assortment of goods that revolved, popped, flashed, bounced, and shrieked; Harry's eyes began to water just looking at it. The right-hand window was covered with a gigantic poster, purple like those of the Ministry, but emblazoned with flashing yellow letters:

**WHY ARE YOU WORRYING ABOUT
YOU-KNOW-WHO?
YOU SHOULD BE WORRYING ABOUT
U-NO-POO —
THE CONSTIPATION SENSATION
THAT'S GRIPPING THE NATION!**

Harry started to laugh. He heard a weak sort of moan beside him and looked around to see Mrs. Weasley gazing, dumbfounded, at the poster. Her lips moved silently, mouthing the name "U-No-Poo."

"They'll be murdered in their beds!" she whispered.

"No they won't!" said Ron, who, like Harry, was laughing. "This is brilliant!"

And he and Harry led the way into the shop. It was packed with customers; Harry could not get near the shelves. He stared around, looking up at the boxes piled to the ceiling: Here were the Skiving Snackboxes that the twins had perfected during their last, unfinished year at Hogwarts; Harry noticed that the Nosebleed Nougat was most popular, with only one battered box left on the shelf. There were bins full of trick wands, the cheapest merely turning into rubber chickens or pairs of briefs when waved, the most expensive beating the unwary user around the head and neck, and boxes of quills, which came in Self-Inking, Spell-Checking, and Smart-Answer varieties. A space cleared in the crowd, and Harry pushed his way toward the counter, where a gaggle of delighted ten-year-olds was watching a tiny little wooden man slowly ascending the steps to a real set of gallows, both perched on a box that read: REUSABLE HANGMAN — SPELL IT OR HE'LL SWING!

"'Patented Daydream Charms . . .'"

Hermione had managed to squeeze through to a large display near the counter and was reading the information on the back of a box bearing a highly colored picture of a handsome youth and a swooning girl who were standing on the deck of a pirate ship.

"'One simple incantation and you will enter a top-quality, highly realistic, thirty-minute daydream, easy to fit into the average school lesson and virtually undetectable (side effects include vacant expression and minor drooling). Not for sale to under-sixteens.' You know," said Hermione, looking up at Harry, "that really is extraordinary magic!"

"For that, Hermione," said a voice behind them, "you can have one for free."

A beaming Fred stood before them, wearing a set of magenta robes that clashed magnificently with his flaming hair.

"How are you, Harry?" They shook hands. "And what's happened to your eye, Hermione?"

"Your punching telescope," she said ruefully.

"Oh blimey, I forgot about those," said Fred. "Here —"

He pulled a tub out of his pocket and handed it to her; she unscrewed it gingerly to reveal a thick yellow paste.

"Just dab it on, that bruise'll be gone within the hour," said Fred. "We had to find a decent bruise remover. We're testing most of our products on ourselves."

Hermione looked nervous. "It is *safe,* isn't it?" she asked.

"'Course it is," said Fred bracingly. "Come on, Harry, I'll give you a tour."

Harry left Hermione dabbing her black eye with paste and followed Fred toward the back of the shop, where he saw a stand of card and rope tricks.

"Muggle magic tricks!" said Fred happily, pointing them out. "For freaks like Dad, you know, who love Muggle stuff. It's not a big earner, but we do fairly steady business, they're great novelties. . . . Oh, here's George. . . ."

Fred's twin shook Harry's hand energetically.

"Giving him the tour? Come through the back, Harry, that's where we're making the real money — *pocket anything, you, and you'll pay in more than Galleons!*" he added warningly to a small boy who hastily whipped his hand out of the tub labeled EDIBLE DARK MARKS — THEY'LL MAKE ANYONE SICK!

George pushed back a curtain beside the Muggle tricks and Harry saw a darker, less crowded room. The packaging on the products lining these shelves was more subdued.

"We've just developed this more serious line," said Fred. "Funny how it happened . . ."

"You wouldn't believe how many people, even people who work at the Ministry, can't do a decent Shield Charm," said George. "'Course, they didn't have you teaching them, Harry."

"That's right. . . . Well, we thought Shield Hats were a bit of a laugh, you know, challenge your mate to jinx you while wearing it and watch his face when the jinx just bounces off. But the Ministry bought five hundred for all its support staff! And we're still getting massive orders!"

"So we've expanded into a range of Shield Cloaks, Shield Gloves . . ."

". . . I mean, they wouldn't help much against the Unforgivable Curses, but for minor to moderate hexes or jinxes . . ."

"And then we thought we'd get into the whole area of Defense Against the Dark Arts, because it's such a money spinner," continued George enthusiastically. "This is cool. Look, Instant Darkness Powder, we're importing it from Peru. Handy if you want to make a quick escape."

"And our Decoy Detonators are just walking off the shelves, look," said Fred, pointing at a number of weird-looking black horn-type objects that were indeed attempting to scurry out of sight. "You just drop one surreptitiously and it'll run off and make a nice loud noise out of sight, giving you a diversion if you need one."

"Handy," said Harry, impressed.

"Here," said George, catching a couple and throwing them to Harry.

A young witch with short blonde hair poked her head around the curtain; Harry saw that she too was wearing magenta staff robes.

"There's a customer out here looking for a joke cauldron, Mr. Weasley and Mr. Weasley," she said.

Harry found it very odd to hear Fred and George called "Mr. Weasley," but they took it in their stride.

"Right you are, Verity, I'm coming," said George promptly. "Harry, you help yourself to anything you want, all right? No charge."

"I can't do that!" said Harry, who had already pulled out his money bag to pay for the Decoy Detonators.

"You don't pay here," said Fred firmly, waving away Harry's gold.

"But —"

"You gave us our start-up loan, we haven't forgotten," said George sternly. "Take whatever you like, and just remember to tell people where you got it, if they ask."

George swept off through the curtain to help with the customers, and Fred led Harry back into the main part of the shop to find Hermione and Ginny still poring over the Patented Daydream Charms.

"Haven't you girls found our special WonderWitch products yet?" asked Fred. "Follow me, ladies. . . ."

Near the window was an array of violently pink products around which a cluster of excited girls was giggling enthusiastically. Hermione and Ginny both hung back, looking wary.

"There you go," said Fred proudly. "Best range of love potions you'll find anywhere."

Ginny raised an eyebrow skeptically. "Do they work?" she asked.

"Certainly they work, for up to twenty-four hours at a time depending on the weight of the boy in question —"

"— and the attractiveness of the girl," said George, reappearing suddenly at their side. "But we're not selling them to our sister," he added, becoming suddenly stern, "not when she's already got about five boys on the go from what we've —"

"Whatever you've heard from Ron is a big fat lie," said Ginny calmly, leaning forward to take a small pink pot off the shelf. "What's this?"

"Guaranteed ten-second pimple vanisher," said Fred. "Excellent on everything from boils to blackheads, but don't change the subject. Are you or are you not currently going out with a boy called Dean Thomas?"

"Yes, I am," said Ginny. "And last time I looked, he was definitely one boy, not five. What are those?"

She was pointing at a number of round balls of fluff in shades of pink and purple, all rolling around the bottom of a cage and emitting high-pitched squeaks.

"Pygmy Puffs," said George. "Miniature puffskeins, we can't breed them fast enough. So what about Michael Corner?"

"I dumped him, he was a bad loser," said Ginny, putting a finger through the bars of the cage and watching the Pygmy Puffs crowd around it. "They're really cute!"

"They're fairly cuddly, yes," conceded Fred. "But you're moving through boyfriends a bit fast, aren't you?"

Ginny turned to look at him, her hands on her hips. There was such a Mrs. Weasley-ish glare on her face that Harry was surprised Fred didn't recoil.

"It's none of your business. And I'll thank *you*," she added angrily to Ron, who had just appeared at George's elbow, laden with merchandise, "not to tell tales about me to these two!"

"That's three Galleons, nine Sickles, and a Knut," said Fred, examining the many boxes in Ron's arms. "Cough up."

"I'm your brother!"

"And that's our stuff you're nicking. Three Galleons, nine Sickles. I'll knock off the Knut."

"But I haven't got three Galleons, nine Sickles!"

"You'd better put it back then, and mind you put it on the right shelves."

Ron dropped several boxes, swore, and made a rude hand gesture at Fred that was unfortunately spotted by Mrs. Weasley, who had chosen that moment to appear.

"If I see you do that again I'll jinx your fingers together," she said sharply.

"Mum, can I have a Pygmy Puff?" said Ginny at once.

"A what?" said Mrs. Weasley warily.

"Look, they're so sweet. . . ."

Mrs. Weasley moved aside to look at the Pygmy Puffs, and Harry, Ron, and Hermione momentarily had an unimpeded view out of the window. Draco Malfoy was hurrying up the street alone. As he passed Weasleys' Wizard Wheezes, he glanced over his shoulder. Seconds later, he moved beyond the scope of the window and they lost sight of him.

"Wonder where his mummy is?" said Harry, frowning.

"Given her the slip by the looks of it," said Ron.

"Why, though?" said Hermione.

Harry said nothing; he was thinking too hard. Narcissa Malfoy would not have let her precious son out of her sight willingly; Malfoy must have made a real effort to free himself from her clutches.

Harry, knowing and loathing Malfoy, was sure the reason could not be innocent.

He glanced around. Mrs. Weasley and Ginny were bending over the Pygmy Puffs. Mr. Weasley was delightedly examining a pack of Muggle marked playing cards. Fred and George were both helping customers. On the other side of the glass, Hagrid was standing with his back to them, looking up and down the street.

"Get under here, quick," said Harry, pulling his Invisibility Cloak out of his bag.

"Oh — I don't know, Harry," said Hermione, looking uncertainly toward Mrs. Weasley.

"Come *on*!" said Ron.

She hesitated for a second longer, then ducked under the cloak with Harry and Ron. Nobody noticed them vanish; they were all too interested in Fred and George's products. Harry, Ron, and Hermione squeezed their way out of the door as quickly as they could, but by the time they gained the street, Malfoy had disappeared just as successfully as they had.

"He was going in that direction," murmured Harry as quietly as possible, so that the humming Hagrid would not hear them. "C'mon."

They scurried along, peering left and right, through shop windows and doors, until Hermione pointed ahead.

"That's him, isn't it?" she whispered. "Turning left?"

"Big surprise," whispered Ron.

For Malfoy had glanced around, then slid into Knockturn Alley and out of sight.

"Quick, or we'll lose him," said Harry, speeding up.

"Our feet'll be seen!" said Hermione anxiously, as the cloak flapped a little around their ankles; it was much more difficult hiding all three of them under the cloak nowadays.

"It doesn't matter," said Harry impatiently. "Just hurry!"

But Knockturn Alley, the side street devoted to the Dark Arts, looked completely deserted. They peered into windows as they passed, but none of the shops seemed to have any customers at all. Harry supposed it was a bit of a giveaway in these dangerous and suspicious times to buy Dark artifacts — or at least, to be seen buying them.

Hermione gave his arm a hard pinch.

"Ouch!"

"Shh! Look! He's in there!" she breathed in Harry's ear.

They had drawn level with the only shop in Knockturn Alley that Harry had ever visited, Borgin and Burkes, which sold a wide variety of sinister objects. There in the midst of the cases full of skulls and old bottles stood Draco Malfoy with his back to them, just visible beyond the very same large black cabinet in which Harry had once hidden to avoid Malfoy and his father. Judging by the movements of Malfoy's hands, he was talking animatedly. The proprietor of the shop, Mr. Borgin, an oily-haired, stooping man, stood facing Malfoy. He was wearing a curious expression of mingled resentment and fear.

"If only we could hear what they're saying!" said Hermione.

"We can!" said Ron excitedly. "Hang on — damn —"

He dropped a couple more of the boxes he was still clutching as he fumbled with the largest.

"Extendable Ears, look!"

"Fantastic!" said Hermione, as Ron unraveled the long, flesh-colored strings and began to feed them toward the bottom of the door. "Oh, I hope the door isn't Imperturbable —"

"No!" said Ron gleefully. "Listen!"

They put their heads together and listened intently to the ends of the strings, through which Malfoy's voice could be heard loud and clear, as though a radio had been turned on.

". . . you know how to fix it?"

"Possibly," said Borgin, in a tone that suggested he was unwilling to commit himself. "I'll need to see it, though. Why don't you bring it into the shop?"

"I can't," said Malfoy. "It's got to stay put. I just need you to tell me how to do it."

Harry saw Borgin lick his lips nervously.

"Well, without seeing it, I must say it will be a very difficult job, perhaps impossible. I couldn't guarantee anything."

"No?" said Malfoy, and Harry knew, just by his tone, that Malfoy was sneering. "Perhaps this will make you more confident."

He moved toward Borgin and was blocked from view by the cabinet. Harry, Ron, and Hermione shuffled sideways to try and keep him in sight, but all they could see was Borgin, looking very frightened.

"Tell anyone," said Malfoy, "and there will be retribution. You know Fenrir Greyback? He's a family friend. He'll be dropping in from time to time to make sure you're giving the problem your full attention."

"There will be no need for —"

"I'll decide that," said Malfoy. "Well, I'd better be off. And don't forget to keep *that* one safe, I'll need it."

"Perhaps you'd like to take it now?"

"No, of course I wouldn't, you stupid little man, how would I look carrying that down the street? Just don't sell it."

"Of course not . . . sir."

Borgin made a bow as deep as the one Harry had once seen him give Lucius Malfoy.

"Not a word to anyone, Borgin, and that includes my mother, understand?"

"Naturally, naturally," murmured Borgin, bowing again.

Next moment, the bell over the door tinkled loudly as Malfoy stalked out of the shop looking very pleased with himself. He passed so close to Harry, Ron, and Hermione that they felt the cloak flutter around their knees again. Inside the shop, Borgin remained frozen; his unctuous smile had vanished; he looked worried.

"What was that about?" whispered Ron, reeling in the Extendable Ears.

"Dunno," said Harry, thinking hard. "He wants something mended . . . and he wants to reserve something in there. . . . Could you see what he pointed at when he said 'that one'?"

"No, he was behind that cabinet —"

"You two stay here," whispered Hermione.

"What are you — ?"

But Hermione had already ducked out from under the cloak. She checked her hair in the reflection in the glass, then marched into the shop, setting the bell tinkling again. Ron hastily fed the Extendable Ears back under the door and passed one of the strings to Harry.

"Hello, horrible morning, isn't it?" Hermione said brightly to Borgin, who did not answer, but cast her a suspicious look. Humming cheerily, Hermione strolled through the jumble of objects on display.

"Is this necklace for sale?" she asked, pausing beside a glass-fronted case.

"If you've got one and a half thousand Galleons," said Mr. Borgin coldly.

"Oh — er — no, I haven't got quite that much," said Hermione, walking on. "And . . . what about this lovely — um — skull?"

"Sixteen Galleons."

"So it's for sale, then? It isn't being . . . kept for anyone?"

Mr. Borgin squinted at her. Harry had the nasty feeling he knew exactly what Hermione was up to. Apparently Hermione felt she had been rumbled too because she suddenly threw caution to the winds.

"The thing is, that — er — boy who was in here just now, Draco Malfoy, well, he's a friend of mine, and I want to get him a birthday present, but if he's already reserved anything, I obviously don't want to get him the same thing, so . . . um . . ."

It was a pretty lame story in Harry's opinion, and apparently Borgin thought so too.

"Out," he said sharply. "Get out!"

Hermione did not wait to be asked twice, but hurried to the door with Borgin at her heels. As the bell tinkled again, Borgin slammed the door behind her and put up the CLOSED sign.

"Ah well," said Ron, throwing the cloak back over Hermione. "Worth a try, but you were a bit obvious —"

"Well, next time you can show me how it's done, Master of Mystery!" she snapped.

Ron and Hermione bickered all the way back to Weasleys'

Wizard Wheezes, where they were forced to stop so that they could dodge undetected around a very anxious-looking Mrs. Weasley and Hagrid, who had clearly noticed their absence. Once in the shop, Harry whipped off the Invisibility Cloak, hid it in his bag, and joined in with the other two when they insisted, in answer to Mrs. Weasley's accusations, that they had been in the back room all along, and that she could not have looked properly.

THE SLUG CLUB

Harry spent a lot of the last week of the holidays pondering the meaning of Malfoy's behavior in Knockturn Alley. What disturbed him most was the satisfied look on Malfoy's face as he had left the shop. Nothing that made Malfoy look that happy could be good news. To his slight annoyance, however, neither Ron nor Hermione seemed quite as curious about Malfoy's activities as he was; or at least, they seemed to get bored of discussing it after a few days.

"Yes, I've already agreed it was fishy, Harry," said Hermione a little impatiently. She was sitting on the windowsill in Fred and George's room with her feet up on one of the cardboard boxes and had only grudgingly looked up from her new copy of *Advanced Rune Translation*. "But haven't we agreed there could be a lot of explanations?"

"Maybe he's broken his Hand of Glory," said Ron vaguely, as he attempted to straighten his broomstick's bent tail twigs. "Remember that shriveled-up arm Malfoy had?"

"But what about when he said, 'Don't forget to keep *that* one safe'?" asked Harry for the umpteenth time. "That sounded to me like Borgin's got another one of the broken objects, and Malfoy wants both."

"You reckon?" said Ron, now trying to scrape some dirt off his broom handle.

"Yeah, I do," said Harry. When neither Ron nor Hermione answered, he said, "Malfoy's father's in Azkaban. Don't you think Malfoy'd like revenge?"

Ron looked up, blinking.

"Malfoy, revenge? What can he do about it?"

"That's my point, I don't know!" said Harry, frustrated. "But he's up to something and I think we should take it seriously. His father's a Death Eater and —"

Harry broke off, his eyes fixed on the window behind Hermione, his mouth open. A startling thought had just occurred to him.

"Harry?" said Hermione in an anxious voice. "What's wrong?"

"Your scar's not hurting again, is it?" asked Ron nervously.

"He's a Death Eater," said Harry slowly. "He's replaced his father as a Death Eater!"

There was a silence; then Ron erupted in laughter. "*Malfoy?* He's sixteen, Harry! You think You-Know-Who would let *Malfoy* join?"

"It seems very unlikely, Harry," said Hermione in a repressive sort of voice. "What makes you think — ?"

"In Madam Malkin's. She didn't touch him, but he yelled and jerked his arm away from her when she went to roll up his sleeve. It was his left arm. He's been branded with the Dark Mark."

Ron and Hermione looked at each other.

"Well . . ." said Ron, sounding thoroughly unconvinced.

"I think he just wanted to get out of there, Harry," said Hermione.

"He showed Borgin something we couldn't see," Harry pressed on stubbornly. "Something that seriously scared Borgin. It was the Mark, I know it — he was showing Borgin who he was dealing with, you saw how seriously Borgin took him!"

Ron and Hermione exchanged another look.

"I'm not sure, Harry. . . ."

"Yeah, I still don't reckon You-Know-Who would let Malfoy join. . . ."

Annoyed, but absolutely convinced he was right, Harry snatched up a pile of filthy Quidditch robes and left the room; Mrs. Weasley had been urging them for days not to leave their washing and packing until the last moment. On the landing he bumped into Ginny, who was returning to her room carrying a pile of freshly laundered clothes.

"I wouldn't go in the kitchen just now," she warned him. "There's a lot of Phlegm around."

"I'll be careful not to slip in it." Harry smiled.

Sure enough, when he entered the kitchen it was to find Fleur sitting at the kitchen table, in full flow about plans for her wedding to Bill, while Mrs. Weasley kept watch over a pile of self-peeling sprouts, looking bad-tempered.

". . . Bill and I 'ave almost decided on only two bridesmaids, Ginny and Gabrielle will look very sweet togezzer. I am theenking of dressing zem in pale gold — pink would of course be 'orrible with Ginny's 'air —"

"Ah, Harry!" said Mrs. Weasley loudly, cutting across Fleur's monologue. "Good, I wanted to explain about the security arrangements for the journey to Hogwarts tomorrow. We've got Ministry cars again, and there will be Aurors waiting at the station —"

"Is Tonks going to be there?" asked Harry, handing over his Quidditch things.

"No, I don't think so, she's been stationed somewhere else from what Arthur said."

"She has let 'erself go, zat Tonks," Fleur mused, examining her own stunning reflection in the back of a teaspoon. "A big mistake if you ask —"

"Yes, *thank* you," said Mrs. Weasley tartly, cutting across Fleur again. "You'd better get on, Harry, I want the trunks ready tonight, if possible, so we don't have the usual last-minute scramble."

And in fact, their departure the following morning was smoother than usual. The Ministry cars glided up to the front of the Burrow to find them waiting, trunks packed; Hermione's cat, Crookshanks, safely enclosed in his traveling basket; and Hedwig; Ron's owl, Pigwidgeon; and Ginny's new purple Pygmy Puff, Arnold, in cages.

"Au revoir, 'Arry," said Fleur throatily, kissing him good-bye. Ron hurried forward, looking hopeful, but Ginny stuck out her foot and Ron fell, sprawling in the dust at Fleur's feet. Furious, red-faced, and dirt-spattered, he hurried into the car without saying good-bye.

There was no cheerful Hagrid waiting for them at King's Cross Station. Instead, two grim-faced, bearded Aurors in dark Muggle suits moved forward the moment the cars stopped and, flanking the party, marched them into the station without speaking.

"Quick, quick, through the barrier," said Mrs. Weasley, who

seemed a little flustered by this austere efficiency. "Harry had better go first, with —"

She looked inquiringly at one of the Aurors, who nodded briefly,
seized Harry's upper arm, and attempted to steer him toward the
barrier between platforms nine and ten.

"I can walk, thanks," said Harry irritably, jerking his arm out of
the Auror's grip. He pushed his trolley directly at the solid barrier,
ignoring his silent companion, and found himself, a second later,
standing on platform nine and three-quarters, where the scarlet
Hogwarts Express stood belching steam over the crowd.

Hermione and the Weasleys joined him within seconds. Without waiting to consult his grim-faced Auror, Harry motioned to
Ron and Hermione to follow him up the platform, looking for an
empty compartment.

"We can't, Harry," said Hermione, looking apologetic. "Ron and
I've got to go to the prefects' carriage first and then patrol the corridors for a bit."

"Oh yeah, I forgot," said Harry.

"You'd better get straight on the train, all of you, you've only got
a few minutes to go," said Mrs. Weasley, consulting her watch.
"Well, have a lovely term, Ron. . . ."

"Mr. Weasley, can I have a quick word?" said Harry, making up
his mind on the spur of the moment.

"Of course," said Mr. Weasley, who looked slightly surprised,
but followed Harry out of earshot of the others nevertheless.

Harry had thought it through carefully and come to the conclusion that, if he was to tell anyone, Mr. Weasley was the right person; firstly, because he worked at the Ministry and was therefore in
the best position to make further investigations, and secondly,

because he thought that there was not too much risk of Mr. Weasley exploding with anger.

He could see Mrs. Weasley and the grim-faced Auror casting the pair of them suspicious looks as they moved away.

"When we were in Diagon Alley," Harry began, but Mr. Weasley forestalled him with a grimace.

"Am I about to discover where you, Ron, and Hermione disappeared to while you were supposed to be in the back room of Fred and George's shop?"

"How did you — ?"

"Harry, please. You're talking to the man who raised Fred and George."

"Er . . . yeah, all right, we weren't in the back room."

"Very well, then, let's hear the worst."

"Well, we followed Draco Malfoy. We used my Invisibility Cloak."

"Did you have any particular reason for doing so, or was it a mere whim?"

"Because I thought Malfoy was up to something," said Harry, disregarding Mr. Weasley's look of mingled exasperation and amusement. "He'd given his mother the slip and I wanted to know why."

"Of course you did," said Mr. Weasley, sounding resigned. "Well? Did you find out why?"

"He went into Borgin and Burkes," said Harry, "and started bullying the bloke in there, Borgin, to help him fix something. And he said he wanted Borgin to keep something else for him. He made it sound like it was the same kind of thing that needed fixing. Like they were a pair. And . . ."

Harry took a deep breath.

"There's something else. We saw Malfoy jump about a mile when Madam Malkin tried to touch his left arm. I think he's been branded with the Dark Mark. I think he's replaced his father as a Death Eater."

Mr. Weasley looked taken aback. After a moment he said, "Harry, I doubt whether You-Know-Who would allow a sixteen-year-old —"

"Does anyone really know what You-Know-Who would or wouldn't do?" asked Harry angrily. "Mr. Weasley, I'm sorry, but isn't it worth investigating? If Malfoy wants something fixing, and he needs to threaten Borgin to get it done, it's probably something Dark or dangerous, isn't it?"

"I doubt it, to be honest, Harry," said Mr. Weasley slowly. "You see, when Lucius Malfoy was arrested, we raided his house. We took away everything that might have been dangerous."

"I think you missed something," said Harry stubbornly.

"Well, maybe," said Mr. Weasley, but Harry could tell that Mr. Weasley was humoring him.

There was a whistle behind them; nearly everyone had boarded the train and the doors were closing.

"You'd better hurry," said Mr. Weasley, as Mrs. Weasley cried, "Harry, quickly!"

He hurried forward and Mr. and Mrs. Weasley helped him load his trunk onto the train.

"Now, dear, you're coming to us for Christmas, it's all fixed with Dumbledore, so we'll see you quite soon," said Mrs. Weasley through the window, as Harry slammed the door shut behind him and the train began to move. "You make sure you look after yourself and —"

The train was gathering speed.

"— be good and —"

She was jogging to keep up now.

"— stay safe!"

Harry waved until the train had turned a corner and Mr. and Mrs. Weasley were lost to view, then turned to see where the others had got to. He supposed Ron and Hermione were cloistered in the prefects' carriage, but Ginny was a little way along the corridor, chatting to some friends. He made his way toward her, dragging his trunk.

People stared shamelessly as he approached. They even pressed their faces against the windows of their compartments to get a look at him. He had expected an upswing in the amount of gaping and gawping he would have to endure this term after all the "Chosen One" rumors in the *Daily Prophet,* but he did not enjoy the sensation of standing in a very bright spotlight. He tapped Ginny on the shoulder.

"Fancy trying to find a compartment?"

"I can't, Harry, I said I'd meet Dean," said Ginny brightly. "See you later."

"Right," said Harry. He felt a strange twinge of annoyance as she walked away, her long red hair dancing behind her; he had become so used to her presence over the summer that he had almost forgotten that Ginny did not hang around with him, Ron, and Hermione while at school. Then he blinked and looked around: He was surrounded by mesmerized girls.

"Hi, Harry!" said a familiar voice from behind him.

"Neville!" said Harry in relief, turning to see a round-faced boy struggling toward him.

"Hello, Harry," said a girl with long hair and large misty eyes, who was just behind Neville.

"Luna, hi, how are you?"

"Very well, thank you," said Luna. She was clutching a magazine to her chest; large letters on the front announced that there was a pair of free Spectrespecs inside.

"*Quibbler* still going strong, then?" asked Harry, who felt a certain fondness for the magazine, having given it an exclusive interview the previous year.

"Oh yes, circulation's well up," said Luna happily.

"Let's find seats," said Harry, and the three of them set off along the train through hordes of silently staring students. At last they found an empty compartment, and Harry hurried inside gratefully.

"They're even staring at *us*!" said Neville, indicating himself and Luna. "Because we're with you!"

"They're staring at you because you were at the Ministry too," said Harry, as he hoisted his trunk into the luggage rack. "Our little adventure there was all over the *Daily Prophet,* you must've seen it."

"Yes, I thought Gran would be angry about all the publicity," said Neville, "but she was really pleased. Says I'm starting to live up to my dad at long last. She bought me a new wand, look!"

He pulled it out and showed it to Harry.

"Cherry and unicorn hair," he said proudly. "We think it was one of the last Ollivander ever sold, he vanished next day — oi, come back here, Trevor!"

And he dived under the seat to retrieve his toad as it made one of its frequent bids for freedom.

"Are we still doing D.A. meetings this year, Harry?" asked Luna, who was detaching a pair of psychedelic spectacles from the middle of *The Quibbler.*

"No point now we've got rid of Umbridge, is there?" said Harry, sitting down. Neville bumped his head against the seat as he emerged from under it. He looked most disappointed.

"I liked the D.A.! I learned loads with you!"

"I enjoyed the meetings too," said Luna serenely. "It was like having friends."

This was one of those uncomfortable things Luna often said and which made Harry feel a squirming mixture of pity and embarrassment. Before he could respond, however, there was a disturbance outside their compartment door; a group of fourth-year girls was whispering and giggling together on the other side of the glass.

"You ask him!"

"No, you!"

"I'll do it!"

And one of them, a bold-looking girl with large dark eyes, a prominent chin, and long black hair pushed her way through the door.

"Hi, Harry, I'm Romilda, Romilda Vane," she said loudly and confidently. "Why don't you join us in our compartment? You don't have to sit with *them,*" she added in a stage whisper, indicating Neville's bottom, which was sticking out from under the seat again as he groped around for Trevor, and Luna, who was now wearing her free Spectrespecs, which gave her the look of a demented, multicolored owl.

"They're friends of mine," said Harry coldly.

"Oh," said the girl, looking very surprised. "Oh. Okay."

And she withdrew, sliding the door closed behind her.

"People expect you to have cooler friends than us," said Luna, once again displaying her knack for embarrassing honesty.

"You are cool," said Harry shortly. "None of them was at the Ministry. They didn't fight with me."

"That's a very nice thing to say," beamed Luna. Then she pushed her Spectrespecs farther up her nose and settled down to read *The Quibbler.*

"We didn't face *him,* though," said Neville, emerging from under the seat with fluff and dust in his hair and a resigned-looking Trevor in his hand. "You did. You should hear my gran talk about you. *'That Harry Potter's got more backbone than the whole Ministry of Magic put together!'* She'd give anything to have you as a grandson. . . ."

Harry laughed uncomfortably and changed the subject to O.W.L. results as soon as he could. While Neville recited his grades and wondered aloud whether he would be allowed to take a Transfiguration N.E.W.T. with only an "Acceptable," Harry watched him without really listening.

Neville's childhood had been blighted by Voldemort just as much as Harry's had, but Neville had no idea how close he had come to having Harry's destiny. The prophecy could have referred to either of them, yet, for his own inscrutable reasons, Voldemort had chosen to believe that Harry was the one meant.

Had Voldemort chosen Neville, it would be Neville sitting opposite Harry bearing the lightning-shaped scar and the weight of the prophecy. . . . Or would it? Would Neville's mother have died to save him, as Lily had died for Harry? Surely she would. . . . But what if she had been unable to stand between her son and Voldemort? Would there then have been no "Chosen One" at all? An empty seat where Neville now sat and a scarless Harry who would have been kissed good-bye by his own mother, not Ron's?

"You all right, Harry? You look funny," said Neville.

Harry started. "Sorry — I —"

"Wrackspurt got you?" asked Luna sympathetically, peering at Harry through her enormous colored spectacles.

"I — what?"

"A Wrackspurt . . . They're invisible. They float in through your ears and make your brain go fuzzy," she said. "I thought I felt one zooming around in here."

She flapped her hands at thin air, as though beating off large invisible moths. Harry and Neville caught each other's eyes and hastily began to talk of Quidditch.

The weather beyond the train windows was as patchy as it had been all summer; they passed through stretches of the chilling mist, then out into weak, clear sunlight. It was during one of the clear spells, when the sun was visible almost directly overhead, that Ron and Hermione entered the compartment at last.

"Wish the lunch trolley would hurry up, I'm starving," said Ron longingly, slumping into the seat beside Harry and rubbing his stomach. "Hi, Neville. Hi, Luna. Guess what?" he added, turning to Harry. "Malfoy's not doing prefect duty. He's just sitting in his compartment with the other Slytherins, we saw him when we passed."

Harry sat up straight, interested. It was not like Malfoy to pass up the chance to demonstrate his power as prefect, which he had happily abused all the previous year.

"What did he do when he saw you?"

"The usual," said Ron indifferently, demonstrating a rude hand gesture. "Not like him, though, is it? Well — *that* is" — he did the hand gesture again — "but why isn't he out there bullying first years?"

"Dunno," said Harry, but his mind was racing. Didn't this look as though Malfoy had more important things on his mind than bullying younger students?

"Maybe he preferred the Inquisitorial Squad," said Hermione. "Maybe being a prefect seems a bit tame after that."

"I don't think so," said Harry. "I think he's —"

But before he could expound on his theory, the compartment door slid open again and a breathless third-year girl stepped inside.

"I'm supposed to deliver these to Neville Longbottom and Harry P-Potter," she faltered, as her eyes met Harry's and she turned scarlet. She was holding out two scrolls of parchment tied with violet ribbon. Perplexed, Harry and Neville took the scroll addressed to each of them and the girl stumbled back out of the compartment.

"What is it?" Ron demanded, as Harry unrolled his.

"An invitation," said Harry.

> *Harry,*
> *I would be delighted if you would join me for a bite of lunch in compartment C.*
> *Sincerely,*
> *Professor H. E. F. Slughorn*

"Who's Professor Slughorn?" asked Neville, looking perplexedly at his own invitation.

"New teacher," said Harry. "Well, I suppose we'll have to go, won't we?"

"But what does he want me for?" asked Neville nervously, as though he was expecting detention.

"No idea," said Harry, which was not entirely true, though he had no proof yet that his hunch was correct. "Listen," he added, seized by a sudden brain wave, "let's go under the Invisibility Cloak, then we might get a good look at Malfoy on the way, see what he's up to."

This idea, however, came to nothing: The corridors, which were packed with people on the lookout for the lunch trolley, were impossible to negotiate while wearing the cloak. Harry stowed it regretfully back in his bag, reflecting that it would have been nice to wear it just to avoid all the staring, which seemed to have increased in intensity even since he had last walked down the train. Every now and then, students would hurtle out of their compartments to get a better look at him. The exception was Cho Chang, who darted into her compartment when she saw Harry coming. As Harry passed the window, he saw her deep in determined conversation with her friend Marietta, who was wearing a very thick layer of makeup that did not entirely obscure the odd formation of pimples still etched across her face. Smirking slightly, Harry pushed on.

When they reached compartment C, they saw at once that they were not Slughorn's only invitees, although judging by the enthusiasm of Slughorn's welcome, Harry was the most warmly anticipated.

"Harry, m'boy!" said Slughorn, jumping up at the sight of him so that his great velvet-covered belly seemed to fill all the remaining space in the compartment. His shiny bald head and great silvery mustache gleamed as brightly in the sunlight as the golden buttons on his waistcoat. "Good to see you, good to see you! And you must be Mr. Longbottom!"

Neville nodded, looking scared. At a gesture from Slughorn, they sat down opposite each other in the only two empty seats, which were nearest the door. Harry glanced around at their fellow guests. He recognized a Slytherin from their year, a tall black boy with high cheekbones and long, slanting eyes; there were also two seventh-year boys Harry did not know and, squashed in the corner beside Slughorn and looking as though she was not entirely sure how she had got there, Ginny.

"Now, do you know everyone?" Slughorn asked Harry and Neville. "Blaise Zabini is in your year, of course —"

Zabini did not make any sign of recognition or greeting, nor did Harry or Neville: Gryffindor and Slytherin students loathed each other on principle.

"This is Cormac McLaggen, perhaps you've come across each other — ? No?"

McLaggen, a large, wiry-haired youth, raised a hand, and Harry and Neville nodded back at him.

"— and this is Marcus Belby, I don't know whether — ?"

Belby, who was thin and nervous-looking, gave a strained smile.

"— and *this* charming young lady tells me she knows you!" Slughorn finished.

Ginny grimaced at Harry and Neville from behind Slughorn's back.

"Well now, this is most pleasant," said Slughorn cozily. "A chance to get to know you all a little better. Here, take a napkin. I've packed my own lunch; the trolley, as I remember it, is heavy on licorice wands, and a poor old man's digestive system isn't quite up to such things. . . . Pheasant, Belby?"

Belby started and accepted what looked like half a cold pheasant.

"I was just telling young Marcus here that I had the pleasure of teaching his Uncle Damocles," Slughorn told Harry and Neville, now passing around a basket of rolls. "Outstanding wizard, outstanding, and his Order of Merlin most well-deserved. Do you see much of your uncle, Marcus?"

Unfortunately, Belby had just taken a large mouthful of pheasant; in his haste to answer Slughorn he swallowed too fast, turned purple, and began to choke.

"*Anapneo,*" said Slughorn calmly, pointing his wand at Belby, whose airway seemed to clear at once.

"Not . . . not much of him, no," gasped Belby, his eyes streaming.

"Well, of course, I daresay he's busy," said Slughorn, looking questioningly at Belby. "I doubt he invented the Wolfsbane Potion without considerable hard work!"

"I suppose . . ." said Belby, who seemed afraid to take another bite of pheasant until he was sure that Slughorn had finished with him. "Er . . . he and my dad don't get on very well, you see, so I don't really know much about . . ."

His voice tailed away as Slughorn gave him a cold smile and turned to McLaggen instead.

"Now, *you,* Cormac," said Slughorn, "I happen to know you see a lot of your Uncle Tiberius, because he has a rather splendid picture of the two of you hunting nogtails in, I think, Norfolk?"

"Oh, yeah, that was fun, that was," said McLaggen. "We went with Bertie Higgs and Rufus Scrimgeour — this was before he became Minister, obviously —"

"Ah, you know Bertie and Rufus too?" beamed Slughorn, now offering around a small tray of pies; somehow, Belby was missed out. "Now tell me . . ."

It was as Harry had suspected. Everyone here seemed to have been invited because they were connected to somebody well-known or influential — everyone except Ginny. Zabini, who was interrogated after McLaggen, turned out to have a famously beautiful witch for a mother (from what Harry could make out, she had been married seven times, each of her husbands dying mysteriously and leaving her mounds of gold). It was Neville's turn next: This was a very uncomfortable ten minutes, for Neville's parents, well-known Aurors, had been tortured into insanity by Bellatrix Lestrange and a couple of Death Eater cronies. At the end of Neville's interview, Harry had the impression that Slughorn was reserving judgment on Neville, yet to see whether he had any of his parents' flair.

"And now," said Slughorn, shifting massively in his seat with the air of a compere introducing his star act. "Harry Potter! *Where* to begin? I feel I barely scratched the surface when we met over the summer!" He contemplated Harry for a moment as though he was a particularly large and succulent piece of pheasant, then said, "'The Chosen One,' they're calling you now!"

Harry said nothing. Belby, McLaggen, and Zabini were all staring at him.

"Of course," said Slughorn, watching Harry closely, "there have been rumors for years. . . . I remember when — well — after that *terrible* night — Lily — James — and you survived — and the word was that you must have powers beyond the ordinary —"

Zabini gave a tiny little cough that was clearly supposed to indicate amused skepticism. An angry voice burst out from behind Slughorn.

"Yeah, Zabini, because *you're* so talented . . . at posing. . . ."

"Oh dear!" chuckled Slughorn comfortably, looking around at Ginny, who was glaring at Zabini around Slughorn's great belly. "You want to be careful, Blaise! I saw this young lady perform the most marvelous Bat-Bogey Hex as I was passing her carriage! I wouldn't cross her!"

Zabini merely looked contemptuous.

"Anyway," said Slughorn, turning back to Harry. "*Such* rumors this summer. Of course, one doesn't know what to believe, the *Prophet* has been known to print inaccuracies, make mistakes — but there seems little doubt, given the number of witnesses, that there was *quite* a disturbance at the Ministry and that you were there in the thick of it all!"

Harry, who could not see any way out of this without flatly lying, nodded but still said nothing. Slughorn beamed at him.

"So modest, so modest, no wonder Dumbledore is so fond — you *were* there, then? But the rest of the stories — so sensational, of course, one doesn't know quite what to believe — this fabled prophecy, for instance —"

"We never heard a prophecy," said Neville, turning geranium pink as he said it.

"That's right," said Ginny staunchly. "Neville and I were both there too, and all this 'Chosen One' rubbish is just the *Prophet* making things up as usual."

"You were both there too, were you?" said Slughorn with great interest, looking from Ginny to Neville, but both of them sat clam-like before his encouraging smile.

"Yes . . . well . . . it is true that the *Prophet* often exaggerates, of course. . . ." Slughorn said, sounding a little disappointed. "I remember dear Gwenog telling me (Gwenog Jones, I mean, of course, Captain of the Holyhead Harpies) —"

He meandered off into a long-winded reminiscence, but Harry had the distinct impression that Slughorn had not finished with him, and that he had not been convinced by Neville and Ginny.

The afternoon wore on with more anecdotes about illustrious wizards Slughorn had taught, all of whom had been delighted to join what he called the "Slug Club" at Hogwarts. Harry could not wait to leave, but couldn't see how to do so politely. Finally the train emerged from yet another long misty stretch into a red sunset, and Slughorn looked around, blinking in the twilight.

"Good gracious, it's getting dark already! I didn't notice that they'd lit the lamps! You'd better go and change into your robes, all of you. McLaggen, you must drop by and borrow that book on nogtails. Harry, Blaise — any time you're passing. Same goes for you, miss," he twinkled at Ginny. "Well, off you go, off you go!"

As he pushed past Harry into the darkening corridor, Zabini shot him a filthy look that Harry returned with interest. He, Ginny, and Neville followed Zabini back along the train.

"I'm glad that's over," muttered Neville. "Strange man, isn't he?"

"Yeah, he is a bit," said Harry, his eyes on Zabini. "How come you ended up in there, Ginny?"

"He saw me hex Zacharias Smith," said Ginny. "You remember that idiot from Hufflepuff who was in the D.A.? He kept on and on asking about what happened at the Ministry and in the end he annoyed me so much I hexed him — when Slughorn came in I thought I was going to get detention, but he just thought it was a really good hex and invited me to lunch! Mad, eh?"

"Better reason for inviting someone than because their mother's famous," said Harry, scowling at the back of Zabini's head, "or because their uncle —"

But he broke off. An idea had just occurred to him, a reckless but potentially wonderful idea. . . . In a minute's time, Zabini was going to reenter the Slytherin sixth-year compartment and Malfoy would be sitting there, thinking himself unheard by anybody except fellow Slytherins. . . . If Harry could only enter, unseen, behind him, what might he not see or hear? True, there was little of the journey left — Hogsmeade Station had to be less than half an hour away, judging by the wildness of the scenery flashing by the windows — but nobody else seemed prepared to take Harry's suspicions seriously, so it was down to him to prove them.

"I'll see you two later," said Harry under his breath, pulling out his Invisibility Cloak and flinging it over himself.

"But what're you — ?" asked Neville.

"Later!" whispered Harry, darting after Zabini as quietly as possible, though the rattling of the train made such caution almost pointless.

The corridors were almost completely empty now. Nearly everyone had returned to their carriages to change into their school robes and pack up their possessions. Though he was as close as he could get to Zabini without touching him, Harry was not quick enough to slip into the compartment when Zabini opened the door. Zabini was already sliding it shut when Harry hastily stuck out his foot to prevent it closing.

"What's wrong with this thing?" said Zabini angrily as he smashed the sliding door repeatedly into Harry's foot.

Harry seized the door and pushed it open, hard; Zabini, still clinging on to the handle, toppled over sideways into Gregory Goyle's lap, and in the ensuing ruckus, Harry darted into the compartment, leapt onto Zabini's temporarily empty seat, and hoisted himself up into the luggage rack. It was fortunate that Goyle and Zabini were snarling at each other, drawing all eyes onto them, for Harry was quite sure his feet and ankles had been revealed as the cloak had flapped around them; indeed, for one horrible moment he thought he saw Malfoy's eyes follow his trainer as it whipped upward out of sight. But then Goyle slammed the door shut and flung Zabini off him; Zabini collapsed into his own seat looking ruffled, Vincent Crabbe returned to his comic, and Malfoy, sniggering, lay back down across two seats with his head in Pansy Parkinson's lap. Harry lay curled uncomfortably under the cloak to ensure that every inch of him remained hidden, and watched Pansy stroke the sleek blond hair off Malfoy's forehead, smirking as she did so, as though anyone would have loved to have been in her place. The lanterns swinging from the carriage ceiling cast a bright light over the scene: Harry could read every word of Crabbe's comic directly below him.

"So, Zabini," said Malfoy, "what did Slughorn want?"

"Just trying to make up to well-connected people," said Zabini, who was still glowering at Goyle. "Not that he managed to find many."

This information did not seem to please Malfoy.

"Who else had he invited?" he demanded.

"McLaggen from Gryffindor," said Zabini.

"Oh yeah, his uncle's big in the Ministry," said Malfoy.

"— someone else called Belby, from Ravenclaw —"

"Not him, he's a prat!" said Pansy.

"— and Longbottom, Potter, and that Weasley girl," finished Zabini.

Malfoy sat up very suddenly, knocking Pansy's hand aside.

"He invited *Longbottom*?"

"Well, I assume so, as Longbottom was there," said Zabini indifferently.

"What's Longbottom got to interest Slughorn?"

Zabini shrugged.

"Potter, precious Potter, obviously he wanted a look at '*the Chosen One*,'" sneered Malfoy, "but that Weasley girl! What's so special about *her*?"

"A lot of boys like her," said Pansy, watching Malfoy out of the corner of her eyes for his reaction. "Even you think she's good-looking, don't you, Blaise, and we all know how hard you are to please!"

"I wouldn't touch a filthy little blood traitor like her whatever she looked like," said Zabini coldly, and Pansy looked pleased. Malfoy sank back across her lap and allowed her to resume the stroking of his hair.

"Well, I pity Slughorn's taste. Maybe he's going a bit senile. Shame, my father always said he was a good wizard in his day. My father used to be a bit of a favorite of his. Slughorn probably hasn't heard I'm on the train, or —"

"I wouldn't bank on an invitation," said Zabini. "He asked me about Nott's father when I first arrived. They used to be old friends, apparently, but when he heard he'd been caught at the Ministry he didn't look happy, and Nott didn't get an invitation, did he? I don't think Slughorn's interested in Death Eaters."

Malfoy looked angry, but forced out a singularly humorless laugh.

"Well, who cares what he's interested in? What is he, when you come down to it? Just some stupid teacher." Malfoy yawned ostentatiously. "I mean, I might not even be at Hogwarts next year, what's it matter to me if some fat old has-been likes me or not?"

"What do you mean, you might not be at Hogwarts next year?" said Pansy indignantly, ceasing grooming Malfoy at once.

"Well, you never know," said Malfoy with the ghost of a smirk. "I might have — er — moved on to bigger and better things."

Crouched in the luggage rack under his cloak, Harry's heart began to race. What would Ron and Hermione say about this? Crabbe and Goyle were gawping at Malfoy; apparently they had had no inkling of any plans to move on to bigger and better things. Even Zabini had allowed a look of curiosity to mar his haughty features. Pansy resumed the slow stroking of Malfoy's hair, looking dumbfounded.

"Do you mean — *Him*?"

Malfoy shrugged.

"Mother wants me to complete my education, but personally, I don't see it as that important these days. I mean, think about it. . . . When the Dark Lord takes over, is he going to care how many O.W.L.s or N.E.W.T.s anyone's got? Of course he isn't. . . . It'll be all about the kind of service he received, the level of devotion he was shown."

"And you think *you'll* be able to do something for him?" asked

Zabini scathingly. "Sixteen years old and not even fully qualified yet?"

"I've just said, haven't I? Maybe he doesn't care if I'm qualified. Maybe the job he wants me to do isn't something that you need to be qualified for," said Malfoy quietly.

Crabbe and Goyle were both sitting with their mouths open like gargoyles. Pansy was gazing down at Malfoy as though she had never seen anything so awe-inspiring.

"I can see Hogwarts," said Malfoy, clearly relishing the effect he had created as he pointed out of the blackened window. "We'd better get our robes on."

Harry was so busy staring at Malfoy, he did not notice Goyle reaching up for his trunk; as he swung it down, it hit Harry hard on the side of the head. He let out an involuntary gasp of pain, and Malfoy looked up at the luggage rack, frowning.

Harry was not afraid of Malfoy, but he still did not much like the idea of being discovered hiding under his Invisibility Cloak by a group of unfriendly Slytherins. Eyes still watering and head still throbbing, he drew his wand, careful not to disarrange the cloak, and waited, breath held. To his relief, Malfoy seemed to decide that he had imagined the noise; he pulled on his robes like the others, locked his trunk, and as the train slowed to a jerky crawl, fastened a thick new traveling cloak round his neck.

Harry could see the corridors filling up again and hoped that Hermione and Ron would take his things out onto the platform for him; he was stuck where he was until the compartment had quite emptied. At last, with a final lurch, the train came to a complete halt. Goyle threw the door open and muscled his way out

into a crowd of second years, punching them aside; Crabbe and
Zabini followed.

"You go on," Malfoy told Pansy, who was waiting for him with
her hand held out as though hoping he would hold it. "I just want
to check something."

Pansy left. Now Harry and Malfoy were alone in the compartment. People were filing past, descending onto the dark platform.
Malfoy moved over to the compartment door and let down the
blinds, so that people in the corridor beyond could not peer in. He
then bent down over his trunk and opened it again.

Harry peered down over the edge of the luggage rack, his heart
pumping a little faster. What had Malfoy wanted to hide from
Pansy? Was he about to see the mysterious broken object it was so
important to mend?

"*Petrificus Totalus!*"

Without warning, Malfoy pointed his wand at Harry, who was
instantly paralyzed. As though in slow motion, he toppled out of
the luggage rack and fell, with an agonizing, floor-shaking crash, at
Malfoy's feet, the Invisibility Cloak trapped beneath him, his
whole body revealed with his legs still curled absurdly into the
cramped kneeling position. He couldn't move a muscle; he could
only gaze up at Malfoy, who smiled broadly.

"I thought so," he said jubilantly. "I heard Goyle's trunk hit you.
And I thought I saw something white flash through the air after
Zabini came back. . . ."

His eyes lingered for a moment upon Harry's trainers.

"You didn't hear anything I care about, Potter. But while I've got
you here . . ."

And he stamped, hard, on Harry's face. Harry felt his nose break; blood spurted everywhere.

"That's from my father. Now, let's see. . . ."

Malfoy dragged the cloak out from under Harry's immobilized body and threw it over him.

"I don't reckon they'll find you till the train's back in London," he said quietly. "See you around, Potter . . . or not."

And taking care to tread on Harry's fingers, Malfoy left the compartment.

SNAPE VICTORIOUS

arry could not move a muscle. He lay there beneath the Invisibility Cloak feeling the blood from his nose flow, hot and wet, over his face, listening to the voices and footsteps in the corridor beyond. His immediate thought was that someone, surely, would check the compartments before the train departed again. But at once came the dispiriting realization that even if somebody looked into the compartment, he would be neither seen nor heard. His best hope was that somebody else would walk in and step on him.

Harry had never hated Malfoy more than as he lay there, like an absurd turtle on its back, blood dripping sickeningly into his open mouth. What a stupid situation to have landed himself in . . . and now the last few footsteps were dying away; everyone was shuffling along the dark platform outside; he could hear the scraping of trunks and the loud babble of talk.

Ron and Hermione would think that he had left the train

without them. Once they arrived at Hogwarts and took their places in the Great Hall, looked up and down the Gryffindor table a few times, and finally realized that he was not there, he, no doubt, would be halfway back to London.

He tried to make a sound, even a grunt, but it was impossible. Then he remembered that some wizards, like Dumbledore, could perform spells without speaking, so he tried to summon his wand, which had fallen out of his hand, by saying the words *"Accio Wand!"* over and over again in his head, but nothing happened.

He thought he could hear the rustling of the trees that surrounded the lake, and the far-off hoot of an owl, but no hint of a search being made or even (he despised himself slightly for hoping it) panicked voices wondering where Harry Potter had gone. A feeling of hopelessness spread through him as he imagined the convoy of thestral-drawn carriages trundling up to the school and the muffled yells of laughter issuing from whichever carriage Malfoy was riding in, where he could be recounting his attack on Harry to Crabbe, Goyle, Zabini, and Pansy Parkinson.

The train lurched, causing Harry to roll over onto his side. Now he was staring at the dusty underside of the seats instead of the ceiling. The floor began to vibrate as the engine roared into life. The Express was leaving and nobody knew he was still on it. . . .

Then he felt his Invisibility Cloak fly off him and a voice overhead said, "Wotcher, Harry."

There was a flash of red light and Harry's body unfroze; he was able to push himself into a more dignified sitting position, hastily wipe the blood off his bruised face with the back of his hand, and raise his head to look up at Tonks, who was holding the Invisibility Cloak she had just pulled away.

"We'd better get out of here, quickly," she said, as the train windows became obscured with steam and they began to move out of the station. "Come on, we'll jump."

Harry hurried after her into the corridor. She pulled open the train door and leapt onto the platform, which seemed to be sliding underneath them as the train gathered momentum. He followed her, staggered a little on landing, then straightened up in time to see the gleaming scarlet steam engine pick up speed, round the corner, and disappear from view.

The cold night air was soothing on his throbbing nose. Tonks was looking at him; he felt angry and embarrassed that he had been discovered in such a ridiculous position. Silently she handed him back the Invisibility Cloak.

"Who did it?"

"Draco Malfoy," said Harry bitterly. "Thanks for . . . well . . ."

"No problem," said Tonks, without smiling. From what Harry could see in the darkness, she was as mousy-haired and miserable-looking as she had been when he had met her at the Burrow. "I can fix your nose if you stand still."

Harry did not think much of this idea; he had been intending to visit Madam Pomfrey, the matron, in whom he had a little more confidence when it came to Healing Spells, but it seemed rude to say this, so he stayed stock-still and closed his eyes.

"*Episkey,*" said Tonks.

Harry's nose felt very hot, and then very cold. He raised a hand and felt it gingerly. It seemed to be mended.

"Thanks a lot!"

"You'd better put that cloak back on, and we can walk up to the school," said Tonks, still unsmiling. As Harry swung the cloak back over himself, she waved her wand; an immense silvery four-legged creature erupted from it and streaked off into the darkness.

"Was that a Patronus?" asked Harry, who had seen Dumbledore send messages like this.

"Yes, I'm sending word to the castle that I've got you or they'll worry. Come on, we'd better not dawdle."

They set off toward the lane that led to the school.

"How did you find me?"

"I noticed you hadn't left the train and I knew you had that cloak. I thought you might be hiding for some reason. When I saw the blinds were drawn down on that compartment I thought I'd check."

"But what are you doing here, anyway?" Harry asked.

"I'm stationed in Hogsmeade now, to give the school extra protection," said Tonks.

"Is it just you who's stationed up here, or — ?"

"No, Proudfoot, Savage, and Dawlish are here too."

"Dawlish, that Auror Dumbledore attacked last year?"

"That's right."

They trudged up the dark, deserted lane, following the freshly made carriage tracks. Harry looked sideways at Tonks under his cloak. Last year she had been inquisitive (to the point of being a little annoying at times), she had laughed easily, she had made jokes. Now she seemed older and much more serious and purposeful. Was this all the effect of what had happened at the Ministry? He reflected uncomfortably that Hermione would have suggested he say something consoling about Sirius to her, that it hadn't been her fault at all, but he couldn't bring himself to do it. He was far from blaming her for Sirius's death; it was no more her fault than anyone else's (and much less than his), but he did not like talking about Sirius if he could avoid it. And so they tramped on through the cold night in silence, Tonks's long cloak whispering on the ground behind them.

Having always traveled there by carriage, Harry had never before appreciated just how far Hogwarts was from Hogsmeade Station. With great relief he finally saw the tall pillars on either side of the gates, each topped with a winged boar. He was cold, he was hungry, and he was quite keen to leave this new, gloomy Tonks behind. But when he put out a hand to push open the gates, he found them chained shut.

"Alohomora!" he said confidently, pointing his wand at the padlock, but nothing happened.

"That won't work on these," said Tonks. "Dumbledore bewitched them himself."

Harry looked around.

"I could climb a wall," he suggested.

"No, you couldn't," said Tonks flatly. "Anti-intruder jinxes on all of them. Security's been tightened a hundredfold this summer."

"Well then," said Harry, starting to feel annoyed at her lack of helpfulness, "I suppose I'll just have to sleep out here and wait for morning."

"Someone's coming down for you," said Tonks. "Look."

A lantern was bobbing at the distant foot of the castle. Harry was so pleased to see it he felt he could even endure Filch's wheezy criticisms of his tardiness and rants about how his timekeeping would improve with the regular application of thumbscrews. It was not until the glowing yellow light was ten feet away from them, and Harry had pulled off his Invisibility Cloak so that he could be seen, that he recognized, with a rush of pure loathing, the uplit hooked nose and long, black, greasy hair of Severus Snape.

"Well, well, well," sneered Snape, taking out his wand and tapping the padlock once, so that the chains snaked backward and the gates creaked open. "Nice of you to turn up, Potter, although you have evidently decided that the wearing of school robes would detract from your appearance."

"I couldn't change, I didn't have my —" Harry began, but Snape cut across him.

"There is no need to wait, Nymphadora, Potter is quite — ah — safe in my hands."

"I meant Hagrid to get the message," said Tonks, frowning.

"Hagrid was late for the start-of-term feast, just like Potter here, so I took it instead. And incidentally," said Snape, standing back to allow Harry to pass him, "I was interested to see your new Patronus."

He shut the gates in her face with a loud clang and tapped the chains with his wand again, so that they slithered, clinking, back into place.

"I think you were better off with the old one," said Snape, the malice in his voice unmistakable. "The new one looks weak."

As Snape swung the lantern about, Harry saw, fleetingly, a look of shock and anger on Tonks's face. Then she was covered in darkness once more.

"Good night," Harry called to her over his shoulder, as he began the walk up to the school with Snape. "Thanks for . . . everything."

"See you, Harry."

Snape did not speak for a minute or so. Harry felt as though his body was generating waves of hatred so powerful that it seemed incredible that Snape could not feel them burning him. He had loathed Snape from their first encounter, but Snape had placed himself forever and irrevocably beyond the possibility of Harry's forgiveness by his attitude toward Sirius. Whatever Dumbledore said, Harry had had time to think over the summer, and had concluded that Snape's snide remarks to Sirius about remaining safely hidden while the rest of the Order of the Phoenix were off fighting Voldemort had probably been a powerful factor in Sirius rushing off to the Ministry the night that he had died. Harry clung to this notion, because it enabled him to blame Snape, which felt satisfying, and also because he knew that if anyone was not sorry that Sirius was dead, it was the man now striding next to him in the darkness.

"Fifty points from Gryffindor for lateness, I think," said Snape. "And, let me see, another twenty for your Muggle attire. You know, I don't believe any House has ever been in negative figures this early in the term: We haven't even started pudding. You might have set a record, Potter."

The fury and hatred bubbling inside Harry seemed to blaze white-hot, but he would rather have been immobilized all the way back to London than tell Snape why he was late.

"I suppose you wanted to make an entrance, did you?" Snape continued. "And with no flying car available you decided that bursting into the Great Hall halfway through the feast ought to create a dramatic effect."

Still Harry remained silent, though he thought his chest might explode. He knew that Snape had come to fetch him for this, for the few minutes when he could needle and torment Harry without anyone else listening.

They reached the castle steps at last and as the great oaken front doors swung open into the vast flagged entrance hall, a burst of talk and laughter and of tinkling plates and glasses greeted them through the doors standing open into the Great Hall. Harry wondered whether he could slip his Invisibility Cloak back on, thereby gaining his seat at the long Gryffindor table (which, inconveniently, was the farthest from the entrance hall) without being noticed. As though he had read Harry's mind, however, Snape said, "No cloak. You can walk in so that everyone sees you, which is what you wanted, I'm sure."

Harry turned on the spot and marched straight through the open doors: anything to get away from Snape. The Great Hall, with its four long House tables and its staff table set at the top of the room, was decorated as usual with floating candles that made the plates below glitter and glow. It was all a shimmering blur to Harry, however, who walked so fast that he was passing the Hufflepuff table before people really started to stare, and by the time they were standing up to get a good look at him, he had spotted Ron and Hermione, sped along the benches toward them, and forced his way in between them.

"Where've you — blimey, what've you done to your face?" said Ron, goggling at him along with everyone else in the vicinity.

"Why, what's wrong with it?" said Harry, grabbing a spoon and squinting at his distorted reflection.

"You're covered in blood!" said Hermione. "Come here —"

She raised her wand, said *"Tergeo!"* and siphoned off the dried blood.

"Thanks," said Harry, feeling his now clean face. "How's my nose looking?"

"Normal," said Hermione anxiously. "Why shouldn't it? Harry, what happened? We've been terrified!"

"I'll tell you later," said Harry curtly. He was very conscious that Ginny, Neville, Dean, and Seamus were listening in; even Nearly Headless Nick, the Gryffindor ghost, had come floating along the bench to eavesdrop.

"But —" said Hermione.

"Not now, Hermione," said Harry, in a darkly significant voice. He hoped very much that they would all assume he had been involved in something heroic, preferably involving a couple of Death Eaters and a dementor. Of course, Malfoy would spread the story as far and wide as he could, but there was always a chance it wouldn't reach too many Gryffindor ears.

He reached across Ron for a couple of chicken legs and a handful of chips, but before he could take them they vanished, to be replaced with puddings.

"You missed the Sorting, anyway," said Hermione, as Ron dived for a large chocolate gateau.

"Hat say anything interesting?" asked Harry, taking a piece of treacle tart.

"More of the same, really . . . advising us all to unite in the face of our enemies, you know."

"Dumbledore mentioned Voldemort at all?"

"Not yet, but he always saves his proper speech for after the feast, doesn't he? It can't be long now."

"Snape said Hagrid was late for the feast —"

"You've seen Snape? How come?" said Ron between frenzied mouthfuls of gateau.

"Bumped into him," said Harry evasively.

"Hagrid was only a few minutes late," said Hermione. "Look, he's waving at you, Harry."

Harry looked up at the staff table and grinned at Hagrid, who was indeed waving at him. Hagrid had never quite managed to comport himself with the dignity of Professor McGonagall, Head of Gryffindor House, the top of whose head came up to somewhere between Hagrid's elbow and shoulder as they were sitting side by side, and who was looking disapprovingly at this enthusiastic greeting. Harry was surprised to see the Divination teacher, Professor Trelawney, sitting on Hagrid's other side; she rarely left her tower room, and he had never seen her at the start-of-term feast before. She looked as odd as ever, glittering with beads and trailing shawls, her eyes magnified to enormous size by her spectacles. Having always considered her a bit of a fraud, Harry had been shocked to discover at the end of the previous term that it had been she who had made the prediction that caused Lord Voldemort to kill Harry's parents and attack Harry himself. The knowledge had made him even less eager to find himself in her company, but thankfully, this year he would be dropping Divination. Her great beaconlike eyes swiveled in his direction; he hastily looked away toward the Slytherin table. Draco Malfoy was miming the shattering of a nose to raucous laughter and applause. Harry dropped his gaze to his treacle tart, his insides burning again. What he would not give to fight Malfoy one-on-one . . .

"So what did Professor Slughorn want?" Hermione asked.

"To know what really happened at the Ministry," said Harry.

"Him and everyone else here," sniffed Hermione. "People were interrogating us about it on the train, weren't they, Ron?"

"Yeah," said Ron. "All wanting to know if you really are 'the Chosen One' —"

"There has been much talk on that very subject even amongst the ghosts," interrupted Nearly Headless Nick, inclining his barely connected head toward Harry so that it wobbled dangerously on its ruff. "I am considered something of a Potter authority; it is widely known that we are friendly. I have assured the spirit community that I will not pester you for information, however. 'Harry Potter knows that he can confide in me with complete confidence,' I told them. 'I would rather die than betray his trust.'"

"That's not saying much, seeing as you're already dead," Ron observed.

"Once again, you show all the sensitivity of a blunt axe," said Nearly Headless Nick in affronted tones, and he rose into the air and glided back toward the far end of the Gryffindor table just as Dumbledore got to his feet at the staff table. The talk and laughter echoing around the Hall died away almost instantly.

"The very best of evenings to you!" he said, smiling broadly, his arms opened wide as though to embrace the whole room.

"What happened to his hand?" gasped Hermione.

She was not the only one who had noticed. Dumbledore's right hand was as blackened and dead-looking as it had been on the night he had come to fetch Harry from the Dursleys. Whispers swept the room; Dumbledore, interpreting them correctly, merely smiled and shook his purple-and-gold sleeve over his injury.

"Nothing to worry about," he said airily. "Now . . . to our new students, welcome, to our old students, welcome back! Another year full of magical education awaits you . . ."

"His hand was like that when I saw him over the summer,"

Harry whispered to Hermione. "I thought he'd have cured it by now, though . . . or Madam Pomfrey would've done."

"It looks as if it's died," said Hermione, with a nauseated expression. "But there are some injuries you can't cure . . . old curses . . . and there are poisons without antidotes. . . ."

". . . and Mr. Filch, our caretaker, has asked me to say that there is a blanket ban on any joke items bought at the shop called Weasleys' Wizard Wheezes.

"Those wishing to play for their House Quidditch teams should give their names to their Heads of House as usual. We are also looking for new Quidditch commentators, who should do likewise.

"We are pleased to welcome a new member of staff this year. Professor Slughorn" — Slughorn stood up, his bald head gleaming in the candlelight, his big waistcoated belly casting the table below into shadow — "is a former colleague of mine who has agreed to resume his old post of Potions master."

"Potions?"

"Potions?"

The word echoed all over the Hall as people wondered whether they had heard right.

"Potions?" said Ron and Hermione together, turning to stare at Harry. "But you said —"

"Professor Snape, meanwhile," said Dumbledore, raising his voice so that it carried over all the muttering, "will be taking over the position of Defense Against the Dark Arts teacher."

"No!" said Harry, so loudly that many heads turned in his direction. He did not care; he was staring up at the staff table, incensed. How could Snape be given the Defense Against the Dark Arts job after all this time? Hadn't it been widely known for years that Dumbledore did not trust him to do it?

"But Harry, you said that Slughorn was going to be teaching Defense Against the Dark Arts!" said Hermione.

"I thought he was!" said Harry, racking his brains to remember when Dumbledore had told him this, but now that he came to think of it, he was unable to recall Dumbledore ever telling him what Slughorn would be teaching.

Snape, who was sitting on Dumbledore's right, did not stand up at the mention of his name; he merely raised a hand in lazy acknowledgment of the applause from the Slytherin table, yet Harry was sure he could detect a look of triumph on the features he loathed so much.

"Well, there's one good thing," he said savagely. "Snape'll be gone by the end of the year."

"What do you mean?" asked Ron.

"That job's jinxed. No one's lasted more than a year. . . . Quirrell actually died doing it. . . . Personally, I'm going to keep my fingers crossed for another death. . . ."

"Harry!" said Hermione, shocked and reproachful.

"He might just go back to teaching Potions at the end of the year," said Ron reasonably. "That Slughorn bloke might not want to stay long-term. Moody didn't."

Dumbledore cleared his throat. Harry, Ron, and Hermione were not the only ones who had been talking; the whole Hall had erupted in a buzz of conversation at the news that Snape had finally achieved his heart's desire. Seemingly oblivious to the sensational nature of the news he had just imparted, Dumbledore said nothing more about staff appointments, but waited a few seconds to ensure that the silence was absolute before continuing.

"Now, as everybody in this Hall knows, Lord Voldemort and his followers are once more at large and gaining in strength."

The silence seemed to tauten and strain as Dumbledore spoke. Harry glanced at Malfoy. Malfoy was not looking at Dumbledore, but making his fork hover in midair with his wand, as though he found the headmaster's words unworthy of his attention.

"I cannot emphasize strongly enough how dangerous the present situation is, and how much care each of us at Hogwarts must take to ensure that we remain safe. The castle's magical fortifications have been strengthened over the summer, we are protected in new and more powerful ways, but we must still guard scrupulously against carelessness on the part of any student or member of staff. I urge you, therefore, to abide by any security restrictions that your teachers might impose upon you, however irksome you might find them — in particular, the rule that you are not to be out of bed after hours. I implore you, should you notice anything strange or suspicious within or outside the castle, to report it to a member of staff immediately. I trust you to conduct yourselves, always, with the utmost regard for your own and others' safety."

Dumbledore's blue eyes swept over the students before he smiled once more.

"But now, your beds await, as warm and comfortable as you could possibly wish, and I know that your top priority is to be well-rested for your lessons tomorrow. Let us therefore say good night. Pip pip!"

With the usual deafening scraping noise, the benches were moved back and the hundreds of students began to file out of the

Great Hall toward their dormitories. Harry, who was in no hurry at all to leave with the gawping crowd, nor to get near enough to Malfoy to allow him to retell the story of the nose-stamping, lagged behind, pretending to retie the lace on his trainer, allowing most of the Gryffindors to draw ahead of him. Hermione had darted ahead to fulfill her prefect's duty of shepherding the first years, but Ron remained with Harry.

"What really happened to your nose?" he asked, once they were at the very back of the throng pressing out of the Hall, and out of earshot of anyone else.

Harry told him. It was a mark of the strength of their friendship that Ron did not laugh.

"I saw Malfoy miming something to do with a nose," he said darkly.

"Yeah, well, never mind that," said Harry bitterly. "Listen to what he was saying before he found out I was there. . . ."

Harry had expected Ron to be stunned by Malfoy's boasts. With what Harry considered pure pigheadedness, however, Ron was unimpressed.

"Come on, Harry, he was just showing off for Parkinson. . . . What kind of mission would You-Know-Who have given him?"

"How d'you know Voldemort doesn't need someone at Hogwarts? It wouldn't be the first —"

"I wish yeh'd stop sayin' tha' name, Harry," said a reproachful voice behind them. Harry looked over his shoulder to see Hagrid shaking his head.

"Dumbledore uses that name," said Harry stubbornly.

"Yeah, well, tha's Dumbledore, innit?" said Hagrid mysteriously. "So how come yeh were late, Harry? I was worried."

"Got held up on the train," said Harry. "Why were *you* late?"

"I was with Grawp," said Hagrid happily. "Los' track o' the time. He's got a new home up in the mountains now, Dumbledore fixed it — nice big cave. He's much happier than he was in the forest. We were havin' a good chat."

"Really?" said Harry, taking care not to catch Ron's eye; the last time he had met Hagrid's half-brother, a vicious giant with a talent for ripping up trees by the roots, his vocabulary had comprised five words, two of which he was unable to pronounce properly.

"Oh yeah, he's really come on," said Hagrid proudly. "Yeh'll be amazed. I'm thinkin' o' trainin' him up as me assistant."

Ron snorted loudly, but managed to pass it off as a violent sneeze. They were now standing beside the oak front doors.

"Anyway, I'll see yeh tomorrow, firs' lesson's straight after lunch. Come early an' yeh can say hello ter Buck — I mean, Witherwings!"

Raising an arm in cheery farewell, he headed out of the front doors into the darkness.

Harry and Ron looked at each other. Harry could tell that Ron was experiencing the same sinking feeling as himself.

"You're not taking Care of Magical Creatures, are you?"

Ron shook his head. "And you're not either, are you?"

Harry shook his head too.

"And Hermione," said Ron, "she's not, is she?"

Harry shook his head again. Exactly what Hagrid would say when he realized his three favorite students had given up his subject, he did not like to think.

THE HALF-BLOOD PRINCE

arry and Ron met Hermione in the common room before breakfast next morning. Hoping for some support
for his theory, Harry lost no time in telling Hermione what he had
overheard Malfoy saying on the Hogwarts Express.

"But he was obviously showing off for Parkinson, wasn't he?" interjected Ron quickly, before Hermione could say anything.

"Well," she said uncertainly, "I don't know. . . . It would be like
Malfoy to make himself seem more important than he is . . . but
that's a big lie to tell. . . ."

"Exactly," said Harry, but he could not press the point, because
so many people were trying to listen in to his conversation, not to
mention staring at him and whispering behind their hands.

"It's rude to point," Ron snapped at a particularly minuscule
first-year boy as they joined the queue to climb out of the portrait
hole. The boy, who had been muttering something about Harry

behind his hand to his friend, promptly turned scarlet and toppled out of the hole in alarm. Ron sniggered.

"I love being a sixth year. *And* we're going to be getting free time this year. Whole periods when we can just sit up here and relax."

"We're going to need that time for studying, Ron!" said Hermione, as they set off down the corridor.

"Yeah, but not today," said Ron. "Today's going to be a real doss, I reckon."

"Hold it!" said Hermione, throwing out an arm and halting a passing fourth year, who was attempting to push past her with a lime-green disk clutched tightly in his hand. "Fanged Frisbees are banned, hand it over," she told him sternly. The scowling boy handed over the snarling Frisbee, ducked under her arm, and took off after his friends. Ron waited for him to vanish, then tugged the Frisbee from Hermione's grip.

"Excellent, I've always wanted one of these."

Hermione's remonstration was drowned by a loud giggle; Lavender Brown had apparently found Ron's remark highly amusing. She continued to laugh as she passed them, glancing back at Ron over her shoulder. Ron looked rather pleased with himself.

The ceiling of the Great Hall was serenely blue and streaked with frail, wispy clouds, just like the squares of sky visible through the high mullioned windows. While they tucked into porridge and eggs and bacon, Harry and Ron told Hermione about their embarrassing conversation with Hagrid the previous evening.

"But he can't really think we'd continue Care of Magical Creatures!" she said, looking distressed. "I mean, when has any of us expressed . . . you know . . . any enthusiasm?"

"That's it, though, innit?" said Ron, swallowing an entire fried egg whole. "We were the ones who made the most effort in classes because we like Hagrid. But he thinks we liked the stupid *subject*. D'you reckon anyone's going to go on to N.E.W.T.?"

Neither Harry nor Hermione answered; there was no need. They knew perfectly well that nobody in their year would want to continue Care of Magical Creatures. They avoided Hagrid's eye and returned his cheery wave only halfheartedly when he left the staff table ten minutes later.

After they had eaten, they remained in their places, awaiting Professor McGonagall's descent from the staff table. The distribution of class schedules was more complicated than usual this year, for Professor McGonagall needed first to confirm that everybody had achieved the necessary O.W.L. grades to continue with their chosen N.E.W.T.s.

Hermione was immediately cleared to continue with Charms, Defense Against the Dark Arts, Transfiguration, Herbology, Arithmancy, Ancient Runes, and Potions, and shot off to a first-period Ancient Runes class without further ado. Neville took a little longer to sort out; his round face was anxious as Professor McGonagall looked down his application and then consulted his O.W.L. results.

"Herbology, fine," she said. "Professor Sprout will be delighted to see you back with an 'Outstanding' O.W.L. And you qualify for Defense Against the Dark Arts with 'Exceeds Expectations.' But the problem is Transfiguration. I'm sorry, Longbottom, but an 'Acceptable' really isn't good enough to continue to N.E.W.T. level. I just don't think you'd be able to cope with the coursework."

Neville hung his head. Professor McGonagall peered at him through her square spectacles.

"Why do you want to continue with Transfiguration, anyway? I've never had the impression that you particularly enjoyed it."

Neville looked miserable and muttered something about "my grandmother wants."

"Hmph," snorted Professor McGonagall. "It's high time your grandmother learned to be proud of the grandson she's got, rather than the one she thinks she ought to have — particularly after what happened at the Ministry."

Neville turned very pink and blinked confusedly; Professor McGonagall had never paid him a compliment before.

"I'm sorry, Longbottom, but I cannot let you into my N.E.W.T. class. I see that you have an 'Exceeds Expectations' in Charms, however — why not try for a N.E.W.T. in Charms?"

"My grandmother thinks Charms is a soft option," mumbled Neville.

"Take Charms," said Professor McGonagall, "and I shall drop Augusta a line reminding her that just because she failed *her* Charms O.W.L., the subject is not necessarily worthless." Smiling slightly at the look of delighted incredulity on Neville's face, Professor McGonagall tapped a blank schedule with the tip of her wand and handed it, now carrying details of his new classes, to Neville.

Professor McGonagall turned next to Parvati Patil, whose first question was whether Firenze, the handsome centaur, was still teaching Divination.

"He and Professor Trelawney are dividing classes between them this year," said Professor McGonagall, a hint of disapproval in her voice; it was common knowledge that she despised the subject of Divination. "The sixth year is being taken by Professor Trelawney."

Parvati set off for Divination five minutes later looking slightly crestfallen.

"So, Potter, Potter . . ." said Professor McGonagall, consulting her notes as she turned to Harry. "Charms, Defense Against the Dark Arts, Herbology, Transfiguration . . . all fine. I must say, I was pleased with your Transfiguration mark, Potter, very pleased. Now, why haven't you applied to continue with Potions? I thought it was your ambition to become an Auror?"

"It was, but you told me I had to get an 'Outstanding' in my O.W.L., Professor."

"And so you did when Professor Snape was teaching the subject. Professor Slughorn, however, is perfectly happy to accept N.E.W.T. students with 'Exceeds Expectations' at O.W.L. Do you wish to proceed with Potions?"

"Yes," said Harry, "but I didn't buy the books or any ingredients or anything —"

"I'm sure Professor Slughorn will be able to lend you some," said Professor McGonagall. "Very well, Potter, here is your schedule. Oh, by the way — twenty hopefuls have already put down their names for the Gryffindor Quidditch team. I shall pass the list to you in due course and you can fix up trials at your leisure."

A few minutes later, Ron was cleared to do the same subjects as Harry, and the two of them left the table together.

"Look," said Ron delightedly, gazing at his schedule, "we've got a free period now . . . and a free period after break . . . and after lunch . . . *excellent!*"

They returned to the common room, which was empty apart from a half dozen seventh years, including Katie Bell, the only remaining member of the original Gryffindor Quidditch team that Harry had joined in his first year.

"I thought you'd get that, well done," she called over, pointing at the Captain's badge on Harry's chest. "Tell me when you call trials!"

"Don't be stupid," said Harry, "you don't need to try out, I've watched you play for five years. . . ."

"You mustn't start off like that," she said warningly. "For all you know, there's someone much better than me out there. Good teams have been ruined before now because Captains just kept playing the old faces, or letting in their friends. . . ."

Ron looked a little uncomfortable and began playing with the Fanged Frisbee Hermione had taken from the fourth-year student. It zoomed around the common room, snarling and attempting to take bites of the tapestry. Crookshanks's yellow eyes followed it and he hissed when it came too close.

An hour later they reluctantly left the sunlit common room for the Defense Against the Dark Arts classroom four floors below. Hermione was already queuing outside, carrying an armful of heavy books and looking put-upon.

"We got so much homework for Runes," she said anxiously, when Harry and Ron joined her. "A fifteen-inch essay, two translations, and I've got to read these by Wednesday!"

"Shame," yawned Ron.

"You wait," she said resentfully. "I bet Snape gives us loads."

The classroom door opened as she spoke, and Snape stepped into the corridor, his sallow face framed as ever by two curtains of greasy black hair. Silence fell over the queue immediately.

"Inside," he said.

Harry looked around as they entered. Snape had imposed his personality upon the room already; it was gloomier than usual, as curtains had been drawn over the windows, and was lit by candle-light. New pictures adorned the walls, many of them showing peo-ple who appeared to be in pain, sporting grisly injuries or strangely contorted body parts. Nobody spoke as they settled down, looking around at the shadowy, gruesome pictures.

"I have not asked you to take out your books," said Snape, clos-ing the door and moving to face the class from behind his desk; Hermione hastily dropped her copy of *Confronting the Faceless* back into her bag and stowed it under her chair. "I wish to speak to you, and I want your fullest attention."

His black eyes roved over their upturned faces, lingering for a fraction of a second longer on Harry's than anyone else's.

"You have had five teachers in this subject so far, I believe."

You believe . . . like you haven't watched them all come and go, Snape, hoping you'd be next, thought Harry scathingly.

"Naturally, these teachers will all have had their own methods and priorities. Given this confusion I am surprised so many of you scraped an O.W.L. in this subject. I shall be even more surprised if all of you manage to keep up with the N.E.W.T. work, which will be much more advanced."

Snape set off around the edge of the room, speaking now in a lower voice; the class craned their necks to keep him in view.

"The Dark Arts," said Snape, "are many, varied, ever-changing, and eternal. Fighting them is like fighting a many-headed monster, which, each time a neck is severed, sprouts a head even fiercer and cleverer than before. You are fighting that which is unfixed, mutat-ing, indestructible."

Harry stared at Snape. It was surely one thing to respect the Dark Arts as a dangerous enemy, another to speak of them, as Snape was doing, with a loving caress in his voice?

"Your defenses," said Snape, a little louder, "must therefore be as flexible and inventive as the arts you seek to undo. These pictures" — he indicated a few of them as he swept past — "give a fair representation of what happens to those who suffer, for instance, the Cruciatus Curse" — he waved a hand toward a witch who was clearly shrieking in agony — "feel the Dementor's Kiss" — a wizard lying huddled and blank-eyed, slumped against a wall — "or provoke the aggression of the Inferius" — a bloody mass upon the ground.

"Has an Inferius been seen, then?" said Parvati Patil in a high-pitched voice. "Is it definite, is he using them?"

"The Dark Lord has used Inferi in the past," said Snape, "which means you would be well-advised to assume he might use them again. Now . . ."

He set off again around the other side of the classroom toward his desk, and again, they watched him as he walked, his dark robes billowing behind him.

". . . you are, I believe, complete novices in the use of nonverbal spells. What is the advantage of a nonverbal spell?"

Hermione's hand shot into the air. Snape took his time looking around at everybody else, making sure he had no choice, before saying curtly, "Very well — Miss Granger?"

"Your adversary has no warning about what kind of magic you're about to perform," said Hermione, "which gives you a split-second advantage."

"An answer copied almost word for word from *The Standard Book of Spells, Grade Six,*" said Snape dismissively (over in the corner, Malfoy sniggered), "but correct in essentials. Yes, those who progress to using magic without shouting incantations gain an element of surprise in their spell-casting. Not all wizards can do this, of course; it is a question of concentration and mind power which some" — his gaze lingered maliciously upon Harry once more — "lack."

Harry knew Snape was thinking of their disastrous Occlumency lessons of the previous year. He refused to drop his gaze, but glowered at Snape until Snape looked away.

"You will now divide," Snape went on, "into pairs. One partner will attempt to jinx the other *without speaking.* The other will attempt to repel the jinx *in equal silence.* Carry on."

Although Snape did not know it, Harry had taught at least half the class (everyone who had been a member of the D.A.) how to perform a Shield Charm the previous year. None of them had ever cast the charm without speaking, however. A reasonable amount of cheating ensued; many people were merely whispering the incantation instead of saying it aloud. Typically, ten minutes into the lesson Hermione managed to repel Neville's muttered Jelly-Legs Jinx without uttering a single word, a feat that would surely have earned her twenty points for Gryffindor from any reasonable teacher, thought Harry bitterly, but which Snape ignored. He swept between them as they practiced, looking just as much like an overgrown bat as ever, lingering to watch Harry and Ron struggling with the task.

Ron, who was supposed to be jinxing Harry, was purple in the face, his lips tightly compressed to save himself from the temptation of muttering the incantation. Harry had his wand raised, waiting on tenterhooks to repel a jinx that seemed unlikely ever to come.

"Pathetic, Weasley," said Snape, after a while. "Here — let me show you —"

He turned his wand on Harry so fast that Harry reacted instinctively; all thought of nonverbal spells forgotten, he yelled, *"Protego!"*

His Shield Charm was so strong Snape was knocked off-balance and hit a desk. The whole class had looked around and now watched as Snape righted himself, scowling.

"Do you remember me telling you we are practicing *nonverbal* spells, Potter?"

"Yes," said Harry stiffly.

"Yes, *sir.*"

"There's no need to call me 'sir,' Professor."

The words had escaped him before he knew what he was saying. Several people gasped, including Hermione. Behind Snape, however, Ron, Dean, and Seamus grinned appreciatively.

"Detention, Saturday night, my office," said Snape. "I do not take cheek from anyone, Potter . . . not even *'the Chosen One.'*"

"That was brilliant, Harry!" chortled Ron, once they were safely on their way to break a short while later.

"You really shouldn't have said it," said Hermione, frowning at Ron. "What made you?"

"He tried to jinx me, in case you didn't notice!" fumed Harry. "I had enough of that during those Occlumency lessons! Why doesn't he use another guinea pig for a change? What's Dumbledore playing at, anyway, letting him teach Defense? Did you hear him talking about the Dark Arts? He loves them! All that *unfixed, indestructible* stuff —"

"Well," said Hermione, "I thought he sounded a bit like you."

"Like *me*?"

"Yes, when you were telling us what it's like to face Voldemort. You said it wasn't just memorizing a bunch of spells, you said it was just you and your brains and your guts — well, wasn't that what Snape was saying? That it really comes down to being brave and quick-thinking?"

Harry was so disarmed that she had thought his words as well worth memorizing as *The Standard Book of Spells* that he did not argue.

"Harry! Hey, Harry!"

Harry looked around; Jack Sloper, one of the Beaters on last year's Gryffindor Quidditch team, was hurrying toward him holding a roll of parchment.

"For you," panted Sloper. "Listen, I heard you're the new Captain. When're you holding trials?"

"I'm not sure yet," said Harry, thinking privately that Sloper would be very lucky to get back on the team. "I'll let you know."

"Oh, right. I was hoping it'd be this weekend —"

But Harry was not listening; he had just recognized the thin, slanting writing on the parchment. Leaving Sloper in mid-sentence, he hurried away with Ron and Hermione, unrolling the parchment as he went.

Dear Harry,

I would like to start our private lessons this Saturday. Kindly come along to my office at 8 P.M. I hope you are enjoying your first day back at school.

Yours sincerely,

Albus Dumbledore

P.S. I enjoy Acid Pops.

"He enjoys Acid Pops?" said Ron, who had read the message over Harry's shoulder and was looking perplexed.

"It's the password to get past the gargoyle outside his study," said Harry in a low voice. "Ha! Snape's not going to be pleased. . . . I won't be able to do his detention!"

He, Ron, and Hermione spent the whole of break speculating on what Dumbledore would teach Harry. Ron thought it most likely to be spectacular jinxes and hexes of the type the Death Eaters would not know. Hermione said such things were illegal, and thought it much more likely that Dumbledore wanted to teach Harry advanced Defensive magic. After break, she went off to Arithmancy while Harry and Ron returned to the common room, where they grudgingly started Snape's homework. This turned out to be so complex that they still had not finished when Hermione joined them for their after-lunch free period (though she considerably speeded up the process). They had only just finished when the bell rang for the afternoon's double Potions and they beat the familiar path down to the dungeon classroom that had, for so long, been Snape's.

When they arrived in the corridor they saw that there were only a dozen people progressing to N.E.W.T. level. Crabbe and Goyle had evidently failed to achieve the required O.W.L. grade, but four Slytherins had made it through, including Malfoy. Four Ravenclaws were there, and one Hufflepuff, Ernie Macmillan, whom Harry liked despite his rather pompous manner.

"Harry," Ernie said portentously, holding out his hand as Harry approached, "didn't get a chance to speak in Defense Against the Dark Arts this morning. Good lesson, I thought, but Shield

Charms are old hat, of course, for us old D. A. lags . . . And how are you, Ron — Hermione?"

Before they could say more than "fine," the dungeon door opened and Slughorn's belly preceded him out of the door. As they filed into the room, his great walrus mustache curved above his beaming mouth, and he greeted Harry and Zabini with particular enthusiasm.

The dungeon was, most unusually, already full of vapors and odd smells. Harry, Ron, and Hermione sniffed interestedly as they passed large, bubbling cauldrons. The four Slytherins took a table together, as did the four Ravenclaws. This left Harry, Ron, and Hermione to share a table with Ernie. They chose the one nearest a gold-colored cauldron that was emitting one of the most seductive scents Harry had ever inhaled: Somehow it reminded him simultaneously of treacle tart, the woody smell of a broomstick handle, and something flowery he thought he might have smelled at the Burrow. He found that he was breathing very slowly and deeply and that the potion's fumes seemed to be filling him up like drink. A great contentment stole over him; he grinned across at Ron, who grinned back lazily.

"Now then, now then, now then," said Slughorn, whose massive outline was quivering through the many shimmering vapors. "Scales out, everyone, and potion kits, and don't forget your copies of *Advanced Potion-Making.* . . ."

"Sir?" said Harry, raising his hand.

"Harry, m'boy?"

"I haven't got a book or scales or anything — nor's Ron — we didn't realize we'd be able to do the N.E.W.T., you see —"

"Ah, yes, Professor McGonagall did mention . . . not to worry, my dear boy, not to worry at all. You can use ingredients from the store cupboard today, and I'm sure we can lend you some scales, and we've got a small stock of old books here, they'll do until you can write to Flourish and Blotts. . . ."

Slughorn strode over to a corner cupboard and, after a moment's foraging, emerged with two very battered-looking copies of *Advanced Potion-Making* by Libatius Borage, which he gave to Harry and Ron along with two sets of tarnished scales.

"Now then," said Slughorn, returning to the front of the class and inflating his already bulging chest so that the buttons on his waistcoat threatened to burst off, "I've prepared a few potions for you to have a look at, just out of interest, you know. These are the kind of thing you ought to be able to make after completing your N.E.W.T.s. You ought to have heard of 'em, even if you haven't made 'em yet. Anyone tell me what this one is?"

He indicated the cauldron nearest the Slytherin table. Harry raised himself slightly in his seat and saw what looked like plain water boiling away inside it.

Hermione's well-practiced hand hit the air before anybody else's; Slughorn pointed at her.

"It's Veritaserum, a colorless, odorless potion that forces the drinker to tell the truth," said Hermione.

"Very good, very good!" said Slughorn happily. "Now," he continued, pointing at the cauldron nearest the Ravenclaw table, "this one here is pretty well known. . . . Featured in a few Ministry leaflets lately too . . . Who can — ?"

Hermione's hand was fastest once more.

"It's Polyjuice Potion, sir," she said.

Harry too had recognized the slow-bubbling, mudlike substance in the second cauldron, but did not resent Hermione getting the credit for answering the question; she, after all, was the one who had succeeded in making it, back in their second year.

"Excellent, excellent! Now, this one here . . . yes, my dear?" said Slughorn, now looking slightly bemused, as Hermione's hand punched the air again.

"It's Amortentia!"

"It is indeed. It seems almost foolish to ask," said Slughorn, who was looking mightily impressed, "but I assume you know what it does?"

"It's the most powerful love potion in the world!" said Hermione.

"Quite right! You recognized it, I suppose, by its distinctive mother-of-pearl sheen?"

"And the steam rising in characteristic spirals," said Hermione enthusiastically, "and it's supposed to smell differently to each of us, according to what attracts us, and I can smell freshly mown grass and new parchment and —"

But she turned slightly pink and did not complete the sentence.

"May I ask your name, my dear?" said Slughorn, ignoring Hermione's embarrassment.

"Hermione Granger, sir."

"Granger? Granger? Can you possibly be related to Hector Dagworth-Granger, who founded the Most Extraordinary Society of Potioneers?"

"No, I don't think so, sir. I'm Muggle-born, you see."

Harry saw Malfoy lean close to Nott and whisper something;

both of them sniggered, but Slughorn showed no dismay; on the contrary, he beamed and looked from Hermione to Harry, who was sitting next to her.

"Oho! *'One of my best friends is Muggle-born, and she's the best in our year!'* I'm assuming this is the very friend of whom you spoke, Harry?"

"Yes, sir," said Harry.

"Well, well, take twenty well-earned points for Gryffindor, Miss Granger," said Slughorn genially.

Malfoy looked rather as he had done the time Hermione had punched him in the face. Hermione turned to Harry with a radiant expression and whispered, "Did you really tell him I'm the best in the year? Oh, Harry!"

"Well, what's so impressive about that?" whispered Ron, who for some reason looked annoyed. "You *are* the best in the year — I'd've told him so if he'd asked me!"

Hermione smiled but made a "shhing" gesture, so that they could hear what Slughorn was saying. Ron looked slightly disgruntled.

"Amortentia doesn't really create *love,* of course. It is impossible to manufacture or imitate love. No, this will simply cause a powerful infatuation or obsession. It is probably the most dangerous and powerful potion in this room — oh yes," he said, nodding gravely at Malfoy and Nott, both of whom were smirking skeptically. "When you have seen as much of life as I have, you will not underestimate the power of obsessive love. . . ."

"And now," said Slughorn, "it is time for us to start work."

"Sir, you haven't told us what's in this one," said Ernie Macmillan, pointing at a small black cauldron standing on Slughorn's desk. The potion within was splashing about merrily; it was the color of molten gold, and large drops were leaping like goldfish above the surface, though not a particle had spilled.

"Oho," said Slughorn again. Harry was sure that Slughorn had not forgotten the potion at all, but had waited to be asked for dramatic effect. "Yes. That. Well, *that* one, ladies and gentlemen, is a most curious little potion called Felix Felicis. I take it," he turned, smiling, to look at Hermione, who had let out an audible gasp, "that you know what Felix Felicis does, Miss Granger?"

"It's liquid luck," said Hermione excitedly. "It makes you lucky!"

The whole class seemed to sit up a little straighter. Now all Harry could see of Malfoy was the back of his sleek blond head, because he was at last giving Slughorn his full and undivided attention.

"Quite right, take another ten points for Gryffindor. Yes, it's a funny little potion, Felix Felicis," said Slughorn. "Desperately tricky to make, and disastrous to get wrong. However, if brewed correctly, as this has been, you will find that all your endeavors tend to succeed . . . at least until the effects wear off."

"Why don't people drink it all the time, sir?" said Terry Boot eagerly.

"Because if taken in excess, it causes giddiness, recklessness, and dangerous overconfidence," said Slughorn. "Too much of a good thing, you know . . . highly toxic in large quantities. But taken sparingly, and very occasionally . . ."

"Have you ever taken it, sir?" asked Michael Corner with great interest.

"Twice in my life," said Slughorn. "Once when I was twenty-four, once when I was fifty-seven. Two tablespoonfuls taken with breakfast. Two perfect days."

He gazed dreamily into the distance. Whether he was playacting or not, thought Harry, the effect was good.

"And that," said Slughorn, apparently coming back to earth, "is what I shall be offering as a prize in this lesson."

There was silence in which every bubble and gurgle of the surrounding potions seemed magnified tenfold.

"One tiny bottle of Felix Felicis," said Slughorn, taking a minuscule glass bottle with a cork in it out of his pocket and showing it to them all. "Enough for twelve hours' luck. From dawn till dusk, you will be lucky in everything you attempt.

"Now, I must give you warning that Felix Felicis is a banned substance in organized competitions . . . sporting events, for instance, examinations, or elections. So the winner is to use it on an ordinary day only . . . and watch how that ordinary day becomes extraordinary!

"So," said Slughorn, suddenly brisk, "how are you to win my fabulous prize? Well, by turning to page ten of *Advanced Potion-Making*. We have a little over an hour left to us, which should be time for you to make a decent attempt at the Draught of Living Death. I know it is more complex than anything you have attempted before, and I do not expect a perfect potion from anybody. The person who does best, however, will win little Felix here. Off you go!"

There was a scraping as everyone drew their cauldrons toward them and some loud clunks as people began adding weights to their scales, but nobody spoke. The concentration within the room was almost tangible. Harry saw Malfoy riffling feverishly through his copy of *Advanced Potion-Making*. It could not have been clearer that Malfoy really wanted that lucky day. Harry bent swiftly over the tattered book Slughorn had lent him.

To his annoyance he saw that the previous owner had scribbled all over the pages, so that the margins were as black as the printed portions. Bending low to decipher the ingredients (even here, the previous owner had made annotations and crossed things out) Harry hurried off toward the store cupboard to find what he needed. As he dashed back to his cauldron, he saw Malfoy cutting up valerian roots as fast as he could.

Everyone kept glancing around at what the rest of the class was doing; this was both an advantage and a disadvantage of Potions, that it was hard to keep your work private. Within ten minutes, the whole place was full of bluish steam. Hermione, of course, seemed to have progressed furthest. Her potion already resembled the "smooth, black currant–colored liquid" mentioned as the ideal halfway stage.

Having finished chopping his roots, Harry bent low over his book again. It was really very irritating, having to try and decipher the directions under all the stupid scribbles of the previous owner, who for some reason had taken issue with the order to cut up the sopophorous bean and had written in the alternative instruction:

> *Crush with flat side of silver dagger, releases juice better than cutting.*

"Sir, I think you knew my grandfather, Abraxas Malfoy?"

Harry looked up; Slughorn was just passing the Slytherin table.

"Yes," said Slughorn, without looking at Malfoy, "I was sorry to hear he had died, although of course it wasn't unexpected, dragon pox at his age. . . ."

And he walked away. Harry bent back over his cauldron, smirking. He could tell that Malfoy had expected to be treated like Harry or Zabini; perhaps even hoped for some preferential treatment of the type he had learned to expect from Snape. It looked as though Malfoy would have to rely on nothing but talent to win the bottle of Felix Felicis.

The sopophorous bean was proving very difficult to cut up. Harry turned to Hermione.

"Can I borrow your silver knife?"

She nodded impatiently, not taking her eyes off her potion, which was still deep purple, though according to the book ought to be turning a light shade of lilac by now.

Harry crushed his bean with the flat side of the dagger. To his astonishment, it immediately exuded so much juice he was amazed the shriveled bean could have held it all. Hastily scooping it all into the cauldron he saw, to his surprise, that the potion immediately turned exactly the shade of lilac described by the textbook.

His annoyance with the previous owner vanishing on the spot, Harry now squinted at the next line of instructions. According to the book, he had to stir counterclockwise until the potion turned clear as water. According to the addition the previous owner had made, however, he ought to add a clockwise stir after every seventh counterclockwise stir. Could the old owner be right twice?

Harry stirred counterclockwise, held his breath, and stirred once clockwise. The effect was immediate. The potion turned palest pink.

"How are you doing that?" demanded Hermione, who was red-faced and whose hair was growing bushier and bushier in the fumes from her cauldron; her potion was still resolutely purple.

"Add a clockwise stir —"

"No, no, the book says counterclockwise!" she snapped.

Harry shrugged and continued what he was doing. Seven stirs counterclockwise, one clockwise, pause . . . seven stirs counterclockwise, one stir clockwise . . .

Across the table, Ron was cursing fluently under his breath; his potion looked like liquid licorice. Harry glanced around. As far as he could see, no one else's potion had turned as pale as his. He felt elated, something that had certainly never happened before in this dungeon.

"And time's . . . up!" called Slughorn. "Stop stirring, please!"

Slughorn moved slowly among the tables, peering into cauldrons. He made no comment, but occasionally gave the potions a stir or a sniff. At last he reached the table where Harry, Ron, Hermione, and Ernie were sitting. He smiled ruefully at the tarlike substance in Ron's cauldron. He passed over Ernie's navy concoction. Hermione's potion he gave an approving nod. Then he saw Harry's, and a look of incredulous delight spread over his face.

"The clear winner!" he cried to the dungeon. "Excellent, excellent, Harry! Good lord, it's clear you've inherited your mother's talent. She was a dab hand at Potions, Lily was! Here you are, then, here you are — one bottle of Felix Felicis, as promised, and use it well!"

Harry slipped the tiny bottle of golden liquid into his inner pocket, feeling an odd combination of delight at the furious looks on the Slytherins' faces and guilt at the disappointed expression on Hermione's. Ron looked simply dumbfounded.

"How did you do that?" he whispered to Harry as they left the dungeon.

"Got lucky, I suppose," said Harry, because Malfoy was within earshot.

Once they were securely ensconced at the Gryffindor table for dinner, however, he felt safe enough to tell them. Hermione's face became stonier with every word he uttered.

"I s'pose you think I cheated?" he finished, aggravated by her expression.

"Well, it wasn't exactly your own work, was it?" she said stiffly.

"He only followed different instructions to ours," said Ron. "Could've been a catastrophe, couldn't it? But he took a risk and it paid off." He heaved a sigh. "Slughorn could've handed me that book, but no, I get the one no one's ever written on. *Puked* on, by the look of page fifty-two, but —"

"Hang on," said a voice close by Harry's left ear and he caught a sudden waft of that flowery smell he had picked up in Slughorn's dungeon. He looked around and saw that Ginny had joined them. "Did I hear right? You've been taking orders from something some-one wrote in a book, Harry?"

She looked alarmed and angry. Harry knew what was on her mind at once.

"It's nothing," he said reassuringly, lowering his voice. "It's not like, you know, Riddle's diary. It's just an old textbook someone's scribbled on."

"But you're doing what it says?"

"I just tried a few of the tips written in the margins, honestly, Ginny, there's nothing funny —"

"Ginny's got a point," said Hermione, perking up at once. "We ought to check that there's nothing odd about it. I mean, all these funny instructions, who knows?"

"Hey!" said Harry indignantly, as she pulled his copy of *Advanced Potion-Making* out of his bag and raised her wand.

"Specialis Revelio!" she said, rapping it smartly on the front cover.

Nothing whatsoever happened. The book simply lay there, looking old and dirty and dog-eared.

"Finished?" said Harry irritably. "Or d'you want to wait and see if it does a few backflips?"

"It seems all right," said Hermione, still staring at the book suspiciously. "I mean, it really does seem to be . . . just a textbook."

"Good. Then I'll have it back," said Harry, snatching it off the table, but it slipped from his hand and landed open on the floor.

Nobody else was looking. Harry bent low to retrieve the book, and as he did so, he saw something scribbled along the bottom of the back cover in the same small, cramped handwriting as the instructions that had won him his bottle of Felix Felicis, now safely hidden inside a pair of socks in his trunk upstairs.

This Book is the Property of the Half-Blood Prince.

THE HOUSE OF GAUNT

or the rest of the week's Potions lessons Harry continued to
follow the Half-Blood Prince's instructions wherever they de-
viated from Libatius Borage's, with the result that by their fourth
lesson Slughorn was raving about Harry's abilities, saying that he
had rarely taught anyone so talented. Neither Ron nor Hermione
was delighted by this. Although Harry had offered to share his
book with both of them, Ron had more difficulty deciphering the
handwriting than Harry did, and could not keep asking Harry to
read aloud or it might look suspicious. Hermione, meanwhile, was
resolutely plowing on with what she called the "official" instructions, but becoming increasingly bad-tempered as they yielded
poorer results than the Prince's.

Harry wondered vaguely who the Half-Blood Prince had been.
Although the amount of homework they had been given prevented
him from reading the whole of his copy of *Advanced Potion-Making*,
he had skimmed through it sufficiently to see that there was barely

a page on which the Prince had not made additional notes, not all of them concerned with potion-making. Here and there were directions for what looked like spells that the Prince had made up himself.

"Or herself," said Hermione irritably, overhearing Harry pointing some of these out to Ron in the common room on Saturday evening. "It might have been a girl. I think the handwriting looks more like a girl's than a boy's."

"The Half-Blood *Prince,* he was called," Harry said. "How many girls have been Princes?"

Hermione seemed to have no answer to this. She merely scowled and twitched her essay on *The Principles of Rematerialization* away from Ron, who was trying to read it upside down.

Harry looked at his watch and hurriedly put the old copy of *Advanced Potion-Making* back into his bag.

"It's five to eight, I'd better go, I'll be late for Dumbledore."

"Ooooh!" gasped Hermione, looking up at once. "Good luck! We'll wait up, we want to hear what he teaches you!"

"Hope it goes okay," said Ron, and the pair of them watched Harry leave through the portrait hole.

Harry proceeded through deserted corridors, though he had to step hastily behind a statue when Professor Trelawney appeared around a corner, muttering to herself as she shuffled a pack of dirty-looking playing cards, reading them as she walked.

"Two of spades: conflict," she murmured, as she passed the place where Harry crouched, hidden. "Seven of spades: an ill omen. Ten of spades: violence. Knave of spades: a dark young man, possibly troubled, one who dislikes the questioner —"

She stopped dead, right on the other side of Harry's statue.

"Well, that can't be right," she said, annoyed, and Harry heard her reshuffling vigorously as she set off again, leaving nothing but a whiff of cooking sherry behind her. Harry waited until he was quite sure she had gone, then hurried off again until he reached the spot in the seventh-floor corridor where a single gargoyle stood against the wall.

"Acid Pops," said Harry, and the gargoyle leapt aside; the wall behind it slid apart, and a moving spiral stone staircase was revealed, onto which Harry stepped, so that he was carried in smooth circles up to the door with the brass knocker that led to Dumbledore's office.

Harry knocked.

"Come in," said Dumbledore's voice.

"Good evening, sir," said Harry, walking into the headmaster's office.

"Ah, good evening, Harry. Sit down," said Dumbledore, smiling. "I hope you've had an enjoyable first week back at school?"

"Yes, thanks, sir," said Harry.

"You must have been busy, a detention under your belt already!"

"Er," began Harry awkwardly, but Dumbledore did not look too stern.

"I have arranged with Professor Snape that you will do your detention next Saturday instead."

"Right," said Harry, who had more pressing matters on his mind than Snape's detention, and now looked around surreptitiously for some indication of what Dumbledore was planning to do with him this evening. The circular office looked just as it always did; the delicate silver instruments stood on spindle-legged tables, puffing smoke and whirring; portraits of previous headmasters and headmistresses dozed in their frames, and Dumbledore's magnificent phoenix, Fawkes, stood on his perch behind the door, watching Harry with bright interest. It did not even look as though Dumbledore had cleared a space for dueling practice.

"So, Harry," said Dumbledore, in a businesslike voice. "You have been wondering, I am sure, what I have planned for you during these — for want of a better word — lessons?"

"Yes, sir."

"Well, I have decided that it is time, now that you know what prompted Lord Voldemort to try and kill you fifteen years ago, for you to be given certain information."

There was a pause.

"You said, at the end of last term, you were going to tell me everything," said Harry. It was hard to keep a note of accusation from his voice. "Sir," he added.

"And so I did," said Dumbledore placidly. "I told you everything I know. From this point forth, we shall be leaving the firm foundation of fact and journeying together through the murky marshes of memory into thickets of wildest guesswork. From here on in, Harry, I may be as woefully wrong as Humphrey Belcher, who believed the time was ripe for a cheese cauldron."

"But you think you're right?" said Harry.

"Naturally I do, but as I have already proven to you, I make mistakes like the next man. In fact, being — forgive me — rather cleverer than most men, my mistakes tend to be correspondingly huger."

"Sir," said Harry tentatively, "does what you're going to tell me have anything to do with the prophecy? Will it help me . . . survive?"

"It has a very great deal to do with the prophecy," said Dumbledore, as casually as if Harry had asked him about the next day's weather, "and I certainly hope that it will help you to survive."

Dumbledore got to his feet and walked around the desk, past Harry, who turned eagerly in his seat to watch Dumbledore bending over the cabinet beside the door. When Dumbledore straightened up, he was holding a familiar shallow stone basin etched with odd markings around its rim. He placed the Pensieve on the desk in front of Harry.

"You look worried."

Harry had indeed been eyeing the Pensieve with some apprehension. His previous experiences with the odd device that stored and revealed thoughts and memories, though highly instructive, had also been uncomfortable. The last time he had disturbed its contents, he had seen much more than he would have wished. But Dumbledore was smiling.

"This time, you enter the Pensieve with me . . . and, even more unusually, with permission."

"Where are we going, sir?"

"For a trip down Bob Ogden's memory lane," said Dumbledore, pulling from his pocket a crystal bottle containing a swirling silvery-white substance.

"Who was Bob Ogden?"

"He was employed by the Department of Magical Law Enforcement," said Dumbledore. "He died some time ago, but not before I had tracked him down and persuaded him to confide these recollections to me. We are about to accompany him on a visit he made in the course of his duties. If you will stand, Harry . . ."

But Dumbledore was having difficulty pulling out the stopper of the crystal bottle: His injured hand seemed stiff and painful.

"Shall — shall I, sir?"

"No matter, Harry —"

Dumbledore pointed his wand at the bottle and the cork flew out.

"Sir — how did you injure your hand?" Harry asked again, looking at the blackened fingers with a mixture of revulsion and pity.

"Now is not the moment for that story, Harry. Not yet. We have an appointment with Bob Ogden."

Dumbledore tipped the silvery contents of the bottle into the Pensieve, where they swirled and shimmered, neither liquid nor gas.

"After you," said Dumbledore, gesturing toward the bowl.

Harry bent forward, took a deep breath, and plunged his face into the silvery substance. He felt his feet leave the office floor; he was falling, falling through whirling darkness and then, quite suddenly, he was blinking in dazzling sunlight. Before his eyes had adjusted, Dumbledore landed beside him.

They were standing in a country lane bordered by high, tangled hedgerows, beneath a summer sky as bright and blue as a forget-me-not. Some ten feet in front of them stood a short, plump man wearing enormously thick glasses that reduced his eyes to molelike specks. He was reading a wooden signpost that was sticking out of the brambles on the left-hand side of the road. Harry knew this must be Ogden; he was the only person in sight, and he was also wearing the strange assortment of clothes so often chosen by inexperienced wizards trying to look like Muggles: in this case, a frock coat and spats over a striped one-piece bathing costume. Before

Harry had time to do more than register his bizarre appearance, however, Ogden had set off at a brisk walk down the lane.

Dumbledore and Harry followed. As they passed the wooden sign, Harry looked up at its two arms. The one pointing back the way they had come read: GREAT HANGLETON, 5 MILES. The arm pointing after Ogden said LITTLE HANGLETON, 1 MILE.

They walked a short way with nothing to see but the hedgerows, the wide blue sky overhead and the swishing, frock-coated figure ahead. Then the lane curved to the left and fell away, sloping steeply down a hillside, so that they had a sudden, unexpected view of a whole valley laid out in front of them. Harry could see a village, undoubtedly Little Hangleton, nestled between two steep hills, its church and graveyard clearly visible. Across the valley, set on the opposite hillside, was a handsome manor house surrounded by a wide expanse of velvety green lawn.

Ogden had broken into a reluctant trot due to the steep downward slope. Dumbledore lengthened his stride, and Harry hurried to keep up. He thought Little Hangleton must be their final destination and wondered, as he had done on the night they had found Slughorn, why they had to approach it from such a distance. He soon discovered that he was mistaken in thinking that they were going to the village, however. The lane curved to the right and when they rounded the corner, it was to see the very edge of Ogden's frock coat vanishing through a gap in the hedge.

Dumbledore and Harry followed him onto a narrow dirt track bordered by higher and wilder hedgerows than those they had left behind. The path was crooked, rocky, and potholed, sloping downhill like the last one, and it seemed to be heading for a patch of dark trees a little below them. Sure enough, the track soon opened up at the copse, and Dumbledore and Harry came to a halt behind Ogden, who had stopped and drawn his wand.

Despite the cloudless sky, the old trees ahead cast deep, dark, cool shadows, and it was a few seconds before Harry's eyes discerned the building half-hidden amongst the tangle of trunks. It seemed to him a very strange location to choose for a house, or else an odd decision to leave the trees growing nearby, blocking all light and the view of the valley below. He wondered whether it was inhabited; its walls were mossy and so many tiles had fallen off the roof that the rafters were visible in places. Nettles grew all around it, their tips reaching the windows, which were tiny and thick with grime. Just as he had concluded that nobody could possibly live there, however, one of the windows was thrown open with a clatter, and a thin trickle of steam or smoke issued from it, as though somebody was cooking.

Ogden moved forward quietly and, it seemed to Harry, rather cautiously. As the dark shadows of the trees slid over him, he stopped again, staring at the front door, to which somebody had nailed a dead snake.

Then there was a rustle and a crack, and a man in rags dropped from the nearest tree, landing on his feet right in front of Ogden, who leapt backward so fast he stood on the tails of his frock coat and stumbled.

"You're not welcome."

The man standing before them had thick hair so matted with dirt it could have been any color. Several of his teeth were missing. His eyes were small and dark and stared in opposite directions. He might have looked comical, but he did not; the effect was frightening, and Harry could not blame Ogden for backing away several more paces before he spoke.

"Er — good morning. I'm from the Ministry of Magic —"

"You're not welcome."

"Er — I'm sorry — I don't understand you," said Ogden nervously.

Harry thought Ogden was being extremely dim; the stranger was making himself very clear in Harry's opinion, particularly as he was brandishing a wand in one hand and a short and rather bloody knife in the other.

"You understand him, I'm sure, Harry?" said Dumbledore quietly.

"Yes, of course," said Harry, slightly nonplussed. "Why can't Ogden — ?"

But as his eyes found the dead snake on the door again, he suddenly understood.

"He's speaking Parseltongue?"

"Very good," said Dumbledore, nodding and smiling.

The man in rags was now advancing on Ogden, knife in one hand, wand in the other.

"Now, look —" Ogden began, but too late: There was a bang, and Ogden was on the ground, clutching his nose, while a nasty yellowish goo squirted from between his fingers.

"Morfin!" said a loud voice.

An elderly man had come hurrying out of the cottage, banging the door behind him so that the dead snake swung pathetically. This man was shorter than the first, and oddly proportioned; his shoulders were very broad and his arms overlong, which, with his bright brown eyes, short scrubby hair, and wrinkled face, gave him the look of a powerful, aged monkey. He came to a halt beside the man with the knife, who was now cackling with laughter at the sight of Ogden on the ground.

"Ministry, is it?" said the older man, looking down at Ogden.

"Correct!" said Ogden angrily, dabbing his face. "And you, I take it, are Mr. Gaunt?"

"S'right," said Gaunt. "Got you in the face, did he?"

"Yes, he did!" snapped Ogden.

"Should've made your presence known, shouldn't you?" said Gaunt aggressively. "This is private property. Can't just walk in here and not expect my son to defend himself."

"Defend himself against what, man?" said Ogden, clambering back to his feet.

"Busybodies. Intruders. Muggles and filth."

Ogden pointed his wand at his own nose, which was still issuing large amounts of what looked like yellow pus, and the flow stopped at once. Mr. Gaunt spoke out of the corner of his mouth to Morfin.

"Get in the house. Don't argue."

This time, ready for it, Harry recognized Parseltongue; even while he could understand what was being said, he distinguished the weird hissing noise that was all Ogden could hear. Morfin seemed to be on the point of disagreeing, but when his father cast him a threatening look he changed his mind, lumbering away to the cottage with an odd rolling gait and slamming the front door behind him, so that the snake swung sadly again.

"It's your son I'm here to see, Mr. Gaunt," said Ogden, as he mopped the last of the pus from the front of his coat. "That was Morfin, wasn't it?"

"Ar, that was Morfin," said the old man indifferently. "Are you pure-blood?" he asked, suddenly aggressive.

"That's neither here nor there," said Ogden coldly, and Harry felt his respect for Ogden rise. Apparently Gaunt felt rather differently. He squinted into Ogden's face and muttered, in what was clearly supposed to be an offensive tone, "Now I come to think about it, I've seen noses like yours down in the village."

"I don't doubt it, if your son's been let loose on them," said Ogden. "Perhaps we could continue this discussion inside?"

"Inside?"

"Yes, Mr. Gaunt. I've already told you. I'm here about Morfin. We sent an owl —"

"I've no use for owls," said Gaunt. "I don't open letters."

"Then you can hardly complain that you get no warning of visitors," said Ogden tartly. "I am here following a serious breach of Wizarding law, which occurred here in the early hours of this morning —"

"All right, all right, all right!" bellowed Gaunt. "Come in the bleeding house, then, and much good it'll do you!"

The house seemed to contain three tiny rooms. Two doors led off the main room, which served as kitchen and living room combined. Morfin was sitting in a filthy armchair beside the smoking fire, twisting a live adder between his thick fingers and crooning softly at it in Parseltongue:

> *Hissy, hissy, little snakey,*
> *Slither on the floor,*
> *You be good to Morfin*
> *Or he'll nail you to the door.*

There was a scuffling noise in the corner beside the open window, and Harry realized that there was somebody else in the room, a girl whose ragged gray dress was the exact color of the dirty stone wall behind her. She was standing beside a steaming pot on a grimy black stove, and was fiddling around with the shelf of squalid-looking pots and pans above it. Her hair was lank and dull and she had a plain, pale, rather heavy face. Her eyes, like her brother's, stared in opposite directions. She looked a little cleaner than the two men, but Harry thought he had never seen a more defeated-looking person.

"M'daughter, Merope," said Gaunt grudgingly, as Ogden looked inquiringly toward her.

"Good morning," said Ogden.

She did not answer, but with a frightened glance at her father turned her back on the room and continued shifting the pots on the shelf behind her.

"Well, Mr. Gaunt," said Ogden, "to get straight to the point, we have reason to believe that your son, Morfin, performed magic in front of a Muggle late last night."

There was a deafening clang. Merope had dropped one of the pots.

"Pick it up!" Gaunt bellowed at her. "That's it, grub on the floor like some filthy Muggle, what's your wand for, you useless sack of muck?"

"Mr. Gaunt, please!" said Ogden in a shocked voice, as Merope, who had already picked up the pot, flushed blotchily scarlet, lost her grip on the pot again, drew her wand shakily from her pocket, pointed it at the pot, and muttered a hasty, inaudible spell that caused the pot to shoot across the floor away from her, hit the opposite wall, and crack in two.

Morfin let out a mad cackle of laughter. Gaunt screamed, "Mend it, you pointless lump, mend it!"

Merope stumbled across the room, but before she had time to raise her wand, Ogden had lifted his own and said firmly, *"Reparo."* The pot mended itself instantly.

Gaunt looked for a moment as though he was going to shout at Ogden, but seemed to think better of it: Instead, he jeered at his daughter, "Lucky the nice man from the Ministry's here, isn't it? Perhaps he'll take you off my hands, perhaps he doesn't mind dirty Squibs. . . ."

Without looking at anybody or thanking Ogden, Merope picked up the pot and returned it, hands trembling, to its shelf. She then stood quite still, her back against the wall between the filthy window and the stove, as though she wished for nothing more than to sink into the stone and vanish.

"Mr. Gaunt," Ogden began again, "as I've said: the reason for my visit —"

"I heard you the first time!" snapped Gaunt. "And so what? Morfin gave a Muggle a bit of what was coming to him — what about it, then?"

"Morfin has broken Wizarding law," said Ogden sternly.

"'Morfin has broken Wizarding law.'" Gaunt imitated Ogden's voice, making it pompous and singsong. Morfin cackled again. "He taught a filthy Muggle a lesson, that's illegal now, is it?"

"Yes," said Ogden. "I'm afraid it is."

He pulled from an inside pocket a small scroll of parchment and unrolled it.

"What's that, then, his sentence?" said Gaunt, his voice rising angrily.

"It is a summons to the Ministry for a hearing —"

"Summons! *Summons?* Who do you think you are, summoning my son anywhere?"

"I'm Head of the Magical Law Enforcement Squad," said Ogden.

"And you think we're scum, do you?" screamed Gaunt, advancing on Ogden now, with a dirty yellow-nailed finger pointing at his chest. "Scum who'll come running when the Ministry tells 'em to? Do you know who you're talking to, you filthy little Mudblood, do you?"

"I was under the impression that I was speaking to Mr. Gaunt," said Ogden, looking wary, but standing his ground.

"That's right!" roared Gaunt. For a moment, Harry thought Gaunt was making an obscene hand gesture, but then realized that he was showing Ogden the ugly, black-stoned ring he was wearing on his middle finger, waving it before Ogden's eyes. "See this? See this? Know what it is? Know where it came from? Centuries it's been in our family, that's how far back we go, and pure-blood all the way! Know how much I've been offered for this, with the Peverell coat of arms engraved on the stone?"

"I've really no idea," said Ogden, blinking as the ring sailed within an inch of his nose, "and it's quite beside the point, Mr. Gaunt. Your son has committed —"

With a howl of rage, Gaunt ran toward his daughter. For a split second, Harry thought he was going to throttle her as his hand flew to her throat; next moment, he was dragging her toward Ogden by a gold chain around her neck.

"See this?" he bellowed at Ogden, shaking a heavy gold locket at him, while Merope spluttered and gasped for breath.

"I see it, I see it!" said Ogden hastily.

"Slytherin's!" yelled Gaunt. "Salazar Slytherin's! We're his last living descendants, what do you say to that, eh?"

"Mr. Gaunt, your daughter!" said Ogden in alarm, but Gaunt had already released Merope; she staggered away from him, back to her corner, massaging her neck and gulping for air.

"So!" said Gaunt triumphantly, as though he had just proved a complicated point beyond all possible dispute. "Don't you go talking to us as if we're dirt on your shoes! Generations of purebloods, wizards all — more than *you* can say, I don't doubt!"

And he spat on the floor at Ogden's feet. Morfin cackled again. Merope, huddled beside the window, her head bowed and her face hidden by her lank hair, said nothing.

"Mr. Gaunt," said Ogden doggedly, "I am afraid that neither your ancestors nor mine have anything to do with the matter in hand. I am here because of Morfin, Morfin and the Muggle he accosted late last night. Our information" — he glanced down at his scroll of parchment — "is that Morfin performed a jinx or hex on the said Muggle, causing him to erupt in highly painful hives."

Morfin giggled.

"Be quiet, boy," snarled Gaunt in Parseltongue, and Morfin fell silent again.

"And so what if he did, then?" Gaunt said defiantly to Ogden. "I expect you've wiped the Muggle's filthy face clean for him, and his memory to boot —"

"That's hardly the point, is it, Mr. Gaunt?" said Ogden. "This was an unprovoked attack on a defenseless —"

"Ar, I had you marked out as a Muggle-lover the moment I saw you," sneered Gaunt, and he spat on the floor again.

"This discussion is getting us nowhere," said Ogden firmly. "It is clear from your son's attitude that he feels no remorse for his actions." He glanced down at his scroll of parchment again. "Morfin will attend a hearing on the fourteenth of September to answer the charges of using magic in front of a Muggle and causing harm and distress to that same Mugg —"

Ogden broke off. The jingling, clopping sounds of horses and loud, laughing voices were drifting in through the open window. Apparently the winding lane to the village passed very close to the copse where the house stood. Gaunt froze, listening, his eyes wide. Morfin hissed and turned his face toward the sounds, his expression hungry. Merope raised her head. Her face, Harry saw, was starkly white.

"My God, what an eyesore!" rang out a girl's voice, as clearly audible through the open window as if she had stood in the room beside them. "Couldn't your father have that hovel cleared away, Tom?"

"It's not ours," said a young man's voice. "Everything on the other side of the valley belongs to us, but that cottage belongs to an old tramp called Gaunt, and his children. The son's quite mad, you should hear some of the stories they tell in the village —"

The girl laughed. The jingling, clopping noises were growing louder and louder. Morfin made to get out of his armchair.

"Keep your seat," said his father warningly, in Parseltongue.

"Tom," said the girl's voice again, now so close they were clearly right beside the house, "I might be wrong — but has somebody nailed a snake to that door?"

"Good lord, you're right!" said the man's voice. "That'll be the son, I told you he's not right in the head. Don't look at it, Cecilia, darling."

The jingling and clopping sounds were now growing fainter again.

"*Darling,*'" whispered Morfin in Parseltongue, looking at his sister. "*'Darling,' he called her. So he wouldn't have you anyway.*"

Merope was so white Harry felt sure she was going to faint.

"*What's that?*" said Gaunt sharply, also in Parseltongue, looking from his son to his daughter. "*What did you say, Morfin?*"

"*She likes looking at that Muggle,*" said Morfin, a vicious expression on his face as he stared at his sister, who now looked terrified. "*Always in the garden when he passes, peering through the hedge at him, isn't she? And last night —*"

Merope shook her head jerkily, imploringly, but Morfin went on ruthlessly, "*Hanging out of the window waiting for him to ride home, wasn't she?*"

"*Hanging out of the window to look at a Muggle?*" said Gaunt quietly.

All three of the Gaunts seemed to have forgotten Ogden, who was looking both bewildered and irritated at this renewed outbreak of incomprehensible hissing and rasping.

"*Is it true?*" said Gaunt in a deadly voice, advancing a step or two toward the terrified girl. "*My daughter — pure-blooded descendant of Salazar Slytherin — hankering after a filthy, dirt-veined Muggle?*"

Merope shook her head frantically, pressing herself into the wall, apparently unable to speak.

"*But I got him, Father!*" cackled Morfin. "*I got him as he went by and he didn't look so pretty with hives all over him, did he, Merope?*"

"*You disgusting little Squib, you filthy little blood traitor!*" roared Gaunt, losing control, and his hands closed around his daughter's throat.

Both Harry and Ogden yelled "No!" at the same time; Ogden raised his wand and cried, *"Relashio!"* Gaunt was thrown backward, away from his daughter; he tripped over a chair and fell flat on his back. With a roar of rage, Morfin leapt out of his chair and ran at Ogden, brandishing his bloody knife and firing hexes indiscriminately from his wand.

Ogden ran for his life. Dumbledore indicated that they ought to follow and Harry obeyed, Merope's screams echoing in his ears.

Ogden hurtled up the path and erupted onto the main lane, his arms over his head, where he collided with the glossy chestnut horse ridden by a very handsome, dark-haired young man. Both he and the pretty girl riding beside him on a gray horse roared with laughter at the sight of Ogden, who bounced off the horse's flank and set off again, his frock coat flying, covered from head to foot in dust, running pell-mell up the lane.

"I think that will do, Harry," said Dumbledore. He took Harry by the elbow and tugged. Next moment, they were both soaring weightlessly through darkness, until they landed squarely on their feet, back in Dumbledore's now twilit office.

"What happened to the girl in the cottage?" said Harry at once, as Dumbledore lit extra lamps with a flick of his wand. "Merope, or whatever her name was?"

"Oh, she survived," said Dumbledore, reseating himself behind his desk and indicating that Harry should sit down too. "Ogden Apparated back to the Ministry and returned with reinforcements within fifteen minutes. Morfin and his father attempted to fight, but both were overpowered, removed from the cottage, and subsequently convicted by the Wizengamot. Morfin, who already had a record of Muggle attacks, was sentenced to three years in Azkaban.

Marvolo, who had injured several Ministry employees in addition to Ogden, received six months."

"Marvolo?" Harry repeated wonderingly.

"That's right," said Dumbledore, smiling in approval. "I am glad to see you're keeping up."

"That old man was — ?"

"Voldemort's grandfather, yes," said Dumbledore. "Marvolo, his son, Morfin, and his daughter, Merope, were the last of the Gaunts, a very ancient Wizarding family noted for a vein of instability and violence that flourished through the generations due to their habit of marrying their own cousins. Lack of sense coupled with a great liking for grandeur meant that the family gold was squandered several generations before Marvolo was born. He, as you saw, was left in squalor and poverty, with a very nasty temper, a fantastic amount of arrogance and pride, and a couple of family heirlooms that he treasured just as much as his son, and rather more than his daughter."

"So Merope," said Harry, leaning forward in his chair and staring at Dumbledore, "so Merope was . . . Sir, does that mean she was . . . *Voldemort's mother*?"

"It does," said Dumbledore. "And it so happens that we also had a glimpse of Voldemort's father. I wonder whether you noticed?"

"The Muggle Morfin attacked? The man on the horse?"

"Very good indeed," said Dumbledore, beaming. "Yes, that was Tom Riddle senior, the handsome Muggle who used to go riding past the Gaunt cottage and for whom Merope Gaunt cherished a secret, burning passion."

"And they ended up married?" Harry said in disbelief, unable to imagine two people less likely to fall in love.

"I think you are forgetting," said Dumbledore, "that Merope was a witch. I do not believe that her magical powers appeared to their best advantage when she was being terrorized by her father. Once Marvolo and Morfin were safely in Azkaban, once she was alone and free for the first time in her life, then, I am sure, she was able to give full rein to her abilities and to plot her escape from the desperate life she had led for eighteen years.

"Can you not think of any measure Merope could have taken to make Tom Riddle forget his Muggle companion, and fall in love with her instead?"

"The Imperius Curse?" Harry suggested. "Or a love potion?"

"Very good. Personally, I am inclined to think that she used a love potion. I am sure it would have seemed more romantic to her, and I do not think it would have been very difficult, some hot day, when Riddle was riding alone, to persuade him to take a drink of water. In any case, within a few months of the scene we have just witnessed, the village of Little Hangleton enjoyed a tremendous scandal. You can imagine the gossip it caused when the squire's son ran off with the tramp's daughter, Merope.

"But the villagers' shock was nothing to Marvolo's. He returned from Azkaban, expecting to find his daughter dutifully awaiting his return with a hot meal ready on his table. Instead, he found a clear inch of dust and her note of farewell, explaining what she had done.

"From all that I have been able to discover, he never mentioned her name or existence from that time forth. The shock of her desertion may have contributed to his early death — or perhaps he had simply never learned to feed himself. Azkaban had greatly weakened Marvolo, and he did not live to see Morfin return to the cottage."

"And Merope? She . . . she died, didn't she? Wasn't Voldemort brought up in an orphanage?"

"Yes, indeed," said Dumbledore. "We must do a certain amount of guessing here, although I do not think it is difficult to deduce what happened. You see, within a few months of their runaway marriage, Tom Riddle reappeared at the manor house in Little Hangleton without his wife. The rumor flew around the neighborhood that he was talking of being 'hoodwinked' and 'taken in.' What he meant, I am sure, is that he had been under an enchantment that had now lifted, though I daresay he did not dare use those precise words for fear of being thought insane. When they heard what he was saying, however, the villagers guessed that Merope had lied to Tom Riddle, pretending that she was going to have his baby, and that he had married her for this reason."

"But she *did* have his baby."

"But not until a year after they were married. Tom Riddle left her while she was still pregnant."

"What went wrong?" asked Harry. "Why did the love potion stop working?"

"Again, this is guesswork," said Dumbledore, "but I believe that Merope, who was deeply in love with her husband, could not bear to continue enslaving him by magical means. I believe that she made the choice to stop giving him the potion. Perhaps, besotted as she was, she had convinced herself that he would by now have fallen in love with her in return. Perhaps she thought he would stay for the baby's sake. If so, she was wrong on both counts. He left her, never saw her again, and never troubled to discover what became of his son."

The sky outside was inky black and the lamps in Dumbledore's office seemed to glow more brightly than before.

"I think that will do for tonight, Harry," said Dumbledore after a moment or two.

"Yes, sir," said Harry.

He got to his feet, but did not leave.

"Sir . . . is it important to know all this about Voldemort's past?"

"Very important, I think," said Dumbledore.

"And it . . . it's got something to do with the prophecy?"

"It has everything to do with the prophecy."

"Right," said Harry, a little confused, but reassured all the same.

He turned to go, then another question occurred to him, and he turned back again. "Sir, am I allowed to tell Ron and Hermione everything you've told me?"

Dumbledore considered him for a moment, then said, "Yes, I think Mr. Weasley and Miss Granger have proved themselves trustworthy. But Harry, I am going to ask you to ask them not to repeat any of this to anybody else. It would not be a good idea if word got around how much I know, or suspect, about Lord Voldemort's secrets."

"No, sir, I'll make sure it's just Ron and Hermione. Good night."

He turned away again, and was almost at the door when he saw it. Sitting on one of the little spindle-legged tables that supported so many frail-looking silver instruments, was an ugly gold ring set with a large, cracked, black stone.

"Sir," said Harry, staring at it. "That ring —"

"Yes?" said Dumbledore.

"You were wearing it when we visited Professor Slughorn that night."

"So I was," Dumbledore agreed.

"But isn't it . . . sir, isn't it the same ring Marvolo Gaunt showed Ogden?"

Dumbledore bowed his head. "The very same."

"But how come — ? Have you always had it?"

"No, I acquired it very recently," said Dumbledore. "A few days before I came to fetch you from your aunt and uncle's, in fact."

"That would be around the time you injured your hand, then, sir?"

"Around that time, yes, Harry."

Harry hesitated. Dumbledore was smiling.

"Sir, how exactly — ?"

"Too late, Harry! You shall hear the story another time. Good night."

"Good night, sir."

HERMIONE'S HELPING HAND

As Hermione had predicted, the sixth years' free periods were not the hours of blissful relaxation Ron had antici- pated, but times in which to attempt to keep up with the vast amount of homework they were being set. Not only were they studying as though they had exams every day, but the lessons them- selves had become more demanding than ever before. Harry barely understood half of what Professor McGonagall said to them these days; even Hermione had had to ask her to repeat instructions once or twice. Incredibly, and to Hermione's increasing resentment, Harry's best subject had suddenly become Potions, thanks to the Half-Blood Prince.

Nonverbal spells were now expected, not only in Defense Against the Dark Arts, but in Charms and Transfiguration too. Harry frequently looked over at his classmates in the common room or at mealtimes to see them purple in the face and straining as though they had overdosed on U-No-Poo; but he knew that they were really struggling to make spells work without saying incantations aloud. It was a relief to get outside into the greenhouses; they were dealing with more dangerous plants than ever in Herbology, but at least they were still allowed to swear loudly if the Venomous Tentacula seized them unexpectedly from behind.

One result of their enormous workload and the frantic hours of practicing nonverbal spells was that Harry, Ron, and Hermione had so far been unable to find time to go and visit Hagrid. He had stopped coming to meals at the staff table, an ominous sign, and on the few occasions when they had passed him in the corridors or out in the grounds, he had mysteriously failed to notice them or hear their greetings.

"We've got to go and explain," said Hermione, looking up at Hagrid's huge empty chair at the staff table the following Saturday at breakfast.

"We've got Quidditch tryouts this morning!" said Ron. "*And* we're supposed to be practicing that Aguamenti Charm from Flitwick! Anyway, explain what? How are we going to tell him we hated his stupid subject?"

"We didn't hate it!" said Hermione.

"Speak for yourself, I haven't forgotten the skrewts," said Ron darkly. "And I'm telling you now, we've had a narrow escape. You didn't hear him going on about his gormless brother — we'd have been teaching Grawp how to tie his shoelaces if we'd stayed."

"I hate not talking to Hagrid," said Hermione, looking upset.

"We'll go down after Quidditch," Harry assured her. He too was missing Hagrid, although like Ron he thought that they were better off without Grawp in their lives. "But trials might take all morning, the number of people who have applied." He felt slightly nervous at confronting the first hurdle of his Captaincy. "I dunno why the team's this popular all of a sudden."

"Oh, come on, Harry," said Hermione, suddenly impatient. "It's not *Quidditch* that's popular, it's you! You've never been more interesting, and frankly, you've never been more fanciable."

Ron gagged on a large piece of kipper. Hermione spared him one look of disdain before turning back to Harry.

"Everyone knows you've been telling the truth now, don't they? The whole Wizarding world has had to admit that you were right about Voldemort being back and that you really have fought him twice in the last two years and escaped both times. And now they're calling you 'the Chosen One' — well, come on, can't you see why people are fascinated by you?"

Harry was finding the Great Hall very hot all of a sudden, even though the ceiling still looked cold and rainy.

"*And* you've been through all that persecution from the Ministry when they were trying to make out you were unstable and a liar. You can still see the marks on the back of your hand where that evil woman made you write with your own blood, but you stuck to your story anyway. . . ."

"You can still see where those brains got hold of me in the Ministry, look," said Ron, shaking back his sleeves.

"And it doesn't hurt that you've grown about a foot over the summer either," Hermione finished, ignoring Ron.

"I'm tall," said Ron inconsequentially.

The post owls arrived, swooping down through rain-flecked windows, scattering everyone with droplets of water. Most people were receiving more post than usual; anxious parents were keen to hear from their children and to reassure them, in turn, that all was well at home. Harry had received no mail since the start of term; his only regular correspondent was now dead and although he had hoped that Lupin might write occasionally, he had so far been disappointed. He was very surprised, therefore, to see the snowy white Hedwig circling amongst all the brown and gray owls. She landed in front of him carrying a large, square package. A moment later, an identical package landed in front of Ron, crushing beneath it his minuscule and exhausted owl, Pigwidgeon.

"Ha!" said Harry, unwrapping the parcel to reveal a new copy of *Advanced Potion-Making,* fresh from Flourish and Blotts.

"Oh good," said Hermione, delighted. "Now you can give that graffitied copy back."

"Are you mad?" said Harry. "I'm keeping it! Look, I've thought it out —"

He pulled the old copy of *Advanced Potion-Making* out of his bag and tapped the cover with his wand, muttering, *"Diffindo!"* The cover fell off. He did the same thing with the brand-new book (Hermione looked scandalized). He then swapped the covers, tapped each, and said, *"Reparo!"*

There sat the Prince's copy, disguised as a new book, and there sat the fresh copy from Flourish and Blotts, looking thoroughly secondhand.

"I'll give Slughorn back the new one, he can't complain, it cost nine Galleons."

Hermione pressed her lips together, looking angry and disapproving, but was distracted by a third owl landing in front of her carrying that day's copy of the *Daily Prophet.* She unfolded it hastily and scanned the front page.

"Anyone we know dead?" asked Ron in a determinedly casual voice; he posed the same question every time Hermione opened her paper.

"No, but there have been more dementor attacks," said Hermione. "And an arrest."

"Excellent, who?" said Harry, thinking of Bellatrix Lestrange.

"Stan Shunpike," said Hermione.

"What?" said Harry, startled.

"*'Stanley Shunpike, conductor on the popular Wizarding conveyance the Knight Bus, has been arrested on suspicion of Death Eater activity. Mr. Shunpike, 21, was taken into custody late last night after a raid on his Clapham home . . .'*"

"Stan Shunpike, a Death Eater?" said Harry, remembering the spotty youth he had first met three years before. "No way!"

"He might have been put under the Imperius Curse," said Ron reasonably. "You never can tell."

"It doesn't look like it," said Hermione, who was still reading. "It says here he was arrested after he was overheard talking about the Death Eaters' secret plans in a pub." She looked up with a troubled expression on her face. "If he was under the Imperius Curse, he'd hardly stand around gossiping about their plans, would he?"

"It sounds like he was trying to make out he knew more than he did," said Ron. "Isn't he the one who claimed he was going to become Minister of Magic when he was trying to chat up those veela?"

"Yeah, that's him," said Harry. "I dunno what they're playing at, taking Stan seriously."

"They probably want to look as though they're doing something," said Hermione, frowning. "People are terrified — you know the Patil twins' parents want them to go home? And Eloise Midgen has already been withdrawn. Her father picked her up last night."

"What!" said Ron, goggling at Hermione. "But Hogwarts is safer than their homes, bound to be! We've got Aurors, and all those extra protective spells, and we've got Dumbledore!"

"I don't think we've got him all the time," said Hermione very quietly, glancing toward the staff table over the top of the *Prophet*. "Haven't you noticed? His seat's been empty as often as Hagrid's this past week."

Harry and Ron looked up at the staff table. The headmaster's chair was indeed empty. Now Harry came to think of it, he had not seen Dumbledore since their private lesson a week ago.

"I think he's left the school to do something with the Order," said Hermione in a low voice. "I mean . . . it's all looking serious, isn't it?"

Harry and Ron did not answer, but Harry knew that they were all thinking the same thing. There had been a horrible incident the day before, when Hannah Abbott had been taken out of Herbology to be told her mother had been found dead. They had not seen Hannah since.

When they left the Gryffindor table five minutes later to head down to the Quidditch pitch, they passed Lavender Brown and Parvati Patil. Remembering what Hermione had said about the Patil twins' parents wanting them to leave Hogwarts, Harry was unsurprised to see that the two best friends were whispering together, looking distressed. What did surprise him was that when Ron drew level with them, Parvati suddenly nudged Lavender, who looked around and gave Ron a wide smile. Ron blinked at her, then returned the smile uncertainly. His walk instantly became some-

thing more like a strut. Harry resisted the temptation to laugh, remembering that Ron had refrained from doing so after Malfoy had
broken Harry's nose; Hermione, however, looked cold and distant
all the way down to the stadium through the cool, misty drizzle,
and departed to find a place in the stands without wishing Ron
good luck.

As Harry had expected, the trials took most of the morning.
Half of Gryffindor House seemed to have turned up, from first
years who were nervously clutching a selection of the dreadful old
school brooms, to seventh years who towered over the rest, looking
coolly intimidating. The latter included a large, wiry-haired boy
Harry recognized immediately from the Hogwarts Express.

"We met on the train, in old Sluggy's compartment," he said
confidently, stepping out of the crowd to shake Harry's hand.
"Cormac McLaggen, Keeper."

"You didn't try out last year, did you?" asked Harry, taking note
of the breadth of McLaggen and thinking that he would probably
block all three goal hoops without even moving.

"I was in the hospital wing when they held the trials," said
McLaggen, with something of a swagger. "Ate a pound of doxy eggs
for a bet."

"Right," said Harry. "Well . . . if you wait over there . . ."

He pointed over to the edge of the pitch, close to where Hermione was sitting. He thought he saw a flicker of annoyance pass over
McLaggen's face and wondered whether McLaggen expected preferential treatment because they were both "old Sluggy's" favorites.

Harry decided to start with a basic test, asking all applicants for
the team to divide into groups of ten and fly once around the pitch.
This was a good decision: The first ten was made up of first years

and it could not have been plainer that they had hardly ever flown before. Only one boy managed to remain airborne for more than a few seconds, and he was so surprised he promptly crashed into one of the goal posts.

The second group was comprised of ten of the silliest girls Harry had ever encountered, who, when he blew his whistle, merely fell about giggling and clutching one another. Romilda Vane was amongst them. When he told them to leave the pitch, they did so quite cheerfully and went to sit in the stands to heckle everyone else.

The third group had a pileup halfway around the pitch. Most of the fourth group had come without broomsticks. The fifth group were Hufflepuffs.

"If there's anyone else here who's not from Gryffindor," roared Harry, who was starting to get seriously annoyed, "leave now, please!"

There was a pause, then a couple of little Ravenclaws went sprinting off the pitch, snorting with laughter.

After two hours, many complaints, and several tantrums, one involving a crashed Comet Two Sixty and several broken teeth, Harry had found himself three Chasers: Katie Bell, returned to the team after an excellent trial; a new find called Demelza Robins, who was particularly good at dodging Bludgers; and Ginny Weasley, who had outflown all the competition and scored seventeen goals to boot. Pleased though he was with his choices, Harry had also shouted himself hoarse at the many complainers and was now enduring a similar battle with the rejected Beaters.

"That's my final decision and if you don't get out of the way for the Keepers I'll hex you," he bellowed.

Neither of his chosen Beaters had the old brilliance of Fred and George, but he was still reasonably pleased with them: Jimmy Peakes, a short but broad-chested third-year boy who had managed to raise a lump the size of an egg on the back of Harry's head with a ferociously hit Bludger, and Ritchie Coote, who looked weedy but aimed well. They now joined the spectators in the stands to watch the selection of their last team member.

Harry had deliberately left the trial of the Keepers until last, hoping for an emptier stadium and less pressure on all concerned. Unfortunately, however, all the rejected players and a number of people who had come down to watch after a lengthy breakfast had joined the crowd by now, so that it was larger than ever. As each Keeper flew up to the goal hoops, the crowd roared and jeered in equal measure. Harry glanced over at Ron, who had always had a problem with nerves; Harry had hoped that winning their final match last term might have cured it, but apparently not: Ron was a delicate shade of green.

None of the first five applicants saved more than two goals apiece. To Harry's great disappointment, Cormac McLaggen saved four penalties out of five. On the last one, however, he shot off in completely the wrong direction; the crowd laughed and booed and McLaggen returned to the ground grinding his teeth.

Ron looked ready to pass out as he mounted his Cleansweep Eleven. "Good luck!" cried a voice from the stands. Harry looked around, expecting to see Hermione, but it was Lavender Brown. He would have quite liked to have hidden his face in his hands, as she did a moment later, but thought that as the Captain he ought to show slightly more grit, and so turned to watch Ron do his trial.

Yet he need not have worried: Ron saved one, two, three, four, five penalties in a row. Delighted, and resisting joining in the cheers of the crowd with difficulty, Harry turned to McLaggen to tell him that, most unfortunately, Ron had beaten him, only to find McLaggen's red face inches from his own. He stepped back hastily.

"His sister didn't really try," said McLaggen menacingly. There was a vein pulsing in his temple like the one Harry had often admired in Uncle Vernon's. "She gave him an easy save."

"Rubbish," said Harry coldly. "That was the one he nearly missed."

McLaggen took a step nearer Harry, who stood his ground this time.

"Give me another go."

"No," said Harry. "You've had your go. You saved four. Ron saved five. Ron's Keeper, he won it fair and square. Get out of my way."

He thought for a moment that McLaggen might punch him, but he contented himself with an ugly grimace and stormed away, growling what sounded like threats to thin air.

Harry turned around to find his new team beaming at him.

"Well done," he croaked. "You flew really well —"

"You did brilliantly, Ron!"

This time it really was Hermione running toward them from the stands; Harry saw Lavender walking off the pitch, arm in arm with Parvati, a rather grumpy expression on her face. Ron looked extremely pleased with himself and even taller than usual as he grinned at the team and at Hermione.

After fixing the time of their first full practice for the following Thursday, Harry, Ron, and Hermione bade good-bye to the rest of the team and headed off toward Hagrid's. A watery sun was trying to break through the clouds now and it had stopped drizzling at last. Harry felt extremely hungry; he hoped there would be something to eat at Hagrid's.

"I thought I was going to miss that fourth penalty," Ron was saying happily. "Tricky shot from Demelza, did you see, had a bit of spin on it —"

"Yes, yes, you were magnificent," said Hermione, looking amused.

"I was better than that McLaggen anyway," said Ron in a highly satisfied voice. "Did you see him lumbering off in the wrong direction on his fifth? Looked like he'd been Confunded. . . ."

To Harry's surprise, Hermione turned a very deep shade of pink at these words. Ron noticed nothing; he was too busy describing each of his other penalties in loving detail.

The great gray hippogriff, Buckbeak, was tethered in front of Hagrid's cabin. He clicked his razor-sharp beak at their approach and turned his huge head toward them.

"Oh dear," said Hermione nervously. "He's still a bit scary, isn't he?"

"Come off it, you've ridden him, haven't you?" said Ron.

Harry stepped forward and bowed low to the hippogriff without breaking eye contact or blinking. After a few seconds, Buckbeak sank into a bow too.

"How are you?" Harry asked him in a low voice, moving forward to stroke the feathery head. "Missing him? But you're okay here with Hagrid, aren't you?"

"Oi!" said a loud voice.

Hagrid had come striding around the corner of his cabin wearing a large flowery apron and carrying a sack of potatoes. His enormous boarhound, Fang, was at his heels; Fang gave a booming bark and bounded forward.

"Git away from him! He'll have yer fingers — oh. It's yeh lot."

Fang was jumping up at Hermione and Ron, attempting to lick their ears. Hagrid stood and looked at them all for a split second, then turned and strode into his cabin, slamming the door behind him.

"Oh dear!" said Hermione, looking stricken.

"Don't worry about it," said Harry grimly. He walked over to the door and knocked loudly.

"Hagrid! Open up, we want to talk to you!"

There was no sound from within.

"If you don't open the door, we'll blast it open!" Harry said, pulling out his wand.

"Harry!" said Hermione, sounding shocked. "You can't possibly —"

"Yeah, I can!" said Harry. "Stand back —"

But before he could say anything else, the door flew open again as Harry had known it would, and there stood Hagrid, glowering down at him and looking, despite the flowery apron, positively alarming.

"I'm a teacher!" he roared at Harry. "A teacher, Potter! How dare yeh threaten ter break down my door!"

"I'm sorry, *sir*," said Harry, emphasizing the last word as he stowed his wand inside his robes.

Hagrid looked stunned. "Since when have yeh called me 'sir'?"

"Since when have you called me 'Potter'?"

"Oh, very clever," growled Hagrid. "Very amusin'. That's me outsmarted, innit? All righ', come in then, yeh ungrateful little . . ."

Mumbling darkly, he stood back to let them pass. Hermione scurried in after Harry, looking rather frightened.

"Well?" said Hagrid grumpily, as Harry, Ron, and Hermione sat down around his enormous wooden table, Fang laying his head immediately upon Harry's knee and drooling all over his robes. "What's this? Feelin' sorry for me? Reckon I'm lonely or summat?"

"No," said Harry at once. "We wanted to see you."

"We've missed you!" said Hermione tremulously.

"Missed me, have yeh?" snorted Hagrid. "Yeah. Righ'."

He stomped around, brewing up tea in his enormous copper kettle, muttering all the while. Finally he slammed down three bucket-sized mugs of mahogany-brown tea in front of them and a plate of his rock cakes. Harry was hungry enough even for Hagrid's cooking, and took one at once.

"Hagrid," said Hermione timidly, when he joined them at the table and started peeling his potatoes with a brutality that suggested that each tuber had done him a great personal wrong, "we really wanted to carry on with Care of Magical Creatures, you know."

Hagrid gave another great snort. Harry rather thought some bogeys landed on the potatoes, and was inwardly thankful that they were not staying for dinner.

"We did!" said Hermione. "But none of us could fit it into our schedules!"

"Yeah. Righ'," said Hagrid again.

There was a funny squelching sound and they all looked around: Hermione let out a tiny shriek, and Ron leapt out of his seat and hurried around the table away from the large barrel standing in the corner that they had only just noticed. It was full of what looked like foot-long maggots, slimy, white, and writhing.

"What are they, Hagrid?" asked Harry, trying to sound interested rather than revolted, but putting down his rock cake all the same.

"Jus' giant grubs," said Hagrid.

"And they grow into . . . ?" said Ron, looking apprehensive.

"They won' grow inter nuthin'," said Hagrid. "I got 'em ter feed ter Aragog."

And without warning, he burst into tears.

"Hagrid!" cried Hermione, leaping up, hurrying around the table the long way to avoid the barrel of maggots, and putting an arm around his shaking shoulders. "What is it?"

"It's . . . him . . ." gulped Hagrid, his beetle-black eyes streaming as he mopped his face with his apron. "It's . . . Aragog. . . . I think he's dyin'. . . . He got ill over the summer an' he's not gettin' better. . . . I don' know what I'll do if he . . . if he . . . We've bin tergether so long. . . ."

Hermione patted Hagrid's shoulder, looking at a complete loss for anything to say. Harry knew how she felt. He had known Hagrid to present a vicious baby dragon with a teddy bear, seen him croon over giant scorpions with suckers and stingers, attempt to reason with his brutal giant of a half-brother, but this was perhaps the most incomprehensible of all his monster fancies: the gigantic talking spider, Aragog, who dwelled deep in the Forbidden Forest and which he and Ron had only narrowly escaped four years previously.

"Is there — is there anything we can do?" Hermione asked, ignoring Ron's frantic grimaces and head-shakings.

"I don' think there is, Hermione," choked Hagrid, attempting to stem the flood of his tears. "See, the rest o' the tribe . . . Aragog's family . . . they're gettin' a bit funny now he's ill . . . bit restive . . ."

"Yeah, I think we saw a bit of that side of them," said Ron in an undertone.

". . . I don' reckon it'd be safe fer anyone but me ter go near the colony at the mo'," Hagrid finished, blowing his nose hard on his apron and looking up. "But thanks fer offerin', Hermione. . . . It means a lot. . . ."

After that, the atmosphere lightened considerably, for although neither Harry nor Ron had shown any inclination to go and feed giant grubs to a murderous, gargantuan spider, Hagrid seemed to take it for granted that they would have liked to have done and became his usual self once more.

"Ar, I always knew yeh'd find it hard ter squeeze me inter yer timetables," he said gruffly, pouring them more tea. "Even if yeh applied fer Time-Turners —"

"We couldn't have done," said Hermione. "We smashed the entire stock of Ministry Time-Turners when we were there last summer. It was in the *Daily Prophet*."

"Ar, well then," said Hagrid. "There's no way yeh could've done it. . . . I'm sorry I've bin — yeh know — I've jus' bin worried abou' Aragog . . . an' I did wonder whether, if Professor Grubbly-Plank had bin teachin' yeh —"

At which all three of them stated categorically and untruthfully that Professor Grubbly-Plank, who had substituted for Hagrid a few times, was a dreadful teacher, with the result that by the time Hagrid waved them off the premises at dusk, he looked quite cheerful.

"I'm starving," said Harry, once the door had closed behind them and they were hurrying through the dark and deserted grounds; he had abandoned the rock cake after an ominous cracking noise from one of his back teeth. "And I've got that detention with Snape tonight, I haven't got much time for dinner. . . ."

As they came into the castle they spotted Cormac McLaggen entering the Great Hall. It took him two attempts to get through the doors; he ricocheted off the frame on the first attempt. Ron merely guffawed gloatingly and strode off into the Hall after him, but Harry caught Hermione's arm and held her back.

"What?" said Hermione defensively.

"If you ask me," said Harry quietly, "McLaggen looks like he *was* Confunded this morning. And he was standing right in front of where you were sitting."

Hermione blushed.

"Oh, all right then, I did it," she whispered. "But you should have heard the way he was talking about Ron and Ginny! Anyway, he's got a nasty temper, you saw how he reacted when he didn't get in — you wouldn't have wanted someone like that on the team."

"No," said Harry. "No, I suppose that's true. But wasn't that dishonest, Hermione? I mean, you're a prefect, aren't you?"

"Oh, be quiet," she snapped, as he smirked.

"What are you two doing?" demanded Ron, reappearing in the doorway to the Great Hall and looking suspicious.

"Nothing," said Harry and Hermione together, and they hurried after Ron. The smell of roast beef made Harry's stomach ache with hunger, but they had barely taken three steps toward the Gryffindor table when Professor Slughorn appeared in front of them, blocking their path.

"Harry, Harry, just the man I was hoping to see!" he boomed genially, twiddling the ends of his walrus mustache and puffing out his enormous belly. "I was hoping to catch you before dinner! What do you say to a spot of supper tonight in my rooms instead? We're having a little party, just a few rising stars, I've got McLaggen coming and Zabini, the charming Melinda Bobbin — I don't know whether you know her? Her family owns a large chain of apothecaries — and, of course, I hope very much that Miss Granger will favor me by coming too."

Slughorn made Hermione a little bow as he finished speaking. It was as though Ron was not present; Slughorn did not so much as look at him.

"I can't come, Professor," said Harry at once. "I've got a detention with Professor Snape."

"Oh dear!" said Slughorn, his face falling comically. "Dear, dear, I was counting on you, Harry! Well, now, I'll just have to have a word with Severus and explain the situation. I'm sure I'll be able to persuade him to postpone your detention. Yes, I'll see you both later!"

He bustled away out of the Hall.

"He's got no chance of persuading Snape," said Harry, the moment Slughorn was out of earshot. "This detention's already been postponed once; Snape did it for Dumbledore, but he won't do it for anyone else."

"Oh, I wish you could come, I don't want to go on my own!" said Hermione anxiously; Harry knew that she was thinking about McLaggen.

"I doubt you'll be alone, Ginny'll probably be invited," snapped Ron, who did not seem to have taken kindly to being ignored by Slughorn.

After dinner they made their way back to Gryffindor Tower. The common room was very crowded, as most people had finished dinner by now, but they managed to find a free table and sat down; Ron, who had been in a bad mood ever since the encounter with Slughorn, folded his arms and frowned at the ceiling. Hermione reached out for a copy of the *Evening Prophet,* which somebody had left abandoned on a chair.

"Anything new?" said Harry.

"Not really . . ." Hermione had opened the newspaper and was scanning the inside pages. "Oh, look, your dad's in here, Ron — he's all right!" she added quickly, for Ron had looked around in alarm. "It just says he's been to visit the Malfoys' house. *'This second search of the Death Eater's residence does not seem to have yielded any results. Arthur Weasley of the Office for the Detection and Confiscation of Counterfeit Defensive Spells and Protective Objects said that his team had been acting upon a confidential tip-off.'"*

"Yeah, mine!" said Harry. "I told him at King's Cross about Malfoy and that thing he was trying to get Borgin to fix! Well, if it's not at their house, he must have brought whatever it is to Hogwarts with him —"

"But how can he have done, Harry?" said Hermione, putting down the newspaper with a surprised look. "We were all searched when we arrived, weren't we?"

"Were you?" said Harry, taken aback. "I wasn't!"

"Oh no, of course you weren't, I forgot you were late. . . . Well, Filch ran over all of us with Secrecy Sensors when we got into the entrance hall. Any Dark object would have been found, I know for a fact Crabbe had a shrunken head confiscated. So you see, Malfoy can't have brought in anything dangerous!"

Momentarily stymied, Harry watched Ginny Weasley playing with Arnold the Pygmy Puff for a while before seeing a way around this objection.

"Someone's sent it to him by owl, then," he said. "His mother or someone."

"All the owls are being checked too," said Hermione. "Filch told us so when he was jabbing those Secrecy Sensors everywhere he could reach."

Really stumped this time, Harry found nothing else to say. There did not seem to be any way Malfoy could have brought a dangerous or Dark object into the school. He looked hopefully at Ron, who was sitting with his arms folded, staring over at Lavender Brown.

"Can you think of any way Malfoy — ?"

"Oh, drop it, Harry," said Ron.

"Listen, it's not my fault Slughorn invited Hermione and me to his stupid party, neither of us wanted to go, you know!" said Harry, firing up.

"Well, as I'm not invited to any parties," said Ron, getting to his feet again, "I think I'll go to bed."

He stomped off toward the door to the boys' dormitories, leaving Harry and Hermione staring after him.

"Harry?" said the new Chaser, Demelza Robins, appearing suddenly at his shoulder. "I've got a message for you."

"From Professor Slughorn?" asked Harry, sitting up hopefully.

"No . . . from Professor Snape," said Demelza. Harry's heart sank. "He says you're to come to his office at half past eight tonight to do your detention — er — no matter how many party invitations you've received. And he wanted you to know you'll be sorting out rotten flobberworms from good ones, to use in Potions and — and he says there's no need to bring protective gloves."

"Right," said Harry grimly. "Thanks a lot, Demelza."

CHAPTER TWELVE

SILVER AND OPALS

Where was Dumbledore, and what was he doing? Harry caught sight of the headmaster only twice over the next few weeks. He rarely appeared at meals anymore, and Harry was sure Hermione was right in thinking that he was leaving the school for days at a time. Had Dumbledore forgotten the lessons he was supposed to be giving Harry? Dumbledore had said that the lessons were leading to something to do with the prophecy; Harry had felt bolstered, comforted, and now he felt slightly abandoned.

Halfway through October came their first trip of the term to Hogsmeade. Harry had wondered whether these trips would still be allowed, given the increasingly tight security measures around the school, but was pleased to know that they were going ahead; it was always good to get out of the castle grounds for a few hours.

Harry woke early on the morning of the trip, which was proving stormy, and whiled away the time until breakfast by reading his copy of *Advanced Potion-Making*. He did not usually lie in bed reading his textbooks; that sort of behavior, as Ron rightly said, was indecent in anybody except Hermione, who was simply weird that way. Harry felt, however, that the Half-Blood Prince's copy of *Advanced Potion-Making* hardly qualified as a textbook. The more Harry pored over the book, the more he realized how much was in there, not only the handy hints and shortcuts on potions that were earning him such a glowing reputation with Slughorn, but also the imaginative little jinxes and hexes scribbled in the margins, which Harry was sure, judging by the crossings-out and revisions, that the Prince had invented himself.

Harry had already attempted a few of the Prince's self-invented spells. There had been a hex that caused toenails to grow alarmingly fast (he had tried this on Crabbe in the corridor, with very entertaining results); a jinx that glued the tongue to the roof of the mouth (which he had twice used, to general applause, on an unsuspecting Argus Filch); and, perhaps most useful of all, *Muffliato*, a spell that filled the ears of anyone nearby with an unidentifiable buzzing, so that lengthy conversations could be held in class without being overheard. The only person who did not find these charms amusing was Hermione, who maintained a rigidly disapproving expression throughout and refused to talk at all if Harry had used the *Muffliato* spell on anyone in the vicinity.

Sitting up in bed, Harry turned the book sideways so as to examine more closely the scribbled instructions for a spell that seemed to have caused the Prince some trouble. There were many crossings-out and alterations, but finally, crammed into a corner of the page, the scribble:

Levicorpus (nvbl)

While the wind and sleet pounded relentlessly on the windows, and Neville snored loudly, Harry stared at the letters in brackets. *Nvbl* . . . that had to mean "nonverbal." Harry rather doubted he would be able to bring off this particular spell; he was still having difficulty with nonverbal spells, something Snape had been quick to comment on in every D.A.D.A. class. On the other hand, the Prince had proved a much more effective teacher than Snape so far.

Pointing his wand at nothing in particular, he gave it an upward flick and said *Levicorpus!* inside his head.

"Aaaaaaaargh!"

There was a flash of light and the room was full of voices: Every-one had woken up as Ron had let out a yell. Harry sent *Advanced Potion-Making* flying in panic; Ron was dangling upside down in midair as though an invisible hook had hoisted him up by the ankle.

"Sorry!" yelled Harry, as Dean and Seamus roared with laughter, and Neville picked himself up from the floor, having fallen out of bed. "Hang on — I'll let you down —"

He groped for the potion book and riffled through it in a panic, trying to find the right page; at last he located it and deciphered one cramped word underneath the spell: Praying that this was the counter-jinx, Harry thought *Liberacorpus!* with all his might.

There was another flash of light, and Ron fell in a heap onto his mattress.

"Sorry," repeated Harry weakly, while Dean and Seamus contin-ued to roar with laughter.

"Tomorrow," said Ron in a muffled voice, "I'd rather you set the alarm clock."

By the time they had got dressed, padding themselves out with several of Mrs. Weasley's hand-knitted sweaters and carrying cloaks, scarves, and gloves, Ron's shock had subsided and he had decided that Harry's new spell was highly amusing; so amusing, in fact, that he lost no time in regaling Hermione with the story as they sat down for breakfast.

". . . and then there was another flash of light and I landed on the bed again!" Ron grinned, helping himself to sausages.

Hermione had not cracked a smile during this anecdote, and now turned an expression of wintry disapproval upon Harry.

"Was this spell, by any chance, another one from that potion book of yours?" she asked.

Harry frowned at her.

"Always jump to the worst conclusion, don't you?"

"Was it?"

"Well . . . yeah, it was, but so what?"

"So you just decided to try out an unknown, handwritten incantation and see what would happen?"

"Why does it matter if it's handwritten?" said Harry, preferring not to answer the rest of the question.

"Because it's probably not Ministry of Magic–approved," said Hermione. "And also," she added, as Harry and Ron rolled their eyes, "because I'm starting to think this Prince character was a bit dodgy."

Both Harry and Ron shouted her down at once.

"It was a laugh!" said Ron, upending a ketchup bottle over his sausages. "Just a laugh, Hermione, that's all!"

"Dangling people upside down by the ankle?" said Hermione. "Who puts their time and energy into making up spells like that?"

"Fred and George," said Ron, shrugging, "it's their kind of thing. And, er —"

"My dad," said Harry. He had only just remembered.

"What?" said Ron and Hermione together.

"My dad used this spell," said Harry. "I — Lupin told me."

This last part was not true; in fact, Harry had seen his father use the spell on Snape, but he had never told Ron and Hermione about that particular excursion into the Pensieve. Now, however, a wonderful possibility occurred to him. Could the Half-Blood Prince possibly be — ?

"Maybe your dad did use it, Harry," said Hermione, "but he's not the only one. We've seen a whole bunch of people use it, in case you've forgotten. Dangling people in the air. Making them float along, asleep, helpless."

Harry stared at her. With a sinking feeling, he too remembered the behavior of the Death Eaters at the Quidditch World Cup. Ron came to his aid.

"That was different," he said robustly. "They were abusing it. Harry and his dad were just having a laugh. You don't like the Prince, Hermione," he added, pointing a sausage at her sternly, "because he's better than you at Potions —"

"It's got nothing to do with that!" said Hermione, her cheeks reddening. "I just think it's very irresponsible to start performing spells when you don't even know what they're for, and stop talking about 'the Prince' as if it's his title, I bet it's just a stupid nickname, and it doesn't seem as though he was a very nice person to me!"

"I don't see where you get that from," said Harry heatedly. "If he'd been a budding Death Eater he wouldn't have been boasting about being 'half-blood,' would he?"

Even as he said it, Harry remembered that his father had been pure-blood, but he pushed the thought out of his mind; he would worry about that later. . . .

"The Death Eaters can't all be pure-blood, there aren't enough pure-blood wizards left," said Hermione stubbornly. "I expect most of them are half-bloods pretending to be pure. It's only Muggle-borns they hate, they'd be quite happy to let you and Ron join up."

"There is no way they'd let me be a Death Eater!" said Ron indignantly, a bit of sausage flying off the fork he was now brandishing at Hermione and hitting Ernie Macmillan on the head. "My whole family are blood traitors! That's as bad as Muggle-borns to Death Eaters!"

"And they'd love to have me," said Harry sarcastically. "We'd be best pals if they didn't keep trying to do me in."

This made Ron laugh; even Hermione gave a grudging smile, and a distraction arrived in the shape of Ginny.

"Hey, Harry, I'm supposed to give you this."

It was a scroll of parchment with Harry's name written upon it in familiar thin, slanting writing.

"Thanks, Ginny . . . It's Dumbledore's next lesson!" Harry told Ron and Hermione, pulling open the parchment and quickly reading its contents. "Monday evening!" He felt suddenly light and happy. "Want to join us in Hogsmeade, Ginny?" he asked.

"I'm going with Dean — might see you there," she replied, waving at them as she left.

Filch was standing at the oak front doors as usual, checking off the names of people who had permission to go into Hogsmeade. The process took even longer than normal as Filch was triple-checking everybody with his Secrecy Sensor.

"What does it matter if we're smuggling Dark stuff OUT?" demanded Ron, eyeing the long thin Secrecy Sensor with apprehension. "Surely you ought to be checking what we bring back IN?"

His cheek earned him a few extra jabs with the Sensor, and he was still wincing as they stepped out into the wind and sleet.

The walk into Hogsmeade was not enjoyable. Harry wrapped his scarf over his lower face; the exposed part soon felt both raw and numb. The road to the village was full of students bent double against the bitter wind. More than once Harry wondered whether they might not have had a better time in the warm common room, and when they finally reached Hogsmeade and saw that Zonko's Joke Shop had been boarded up, Harry took it as confirmation that this trip was not destined to be fun. Ron pointed, with a thickly gloved hand, toward Honeydukes, which was mercifully open, and Harry and Hermione staggered in his wake into the crowded shop.

"Thank God," shivered Ron as they were enveloped by warm, toffee-scented air. "Let's stay here all afternoon."

"Harry, m'boy!" said a booming voice from behind them.

"Oh no," muttered Harry. The three of them turned to see Professor Slughorn, who was wearing an enormous furry hat and an overcoat with matching fur collar, clutching a large bag of crystalized pineapple, and occupying at least a quarter of the shop.

"Harry, that's three of my little suppers you've missed now!" said Slughorn, poking him genially in the chest. "It won't do, m'boy, I'm determined to have you! Miss Granger loves them, don't you?"

"Yes," said Hermione helplessly, "they're really —"

"So why don't you come along, Harry?" demanded Slughorn.

"Well, I've had Quidditch practice, Professor," said Harry, who had indeed been scheduling practices every time Slughorn had sent him a little, violet ribbon-adorned invitation. This strategy meant that Ron was not left out, and they usually had a laugh with Ginny, imagining Hermione shut up with McLaggen and Zabini.

"Well, I certainly expect you to win your first match after all this hard work!" said Slughorn. "But a little recreation never hurt anybody. Now, how about Monday night, you can't possibly want to practice in this weather. . . ."

"I can't, Professor, I've got — er — an appointment with Professor Dumbledore that evening."

"Unlucky again!" cried Slughorn dramatically. "Ah, well . . . you can't evade me forever, Harry!"

And with a regal wave, he waddled out of the shop, taking as little notice of Ron as though he had been a display of Cockroach Clusters.

"I can't believe you've wriggled out of another one," said Hermione, shaking her head. "They're not *that* bad, you know. . . . They're even quite fun sometimes. . . ." But then she caught sight of Ron's expression. "Oh, look — they've got deluxe sugar quills — those would last hours!"

Glad that Hermione had changed the subject, Harry showed much more interest in the new extra-large sugar quills than he would normally have done, but Ron continued to look moody and merely shrugged when Hermione asked him where he wanted to go next.

"Let's go to the Three Broomsticks," said Harry. "It'll be warm."

They bundled their scarves back over their faces and left the sweetshop. The bitter wind was like knives on their faces after the sugary warmth of Honeydukes. The street was not very busy; nobody was lingering to chat, just hurrying toward their destinations. The exceptions were two men a little ahead of them, standing just outside the Three Broomsticks. One was very tall and thin; squinting through his rain-washed glasses Harry recognized the barman who worked in the other Hogsmeade pub, the Hog's Head. As Harry, Ron, and Hermione drew closer, the barman drew his cloak more tightly around his neck and walked away, leaving the shorter man to fumble with something in his arms. They were barely feet from him when Harry realized who the man was.

"Mundungus!"

The squat, bandy-legged man with long, straggly, ginger hair jumped and dropped an ancient suitcase, which burst open, releasing what looked like the entire contents of a junk shop window.

"Oh, 'ello, 'Arry," said Mundungus Fletcher, with a most unconvincing stab at airiness. "Well, don't let me keep ya."

And he began scrabbling on the ground to retrieve the contents of his suitcase with every appearance of a man eager to be gone.

"Are you selling this stuff?" asked Harry, watching Mundungus grab an assortment of grubby-looking objects from the ground.

"Oh, well, gotta scrape a living," said Mundungus. "Gimme that!"

Ron had stooped down and picked up something silver.

"Hang on," Ron said slowly. "This looks familiar —"

"Thank you!" said Mundungus, snatching the goblet out of Ron's hand and stuffing it back into the case. "Well, I'll see you all — OUCH!"

Harry had pinned Mundungus against the wall of the pub by the throat. Holding him fast with one hand, he pulled out his wand.

"Harry!" squealed Hermione.

"You took that from Sirius's house," said Harry, who was almost nose to nose with Mundungus and was breathing in an unpleasant smell of old tobacco and spirits. "That had the Black family crest on it."

"I — no — what — ?" spluttered Mundungus, who was slowly turning purple.

"What did you do, go back the night he died and strip the place?" snarled Harry.

"I — no —"

"Give it to me!"

"Harry, you mustn't!" shrieked Hermione, as Mundungus started to turn blue.

There was a bang, and Harry felt his hands fly off Mundungus's throat. Gasping and spluttering, Mundungus seized his fallen case, then — *CRACK* — he Disapparated.

Harry swore at the top of his voice, spinning on the spot to see where Mundungus had gone.

"COME BACK, YOU THIEVING — !"

"There's no point, Harry."

Tonks had appeared out of nowhere, her mousy hair wet with sleet.

"Mundungus will probably be in London by now. There's no point yelling."

"He's nicked Sirius's stuff! Nicked it!"

"Yes, but still," said Tonks, who seemed perfectly untroubled by this piece of information. "You should get out of the cold."

She watched them go through the door of the Three Broomsticks.

The moment he was inside, Harry burst out, *"He was nicking Sirius's stuff!"*

"I know, Harry, but please don't shout, people are staring," whispered Hermione. "Go and sit down, I'll get you a drink."

Harry was still fuming when Hermione returned to their table a few minutes later holding three bottles of butterbeer.

"Can't the Order control Mundungus?" Harry demanded of the other two in a furious whisper. "Can't they at least stop him stealing everything that's not fixed down when he's at headquarters?"

"Shh!" said Hermione desperately, looking around to make sure nobody was listening; there were a couple of warlocks sitting close by who were staring at Harry with great interest, and Zabini was lolling against a pillar not far away. "Harry, I'd be annoyed too, I know it's your things he's stealing —"

Harry gagged on his butterbeer; he had momentarily forgotten that he owned number twelve, Grimmauld Place.

"Yeah, it's my stuff!" he said. "No wonder he wasn't pleased to see me! Well, I'm going to tell Dumbledore what's going on, he's the only one who scares Mundungus."

"Good idea," whispered Hermione, clearly pleased that Harry was calming down. "Ron, what are you staring at?"

"Nothing," said Ron, hastily looking away from the bar, but Harry knew he was trying to catch the eye of the curvy and attractive barmaid, Madam Rosmerta, for whom he had long nursed a soft spot.

"I expect 'nothing's' in the back getting more firewhisky," said Hermione waspishly.

Ron ignored this jibe, sipping his drink in what he evidently considered to be a dignified silence. Harry was thinking about Sirius, and how he had hated those silver goblets anyway. Hermione drummed her fingers on the table, her eyes flickering between Ron and the bar. The moment Harry drained the last drops in his bottle she said, "Shall we call it a day and go back to school, then?"

The other two nodded; it had not been a fun trip and the weather was getting worse the longer they stayed. Once again they drew their cloaks tightly around them, rearranged their scarves, pulled on their gloves, then followed Katie Bell and a friend out of the pub and back up the High Street. Harry's thoughts strayed to Ginny as they trudged up the road to Hogwarts through the frozen slush. They had not met up with her, undoubtedly, thought Harry, because she and Dean were cozily closeted in Madam Puddifoot's Tea Shop, that haunt of happy couples. Scowling, he bowed his head against the swirling sleet and trudged on.

It was a little while before Harry became aware that the voices of Katie Bell and her friend, which were being carried back to him on the wind, had become shriller and louder. Harry squinted at their indistinct figures. The two girls were having an argument about something Katie was holding in her hand. "It's nothing to do with you, Leanne!" Harry heard Katie say.

They rounded a corner in the lane, sleet coming thick and fast, blurring Harry's glasses. Just as he raised a gloved hand to wipe them, Leanne made to grab hold of the package Katie was holding; Katie tugged it back and the package fell to the ground.

At once, Katie rose into the air, not as Ron had done, suspended comically by the ankle, but gracefully, her arms outstretched, as though she was about to fly. Yet there was something wrong, something eerie. . . . Her hair was whipped around her by the fierce wind, but her eyes were closed and her face was quite empty of expression. Harry, Ron, Hermione, and Leanne had all halted in their tracks, watching.

Then, six feet above the ground, Katie let out a terrible scream. Her eyes flew open but whatever she could see, or whatever she was feeling, was clearly causing her terrible anguish. She screamed and screamed; Leanne started to scream too and seized Katie's ankles, trying to tug her back to the ground. Harry, Ron, and Hermione rushed forward to help, but even as they grabbed Katie's legs, she fell on top of them; Harry and Ron managed to catch her but she was writhing so much they could hardly hold her. Instead they lowered her to the ground where she thrashed and screamed, apparently unable to recognize any of them.

Harry looked around; the landscape seemed deserted.

"Stay there!" he shouted at the others over the howling wind. "I'm going for help!"

He began to sprint toward the school; he had never seen anyone behave as Katie had just behaved and could not think what had caused it; he hurtled around a bend in the lane and collided with what seemed to be an enormous bear on its hind legs.

"Hagrid!" he panted, disentangling himself from the hedgerow into which he had fallen.

"Harry!" said Hagrid, who had sleet trapped in his eyebrows and beard, and was wearing his great, shaggy beaverskin coat. "Jus' bin visitin' Grawp, he's comin' on so well yeh wouldn' —"

"Hagrid, someone's hurt back there, or cursed, or something —"

"Wha'?" said Hagrid, bending lower to hear what Harry was saying over the raging wind.

"Someone's been cursed!" bellowed Harry.

"Cursed? Who's bin cursed — not Ron? Hermione?"

"No, it's not them, it's Katie Bell — this way . . ."

Together they ran back along the lane. It took them no time to find the little group of people around Katie, who was still writhing and screaming on the ground; Ron, Hermione, and Leanne were all trying to quiet her.

"Get back!" shouted Hagrid. "Lemme see her!"

"Something's happened to her!" sobbed Leanne. "I don't know what —"

Hagrid stared at Katie for a second, then without a word, bent down, scooped her into his arms, and ran off toward the castle with her. Within seconds, Katie's piercing screams had died away and the only sound was the roar of the wind.

Hermione hurried over to Katie's wailing friend and put an arm around her.

"It's Leanne, isn't it?"

The girl nodded.

"Did it just happen all of a sudden, or — ?"

"It was when that package tore," sobbed Leanne, pointing at the now sodden brown-paper package on the ground, which had split open to reveal a greenish glitter. Ron bent down, his hand outstretched, but Harry seized his arm and pulled him back.

"Don't touch it!"

He crouched down. An ornate opal necklace was visible, poking out of the paper.

"I've seen that before," said Harry, staring at the thing. "It was on display in Borgin and Burkes ages ago. The label said it was cursed. Katie must have touched it." He looked up at Leanne, who had started to shake uncontrollably. "How did Katie get hold of this?"

"Well, that's why we were arguing. She came back from the bathroom in the Three Broomsticks holding it, said it was a surprise for somebody at Hogwarts and she had to deliver it. She looked all funny when she said it. . . . Oh no, oh no, I bet she'd been Imperiused and I didn't realize!"

Leanne shook with renewed sobs. Hermione patted her shoulder gently.

"She didn't say who'd given it to her, Leanne?"

"No . . . she wouldn't tell me . . . and I said she was being stupid and not to take it up to school, but she just wouldn't listen and . . . and then I tried to grab it from her . . . and — and —"

Leanne let out a wail of despair.

"We'd better get up to school," said Hermione, her arm still around Leanne. "We'll be able to find out how she is. Come on. . . ."

Harry hesitated for a moment, then pulled his scarf from around his face and, ignoring Ron's gasp, carefully covered the necklace in it and picked it up.

"We'll need to show this to Madam Pomfrey," he said.

As they followed Hermione and Leanne up the road, Harry was thinking furiously. They had just entered the grounds when he spoke, unable to keep his thoughts to himself any longer.

"Malfoy knows about this necklace. It was in a case at Borgin and Burkes four years ago, I saw him having a good look at it while I was hiding from him and his dad. *This* is what he was buying that day when we followed him! He remembered it and he went back for it!"

"I — I dunno, Harry," said Ron hesitantly. "Loads of people go to Borgin and Burkes . . . and didn't that girl say Katie got it in the girls' bathroom?"

"She said she came back from the bathroom with it, she didn't necessarily get it in the bathroom itself —"

"McGonagall!" said Ron warningly.

Harry looked up. Sure enough, Professor McGonagall was hurrying down the stone steps through swirling sleet to meet them.

"Hagrid says you four saw what happened to Katie Bell — upstairs to my office at once, please! What's that you're holding, Potter?"

"It's the thing she touched," said Harry.

"Good lord," said Professor McGonagall, looking alarmed as she took the necklace from Harry. "No, no, Filch, they're with me!" she added hastily, as Filch came shuffling eagerly across the entrance hall holding his Secrecy Sensor aloft. "Take this necklace to Professor Snape at once, but be sure not to touch it, keep it wrapped in the scarf!"

Harry and the others followed Professor McGonagall upstairs and into her office. The sleet-spattered windows were rattling in their frames, and the room was chilly despite the fire crackling in the grate. Professor McGonagall closed the door and swept around her desk to face Harry, Ron, Hermione, and the still sobbing Leanne.

"Well?" she said sharply. "What happened?"

Haltingly, and with many pauses while she attempted to control her crying, Leanne told Professor McGonagall how Katie had gone to the bathroom in the Three Broomsticks and returned holding the unmarked package, how Katie had seemed a little odd, and how they had argued about the advisability of agreeing to deliver unknown objects, the argument culminating in the tussle over the parcel, which tore open. At this point, Leanne was so overcome, there was no getting another word out of her.

"All right," said Professor McGonagall, not unkindly, "go up to the hospital wing, please, Leanne, and get Madam Pomfrey to give you something for shock."

When she had left the room, Professor McGonagall turned back to Harry, Ron, and Hermione.

"What happened when Katie touched the necklace?"

"She rose up in the air," said Harry, before either Ron or Hermione could speak, "and then began to scream, and collapsed. Professor, can I see Professor Dumbledore, please?"

"The headmaster is away until Monday, Potter," said Professor McGonagall, looking surprised.

"Away?" Harry repeated angrily.

"Yes, Potter, away!" said Professor McGonagall tartly. "But anything you have to say about this horrible business can be said to me, I'm sure!"

For a split second, Harry hesitated. Professor McGonagall did not invite confidences; Dumbledore, though in many ways more intimidating, still seemed less likely to scorn a theory, however wild. This was a life-and-death matter, though, and no moment to worry about being laughed at.

"I think Draco Malfoy gave Katie that necklace, Professor."

On one side of him, Ron rubbed his nose in apparent embarrassment; on the other, Hermione shuffled her feet as though quite keen to put a bit of distance between herself and Harry.

"That is a very serious accusation, Potter," said Professor McGonagall, after a shocked pause. "Do you have any proof?"

"No," said Harry, "but . . ." and he told her about following Malfoy to Borgin and Burkes and the conversation they had overheard between him and Mr. Borgin.

When he had finished speaking, Professor McGonagall looked slightly confused.

"Malfoy took something to Borgin and Burkes for repair?"

"No, Professor, he just wanted Borgin to tell him how to mend something, he didn't have it with him. But that's not the point, the thing is that he bought something at the same time, and I think it was that necklace —"

"You saw Malfoy leaving the shop with a similar package?"

"No, Professor, he told Borgin to keep it in the shop for him —"

"But Harry," Hermione interrupted, "Borgin asked him if he wanted to take it with him, and Malfoy said no —"

"Because he didn't want to touch it, obviously!" said Harry angrily.

"What he actually said was, 'How would I look carrying that down the street?'" said Hermione.

"Well, he would look a bit of a prat carrying a necklace," interjected Ron.

"Oh, Ron," said Hermione despairingly, "it would be all wrapped up, so he wouldn't have to touch it, and quite easy to hide inside a cloak, so nobody would see it! I think whatever he reserved at Borgin and Burkes was noisy or bulky, something he knew would draw attention to him if he carried it down the street — and in any case," she pressed on loudly, before Harry could interrupt, "I asked Borgin about the necklace, don't you remember? When I went in to try and find out what Malfoy had asked him to keep, I saw it there. And Borgin just told me the price, he didn't say it was already sold or anything —"

"Well, you were being really obvious, he realized what you were up to within about five seconds, of course he wasn't going to tell you — anyway, Malfoy could've sent off for it since —"

"That's enough!" said Professor McGonagall, as Hermione opened her mouth to retort, looking furious. "Potter, I appreciate you telling me this, but we cannot point the finger of blame at Mr. Malfoy purely because he visited the shop where this necklace might have been purchased. The same is probably true of hundreds of people —"

"— that's what I said —" muttered Ron.

"— and in any case, we have put stringent security measures in place this year. I do not believe that necklace can possibly have entered this school without our knowledge —"

"But —"

"— and what is more," said Professor McGonagall, with an air of awful finality, "Mr. Malfoy was not in Hogsmeade today."

Harry gaped at her, deflating.

"How do you know, Professor?"

"Because he was doing detention with me. He has now failed to complete his Transfiguration homework twice in a row. So, thank you for telling me your suspicions, Potter," she said as she marched past them, "but I need to go up to the hospital wing now to check on Katie Bell. Good day to you all."

She held open her office door. They had no choice but to file past her without another word.

Harry was angry with the other two for siding with McGonagall;

nevertheless, he felt compelled to join in once they started discussing what had happened.

"So who do you reckon Katie was supposed to give the necklace to?" asked Ron, as they climbed the stairs to the common room.

"Goodness only knows," said Hermione. "But whoever it was has had a narrow escape. No one could have opened that package without touching the necklace."

"It could've been meant for loads of people," said Harry. "Dumbledore — the Death Eaters would love to get rid of him, he must be one of their top targets. Or Slughorn — Dumbledore reckons Voldemort really wanted him and they can't be pleased that he's sided with Dumbledore. Or —"

"Or you," said Hermione, looking troubled.

"Couldn't have been," said Harry, "or Katie would've just turned around in the lane and given it to me, wouldn't she? I was behind her all the way out of the Three Broomsticks. It would have made much more sense to deliver the parcel outside Hogwarts, what with Filch searching everyone who goes in and out. I wonder why Malfoy told her to take it into the castle?"

"Harry, Malfoy wasn't in Hogsmeade!" said Hermione, actually stamping her foot in frustration.

"He must have used an accomplice, then," said Harry. "Crabbe or Goyle — or, come to think of it, another Death Eater, he'll have loads better cronies than Crabbe and Goyle now he's joined up —"

Ron and Hermione exchanged looks that plainly said *There's no point arguing with him.*

"Dilligrout," said Hermione firmly as they reached the Fat Lady.

The portrait swung open to admit them to the common room. It was quite full and smelled of damp clothing; many people seemed to have returned from Hogsmeade early because of the bad weather. There was no buzz of fear or speculation, however: Clearly, the news of Katie's fate had not yet spread.

"It wasn't a very slick attack, really, when you stop and think about it," said Ron, casually turfing a first year out of one of the good armchairs by the fire so that he could sit down. "The curse didn't even make it into the castle. Not what you'd call foolproof."

"You're right," said Hermione, prodding Ron out of the chair with her foot and offering it to the first year again. "It wasn't very well thought-out at all."

"But since when has Malfoy been one of the world's great thinkers?" asked Harry.

Neither Ron nor Hermione answered him.

THE SECRET RIDDLE

atie was removed to St. Mungo's Hospital for Magical Maladies and Injuries the following day, by which time the news that she had been cursed had spread all over the school, though the details were confused and nobody other than Harry, Ron, Hermione, and Leanne seemed to know that Katie herself had not been the intended target.

"Oh, and Malfoy knows, of course," said Harry to Ron and Hermione, who continued their new policy of feigning deafness whenever Harry mentioned his Malfoy-Is-a-Death-Eater theory.

Harry had wondered whether Dumbledore would return from wherever he had been in time for Monday night's lesson, but having had no word to the contrary, he presented himself outside Dumbledore's office at eight o'clock, knocked, and was told to enter. There sat Dumbledore looking unusually tired; his hand was as black and burned as ever, but he smiled when he gestured to Harry to sit down. The Pensieve was sitting on the desk again, casting silvery specks of light over the ceiling.

"You have had a busy time while I have been away," Dumbledore said. "I believe you witnessed Katie's accident."

"Yes, sir. How is she?"

"Still very unwell, although she was relatively lucky. She appears to have brushed the necklace with the smallest possible amount of skin: There was a tiny hole in her glove. Had she put it on, had she even held it in her ungloved hand, she would have died, perhaps instantly. Luckily Professor Snape was able to do enough to prevent a rapid spread of the curse —"

"Why him?" asked Harry quickly. "Why not Madam Pomfrey?"

"Impertinent," said a soft voice from one of the portraits on the wall, and Phineas Nigellus Black, Sirius's great-great-grandfather, raised his head from his arms where he had appeared to be sleeping. "I would not have permitted a student to question the way Hogwarts operated in my day."

"Yes, thank you, Phineas," said Dumbledore quellingly. "Professor Snape knows much more about the Dark Arts than Madam Pomfrey, Harry. Anyway, the St. Mungo's staff are sending me hourly reports, and I am hopeful that Katie will make a full recovery in time."

"Where were you this weekend, sir?" Harry asked, disregarding a strong feeling that he might be pushing his luck, a feeling apparently shared by Phineas Nigellus, who hissed softly.

"I would rather not say just now," said Dumbledore. "However, I shall tell you in due course."

"You will?" said Harry, startled.

"Yes, I expect so," said Dumbledore, withdrawing a fresh bottle of silver memories from inside his robes and uncorking it with a prod of his wand.

"Sir," said Harry tentatively, "I met Mundungus in Hogsmeade."

"Ah yes, I am already aware that Mundungus has been treating your inheritance with light-fingered contempt," said Dumbledore, frowning a little. "He has gone to ground since you accosted him outside the Three Broomsticks; I rather think he dreads facing me. However, rest assured that he will not be making away with any more of Sirius's old possessions."

"That mangy old half-blood has been stealing Black heirlooms?" said Phineas Nigellus, incensed; and he stalked out of his frame, undoubtedly to visit his portrait in number twelve, Grimmauld Place.

"Professor," said Harry, after a short pause, "did Professor McGonagall tell you what I told her after Katie got hurt? About Draco Malfoy?"

"She told me of your suspicions, yes," said Dumbledore.

"And do you — ?"

"I shall take all appropriate measures to investigate anyone who might have had a hand in Katie's accident," said Dumbledore. "But what concerns me now, Harry, is our lesson."

Harry felt slightly resentful at this: If their lessons were so very important, why had there been such a long gap between the first and second? However, he said no more about Draco Malfoy, but watched as Dumbledore poured the fresh memories into the Pensieve and began swirling the stone basin once more between his long-fingered hands.

"You will remember, I am sure, that we left the tale of Lord

Voldemort's beginnings at the point where the handsome Muggle, Tom Riddle, had abandoned his witch wife, Merope, and returned to his family home in Little Hangleton. Merope was left alone in London, expecting the baby who would one day become Lord Voldemort."

"How do you know she was in London, sir?"

"Because of the evidence of one Caractacus Burke," said Dumbledore, "who, by an odd coincidence, helped found the very shop whence came the necklace we have just been discussing."

He swilled the contents of the Pensieve as Harry had seen him swill them before, much as a gold prospector sifts for gold. Up out of the swirling, silvery mass rose a little old man revolving slowly in the Pensieve, silver as a ghost but much more solid, with a thatch of hair that completely covered his eyes.

"Yes, we acquired it in curious circumstances. It was brought in by a young witch just before Christmas, oh, many years ago now. She said she needed the gold badly, well, that much was obvious. Covered in rags and pretty far along . . . Going to have a baby, see. She said the locket had been Slytherin's. Well, we hear that sort of story all the time, 'Oh, this was Merlin's, this was, his favorite teapot,' but when I looked at it, it had his mark all right, and a few simple spells were enough to tell me the truth. Of course, that made it near enough priceless. She didn't seem to have any idea how much it was worth. Happy to get ten Galleons for it. Best bargain we ever made!"

Dumbledore gave the Pensieve an extra-vigorous shake and Caractacus Burke descended back into the swirling mass of memory from whence he had come.

"He only gave her ten Galleons?" said Harry indignantly.

"Caractacus Burke was not famed for his generosity," said Dumbledore. "So we know that, near the end of her pregnancy, Merope was alone in London and in desperate need of gold, desperate enough to sell her one and only valuable possession, the locket that was one of Marvolo's treasured family heirlooms."

"But she could do magic!" said Harry impatiently. "She could have got food and everything for herself by magic, couldn't she?"

"Ah," said Dumbledore, "perhaps she could. But it is my belief — I am guessing again, but I am sure I am right — that when her husband abandoned her, Merope stopped using magic. I do not think that she wanted to be a witch any longer. Of course, it is also possible that her unrequited love and the attendant despair sapped her of her powers; that can happen. In any case, as you are about to see, Merope refused to raise her wand even to save her own life."

"She wouldn't even stay alive for her son?"

Dumbledore raised his eyebrows. "Could you possibly be feeling sorry for Lord Voldemort?"

"No," said Harry quickly, "but she had a choice, didn't she, not like my mother —"

"Your mother had a choice too," said Dumbledore gently. "Yes, Merope Riddle chose death in spite of a son who needed her, but do not judge her too harshly, Harry. She was greatly weakened by long suffering and she never had your mother's courage. And now, if you will stand . . ."

"Where are we going?" Harry asked, as Dumbledore joined him at the front of the desk.

"This time," said Dumbledore, "we are going to enter *my*

memory. I think you will find it both rich in detail and satisfyingly accurate. After you, Harry . . ."

Harry bent over the Pensieve; his face broke the cool surface of the memory and then he was falling through darkness again. . . . Seconds later, his feet hit firm ground; he opened his eyes and found that he and Dumbledore were standing in a bustling, old-fashioned London street.

"There I am," said Dumbledore brightly, pointing ahead of them to a tall figure crossing the road in front of a horse-drawn milk cart.

This younger Albus Dumbledore's long hair and beard were auburn. Having reached their side of the street, he strode off along the pavement, drawing many curious glances due to the flamboyantly cut suit of plum velvet that he was wearing.

"Nice suit, sir," said Harry, before he could stop himself, but Dumbledore merely chuckled as they followed his younger self a short distance, finally passing through a set of iron gates into a bare courtyard that fronted a rather grim, square building surrounded by high railings. He mounted the few steps leading to the front door and knocked once. After a moment or two, the door was opened by a scruffy girl wearing an apron.

"Good afternoon. I have an appointment with a Mrs. Cole, who, I believe, is the matron here?"

"Oh," said the bewildered-looking girl, taking in Dumbledore's eccentric appearance. "Um . . . just a mo' . . . MRS. COLE!" she bellowed over her shoulder.

Harry heard a distant voice shouting something in response. The girl turned back to Dumbledore. "Come in, she's on 'er way."

Dumbledore stepped into a hallway tiled in black and white; the whole place was shabby but spotlessly clean. Harry and the older Dumbledore followed. Before the front door had closed behind them, a skinny, harassed-looking woman came scurrying toward them. She had a sharp-featured face that appeared more anxious than unkind, and she was talking over her shoulder to another aproned helper as she walked toward Dumbledore.

". . . and take the iodine upstairs to Martha, Billy Stubbs has been picking his scabs and Eric Whalley's oozing all over his sheets — chicken pox on top of everything else," she said to no-body in particular, and then her eyes fell upon Dumbledore and she stopped dead in her tracks, looking as astonished as if a giraffe had just crossed her threshold.

"Good afternoon," said Dumbledore, holding out his hand.

Mrs. Cole simply gaped.

"My name is Albus Dumbledore. I sent you a letter requesting an appointment and you very kindly invited me here today."

Mrs. Cole blinked. Apparently deciding that Dumbledore was not a hallucination, she said feebly, "Oh yes. Well — well then — you'd better come into my room. Yes."

She led Dumbledore into a small room that seemed part sitting room, part office. It was as shabby as the hallway and the furniture was old and mismatched. She invited Dumbledore to sit on a rick-ety chair and seated herself behind a cluttered desk, eyeing him nervously.

"I am here, as I told you in my letter, to discuss Tom Riddle and arrangements for his future," said Dumbledore.

"Are you family?" asked Mrs. Cole.

"No, I am a teacher," said Dumbledore. "I have come to offer Tom a place at my school."

"What school's this, then?"

"It is called Hogwarts," said Dumbledore.

"And how come you're interested in Tom?"

"We believe he has qualities we are looking for."

"You mean he's won a scholarship? How can he have done? He's never been entered for one."

"Well, his name has been down for our school since birth —"

"Who registered him? His parents?"

There was no doubt that Mrs. Cole was an inconveniently sharp woman. Apparently Dumbledore thought so too, for Harry now saw him slip his wand out of the pocket of his velvet suit, at the same time picking up a piece of perfectly blank paper from Mrs. Cole's desktop.

"Here," said Dumbledore, waving his wand once as he passed her the piece of paper, "I think this will make everything clear."

Mrs. Cole's eyes slid out of focus and back again as she gazed intently at the blank paper for a moment.

"That seems perfectly in order," she said placidly, handing it back. Then her eyes fell upon a bottle of gin and two glasses that had certainly not been present a few seconds before.

"Er — may I offer you a glass of gin?" she said in an extra-refined voice.

"Thank you very much," said Dumbledore, beaming.

It soon became clear that Mrs. Cole was no novice when it came to gin drinking. Pouring both of them a generous measure, she drained her own glass in one gulp. Smacking her lips frankly, she smiled at Dumbledore for the first time, and he didn't hesitate to press his advantage.

"I was wondering whether you could tell me anything of Tom Riddle's history? I think he was born here in the orphanage?"

"That's right," said Mrs. Cole, helping herself to more gin. "I remember it clear as anything, because I'd just started here myself. New Year's Eve and bitter cold, snowing, you know. Nasty night. And this girl, not much older than I was myself at the time, came staggering up the front steps. Well, she wasn't the first. We took her in, and she had the baby within the hour. And she was dead in another hour."

Mrs. Cole nodded impressively and took another generous gulp of gin.

"Did she say anything before she died?" asked Dumbledore. "Anything about the boy's father, for instance?"

"Now, as it happens, she did," said Mrs. Cole, who seemed to be rather enjoying herself now, with the gin in her hand and an eager audience for her story. "I remember she said to me, 'I hope he looks like his papa,' and I won't lie, she was right to hope it, because she was no beauty — and then she told me he was to be named Tom, for his father, and Marvolo, for *her* father — yes, I know, funny name, isn't it? We wondered whether she came from a circus — and she said the boy's surname was to be Riddle. And she died soon after that without another word.

"Well, we named him just as she'd said, it seemed so important to the poor girl, but no Tom nor Marvolo nor any kind of Riddle ever came looking for him, nor any family at all, so he stayed in the orphanage and he's been here ever since."

Mrs. Cole helped herself, almost absentmindedly, to another

healthy measure of gin. Two pink spots had appeared high on her cheekbones. Then she said, "He's a funny boy."

"Yes," said Dumbledore. "I thought he might be."

"He was a funny baby too. He hardly ever cried, you know. And then, when he got a little older, he was . . . odd."

"Odd in what way?" asked Dumbledore gently.

"Well, he —"

But Mrs. Cole pulled up short, and there was nothing blurry or vague about the inquisitorial glance she shot Dumbledore over her gin glass.

"He's definitely got a place at your school, you say?"

"Definitely," said Dumbledore.

"And nothing I say can change that?"

"Nothing," said Dumbledore.

"You'll be taking him away, whatever?"

"Whatever," repeated Dumbledore gravely.

She squinted at him as though deciding whether or not to trust him. Apparently she decided she could, because she said in a sudden rush, "He scares the other children."

"You mean he is a bully?" asked Dumbledore.

"I think he must be," said Mrs. Cole, frowning slightly, "but it's very hard to catch him at it. There have been incidents. . . . Nasty things . . ."

Dumbledore did not press her, though Harry could tell that he was interested. She took yet another gulp of gin and her rosy cheeks grew rosier still.

"Billy Stubbs's rabbit . . . well, Tom *said* he didn't do it and I don't see how he could have done, but even so, it didn't hang itself from the rafters, did it?"

"I shouldn't think so, no," said Dumbledore quietly.

"But I'm jiggered if I know how he got up there to do it. All I know is he and Billy had argued the day before. And then" — Mrs. Cole took another swig of gin, slopping a little over her chin this time — "on the summer outing — we take them out, you know, once a year, to the countryside or to the seaside — well, Amy Benson and Dennis Bishop were never quite right afterwards, and all we ever got out of them was that they'd gone into a cave with Tom Riddle. He swore they'd just gone exploring, but *something* happened in there, I'm sure of it. And, well, there have been a lot of things, funny things. . . ."

She looked around at Dumbledore again, and though her cheeks were flushed, her gaze was steady. "I don't think many people will be sorry to see the back of him."

"You understand, I'm sure, that we will not be keeping him permanently?" said Dumbledore. "He will have to return here, at the very least, every summer."

"Oh, well, that's better than a whack on the nose with a rusty poker," said Mrs. Cole with a slight hiccup. She got to her feet, and Harry was impressed to see that she was quite steady, even though two-thirds of the gin was now gone. "I suppose you'd like to see him?"

"Very much," said Dumbledore, rising too.

She led him out of her office and up the stone stairs, calling out instructions and admonitions to helpers and children as she passed. The orphans, Harry saw, were all wearing the same kind of grayish tunic. They looked reasonably well-cared for, but there was no denying that this was a grim place in which to grow up.

"Here we are," said Mrs. Cole, as they turned off the second landing and stopped outside the first door in a long corridor. She knocked twice and entered.

"Tom? You've got a visitor. This is Mr. Dumberton — sorry, Dunderbore. He's come to tell you — well, I'll let him do it."

Harry and the two Dumbledores entered the room, and Mrs. Cole closed the door on them. It was a small bare room with nothing in it except an old wardrobe, a wooden chair, and an iron bedstead. A boy was sitting on top of the gray blankets, his legs stretched out in front of him, holding a book.

There was no trace of the Gaunts in Tom Riddle's face. Merope had got her dying wish: He was his handsome father in miniature, tall for eleven years old, dark-haired, and pale. His eyes narrowed slightly as he took in Dumbledore's eccentric appearance. There was a moment's silence.

"How do you do, Tom?" said Dumbledore, walking forward and holding out his hand.

The boy hesitated, then took it, and they shook hands. Dumbledore drew up the hard wooden chair beside Riddle, so that the pair of them looked rather like a hospital patient and visitor.

"I am Professor Dumbledore."

"'Professor'?" repeated Riddle. He looked wary. "Is that like 'doctor'? What are you here for? Did *she* get you in to have a look at me?"

He was pointing at the door through which Mrs. Cole had just left.

"No, no," said Dumbledore, smiling.

"I don't believe you," said Riddle. "She wants me looked at, doesn't she? Tell the truth!"

He spoke the last three words with a ringing force that was

almost shocking. It was a command, and it sounded as though he had given it many times before. His eyes had widened and he was glaring at Dumbledore, who made no response except to continue smiling pleasantly. After a few seconds Riddle stopped glaring, though he looked, if anything, warier still.

"Who are you?"

"I have told you. My name is Professor Dumbledore and I work at a school called Hogwarts. I have come to offer you a place at my school — your new school, if you would like to come."

Riddle's reaction to this was most surprising. He leapt from the bed and backed away from Dumbledore, looking furious.

"You can't kid me! The asylum, that's where you're from, isn't it? 'Professor,' yes, of course — well, I'm not going, see? That old cat's the one who should be in the asylum. I never did anything to little Amy Benson or Dennis Bishop, and you can ask them, they'll tell you!"

"I am not from the asylum," said Dumbledore patiently. "I am a teacher and, if you will sit down calmly, I shall tell you about Hogwarts. Of course, if you would rather not come to the school, nobody will force you —"

"I'd like to see them try," sneered Riddle.

"Hogwarts," Dumbledore went on, as though he had not heard Riddle's last words, "is a school for people with special abilities —"

"I'm not mad!"

"I know that you are not mad. Hogwarts is not a school for mad people. It is a school of magic."

There was silence. Riddle had frozen, his face expressionless, but his eyes were flickering back and forth between each of Dumbledore's, as though trying to catch one of them lying.

"Magic?" he repeated in a whisper.

"That's right," said Dumbledore.

"It's . . . it's magic, what I can do?"

"What is it that you can do?"

"All sorts," breathed Riddle. A flush of excitement was rising up his neck into his hollow cheeks; he looked fevered. "I can make things move without touching them. I can make animals do what I want them to do, without training them. I can make bad things happen to people who annoy me. I can make them hurt if I want to."

His legs were trembling. He stumbled forward and sat down on the bed again, staring at his hands, his head bowed as though in prayer.

"I knew I was different," he whispered to his own quivering fingers. "I knew I was special. Always, I knew there was something."

"Well, you were quite right," said Dumbledore, who was no longer smiling, but watching Riddle intently. "You are a wizard."

Riddle lifted his head. His face was transfigured: There was a wild happiness upon it, yet for some reason it did not make him better looking; on the contrary, his finely carved features seemed somehow rougher, his expression almost bestial.

"Are you a wizard too?"

"Yes, I am."

"Prove it," said Riddle at once, in the same commanding tone he had used when he had said, "Tell the truth."

Dumbledore raised his eyebrows. "If, as I take it, you are accepting your place at Hogwarts —"

"Of course I am!"

"Then you will address me as 'Professor' or 'sir.'"

Riddle's expression hardened for the most fleeting moment before he said, in an unrecognizably polite voice, "I'm sorry, sir. I meant — please, Professor, could you show me — ?"

Harry was sure that Dumbledore was going to refuse, that he would tell Riddle there would be plenty of time for practical demonstrations at Hogwarts, that they were currently in a building full of Muggles and must therefore be cautious. To his great surprise, however, Dumbledore drew his wand from an inside pocket of his suit jacket, pointed it at the shabby wardrobe in the corner, and gave the wand a casual flick.

The wardrobe burst into flames.

Riddle jumped to his feet; Harry could hardly blame him for howling in shock and rage; all his worldly possessions must be in there. But even as Riddle rounded on Dumbledore, the flames vanished, leaving the wardrobe completely undamaged.

Riddle stared from the wardrobe to Dumbledore; then, his expression greedy, he pointed at the wand. "Where can I get one of them?"

"All in good time," said Dumbledore. "I think there is something trying to get out of your wardrobe."

And sure enough, a faint rattling could be heard from inside it. For the first time, Riddle looked frightened.

"Open the door," said Dumbledore.

Riddle hesitated, then crossed the room and threw open the wardrobe door. On the topmost shelf, above a rail of threadbare clothes, a small cardboard box was shaking and rattling as though there were several frantic mice trapped inside it.

"Take it out," said Dumbledore.

Riddle took down the quaking box. He looked unnerved.

"Is there anything in that box that you ought not to have?" asked Dumbledore.

Riddle threw Dumbledore a long, clear, calculating look. "Yes, I suppose so, sir," he said finally, in an expressionless voice.

"Open it," said Dumbledore.

Riddle took off the lid and tipped the contents onto his bed without looking at them. Harry, who had expected something much more exciting, saw a mess of small, everyday objects: a yo-yo, a silver thimble, and a tarnished mouth organ among them. Once free of the box, they stopped quivering and lay quite still upon the thin blankets.

"You will return them to their owners with your apologies," said Dumbledore calmly, putting his wand back into his jacket. "I shall know whether it has been done. And be warned: Thieving is not tolerated at Hogwarts."

Riddle did not look remotely abashed; he was still staring coldly and appraisingly at Dumbledore. At last he said in a colorless voice, "Yes, sir."

"At Hogwarts," Dumbledore went on, "we teach you not only to use magic, but to control it. You have — inadvertently, I am sure — been using your powers in a way that is neither taught nor tolerated at our school. You are not the first, nor will you be the last, to allow your magic to run away with you. But you should know that Hogwarts can expel students, and the Ministry of Magic — yes, there is a Ministry — will punish lawbreakers still more severely. All new wizards must accept that, in entering our world, they abide by our laws."

"Yes, sir," said Riddle again.

It was impossible to tell what he was thinking; his face remained quite blank as he put the little cache of stolen objects back into the cardboard box. When he had finished, he turned to Dumbledore and said baldly, "I haven't got any money."

"That is easily remedied," said Dumbledore, drawing a leather money-pouch from his pocket. "There is a fund at Hogwarts for those who require assistance to buy books and robes. You might have to buy some of your spellbooks and so on secondhand, but —"

"Where do you buy spellbooks?" interrupted Riddle, who had taken the heavy money bag without thanking Dumbledore, and was now examining a fat gold Galleon.

"In Diagon Alley," said Dumbledore. "I have your list of books and school equipment with me. I can help you find everything —"

"You're coming with me?" asked Riddle, looking up.

"Certainly, if you —"

"I don't need you," said Riddle. "I'm used to doing things for myself, I go round London on my own all the time. How do you get to this Diagon Alley — sir?" he added, catching Dumbledore's eye.

Harry thought that Dumbledore would insist upon accompanying Riddle, but once again he was surprised. Dumbledore handed Riddle the envelope containing his list of equipment, and after telling Riddle exactly how to get to the Leaky Cauldron from the orphanage, he said, "You will be able to see it, although Muggles around you — non-magical people, that is — will not. Ask for Tom the barman — easy enough to remember, as he shares your name —"

Riddle gave an irritable twitch, as though trying to displace an irksome fly.

"You dislike the name 'Tom'?"

"There are a lot of Toms," muttered Riddle. Then, as though he could not suppress the question, as though it burst from him in spite of himself, he asked, "Was my father a wizard? He was called Tom Riddle too, they've told me."

"I'm afraid I don't know," said Dumbledore, his voice gentle.

"My mother can't have been magic, or she wouldn't have died," said Riddle, more to himself than Dumbledore. "It must've been him. So — when I've got all my stuff — when do I come to this Hogwarts?"

"All the details are on the second piece of parchment in your envelope," said Dumbledore. "You will leave from King's Cross Station on the first of September. There is a train ticket in there too."

Riddle nodded. Dumbledore got to his feet and held out his hand again. Taking it, Riddle said, "I can speak to snakes. I found out when we've been to the country on trips — they find me, they whisper to me. Is that normal for a wizard?"

Harry could tell that he had withheld mention of this strangest power until that moment, determined to impress.

"It is unusual," said Dumbledore, after a moment's hesitation, "but not unheard of."

His tone was casual but his eyes moved curiously over Riddle's face. They stood for a moment, man and boy, staring at each other. Then the handshake was broken; Dumbledore was at the door.

"Good-bye, Tom. I shall see you at Hogwarts."

"I think that will do," said the white-haired Dumbledore at Harry's side, and seconds later, they were soaring weightlessly through darkness once more, before landing squarely in the present-day office.

"Sit down," said Dumbledore, landing beside Harry.

Harry obeyed, his mind still full of what he had just seen.

"He believed it much quicker than I did — I mean, when you told him he was a wizard," said Harry. "I didn't believe Hagrid at first, when he told me."

"Yes, Riddle was perfectly ready to believe that he was — to use his word — 'special,'" said Dumbledore.

"Did you know — then?" asked Harry.

"Did I know that I had just met the most dangerous Dark wizard of all time?" said Dumbledore. "No, I had no idea that he was to grow up to be what he is. However, I was certainly intrigued by him. I returned to Hogwarts intending to keep an eye upon him, something I should have done in any case, given that he was alone and friendless, but which, already, I felt I ought to do for others' sake as much as his.

"His powers, as you heard, were surprisingly well-developed for such a young wizard and — most interestingly and ominously of all — he had already discovered that he had some measure of control over them, and begun to use them consciously. And as you saw, they were not the random experiments typical of young wizards: He was already using magic against other people, to frighten, to punish, to control. The little stories of the strangled rabbit and the young boy and girl he lured into a cave were most suggestive. . . . *'I can make them hurt if I want to. . . .'*"

"And he was a Parselmouth," interjected Harry.

"Yes, indeed; a rare ability, and one supposedly connected with the Dark Arts, although as we know, there are Parselmouths among the great and the good too. In fact, his ability to speak to serpents did not make me nearly as uneasy as his obvious instincts for cruelty, secrecy, and domination.

"Time is making fools of us again," said Dumbledore, indicating the dark sky beyond the windows. "But before we part, I want to draw your attention to certain features of the scene we have just witnessed, for they have a great bearing on the matters we shall be discussing in future meetings.

"Firstly, I hope you noticed Riddle's reaction when I mentioned that another shared his first name, 'Tom'?"

Harry nodded.

"There he showed his contempt for anything that tied him to other people, anything that made him ordinary. Even then, he wished to be different, separate, notorious. He shed his name, as you know, within a few short years of that conversation and created the mask of 'Lord Voldemort' behind which he has been hidden for so long.

"I trust that you also noticed that Tom Riddle was already highly self-sufficient, secretive, and, apparently, friendless? He did not want help or companionship on his trip to Diagon Alley. He preferred to operate alone. The adult Voldemort is the same. You will hear many of his Death Eaters claiming that they are in his confidence, that they alone are close to him, even understand him. They are deluded. Lord Voldemort has never had a friend, nor do I believe that he has ever wanted one.

"And lastly — I hope you are not too sleepy to pay attention to this, Harry — the young Tom Riddle liked to collect trophies. You saw the box of stolen articles he had hidden in his room. These were taken from victims of his bullying behavior, souvenirs, if you will, of particularly unpleasant bits of magic. Bear in mind this magpie-like tendency, for this, particularly, will be important later.

"And now, it really is time for bed."

Harry got to his feet. As he walked across the room, his eyes fell upon the little table on which Marvolo Gaunt's ring had rested last time, but the ring was no longer there.

"Yes, Harry?" said Dumbledore, for Harry had come to a halt.

"The ring's gone," said Harry, looking around. "But I thought you might have the mouth organ or something."

Dumbledore beamed at him, peering over the top of his half-moon spectacles.

"Very astute, Harry, but the mouth organ was only ever a mouth organ."

And on that enigmatic note he waved to Harry, who understood himself to be dismissed.

FELIX FELICIS

Harry had Herbology first thing the following morning. He had been unable to tell Ron and Hermione about his lesson with Dumbledore over breakfast for fear of being overheard, but he filled them in as they walked across the vegetable patch toward the greenhouses. The weekend's brutal wind had died out at last; the weird mist had returned and it took them a little longer than usual to find the correct greenhouse.

"Wow, scary thought, the boy You-Know-Who," said Ron quietly, as they took their places around one of the gnarled Snargaluff stumps that formed this term's project, and began pulling on their protective gloves. "But I still don't get why Dumbledore's showing you all this. I mean, it's really interesting and everything, but what's the point?"

"Dunno," said Harry, inserting a gum shield. "But he says it's all important and it'll help me survive."

"I think it's fascinating," said Hermione earnestly. "It makes absolute sense to know as much about Voldemort as possible. How else will you find out his weaknesses?"

"So how was Slughorn's latest party?" Harry asked her thickly through the gum shield.

"Oh, it was quite fun, really," said Hermione, now putting on protective goggles. "I mean, he drones on about famous ex-pupils a bit, and he absolutely *fawns* on McLaggen because he's so well-connected, but he gave us some really nice food and he introduced us to Gwenog Jones."

"Gwenog Jones?" said Ron, his eyes widening under his own goggles. "*The* Gwenog Jones? Captain of the Holyhead Harpies?"

"That's right," said Hermione. "Personally, I thought she was a bit full of herself, but —"

"*Quite* enough chat over here!" said Professor Sprout briskly, bustling over and looking stern. "You're lagging behind, everybody else has started, and Neville's already got his first pod!"

They looked around; sure enough, there sat Neville with a bloody lip and several nasty scratches along the side of his face, but clutching an unpleasantly pulsating green object about the size of a grapefruit.

"Okay, Professor, we're starting now!" said Ron, adding quietly, when she had turned away again, "should've used Muffliato, Harry."

"No, we shouldn't!" said Hermione at once, looking, as she always did, intensely cross at the thought of the Half-Blood Prince and his spells. "Well, come on . . . we'd better get going. . . ."

She gave the other two an apprehensive look; they all took deep breaths and then dived at the gnarled stump between them.

It sprang to life at once; long, prickly, bramblelike vines flew out of the top and whipped through the air. One tangled itself in

Hermione's hair, and Ron beat it back with a pair of secateurs; Harry succeeded in trapping a couple of vines and knotting them together; a hole opened in the middle of all the tentaclelike branches; Hermione plunged her arm bravely into this hole, which closed like a trap around her elbow; Harry and Ron tugged and wrenched at the vines, forcing the hole to open again, and Hermione snatched her arm free, clutching in her fingers a pod just like Neville's. At once, the prickly vines shot back inside, and the gnarled stump sat there looking like an innocently dead lump of wood.

"You know, I don't think I'll be having any of these in my garden when I've got my own place," said Ron, pushing his goggles up onto his forehead and wiping sweat from his face.

"Pass me a bowl," said Hermione, holding the pulsating pod at arm's length; Harry handed one over and she dropped the pod into it with a look of disgust on her face.

"Don't be squeamish, squeeze it out, they're best when they're fresh!" called Professor Sprout.

"Anyway," said Hermione, continuing their interrupted conversation as though a lump of wood had not just attacked them, "Slughorn's going to have a Christmas party, Harry, and there's no way you'll be able to wriggle out of this one because he actually asked me to check your free evenings, so he could be sure to have it on a night you can come."

Harry groaned. Meanwhile, Ron, who was attempting to burst the pod in the bowl by putting both hands on it, standing up, and squashing it as hard as he could, said angrily, "And this is another party just for Slughorn's favorites, is it?"

"Just for the Slug Club, yes," said Hermione.

The pod flew out from under Ron's fingers and hit the greenhouse glass, rebounding onto the back of Professor Sprout's head and knocking off her old, patched hat. Harry went to retrieve the pod; when he got back, Hermione was saying, "Look, *I* didn't make up the name 'Slug Club' —"

"'*Slug Club,*'" repeated Ron with a sneer worthy of Malfoy. "It's pathetic. Well, I hope you enjoy your party. Why don't you try hooking up with McLaggen, then Slughorn can make you King and Queen Slug —"

"We're allowed to bring guests," said Hermione, who for some reason had turned a bright, boiling scarlet, "and I was *going* to ask you to come, but if you think it's that stupid then I won't bother!"

Harry suddenly wished the pod had flown a little farther, so that he need not have been sitting here with the pair of them. Unnoticed by either, he seized the bowl that contained the pod and began to try and open it by the noisiest and most energetic means he could think of; unfortunately, he could still hear every word of their conversation.

"You were going to ask me?" asked Ron, in a completely different voice.

"Yes," said Hermione angrily. "But obviously if you'd rather I *hooked up with McLaggen . . .*"

There was a pause while Harry continued to pound the resilient pod with a trowel.

"No, I wouldn't," said Ron, in a very quiet voice.

Harry missed the pod, hit the bowl, and shattered it.

"*Reparo,*" he said hastily, poking the pieces with his wand, and the bowl sprang back together again. The crash, however, appeared to have awoken Ron and Hermione to Harry's presence. Hermione looked flustered and immediately started fussing about for her copy of *Flesh-Eating Trees of the World* to find out the correct way to juice Snargaluff pods; Ron, on the other hand, looked sheepish but also rather pleased with himself.

"Hand that over, Harry," said Hermione hurriedly. "It says we're supposed to puncture them with something sharp. . . ."

Harry passed her the pod in the bowl; he and Ron both snapped their goggles back over their eyes and dived, once more, for the stump.

It was not as though he was really surprised, thought Harry, as he wrestled with a thorny vine intent upon throttling him; he had had an inkling that this might happen sooner or later. But he was not sure how he felt about it. . . . He and Cho were now too embarrassed to look at each other, let alone talk to each other; what if Ron and Hermione started going out together, then split up? Could their friendship survive it? Harry remembered the few weeks when they had not been talking to each other in the third year; he had not enjoyed trying to bridge the distance between them. And then, what if they didn't split up? What if they became like Bill and Fleur, and it became excruciatingly embarrassing to be in their presence, so that he was shut out for good?

"Gotcha!" yelled Ron, pulling a second pod from the stump just as Hermione managed to burst the first one open, so that the bowl was full of tubers wriggling like pale green worms.

The rest of the lesson passed without further mention of Slughorn's party. Although Harry watched his two friends more closely over the next few days, Ron and Hermione did not seem any different except that they were a little politer to each other than usual. Harry supposed he would just have to wait to see what happened under the influence of butterbeer in Slughorn's dimly lit room on the night of the party. In the meantime, however, he had more pressing worries.

Katie Bell was still in St. Mungo's Hospital with no prospect of leaving, which meant that the promising Gryffindor team Harry had been training so carefully since September was one Chaser short. He kept putting off replacing Katie in the hope that she would return, but their opening match against Slytherin was looming, and he finally had to accept that she would not be back in time to play.

Harry did not think he could stand another full-House tryout. With a sinking feeling that had little to do with Quidditch, he cornered Dean Thomas after Transfiguration one day. Most of the class had already left, although several twittering yellow birds were still zooming around the room, all of Hermione's creation; nobody else had succeeded in conjuring so much as a feather from thin air.

"Are you still interested in playing Chaser?"

"Wha — ? Yeah, of course!" said Dean excitedly. Over Dean's shoulder, Harry saw Seamus Finnigan slamming his books into his bag, looking sour. One of the reasons why Harry would have preferred not to have to ask Dean to play was that he knew Seamus would not like it. On the other hand, he had to do what was best for the team, and Dean had outflown Seamus at the tryouts.

"Well then, you're in," said Harry. "There's a practice tonight, seven o'clock."

"Right," said Dean. "Cheers, Harry! Blimey, I can't wait to tell Ginny!"

He sprinted out of the room, leaving Harry and Seamus alone together, an uncomfortable moment made no easier when a bird dropping landed on Seamus's head as one of Hermione's canaries whizzed over them.

Seamus was not the only person disgruntled by the choice of Katie's substitute. There was much muttering in the common room about the fact that Harry had now chosen two of his classmates for the team. As Harry had endured much worse mutterings than this in his school career, he was not particularly bothered, but all the same, the pressure was increasing to provide a win in the upcoming match against Slytherin. If Gryffindor won, Harry knew that the whole House would forget that they had criticized him and swear that they had always known it was a great team. If they lost . . . well, Harry thought wryly, he had still endured worse mutterings. . . .

Harry had no reason to regret his choice once he saw Dean fly that evening; he worked well with Ginny and Demelza. The Beaters, Peakes and Coote, were getting better all the time. The only problem was Ron.

Harry had known all along that Ron was an inconsistent player who suffered from nerves and a lack of confidence, and unfortunately, the looming prospect of the opening game of the season seemed to have brought out all his old insecurities. After letting in half a dozen goals, most of them scored by Ginny, his technique became wilder and wilder, until he finally punched an oncoming Demelza Robins in the mouth.

"It was an accident, I'm sorry, Demelza, really sorry!" Ron shouted after her as she zigzagged back to the ground, dripping blood everywhere. "I just —"

"Panicked," Ginny said angrily, landing next to Demelza and examining her fat lip. "You prat, Ron, look at the state of her!"

"I can fix that," said Harry, landing beside the two girls, pointing his wand at Demelza's mouth, and saying *"Episkey."* "And Ginny, don't call Ron a prat, you're not the Captain of this team —"

"Well, you seemed too busy to call him a prat and I thought someone should —"

Harry forced himself not to laugh.

"In the air, everyone, let's go. . . ."

Overall it was one of the worst practices they had had all term, though Harry did not feel that honesty was the best policy when they were this close to the match.

"Good work, everyone, I think we'll flatten Slytherin," he said bracingly, and the Chasers and Beaters left the changing room looking reasonably happy with themselves.

"I played like a sack of dragon dung," said Ron in a hollow voice when the door had swung shut behind Ginny.

"No, you didn't," said Harry firmly. "You're the best Keeper I tried out, Ron. Your only problem is nerves."

He kept up a relentless flow of encouragement all the way back to the castle, and by the time they reached the second floor, Ron was looking marginally more cheerful. When Harry pushed open the tapestry to take their usual shortcut up to Gryffindor Tower, however, they found themselves looking at Dean and Ginny, who were locked in a close embrace and kissing fiercely as though glued together.

It was as though something large and scaly erupted into life in Harry's stomach, clawing at his insides: Hot blood seemed to flood his brain, so that all thought was extinguished, replaced by a savage urge to jinx Dean into a jelly. Wrestling with this sudden madness, he heard Ron's voice as though from a great distance away.

"Oi!"

Dean and Ginny broke apart and looked around.

"What?" said Ginny.

"I don't want to find my own sister snogging people in public!"

"This was a deserted corridor till you came butting in!" said Ginny.

Dean was looking embarrassed. He gave Harry a shifty grin that Harry did not return, as the newborn monster inside him was roaring for Dean's instant dismissal from the team.

"Er . . . c'mon, Ginny," said Dean, "let's go back to the common room. . . ."

"You go!" said Ginny. "I want a word with my dear brother!"

Dean left, looking as though he was not sorry to depart the scene.

"Right," said Ginny, tossing her long red hair out of her face and glaring at Ron, "let's get this straight once and for all. It is none of your business who I go out with or what I do with them, Ron —"

"Yeah, it is!" said Ron, just as angrily. "D'you think I want people saying my sister's a —"

"A what?" shouted Ginny, drawing her wand. "A *what*, exactly?"

"He doesn't mean anything, Ginny —" said Harry automatically, though the monster was roaring its approval of Ron's words.

"Oh yes he does!" she said, flaring up at Harry. "Just because *he's* never snogged anyone in his life, just because the best kiss *he's* ever had is from our Auntie Muriel —"

"Shut your mouth!" bellowed Ron, bypassing red and turning maroon.

"No, I will not!" yelled Ginny, beside herself. "I've seen you with Phlegm, hoping she'll kiss you on the cheek every time you see her, it's pathetic! If you went out and got a bit of snogging done yourself, you wouldn't mind so much that everyone else does it!"

Ron had pulled out his wand too; Harry stepped swiftly between them.

"You don't know what you're talking about!" Ron roared, trying to get a clear shot at Ginny around Harry, who was now standing in front of her with his arms outstretched. "Just because I don't do it in public — !"

Ginny screamed with derisive laughter, trying to push Harry out of the way.

"Been kissing Pigwidgeon, have you? Or have you got a picture of Auntie Muriel stashed under your pillow?"

"You —"

A streak of orange light flew under Harry's left arm and missed Ginny by inches; Harry pushed Ron up against the wall.

"Don't be stupid —"

"Harry's snogged Cho Chang!" shouted Ginny, who sounded close to tears now. "And Hermione snogged Viktor Krum, it's only you who acts like it's something disgusting, Ron, and that's because you've got about as much experience as a twelve-year-old!"

And with that, she stormed away. Harry quickly let go of Ron; the look on his face was murderous. They both stood there, breathing heavily, until Mrs. Norris, Filch's cat, appeared around the corner, which broke the tension.

"C'mon," said Harry, as the sound of Filch's shuffling feet reached their ears.

They hurried up the stairs and along a seventh-floor corridor. "Oi, out of the way!" Ron barked at a small girl who jumped in fright and dropped a bottle of toadspawn.

Harry hardly noticed the sound of shattering glass; he felt disoriented, dizzy; being struck by a lightning bolt must be something like this. *It's just because she's Ron's sister,* he told himself. *You just didn't like seeing her kissing Dean because she's Ron's sister. . . .*

But unbidden into his mind came an image of that same deserted corridor with himself kissing Ginny instead. . . . The monster in his chest purred . . . but then he saw Ron ripping open the tapestry curtain and drawing his wand on Harry, shouting things like "betrayal of trust" . . . "supposed to be my friend" . . .

"D'you think Hermione did snog Krum?" Ron asked abruptly, as they approached the Fat Lady. Harry gave a guilty start and wrenched his imagination away from a corridor in which no Ron intruded, in which he and Ginny were quite alone —

"What?" he said confusedly. "Oh . . . er . . ."

The honest answer was "yes," but he did not want to give it. However, Ron seemed to gather the worst from the look on Harry's face.

"Dilligrout," he said darkly to the Fat Lady, and they climbed through the portrait hole into the common room.

Neither of them mentioned Ginny or Hermione again; indeed, they barely spoke to each other that evening and got into bed in silence, each absorbed in his own thoughts.

Harry lay awake for a long time, looking up at the canopy of his four-poster and trying to convince himself that his feelings for Ginny were entirely elder-brotherly. They had lived, had they not, like brother and sister all summer, playing Quidditch, teasing Ron, and having a laugh about Bill and Phlegm? He had known Ginny for years now. . . . It was natural that he should feel protective . . . natural that he should want to look out for her . . . want to rip

Dean limb from limb for kissing her . . . No . . . he would have to control that particular brotherly feeling. . . .

Ron gave a great grunting snore.

She's Ron's sister, Harry told himself firmly. *Ron's sister. She's out-of-bounds.* He would not risk his friendship with Ron for anything. He punched his pillow into a more comfortable shape and waited for sleep to come, trying his utmost not to allow his thoughts to stray anywhere near Ginny.

Harry awoke next morning feeling slightly dazed and confused by a series of dreams in which Ron had chased him with a Beater's bat, but by midday he would have happily exchanged the dream Ron for the real one, who was not only cold-shouldering Ginny and Dean, but also treating a hurt and bewildered Hermione with an icy, sneering indifference. What was more, Ron seemed to have become, overnight, as touchy and ready to lash out as the average Blast-Ended Skrewt. Harry spent the day attempting to keep the peace between Ron and Hermione with no success; finally, Hermione departed for bed in high dudgeon, and Ron stalked off to the boys' dormitory after swearing angrily at several frightened first years for looking at him.

To Harry's dismay, Ron's new aggression did not wear off over the next few days. Worse still, it coincided with an even deeper dip in his Keeping skills, which made him still more aggressive, so that during the final Quidditch practice before Saturday's match, he failed to save every single goal the Chasers aimed at him, but bellowed at everybody so much that he reduced Demelza Robins to tears.

"You shut up and leave her alone!" shouted Peakes, who was about two-thirds Ron's height, though admittedly carrying a heavy bat.

"ENOUGH!" bellowed Harry, who had seen Ginny glowering in Ron's direction and, remembering her reputation as an accomplished caster of the Bat-Bogey Hex, soared over to intervene before things got out of hand. "Peakes, go and pack up the Bludgers. Demelza, pull yourself together, you played really well today. Ron . . ." he waited until the rest of the team were out of earshot before saying it, "you're my best mate, but carry on treating the rest of them like this and I'm going to kick you off the team."

He really thought for a moment that Ron might hit him, but then something much worse happened: Ron seemed to sag on his broom; all the fight went out of him and he said, "I resign. I'm pathetic."

"You're not pathetic and you're not resigning!" said Harry fiercely, seizing Ron by the front of his robes. "You can save anything when you're on form, it's a mental problem you've got!"

"You calling me mental?"

"Yeah, maybe I am!"

They glared at each other for a moment, then Ron shook his head wearily. "I know you haven't got any time to find another Keeper, so I'll play tomorrow, but if we lose, and we will, I'm taking myself off the team."

Nothing Harry said made any difference. He tried boosting Ron's confidence all through dinner, but Ron was too busy being grumpy and surly with Hermione to notice. Harry persisted in the common room that evening, but his assertion that the whole team would be devastated if Ron left was somewhat undermined by the fact that the rest of the team was sitting in a huddle in a distant corner, clearly muttering about Ron and casting him nasty looks. Finally Harry tried getting angry again in the hope of provoking Ron into a defiant, and hopefully goal-saving, attitude, but this strategy did not appear to work any better than encouragement; Ron went to bed as dejected and hopeless as ever.

Harry lay awake for a very long time in the darkness. He did not want to lose the upcoming match; not only was it his first as Captain, but he was determined to beat Draco Malfoy at Quidditch even if he could not yet prove his suspicions about him. Yet if Ron played as he had done in the last few practices, their chances of winning were very slim. . . .

If only there was something he could do to make Ron pull himself together . . . make him play at the top of his form . . . something that would ensure that Ron had a really good day. . . .

And the answer came to Harry in one, sudden, glorious stroke of inspiration.

Breakfast was the usual excitable affair next morning; the Slytherins hissed and booed loudly as every member of the Gryffindor team entered the Great Hall. Harry glanced at the ceiling and saw a clear, pale blue sky: a good omen.

The Gryffindor table, a solid mass of red and gold, cheered as Harry and Ron approached. Harry grinned and waved; Ron grimaced weakly and shook his head.

"Cheer up, Ron!" called Lavender. "I know you'll be brilliant!"

Ron ignored her.

"Tea?" Harry asked him. "Coffee? Pumpkin juice?"

"Anything," said Ron glumly, taking a moody bite of toast.

A few minutes later Hermione, who had become so tired of Ron's recent unpleasant behavior that she had not come down to breakfast with them, paused on her way up the table.

"How are you both feeling?" she asked tentatively, her eyes on the back of Ron's head.

"Fine," said Harry, who was concentrating on handing Ron a glass of pumpkin juice. "There you go, Ron. Drink up."

Ron had just raised the glass to his lips when Hermione spoke sharply.

"Don't drink that, Ron!"

Both Harry and Ron looked up at her.

"Why not?" said Ron.

Hermione was now staring at Harry as though she could not believe her eyes.

"You just put something in that drink."

"Excuse me?" said Harry.

"You heard me. I saw you. You just tipped something into Ron's drink. You've got the bottle in your hand right now!"

"I don't know what you're talking about," said Harry, stowing the little bottle hastily in his pocket.

"Ron, I warn you, don't drink it!" Hermione said again, alarmed, but Ron picked up the glass, drained it in one gulp, and said, "Stop bossing me around, Hermione."

She looked scandalized. Bending low so that only Harry could hear her, she hissed, "You should be expelled for that. I'd never have believed it of you, Harry!"

"Hark who's talking," he whispered back. "Confunded anyone lately?"

She stormed up the table away from them. Harry watched her go without regret. Hermione had never really understood what a serious business Quidditch was. He then looked around at Ron, who was smacking his lips.

"Nearly time," said Harry blithely.

The frosty grass crunched underfoot as they strode down to the stadium.

"Pretty lucky the weather's this good, eh?" Harry asked Ron.

"Yeah," said Ron, who was pale and sick-looking.

Ginny and Demelza were already wearing their Quidditch robes and waiting in the changing room.

"Conditions look ideal," said Ginny, ignoring Ron. "And guess what? That Slytherin Chaser Vaisey — he took a Bludger in the head yesterday during their practice, and he's too sore to play! And even better than that — Malfoy's gone off sick too!"

"*What?*" said Harry, wheeling around to stare at her. "He's ill? What's wrong with him?"

"No idea, but it's great for us," said Ginny brightly. "They're playing Harper instead; he's in my year and he's an idiot."

Harry smiled back vaguely, but as he pulled on his scarlet robes his mind was far from Quidditch. Malfoy had once before claimed he could not play due to injury, but on that occasion he had made sure the whole match was rescheduled for a time that suited the Slytherins better. Why was he now happy to let a substitute go on? Was he really ill, or was he faking?

"Fishy, isn't it?" he said in an undertone to Ron. "Malfoy not playing?"

"Lucky, I call it," said Ron, looking slightly more animated. "And Vaisey off too, he's their best goal scorer, I didn't fancy — hey!" he said suddenly, freezing halfway through pulling on his Keeper's gloves and staring at Harry.

"What?"

"I . . . you . . . ." Ron had dropped his voice, he looked both scared and excited. "My drink . . . my pumpkin juice . . . you didn't . . . ?"

Harry raised his eyebrows, but said nothing except, "We'll be starting in about five minutes, you'd better get your boots on."

They walked out onto the pitch to tumultuous roars and boos. One end of the stadium was solid red and gold; the other, a sea of green and silver. Many Hufflepuffs and Ravenclaws had taken sides too: Amidst all the yelling and clapping Harry could distinctly hear the roar of Luna Lovegood's famous lion-topped hat.

Harry stepped up to Madam Hooch, the referee, who was standing ready to release the balls from the crate.

"Captains shake hands," she said, and Harry had his hand crushed by the new Slytherin Captain, Urquhart. "Mount your brooms. On the whistle . . . three . . . two . . . one . . . ."

The whistle sounded, Harry and the others kicked off hard from the frozen ground, and they were away.

Harry soared around the perimeter of the grounds, looking around for the Snitch and keeping one eye on Harper, who was zigzagging far below him. Then a voice that was jarringly different to the usual commentator's started up.

"Well, there they go, and I think we're all surprised to see the team that Potter's put together this year. Many thought, given Ronald Weasley's patchy performance as Keeper last year, that he might be off the team, but of course, a close personal friendship with the Captain does help. . . ."

These words were greeted with jeers and applause from the Slytherin end of the pitch. Harry craned around on his broom to look toward the commentator's podium. A tall, skinny blond boy with an upturned nose was standing there, talking into the magical megaphone that had once been Lee Jordan's; Harry recognized Zacharias Smith, a Hufflepuff player whom he heartily disliked.

"Oh, and here comes Slytherin's first attempt on goal, it's Urquhart streaking down the pitch and —"

Harry's stomach turned over.

"— Weasley saves it, well, he's bound to get lucky sometimes, I suppose. . . ."

"That's right, Smith, he is," muttered Harry, grinning to himself, as he dived amongst the Chasers with his eyes searching all around for some hint of the elusive Snitch.

With half an hour of the game gone, Gryffindor were leading sixty points to zero, Ron having made some truly spectacular saves, some by the very tips of his gloves, and Ginny having scored four of Gryffindor's six goals. This effectively stopped Zacharias wondering loudly whether the two Weasleys were only there because Harry liked them, and he started on Peakes and Coote instead.

"Of course, Coote isn't really the usual build for a Beater," said Zacharias loftily, "they've generally got a bit more muscle —"

"Hit a Bludger at him!" Harry called to Coote as he zoomed past, but Coote, grinning broadly, chose to aim the next Bludger at Harper instead, who was just passing Harry in the opposite direction. Harry was pleased to hear the dull thunk that meant the Bludger had found its mark.

It seemed as though Gryffindor could do no wrong. Again and again they scored, and again and again, at the other end of the pitch, Ron saved goals with apparent ease. He was actually smiling now, and when the crowd greeted a particularly good save with a rousing chorus of the old favorite "Weasley Is Our King," he pretended to conduct them from on high.

"Thinks he's something special today, doesn't he?" said a snide voice, and Harry was nearly knocked off his broom as Harper collided with him hard and deliberately. "Your blood-traitor pal . . ."

Madam Hooch's back was turned, and though Gryffindors below shouted in anger, by the time she looked around, Harper had already sped off. His shoulder aching, Harry raced after him, determined to ram him back. . . .

"And I think Harper of Slytherin's seen the Snitch!" said Zacharias Smith through his megaphone. "Yes, he's certainly seen something Potter hasn't!"

Smith really was an idiot, thought Harry, hadn't he noticed them collide? But next moment, his stomach seemed to drop out of the sky — Smith was right and Harry was wrong: Harper had not sped upward at random; he had spotted what Harry had not: The Snitch was speeding along high above them, glinting brightly against the clear blue sky.

Harry accelerated; the wind was whistling in his ears so that it drowned all sound of Smith's commentary or the crowd, but Harper was still ahead of him, and Gryffindor was only a hundred points up; if Harper got there first Gryffindor had lost . . . and now Harper was feet from it, his hand outstretched. . . .

"Oi, Harper!" yelled Harry in desperation. "How much did Malfoy pay you to come on instead of him?"

He did not know what made him say it, but Harper did a double-take; he fumbled the Snitch, let it slip through his fingers, and shot right past it. Harry made a great swipe for the tiny, fluttering ball and caught it.

"YES!" Harry yelled. Wheeling around, he hurtled back toward the ground, the Snitch held high in his hand. As the crowd realized what had happened, a great shout went up that almost drowned the sound of the whistle that signaled the end of the game.

"Ginny, where're you going?" yelled Harry, who had found himself trapped in the midst of a mass midair hug with the rest of the team, but Ginny sped right on past them until, with an almighty crash, she collided with the commentator's podium. As the crowd shrieked and laughed, the Gryffindor team landed beside the wreckage of wood under which Zacharias was feebly stirring; Harry heard Ginny saying blithely to an irate Professor McGonagall, "Forgot to brake, Professor, sorry."

Laughing, Harry broke free of the rest of the team and hugged Ginny, but let go very quickly. Avoiding her gaze, he clapped a cheering Ron on the back instead as, all enmity forgotten, the Gryffindor team left the pitch arm in arm, punching the air and waving to their supporters.

The atmosphere in the changing room was jubilant.

"Party up in the common room, Seamus said!" yelled Dean exuberantly. "C'mon, Ginny, Demelza!"

Ron and Harry were the last two in the changing room. They were just about to leave when Hermione entered. She was twisting her Gryffindor scarf in her hands and looked upset but determined.

"I want a word with you, Harry." She took a deep breath. "You shouldn't have done it. You heard Slughorn, it's illegal."

"What are you going to do, turn us in?" demanded Ron.

"What are you two talking about?" asked Harry, turning away to hang up his robes so that neither of them would see him grinning.

"You know perfectly well what we're talking about!" said Hermione shrilly. "You spiked Ron's juice with lucky potion at breakfast! Felix Felicis!"

"No, I didn't," said Harry, turning back to face them both.

"Yes you did, Harry, and that's why everything went right, there were Slytherin players missing and Ron saved everything!"

"I didn't put it in!" said Harry, grinning broadly. He slipped his hand inside his jacket pocket and drew out the tiny bottle that Hermione had seen in his hand that morning. It was full of golden potion and the cork was still tightly sealed with wax. "I wanted Ron to think I'd done it, so I faked it when I knew you were looking." He looked at Ron. "You saved everything because you felt lucky. You did it all yourself."

He pocketed the potion again.

"There really wasn't anything in my pumpkin juice?" Ron said, astounded. "But the weather's good . . . and Vaisey couldn't play. . . . I honestly haven't been given lucky potion?"

Harry shook his head. Ron gaped at him for a moment, then rounded on Hermione, imitating her voice. "*You added Felix Felicis to Ron's juice this morning, that's why he saved everything!* See! I can save goals without help, Hermione!"

"I never said you couldn't — Ron, *you* thought you'd been given it too!"

But Ron had already strode past her out of the door with his broomstick over his shoulder.

"Er," said Harry into the sudden silence; he had not expected his plan to backfire like this, "shall . . . shall we go up to the party, then?"

"You go!" said Hermione, blinking back tears. "I'm *sick* of Ron at the moment, I don't know what I'm supposed to have done. . . ."

And she stormed out of the changing room too.

Harry walked slowly back up the grounds toward the castle through the crowd, many of whom shouted congratulations at him, but he felt a great sense of letdown; he had been sure that if Ron won the match, he and Hermione would be friends again immediately. He did not see how he could possibly explain to Hermione that what she had done to offend Ron was kiss Viktor Krum, not when the offense had occurred so long ago.

Harry could not see Hermione at the Gryffindor celebration party, which was in full swing when he arrived. Renewed cheers and clapping greeted his appearance, and he was soon surrounded by a mob of people congratulating him. What with trying to shake off the Creevey brothers, who wanted a blow-by-blow match analysis, and the large group of girls that encircled him, laughing at his least amusing comments and batting their eyelids, it was some time before he could try to find Ron. At last, he extricated himself from Romilda Vane, who was hinting heavily that she would like to go to Slughorn's Christmas party with him. As he was ducking toward the drinks table, he walked straight into Ginny, Arnold the Pygmy Puff riding on her shoulder and Crookshanks mewing hopefully at her heels.

"Looking for Ron?" she asked, smirking. "He's over there, the filthy hypocrite."

Harry looked into the corner she was indicating. There, in full view of the whole room, stood Ron wrapped so closely around Lavender Brown it was hard to tell whose hands were whose.

"It looks like he's eating her face, doesn't it?" said Ginny dispassionately. "But I suppose he's got to refine his technique somehow. Good game, Harry."

She patted him on the arm; Harry felt a swooping sensation in his stomach, but then she walked off to help herself to more butterbeer. Crookshanks trotted after her, his yellow eyes fixed upon Arnold.

Harry turned away from Ron, who did not look like he would be surfacing soon, just as the portrait hole was closing. With a sinking feeling, he thought he saw a mane of bushy brown hair whipping out of sight.

He darted forward, sidestepped Romilda Vane again, and pushed open the portrait of the Fat Lady. The corridor outside seemed to be deserted.

"Hermione?"

He found her in the first unlocked classroom he tried. She was sitting on the teacher's desk, alone except for a small ring of twittering yellow birds circling her head, which she had clearly just conjured out of midair. Harry could not help admiring her spellwork at a time like this.

"Oh, hello, Harry," she said in a brittle voice. "I was just practicing."

"Yeah . . . they're — er — really good. . . ." said Harry.

He had no idea what to say to her. He was just wondering whether there was any chance that she had not noticed Ron, that she had merely left the room because the party was a little too rowdy, when she said, in an unnaturally high-pitched voice, "Ron seems to be enjoying the celebrations."

"Er . . . does he?" said Harry.

"Don't pretend you didn't see him," said Hermione. "He wasn't exactly hiding it, was — ?"

The door behind them burst open. To Harry's horror, Ron came in, laughing, pulling Lavender by the hand.

"Oh," he said, drawing up short at the sight of Harry and Hermione.

"Oops!" said Lavender, and she backed out of the room, giggling. The door swung shut behind her.

There was a horrible, swelling, billowing silence. Hermione was staring at Ron, who refused to look at her, but said with an odd mixture of bravado and awkwardness, "Hi, Harry! Wondered where you'd got to!"

Hermione slid off the desk. The little flock of golden birds continued to twitter in circles around her head so that she looked like a strange, feathery model of the solar system.

"You shouldn't leave Lavender waiting outside," she said quietly. "She'll wonder where you've gone."

She walked very slowly and erectly toward the door. Harry glanced at Ron, who was looking relieved that nothing worse had happened.

"*Oppugno!*" came a shriek from the doorway.

Harry spun around to see Hermione pointing her wand at Ron, her expression wild: The little flock of birds was speeding like a hail of fat golden bullets toward Ron, who yelped and covered his face with his hands, but the birds attacked, pecking and clawing at every bit of flesh they could reach.

"Gerremoffme!" he yelled, but with one last look of vindictive fury, Hermione wrenched open the door and disappeared through it. Harry thought he heard a sob before it slammed.

CHAPTER FIFTEEN

THE UNBREAKABLE VOW

Snow was swirling against the icy windows once more; Christmas was approaching fast. Hagrid had already single-handedly delivered the usual twelve Christmas trees for the Great Hall; garlands of holly and tinsel had been twisted around the banisters of the stairs; everlasting candles glowed from inside the helmets of suits of armor and great bunches of mistletoe had been hung at intervals along the corridors. Large groups of girls tended to converge underneath the mistletoe bunches every time Harry went past, which caused blockages in the corridors; fortunately, however, Harry's frequent nighttime wanderings had given him an unusually good knowledge of the castle's secret passageways, so that he was able, without too much difficulty, to navigate mistletoe-free routes between classes.

Ron, who might once have found the necessity of these detours a cause for jealousy rather than hilarity, simply roared with laughter about it all. Although Harry much preferred this new laughing, joking Ron to the moody, aggressive model he had been enduring for the last few weeks, the improved Ron came at a heavy price. Firstly, Harry had to put up with the frequent presence of Lavender Brown, who seemed to regard any moment that she was not kissing Ron as a moment wasted; and secondly, Harry found himself once more the best friend of two people who seemed unlikely ever to speak to each other again.

Ron, whose hands and forearms still bore scratches and cuts from Hermione's bird attack, was taking a defensive and resentful tone.

"She can't complain," he told Harry. "She snogged Krum. So she's found out someone wants to snog me too. Well, it's a free country. I haven't done anything wrong."

Harry did not answer, but pretended to be absorbed in the book they were supposed to have read before Charms next morning (*Quintessence: A Quest*). Determined as he was to remain friends with both Ron and Hermione, he was spending a lot of time with his mouth shut tight.

"I never promised Hermione anything," Ron mumbled. "I mean, all right, I was going to go to Slughorn's Christmas party with her, but she never said . . . just as friends . . . I'm a free agent. . . ."

Harry turned a page of *Quintessence,* aware that Ron was watching him. Ron's voice tailed away in mutters, barely audible over the loud crackling of the fire, though Harry thought he caught the words "Krum" and "can't complain" again.

Hermione's schedule was so full that Harry could only talk to her properly in the evenings, when Ron was, in any case, so tightly wrapped around Lavender that he did not notice what Harry was doing. Hermione refused to sit in the common room while Ron was there, so Harry generally joined her in the library, which meant that their conversations were held in whispers.

"He's at perfect liberty to kiss whomever he likes," said Hermione, while the librarian, Madam Pince, prowled the shelves behind them. "I really couldn't care less."

She raised her quill and dotted an *i* so ferociously that she punctured a hole in her parchment. Harry said nothing. He thought his voice might soon vanish from lack of use. He bent a little lower over *Advanced Potion-Making* and continued to make notes on Everlasting Elixirs, occasionally pausing to decipher the Prince's useful additions to Libatius Borage's text.

"And incidentally," said Hermione, after a few moments, "you need to be careful."

"For the last time," said Harry, speaking in a slightly hoarse whisper after three-quarters of an hour of silence, "I am not giving back this book, I've learned more from the Half-Blood Prince than Snape or Slughorn have taught me in —"

"I'm not talking about your stupid so-called Prince," said Hermione, giving his book a nasty look as though it had been rude to her. "I'm talking about earlier. I went into the girls' bathroom just before I came in here and there were about a dozen girls in there, including that Romilda Vane, trying to decide how to slip you a love potion. They're all hoping they're going to get you to take them to Slughorn's party, and they all seem to have bought Fred and George's love potions, which I'm afraid to say probably work —"

"Why didn't you confiscate them then?" demanded Harry. It seemed extraordinary that Hermione's mania for upholding rules could have abandoned her at this crucial juncture.

"They didn't have the potions with them in the bathroom," said Hermione scornfully. "They were just discussing tactics. As I doubt whether even the *Half-Blood Prince*" — she gave the book another nasty look — "could dream up an antidote for a dozen different love potions at once, I'd just invite someone to go with you, that'll stop all the others thinking they've still got a chance. It's tomorrow night, they're getting desperate."

"There isn't anyone I want to invite," mumbled Harry, who was still trying not to think about Ginny any more than he could help, despite the fact that she kept cropping up in his dreams in ways that made him devoutly thankful that Ron could not perform Legilimency.

"Well, just be careful what you drink, because Romilda Vane looked like she meant business," said Hermione grimly.

She hitched up the long roll of parchment on which she was writing her Arithmancy essay and continued to scratch away with her quill. Harry watched her with his mind a long way away.

"Hang on a moment," he said slowly. "I thought Filch had banned anything bought at Weasleys' Wizard Wheezes?"

"And when has anyone ever paid attention to what Filch has banned?" asked Hermione, still concentrating on her essay.

"But I thought all the owls were being searched. So how come these girls are able to bring love potions into school?"

"Fred and George send them disguised as perfumes and cough potions," said Hermione. "It's part of their Owl Order Service."

"You know a lot about it."

Hermione gave him the kind of nasty look she had just given his copy of *Advanced Potion-Making.*

"It was all on the back of the bottles they showed Ginny and me in the summer," she said coldly. "I don't go around putting potions in people's drinks . . . or pretending to, either, which is just as bad. . . ."

"Yeah, well, never mind that," said Harry quickly. "The point is, Filch is being fooled, isn't he? These girls are getting stuff into the school disguised as something else! So why couldn't Malfoy have brought the necklace into the school — ?"

"Oh, Harry . . . not that again . . ."

"Come on, why not?" demanded Harry.

"Look," sighed Hermione, "Secrecy Sensors detect jinxes, curses, and concealment charms, don't they? They're used to find Dark Magic and Dark objects. They'd have picked up a powerful curse, like the one on that necklace, within seconds. But something that's just been put in the wrong bottle wouldn't register — and anyway, love potions aren't Dark or dangerous —"

"Easy for you to say," muttered Harry, thinking of Romilda Vane.

"— so it would be down to Filch to realize it wasn't a cough potion, and he's not a very good wizard, I doubt he can tell one potion from —"

Hermione stopped dead; Harry had heard it too. Somebody had moved close behind them among the dark bookshelves. They waited, and a moment later the vulturelike countenance of Madam Pince appeared around the corner, her sunken cheeks, her skin like parchment, and her long hooked nose illuminated unflatteringly by the lamp she was carrying.

"The library is now closed," she said. "Mind you return anything you have borrowed to the correct — *what have you been doing to that book, you depraved boy?*"

"It isn't the library's, it's mine!" said Harry hastily, snatching his copy of *Advanced Potion-Making* off the table as she lunged at it with a clawlike hand.

"Despoiled!" she hissed. "Desecrated! Befouled!"

"It's just a book that's been written on!" said Harry, tugging it out of her grip.

She looked as though she might have a seizure; Hermione, who had hastily packed her things, grabbed Harry by the arm and frog-marched him away.

"She'll ban you from the library if you're not careful. Why did you have to bring that stupid book?"

"It's not my fault she's barking mad, Hermione. Or d'you think she overheard you being rude about Filch? I've always thought there might be something going on between them. . . ."

"Oh, ha ha . . ."

Enjoying the fact that they could speak normally again, they made their way along the deserted, lamp-lit corridors back to the common room, arguing about whether or not Filch and Madam Pince were secretly in love with each other.

"Baubles," said Harry to the Fat Lady, this being the new, festive password.

"Same to you," said the Fat Lady with a roguish grin, and she swung forward to admit them.

"Hi, Harry!" said Romilda Vane, the moment he had climbed through the portrait hole. "Fancy a gillywater?"

Hermione gave him a "what-did-I-tell-you?" look over her shoulder.

"No thanks," said Harry quickly. "I don't like it much."

"Well, take these anyway," said Romilda, thrusting a box into his hands. "Chocolate Cauldrons, they've got firewhisky in them. My gran sent them to me, but I don't like them."

"Oh — right — thanks a lot," said Harry, who could not think what else to say. "Er — I'm just going over here with . . ."

He hurried off behind Hermione, his voice tailing away feebly.

"Told you," said Hermione succinctly. "Sooner you ask someone, sooner they'll all leave you alone and you can —"

But her face suddenly turned blank; she had just spotted Ron and Lavender, who were entwined in the same armchair.

"Well, good night, Harry," said Hermione, though it was only seven o'clock in the evening, and she left for the girls' dormitory without another word.

Harry went to bed comforting himself that there was only one more day of lessons to struggle through, plus Slughorn's party, after which he and Ron would depart together for the Burrow. It now seemed impossible that Ron and Hermione would make up with each other before the holidays began, but perhaps, somehow, the break would give them time to calm down, think better of their behavior. . . .

But his hopes were not high, and they sank still lower after enduring a Transfiguration lesson with them both next day. They had just embarked upon the immensely difficult topic of human Transfiguration; working in front of mirrors, they were supposed to be changing the color of their own eyebrows. Hermione laughed

unkindly at Ron's disastrous first attempt, during which he somehow managed to give himself a spectacular handlebar mustache;
Ron retaliated by doing a cruel but accurate impression of Hermione jumping up and down in her seat every time Professor McGonagall asked a question, which Lavender and Parvati found deeply
amusing and which reduced Hermione to the verge of tears again.
She raced out of the classroom on the bell, leaving half her things
behind; Harry, deciding that her need was greater than Ron's just
now, scooped up her remaining possessions and followed her.

He finally tracked her down as she emerged from a girls' bathroom on the floor below. She was accompanied by Luna Lovegood,
who was patting her vaguely on the back.

"Oh, hello, Harry," said Luna. "Did you know one of your eyebrows is bright yellow?"

"Hi, Luna. Hermione, you left your stuff. . . ."

He held out her books.

"Oh yes," said Hermione in a choked voice, taking her things
and turning away quickly to hide the fact that she was wiping her
eyes on her pencil case. "Thank you, Harry. Well, I'd better get going. . . ."

And she hurried off, without giving Harry any time to offer
words of comfort, though admittedly he could not think of any.

"She's a bit upset," said Luna. "I thought at first it was Moaning
Myrtle in there, but it turned out to be Hermione. She said something about that Ron Weasley. . . ."

"Yeah, they've had a row," said Harry.

"He says very funny things sometimes, doesn't he?" said Luna, as
they set off down the corridor together. "But he can be a bit unkind. I noticed that last year."

"I s'pose," said Harry. Luna was demonstrating her usual knack of speaking uncomfortable truths; he had never met anyone quite like her. "So have you had a good term?"

"Oh, it's been all right," said Luna. "A bit lonely without the D.A. Ginny's been nice, though. She stopped two boys in our Transfiguration class calling me 'Loony' the other day —"

"How would you like to come to Slughorn's party with me tonight?"

The words were out of Harry's mouth before he could stop them; he heard himself say them as though it were a stranger speaking.

Luna turned her protuberant eyes upon him in surprise.

"Slughorn's party? With you?"

"Yeah," said Harry. "We're supposed to bring guests, so I thought you might like . . . I mean . . ." He was keen to make his intentions perfectly clear. "I mean, just as friends, you know. But if you don't want to . . ."

He was already half hoping that she didn't want to.

"Oh, no, I'd love to go with you as friends!" said Luna, beaming as he had never seen her beam before. "Nobody's ever asked me to a party before, as a friend! Is that why you dyed your eyebrow, for the party? Should I do mine too?"

"No," said Harry firmly, "that was a mistake. I'll get Hermione to put it right for me. So, I'll meet you in the entrance hall at eight o'clock then."

"AHA!" screamed a voice from overhead and both of them jumped; unnoticed by either of them, they had just passed right underneath Peeves, who was hanging upside down from a chandelier and grinning maliciously at them.

"Potty asked Loony to go to the party! Potty lurves Loony! Potty luuuuurves Loooooooony!"

And he zoomed away, cackling and shrieking, "Potty loves Loony!"

"Nice to keep these things private," said Harry. And sure enough, in no time at all the whole school seemed to know that Harry Potter was taking Luna Lovegood to Slughorn's party.

"You could've taken *anyone*!" said Ron in disbelief over dinner. "*Anyone!* And you chose Loony Lovegood?"

"Don't call her that, Ron," snapped Ginny, pausing behind Harry on her way to join friends. "I'm really glad you're taking her, Harry, she's so excited."

And she moved on down the table to sit with Dean. Harry tried to feel pleased that Ginny was glad he was taking Luna to the party, but could not quite manage it. A long way along the table, Hermione was sitting alone, playing with her stew. Harry noticed Ron looking at her furtively.

"You could say sorry," suggested Harry bluntly.

"What, and get attacked by another flock of canaries?" muttered Ron.

"What did you have to imitate her for?"

"She laughed at my mustache!"

"So did I, it was the stupidest thing I've ever seen."

But Ron did not seem to have heard; Lavender had just arrived with Parvati. Squeezing herself in between Harry and Ron, Lavender flung her arms around Ron's neck.

"Hi, Harry," said Parvati who, like him, looked faintly embarrassed and bored by the behavior of their two friends.

"Hi," said Harry. "How're you? You're staying at Hogwarts, then? I heard your parents wanted you to leave."

"I managed to talk them out of it for the time being," said Parvati. "That Katie thing really freaked them out, but as there hasn't been anything since . . . Oh, hi, Hermione!"

Parvati positively beamed. Harry could tell that she was feeling guilty for having laughed at Hermione in Transfiguration. He looked around and saw that Hermione was beaming back, if possible even more brightly. Girls were very strange sometimes.

"Hi, Parvati!" said Hermione, ignoring Ron and Lavender completely. "Are you going to Slughorn's party tonight?"

"No invite," said Parvati gloomily. "I'd love to go, though, it sounds like it's going to be really good. . . . You're going, aren't you?"

"Yes, I'm meeting Cormac at eight, and we're —"

There was a noise like a plunger being withdrawn from a blocked sink and Ron surfaced. Hermione acted as though she had not seen or heard anything.

"— we're going up to the party together."

"Cormac?" said Parvati. "Cormac McLaggen, you mean?"

"That's right," said Hermione sweetly. "The one who *almost*" — she put a great deal of emphasis on the word — "became Gryffindor Keeper."

"Are you going out with him, then?" asked Parvati, wide-eyed.

"Oh — yes — didn't you know?" said Hermione, with a most un-Hermione-ish giggle.

"No!" said Parvati, looking positively agog at this piece of gossip. "Wow, you like your Quidditch players, don't you? First Krum, then McLaggen . . ."

"I like *really good* Quidditch players," Hermione corrected her, still smiling. "Well, see you . . . Got to go and get ready for the party. . . ."

She left. At once Lavender and Parvati put their heads together to discuss this new development, with everything they had ever heard about McLaggen, and all they had ever guessed about Hermione. Ron looked strangely blank and said nothing. Harry was left to ponder in silence the depths to which girls would sink to get revenge.

When he arrived in the entrance hall at eight o'clock that night, he found an unusually large number of girls lurking there, all of whom seemed to be staring at him resentfully as he approached Luna. She was wearing a set of spangled silver robes that were attracting a certain amount of giggles from the onlookers, but otherwise she looked quite nice. Harry was glad, in any case, that she had left off her radish earrings, her butterbeer cork necklace, and her Spectrespecs.

"Hi," he said. "Shall we get going then?"

"Oh yes," she said happily. "Where is the party?"

"Slughorn's office," said Harry, leading her up the marble staircase away from all the staring and muttering. "Did you hear, there's supposed to be a vampire coming?"

"Rufus Scrimgeour?" asked Luna.

"I — what?" said Harry, disconcerted. "You mean the Minister of Magic?"

"Yes, he's a vampire," said Luna matter-of-factly. "Father wrote a very long article about it when Scrimgeour first took over from Cornelius Fudge, but he was forced not to publish by somebody from the Ministry. Obviously, they didn't want the truth to get out!"

Harry, who thought it most unlikely that Rufus Scrimgeour was a vampire, but who was used to Luna repeating her father's bizarre views as though they were fact, did not reply; they were already approaching Slughorn's office and the sounds of laughter, music, and loud conversation were growing louder with every step they took.

Whether it had been built that way, or because he had used magical trickery to make it so, Slughorn's office was much larger than the usual teacher's study. The ceiling and walls had been draped with emerald, crimson, and gold hangings, so that it looked as though they were all inside a vast tent. The room was crowded and stuffy and bathed in the red light cast by an ornate golden lamp dangling from the center of the ceiling in which real fairies were fluttering, each a brilliant speck of light. Loud singing accompanied by what sounded like mandolins issued from a distant corner; a haze of pipe smoke hung over several elderly warlocks deep in conversation, and a number of house-elves were negotiating their way squeakily through the forest of knees, obscured by the heavy silver platters of food they were bearing, so that they looked like little roving tables.

"Harry, m'boy!" boomed Slughorn, almost as soon as Harry and Luna had squeezed in through the door. "Come in, come in, so many people I'd like you to meet!"

Slughorn was wearing a tasseled velvet hat to match his smoking jacket. Gripping Harry's arm so tightly he might have been hoping to Disapparate with him, Slughorn led him purposefully into the party; Harry seized Luna's hand and dragged her along with him.

"Harry, I'd like you to meet Eldred Worple, an old student of mine, author of *Blood Brothers: My Life Amongst the Vampires* — and, of course, his friend Sanguini."

Worple, who was a small, stout, bespectacled man, grabbed

Harry's hand and shook it enthusiastically; the vampire Sanguini, who was tall and emaciated with dark shadows under his eyes, merely nodded. He looked rather bored. A gaggle of girls was standing close to him, looking curious and excited.

"Harry Potter, I am simply delighted!" said Worple, peering shortsightedly up into Harry's face. "I was saying to Professor Slughorn only the other day, *'Where is the biography of Harry Potter for which we have all been waiting?'*"

"Er," said Harry, "were you?"

"Just as modest as Horace described!" said Worple. "But seriously" — his manner changed; it became suddenly businesslike — "I would be delighted to write it myself — people are craving to know more about you, dear boy, craving! If you were prepared to grant me a few interviews, say in four- or five-hour sessions, why, we could have the book finished within months. And all with very little effort on your part, I assure you — ask Sanguini here if it isn't quite — *Sanguini, stay here!*" added Worple, suddenly stern, for the vampire had been edging toward the nearby group of girls, a rather hungry look in his eye. "Here, have a pasty," said Worple, seizing one from a passing elf and stuffing it into Sanguini's hand before turning his attention back to Harry.

"My dear boy, the gold you could make, you have no idea —"

"I'm definitely not interested," said Harry firmly, "and I've just seen a friend of mine, sorry."

He pulled Luna after him into the crowd; he had indeed just seen a long mane of brown hair disappear between what looked like two members of the Weird Sisters.

"Hermione! *Hermione!*"

"Harry! There you are, thank goodness! Hi, Luna!"

"What's happened to you?" asked Harry, for Hermione looked distinctly disheveled, rather as though she had just fought her way out of a thicket of Devil's Snare.

"Oh, I've just escaped — I mean, I've just left Cormac," she said. "Under the mistletoe," she added in explanation, as Harry continued to look questioningly at her.

"Serves you right for coming with him," he told her severely.

"I thought he'd annoy Ron most," said Hermione dispassionately. "I debated for a while about Zacharias Smith, but I thought, on the whole —"

"*You considered Smith?*" said Harry, revolted.

"Yes, I did, and I'm starting to wish I'd chosen him, McLaggen makes Grawp look a gentleman. Let's go this way, we'll be able to see him coming, he's so tall. . . ."

The three of them made their way over to the other side of the room, scooping up goblets of mead on the way, realizing too late that Professor Trelawney was standing there alone.

"Hello," said Luna politely to Professor Trelawney.

"Good evening, my dear," said Professor Trelawney, focusing upon Luna with some difficulty. Harry could smell cooking sherry again. "I haven't seen you in my classes lately. . . ."

"No, I've got Firenze this year," said Luna.

"Oh, of course," said Professor Trelawney with an angry, drunken titter. "Or Dobbin, as I prefer to think of him. You would have thought, would you not, that now I am returned to the school Professor Dumbledore might have got rid of the horse? But no . . . we share classes. . . . It's an insult, frankly, an insult. Do you know . . ."

Professor Trelawney seemed too tipsy to have recognized Harry.

Under cover of her furious criticisms of Firenze, Harry drew closer to Hermione and said, "Let's get something straight. Are you planning to tell Ron that you interfered at Keeper tryouts?"

Hermione raised her eyebrows. "Do you really think I'd stoop that low?"

Harry looked at her shrewdly. "Hermione, if you can ask out McLaggen —"

"There's a difference," said Hermione with dignity. "I've got no plans to tell Ron anything about what might, or might not, have happened at Keeper tryouts."

"Good," said Harry fervently. "Because he'll just fall apart again, and we'll lose the next match —"

"Quidditch!" said Hermione angrily. "Is that all boys care about? Cormac hasn't asked me one single question about myself, no, I've just been treated to 'A Hundred Great Saves Made by Cormac McLaggen' nonstop ever since — oh no, here he comes!"

She moved so fast it was as though she had Disapparated; one moment she was there, the next, she had squeezed between two guffawing witches and vanished.

"Seen Hermione?" asked McLaggen, forcing his way through the throng a minute later.

"No, sorry," said Harry, and he turned quickly to join in Luna's conversation, forgetting for a split second to whom she was talking.

"Harry Potter!" said Professor Trelawney in deep, vibrant tones, noticing him for the first time.

"Oh, hello," said Harry unenthusiastically.

"My dear boy!" she said in a very carrying whisper. "The rumors! The stories! 'The Chosen One'! Of course, I have known for a very long time. . . . The omens were never good, Harry. . . . But why have you not returned to Divination? For you, of all people, the subject is of the utmost importance!"

"Ah, Sybill, we all think our subject's most important!" said a loud voice, and Slughorn appeared at Professor Trelawney's other side, his face very red, his velvet hat a little askew, a glass of mead in one hand and an enormous mince pie in the other. "But I don't think I've ever known such a natural at Potions!" said Slughorn, regarding Harry with a fond, if bloodshot, eye. "Instinctive, you know — like his mother! I've only ever taught a few with this kind of ability, I can tell you that, Sybill — why even Severus —"

And to Harry's horror, Slughorn threw out an arm and seemed to scoop Snape out of thin air toward them.

"Stop skulking and come and join us, Severus!" hiccuped Slughorn happily. "I was just talking about Harry's exceptional potion-making! Some credit must go to you, of course, you taught him for five years!"

Trapped, with Slughorn's arm around his shoulders, Snape looked down his hooked nose at Harry, his black eyes narrowed.

"Funny, I never had the impression that I managed to teach Potter anything at all."

"Well, then, it's natural ability!" shouted Slughorn. "You should have seen what he gave me, first lesson, Draught of Living Death — never had a student produce finer on a first attempt, I don't think even you, Severus —"

"Really?" said Snape quietly, his eyes still boring into Harry, who felt a certain disquiet. The last thing he wanted was for Snape to start investigating the source of his newfound brilliance at Potions.

"Remind me what other subjects you're taking, Harry?" asked Slughorn.

"Defense Against the Dark Arts, Charms, Transfiguration, Herbology . . ."

"All the subjects required, in short, for an Auror," said Snape, with the faintest sneer.

"Yeah, well, that's what I'd like to do," said Harry defiantly.

"And a great one you'll make too!" boomed Slughorn.

"I don't think you should be an Auror, Harry," said Luna unexpectedly. Everybody looked at her. "The Aurors are part of the Rotfang Conspiracy, I thought everyone knew that. They're working to bring down the Ministry of Magic from within using a combination of Dark Magic and gum disease."

Harry inhaled half his mead up his nose as he started to laugh. Really, it had been worth bringing Luna just for this. Emerging from his goblet, coughing, sopping wet but still grinning, he saw something calculated to raise his spirits even higher: Draco Malfoy being dragged by the ear toward them by Argus Filch.

"Professor Slughorn," wheezed Filch, his jowls aquiver and the maniacal light of mischief-detection in his bulging eyes, "I discovered this boy lurking in an upstairs corridor. He claims to have been invited to your party and to have been delayed in setting out. Did you issue him with an invitation?"

Malfoy pulled himself free of Filch's grip, looking furious.

"All right, I wasn't invited!" he said angrily. "I was trying to gate-crash, happy?"

"No, I'm not!" said Filch, a statement at complete odds with the glee on his face. "You're in trouble, you are! Didn't the headmaster say that nighttime prowling's out, unless you've got permission, didn't he, eh?"

"That's all right, Argus, that's all right," said Slughorn, waving a hand. "It's Christmas, and it's not a crime to want to come to a party. Just this once, we'll forget any punishment; you may stay, Draco."

Filch's expression of outraged disappointment was perfectly predictable; but why, Harry wondered, watching him, did Malfoy look almost equally unhappy? And why was Snape looking at Malfoy as though both angry and . . . was it possible? . . . a little afraid?

But almost before Harry had registered what he had seen, Filch had turned and shuffled away, muttering under his breath; Malfoy had composed his face into a smile and was thanking Slughorn for his generosity, and Snape's face was smoothly inscrutable again.

"It's nothing, nothing," said Slughorn, waving away Malfoy's thanks. "I did know your grandfather, after all. . . ."

"He always spoke very highly of you, sir," said Malfoy quickly. "Said you were the best potion-maker he'd ever known. . . ."

Harry stared at Malfoy. It was not the sucking-up that intrigued him; he had watched Malfoy do that to Snape for a long time. It was the fact that Malfoy did, after all, look a little ill. This was the first time he had seen Malfoy close up for ages; he now saw that Malfoy had dark shadows under his eyes and a distinctly grayish tinge to his skin.

"I'd like a word with you, Draco," said Snape suddenly.

"Oh, now, Severus," said Slughorn, hiccuping again, "it's Christmas, don't be too hard —"

"I'm his Head of House, and I shall decide how hard, or otherwise, to be," said Snape curtly. "Follow me, Draco."

They left, Snape leading the way, Malfoy looking resentful. Harry stood there for a moment, irresolute, then said, "I'll be back in a bit, Luna — er — bathroom."

"All right," she said cheerfully, and he thought he heard her, as he hurried off into the crowd, resume the subject of the Rotfang Conspiracy with Professor Trelawney, who seemed sincerely interested.

It was easy, once out of the party, to pull his Invisibility Cloak out of his pocket and throw it over himself, for the corridor was quite deserted. What was more difficult was finding Snape and Malfoy. Harry ran down the corridor, the noise of his feet masked by the music and loud talk still issuing from Slughorn's office behind him. Perhaps Snape had taken Malfoy to his office in the dungeons . . . or perhaps he was escorting him back to the Slytherin common room. . . . Harry pressed his ear against door after door as he dashed down the corridor until, with a great jolt of excitement, he crouched down to the keyhole of the last classroom in the corridor and heard voices.

". . . cannot afford mistakes, Draco, because if you are expelled —"

"I didn't have anything to do with it, all right?"

"I hope you are telling the truth, because it was both clumsy and foolish. Already you are suspected of having a hand in it."

"Who suspects me?" said Malfoy angrily. "For the last time, I didn't do it, okay? That Bell girl must've had an enemy no one knows about — don't look at me like that! I know what you're doing, I'm not stupid, but it won't work — I can stop you!"

There was a pause and then Snape said quietly, "Ah . . . Aunt Bellatrix has been teaching you Occlumency, I see. What thoughts are you trying to conceal from your master, Draco?"

"I'm not trying to conceal anything from *him,* I just don't want *you* butting in!"

Harry pressed his ear still more closely against the keyhole. . . . What had happened to make Malfoy speak to Snape like this — Snape, toward whom he had always shown respect, even liking?

"So that is why you have been avoiding me this term? You have feared my interference? You realize that, had anybody else failed to come to my office when I had told them repeatedly to be there, Draco —"

"So put me in detention! Report me to Dumbledore!" jeered Malfoy.

There was another pause. Then Snape said, "You know perfectly well that I do not wish to do either of those things."

"You'd better stop telling me to come to your office then!"

"Listen to me," said Snape, his voice so low now that Harry had to push his ear very hard against the keyhole to hear. "I am trying to help you. I swore to your mother I would protect you. I made the Unbreakable Vow, Draco —"

"Looks like you'll have to break it, then, because I don't need your protection! It's my job, he gave it to me and I'm doing it, I've got a plan and it's going to work, it's just taking a bit longer than I thought it would!"

"What is your plan?"

"It's none of your business!"

"If you tell me what you are trying to do, I can assist you —"

"I've got all the assistance I need, thanks, I'm not alone!"

"You were certainly alone tonight, which was foolish in the extreme, wandering the corridors without lookouts or backup, these are elementary mistakes —"

"I would've had Crabbe and Goyle with me if you hadn't put them in detention!"

"Keep your voice down!" spat Snape, for Malfoy's voice had risen excitedly. "If your friends Crabbe and Goyle intend to pass their Defense Against the Dark Arts O.W.L. this time around, they will need to work a little harder than they are doing at pres —"

"What does it matter?" said Malfoy. "Defense Against the Dark Arts — it's all just a joke, isn't it, an act? Like any of us need protecting against the Dark Arts —"

"It is an act that is crucial to success, Draco!" said Snape. "Where do you think I would have been all these years, if I had not known how to act? Now listen to me! You are being incautious, wandering around at night, getting yourself caught, and if you are placing your reliance in assistants like Crabbe and Goyle —"

"They're not the only ones, I've got other people on my side, better people!"

"Then why not confide in me, and I can —"

"I know what you're up to! You want to steal my glory!"

There was another pause, then Snape said coldly, "You are speaking like a child. I quite understand that your father's capture and imprisonment has upset you, but —"

Harry had barely a second's warning; he heard Malfoy's footsteps on the other side of the door and flung himself out of the way just as it burst open; Malfoy was striding away down the corridor, past the open door of Slughorn's office, around the distant corner, and out of sight.

Hardly daring to breathe, Harry remained crouched down as Snape emerged slowly from the classroom. His expression unfathomable, he returned to the party. Harry remained on the floor, hidden beneath the cloak, his mind racing.

A VERY FROSTY
CHRISTMAS

"So Snape was offering to help him? He was definitely *offering to help him?*"

"If you ask that once more," said Harry, "I'm going to stick this sprout —"

"I'm only checking!" said Ron. They were standing alone at the Burrow's kitchen sink, peeling a mountain of sprouts for Mrs. Weasley. Snow was drifting past the window in front of them.

"Yes, Snape was offering to help him!" said Harry. "He said he'd promised Malfoy's mother to protect him, that he'd made an Unbreakable Oath or something —"

"An Unbreakable Vow?" said Ron, looking stunned. "Nah, he can't have. . . . Are you sure?"

"Yes, I'm sure," said Harry. "Why, what does it mean?"

"Well, you can't break an Unbreakable Vow. . . ."

"I'd worked that much out for myself, funnily enough. What happens if you break it, then?"

"You die," said Ron simply. "Fred and George tried to get me to make one when I was about five. I nearly did too, I was holding hands with Fred and everything when Dad found us. He went mental," said Ron, with a reminiscent gleam in his eyes. "Only time I've ever seen Dad as angry as Mum. Fred reckons his left buttock has never been the same since."

"Yeah, well, passing over Fred's left buttock —"

"I beg your pardon?" said Fred's voice as the twins entered the kitchen.

"Aaah, George, look at this. They're using knives and everything. Bless them."

"I'll be seventeen in two and a bit months' time," said Ron grumpily, "and then I'll be able to do it by magic!"

"But meanwhile," said George, sitting down at the kitchen table and putting his feet up on it, "we can enjoy watching you demonstrate the correct use of a — whoops-a-daisy!"

"You made me do that!" said Ron angrily, sucking his cut thumb. "You wait, when I'm seventeen —"

"I'm sure you'll dazzle us all with hitherto unsuspected magical skills," yawned Fred.

"And speaking of hitherto unsuspected skills, Ronald," said George, "what is this we hear from Ginny about you and a young lady called — unless our information is faulty — Lavender Brown?"

Ron turned a little pink, but did not look displeased as he turned back to the sprouts. "Mind your own business."

"What a snappy retort," said Fred. "I really don't know how you think of them. No, what we wanted to know was . . . how did it happen?"

"What d'you mean?"

"Did she have an accident or something?"

"What?"

"Well, how did she sustain such extensive brain damage? Careful, now!"

Mrs. Weasley entered the room just in time to see Ron throw the sprout knife at Fred, who had turned it into a paper airplane with one lazy flick of his wand.

"Ron!" she said furiously. "Don't you ever let me see you throwing knives again!"

"I won't," said Ron, "let you see," he added under his breath, as he turned back to the sprout mountain.

"Fred, George, I'm sorry, dears, but Remus is arriving tonight, so Bill will have to squeeze in with you two."

"No problem," said George.

"Then, as Charlie isn't coming home, that just leaves Harry and Ron in the attic, and if Fleur shares with Ginny —"

"— that'll make Ginny's Christmas —" muttered Fred.

"— everyone should be comfortable. Well, they'll have a bed, anyway," said Mrs. Weasley, sounding slightly harassed.

"Percy definitely not showing his ugly face, then?" asked Fred.

Mrs. Weasley turned away before she answered. "No, he's busy, I expect, at the Ministry."

"Or he's the world's biggest prat," said Fred, as Mrs. Weasley left the kitchen. "One of the two. Well, let's get going, then, George."

"What are you two up to?" asked Ron. "Can't you help us with these sprouts? You could just use your wand and then we'll be free too!"

"No, I don't think we can do that," said Fred seriously. "It's very character-building stuff, learning to peel sprouts without magic, makes you appreciate how difficult it is for Muggles and Squibs —"

"— and if you want people to help you, Ron," added George, throwing the paper airplane at him, "I wouldn't chuck knives at them. Just a little hint. We're off to the village, there's a very pretty girl working in the paper shop who thinks my card tricks are something marvelous . . . almost like real magic. . . ."

"Gits," said Ron darkly, watching Fred and George setting off across the snowy yard. "Would've only taken them ten seconds and then we could've gone too."

"I couldn't," said Harry. "I promised Dumbledore I wouldn't wander off while I'm staying here."

"Oh yeah," said Ron. He peeled a few more sprouts and then said, "Are you going to tell Dumbledore what you heard Snape and Malfoy saying to each other?"

"Yep," said Harry. "I'm going to tell anyone who can put a stop to it, and Dumbledore's top of the list. I might have another word with your dad too."

"Pity you didn't hear what Malfoy's actually doing, though."

"I couldn't have done, could I? That was the whole point, he was refusing to tell Snape."

There was silence for a moment or two, then Ron said, "'Course, you know what they'll all say? Dad and Dumbledore and all of them? They'll say Snape isn't really trying to help Malfoy, he was just trying to find out what Malfoy's up to."

"They didn't hear him," said Harry flatly. "No one's that good an actor, not even Snape."

"Yeah . . . I'm just saying, though," said Ron.

Harry turned to face him, frowning. "You think I'm right, though?"

"Yeah, I do!" said Ron hastily. "Seriously, I do! But they're all convinced Snape's in the Order, aren't they?"

Harry said nothing. It had already occurred to him that this would be the most likely objection to his new evidence; he could hear Hermione now: *Obviously, Harry, he was pretending to offer help so he could trick Malfoy into telling him what he's doing. . . .*

This was pure imagination, however, as he had had no opportunity to tell Hermione what he had overheard. She had disappeared from Slughorn's party before he returned to it, or so he had been informed by an irate McLaggen, and she had already gone to bed by the time he returned to the common room. As he and Ron had left for the Burrow early the next day, he had barely had time to wish her a happy Christmas and to tell her that he had some very important news when they got back from the holidays. He was not entirely sure that she had heard him, though; Ron and Lavender had been saying a thoroughly nonverbal good-bye just behind him at the time.

Still, even Hermione would not be able to deny one thing: Malfoy was definitely up to something, and Snape knew it, so Harry felt fully justified in saying "I told you so," which he had done several times to Ron already.

Harry did not get the chance to speak to Mr. Weasley, who was working very long hours at the Ministry, until Christmas Eve night. The Weasleys and their guests were sitting in the living room, which Ginny had decorated so lavishly that it was rather like sitting in a paper-chain explosion. Fred, George, Harry, and Ron were the only ones who knew that the angel on top of the tree was actually a garden gnome that had bitten Fred on the ankle as he pulled up carrots for Christmas dinner. Stupefied, painted gold, stuffed into a miniature tutu and with small wings glued to its back, it glowered down at them all, the ugliest angel Harry had ever seen, with a large bald head like a potato and rather hairy feet.

They were all supposed to be listening to a Christmas broadcast by Mrs. Weasley's favorite singer, Celestina Warbeck, whose voice was warbling out of the large wooden wireless set. Fleur, who seemed to find Celestina very dull, was talking so loudly in the corner that a scowling Mrs. Weasley kept pointing her wand at the volume control, so that Celestina grew louder and louder. Under cover of a particularly jazzy number called "A Cauldron Full of Hot, Strong Love," Fred and George started a game of Exploding Snap with Ginny. Ron kept shooting Bill and Fleur covert looks, as though hoping to pick up tips. Meanwhile, Remus Lupin, who was thinner and more ragged-looking than ever, was sitting beside the fire, staring into its depths as though he could not hear Celestina's voice.

> *Oh, come and stir my cauldron,*
> *And if you do it right,*
> *I'll boil you up some hot strong love*
> *To keep you warm tonight.*

"We danced to this when we were eighteen!" said Mrs. Weasley, wiping her eyes on her knitting. "Do you remember, Arthur?"

"Mphf?" said Mr. Weasley, whose head had been nodding over the satsuma he was peeling. "Oh yes . . . marvelous tune . . ."

With an effort, he sat up a little straighter and looked around at Harry, who was sitting next to him.

"Sorry about this," he said, jerking his head toward the wireless as Celestina broke into the chorus. "Be over soon."

"No problem," said Harry, grinning. "Has it been busy at the Ministry?"

"Very," said Mr. Weasley. "I wouldn't mind if we were getting anywhere, but of the three arrests we've made in the last couple of months, I doubt that one of them is a genuine Death Eater — only don't repeat that, Harry," he added quickly, looking much more awake all of a sudden.

"They're not still holding Stan Shunpike, are they?" asked Harry.

"I'm afraid so," said Mr. Weasley. "I know Dumbledore's tried appealing directly to Scrimgeour about Stan. . . . I mean, anybody who has actually interviewed him agrees that he's about as much a Death Eater as this satsuma . . . but the top levels want to look as though they're making some progress, and 'three arrests' sounds better than 'three mistaken arrests and releases'. . . but again, this is all top secret. . . ."

"I won't say anything," said Harry. He hesitated for a moment, wondering how best to embark on what he wanted to say; as he marshaled his thoughts, Celestina Warbeck began a ballad called "You Charmed the Heart Right Out of Me."

"Mr. Weasley, you know what I told you at the station when we were setting off for school?"

"I checked, Harry," said Mr. Weasley at once. "I went and searched the Malfoys' house. There was nothing, either broken or whole, that shouldn't have been there."

"Yeah, I know, I saw in the *Prophet* that you'd looked . . . but this is something different. . . . Well, something more . . ."

And he told Mr. Weasley everything he had overheard between

Malfoy and Snape. As Harry spoke, he saw Lupin's head turn a little toward him, taking in every word. When he had finished, there was silence, except for Celestina's crooning.

> *Oh, my poor heart, where has it gone?*
> *It's left me for a spell . . .*

"Has it occurred to you, Harry," said Mr. Weasley, "that Snape was simply pretending — ?"

"Pretending to offer help, so that he could find out what Malfoy's up to?" said Harry quickly. "Yeah, I thought you'd say that. But how do we know?"

"It isn't our business to know," said Lupin unexpectedly. He had turned his back on the fire now and faced Harry across Mr. Weasley. "It's Dumbledore's business. Dumbledore trusts Severus, and that ought to be good enough for all of us."

"But," said Harry, "just say — just say Dumbledore's wrong about Snape —"

"People have said it, many times. It comes down to whether or not you trust Dumbledore's judgment. I do; therefore, I trust Severus."

"But Dumbledore can make mistakes," argued Harry. "He says it himself. And you" — he looked Lupin straight in the eye — "do you honestly like Snape?"

"I neither like nor dislike Severus," said Lupin. "No, Harry, I am speaking the truth," he added, as Harry pulled a skeptical expression. "We shall never be bosom friends, perhaps; after all that happened between James and Sirius and Severus, there is too much bitterness there. But I do not forget that during the year I taught at

Hogwarts, Severus made the Wolfsbane Potion for me every month, made it perfectly, so that I did not have to suffer as I usually do at the full moon."

"But he 'accidentally' let it slip that you're a werewolf, so you had to leave!" said Harry angrily.

Lupin shrugged. "The news would have leaked out anyway. We both know he wanted my job, but he could have wreaked much worse damage on me by tampering with the potion. He kept me healthy. I must be grateful."

"Maybe he didn't dare mess with the potion with Dumbledore watching him!" said Harry.

"You are determined to hate him, Harry," said Lupin with a faint smile. "And I understand; with James as your father, with Sirius as your godfather, you have inherited an old prejudice. By all means tell Dumbledore what you have told Arthur and me, but do not expect him to share your view of the matter; do not even expect him to be surprised by what you tell him. It might have been on Dumbledore's orders that Severus questioned Draco."

. . . and now you've torn it quite apart
I'll thank you to give back my heart!

Celestina ended her song on a very long, high-pitched note and loud applause issued out of the wireless, which Mrs. Weasley joined in with enthusiastically.

"Eez eet over?" said Fleur loudly. "Thank goodness, what an 'orrible —"

"Shall we have a nightcap, then?" asked Mr. Weasley loudly, leaping to his feet. "Who wants eggnog?"

"What have you been up to lately?" Harry asked Lupin, as Mr. Weasley bustled off to fetch the eggnog, and everybody else stretched and broke into conversation.

"Oh, I've been underground," said Lupin. "Almost literally. That's why I haven't been able to write, Harry; sending letters to you would have been something of a giveaway."

"What do you mean?"

"I've been living among my fellows, my equals," said Lupin. "Werewolves," he added, at Harry's look of incomprehension. "Nearly all of them are on Voldemort's side. Dumbledore wanted a spy and here I was . . . ready-made."

He sounded a little bitter, and perhaps realized it, for he smiled more warmly as he went on, "I am not complaining; it is necessary work and who can do it better than I? However, it has been difficult gaining their trust. I bear the unmistakable signs of having tried to live among wizards, you see, whereas they have shunned normal society and live on the margins, stealing — and sometimes killing — to eat."

"How come they like Voldemort?"

"They think that, under his rule, they will have a better life," said Lupin. "And it is hard to argue with Greyback out there. . . ."

"Who's Greyback?"

"You haven't heard of him?" Lupin's hands closed convulsively in his lap. "Fenrir Greyback is, perhaps, the most savage werewolf alive today. He regards it as his mission in life to bite and to contaminate as many people as possible; he wants to create enough werewolves to overcome the wizards. Voldemort has promised him prey in return for his services. Greyback specializes in children. . . . Bite them young, he says, and raise them away from their parents, raise them to hate normal wizards. Voldemort has threatened to unleash him upon people's sons and daughters; it is a threat that usually produces good results."

Lupin paused and then said, "It was Greyback who bit me."

"What?" said Harry, astonished. "When — when you were a kid, you mean?"

"Yes. My father had offended him. I did not know, for a very long time, the identity of the werewolf who had attacked me; I even felt pity for him, thinking that he had had no control, knowing by then how it felt to transform. But Greyback is not like that. At the full moon, he positions himself close to victims, ensuring that he is near enough to strike. He plans it all. And this is the man Voldemort is using to marshal the werewolves. I cannot pretend that my particular brand of reasoned argument is making much headway against Greyback's insistence that we werewolves deserve blood, that we ought to revenge ourselves on normal people."

"But you are normal!" said Harry fiercely. "You've just got a — a problem —"

Lupin burst out laughing. "Sometimes you remind me a lot of James. He called it my 'furry little problem' in company. Many people were under the impression that I owned a badly behaved rabbit."

He accepted a glass of eggnog from Mr. Weasley with a word of thanks, looking slightly more cheerful. Harry, meanwhile, felt a rush of excitement: This last mention of his father had reminded him that there was something he had been looking forward to asking Lupin.

"Have you ever heard of someone called the Half-Blood Prince?"

"The Half-Blood what?"

"Prince," said Harry, watching him closely for signs of recognition.

"There are no Wizarding princes," said Lupin, now smiling. "Is this a title you're thinking of adopting? I should have thought being 'the Chosen One' would be enough."

"It's nothing to do with me!" said Harry indignantly. "The Half-Blood Prince is someone who used to go to Hogwarts, I've got his old Potions book. He wrote spells all over it, spells he invented. One of them was Levicorpus —"

"Oh, that one had a great vogue during my time at Hogwarts," said Lupin reminiscently. "There were a few months in my fifth year when you couldn't move for being hoisted into the air by your ankle."

"My dad used it," said Harry. "I saw him in the Pensieve, he used it on Snape."

He tried to sound casual, as though this was a throwaway comment of no real importance, but he was not sure he had achieved the right effect; Lupin's smile was a little too understanding.

"Yes," he said, "but he wasn't the only one. As I say, it was very popular. . . . You know how these spells come and go. . . ."

"But it sounds like it was invented while you were at school," Harry persisted.

"Not necessarily," said Lupin. "Jinxes go in and out of fashion like everything else."

He looked into Harry's face and then said quietly, "James was a pureblood, Harry, and I promise you, he never asked us to call him 'Prince.'"

Abandoning pretense, Harry said, "And it wasn't Sirius? Or you?"

"Definitely not."

"Oh." Harry stared into the fire. "I just thought — well, he's helped me out a lot in Potions classes, the Prince has."

"How old is this book, Harry?"

"I dunno, I've never checked."

"Well, perhaps that will give you some clue as to when the Prince was at Hogwarts," said Lupin.

Shortly after this, Fleur decided to imitate Celestina singing "A Cauldron Full of Hot, Strong Love," which was taken by everyone, once they had glimpsed Mrs. Weasley's expression, to be the cue to go to bed. Harry and Ron climbed all the way up to Ron's attic bedroom, where a camp bed had been added for Harry.

Ron fell asleep almost immediately, but Harry delved into his trunk and pulled out his copy of *Advanced Potion-Making* before getting into bed. There he turned its pages, searching, until he finally found, at the front of the book, the date that it had been published. It was nearly fifty years old. Neither his father, nor his father's friends, had been at Hogwarts fifty years ago. Feeling disappointed, Harry threw the book back into his trunk, turned off the lamp, and rolled over, thinking of werewolves and Snape, Stan Shunpike and the Half-Blood Prince, and finally falling into an uneasy sleep full of creeping shadows and the cries of bitten children. . . .

"She's got to be joking. . . ."

Harry woke with a start to find a bulging stocking lying over the end of his bed. He put on his glasses and looked around; the tiny window was almost completely obscured with snow and, in front of it, Ron was sitting bolt upright in bed and examining what appeared to be a thick gold chain.

"What's that?" asked Harry.

"It's from Lavender," said Ron, sounding revolted. "She can't honestly think I'd wear . . ."

Harry looked more closely and let out a shout of laughter. Dangling from the chain in large gold letters were the words:

My Sweetheart

"Nice," he said. "Classy. You should definitely wear it in front of Fred and George."

"If you tell them," said Ron, shoving the necklace out of sight under his pillow, "I — I — I'll —"

"Stutter at me?" said Harry, grinning. "Come on, would I?"

"How could she think I'd like something like that, though?" Ron demanded of thin air, looking rather shocked.

"Well, think back," said Harry. "Have you ever let it slip that you'd like to go out in public with the words 'My Sweetheart' round your neck?"

"Well . . . we don't really talk much," said Ron. "It's mainly . . ."

"Snogging," said Harry.

"Well, yeah," said Ron. He hesitated a moment, then said, "Is Hermione really going out with McLaggen?"

"I dunno," said Harry. "They were at Slughorn's party together, but I don't think it went that well."

Ron looked slightly more cheerful as he delved deeper into his stocking.

Harry's presents included a sweater with a large Golden Snitch worked onto the front, hand-knitted by Mrs. Weasley, a large box of Weasleys' Wizard Wheezes products from the twins, and a

slightly damp, moldy-smelling package that came with a label reading To Master, From Kreacher.

Harry stared at it. "D'you reckon this is safe to open?" he asked.

"Can't be anything dangerous, all our mail's still being searched
at the Ministry," replied Ron, though he was eyeing the parcel
suspiciously.

"I didn't think of giving Kreacher anything. Do people usually
give their house-elves Christmas presents?" asked Harry, prodding
the parcel cautiously.

"Hermione would," said Ron. "But let's wait and see what it is
before you start feeling guilty."

A moment later, Harry had given a loud yell and leapt out of his
camp bed; the package contained a large number of maggots.

"Nice," said Ron, roaring with laughter. "Very thoughtful."

"I'd rather have them than that necklace," said Harry, which
sobered Ron up at once.

Everybody was wearing new sweaters when they all sat down for
Christmas lunch, everyone except Fleur (on whom, it appeared,
Mrs. Weasley had not wanted to waste one) and Mrs. Weasley
herself, who was sporting a brand-new midnight blue witch's hat
glittering with what looked like tiny starlike diamonds, and a spectacular golden necklace.

"Fred and George gave them to me! Aren't they beautiful?"

"Well, we find we appreciate you more and more, Mum, now
we're washing our own socks," said George, waving an airy hand.
"Parsnips, Remus?"

"Harry, you've got a maggot in your hair," said Ginny cheerfully,
leaning across the table to pick it out; Harry felt goose bumps erupt
up his neck that had nothing to do with the maggot.

"'Ow 'orrible," said Fleur, with an affected little shudder.

"Yes, isn't it?" said Ron. "Gravy, Fleur?"

In his eagerness to help her, he knocked the gravy boat flying; Bill waved his wand and the gravy soared up in the air and returned meekly to the boat.

"You are as bad as zat Tonks," said Fleur to Ron, when she had finished kissing Bill in thanks. "She is always knocking —"

"I invited *dear* Tonks to come along today," said Mrs. Weasley, setting down the carrots with unnecessary force and glaring at Fleur. "But she wouldn't come. Have you spoken to her lately, Remus?"

"No, I haven't been in contact with anybody very much," said Lupin. "But Tonks has got her own family to go to, hasn't she?"

"Hmmm," said Mrs. Weasley. "Maybe. I got the impression she was planning to spend Christmas alone, actually."

She gave Lupin an annoyed look, as though it was all his fault she was getting Fleur for a daughter-in-law instead of Tonks, but Harry, glancing across at Fleur, who was now feeding Bill bits of turkey off her own fork, thought that Mrs. Weasley was fighting a long-lost battle. He was, however, reminded of a question he had with regard to Tonks, and who better to ask than Lupin, the man who knew all about Patronuses?

"Tonks's Patronus has changed its form," he told him. "Snape said so anyway. I didn't know that could happen. Why would your Patronus change?"

Lupin took his time chewing his turkey and swallowing before saying slowly, "Sometimes . . . a great shock . . . an emotional upheaval . . ."

"It looked big, and it had four legs," said Harry, struck by a sudden thought and lowering his voice. "Hey . . . it couldn't be — ?"

"Arthur!" said Mrs. Weasley suddenly. She had risen from her chair; her hand was pressed over her heart and she was staring out of the kitchen window. "Arthur — it's Percy!"

"What?"

Mr. Weasley looked around. Everybody looked quickly at the window; Ginny stood up for a better look. There, sure enough, was Percy Weasley, striding across the snowy yard, his horn-rimmed glasses glinting in the sunlight. He was not, however, alone.

"Arthur, he's — he's with the Minister!"

And sure enough, the man Harry had seen in the *Daily Prophet* was following along in Percy's wake, limping slightly, his mane of graying hair and his black cloak flecked with snow. Before any of them could say anything, before Mr. and Mrs. Weasley could do more than exchange stunned looks, the back door opened and there stood Percy.

There was a moment's painful silence. Then Percy said rather stiffly, "Merry Christmas, Mother."

"Oh, *Percy*!" said Mrs. Weasley, and she threw herself into his arms.

Rufus Scrimgeour paused in the doorway, leaning on his walking stick and smiling as he observed this affecting scene.

"You must forgive this intrusion," he said, when Mrs. Weasley looked around at him, beaming and wiping her eyes. "Percy and I were in the vicinity — working, you know — and he couldn't resist dropping in and seeing you all."

But Percy showed no sign of wanting to greet any of the rest of the family. He stood, poker-straight and awkward-looking, and stared over everybody else's heads. Mr. Weasley, Fred, and George were all observing him, stony-faced.

"Please, come in, sit down, Minister!" fluttered Mrs. Weasley, straightening her hat. "Have a little purkey, or some tooding. . . . I mean —"

"No, no, my dear Molly," said Scrimgeour. Harry guessed that he had checked her name with Percy before they entered the house. "I don't want to intrude, wouldn't be here at all if Percy hadn't wanted to see you all so badly. . . ."

"Oh, Perce!" said Mrs. Weasley tearfully, reaching up to kiss him.

". . . We've only looked in for five minutes, so I'll have a stroll around the yard while you catch up with Percy. No, no, I assure you I don't want to butt in! Well, if anybody cared to show me your charming garden . . . Ah, that young man's finished, why doesn't he take a stroll with me?"

The atmosphere around the table changed perceptibly. Everybody looked from Scrimgeour to Harry. Nobody seemed to find Scrimgeour's pretense that he did not know Harry's name convincing, or find it natural that he should be chosen to accompany the Minister around the garden when Ginny, Fleur, and George also had clean plates.

"Yeah, all right," said Harry into the silence.

He was not fooled; for all Scrimgeour's talk that they had just been in the area, that Percy wanted to look up his family, this must be the real reason that they had come, so that Scrimgeour could speak to Harry alone.

"It's fine," he said quietly, as he passed Lupin, who had half risen from his chair. "Fine," he added, as Mr. Weasley opened his mouth to speak.

"Wonderful!" said Scrimgeour, standing back to let Harry pass through the door ahead of him. "We'll just take a turn around the garden, and Percy and I'll be off. Carry on, everyone!"

Harry walked across the yard toward the Weasleys' overgrown, snow-covered garden, Scrimgeour limping slightly at his side. He had, Harry knew, been Head of the Auror office; he looked tough and battle-scarred, very different from portly Fudge in his bowler hat.

"Charming," said Scrimgeour, stopping at the garden fence and looking out over the snowy lawn and the indistinguishable plants. "Charming."

Harry said nothing. He could tell that Scrimgeour was watching him.

"I've wanted to meet you for a very long time," said Scrimgeour, after a few moments. "Did you know that?"

"No," said Harry truthfully.

"Oh yes, for a very long time. But Dumbledore has been very protective of you," said Scrimgeour. "Natural, of course, natural, after what you've been through. . . . Especially what happened at the Ministry . . ."

He waited for Harry to say something, but Harry did not oblige, so he went on, "I have been hoping for an occasion to talk to you ever since I gained office, but Dumbledore has — most understandably, as I say — prevented this."

Still, Harry said nothing, waiting.

"The rumors that have flown around!" said Scrimgeour. "Well, of course, we both know how these stories get distorted . . . all these whispers of a prophecy . . . of you being 'the Chosen One' . . ."

They were getting near it now, Harry thought, the reason Scrimgeour was here.

". . . I assume that Dumbledore has discussed these matters with you?"

Harry deliberated, wondering whether he ought to lie or not. He looked at the little gnome prints all around the flowerbeds, and the scuffed-up patch that marked the spot where Fred had caught the gnome now wearing the tutu at the top of the Christmas tree. Finally, he decided on the truth . . . or a bit of it.

"Yeah, we've discussed it."

"Have you, have you . . ." said Scrimgeour. Harry could see, out of the corner of his eye, Scrimgeour squinting at him, so he pretended to be very interested in a gnome that had just poked its head out from underneath a frozen rhododendron. "And what has Dumbledore told you, Harry?"

"Sorry, but that's between us," said Harry. He kept his voice as pleasant as he could, and Scrimgeour's tone, too, was light and friendly as he said, "Oh, of course, if it's a question of confidences, I wouldn't want you to divulge . . . no, no . . . and in any case, does it really matter whether you are 'the Chosen One' or not?"

Harry had to mull that one over for a few seconds before responding. "I don't really know what you mean, Minister."

"Well, of course, to *you* it will matter enormously," said Scrimgeour with a laugh. "But to the Wizarding community at large . . . it's all perception, isn't it? It's what people believe that's important."

Harry said nothing. He thought he saw, dimly, where they were heading, but he was not going to help Scrimgeour get there. The gnome under the rhododendron was now digging for worms at its roots, and Harry kept his eyes fixed upon it.

"People believe you *are* 'the Chosen One,' you see," said Scrimgeour. "They think you quite the hero — which, of course, you are, Harry, chosen or not! How many times have you faced He-Who-Must-Not-Be-Named now? Well, anyway," he pressed on, without waiting for a reply, "the point is, you are a symbol of hope for many, Harry. The idea that there is somebody out there who might be able, who might even be *destined,* to destroy He-Who-Must-Not-Be-Named — well, naturally, it gives people a lift. And I can't help but feel that, once you realize this, you might consider it, well, almost a duty, to stand alongside the Ministry, and give everyone a boost."

The gnome had just managed to get hold of a worm. It was now tugging very hard on it, trying to get it out of the frozen ground. Harry was silent so long that Scrimgeour said, looking from Harry to the gnome, "Funny little chaps, aren't they? But what say you, Harry?"

"I don't exactly understand what you want," said Harry slowly. "'Stand alongside the Ministry' . . . What does that mean?"

"Oh, well, nothing at all onerous, I assure you," said Scrimgeour. "If you were to be seen popping in and out of the Ministry from time to time, for instance, that would give the right impression. And of course, while you were there, you would have ample opportunity to speak to Gawain Robards, my successor as Head of the Auror office. Dolores Umbridge has told me that you cherish an ambition to become an Auror. Well, that could be arranged very easily. . . ."

Harry felt anger bubbling in the pit of his stomach: So Dolores Umbridge was still at the Ministry, was she?

"So basically," he said, as though he just wanted to clarify a few points, "you'd like to give the impression that I'm working for the Ministry?"

"It would give everyone a lift to think you were more involved, Harry," said Scrimgeour, sounding relieved that Harry had cottoned on so quickly. "'The Chosen One,' you know . . . It's all about giving people hope, the feeling that exciting things are happening. . . ."

"But if I keep running in and out of the Ministry," said Harry, still endeavoring to keep his voice friendly, "won't that seem as though I approve of what the Ministry's up to?"

"Well," said Scrimgeour, frowning slightly, "well, yes, that's partly why we'd like —"

"No, I don't think that'll work," said Harry pleasantly. "You see, I don't like some of the things the Ministry's doing. Locking up Stan Shunpike, for instance."

Scrimgeour did not speak for a moment but his expression hardened instantly. "I would not expect you to understand," he said, and he was not as successful at keeping anger out of his voice as Harry had been. "These are dangerous times, and certain measures need to be taken. You are sixteen years old —"

"Dumbledore's a lot older than sixteen, and he doesn't think Stan should be in Azkaban either," said Harry. "You're making Stan a scapegoat, just like you want to make me a mascot."

They looked at each other, long and hard. Finally Scrimgeour said, with no pretense at warmth, "I see. You prefer — like your hero, Dumbledore — to disassociate yourself from the Ministry?"

"I don't want to be used," said Harry.

"Some would say it's your duty to be used by the Ministry!"

"Yeah, and others might say it's your duty to check that people really are Death Eaters before you chuck them in prison," said Harry, his temper rising now. "You're doing what Barty Crouch

did. You never get it right, you people, do you? Either we've got
Fudge, pretending everything's lovely while people get murdered
right under his nose, or we've got you, chucking the wrong people
into jail and trying to pretend you've got 'the Chosen One' working for you!"

"So you're not 'the Chosen One'?" said Scrimgeour.

"I thought you said it didn't matter either way?" said Harry, with
a bitter laugh. "Not to you anyway."

"I shouldn't have said that," said Scrimgeour quickly. "It was
tactless —"

"No, it was honest," said Harry. "One of the only honest things
you've said to me. You don't care whether I live or die, but you do
care that I help you convince everyone you're winning the war
against Voldemort. I haven't forgotten, Minister. . . ."

He raised his right fist. There, shining white on the back of his
cold hand, were the scars which Dolores Umbridge had forced him
to carve into his own flesh: *I must not tell lies.*

"I don't remember you rushing to my defense when I was trying
to tell everyone Voldemort was back. The Ministry wasn't so keen
to be pals last year."

They stood in silence as icy as the ground beneath their feet. The
gnome had finally managed to extricate his worm and was now
sucking on it happily, leaning against the bottommost branches of
the rhododendron bush.

"What is Dumbledore up to?" said Scrimgeour brusquely.
"Where does he go when he is absent from Hogwarts?"

"No idea," said Harry.

"And you wouldn't tell me if you knew," said Scrimgeour,
"would you?"

"No, I wouldn't," said Harry.

"Well, then, I shall have to see whether I can't find out by other means."

"You can try," said Harry indifferently. "But you seem cleverer than Fudge, so I'd have thought you'd have learned from his mistakes. He tried interfering at Hogwarts. You might have noticed he's not Minister anymore, but Dumbledore's still headmaster. I'd leave Dumbledore alone, if I were you."

There was a long pause.

"Well, it is clear to me that he has done a very good job on you," said Scrimgeour, his eyes cold and hard behind his wire-rimmed glasses. "Dumbledore's man through and through, aren't you, Potter?"

"Yeah, I am," said Harry. "Glad we straightened that out."

And turning his back on the Minister of Magic, he strode back toward the house.

A SLUGGISH MEMORY

Late in the afternoon, a few days after New Year, Harry, Ron, and Ginny lined up beside the kitchen fire to return to Hogwarts. The Ministry had arranged this one-off connection to the Floo Network to return students quickly and safely to the school. Only Mrs. Weasley was there to say good-bye, as Mr. Weasley, Fred, George, Bill, and Fleur were all at work. Mrs. Weasley dissolved into tears at the moment of parting. Admittedly, it took very little to set her off lately; she had been crying on and off ever since Percy had stormed from the house on Christmas Day with his glasses splattered with mashed parsnip (for which Fred, George, and Ginny all claimed credit).

"Don't cry, Mum," said Ginny, patting her on the back as Mrs. Weasley sobbed into her shoulder. "It's okay. . . ."

"Yeah, don't worry about us," said Ron, permitting his mother to plant a very wet kiss on his cheek, "or about Percy. He's such a prat, it's not really a loss, is it?"

Mrs. Weasley sobbed harder than ever as she enfolded Harry in her arms.

"Promise me you'll look after yourself. . . . Stay out of trouble. . . ."

"I always do, Mrs. Weasley," said Harry. "I like a quiet life, you know me."

She gave a watery chuckle and stood back. "Be good, then, all of you. . . ."

Harry stepped into the emerald fire and shouted "Hogwarts!" He had one last fleeting view of the Weasleys' kitchen and Mrs. Weasley's tearful face before the flames engulfed him; spinning very fast, he caught blurred glimpses of other Wizarding rooms, which were whipped out of sight before he could get a proper look; then he was slowing down, finally stopping squarely in the fireplace in Professor McGonagall's office. She barely glanced up from her work as he clambered out over the grate.

"Evening, Potter. Try not to get too much ash on the carpet."

"No, Professor."

Harry straightened his glasses and flattened his hair as Ron came spinning into view. When Ginny had arrived, all three of them trooped out of McGonagall's office and off toward Gryffindor Tower. Harry glanced out of the corridor windows as they passed; the sun was already sinking over grounds carpeted in deeper snow than had lain over the Burrow garden. In the distance, he could see Hagrid feeding Buckbeak in front of his cabin.

"Baubles," said Ron confidently, when they reached the Fat Lady, who was looking rather paler than usual and winced at his loud voice.

"No," she said.

"What d'you mean, 'no'?"

"There is a new password," she said. "And please don't shout."

"But we've been away, how're we supposed to — ?"

"Harry! Ginny!"

Hermione was hurrying toward them, very pink-faced and wearing a cloak, hat, and gloves.

"I got back a couple of hours ago, I've just been down to visit Hagrid and Buck — I mean Witherwings," she said breathlessly. "Did you have a good Christmas?"

"Yeah," said Ron at once, "pretty eventful, Rufus Scrim —"

"I've got something for you, Harry," said Hermione, neither looking at Ron nor giving any sign that she had heard him. "Oh, hang on — password. *Abstinence*."

"Precisely," said the Fat Lady in a feeble voice, and swung forward to reveal the portrait hole.

"What's up with her?" asked Harry.

"Overindulged over Christmas, apparently," said Hermione, rolling her eyes as she led the way into the packed common room. "She and her friend Violet drank their way through all the wine in that picture of drunk monks down by the Charms corridor. Anyway . . ."

She rummaged in her pocket for a moment, then pulled out a scroll of parchment with Dumbledore's writing on it.

"Great," said Harry, unrolling it at once to discover that his next lesson with Dumbledore was scheduled for the following night. "I've got loads to tell him — and you. Let's sit down —"

But at that moment there was a loud squeal of "Won-Won!" and Lavender Brown came hurtling out of nowhere and flung herself into Ron's arms. Several onlookers sniggered; Hermione gave a tinkling laugh and said, "There's a table over here. . . . Coming, Ginny?"

"No, thanks, I said I'd meet Dean," said Ginny, though Harry could not help noticing that she did not sound very enthusiastic. Leaving Ron and Lavender locked in a kind of vertical wrestling match, Harry led Hermione over to the spare table.

"So how was your Christmas?"

"Oh, fine," she shrugged. "Nothing special. How was it at Won-Won's?"

"I'll tell you in a minute," said Harry. "Look, Hermione, can't you — ?"

"No, I can't," she said flatly. "So don't even ask."

"I thought maybe, you know, over Christmas —"

"It was the Fat Lady who drank a vat of five-hundred-year-old wine, Harry, not me. So what was this important news you wanted to tell me?"

She looked too fierce to argue with at that moment, so Harry dropped the subject of Ron and recounted all that he had overheard between Malfoy and Snape. When he had finished, Hermione sat in thought for a moment and then said, "Don't you think — ?"

"— he was pretending to offer help so that he could trick Malfoy into telling him what he's doing?"

"Well, yes," said Hermione.

"Ron's dad and Lupin think so," Harry said grudgingly. "But this definitely proves Malfoy's planning something, you can't deny that."

"No, I can't," she answered slowly.

"And he's acting on Voldemort's orders, just like I said!"

"Hmm . . . did either of them actually mention Voldemort's name?"

Harry frowned, trying to remember. "I'm not sure . . . Snape definitely said 'your master,' and who else would that be?"

"I don't know," said Hermione, biting her lip. "Maybe his father?"

She stared across the room, apparently lost in thought, not even noticing Lavender tickling Ron. "How's Lupin?"

"Not great," said Harry, and he told her all about Lupin's mission among the werewolves and the difficulties he was facing. "Have you heard of this Fenrir Greyback?"

"Yes, I have!" said Hermione, sounding startled. "And so have you, Harry!"

"When, History of Magic? You know full well I never listened . . ."

"No, no, not History of Magic — Malfoy threatened Borgin with him!" said Hermione. "Back in Knockturn Alley, don't you remember? He told Borgin that Greyback was an old family friend and that he'd be checking up on Borgin's progress!"

Harry gaped at her. "I forgot! But this *proves* Malfoy's a Death Eater, how else could he be in contact with Greyback and telling him what to do?"

"It is pretty suspicious," breathed Hermione. "Unless . . ."

"Oh, come on," said Harry in exasperation, "you can't get round this one!"

"Well . . . there is the possibility it was an empty threat."

"You're unbelievable, you are," said Harry, shaking his head. "We'll see who's right. . . . You'll be eating your words, Hermione, just like the Ministry. Oh yeah, I had a row with Rufus Scrimgeour as well. . . ."

And the rest of the evening passed amicably with both of them abusing the Minister of Magic, for Hermione, like Ron, thought that after all the Ministry had put Harry through the previous year, they had a great deal of nerve asking him for help now.

The new term started next morning with a pleasant surprise for the sixth years: a large sign had been pinned to the common room notice boards overnight.

APPARITION LESSONS

If you are seventeen years of age, or will turn seventeen on or before the 31st August next, you are eligible for a twelve-week course of Apparition Lessons from a Ministry of Magic Apparition instructor. Please sign below if you would like to participate. Cost: 12 Galleons.

Harry and Ron joined the crowd that was jostling around the notice and taking it in turns to write their names at the bottom. Ron was just taking out his quill to sign after Hermione when Lavender crept up behind him, slipped her hands over his eyes, and trilled, "Guess who, Won-Won?" Harry turned to see Hermione stalking off; he caught up with her, having no wish to stay behind with Ron and Lavender, but to his surprise, Ron caught up with them only a little way beyond the portrait hole, his ears bright red and his expression disgruntled. Without a word, Hermione sped up to walk with Neville.

"So — Apparition," said Ron, his tone making it perfectly plain that Harry was not to mention what had just happened. "Should be a laugh, eh?"

"I dunno," said Harry. "Maybe it's better when you do it yourself, I didn't enjoy it much when Dumbledore took me along for the ride."

"I forgot you'd already done it. . . . I'd better pass my test first time," said Ron, looking anxious. "Fred and George did."

"Charlie failed, though, didn't he?"

"Yeah, but Charlie's bigger than me" — Ron held his arms out from his body as though he was a gorilla — "so Fred and George didn't go on about it much . . . not to his face anyway . . ."

"When can we take the actual test?"

"Soon as we're seventeen. That's only March for me!"

"Yeah, but you wouldn't be able to Apparate in here, not in the castle . . ."

"Not the point, is it? Everyone would know I *could* Apparate if I wanted."

Ron was not the only one to be excited at the prospect of Apparition. All that day there was much talk about the forthcoming lessons; a great deal of store was set by being able to vanish and reappear at will.

"How cool will it be when we can just —" Seamus clicked his fingers to indicate disappearance. "Me cousin Fergus does it just to annoy me, you wait till I can do it back . . . He'll never have another peaceful moment. . . ."

Lost in visions of this happy prospect, he flicked his wand a little too enthusiastically, so that instead of producing the fountain of pure water that was the object of today's Charms lesson, he let out a hoselike jet that ricocheted off the ceiling and knocked Professor Flitwick flat on his face.

"Harry's already Apparated," Ron told a slightly abashed Seamus, after Professor Flitwick had dried himself off with a wave of his wand and set Seamus lines: *"I am a wizard, not a baboon brandishing a stick."* "Dum — er — someone took him. Side-Along-Apparition, you know."

"Whoa!" whispered Seamus, and he, Dean, and Neville put their heads a little closer to hear what Apparition felt like. For the rest of the day, Harry was besieged with requests from the other sixth years to describe the sensation of Apparition. All of them seemed awed, rather than put off, when he told them how uncomfortable it was, and he was still answering detailed questions at ten to eight that evening, when he was forced to lie and say that he needed to return a book to the library, so as to escape in time for his lesson with Dumbledore.

The lamps in Dumbledore's office were lit, the portraits of previous headmasters were snoring gently in their frames, and the Pensieve was ready upon the desk once more. Dumbledore's hands lay on either side of it, the right one as blackened and burnt-looking as ever. It did not seem to have healed at all and Harry wondered, for perhaps the hundredth time, what had caused such a distinctive injury, but did not ask; Dumbledore had said that he would know eventually and there was, in any case, another subject he wanted to discuss. But before Harry could say anything about Snape and Malfoy, Dumbledore spoke.

"I hear that you met the Minister of Magic over Christmas?"

"Yes," said Harry. "He's not very happy with me."

"No," sighed Dumbledore. "He is not very happy with me either. We must try not to sink beneath our anguish, Harry, but battle on."

Harry grinned.

"He wanted me to tell the Wizarding community that the Ministry's doing a wonderful job."

Dumbledore smiled.

"It was Fudge's idea originally, you know. During his last days in office, when he was trying desperately to cling to his post, he sought a meeting with you, hoping that you would give him your support —"

"After everything Fudge did last year?" said Harry angrily. "After *Umbridge*?"

"I told Cornelius there was no chance of it, but the idea did not die when he left office. Within hours of Scrimgeour's appointment we met and he demanded that I arrange a meeting with you —"

"So that's why you argued!" Harry blurted out. "It was in the *Daily Prophet*."

"The *Prophet* is bound to report the truth occasionally," said Dumbledore, "if only accidentally. Yes, that was why we argued. Well, it appears that Rufus found a way to corner you at last."

"He accused me of being 'Dumbledore's man through and through.'"

"How very rude of him."

"I told him I was."

Dumbledore opened his mouth to speak and then closed it again. Behind Harry, Fawkes the phoenix let out a low, soft, musical cry. To Harry's intense embarrassment, he suddenly realized that Dumbledore's bright blue eyes looked rather watery, and stared hastily at his own knees. When Dumbledore spoke, however, his voice was quite steady.

"I am very touched, Harry."

"Scrimgeour wanted to know where you go when you're not at Hogwarts," said Harry, still looking fixedly at his knees.

"Yes, he is very nosy about that," said Dumbledore, now sounding cheerful, and Harry thought it safe to look up again. "He has even attempted to have me followed. Amusing, really. He set Dawlish to tail me. It wasn't kind. I have already been forced to jinx Dawlish once; I did it again with the greatest regret."

"So they still don't know where you go?" asked Harry, hoping for more information on this intriguing subject, but Dumbledore merely smiled over the top of his half-moon spectacles.

"No, they don't, and the time is not quite right for you to know either. Now, I suggest we press on, unless there's anything else — ?"

"There is, actually, sir," said Harry. "It's about Malfoy and Snape."

"*Professor* Snape, Harry."

"Yes, sir. I overheard them during Professor Slughorn's party . . . well, I followed them, actually. . . ."

Dumbledore listened to Harry's story with an impassive face. When Harry had finished he did not speak for a few moments, then said, "Thank you for telling me this, Harry, but I suggest that you put it out of your mind. I do not think that it is of great importance."

"Not of great importance?" repeated Harry incredulously. "Professor, did you understand — ?"

"Yes, Harry, blessed as I am with extraordinary brainpower, I understood everything you told me," said Dumbledore, a little sharply. "I think you might even consider the possibility that I understood more than you did. Again, I am glad that you have confided in me, but let me reassure you that you have not told me anything that causes me disquiet."

Harry sat in seething silence, glaring at Dumbledore. What was going on? Did this mean that Dumbledore had indeed ordered Snape to find out what Malfoy was doing, in which case he had already heard everything Harry had just told him from Snape? Or was he really worried by what he had heard, but pretending not to be?

"So, sir," said Harry, in what he hoped was a polite, calm voice, "you definitely still trust — ?"

"I have been tolerant enough to answer that question already," said Dumbledore, but he did not sound very tolerant anymore. "My answer has not changed."

"I should think not," said a snide voice; Phineas Nigellus was evidently only pretending to be asleep. Dumbledore ignored him.

"And now, Harry, I must insist that we press on. I have more important things to discuss with you this evening."

Harry sat there feeling mutinous. How would it be if he refused to permit the change of subject, if he insisted upon arguing the case against Malfoy? As though he had read Harry's mind, Dumbledore shook his head.

"Ah, Harry, how often this happens, even between the best of friends! Each of us believes that what he has to say is much more important than anything the other might have to contribute!"

"I don't think what you've got to say is unimportant, sir," said Harry stiffly.

"Well, you are quite right, because it is not," said Dumbledore briskly. "I have two more memories to show you this evening, both obtained with enormous difficulty, and the second of them is, I think, the most important I have collected."

Harry did not say anything to this; he still felt angry at the reception his confidences had received, but could not see what was to be gained by arguing further.

"So," said Dumbledore, in a ringing voice, "we meet this evening to continue the tale of Tom Riddle, whom we left last lesson poised on the threshold of his years at Hogwarts. You will remember how excited he was to hear that he was a wizard, that he refused my company on a trip to Diagon Alley, and that I, in turn, warned him against continued thievery when he arrived at school.

"Well, the start of the school year arrived and with it came Tom Riddle, a quiet boy in his secondhand robes, who lined up with the other first years to be sorted. He was placed in Slytherin House almost the moment that the Sorting Hat touched his head," continued Dumbledore, waving his blackened hand toward the shelf over his head where the Sorting Hat sat, ancient and unmoving. "How soon Riddle learned that the famous founder of the House could talk to snakes, I do not know — perhaps that very evening. The knowledge can only have excited him and increased his sense of self-importance.

"However, if he was frightening or impressing fellow Slytherins with displays of Parseltongue in their common room, no hint of it reached the staff. He showed no sign of outward arrogance or aggression at all. As an unusually talented and very good-looking orphan, he naturally drew attention and sympathy from the staff almost from the moment of his arrival. He seemed polite, quiet, and thirsty for knowledge. Nearly all were most favorably impressed by him."

"Didn't you tell them, sir, what he'd been like when you met him at the orphanage?" asked Harry.

"No, I did not. Though he had shown no hint of remorse, it was possible that he felt sorry for how he had behaved before and was resolved to turn over a fresh leaf. I chose to give him that chance."

Dumbledore paused and looked inquiringly at Harry, who had opened his mouth to speak. Here, again, was Dumbledore's tendency to trust people in spite of overwhelming evidence that they did not deserve it! But then Harry remembered something. . . .

"But you didn't *really* trust him, sir, did you? He told me . . . the Riddle who came out of that diary said, 'Dumbledore never seemed to like me as much as the other teachers did.'"

"Let us say that I did not take it for granted that he was trustworthy," said Dumbledore. "I had, as I have already indicated, resolved to keep a close eye upon him, and so I did. I cannot pretend that I gleaned a great deal from my observations at first. He was very guarded with me; he felt, I am sure, that in the thrill of discovering his true identity he had told me a little too much. He was careful never to reveal as much again, but he could not take back what he had let slip in his excitement, nor what Mrs. Cole had confided in me. However, he had the sense never to try and charm me as he charmed so many of my colleagues.

"As he moved up the school, he gathered about him a group of dedicated friends; I call them that, for want of a better term, although as I have already indicated, Riddle undoubtedly felt no affection for any of them. This group had a kind of dark glamour within the castle. They were a motley collection; a mixture of the weak seeking protection, the ambitious seeking some shared glory, and the thuggish gravitating toward a leader who could show them more refined forms of cruelty. In other words, they were the forerunners of the Death Eaters, and indeed some of them became the first Death Eaters after leaving Hogwarts.

"Rigidly controlled by Riddle, they were never detected in open wrongdoing, although their seven years at Hogwarts were marked by a number of nasty incidents to which they were never satisfactorily linked, the most serious of which was, of course, the opening of the Chamber of Secrets, which resulted in the death of a girl. As you know, Hagrid was wrongly accused of that crime.

"I have not been able to find many memories of Riddle at Hogwarts," said Dumbledore, placing his withered hand on the Pensieve. "Few who knew him then are prepared to talk about him; they are too terrified. What I know, I found out after he had left Hogwarts, after much painstaking effort, after tracing those few who could be tricked into speaking, after searching old records and questioning Muggle and wizard witnesses alike.

"Those whom I could persuade to talk told me that Riddle was obsessed with his parentage. This is understandable, of course; he had grown up in an orphanage and naturally wished to know how he came to be there. It seems that he searched in vain for some trace of Tom Riddle senior on the shields in the trophy room, on the lists of prefects in the old school records, even in the books of Wizarding history. Finally he was forced to accept that his father had never set foot in Hogwarts. I believe that it was then that he dropped the name forever, assumed the identity of Lord Voldemort, and began his investigations into his previously despised mother's family — the woman whom, you will remember, he had thought could not be a witch if she had succumbed to the shameful human weakness of death.

"All he had to go upon was the single name 'Marvolo,' which he knew from those who ran the orphanage had been his mother's father's name. Finally, after painstaking research through old books of Wizarding families, he discovered the existence of Slytherin's surviving line. In the summer of his sixteenth year, he left the orphanage to which he returned annually and set off to find his Gaunt relatives. And now, Harry, if you will stand . . ."

Dumbledore rose, and Harry saw that he was again holding a small crystal bottle filled with swirling, pearly memory.

"I was very lucky to collect this," he said, as he poured the gleaming mass into the Pensieve. "As you will understand when we have experienced it. Shall we?"

Harry stepped up to the stone basin and bowed obediently until his face sank through the surface of the memory; he felt the familiar sensation of falling through nothingness and then landed upon a dirty stone floor in almost total darkness.

It took him several seconds to recognize the place, by which time Dumbledore had landed beside him. The Gaunts' house was now more indescribably filthy than anywhere Harry had ever seen. The ceiling was thick with cobwebs, the floor coated in grime; moldy and rotting food lay upon the table amidst a mass of crusted pots. The only light came from a single guttering candle placed at the feet of a man with hair and beard so overgrown Harry could see neither eyes nor mouth. He was slumped in an armchair by the fire, and Harry wondered for a moment whether he was dead. But then there came a loud knock on the door and the man jerked awake, raising a wand in his right hand and a short knife in his left.

The door creaked open. There on the threshold, holding an old-fashioned lamp, stood a boy Harry recognized at once: tall, pale, dark-haired, and handsome — the teenage Voldemort.

Voldemort's eyes moved slowly around the hovel and then found the man in the armchair. For a few seconds they looked at each other, then the man staggered upright, the many empty bottles at his feet clattering and tinkling across the floor.

"YOU!" he bellowed. "YOU!"

And he hurtled drunkenly at Riddle, wand and knife held aloft.

"Stop."

Riddle spoke in Parseltongue. The man skidded into the table, sending moldy pots crashing to the floor. He stared at Riddle. There was a long silence while they contemplated each other. The man broke it.

"You speak it?"

"Yes, I speak it," said Riddle. He moved forward into the room, allowing the door to swing shut behind him. Harry could not help but feel a resentful admiration for Voldemort's complete lack of fear. His face merely expressed disgust and, perhaps, disappointment.

"Where is Marvolo?" he asked.

"Dead," said the other. *"Died years ago, didn't he?"*

Riddle frowned.

"Who are you, then?"

"I'm Morfin, ain't I?"

"Marvolo's son?"

"'Course I am, then . . ."

Morfin pushed the hair out of his dirty face, the better to see Riddle, and Harry saw that he wore Marvolo's black-stoned ring on his right hand.

"I thought you was that Muggle," whispered Morfin. "You look mighty like that Muggle."

"What Muggle?" said Riddle sharply.

"That Muggle what my sister took a fancy to, that Muggle what lives in the big house over the way," said Morfin, and he spat unexpectedly upon the floor between them. "You look right like him. Riddle. But he's older now, in 'e? He's older'n you, now I think on it. . . ."

Morfin looked slightly dazed and swayed a little, still clutching the edge of the table for support. "He come back, see," he added stupidly.

Voldemort was gazing at Morfin as though appraising his possibilities. Now he moved a little closer and said, "Riddle came back?"

"Ar, he left her, and serve her right, marrying filth!" said Morfin, spitting on the floor again. "Robbed us, mind, before she ran off! Where's the locket, eh, where's Slytherin's locket?"

Voldemort did not answer. Morfin was working himself into a rage again; he brandished his knife and shouted, "Dishonored us, she did, that little slut! And who're you, coming here and asking questions about all that? It's over, innit. . . . It's over. . . ."

He looked away, staggering slightly, and Voldemort moved forward. As he did so, an unnatural darkness fell, extinguishing Voldemort's lamp and Morfin's candle, extinguishing everything. . . .

Dumbledore's fingers closed tightly around Harry's arm and

they were soaring back into the present again. The soft golden light in Dumbledore's office seemed to dazzle Harry's eyes after that impenetrable darkness.

"Is that all?" said Harry at once. "Why did it go dark, what happened?"

"Because Morfin could not remember anything from that point onward," said Dumbledore, gesturing Harry back into his seat. "When he awoke next morning, he was lying on the floor, quite alone. Marvolo's ring had gone.

"Meanwhile, in the village of Little Hangleton, a maid was running along the High Street, screaming that there were three bodies lying in the drawing room of the big house: Tom Riddle Senior and his mother and father.

"The Muggle authorities were perplexed. As far as I am aware, they do not know to this day how the Riddles died, for the *Avada Kedavra* curse does not usually leave any sign of damage. . . . The exception sits before me," Dumbledore added, with a nod to Harry's scar. "The Ministry, on the other hand, knew at once that this was a wizard's murder. They also knew that a convicted Muggle-hater lived across the valley from the Riddle house, a Muggle-hater who had already been imprisoned once for attacking one of the murdered people.

"So the Ministry called upon Morfin. They did not need to question him, to use Veritaserum or Legilimency. He admitted to the murder on the spot, giving details only the murderer could know. He was proud, he said, to have killed the Muggles, had been awaiting his chance all these years. He handed over his wand, which was proved at once to have been used to kill the Riddles. And he permitted himself to be led off to Azkaban without a fight.

All that disturbed him was the fact that his father's ring had disappeared. 'He'll kill me for losing it,' he told his captors over and over again. 'He'll kill me for losing his ring.' And that, apparently, was all he ever said again. He lived out the remainder of his life in Azkaban, lamenting the loss of Marvolo's last heirloom, and is buried beside the prison, alongside the other poor souls who have expired within its walls."

"So Voldemort stole Morfin's wand and used it?" said Harry, sitting up straight.

"That's right," said Dumbledore. "We have no memories to show us this, but I think we can be fairly sure what happened. Voldemort Stupefied his uncle, took his wand, and proceeded across the valley to 'the big house over the way.' There he murdered the Muggle man who had abandoned his witch mother, and, for good measure, his Muggle grandparents, thus obliterating the last of the unworthy Riddle line and revenging himself upon the father who never wanted him. Then he returned to the Gaunt hovel, performed the complex bit of magic that would implant a false memory in his uncle's mind, laid Morfin's wand beside its unconscious owner, pocketed the ancient ring he wore, and departed."

"And Morfin never realized he hadn't done it?"

"Never," said Dumbledore. "He gave, as I say, a full and boastful confession."

"But he had this real memory in him all the time!"

"Yes, but it took a great deal of skilled Legilimency to coax it out of him," said Dumbledore, "and why should anybody delve further into Morfin's mind when he had already confessed to the crime? However, I was able to secure a visit to Morfin in the last weeks of his life, by which time I was attempting to discover as much as I

could about Voldemort's past. I extracted this memory with difficulty. When I saw what it contained, I attempted to use it to secure
Morfin's release from Azkaban. Before the Ministry reached their
decision, however, Morfin had died."

"But how come the Ministry didn't realize that Voldemort had
done all that to Morfin?" Harry asked angrily. "He was underage at
the time, wasn't he? I thought they could detect underage magic!"

"You are quite right — they can detect magic, but not the per-
petrator: You will remember that you were blamed by the Ministry
for the Hover Charm that was, in fact, cast by —"

"Dobby," growled Harry; this injustice still rankled. "So if you're
underage and you do magic inside an adult witch or wizard's house,
the Ministry won't know?"

"They will certainly be unable to tell who performed the magic,"
said Dumbledore, smiling slightly at the look of great indignation
on Harry's face. "They rely on witch and wizard parents to enforce
their offspring's obedience while within their walls."

"Well, that's rubbish," snapped Harry. "Look what happened
here, look what happened to Morfin!"

"I agree," said Dumbledore. "Whatever Morfin was, he did not
deserve to die as he did, blamed for murders he had not committed. But it is getting late, and I want you to see this other memory
before we part. . . ."

Dumbledore took from an inside pocket another crystal phial
and Harry fell silent at once, remembering that Dumbledore had
said it was the most important one he had collected. Harry noticed
that the contents proved difficult to empty into the Pensieve, as
though they had congealed slightly; did memories go bad?

"This will not take long," said Dumbledore, when he had finally emptied the phial. "We shall be back before you know it. Once more into the Pensieve, then . . ."

And Harry fell again through the silver surface, landing this time right in front of a man he recognized at once.

It was a much younger Horace Slughorn. Harry was so used to him bald that he found the sight of Slughorn with thick, shiny, straw-colored hair quite disconcerting; it looked as though he had had his head thatched, though there was already a shiny Galleon-sized bald patch on his crown. His mustache, less massive than it was these days, was gingery-blond. He was not quite as rotund as the Slughorn Harry knew, though the golden buttons on his richly embroidered waistcoat were taking a fair amount of strain. His little feet resting upon a velvet pouffe, he was sitting well back in a comfortable winged armchair, one hand grasping a small glass of wine, the other searching through a box of crystalized pineapple.

Harry looked around as Dumbledore appeared beside him and saw that they were standing in Slughorn's office. Half a dozen boys were sitting around Slughorn, all on harder or lower seats than his, and all in their mid-teens. Harry recognized Voldemort at once. His was the most handsome face and he looked the most relaxed of all the boys. His right hand lay negligently upon the arm of his chair; with a jolt, Harry saw that he was wearing Marvolo's gold-and-black ring; he had already killed his father.

"Sir, is it true that Professor Merrythought is retiring?" he asked.

"Tom, Tom, if I knew I couldn't tell you," said Slughorn, wagging a reproving, sugar-covered finger at Riddle, though ruining the effect slightly by winking. "I must say, I'd like to know where you get your information, boy, more knowledgeable than half the staff, you are."

Riddle smiled; the other boys laughed and cast him admiring looks.

"What with your uncanny ability to know things you shouldn't, and your careful flattery of the people who matter — thank you for the pineapple, by the way, you're quite right, it is my favorite —"

As several of the boys tittered, something very odd happened. The whole room was suddenly filled with a thick white fog, so that Harry could see nothing but the face of Dumbledore, who was standing beside him. Then Slughorn's voice rang out through the mist, unnaturally loudly, *"You'll go wrong, boy, mark my words."*

The fog cleared as suddenly as it had appeared and yet nobody made any allusion to it, nor did anybody look as though anything unusual had just happened. Bewildered, Harry looked around as a small golden clock standing upon Slughorn's desk chimed eleven o'clock.

"Good gracious, is it that time already?" said Slughorn. "You'd better get going, boys, or we'll all be in trouble. Lestrange, I want your essay by tomorrow or it's detention. Same goes for you, Avery."

Slughorn pulled himself out of his armchair and carried his empty glass over to his desk as the boys filed out. Voldemort, however, stayed behind. Harry could tell he had dawdled deliberately, wanting to be last in the room with Slughorn.

"Look sharp, Tom," said Slughorn, turning around and finding him still present. "You don't want to be caught out of bed out of hours, and you a prefect . . ."

"Sir, I wanted to ask you something."

"Ask away, then, m'boy, ask away. . . ."

"Sir, I wondered what you know about . . . about Horcruxes?"

And it happened all over again: The dense fog filled the room so that Harry could not see Slughorn or Voldemort at all; only Dumbledore, smiling serenely beside him. Then Slughorn's voice boomed out again, just as it had done before.

"*I don't know anything about Horcruxes and I wouldn't tell you if I did! Now get out of here at once and don't let me catch you mentioning them again!*"

"Well, that's that," said Dumbledore placidly beside Harry. "Time to go."

And Harry's feet left the floor to fall, seconds later, back onto the rug in front of Dumbledore's desk.

"That's all there is?" said Harry blankly.

Dumbledore had said that this was the most important memory of all, but he could not see what was so significant about it. Admittedly the fog, and the fact that nobody seemed to have noticed it, was odd, but other than that nothing seemed to have happened except that Voldemort had asked a question and failed to get an answer.

"As you might have noticed," said Dumbledore, reseating himself behind his desk, "that memory has been tampered with."

"Tampered with?" repeated Harry, sitting back down too.

"Certainly," said Dumbledore. "Professor Slughorn has meddled with his own recollections."

"But why would he do that?"

"Because, I think, he is ashamed of what he remembers," said Dumbledore. "He has tried to rework the memory to show himself in a better light, obliterating those parts which he does not wish me to see. It is, as you will have noticed, very crudely done, and that is all to the good, for it shows that the true memory is still there beneath the alterations.

"And so, for the first time, I am giving you homework, Harry. It will be your job to persuade Professor Slughorn to divulge the real memory, which will undoubtedly be our most crucial piece of information of all."

Harry stared at him.

"But surely, sir," he said, keeping his voice as respectful as possible, "you don't need me — you could use Legilimency . . . or Veritaserum. . . ."

"Professor Slughorn is an extremely able wizard who will be expecting both," said Dumbledore. "He is much more accomplished at Occlumency than poor Morfin Gaunt, and I would be astonished if he has not carried an antidote to Veritaserum with him ever since I coerced him into giving me this travesty of a recollection.

"No, I think it would be foolish to attempt to wrest the truth from Professor Slughorn by force, and might do much more harm than good; I do not wish him to leave Hogwarts. However, he has his weaknesses like the rest of us, and I believe that you are the one person who might be able to penetrate his defenses. It is most important that we secure the true memory, Harry. . . . How important, we will only know when we have seen the real thing. So, good luck . . . and good night."

A little taken aback by the abrupt dismissal, Harry got to his feet quickly. "Good night, sir."

As he closed the study door behind him, he distinctly heard Phineas Nigellus say, "I can't see why the boy should be able to do it better than you, Dumbledore."

"I wouldn't expect you to, Phineas," replied Dumbledore, and Fawkes gave another low, musical cry.

BIRTHDAY SURPRISES

The next day Harry confided in both Ron and Hermione the task that Dumbledore had set him, though separately, for Hermione still refused to remain in Ron's presence longer than it took to give him a contemptuous look.

Ron thought that Harry was unlikely to have any trouble with Slughorn at all.

"He loves you," he said over breakfast, waving an airy forkful of fried egg. "Won't refuse you anything, will he? Not his little Potions Prince. Just hang back after class this afternoon and ask him."

Hermione, however, took a gloomier view. "He must be determined to hide what really happened if Dumbledore couldn't get it out of him," she said in a low voice, as they stood in the deserted, snowy courtyard at break. "Horcruxes . . . *Horcruxes* . . . I've never even heard of them. . . ."

"You haven't?" Harry was disappointed; he had hoped that

Hermione might have been able to give him a clue as to what Horcruxes were.

"They must be really advanced Dark Magic, or why would Voldemort have wanted to know about them? I think it's going to be difficult to get the information, Harry, you'll have to be very careful about how you approach Slughorn, think out a strategy. . . ."

"Ron reckons I should just hang back after Potions this afternoon. . . ."

"Oh, well, if *Won-Won* thinks that, you'd better do it," she said, flaring up at once. "After all, when has *Won-Won's* judgment ever been faulty?"

"Hermione, can't you — ?"

"No!" she said angrily, and stormed away, leaving Harry alone and ankle-deep in snow.

Potions lessons were uncomfortable enough these days, seeing as Harry, Ron, and Hermione had to share a desk. Today, Hermione moved her cauldron around the table so that she was close to Ernie, and ignored both Harry and Ron.

"What've *you* done?" Ron muttered to Harry, looking at Hermione's haughty profile.

But before Harry could answer, Slughorn was calling for silence from the front of the room.

"Settle down, settle down, please! Quickly, now, lots of work to get through this afternoon! Golpalott's Third Law . . . who can tell me — ? But Miss Granger can, of course!"

Hermione recited at top speed: "Golpalott's-Third-Law-states-that-the-antidote-for-a-blended-poison-will-be-equal-to-more-than-the-sum-of-the-antidotes-for-each-of-the-separate-components."

"Precisely!" beamed Slughorn. "Ten points for Gryffindor! Now, if we accept Golpalott's Third Law as true . . ."

Harry was going to have to take Slughorn's word for it that Golpalott's Third Law was true, because he had not understood any of it. Nobody apart from Hermione seemed to be following what Slughorn said next either.

". . . which means, of course, that assuming we have achieved correct identification of the potion's ingredients by Scarpin's Revelaspell, our primary aim is not the relatively simple one of selecting antidotes to those ingredients in and of themselves, but to find that added component that will, by an almost alchemical process, transform these disparate elements —"

Ron was sitting beside Harry with his mouth half open, doodling absently on his new copy of *Advanced Potion-Making*. Ron kept forgetting that he could no longer rely on Hermione to help him out of trouble when he failed to grasp what was going on.

". . . and so," finished Slughorn, "I want each of you to come and take one of these phials from my desk. You are to create an antidote for the poison within it before the end of the lesson. Good luck, and don't forget your protective gloves!"

Hermione had left her stool and was halfway toward Slughorn's desk before the rest of the class had realized it was time to move, and by the time Harry, Ron, and Ernie returned to the table, she had already tipped the contents of her phial into her cauldron and was kindling a fire underneath it.

"It's a shame that the Prince won't be able to help you much with this, Harry," she said brightly as she straightened up. "You have to understand the principles involved this time. No shortcuts or cheats!"

Annoyed, Harry uncorked the poison he had taken from Slughorn's desk, which was a garish shade of pink, tipped it into his cauldron, and lit a fire underneath it. He did not have the faintest idea what he was supposed to do next. He glanced around at Ron, who was now standing there looking rather gormless, having copied everything Harry had done.

"You sure the Prince hasn't got any tips?" Ron muttered to Harry.

Harry pulled out his trusty copy of *Advanced Potion-Making* and turned to the chapter on antidotes. There was Golpalott's Third Law, stated word for word as Hermione had recited it, but not a single illuminating note in the Prince's hand to explain what it meant. Apparently the Prince, like Hermione, had had no difficulty understanding it.

"Nothing," said Harry gloomily.

Hermione was now waving her wand enthusiastically over her cauldron. Unfortunately, they could not copy the spell she was doing because she was now so good at nonverbal incantations that she did not need to say the words aloud. Ernie Macmillan, however, was muttering, *"Specialis Revelio!"* over his cauldron, which sounded impressive, so Harry and Ron hastened to imitate him.

It took Harry only five minutes to realize that his reputation as the best potion-maker in the class was crashing around his ears. Slughorn had peered hopefully into his cauldron on his first circuit of the dungeon, preparing to exclaim in delight as he usually did, and instead had withdrawn his head hastily, coughing, as the smell of bad eggs overwhelmed him. Hermione's expression could not have been any smugger; she had loathed being outperformed in every Potions class. She was now decanting the mysteriously separated ingredients of her poison into ten different crystal phials. More to avoid watching this irritating sight than anything else, Harry bent over the Half-Blood Prince's book and turned a few pages with unnecessary force.

And there it was, scrawled right across a long list of antidotes:

Just shove a bezoar down their throats.

Harry stared at these words for a moment. Hadn't he once, long ago, heard of bezoars? Hadn't Snape mentioned them in their first-ever Potions lesson? *"A stone taken from the stomach of a goat, which will protect from most poisons."*

It was not an answer to the Golpalott problem, and had Snape still been their teacher, Harry would not have dared do it, but this was a moment for desperate measures. He hastened toward the store cupboard and rummaged within it, pushing aside unicorn horns and tangles of dried herbs until he found, at the very back, a small cardboard box on which had been scribbled the word BEZOARS.

He opened the box just as Slughorn called, "Two minutes left, everyone!" Inside were half a dozen shriveled brown objects, looking more like dried-up kidneys than real stones. Harry seized one, put the box back in the cupboard, and hurried back to his cauldron.

"Time's . . . UP!" called Slughorn genially. "Well, let's see how you've done! Blaise . . . what have you got for me?"

Slowly, Slughorn moved around the room, examining the various antidotes. Nobody had finished the task, although Hermione was trying to cram a few more ingredients into her bottle before

Slughorn reached her. Ron had given up completely, and was merely trying to avoid breathing in the putrid fumes issuing from his cauldron. Harry stood there waiting, the bezoar clutched in a slightly sweaty hand.

Slughorn reached their table last. He sniffed Ernie's potion and passed on to Ron's with a grimace. He did not linger over Ron's cauldron, but backed away swiftly, retching slightly.

"And you, Harry," he said. "What have you got to show me?"

Harry held out his hand, the bezoar sitting on his palm.

Slughorn looked down at it for a full ten seconds. Harry wondered, for a moment, whether he was going to shout at him. Then he threw back his head and roared with laughter.

"You've got nerve, boy!" he boomed, taking the bezoar and holding it up so that the class could see it. "Oh, you're like your mother. . . . Well, I can't fault you. . . . A bezoar would certainly act as an antidote to all these potions!"

Hermione, who was sweaty-faced and had soot on her nose, looked livid. Her half-finished antidote, comprising fifty-two ingredients, including a chunk of her own hair, bubbled sluggishly behind Slughorn, who had eyes for nobody but Harry.

"And you thought of a bezoar all by yourself, did you, Harry?" she asked through gritted teeth.

"That's the individual spirit a real potion-maker needs!" said Slughorn happily, before Harry could reply. "Just like his mother, she had the same intuitive grasp of potion-making, it's undoubtedly from Lily he gets it. . . . Yes, Harry, yes, if you've got a bezoar to hand, of course that would do the trick . . . although as they don't work on everything, and are pretty rare, it's still worth knowing how to mix antidotes. . . ."

The only person in the room looking angrier than Hermione was Malfoy, who, Harry was pleased to see, had spilled something that looked like cat-sick over himself. Before either of them could express their fury that Harry had come top of the class by not doing any work, however, the bell rang.

"Time to pack up!" said Slughorn. "And an extra ten points to Gryffindor for sheer cheek!"

Still chuckling, he waddled back to his desk at the front of the dungeon.

Harry dawdled behind, taking an inordinate amount of time to do up his bag. Neither Ron nor Hermione wished him luck as they left; both looked rather annoyed. At last Harry and Slughorn were the only two left in the room.

"Come on, now, Harry, you'll be late for your next lesson," said Slughorn affably, snapping the gold clasps shut on his dragon-skin briefcase.

"Sir," said Harry, reminding himself irresistibly of Voldemort, "I wanted to ask you something."

"Ask away, then, my dear boy, ask away. . . ."

"Sir, I wondered what you know about . . . about Horcruxes?"

Slughorn froze. His round face seemed to sink in upon itself. He licked his lips and said hoarsely, "What did you say?"

"I asked whether you know anything about Horcruxes, sir. You see —"

"Dumbledore put you up to this," whispered Slughorn. His voice had changed completely. It was not genial anymore, but shocked, terrified. He fumbled in his breast pocket and pulled out a handkerchief, mopping his sweating brow. "Dumbledore's shown you that — that memory. Well? Hasn't he?"

"Yes," said Harry, deciding on the spot that it was best not to lie.

"Yes, of course," said Slughorn quietly, still dabbing at his white face. "Of course . . . well, if you've seen that memory, Harry, you'll know that I don't know anything — *anything*" — he repeated the word forcefully — "about Horcruxes."

He seized his dragon-skin briefcase, stuffed his handkerchief back into his pocket, and marched to the dungeon door.

"Sir," said Harry desperately, "I just thought there might be a bit more to the memory —"

"Did you?" said Slughorn. "Then you were wrong, weren't you? WRONG!"

He bellowed the last word and, before Harry could say another word, slammed the dungeon door behind him.

Neither Ron nor Hermione was at all sympathetic when Harry told them of this disastrous interview. Hermione was still seething at the way Harry had triumphed without doing the work properly. Ron was resentful that Harry hadn't slipped him a bezoar too.

"It would've just looked stupid if we'd both done it!" said Harry irritably. "Look, I had to try and soften him up so I could ask him about Voldemort, didn't I? Oh, will you *get a grip!*" he added in exasperation, as Ron winced at the sound of the name.

Infuriated by his failure and by Ron's and Hermione's attitudes, Harry brooded for the next few days over what to do next about Slughorn. He decided that, for the time being, he would let Slughorn think that he had forgotten all about Horcruxes; it was surely best to lull him into a false sense of security before returning to the attack.

When Harry did not question Slughorn again, the Potions master reverted to his usual affectionate treatment of him, and appeared to have put the matter from his mind. Harry awaited an invitation to one of his little evening parties, determined to accept this time, even if he had to reschedule Quidditch practice. Unfortunately, however, no such invitation arrived. Harry checked with Hermione and Ginny: Neither of them had received an invitation and nor, as far as they knew, had anybody else. Harry could not help wondering whether this meant that Slughorn was not quite as forgetful as he appeared, simply determined to give Harry no additional opportunities to question him.

Meanwhile, the Hogwarts library had failed Hermione for the first time in living memory. She was so shocked, she even forgot that she was annoyed at Harry for his trick with the bezoar.

"I haven't found one single explanation of what Horcruxes do!" she told him. "Not a single one! I've been right through the restricted section and even in the most *horrible* books, where they tell you how to brew the most *gruesome* potions — nothing! All I could find was this, in the introduction to *Magick Moste Evile* — listen — 'Of the Horcrux, wickedest of magical inventions, we shall not speak nor give direction. . . .' I mean, why mention it then?" she said impatiently, slamming the old book shut; it let out a ghostly wail. "Oh, shut up," she snapped, stuffing it back into her bag.

The snow melted around the school as February arrived, to be replaced by cold, dreary wetness. Purplish-gray clouds hung low over the castle and a constant fall of chilly rain made the lawns slippery and muddy. The upshot of this was that the sixth years' first Apparition lesson, which was scheduled for a Saturday morning so that no normal lessons would be missed, took place in the Great Hall instead of in the grounds.

When Harry and Hermione arrived in the Hall (Ron had come

down with Lavender), they found that the tables had disappeared. Rain lashed against the high windows and the enchanted ceiling swirled darkly above them as they assembled in front of Professors McGonagall, Snape, Flitwick, and Sprout — the Heads of Houses — and a small wizard whom Harry took to be the Apparition instructor from the Ministry. He was oddly colorless, with transparent eyelashes, wispy hair, and an insubstantial air, as though a single gust of wind might blow him away. Harry wondered whether constant disappearances and reappearances had somehow diminished his substance, or whether this frail build was ideal for anyone wishing to vanish.

"Good morning," said the Ministry wizard, when all the students had arrived and the Heads of Houses had called for quiet. "My name is Wilkie Twycross and I shall be your Ministry Apparition instructor for the next twelve weeks. I hope to be able to prepare you for your Apparition Tests in this time —"

"Malfoy, be quiet and pay attention!" barked Professor McGonagall.

Everybody looked around. Malfoy had flushed a dull pink; he looked furious as he stepped away from Crabbe, with whom he appeared to have been having a whispered argument. Harry glanced quickly at Snape, who also looked annoyed, though Harry strongly suspected that this was less because of Malfoy's rudeness than the fact that McGonagall had reprimanded one of his House.

"— by which time, many of you may be ready to take your tests," Twycross continued, as though there had been no interruption.

"As you may know, it is usually impossible to Apparate or Disapparate within Hogwarts. The headmaster has lifted this enchantment, purely within the Great Hall, for one hour, so as to enable you to practice. May I emphasize that you will not be able to Apparate outside the walls of this Hall, and that you would be unwise to try.

"I would like each of you to place yourselves now so that you have a clear five feet of space in front of you."

There was a great scrambling and jostling as people separated, banged into each other, and ordered others out of their space. The Heads of Houses moved among the students, marshaling them into position and breaking up arguments.

"Harry, where are you going?" demanded Hermione.

But Harry did not answer; he was moving quickly through the crowd, past the place where Professor Flitwick was making squeaky attempts to position a few Ravenclaws, all of whom wanted to be near the front, past Professor Sprout, who was chivying the Hufflepuffs into line, until, by dodging around Ernie Macmillan, he managed to position himself right at the back of the crowd, directly behind Malfoy, who was taking advantage of the general upheaval to continue his argument with Crabbe, standing five feet away and looking mutinous.

"I don't know how much longer, all right?" Malfoy shot at him, oblivious to Harry standing right behind him. "It's taking longer than I thought it would."

Crabbe opened his mouth, but Malfoy appeared to second-guess what he was going to say. "Look, it's none of your business what I'm doing, Crabbe, you and Goyle just do as you're told and keep a lookout!"

"I tell my friends what I'm up to, if I want them to keep a lookout for me," Harry said, just loud enough for Malfoy to hear him.

Malfoy spun around on the spot, his hand flying to his wand, but at that precise moment the four Heads of House shouted, "Quiet!" and silence fell again. Malfoy turned slowly to face the front again.

"Thank you," said Twycross. "Now then . . ."

He waved his wand. Old-fashioned wooden hoops instantly appeared on the floor in front of every student.

"The important things to remember when Apparating are the three D's!" said Twycross. "Destination, Determination, Deliberation!

"Step one: Fix your mind firmly upon the desired *destination*," said Twycross. "In this case, the interior of your hoop. Kindly concentrate upon that destination now."

Everybody looked around furtively to check that everyone else was staring into their hoop, then hastily did as they were told. Harry gazed at the circular patch of dusty floor enclosed by his hoop and tried hard to think of nothing else. This proved impossible, as he couldn't stop puzzling over what Malfoy was doing that needed lookouts.

"Step two," said Twycross, "focus your *determination* to occupy the visualized space! Let your yearning to enter it flood from your mind to every particle of your body!"

Harry glanced around surreptitiously. A little way to his left, Ernie Macmillan was contemplating his hoop so hard that his face had turned pink; it looked as though he was straining to lay a Quaffle-sized egg. Harry bit back a laugh and hastily returned his gaze to his own hoop.

"Step three," called Twycross, "and only when I give the command . . . Turn on the spot, feeling your way into nothingness, moving with *deliberation*! On my command, now . . . one —"

Harry glanced around again; lots of people were looking positively alarmed at being asked to Apparate so quickly.

"— two —"

Harry tried to fix his thoughts on his hoop again; he had already forgotten what the three D's stood for.

"— THREE!"

Harry spun on the spot, lost balance, and nearly fell over. He was not the only one. The whole Hall was suddenly full of staggering people; Neville was flat on his back; Ernie Macmillan, on the other hand, had done a kind of pirouetting leap into his hoop and looked momentarily thrilled, until he caught sight of Dean Thomas roaring with laughter at him.

"Never mind, never mind," said Twycross dryly, who did not seem to have expected anything better. "Adjust your hoops, please, and back to your original positions. . . ."

The second attempt was no better than the first. The third was just as bad. Not until the fourth did anything exciting happen. There was a horrible screech of pain and everybody looked around, terrified, to see Susan Bones of Hufflepuff wobbling in her hoop with her left leg still standing five feet away where she had started.

The Heads of House converged on her; there was a great bang and a puff of purple smoke, which cleared to reveal Susan sobbing, reunited with her leg but looking horrified.

"Splinching, or the separation of random body parts," said Wilkie Twycross dispassionately, "occurs when the mind is insufficiently *determined*. You must concentrate continuously upon your *destination,* and move, without haste, but with *deliberation . . .* thus."

Twycross stepped forward, turned gracefully on the spot with his arms outstretched, and vanished in a swirl of robes, reappearing at the back of the Hall.

"Remember the three D's," he said, "and try again . . . one — two — three —"

But an hour later, Susan's Splinching was still the most interesting thing that had happened. Twycross did not seem discouraged. Fastening his cloak at his neck, he merely said, "Until next Saturday, everybody, and do not forget: *Destination. Determination. Deliberation.*"

With that, he waved his wand, Vanishing the hoops, and walked out of the Hall accompanied by Professor McGonagall. Talk broke out at once as people began moving toward the entrance hall.

"How did you do?" asked Ron, hurrying toward Harry. "I think I felt something the last time I tried — a kind of tingling in my feet."

"I expect your trainers are too small, Won-Won," said a voice behind them, and Hermione stalked past, smirking.

"I didn't feel anything," said Harry, ignoring this interruption. "But I don't care about that now —"

"What d'you mean, you don't care? Don't you want to learn to Apparate?" said Ron incredulously.

"I'm not fussed, really, I prefer flying," said Harry, glancing over his shoulder to see where Malfoy was, and speeding up as they came into the entrance hall. "Look, hurry up, will you, there's something I want to do. . . ."

Perplexed, Ron followed Harry back to the Gryffindor Tower at a run. They were temporarily detained by Peeves, who had jammed a door on the fourth floor shut and was refusing to let anyone pass until they set fire to their own pants, but Harry and Ron simply turned back and took one of their trusted shortcuts. Within five minutes, they were climbing through the portrait hole.

"Are you going to tell me what we're doing, then?" asked Ron, panting slightly.

"Up here," said Harry, and he crossed the common room and led the way through the door to the boys' staircase.

Their dormitory was, as Harry had hoped, empty. He flung open his trunk and began to rummage in it, while Ron watched impatiently.

"Harry . . ."

"Malfoy's using Crabbe and Goyle as lookouts. He was arguing with Crabbe just now. I want to know — aha."

He had found it, a folded square of apparently blank parchment, which he now smoothed out and tapped with the tip of his wand.

"*I solemnly swear that I am up to no good* . . . or Malfoy is anyway."

At once, the Marauder's Map appeared on the parchment's surface. Here was a detailed plan of every one of the castle's floors and, moving around it, the tiny, labeled black dots that signified each of the castle's occupants.

"Help me find Malfoy," said Harry urgently.

He laid the map upon his bed, and he and Ron leaned over it, searching.

"*There!*" said Ron, after a minute or so. "He's in the Slytherin common room, look . . . with Parkinson and Zabini and Crabbe and Goyle . . ."

Harry looked down at the map, disappointed, but rallied almost at once.

"Well, I'm keeping an eye on him from now on," he said firmly. "And the moment I see him lurking somewhere with Crabbe and Goyle keeping watch outside, it'll be on with the old Invisibility Cloak and off to find out what he's —"

He broke off as Neville entered the dormitory, bringing with him a strong smell of singed material, and began rummaging in his trunk for a fresh pair of pants.

Despite his determination to catch Malfoy out, Harry had no luck at all over the next couple of weeks. Although he consulted the map as often as he could, sometimes making unnecessary visits to the bathroom between lessons to search it, he did not once see Malfoy anywhere suspicious. Admittedly, he spotted Crabbe and Goyle moving around the castle on their own more often than usual, sometimes remaining stationary in deserted corridors, but at these times Malfoy was not only nowhere near them, but impossible to locate on the map at all. This was most mysterious. Harry toyed with the possibility that Malfoy was actually leaving the school grounds, but could not see how he could be doing it, given the very high level of security now operating within the castle. He could only suppose that he was missing Malfoy amongst the hundreds of tiny black dots upon the map. As for the fact that Malfoy, Crabbe, and Goyle appeared to be going their different ways when they were usually inseparable, these things happened as people got older — Ron and Hermione, Harry reflected sadly, were living proof.

February moved toward March with no change in the weather except that it became windy as well as wet. To general indignation, a sign went up on all common room notice boards that the next trip into Hogsmeade had been canceled. Ron was furious.

"It was on my birthday!" he said. "I was looking forward to that!"

"Not a big surprise, though, is it?" said Harry. "Not after what happened to Katie."

She had still not returned from St. Mungo's. What was more, further disappearances had been reported in the *Daily Prophet,* including several relatives of students at Hogwarts.

"But now all I've got to look forward to is stupid Apparition!" said Ron grumpily. "Big birthday treat . . ."

Three lessons on, Apparition was proving as difficult as ever, though a few more people had managed to Splinch themselves. Frustration was running high and there was a certain amount of ill-feeling toward Wilkie Twycross and his three D's, which had inspired a number of nicknames for him, the politest of which were Dogbreath and Dunghead.

"Happy birthday, Ron," said Harry, when they were woken on the first of March by Seamus and Dean leaving noisily for breakfast. "Have a present."

He threw the package across onto Ron's bed, where it joined a small pile of them that must, Harry assumed, have been delivered by house-elves in the night.

"Cheers," said Ron drowsily and, as he ripped off the paper, Harry got out of bed, opened his own trunk, and began rummaging in it for the Marauder's Map, which he hid after every use. He turfed out half the contents of his trunk before he found it hiding beneath the rolled-up socks in which he was still keeping his bottle of lucky potion, Felix Felicis.

"Right," he murmured, taking it back to bed with him, tapping it quietly and murmuring, *"I solemnly swear that I am up to no good,"* so that Neville, who was passing the foot of his bed at the time, would not hear.

"Nice one, Harry!" said Ron enthusiastically, waving the new pair of Quidditch Keeper's gloves Harry had given him.

"No problem," said Harry absentmindedly, as he searched the Slytherin dormitory closely for Malfoy. "Hey . . . I don't think he's in his bed. . . ."

Ron did not answer; he was too busy unwrapping presents, every now and then letting out an exclamation of pleasure.

"Seriously good haul this year!" he announced, holding up a heavy gold watch with odd symbols around the edge and tiny moving stars instead of hands. "See what Mum and Dad got me? Blimey, I think I'll come of age next year too. . . ."

"Cool," muttered Harry, sparing the watch a glance before peering more closely at the map. Where was Malfoy? He did not seem to be at the Slytherin table in the Great Hall, eating breakfast. . . . He was nowhere near Snape, who was sitting in his study. . . . He wasn't in any of the bathrooms or in the hospital wing. . . .

"Want one?" said Ron thickly, holding out a box of Chocolate Cauldrons.

"No thanks," said Harry, looking up. "Malfoy's gone again!"

"Can't have done," said Ron, stuffing a second Cauldron into his mouth as he slid out of bed to get dressed. "Come on, if you don't hurry up, you'll have to Apparate on an empty stomach. . . . Might make it easier, I suppose . . ." Ron looked thoughtfully at the box of Chocolate Cauldrons, then shrugged and helped himself to a third.

Harry tapped the map with his wand, muttered, "Mischief managed," though it hadn't been, and got dressed, thinking hard. There had to be an explanation for Malfoy's periodic disappearances, but he simply could not think what it could be. The best way of finding out would be to tail him, but even with the Invisibility Cloak this was an impractical idea: Harry had lessons, Quidditch practice, homework, and Apparition; he could not follow Malfoy around school all day without his absence being remarked upon.

"Ready?" he said to Ron.

He was halfway to the dormitory door when he realized that Ron had not moved, but was leaning on his bedpost, staring out of the rain-washed window with a strangely unfocused look on his face.

"Ron? Breakfast."

"I'm not hungry."

Harry stared at him.

"I thought you just said — ?"

"Well, all right, I'll come down with you," sighed Ron, "but I don't want to eat."

Harry scrutinized him suspiciously.

"You've just eaten half a box of Chocolate Cauldrons, haven't you?"

"It's not that," Ron sighed again. "You . . . you wouldn't understand."

"Fair enough," said Harry, albeit puzzled, as he turned to open the door.

"Harry!" said Ron suddenly.

"What?"

"Harry, I can't stand it!"

"You can't stand what?" asked Harry, now starting to feel definitely alarmed. Ron was rather pale and looked as though he was about to be sick.

"I can't stop thinking about her!" said Ron hoarsely.

Harry gaped at him. He had not expected this and was not sure he wanted to hear it. Friends they might be, but if Ron started calling Lavender "Lav-Lav," he would have to put his foot down.

"Why does that stop you having breakfast?" Harry asked, trying to inject a note of common sense into the proceedings.

"I don't think she knows I exist," said Ron with a desperate gesture.

"She definitely knows you exist," said Harry, bewildered. "She keeps snogging you, doesn't she?"

Ron blinked. "Who are you talking about?"

"Who are *you* talking about?" said Harry, with an increasing sense that all reason had dropped out of the conversation.

"Romilda Vane," said Ron softly, and his whole face seemed to illuminate as he said it, as though hit by a ray of purest sunlight.

They stared at each other for almost a whole minute, before Harry said, "This is a joke, right? You're joking."

"I think . . . Harry, I think I love her," said Ron in a strangled voice.

"Okay," said Harry, walking up to Ron to get a better look at the glazed eyes and the pallid complexion, "okay . . . Say that again with a straight face."

"I love her," repeated Ron breathlessly. "Have you seen her hair, it's all black and shiny and silky . . . and her eyes? Her big dark eyes? And her —"

"This is really funny and everything," said Harry impatiently, "but joke's over, all right? Drop it."

He turned to leave; he had got two steps toward the door when a crashing blow hit him on the right ear. Staggering, he looked around. Ron's fist was drawn right back; his face was contorted with rage; he was about to strike again.

Harry reacted instinctively; his wand was out of his pocket and the incantation sprang to mind without conscious thought: *Levicorpus!*

Ron yelled as his heel was wrenched upward once more; he dangled helplessly, upside down, his robes hanging off him.

"What was that for?" Harry bellowed.

"You insulted her, Harry! You said it was a joke!" shouted Ron, who was slowly turning purple in the face as all the blood rushed to his head.

"This is insane!" said Harry. "What's got into — ?"

And then he saw the box lying open on Ron's bed, and the truth hit him with the force of a stampeding troll.

"Where did you get those Chocolate Cauldrons?"

"They were a birthday present!" shouted Ron, revolving slowly in midair as he struggled to get free. "I offered you one, didn't I?"

"You just picked them up off the floor, didn't you?"

"They'd fallen off my bed, all right? Let me go!"

"They didn't fall off your bed, you prat, don't you understand? They were mine, I chucked them out of my trunk when I was looking for the map, they're the Chocolate Cauldrons Romilda gave me before Christmas, and they're all spiked with love potion!"

But only one word of this seemed to have registered with Ron.

"Romilda?" he repeated. "Did you say Romilda? Harry — do you know her? Can you introduce me?"

Harry stared at the dangling Ron, whose face now looked tremendously hopeful, and fought a strong desire to laugh. A part of him — the part closest to his throbbing right ear — was quite keen on the idea of letting Ron down and watching him run amok until the effects of the potion wore off. . . . But on the other hand, they were supposed to be friends, Ron had not been himself when he had attacked, and Harry thought that he would deserve another punching if he permitted Ron to declare undying love for Romilda Vane.

"Yeah, I'll introduce you," said Harry, thinking fast. "I'm going to let you down now, okay?"

He sent Ron crashing back to the floor (his ear did hurt quite a lot), but Ron simply bounded to his feet again, grinning.

"She'll be in Slughorn's office," said Harry confidently, leading the way to the door.

"Why will she be in there?" asked Ron anxiously, hurrying to keep up.

"Oh, she has extra Potions lessons with him," said Harry, inventing wildly.

"Maybe I could ask if I can have them with her?" said Ron eagerly.

"Great idea," said Harry.

Lavender was waiting beside the portrait hole, a complication Harry had not foreseen.

"You're late, Won-Won!" she pouted. "I've got you a birthday —"

"Leave me alone," said Ron impatiently. "Harry's going to introduce me to Romilda Vane."

And without another word to her, he pushed his way out of the portrait hole. Harry tried to make an apologetic face to Lavender, but it might have turned out simply amused, because she looked more offended than ever as the Fat Lady swung shut behind them.

Harry had been slightly worried that Slughorn might be at breakfast, but he answered his office door at the first knock, wearing a green velvet dressing gown and matching nightcap and looking rather bleary-eyed.

"Harry," he mumbled. "This is very early for a call. . . . I generally sleep late on a Saturday. . . ."

"Professor, I'm really sorry to disturb you," said Harry as quietly as possible, while Ron stood on tiptoe, attempting to see past Slughorn into his room, "but my friend Ron's swallowed a love potion by mistake. You couldn't make him an antidote, could you? I'd take him to Madam Pomfrey, but we're not supposed to have anything from Weasleys' Wizard Wheezes and, you know . . . awkward questions . . ."

"I'd have thought you could have whipped him up a remedy, Harry, an expert potioneer like you?" asked Slughorn.

"Er," said Harry, somewhat distracted by the fact that Ron was now elbowing him in the ribs in an attempt to force his way into the room, "well, I've never mixed an antidote for a love potion, sir, and by the time I get it right, Ron might've done something serious —"

Helpfully, Ron chose this moment to moan, "I can't see her, Harry — is he hiding her?"

"Was this potion within date?" asked Slughorn, now eyeing Ron with professional interest. "They can strengthen, you know, the longer they're kept."

"That would explain a lot," panted Harry, now positively wrestling with Ron to keep him from knocking Slughorn over. "It's his birthday, Professor," he added imploringly.

"Oh, all right, come in, then, come in," said Slughorn, relenting. "I've got the necessary here in my bag, it's not a difficult antidote. . . ."

Ron burst through the door into Slughorn's overheated, crowded study, tripped over a tasseled footstool, regained his balance by seizing Harry around the neck, and muttered, "She didn't see that, did she?"

"She's not here yet," said Harry, watching Slughorn opening his potion kit and adding a few pinches of this and that to a small crystal bottle.

"That's good," said Ron fervently. "How do I look?"

"Very handsome," said Slughorn smoothly, handing Ron a glass of clear liquid. "Now drink that up, it's a tonic for the nerves, keep you calm when she arrives, you know."

"Brilliant," said Ron eagerly, and he gulped the antidote down noisily.

Harry and Slughorn watched him. For a moment, Ron beamed at them. Then, very slowly, his grin sagged and vanished, to be replaced by an expression of utmost horror.

"Back to normal, then?" said Harry, grinning. Slughorn chuckled. "Thanks a lot, Professor."

"Don't mention it, m'boy, don't mention it," said Slughorn, as Ron collapsed into a nearby armchair, looking devastated. "Pick-me-up, that's what he needs," Slughorn continued, now bustling over to a table loaded with drinks. "I've got butterbeer, I've got wine, I've got one last bottle of this oak-matured mead . . . hmm . . .

meant to give that to Dumbledore for Christmas . . . ah, well . . ."
He shrugged. "He can't miss what he's never had! Why don't we
open it now and celebrate Mr. Weasley's birthday? Nothing like a
fine spirit to chase away the pangs of disappointed love. . . ."

He chortled again, and Harry joined in. This was the first time
he had found himself almost alone with Slughorn since his disastrous first attempt to extract the true memory from him. Perhaps,
if he could just keep Slughorn in a good mood . . . perhaps if they
got through enough of the oak-matured mead . . .

"There you are then," said Slughorn, handing Harry and Ron a
glass of mead each before raising his own. "Well, a very happy
birthday, Ralph —"

"Ron —" whispered Harry.

But Ron, who did not appear to be listening to the toast, had already thrown the mead into his mouth and swallowed it.

There was one second, hardly more than a heartbeat, in which
Harry knew there was something terribly wrong and Slughorn, it
seemed, did not.

"— and may you have many more —"

"Ron!"

Ron had dropped his glass; he half-rose from his chair and then
crumpled, his extremities jerking uncontrollably. Foam was drib-
bling from his mouth, and his eyes were bulging from their sockets.

"Professor!" Harry bellowed. "Do something!"

But Slughorn seemed paralyzed by shock. Ron twitched and
choked: His skin was turning blue.

"What — but —" spluttered Slughorn.

Harry leapt over a low table and sprinted toward Slughorn's
open potion kit, pulling out jars and pouches, while the terrible

sound of Ron's gargling breath filled the room. Then he found it —
the shriveled kidneylike stone Slughorn had taken from him in
Potions.

He hurtled back to Ron's side, wrenched open his jaw, and
thrust the bezoar into his mouth. Ron gave a great shudder, a rattling gasp, and his body became limp and still.

ELF TAILS

S o, all in all, not one of Ron's better birthdays?" said Fred.

It was evening; the hospital wing was quiet, the windows curtained, the lamps lit. Ron's was the only occupied bed. Harry, Hermione, and Ginny were sitting around him; they had spent all day waiting outside the double doors, trying to see inside whenever somebody went in or out. Madam Pomfrey had only let them enter at eight o'clock. Fred and George had arrived at ten past.

"This isn't how we imagined handing over our present," said George grimly, putting down a large wrapped gift on Ron's bedside cabinet and sitting beside Ginny.

"Yeah, when we pictured the scene, he was conscious," said Fred.

"There we were in Hogsmeade, waiting to surprise him —" said George.

"You were in Hogsmeade?" asked Ginny, looking up.

"We were thinking of buying Zonko's," said Fred gloomily. "A Hogsmeade branch, you know, but a fat lot of good it'll do us if you lot aren't allowed out at weekends to buy our stuff anymore. . . . But never mind that now."

He drew up a chair beside Harry and looked at Ron's pale face.

"How exactly did it happen, Harry?"

Harry retold the story he had already recounted, it felt like a hundred times to Dumbledore, to McGonagall, to Madam Pomfrey, to Hermione, and to Ginny.

". . . and then I got the bezoar down his throat and his breathing eased up a bit, Slughorn ran for help, McGonagall and Madam Pomfrey turned up, and they brought Ron up here. They reckon he'll be all right. Madam Pomfrey says he'll have to stay here a week or so . . . keep taking essence of rue . . ."

"Blimey, it was lucky you thought of a bezoar," said George in a low voice.

"Lucky there was one in the room," said Harry, who kept turning cold at the thought of what would have happened if he had not been able to lay hands on the little stone.

Hermione gave an almost inaudible sniff. She had been exceptionally quiet all day. Having hurtled, white-faced, up to Harry outside the hospital wing and demanded to know what had happened, she had taken almost no part in Harry and Ginny's obsessive discussion about how Ron had been poisoned, but merely stood beside them, clench-jawed and frightened-looking, until at last they had been allowed in to see him.

"Do Mum and Dad know?" Fred asked Ginny.

"They've already seen him, they arrived an hour ago — they're in Dumbledore's office now, but they'll be back soon. . . ."

There was a pause while they all watched Ron mumble a little in his sleep.

"So the poison was in the drink?" said Fred quietly.

"Yes," said Harry at once; he could think of nothing else and was glad for the opportunity to start discussing it again. "Slughorn poured it out —"

"Would he have been able to slip something into Ron's glass without you seeing?"

"Probably," said Harry, "but why would Slughorn want to poison Ron?"

"No idea," said Fred, frowning. "You don't think he could have mixed up the glasses by mistake? Meaning to get you?"

"Why would Slughorn want to poison Harry?" asked Ginny.

"I dunno," said Fred, "but there must be loads of people who'd like to poison Harry, mustn't there? 'The Chosen One' and all that?"

"So you think Slughorn's a Death Eater?" said Ginny.

"Anything's possible," said Fred darkly.

"He could be under the Imperius Curse," said George.

"Or he could be innocent," said Ginny. "The poison could have been in the bottle, in which case it was probably meant for Slughorn himself."

"Who'd want to kill Slughorn?"

"Dumbledore reckons Voldemort wanted Slughorn on his side," said Harry. "Slughorn was in hiding for a year before he came to Hogwarts. And . . ." He thought of the memory Dumbledore had not yet been able to extract from Slughorn. "And maybe Voldemort wants him out of the way, maybe he thinks he could be valuable to Dumbledore."

"But you said Slughorn had been planning to give that bottle to Dumbledore for Christmas," Ginny reminded him. "So the poisoner could just as easily have been after Dumbledore."

"Then the poisoner didn't know Slughorn very well," said Hermione, speaking for the first time in hours and sounding as though she had a bad head cold. "Anyone who knew Slughorn would have known there was a good chance he'd keep something that tasty for himself."

"Er-my-nee," croaked Ron unexpectedly from between them.

They all fell silent, watching him anxiously, but after muttering incomprehensibly for a moment he merely started snoring.

The dormitory doors flew open, making them all jump: Hagrid came striding toward them, his hair rain-flecked, his bearskin coat flapping behind him, a crossbow in his hand, leaving a trail of muddy dolphin-sized footprints all over the floor.

"Bin in the forest all day!" he panted. "Aragog's worse, I bin readin' to him — didn' get up ter dinner till jus' now an' then Professor Sprout told me abou' Ron! How is he?"

"Not bad," said Harry. "They say he'll be okay."

"No more than six visitors at a time!" said Madam Pomfrey, hurrying out of her office.

"Hagrid makes six," George pointed out.

"Oh . . . yes . . ." said Madam Pomfrey, who seemed to have been counting Hagrid as several people due to his vastness. To cover her confusion, she hurried off to clear up his muddy footprints with her wand.

"I don' believe this," said Hagrid hoarsely, shaking his great shaggy head as he stared down at Ron. "Jus' don' believe it . . . Look at him lyin' there. . . . Who'd want ter hurt him, eh?"

"That's just what we were discussing," said Harry. "We don't know."

"Someone-couldn' have a grudge against the Gryffindor Quidditch team, could they?" said Hagrid anxiously. "Firs' Katie, now Ron . . ."

"I can't see anyone trying to bump off a Quidditch team," said George.

"Wood might've done the Slytherins if he could've got away with it," said Fred fairly.

"Well, I don't think it's Quidditch, but I think there's a connection between the attacks," said Hermione quietly.

"How d'you work that out?" asked Fred.

"Well, for one thing, they both ought to have been fatal and weren't, although that was pure luck. And for another, neither the poison nor the necklace seems to have reached the person who was supposed to be killed. Of course," she added broodingly, "that makes the person behind this even more dangerous in a way, because they don't seem to care how many people they finish off before they actually reach their victim."

Before anybody could respond to this ominous pronouncement, the dormitory doors opened again and Mr. and Mrs. Weasley hurried up the ward. They had done no more than satisfy themselves that Ron would make a full recovery on their last visit to the ward; now Mrs. Weasley seized hold of Harry and hugged him very tightly. "Dumbledore's told us how you saved him with the bezoar," she sobbed. "Oh, Harry, what can we say? You saved Ginny . . . you saved Arthur . . . now you've saved Ron . . ."

"Don't be . . . I didn't . . ." muttered Harry awkwardly.

"Half our family does seem to owe you their lives, now I stop and think about it," Mr. Weasley said in a constricted voice. "Well, all I can say is that it was a lucky day for the Weasleys when Ron decided to sit in your compartment on the Hogwarts Express, Harry."

Harry could not think of any reply to this and was almost glad when Madam Pomfrey reminded them that there were only supposed to be six visitors around Ron's bed; he and Hermione rose at once to leave and Hagrid decided to go with them, leaving Ron with his family.

"It's terrible," growled Hagrid into his beard, as the three of them walked back along the corridor to the marble staircase. "All this new security, an' kids are still gettin' hurt. . . . Dumbledore's worried sick. . . . He don' say much, but I can tell. . . ."

"Hasn't he got any ideas, Hagrid?" asked Hermione desperately.

"I 'spect he's got hundreds of ideas, brain like his," said Hagrid. "But he doesn' know who sent that necklace nor put poison in that wine, or they'd've bin caught, wouldn' they? Wha' worries me," said Hagrid, lowering his voice and glancing over his shoulder (Harry, for good measure, checked the ceiling for Peeves), "is how long Hogwarts can stay open if kids are bein' attacked. Chamber o' Secrets all over again, isn' it? There'll be panic, more parents takin' their kids outta school, an' nex' thing yeh know the board o' governors . . ."

Hagrid stopped talking as the ghost of a long-haired woman drifted serenely past, then resumed in a hoarse whisper, ". . . the board o' governors'll be talkin' about shuttin' us up fer good."

"Surely not?" said Hermione, looking worried.

"Gotta see it from their point o' view," said Hagrid heavily. "I mean, it's always bin a bit of a risk sendin' a kid ter Hogwarts, hasn' it? Yer expect accidents, don' yeh, with hundreds of underage wizards all locked up tergether, but attempted murder, tha's diff'rent. 'S'no wonder Dumbledore's angry with Sn —"

Hagrid stopped in his tracks, a familiar, guilty expression on what was visible of his face above his tangled black beard.

"What?" said Harry quickly. "Dumbledore's angry with Snape?"

"I never said tha'," said Hagrid, though his look of panic could not have been a bigger giveaway. "Look at the time, it's gettin' on fer midnight, I need ter —"

"Hagrid, why is Dumbledore angry with Snape?" Harry asked loudly.

"Shhhh!" said Hagrid, looking both nervous and angry. "Don' shout stuff like that, Harry, d'yeh wan' me ter lose me job? Mind, I don' suppose yeh'd care, would yeh, not now yeh've given up Care of Mag —"

"Don't try and make me feel guilty, it won't work!" said Harry forcefully. "What's Snape done?"

"I dunno, Harry, I shouldn'ta heard it at all! I — well, I was comin' outta the forest the other evenin' an' I overheard 'em talking — well, arguin'. Didn't like ter draw attention to meself, so I sorta skulked an' tried not ter listen, but it was a — well, a heated discussion an' it wasn' easy ter block it out."

"Well?" Harry urged him, as Hagrid shuffled his enormous feet uneasily.

"Well — I jus' heard Snape sayin' Dumbledore took too much fer granted an' maybe he — Snape — didn' wan' ter do it any-more —"

"Do what?"

"I dunno, Harry, it sounded like Snape was feelin' a bit over-worked, tha's all — anyway, Dumbledore told him flat out he'd agreed ter do it an' that was all there was to it. Pretty firm with him. An' then he said summat abou' Snape makin' investigations in his House, in Slytherin. Well, there's nothin' strange abou' that!" Hagrid added hastily, as Harry and Hermione exchanged looks full of meaning. "All the Heads o' Houses were asked ter look inter that necklace business —"

"Yeah, but Dumbledore's not having rows with the rest of them, is he?" said Harry.

"Look," Hagrid twisted his crossbow uncomfortably in his hands; there was a loud splintering sound and it snapped in two. "I know what yeh're like abou' Snape, Harry, an' I don' want yeh ter go readin' more inter this than there is."

"Look out," said Hermione tersely.

They turned just in time to see the shadow of Argus Filch looming over the wall behind them before the man himself turned the corner, hunchbacked, his jowls aquiver.

"Oho!" he wheezed. "Out of bed so late, this'll mean detention!"

"No it won', Filch," said Hagrid shortly. "They're with me, aren' they?"

"And what difference does that make?" asked Filch obnoxiously.

"I'm a ruddy teacher, aren' I, yeh sneakin' Squib!" said Hagrid, firing up at once.

There was a nasty hissing noise as Filch swelled with fury; Mrs. Norris had arrived, unseen, and was twisting herself sinuously around Filch's skinny ankles.

"Get goin'," said Hagrid out of the corner of his mouth.

Harry did not need telling twice; he and Hermione both hurried off; Hagrid's and Filch's raised voices echoed behind them as they ran. They passed Peeves near the turning into Gryffindor Tower, but he was streaking happily toward the source of the yelling, cackling and calling,

> When there's strife and when there's trouble
> Call on Peevsie, he'll make double!

The Fat Lady was snoozing and not pleased to be woken, but swung forward grumpily to allow them to clamber into the mercifully peaceful and empty common room. It did not seem that people knew about Ron yet; Harry was very relieved: He had been interrogated enough that day. Hermione bade him good night and set off for the girls' dormitory. Harry, however, remained behind, taking a seat beside the fire and looking down into the dying embers.

So Dumbledore had argued with Snape. In spite of all he had told Harry, in spite of his insistence that he trusted Snape completely, he had lost his temper with him. . . . He did not think that Snape had tried hard enough to investigate the Slytherins . . . or, perhaps, to investigate a single Slytherin: Malfoy?

Was it because Dumbledore did not want Harry to do anything foolish, to take matters into his own hands, that he had pretended there was nothing in Harry's suspicions? That seemed likely. It might even be that Dumbledore did not want anything to distract Harry from their lessons, or from procuring that memory from Slughorn. Perhaps Dumbledore did not think it right to confide suspicions about his staff to sixteen-year-olds. . . .

"There you are, Potter!"

Harry jumped to his feet in shock, his wand at the ready. He had been quite convinced that the common room was empty; he had not been at all prepared for a hulking figure to rise suddenly out of a distant chair. A closer look showed him that it was Cormac McLaggen.

"I've been waiting for you to come back," said McLaggen, disregarding Harry's drawn wand. "Must've fallen asleep. Look, I saw them taking Weasley up to the hospital wing earlier. Didn't look like he'll be fit for next week's match."

It took Harry a few moments to realize what McLaggen was talking about.

"Oh . . . right . . . Quidditch," he said, putting his wand back into the belt of his jeans and running a hand wearily through his hair. "Yeah . . . he might not make it."

"Well, then, I'll be playing Keeper, won't I?" said McLaggen.

"Yeah," said Harry. "Yeah, I suppose so. . . ."

He could not think of an argument against it; after all, McLaggen had certainly performed second-best in the trials.

"Excellent," said McLaggen in a satisfied voice. "So when's practice?"

"What? Oh . . . there's one tomorrow evening."

"Good. Listen, Potter, we should have a talk beforehand. I've got some ideas on strategy you might find useful."

"Right," said Harry unenthusiastically. "Well, I'll hear them tomorrow, then. I'm pretty tired now . . . see you . . ."

The news that Ron had been poisoned spread quickly next day, but it did not cause the sensation that Katie's attack had done. People seemed to think that it might have been an accident, given that he had been in the Potions master's room at the time, and that as he had been given an antidote immediately there was no real harm done. In fact, the Gryffindors were generally much more interested in the upcoming Quidditch match against Hufflepuff, for many of them wanted to see Zacharias Smith, who played Chaser on the Hufflepuff team, punished soundly for his commentary during the opening match against Slytherin.

Harry, however, had never been less interested in Quidditch; he was rapidly becoming obsessed with Draco Malfoy. Still checking the Marauder's Map whenever he got a chance, he sometimes made detours to wherever Malfoy happened to be, but had not yet detected him doing anything out of the ordinary. And still there were those inexplicable times when Malfoy simply vanished from the map. . . .

But Harry did not get a lot of time to consider the problem, what with Quidditch practice, homework, and the fact that he was now being dogged wherever he went by Cormac McLaggen and Lavender Brown.

He could not decide which of them was more annoying. McLaggen kept up a constant stream of hints that he would make a better permanent Keeper for the team than Ron, and that now that Harry was seeing him play regularly he would surely come around to this way of thinking too; he was also keen to criticize the other players and provide Harry with detailed training schemes, so that more than once Harry was forced to remind him who was Captain.

Meanwhile, Lavender kept sidling up to Harry to discuss Ron, which Harry found almost more wearing than McLaggen's Quidditch lectures. At first, Lavender had been very annoyed that nobody had thought to tell her that Ron was in the hospital wing — "I mean, I *am* his girlfriend!" — but unfortunately she had now decided to forgive Harry this lapse of memory and was keen to have lots of in-depth chats with him about Ron's feelings, a most uncomfortable experience that Harry would have happily forgone.

"Look, why don't you talk to Ron about all this?" Harry asked, after a particularly long interrogation from Lavender that took in everything from precisely what Ron had said about her new dress robes to whether or not Harry thought that Ron considered his relationship with Lavender to be "serious."

"Well, I would, but he's always asleep when I go and see him!" said Lavender fretfully.

"Is he?" said Harry, surprised, for he had found Ron perfectly alert every time he had been up to the hospital wing, both highly interested in the news of Dumbledore and Snape's row and keen to abuse McLaggen as much as possible.

"Is Hermione Granger still visiting him?" Lavender demanded suddenly.

"Yeah, I think so. Well, they're friends, aren't they?" said Harry uncomfortably.

"Friends, don't make me laugh," said Lavender scornfully. "She didn't talk to him for weeks after he started going out with me! But I suppose she wants to make up with him now he's all *interesting. . . .* "

"Would you call getting poisoned being interesting?" asked Harry. "Anyway — sorry, got to go — there's McLaggen coming for a talk about Quidditch," said Harry hurriedly, and he dashed sideways through a door pretending to be solid wall and sprinted down the shortcut that would take him off to Potions where, thankfully, neither Lavender nor McLaggen could follow him.

On the morning of the Quidditch match against Hufflepuff, Harry dropped in on the hospital wing before heading down to the pitch. Ron was very agitated; Madam Pomfrey would not let him go down to watch the match, feeling it would overexcite him.

"So how's McLaggen shaping up?" he asked Harry nervously, apparently forgetting that he had already asked the same question twice.

"I've told you," said Harry patiently, "he could be world-class and I wouldn't want to keep him. He keeps trying to tell everyone what to do, he thinks he could play every position better than the rest of us. I can't wait to be shot of him. And speaking of getting shot of people," Harry added, getting to his feet and picking up his Firebolt, "will you stop pretending to be asleep when Lavender comes to see you? She's driving me mad as well."

"Oh," said Ron, looking sheepish. "Yeah. All right."

"If you don't want to go out with her anymore, just tell her," said Harry.

"Yeah . . . well . . . it's not that easy, is it?" said Ron. He paused. "Hermione going to look in before the match?" he added casually.

"No, she's already gone down to the pitch with Ginny."

"Oh," said Ron, looking rather glum. "Right. Well, good luck. Hope you hammer McLag — I mean, Smith."

"I'll try," said Harry, shouldering his broom. "See you after the match."

He hurried down through the deserted corridors; the whole school was outside, either already seated in the stadium or heading down toward it. He was looking out of the windows he passed, trying to gauge how much wind they were facing, when a noise ahead made him glance up and he saw Malfoy walking toward him, accompanied by two girls, both of whom looked sulky and resentful.

Malfoy stopped short at the sight of Harry, then gave a short, humorless laugh and continued walking.

"Where're you going?" Harry demanded.

"Yeah, I'm really going to tell you, because it's your business, Potter," sneered Malfoy. "You'd better hurry up, they'll be waiting for 'the Chosen Captain' — 'the Boy Who Scored' — whatever they call you these days."

One of the girls gave an unwilling giggle. Harry stared at her. She blushed. Malfoy pushed past Harry and she and her friend followed at a trot, turning the corner and vanishing from view.

Harry stood rooted on the spot and watched them disappear. This was infuriating; he was already cutting it fine to get to the match on time and yet there was Malfoy, skulking off while the rest of the school was absent: Harry's best chance yet of discovering what Malfoy was up to. The silent seconds trickled past, and Harry remained where he was, frozen, gazing at the place where Malfoy had vanished. . . .

"Where have you been?" demanded Ginny, as Harry sprinted into the changing rooms. The whole team was changed and ready; Coote and Peakes, the Beaters, were both hitting their clubs nervously against their legs.

"I met Malfoy," Harry told her quietly, as he pulled his scarlet robes over his head. "So?"

"So I wanted to know how come he's up at the castle with a couple of girlfriends while everyone else is down here. . . ."

"Does it matter right now?"

"Well, I'm not likely to find out, am I?" said Harry, seizing his Firebolt and pushing his glasses straight. "Come on then!"

And without another word, he marched out onto the pitch to deafening cheers and boos.

There was little wind; the clouds were patchy; every now and then there were dazzling flashes of bright sunlight.

"Tricky conditions!" McLaggen said bracingly to the team. "Coote, Peakes, you'll want to fly out of the sun, so they don't see you coming —"

"I'm the Captain, McLaggen, shut up giving them instructions," said Harry angrily. "Just get up by the goal posts!"

Once McLaggen had marched off, Harry turned to Coote and Peakes.

"Make sure you *do* fly out of the sun," he told them grudgingly.

He shook hands with the Hufflepuff Captain, and then, on Madam Hooch's whistle, kicked off and rose into the air, higher than the rest of his team, streaking around the pitch in search of the Snitch. If he could catch it good and early, there might be a chance he could get back up to the castle, seize the Marauder's Map, and find out what Malfoy was doing. . . .

"And that's Smith of Hufflepuff with the Quaffle," said a dreamy voice, echoing over the grounds. "He did the commentary last time, of course, and Ginny Weasley flew into him, I think probably on purpose, it looked like it. Smith was being quite rude about Gryffindor, I expect he regrets that now he's playing them — oh, look, he's lost the Quaffle, Ginny took it from him, I do like her, she's very nice. . . ."

Harry stared down at the commentator's podium. Surely nobody in their right mind would have let Luna Lovegood commentate? But even from above there was no mistaking that long, dirty-blonde hair, nor the necklace of butterbeer corks. . . . Beside Luna, Professor McGonagall was looking slightly uncomfortable, as though she was indeed having second thoughts about this appointment.

". . . but now that big Hufflepuff player's got the Quaffle from her, I can't remember his name, it's something like Bibble — no, Buggins —"

"It's Cadwallader!" said Professor McGonagall loudly from beside Luna. The crowd laughed.

Harry stared around for the Snitch; there was no sign of it. Moments later, Cadwallader scored. McLaggen had been shouting criticism at Ginny for allowing the Quaffle out of her possession, with the result that he had not noticed the large red ball soaring past his right ear.

"McLaggen, will you pay attention to what you're supposed to be doing and leave everyone else alone!" bellowed Harry, wheeling around to face his Keeper.

"You're not setting a great example!" McLaggen shouted back, red-faced and furious.

"And Harry Potter's now having an argument with his Keeper," said Luna serenely, while both Hufflepuffs and Slytherins below in the crowd cheered and jeered. "I don't think that'll help him find the Snitch, but maybe it's a clever ruse. . . ."

Swearing angrily, Harry spun round and set off around the pitch again, scanning the skies for some sign of the tiny, winged golden ball.

Ginny and Demelza scored a goal apiece, giving the red-and-gold-clad supporters below something to cheer about. Then Cadwallader scored again, making things level, but Luna did not seem to have noticed; she appeared singularly uninterested in such mundane things as the score, and kept attempting to draw the crowd's attention to such things as interestingly shaped clouds and the possibility that Zacharias Smith, who had so far failed to maintain possession of the Quaffle for longer than a minute, was suffering from something called "Loser's Lurgy."

"Seventy-forty to Hufflepuff!" barked Professor McGonagall into Luna's megaphone.

"Is it, already?" said Luna vaguely. "Oh, look! The Gryffindor Keeper's got hold of one of the Beater's bats."

Harry spun around in midair. Sure enough, McLaggen, for reasons best known to himself, had pulled Peakes's bat from him and appeared to be demonstrating how to hit a Bludger toward an oncoming Cadwallader.

"Will you give him back his bat and get back to the goal posts!" roared Harry, pelting toward McLaggen just as McLaggen took a ferocious swipe at the Bludger and mishit it.

A blinding, sickening pain . . . a flash of light . . . distant screams . . . and the sensation of falling down a long tunnel . . .

And the next thing Harry knew, he was lying in a remarkably warm and comfortable bed and looking up at a lamp that was throwing a circle of golden light onto a shadowy ceiling. He raised his head awkwardly. There on his left was a familiar-looking, freckly, red-haired person.

"Nice of you to drop in," said Ron, grinning.

Harry blinked and looked around. Of course: He was in the hospital wing. The sky outside was indigo streaked with crimson. The match must have finished hours ago . . . as had any hope of cornering Malfoy. Harry's head felt strangely heavy; he raised a hand and felt a stiff turban of bandages.

"What happened?"

"Cracked skull," said Madam Pomfrey, bustling up and pushing him back against his pillows. "Nothing to worry about, I mended it at once, but I'm keeping you in overnight. You shouldn't overexert yourself for a few hours."

"I don't want to stay here overnight," said Harry angrily, sitting up and throwing back his covers. "I want to find McLaggen and kill him."

"I'm afraid that would come under the heading of 'overexertion,'" said Madam Pomfrey, pushing him firmly back onto the bed and raising her wand in a threatening manner. "You will stay here until I discharge you, Potter, or I shall call the headmaster."

She bustled back into her office, and Harry sank back into his pillows, fuming.

"D'you know how much we lost by?" he asked Ron through clenched teeth.

"Well, yeah I do," said Ron apologetically. "Final score was three hundred and twenty to sixty."

"Brilliant," said Harry savagely. "Really brilliant! When I get hold of McLaggen —"

"You don't want to get hold of him, he's the size of a troll," said

Ron reasonably. "Personally, I think there's a lot to be said for hexing him with that toenail thing of the Prince's. Anyway, the rest of the team might've dealt with him before you get out of here, they're not happy. . . ."

There was a note of badly suppressed glee in Ron's voice; Harry could tell he was nothing short of thrilled that McLaggen had messed up so badly. Harry lay there, staring up at the patch of light on the ceiling, his recently mended skull not hurting, precisely, but feeling slightly tender underneath all the bandaging.

"I could hear the match commentary from here," said Ron, his voice now shaking with laughter. "I hope Luna always commentates from now on. . . . *Loser's Lurgy* . . ."

But Harry was still too angry to see much humor in the situation, and after a while Ron's snorts subsided.

"Ginny came in to visit while you were unconscious," he said, after a long pause, and Harry's imagination zoomed into overdrive, rapidly constructing a scene in which Ginny, weeping over his lifeless form, confessed her feelings of deep attraction to him while Ron gave them his blessing. . . . "She reckons you only just arrived on time for the match. How come? You left here early enough."

"Oh . . ." said Harry, as the scene in his mind's eye imploded. "Yeah . . . well, I saw Malfoy sneaking off with a couple of girls who didn't look like they wanted to be with him, and that's the second time he's made sure he isn't down on the Quidditch pitch with the rest of the school; he skipped the last match too, remember?" Harry sighed. "Wish I'd followed him now, the match was such a fiasco. . . ."

"Don't be stupid," said Ron sharply. "You couldn't have missed a Quidditch match just to follow Malfoy, you're the Captain!"

"I want to know what he's up to," said Harry. "And don't tell me it's all in my head, not after what I overheard between him and Snape —"

"I never said it was all in your head," said Ron, hoisting himself up on an elbow in turn and frowning at Harry, "but there's no rule saying only one person at a time can be plotting anything in this place! You're getting a bit obsessed with Malfoy, Harry. I mean, thinking about missing a match just to follow him . . ."

"I want to catch him at it!" said Harry in frustration. "I mean, where's he going when he disappears off the map?"

"I dunno . . . Hogsmeade?" suggested Ron, yawning.

"I've never seen him going along any of the secret passageways on the map. I thought they were being watched now anyway?"

"Well then, I dunno," said Ron.

Silence fell between them. Harry stared up at the circle of lamp-light above him, thinking. . . .

If only he had Rufus Scrimgeour's power, he would have been able to set a tail upon Malfoy, but unfortunately Harry did not have an office full of Aurors at his command. . . . He thought fleetingly of trying to set something up with the D.A., but there again was the problem that people would be missed from lessons; most of them, after all, still had full schedules. . . .

There was a low, rumbling snore from Ron's bed. After a while Madam Pomfrey came out of her office, this time wearing a thick dressing gown. It was easiest to feign sleep; Harry rolled over onto his side and listened to all the curtains closing themselves as she waved her wand. The lamps dimmed, and she returned to her office; he heard the door click behind her and knew that she was off to bed.

This was, Harry reflected in the darkness, the third time that he had been brought to the hospital wing because of a Quidditch injury. Last time he had fallen off his broom due to the presence of dementors around the pitch, and the time before that, all the bones had been removed from his arm by the incurably inept Professor Lockhart. . . . That had been his most painful injury by far . . . he remembered the agony of regrowing an armful of bones in one night, a discomfort not eased by the arrival of an unexpected visitor in the middle of the —

Harry sat bolt upright, his heart pounding, his bandage turban askew. He had the solution at last: There *was* a way to have Malfoy followed — how could he have forgotten, why hadn't he thought of it before?

But the question was, how to call him? What did you do?

Quietly, tentatively, Harry spoke into the darkness.

"Kreacher?"

There was a very loud *crack,* and the sounds of scuffling and squeaks filled the silent room. Ron awoke with a yelp.

"What's going — ?"

Harry pointed his wand hastily at the door of Madam Pomfrey's office and muttered, *"Muffliato!"* so that she would not come running. Then he scrambled to the end of his bed for a better look at what was going on.

Two house-elves were rolling around on the floor in the middle of the dormitory, one wearing a shrunken maroon jumper and several woolly hats, the other, a filthy old rag strung over his hips like a loincloth. Then there was another loud bang, and Peeves the Poltergeist appeared in midair above the wrestling elves.

"I was watching that, Potty!" he told Harry indignantly, pointing at the fight below, before letting out a loud cackle. "Look at the ickle creatures squabbling, bitey bitey, punchy punchy —"

"Kreacher will not insult Harry Potter in front of Dobby, no he won't, or Dobby will shut Kreacher's mouth for him!" cried Dobby in a high-pitched voice.

"— kicky, scratchy!" cried Peeves happily, now pelting bits of chalk at the elves to enrage them further. "Tweaky, pokey!"

"Kreacher will say what he likes about his master, oh yes, and what a master he is, filthy friend of Mudbloods, oh, what would poor Kreacher's mistress say — ?"

Exactly what Kreacher's mistress would have said they did not find out, for at that moment Dobby sank his knobbly little fist into Kreacher's mouth and knocked out half of his teeth. Harry and Ron both leapt out of their beds and wrenched the two elves apart, though they continued to try and kick and punch each other, egged on by Peeves, who swooped around the lamp squealing, "Stick your fingers up his nosey, draw his cork and pull his earsies —"

Harry aimed his wand at Peeves and said, *"Langlock!"* Peeves clutched at his throat, gulped, then swooped from the room making obscene gestures but unable to speak, owing to the fact that his tongue had just glued itself to the roof of his mouth.

"Nice one," said Ron appreciatively, lifting Dobby into the air so that his flailing limbs no longer made contact with Kreacher. "That was another Prince hex, wasn't it?"

"Yeah," said Harry, twisting Kreacher's wizened arm into a half nelson. "Right — I'm forbidding you to fight each other! Well,

Kreacher, you're forbidden to fight Dobby. Dobby, I know I'm not allowed to give you orders —"

"Dobby is a free house-elf and he can obey anyone he likes and Dobby will do whatever Harry Potter wants him to do!" said Dobby, tears now streaming down his shriveled little face onto his jumper.

"Okay then," said Harry, and he and Ron both released the elves, who fell to the floor but did not continue fighting.

"Master called me?" croaked Kreacher, sinking into a bow even as he gave Harry a look that plainly wished him a painful death.

"Yeah, I did," said Harry, glancing toward Madam Pomfrey's office door to check that the *Muffliato* spell was still working; there was no sign that she had heard any of the commotion. "I've got a job for you."

"Kreacher will do whatever Master wants," said Kreacher, sinking so low that his lips almost touched his gnarled toes, "because Kreacher has no choice, but Kreacher is ashamed to have such a master, yes —"

"Dobby will do it, Harry Potter!" squeaked Dobby, his tennis-ball-sized eyes still swimming in tears. "Dobby would be honored to help Harry Potter!"

"Come to think of it, it would be good to have both of you," said Harry. "Okay then . . . I want you to tail Draco Malfoy."

Ignoring the look of mingled surprise and exasperation on Ron's face, Harry went on, "I want to know where he's going, who he's meeting, and what he's doing. I want you to follow him around the clock."

"Yes, Harry Potter!" said Dobby at once, his great eyes shining with excitement. "And if Dobby does it wrong, Dobby will throw himself off the topmost tower, Harry Potter!"

"There won't be any need for that," said Harry hastily.

"Master wants me to follow the youngest of the Malfoys?" croaked Kreacher. "Master wants me to spy upon the pure-blood great-nephew of my old mistress?"

"That's the one," said Harry, foreseeing a great danger and determining to prevent it immediately. "And you're forbidden to tip him off, Kreacher, or to show him what you're up to, or to talk to him at all, or to write him messages or . . . or to contact him in any way. Got it?"

He thought he could see Kreacher struggling to see a loophole in the instructions he had just been given and waited. After a moment or two, and to Harry's great satisfaction, Kreacher bowed deeply again and said, with bitter resentment, "Master thinks of everything, and Kreacher must obey him even though Kreacher would much rather be the servant of the Malfoy boy, oh yes. . . ."

"That's settled, then," said Harry. "I'll want regular reports, but make sure I'm not surrounded by people when you turn up. Ron and Hermione are okay. And don't tell anyone what you're doing. Just stick to Malfoy like a couple of wart plasters."

LORD VOLDEMORT'S REQUEST

Harry and Ron left the hospital wing first thing on Monday morning, restored to full health by the ministrations of Madam Pomfrey and now able to enjoy the benefits of having been knocked out and poisoned, the best of which was that Hermione was friends with Ron again. Hermione even escorted them down to breakfast, bringing with her the news that Ginny had argued with Dean. The drowsing creature in Harry's chest suddenly raised its head, sniffing the air hopefully.

"What did they row about?" he asked, trying to sound casual as they turned onto a seventh-floor corridor that was deserted but for a very small girl who had been examining a tapestry of trolls in tutus. She looked terrified at the sight of the approaching sixth years and dropped the heavy brass scales she was carrying.

"It's all right!" said Hermione kindly, hurrying forward to help her. "Here . . ."

She tapped the broken scales with her wand and said, *"Reparo."* The girl did not say thank you, but remained rooted to the spot as they passed and watched them out of sight; Ron glanced back at her.

"I swear they're getting smaller," he said.

"Never mind her," said Harry, a little impatiently. "What did Ginny and Dean row about, Hermione?"

"Oh, Dean was laughing about McLaggen hitting that Bludger at you," said Hermione.

"It must've looked funny," said Ron reasonably.

"It didn't look funny at all!" said Hermione hotly. "It looked terrible and if Coote and Peakes hadn't caught Harry he could have been very badly hurt!"

"Yeah, well, there was no need for Ginny and Dean to split up over it," said Harry, still trying to sound casual. "Or are they still together?"

"Yes, they are — but why are you so interested?" asked Hermione, giving Harry a sharp look.

"I just don't want my Quidditch team messed up again!" he said hastily, but Hermione continued to look suspicious, and he was most relieved when a voice behind them called, "Harry!" giving him an excuse to turn his back on her.

"Oh, hi, Luna."

"I went to the hospital wing to find you," said Luna, rummaging in her bag. "But they said you'd left. . . ."

She thrust what appeared to be a green onion, a large spotted toadstool, and a considerable amount of what looked like cat litter into Ron's hands, finally pulling out a rather grubby scroll of parchment that she handed to Harry.

". . . I've been told to give you this."

It was a small roll of parchment, which Harry recognized at once as another invitation to a lesson with Dumbledore.

"Tonight," he told Ron and Hermione, once he had unrolled it.

"Nice commentary last match!" said Ron to Luna as she took back the green onion, the toadstool, and the cat litter. Luna smiled vaguely.

"You're making fun of me, aren't you?" she said. "Everyone says I was dreadful."

"No, I'm serious!" said Ron earnestly. "I can't remember enjoying commentary more! What is this, by the way?" he added, holding the onionlike object up to eye level.

"Oh, it's a Gurdyroot," she said, stuffing the cat litter and the toadstool back into her bag. "You can keep it if you like, I've got a few of them. They're really excellent for warding off Gulping Plimpies."

And she walked away, leaving Ron chortling, still clutching the Gurdyroot.

"You know, she's grown on me, Luna," he said, as they set off again for the Great Hall. "I know she's insane, but it's in a good —"

He stopped talking very suddenly. Lavender Brown was standing at the foot of the marble staircase looking thunderous.

"Hi," said Ron nervously.

"C'mon," Harry muttered to Hermione, and they sped past, though not before they had heard Lavender say, "Why didn't you tell me you were getting out today? And why was *she* with you?"

Ron looked both sulky and annoyed when he appeared at breakfast half an hour later, and though he sat with Lavender, Harry did not see them exchange a word all the time they were together. Hermione was acting as though she was quite oblivious to all of this, but once or twice Harry saw an inexplicable smirk cross her face. All that day she seemed to be in a particularly good mood, and that evening in the common room she even consented to look over (in other words, finish writing) Harry's Herbology essay, something she had been resolutely refusing to do up to this point, because she had known that Harry would then let Ron copy his work.

"Thanks a lot, Hermione," said Harry, giving her a hasty pat on the back as he checked his watch and saw that it was nearly eight o'clock. "Listen, I've got to hurry or I'll be late for Dumbledore. . . ."

She did not answer, but merely crossed out a few of his feebler sentences in a weary sort of way. Grinning, Harry hurried out through the portrait hole and off to the headmaster's office. The gargoyle leapt aside at the mention of toffee éclairs, and Harry took the spiral staircase two steps at a time, knocking on the door just as a clock within chimed eight.

"Enter," called Dumbledore, but as Harry put out a hand to push the door, it was wrenched open from inside. There stood Professor Trelawney.

"Aha!" she cried, pointing dramatically at Harry as she blinked at him through her magnifying spectacles. "So this is the reason I am to be thrown unceremoniously from your office, Dumbledore!"

"My dear Sybill," said Dumbledore in a slightly exasperated voice, "there is no question of throwing you unceremoniously from anywhere, but Harry does have an appointment, and I really don't think there is any more to be said —"

"Very well," said Professor Trelawney, in a deeply wounded voice. "If you will not banish the usurping nag, so be it. . . .

Perhaps I shall find a school where my talents are better appreciated. . . ."

She pushed past Harry and disappeared down the spiral staircase; they heard her stumble halfway down, and Harry guessed that she had tripped over one of her trailing shawls.

"Please close the door and sit down, Harry," said Dumbledore, sounding rather tired.

Harry obeyed, noticing as he took his usual seat in front of Dumbledore's desk that the Pensieve lay between them once more, as did two more tiny crystal bottles full of swirling memory.

"Professor Trelawney still isn't happy Firenze is teaching, then?" Harry asked.

"No," said Dumbledore, "Divination is turning out to be much more trouble than I could have foreseen, never having studied the subject myself. I cannot ask Firenze to return to the forest, where he is now an outcast, nor can I ask Sybill Trelawney to leave. Between ourselves, she has no idea of the danger she would be in outside the castle. She does not know — and I think it would be unwise to enlighten her — that she made the prophecy about you and Voldemort, you see."

Dumbledore heaved a deep sigh, then said, "But never mind my staffing problems. We have much more important matters to discuss. Firstly — have you managed the task I set you at the end of our previous lesson?"

"Ah," said Harry, brought up short. What with Apparition lessons and Quidditch and Ron being poisoned and getting his skull cracked and his determination to find out what Draco Malfoy was up to, Harry had almost forgotten about the memory Dumbledore had asked him to extract from Professor Slughorn. "Well, I asked Professor Slughorn about it at the end of Potions, sir, but, er, he wouldn't give it to me."

There was a little silence.

"I see," said Dumbledore eventually, peering at Harry over the top of his half-moon spectacles and giving Harry the usual sensation that he was being X-rayed. "And you feel that you have exerted your very best efforts in this matter, do you? That you have exercised all of your considerable ingenuity? That you have left no depth of cunning unplumbed in your quest to retrieve the memory?"

"Well," Harry stalled, at a loss for what to say next. His single attempt to get hold of the memory suddenly seemed embarrassingly feeble. "Well . . . the day Ron swallowed love potion by mistake I took him to Professor Slughorn. I thought maybe if I got Professor Slughorn in a good enough mood —"

"And did that work?" asked Dumbledore.

"Well, no, sir, because Ron got poisoned —"

"— which, naturally, made you forget all about trying to retrieve the memory; I would have expected nothing else, while your best friend was in danger. Once it became clear that Mr. Weasley was going to make a full recovery, however, I would have hoped that you returned to the task I set you. I thought I made it clear to you how very important that memory is. Indeed, I did my best to impress upon you that it is the most crucial memory of all and that we will be wasting our time without it."

A hot, prickly feeling of shame spread from the top of Harry's head all the way down his body. Dumbledore had not raised his voice, he did not even sound angry, but Harry would have preferred him to yell; this cold disappointment was worse than anything.

"Sir," he said, a little desperately, "it isn't that I wasn't bothered or anything, I've just had other — other things . . ."

"Other things on your mind," Dumbledore finished the sentence for him. "I see."

Silence fell between them again, the most uncomfortable silence Harry had ever experienced with Dumbledore; it seemed to go on and on, punctuated only by the little grunting snores of the portrait of Armando Dippet over Dumbledore's head. Harry felt strangely diminished, as though he had shrunk a little since he had entered the room. When he could stand it no longer he said, "Professor Dumbledore, I'm really sorry. I should have done more. . . . I should have realized you wouldn't have asked me to do it if it wasn't really important."

"Thank you for saying that, Harry," said Dumbledore quietly. "May I hope, then, that you will give this matter higher priority from now on? There will be little point in our meeting after tonight unless we have that memory."

"I'll do it, sir, I'll get it from him," he said earnestly.

"Then we shall say no more about it just now," said Dumbledore more kindly, "but continue with our story where we left off. You remember where that was?"

"Yes, sir," said Harry quickly. "Voldemort killed his father and his grandparents and made it look as though his Uncle Morfin did it. Then he went back to Hogwarts and he asked . . . he asked Professor Slughorn about Horcruxes," he mumbled shamefacedly.

"Very good," said Dumbledore. "Now, you will remember, I hope, that I told you at the very outset of these meetings of ours that we would be entering the realms of guesswork and speculation?"

"Yes, sir."

"Thus far, as I hope you agree, I have shown you reasonably firm sources of fact for my deductions as to what Voldemort did until the age of seventeen?"

Harry nodded.

"But now, Harry," said Dumbledore, "now things become murkier and stranger. If it was difficult to find evidence about the boy Riddle, it has been almost impossible to find anyone prepared to reminisce about the man Voldemort. In fact, I doubt whether there is a soul alive, apart from himself, who could give us a full account of his life since he left Hogwarts. However, I have two last memories that I would like to share with you." Dumbledore indicated the two little crystal bottles gleaming beside the Pensieve. "I shall then be glad of your opinion as to whether the conclusions I have drawn from them seem likely."

The idea that Dumbledore valued his opinion this highly made Harry feel even more deeply ashamed that he had failed in the task of retrieving the Horcrux memory, and he shifted guiltily in his seat as Dumbledore raised the first of the two bottles to the light and examined it.

"I hope you are not tired of diving into other people's memories, for they are curious recollections, these two," he said. "This first one came from a very old house-elf by the name of Hokey. Before we see what Hokey witnessed, I must quickly recount how Lord Voldemort left Hogwarts.

"He reached the seventh year of his schooling with, as you might have expected, top grades in every examination he had taken. All around him, his classmates were deciding which jobs they were to pursue once they had left Hogwarts. Nearly everybody expected spectacular things from Tom Riddle, prefect, Head Boy, winner of the Award for Special Services to the School. I know that several teachers, Professor Slughorn amongst them, suggested that he join the Ministry of Magic, offered to set up appointments, put him in touch with useful contacts. He refused all offers. The next thing the staff knew, Voldemort was working at Borgin and Burkes."

"At Borgin and Burkes?" Harry repeated, stunned.

"At Borgin and Burkes," repeated Dumbledore calmly. "I think you will see what attractions the place held for him when we have entered Hokey's memory. But this was not Voldemort's first choice of job. Hardly anyone knew of it at the time — I was one of the few in whom the then headmaster confided — but Voldemort first approached Professor Dippet and asked whether he could remain at Hogwarts as a teacher."

"He wanted to stay here? Why?" asked Harry, more amazed still.

"I believe he had several reasons, though he confided none of them to Professor Dippet," said Dumbledore. "Firstly, and very importantly, Voldemort was, I believe, more attached to this school than he has ever been to a person. Hogwarts was where he had been happiest; the first and only place he had felt at home."

Harry felt slightly uncomfortable at these words, for this was exactly how he felt about Hogwarts too.

"Secondly, the castle is a stronghold of ancient magic. Undoubtedly Voldemort had penetrated many more of its secrets than most of the students who pass through the place, but he may have felt that there were still mysteries to unravel, stores of magic to tap.

"And thirdly, as a teacher, he would have had great power and influence over young witches and wizards. Perhaps he had gained the idea from Professor Slughorn, the teacher with whom he was on best terms, who had demonstrated how influential a role a teacher can play. I do not imagine for an instant that Voldemort envisaged spending the rest of his life at Hogwarts, but I do think that he saw it as a useful recruiting ground, and a place where he might begin to build himself an army."

"But he didn't get the job, sir?"

"No, he did not. Professor Dippet told him that he was too young at eighteen, but invited him to reapply in a few years, if he still wished to teach."

"How did you feel about that, sir?" asked Harry hesitantly.

"Deeply uneasy," said Dumbledore. "I had advised Armando against the appointment — I did not give the reasons I have given you, for Professor Dippet was very fond of Voldemort and convinced of his honesty. But I did not want Lord Voldemort back at this school, and especially not in a position of power."

"Which job did he want, sir? What subject did he want to teach?"

Somehow, Harry knew the answer even before Dumbledore gave it.

"Defense Against the Dark Arts. It was being taught at the time by an old Professor by the name of Galatea Merrythought, who had been at Hogwarts for nearly fifty years.

"So Voldemort went off to Borgin and Burkes, and all the staff who had admired him said what a waste it was, a brilliant young wizard like that, working in a shop. However, Voldemort was no mere assistant. Polite and handsome and clever, he was soon given particular jobs of the type that only exist in a place like Borgin and Burkes, which specializes, as you know, Harry, in objects with unusual and powerful properties. Voldemort was sent to persuade people to part with their treasures for sale by the partners, and he was, by all accounts, unusually gifted at doing this."

"I'll bet he was," said Harry, unable to contain himself.

"Well, quite," said Dumbledore, with a faint smile. "And now it is time to hear from Hokey the house-elf, who worked for a very old, very rich witch by the name of Hepzibah Smith."

Dumbledore tapped a bottle with his wand, the cork flew out, and he tipped the swirling memory into the Pensieve, saying as he did so, "After you, Harry."

Harry got to his feet and bent once more over the rippling silver contents of the stone basin until his face touched them. He tumbled through dark nothingness and landed in a sitting room in front of an immensely fat old lady wearing an elaborate ginger wig and a brilliant pink set of robes that flowed all around her, giving her the look of a melting iced cake. She was looking into a small jeweled mirror and dabbing rouge onto her already scarlet cheeks with a large powder puff, while the tiniest and oldest house-elf Harry had ever seen laced her fleshy feet into tight satin slippers.

"Hurry up, Hokey!" said Hepzibah imperiously. "He said he'd come at four, it's only a couple of minutes to and he's never been late yet!"

She tucked away her powder puff as the house-elf straightened up. The top of the elf's head barely reached the seat of Hepzibah's chair, and her papery skin hung off her frame just like the crisp linen sheet she wore draped like a toga.

"How do I look?" said Hepzibah, turning her head to admire the various angles of her face in the mirror.

"Lovely, madam," squeaked Hokey.

Harry could only assume that it was down in Hokey's contract that she must lie through her teeth when asked this question, because Hepzibah Smith looked a long way from lovely in his opinion.

A tinkling doorbell rang and both mistress and elf jumped.

"Quick, quick, he's here, Hokey!" cried Hepzibah and the elf scurried out of the room, which was so crammed with objects that it was difficult to see how anybody could navigate their way across it without knocking over at least a dozen things: There were cabinets full of little lacquered boxes, cases full of gold-embossed books, shelves of orbs and celestial globes, and many flourishing potted plants in brass containers. In fact, the room looked like a cross between a magical antique shop and a conservatory.

The house-elf returned within minutes, followed by a tall young man Harry had no difficulty whatsoever in recognizing as Voldemort. He was plainly dressed in a black suit; his hair was a little longer than it had been at school and his cheeks were hollowed, but all of this suited him; he looked more handsome than ever. He picked his way through the cramped room with an air that showed he had visited many times before and bowed low over Hepzibah's fat little hand, brushing it with his lips.

"I brought you flowers," he said quietly, producing a bunch of roses from nowhere.

"You naughty boy, you shouldn't have!" squealed old Hepzibah, though Harry noticed that she had an empty vase standing ready on the nearest little table. "You do spoil this old lady, Tom. . . . Sit down, sit down. . . . Where's Hokey? Ah . . ."

The house-elf had come dashing back into the room carrying a tray of little cakes, which she set at her mistress's elbow.

"Help yourself, Tom," said Hepzibah, "I know how you love my cakes. Now, how are you? You look pale. They overwork you at that shop, I've said it a hundred times. . . ."

Voldemort smiled mechanically and Hepzibah simpered.

"Well, what's your excuse for visiting this time?" she asked, batting her lashes.

"Mr. Burke would like to make an improved offer for the goblin-made armor," said Voldemort. "Five hundred Galleons, he feels it is a more than fair —"

"Now, now, not so fast, or I'll think you're only here for my trinkets!" pouted Hepzibah.

"I am ordered here because of them," said Voldemort quietly. "I am only a poor assistant, madam, who must do as he is told. Mr. Burke wishes me to inquire —"

"Oh, Mr. Burke, phooey!" said Hepzibah, waving a little hand. "I've something to show you that I've never shown Mr. Burke! Can you keep a secret, Tom? Will you promise you won't tell Mr. Burke I've got it? He'd never let me rest if he knew I'd shown it to you, and I'm not selling, not to Burke, not to anyone! But you, Tom, you'll appreciate it for its history, not how many Galleons you can get for it."

"I'd be glad to see anything Miss Hepzibah shows me," said Voldemort quietly, and Hepzibah gave another girlish giggle.

"I had Hokey bring it out for me. . . . Hokey, where are you? I want to show Mr. Riddle our *finest* treasure. . . . In fact, bring both, while you're at it. . . ."

"Here, madam," squeaked the house-elf, and Harry saw two leather boxes, one on top of the other, moving across the room as if of their own volition, though he knew the tiny elf was holding them over her head as she wended her way between tables, pouffes, and footstools.

"Now," said Hepzibah happily, taking the boxes from the elf, laying them in her lap, and preparing to open the topmost one, "I think you'll like this, Tom. . . . Oh, if my family knew I was showing you. . . . They can't wait to get their hands on this!"

She opened the lid. Harry edged forward a little to get a better view and saw what looked like a small golden cup with two finely wrought handles.

"I wonder whether you know what it is, Tom? Pick it up, have a good look!" whispered Hepzibah, and Voldemort stretched out a long-fingered hand and lifted the cup by one handle out of its snug silken wrappings. Harry thought he saw a red gleam in his dark eyes. His greedy expression was curiously mirrored on Hepzibah's face, except that her tiny eyes were fixed upon Voldemort's handsome features.

"A badger," murmured Voldemort, examining the engraving upon the cup. "Then this was . . . ?"

"Helga Hufflepuff's, as you very well know, you clever boy!" said Hepzibah, leaning forward with a loud creaking of corsets and actually pinching his hollow cheek. "Didn't I tell you I was distantly descended? This has been handed down in the family for years and years. Lovely, isn't it? And all sorts of powers it's supposed to possess too, but I haven't tested them thoroughly, I just keep it nice and safe in here. . . ."

She hooked the cup back off Voldemort's long forefinger and restored it gently to its box, too intent upon settling it carefully back into position to notice the shadow that crossed Voldemort's face as the cup was taken away.

"Now then," said Hepzibah happily, "where's Hokey? Oh yes, there you are — take that away now, Hokey."

The elf obediently took the boxed cup, and Hepzibah turned her attention to the much flatter box in her lap.

"I think you'll like this even more, Tom," she whispered. "Lean in a little, dear boy, so you can see. . . . Of course, Burke knows I've got this one, I bought it from him, and I daresay he'd love to get it back when I'm gone. . . ."

She slid back the fine filigree clasp and flipped open the box. There upon the smooth crimson velvet lay a heavy golden locket.

Voldemort reached out his hand, without invitation this time, and held it up to the light, staring at it.

"Slytherin's mark," he said quietly, as the light played upon an ornate, serpentine *S*.

"That's right!" said Hepzibah, delighted, apparently, at the sight of Voldemort gazing at her locket, transfixed. "I had to pay an arm and a leg for it, but I couldn't let it pass, not a real treasure like that, had to have it for my collection. Burke bought it, apparently, from a ragged-looking woman who seemed to have stolen it, but had no idea of its true value —"

There was no mistaking it this time: Voldemort's eyes flashed scarlet at the words, and Harry saw his knuckles whiten on the locket's chain.

"— I daresay Burke paid her a pittance but there you are. . . . Pretty, isn't it? And again, all kinds of powers attributed to it, though I just keep it nice and safe. . . ."

She reached out to take the locket back. For a moment, Harry thought Voldemort was not going to let go of it, but then it had slid through his fingers and was back in its red velvet cushion.

"So there you are, Tom, dear, and I hope you enjoyed that!"

She looked him full in the face and for the first time, Harry saw her foolish smile falter.

"Are you all right, dear?"

"Oh yes," said Voldemort quietly. "Yes, I'm very well. . . ."

"I thought — but a trick of the light, I suppose —" said Hepzibah, looking unnerved, and Harry guessed that she too had seen the momentary red gleam in Voldemort's eyes. "Here, Hokey, take these away and lock them up again. . . . The usual enchantments . . ."

"Time to leave, Harry," said Dumbledore quietly, and as the little elf bobbed away bearing the boxes, Dumbledore grasped Harry once again above the elbow and together they rose up through oblivion and back to Dumbledore's office.

"Hepzibah Smith died two days after that little scene," said Dumbledore, resuming his seat and indicating that Harry should do the same. "Hokey the house-elf was convicted by the Ministry of poisoning her mistress's evening cocoa by accident."

"No way!" said Harry angrily.

"I see we are of one mind," said Dumbledore. "Certainly, there are many similarities between this death and that of the Riddles. In both cases, somebody else took the blame, someone who had a clear memory of having caused the death —"

"Hokey confessed?"

"She remembered putting something in her mistress's cocoa that turned out not to be sugar, but a lethal and little-known poison," said Dumbledore. "It was concluded that she had not meant to do it, but being old and confused —"

"Voldemort modified her memory, just like he did with Morfin!"

"Yes, that is my conclusion too," said Dumbledore. "And, just as with Morfin, the Ministry was predisposed to suspect Hokey —"

"— because she was a house-elf," said Harry. He had rarely felt more in sympathy with the society Hermione had set up, S.P.E.W.

"Precisely," said Dumbledore. "She was old, she admitted to having tampered with the drink, and nobody at the Ministry bothered to inquire further. As in the case of Morfin, by the time I traced her and managed to extract this memory, her life was almost over — but her memory, of course, proves nothing except that Voldemort knew of the existence of the cup and the locket.

"By the time Hokey was convicted, Hepzibah's family had realized that two of her greatest treasures were missing. It took them a while to be sure of this, for she had many hiding places, having always guarded her collection most jealously. But before they were sure beyond doubt that the cup and the locket were both gone, the assistant who had worked at Borgin and Burkes, the young man who had visited Hepzibah so regularly and charmed her so well, had resigned his post and vanished. His superiors had no idea where he had gone; they were as surprised as anyone at his disappearance. And that was the last that was seen or heard of Tom Riddle for a very long time.

"Now," said Dumbledore, "if you don't mind, Harry, I want to pause once more to draw your attention to certain points of our story. Voldemort had committed another murder; whether it was his first since he killed the Riddles, I do not know, but I think it was. This time, as you will have seen, he killed not for revenge, but for gain. He wanted the two fabulous trophies that poor, besotted, old woman showed him. Just as he had once robbed the other children at his orphanage, just as he had stolen his Uncle Morfin's ring, so he ran off now with Hepzibah's cup and locket."

"But," said Harry, frowning, "it seems mad. . . . Risking everything, throwing away his job, just for those . . ."

"Mad to you, perhaps, but not to Voldemort," said Dumbledore. "I hope you will understand in due course exactly what those objects meant to him, Harry, but you must admit that it is not difficult to imagine that he saw the locket, at least, as rightfully his."

"The locket maybe," said Harry, "but why take the cup as well?"

"It had belonged to another of Hogwarts's founders," said Dumbledore. "I think he still felt a great pull toward the school and that he could not resist an object so steeped in Hogwarts history. There were other reasons, I think. . . . I hope to be able to demonstrate them to you in due course.

"And now for the very last recollection I have to show you, at least until you manage to retrieve Professor Slughorn's memory for us. Ten years separate Hokey's memory and this one, ten years during which we can only guess at what Lord Voldemort was doing. . . ."

Harry got to his feet once more as Dumbledore emptied the last memory into the Pensieve.

"Whose memory is it?" he asked.

"Mine," said Dumbledore.

And Harry dived after Dumbledore through the shifting silver mass, landing in the very office he had just left. There was Fawkes slumbering happily on his perch, and there behind the desk was Dumbledore, who looked very similar to the Dumbledore standing beside Harry, though both hands were whole and undamaged and his face was, perhaps, a little less lined. The one difference between the present-day office and this one was that it was snowing in the past; bluish flecks were drifting past the window in the dark and building up on the outside ledge.

The younger Dumbledore seemed to be waiting for something, and sure enough, moments after their arrival, there was a knock on the door and he said, "Enter."

Harry let out a hastily stifled gasp. Voldemort had entered the room. His features were not those Harry had seen emerge from the great stone cauldron almost two years ago: They were not as snake-like, the eyes were not yet scarlet, the face not yet masklike, and yet he was no longer handsome Tom Riddle. It was as though his features had been burned and blurred; they were waxy and oddly distorted, and the whites of the eyes now had a permanently bloody look, though the pupils were not yet the slits that Harry knew they would become. He was wearing a long black cloak, and his face was as pale as the snow glistening on his shoulders.

The Dumbledore behind the desk showed no sign of surprise. Evidently this visit had been made by appointment.

"Good evening, Tom," said Dumbledore easily. "Won't you sit down?"

"Thank you," said Voldemort, and he took the seat to which Dumbledore had gestured — the very seat, by the looks of it, that Harry had just vacated in the present. "I heard that you had become headmaster," he said, and his voice was slightly higher and colder than it had been. "A worthy choice."

"I am glad you approve," said Dumbledore, smiling. "May I offer you a drink?"

"That would be welcome," said Voldemort. "I have come a long way."

Dumbledore stood and swept over to the cabinet where he now kept the Pensieve, but which then was full of bottles. Having handed Voldemort a goblet of wine and poured one for himself, he returned to the seat behind his desk.

"So, Tom . . . to what do I owe the pleasure?"

Voldemort did not answer at once, but merely sipped his wine.

"They do not call me 'Tom' anymore," he said. "These days, I am known as —"

"I know what you are known as," said Dumbledore, smiling pleasantly. "But to me, I'm afraid, you will always be Tom Riddle. It is one of the irritating things about old teachers. I am afraid that they never quite forget their charges' youthful beginnings."

He raised his glass as though toasting Voldemort, whose face remained expressionless. Nevertheless, Harry felt the atmosphere in the room change subtly: Dumbledore's refusal to use Voldemort's chosen name was a refusal to allow Voldemort to dictate the terms of the meeting, and Harry could tell that Voldemort took it as such.

"I am surprised you have remained here so long," said Voldemort after a short pause. "I always wondered why a wizard such as yourself never wished to leave school."

"Well," said Dumbledore, still smiling, "to a wizard such as myself, there can be nothing more important than passing on ancient skills, helping hone young minds. If I remember correctly, you once saw the attraction of teaching too."

"I see it still," said Voldemort. "I merely wondered why you — who are so often asked for advice by the Ministry, and who have twice, I think, been offered the post of Minister —"

"Three times at the last count, actually," said Dumbledore. "But the Ministry never attracted me as a career. Again, something we have in common, I think."

Voldemort inclined his head, unsmiling, and took another sip of wine. Dumbledore did not break the silence that stretched between them now, but waited, with a look of pleasant expectancy, for Voldemort to talk first.

"I have returned," he said, after a little while, "later, perhaps, than Professor Dippet expected . . . but I have returned, nevertheless, to request again what he once told me I was too young to have. I have come to you to ask that you permit me to return to this castle, to teach. I think you must know that I have seen and done much since I left this place. I could show and tell your students things they can gain from no other wizard."

Dumbledore considered Voldemort over the top of his own goblet for a while before speaking.

"Yes, I certainly do know that you have seen and done much since leaving us," he said quietly. "Rumors of your doings have reached your old school, Tom. I should be sorry to believe half of them."

Voldemort's expression remained impassive as he said, "Greatness inspires envy, envy engenders spite, spite spawns lies. You must know this, Dumbledore."

"You call it 'greatness,' what you have been doing, do you?" asked Dumbledore delicately.

"Certainly," said Voldemort, and his eyes seemed to burn red. "I have experimented; I have pushed the boundaries of magic further, perhaps, than they have ever been pushed —"

"Of some kinds of magic," Dumbledore corrected him quietly. "Of some. Of others, you remain . . . forgive me . . . woefully ignorant."

For the first time, Voldemort smiled. It was a taut leer, an evil thing, more threatening than a look of rage.

"The old argument," he said softly. "But nothing I have seen in the world has supported your famous pronouncements that love is more powerful than my kind of magic, Dumbledore."

"Perhaps you have been looking in the wrong places," suggested Dumbledore.

"Well, then, what better place to start my fresh researches than here, at Hogwarts?" said Voldemort. "Will you let me return? Will you let me share my knowledge with your students? I place myself and my talents at your disposal. I am yours to command."

Dumbledore raised his eyebrows. "And what will become of those whom *you* command? What will happen to those who call themselves — or so rumor has it — the Death Eaters?"

Harry could tell that Voldemort had not expected Dumbledore to know this name; he saw Voldemort's eyes flash red again and the slitlike nostrils flare.

"My friends," he said, after a moment's pause, "will carry on without me, I am sure."

"I am glad to hear that you consider them friends," said Dumbledore. "I was under the impression that they are more in the order of servants."

"You are mistaken," said Voldemort.

"Then if I were to go to the Hog's Head tonight, I would not find a group of them — Nott, Rosier, Mulciber, Dolohov — awaiting your return? Devoted friends indeed, to travel this far with you on a snowy night, merely to wish you luck as you attempted to secure a teaching post."

There could be no doubt that Dumbledore's detailed knowledge of those with whom he was traveling was even less welcome to Voldemort; however, he rallied almost at once.

"You are omniscient as ever, Dumbledore."

"Oh no, merely friendly with the local barmen," said Dumbledore lightly. "Now, Tom . . ."

Dumbledore set down his empty glass and drew himself up in his seat, the tips of his fingers together in a very characteristic gesture.

"Let us speak openly. Why have you come here tonight, surrounded by henchmen, to request a job we both know you do not want?"

Voldemort looked coldly surprised. "A job I do not want? On the contrary, Dumbledore, I want it very much."

"Oh, you want to come back to Hogwarts, but you do not want to teach any more than you wanted to when you were eighteen. What is it you're after, Tom? Why not try an open request for once?"

Voldemort sneered. "If you do not want to give me a job —"

"Of course I don't," said Dumbledore. "And I don't think for a moment you expected me to. Nevertheless, you came here, you asked, you must have had a purpose."

Voldemort stood up. He looked less like Tom Riddle than ever, his features thick with rage. "This is your final word?"

"It is," said Dumbledore, also standing.

"Then we have nothing more to say to each other."

"No, nothing," said Dumbledore, and a great sadness filled his face. "The time is long gone when I could frighten you with a burning wardrobe and force you to make repayment for your crimes. But I wish I could, Tom. . . . I wish I could. . . ."

For a second, Harry was on the verge of shouting a pointless warning: He was sure that Voldemort's hand had twitched toward his pocket and his wand; but then the moment had passed, Voldemort had turned away, the door was closing, and he was gone.

Harry felt Dumbledore's hand close over his arm again and moments later, they were standing together on almost the same spot, but there was no snow building on the window ledge, and Dumbledore's hand was blackened and dead-looking once more.

"Why?" said Harry at once, looking up into Dumbledore's face. "Why did he come back? Did you ever find out?"

"I have ideas," said Dumbledore, "but no more than that."

"What ideas, sir?"

"I shall tell you, Harry, when you have retrieved that memory from Professor Slughorn," said Dumbledore. "When you have that last piece of the jigsaw, everything will, I hope, be clear . . . to both of us."

Harry was still burning with curiosity and even though Dumbledore had walked to the door and was holding it open for him, he did not move at once.

"Was he after the Defense Against the Dark Arts job again, sir? He didn't say. . . ."

"Oh, he definitely wanted the Defense Against the Dark Arts job," said Dumbledore. "The aftermath of our little meeting proved that. You see, we have never been able to keep a Defense Against the Dark Arts teacher for longer than a year since I refused the post to Lord Voldemort."

THE UNKNOWABLE ROOM

Harry wracked his brains over the next week as to how he was to persuade Slughorn to hand over the true memory, but nothing in the nature of a brain wave occurred and he was reduced to doing what he did increasingly these days when at a loss: poring over his Potions book, hoping that the Prince would have scribbled something useful in a margin, as he had done so many times before.

"You won't find anything in there," said Hermione firmly, late on Sunday evening.

"Don't start, Hermione," said Harry. "If it hadn't been for the Prince, Ron wouldn't be sitting here now."

"He would if you'd just listened to Snape in our first year," said Hermione dismissively.

Harry ignored her. He had just found an incantation (*"Sectumsempra!"*) scrawled in a margin above the intriguing words "For

Enemies," and was itching to try it out, but thought it best not to in front of Hermione. Instead, he surreptitiously folded down the corner of the page.

They were sitting beside the fire in the common room; the only other people awake were fellow sixth years. There had been a certain amount of excitement earlier when they had come back from dinner to find a new sign on the notice board that announced the date for their Apparition Test. Those who would be seventeen on or before the first test date, the twenty-first of April, had the option of signing up for additional practice sessions, which would take place (heavily supervised) in Hogsmeade.

Ron had panicked on reading this notice; he had still not managed to Apparate and feared he would not be ready for the test. Hermione, who had now achieved Apparition twice, was a little more confident, but Harry, who would not be seventeen for another four months, could not take the test whether ready or not.

"At least you can Apparate, though!" said Ron tensely. "You'll have no trouble come July!"

"I've only done it once," Harry reminded him; he had finally managed to disappear and rematerialize inside his hoop during their previous lesson.

Having wasted a lot of time worrying aloud about Apparition, Ron was now struggling to finish a viciously difficult essay for Snape that Harry and Hermione had already completed. Harry fully expected to receive low marks on his, because he had disagreed with Snape on the best way to tackle dementors, but he did not care: Slughorn's memory was the most important thing to him now.

"I'm telling you, the stupid Prince isn't going to be able to help you with this, Harry!" said Hermione, more loudly. "There's only one way to force someone to do what you want, and that's the Imperius Curse, which is illegal —"

"Yeah, I know that, thanks," said Harry, not looking up from the book. "That's why I'm looking for something different. Dumbledore says Veritaserum won't do it, but there might be something else, a potion or a spell. . . ."

"You're going about it the wrong way," said Hermione. "Only you can get the memory, Dumbledore says. That must mean you can persuade Slughorn where other people can't. It's not a question of slipping him a potion, anyone could do that —"

"How d'you spell 'belligerent'?" said Ron, shaking his quill very hard while staring at his parchment. "It can't be B — U — M —"

"No, it isn't," said Hermione, pulling Ron's essay toward her. "And 'augury' doesn't begin O — R — G either. What kind of quill are you using?"

"It's one of Fred and George's Spell-Check ones . . . but I think the charm must be wearing off. . . ."

"Yes, it must," said Hermione, pointing at the title of his essay, "because we were asked how we'd deal with dementors, not 'Dugbogs,' and I don't remember you changing your name to 'Roonil Wazlib' either."

"Ah no!" said Ron, staring horror-struck at the parchment. "Don't say I'll have to write the whole thing out again!"

"It's okay, we can fix it," said Hermione, pulling the essay toward her and taking out her wand.

"I love you, Hermione," said Ron, sinking back in his chair, rubbing his eyes wearily.

Hermione turned faintly pink, but merely said, "Don't let Lavender hear you saying that."

"I won't," said Ron into his hands. "Or maybe I will . . . then she'll ditch me . . ."

"Why don't you ditch her if you want to finish it?" asked Harry.

"You haven't ever chucked anyone, have you?" said Ron. "You and Cho just —"

"Sort of fell apart, yeah," said Harry.

"Wish that would happen with me and Lavender," said Ron gloomily, watching Hermione silently tapping each of his misspelled words with the end of her wand, so that they corrected themselves on the page. "But the more I hint I want to finish it, the tighter she holds on. It's like going out with the giant squid."

"There," said Hermione, some twenty minutes later, handing back Ron's essay.

"Thanks a million," said Ron. "Can I borrow your quill for the conclusion?"

Harry, who had found nothing useful in the Half-Blood Prince's notes so far, looked around; the three of them were now the only ones left in the common room, Seamus having just gone up to bed cursing Snape and his essay. The only sounds were the crackling of the fire and Ron scratching out one last paragraph on dementors using Hermione's quill. Harry had just closed the Half-Blood Prince's book, yawning, when —

Crack.

Hermione let out a little shriek; Ron spilled ink all over his freshly completed essay, and Harry said, "Kreacher!"

The house-elf bowed low and addressed his own gnarled toes.

"Master said he wanted regular reports on what the Malfoy boy is doing, so Kreacher has come to give —"

Crack.

Dobby appeared alongside Kreacher, his tea-cozy hat askew.

"Dobby has been helping too, Harry Potter!" he squeaked, casting Kreacher a resentful look. "And Kreacher ought to tell Dobby when he is coming to see Harry Potter so they can make their reports together!"

"What is this?" asked Hermione, still looking shocked by these sudden appearances. "What's going on, Harry?"

Harry hesitated before answering, because he had not told Hermione about setting Kreacher and Dobby to tail Malfoy; house-elves were always such a touchy subject with her.

"Well . . . they've been following Malfoy for me," he said.

"Night and day," croaked Kreacher.

"Dobby has not slept for a week, Harry Potter!" said Dobby proudly, swaying where he stood.

Hermione looked indignant.

"You haven't slept, Dobby? But surely, Harry, you didn't tell him not to —"

"No, of course I didn't," said Harry quickly. "Dobby, you can sleep, all right? But has either of you found out anything?" he hastened to ask, before Hermione could intervene again.

"Master Malfoy moves with a nobility that befits his pure blood," croaked Kreacher at once. "His features recall the fine bones of my mistress and his manners are those of —"

"Draco Malfoy is a bad boy!" squeaked Dobby angrily. "A bad boy who — who —"

He shuddered from the tassel of his tea cozy to the toes of his socks and then ran at the fire, as though about to dive into it;

Harry, to whom this was not entirely unexpected, caught him around the middle and held him fast. For a few seconds Dobby struggled, then went limp.

"Thank you, Harry Potter," he panted. "Dobby still finds it difficult to speak ill of his old masters. . . ."

Harry released him; Dobby straightened his tea cozy and said defiantly to Kreacher, "But Kreacher should know that Draco Malfoy is not a good master to a house-elf!"

"Yeah, we don't need to hear about you being in love with Malfoy," Harry told Kreacher. "Let's fast forward to where he's actually been going."

Kreacher bowed again, looking furious, and then said, "Master Malfoy eats in the Great Hall, he sleeps in a dormitory in the dungeons, he attends his classes in a variety of —"

"Dobby, you tell me," said Harry, cutting across Kreacher. "Has he been going anywhere he shouldn't have?"

"Harry Potter, sir," squeaked Dobby, his great orblike eyes shining in the firelight, "the Malfoy boy is breaking no rules that Dobby can discover, but he is still keen to avoid detection. He has been making regular visits to the seventh floor with a variety of other students, who keep watch for him while he enters —"

"The Room of Requirement!" said Harry, smacking himself hard on the forehead with *Advanced Potion-Making*. Hermione and Ron stared at him. "That's where he's been sneaking off to! That's where he's doing . . . whatever he's doing! And I bet that's why he's been disappearing off the map — come to think of it, I've never seen the Room of Requirement on there!"

"Maybe the Marauders never knew the room was there," said Ron.

"I think it'll be part of the magic of the room," said Hermione. "If you need it to be Unplottable, it will be."

"Dobby, have you managed to get in to have a look at what Malfoy's doing?" said Harry eagerly.

"No, Harry Potter, that is impossible," said Dobby.

"No, it's not," said Harry at once. "Malfoy got into our headquarters there last year, so I'll be able to get in and spy on him, no problem."

"But I don't think you will, Harry," said Hermione slowly. "Malfoy already knew exactly how we were using the room, didn't he, because that stupid Marietta had blabbed. He needed the room to become the headquarters of the D.A., so it did. But you don't know what the room becomes when Malfoy goes in there, so you don't know what to ask it to transform into."

"There'll be a way around that," said Harry dismissively. "You've done brilliantly, Dobby."

"Kreacher's done well too," said Hermione kindly; but far from looking grateful, Kreacher averted his huge, bloodshot eyes and croaked at the ceiling, "The Mudblood is speaking to Kreacher, Kreacher will pretend he cannot hear —"

"Get out of it," Harry snapped at him, and Kreacher made one last deep bow and Disapparated. "You'd better go and get some sleep too, Dobby."

"Thank you, Harry Potter, sir!" squeaked Dobby happily, and he too vanished.

"How good's this?" said Harry enthusiastically, turning to Ron and Hermione the moment the room was elf-free again. "We know where Malfoy's going! We've got him cornered now!"

"Yeah, it's great," said Ron glumly, who was attempting to mop up the sodden mass of ink that had recently been an almost completed essay. Hermione pulled it toward her and began siphoning the ink off with her wand.

"But what's all this about him going up there with a 'variety of students'?" said Hermione. "How many people are in on it? You wouldn't think he'd trust lots of them to know what he's doing. . . ."

"Yeah, that is weird," said Harry, frowning. "I heard him telling Crabbe it wasn't Crabbe's business what he was doing . . . so what's he telling all these . . . all these . . ."

Harry's voice tailed away; he was staring at the fire.

"God, I've been stupid," he said quietly. "It's obvious, isn't it? There was a great vat of it down in the dungeon. . . . He could've nicked some any time during that lesson. . . ."

"Nicked what?" said Ron.

"Polyjuice Potion. He stole some of the Polyjuice Potion Slughorn showed us in our first Potions lesson. . . . There aren't a whole variety of students standing guard for Malfoy . . . it's just Crabbe and Goyle as usual. . . . Yeah, it all fits!" said Harry, jumping up and starting to pace in front of the fire. "They're stupid enough to do what they're told even if he won't tell them what he's up to . . . but he doesn't want them to be seen lurking around outside the Room of Requirement, so he's got them taking Polyjuice to make them look like other people. . . . Those two girls I saw him with when he missed Quidditch — ha! Crabbe and Goyle!"

"Do you mean to say," said Hermione in a hushed voice, "that that little girl whose scales I repaired — ?"

"Yeah, of course!" said Harry loudly, staring at her. "Of course! Malfoy must've been inside the room at the time, so she — what am I talking about? — *he* dropped the scales to tell Malfoy not to come out, because there was someone there! And there was that girl who dropped the toadspawn too! We've been walking past him all the time and not realizing it!"

"He's got Crabbe and Goyle transforming into girls?" guffawed Ron. "Blimey . . . No wonder they don't look too happy these days. . . . I'm surprised they don't tell him to stuff it. . . ."

"Well, they wouldn't, would they, if he's shown them his Dark Mark?" said Harry.

"Hmmm . . . the Dark Mark we don't know exists," said Hermione skeptically, rolling up Ron's dried essay before it could come to any more harm and handing it to him.

"We'll see," said Harry confidently.

"Yes, we will," Hermione said, getting to her feet and stretching. "But, Harry, before you get all excited, I still don't think you'll be able to get into the Room of Requirement without knowing what's there first. And I don't think you should forget" — she heaved her bag onto her shoulder and gave him a very serious look — "that what you're *supposed* to be concentrating on is getting that memory from Slughorn. Good night."

Harry watched her go, feeling slightly disgruntled. Once the door to the girls' dormitories had closed behind her he rounded on Ron.

"What d'you think?"

"Wish I could Disapparate like a house-elf," said Ron, staring at the spot where Dobby had vanished. "I'd have that Apparition Test in the bag."

Harry did not sleep well that night. He lay awake for what felt like hours, wondering how Malfoy was using the Room of Requirement and what he, Harry, would see when he went in there the following day, for whatever Hermione said, Harry was sure that if Malfoy had been able to see the headquarters of the D.A., he would be able to see Malfoy's . . . what could it be? A meeting place? A hideout? A storeroom? A workshop? Harry's mind worked feverishly and his dreams, when he finally fell asleep, were broken and disturbed by images of Malfoy, who turned into Slughorn, who turned into Snape. . . .

Harry was in a state of great anticipation over breakfast the following morning; he had a free period before Defense Against the Dark Arts and was determined to spend it trying to get into the Room of Requirement. Hermione was rather ostentatiously showing no interest in his whispered plans for forcing entry into the room, which irritated Harry, because he thought she might be a lot of help if she wanted to.

"Look," he said quietly, leaning forward and putting a hand on the *Daily Prophet,* which she had just removed from a post owl, to stop her from opening it and vanishing behind it. "I haven't forgotten about Slughorn, but I haven't got a clue how to get that memory off him, and until I get a brain wave why shouldn't I find out what Malfoy's doing?"

"I've already told you, you need to *persuade* Slughorn," said Hermione. "It's not a question of tricking him or bewitching him, or Dumbledore could have done it in a second. Instead of messing around outside the Room of Requirement" — she jerked the *Prophet* out from under Harry's hand and unfolded it to look at the front page — "you should go and find Slughorn and start appealing to his better nature."

"Anyone we know — ?" asked Ron, as Hermione scanned the headlines.

"Yes!" said Hermione, causing both Harry and Ron to gag on their breakfast. "But it's all right, he's not dead — it's Mundungus, he's been arrested and sent to Azkaban! Something to do with impersonating an Inferius during an attempted burglary . . . and someone called Octavius Pepper has vanished. . . . Oh, and how horrible, a nine-year-old boy has been arrested for trying to kill his grandparents, they think he was under the Imperius Curse. . . ."

They finished their breakfast in silence. Hermione set off immediately for Ancient Runes; Ron for the common room, where he still had to finish his conclusion on Snape's dementor essay; and Harry for the corridor on the seventh floor and the stretch of wall opposite the tapestry of Barnabas the Barmy teaching trolls to do ballet.

Harry slipped on his Invisibility Cloak once he had found an empty passage, but he need not have bothered. When he reached his destination he found it deserted. Harry was not sure whether his chances of getting inside the room were better with Malfoy inside it or out, but at least his first attempt was not going to be complicated by the presence of Crabbe or Goyle pretending to be an eleven-year-old girl.

He closed his eyes as he approached the place where the Room of Requirement's door was concealed. He knew what he had to do; he had become most accomplished at it last year. Concentrating with all his might he thought, *I need to see what Malfoy's doing in here. . . . I need to see what Malfoy's doing in here. . . . I need to see what Malfoy's doing in here. . . .*

Three times he walked past the door; then, his heart pounding with excitement, he opened his eyes and faced it —

But he was still looking at a stretch of mundanely blank wall.

He moved forward and gave it an experimental push. The stone remained solid and unyielding.

"Okay," said Harry aloud. "Okay . . . I thought the wrong thing. . . ."

He pondered for a moment then set off again, eyes closed, concentrating as hard as he could.

I need to see the place where Malfoy keeps coming secretly. . . . I need to see the place where Malfoy keeps coming secretly. . . .

After three walks past, he opened his eyes expectantly.

There was no door.

"Oh, come off it," he told the wall irritably. "That was a clear instruction. . . . Fine . . ."

He thought hard for several minutes before striding off once more.

I need you to become the place you become for Draco Malfoy. . . .

He did not immediately open his eyes when he had finished his patrolling; he was listening hard, as though he might hear the door pop into existence. He heard nothing, however, except the distant twittering of birds outside. He opened his eyes.

There was still no door.

Harry swore. Someone screamed. He looked around to see a gaggle of first years running back around the corner, apparently under the impression that they had just encountered a particularly foulmouthed ghost.

Harry tried every variation of "I need to see what Draco Malfoy is doing inside you" that he could think of for a whole hour, at the end of which he was forced to concede that Hermione might have had a point: The room simply did not want to open for him. Frustrated and annoyed, he set off for Defense Against the Dark Arts, pulling off his Invisibility Cloak and stuffing it into his bag as he went.

"Late again, Potter," said Snape coldly, as Harry hurried into the candlelit classroom. "Ten points from Gryffindor."

Harry scowled at Snape as he flung himself into the seat beside Ron; half the class was still on its feet, taking out books and organizing their things; he could not be much later than any of them.

"Before we start, I want your dementor essays," said Snape, waving his wand carelessly, so that twenty-five scrolls of parchment soared into the air and landed in a neat pile on his desk. "And I hope for your sakes they are better than the tripe I had to endure on resisting the Imperius Curse. Now, if you will all open your books to page — what is it, Mr. Finnigan?"

"Sir," said Seamus, "I've been wondering, how do you tell the difference between an Inferius and a ghost? Because there was something in the paper about an Inferius —"

"No, there wasn't," said Snape in a bored voice.

"But sir, I heard people talking —"

"If you had actually read the article in question, Mr. Finnigan, you would have known that the so-called Inferius was nothing but a smelly sneak thief by the name of Mundungus Fletcher."

"I thought Snape and Mundungus were on the same side," muttered Harry to Ron and Hermione. "Shouldn't he be upset Mundungus has been arrest —"

"But Potter seems to have a lot to say on the subject," said Snape, pointing suddenly at the back of the room, his black eyes fixed on Harry. "Let us ask Potter how we would tell the difference between an Inferius and a ghost."

The whole class looked around at Harry, who hastily tried to recall what Dumbledore had told him the night that they had gone to visit Slughorn.

"Er — well — ghosts are transparent —" he said.

"Oh, very good," interrupted Snape, his lip curling. "Yes, it is easy to see that nearly six years of magical education have not been wasted on you, Potter. *'Ghosts are transparent.'*"

Pansy Parkinson let out a high-pitched giggle. Several other people were smirking. Harry took a deep breath and continued calmly, though his insides were boiling, "Yeah, ghosts are transparent, but Inferi are dead bodies, aren't they? So they'd be solid —"

"A five-year-old could have told us as much," sneered Snape. "The Inferius is a corpse that has been reanimated by a Dark wizard's spells. It is not alive, it is merely used like a puppet to do the wizard's bidding. A ghost, as I trust that you are all aware by now, is the imprint of a departed soul left upon the earth . . . and of course, as Potter so wisely tells us, *transparent.*"

"Well, what Harry said is the most useful if we're trying to tell them apart!" said Ron. "When we come face-to-face with one down a dark alley, we're going to be having a shufti to see if it's solid, aren't we, we're not going to be asking, 'Excuse me, are you the imprint of a departed soul?'"

There was a ripple of laughter, instantly quelled by the look Snape gave the class.

"Another ten points from Gryffindor," said Snape. "I would expect nothing more sophisticated from you, Ronald Weasley, the boy so solid he cannot Apparate half an inch across a room."

"No!" whispered Hermione, grabbing Harry's arm as he opened his mouth furiously. "There's no point, you'll just end up in detention again, leave it!"

"Now open your books to page two hundred and thirteen," said Snape, smirking a little, "and read the first two paragraphs on the Cruciatus Curse. . . ."

Ron was very subdued all through the class. When the bell sounded at the end of the lesson, Lavender caught up with Ron and Harry (Hermione mysteriously melted out of sight as she approached) and abused Snape hotly for his jibe about Ron's Apparition, but this seemed to merely irritate Ron, and he shook her off by making a detour into the boys' bathroom with Harry.

"Snape's right, though, isn't he?" said Ron, after staring into a cracked mirror for a minute or two. "I dunno whether it's worth me taking the test. I just can't get the hang of Apparition."

"You might as well do the extra practice sessions in Hogsmeade and see where they get you," said Harry reasonably. "It'll be more interesting than trying to get into a stupid hoop anyway. Then, if you're still not — you know — as good as you'd like to be, you can postpone the test, do it with me over the summ — Myrtle, this is the boys' bathroom!"

The ghost of a girl had risen out of the toilet in a cubicle behind them and was now floating in midair, staring at them through thick, white, round glasses.

"Oh," she said glumly. "It's you two."

"Who were you expecting?" said Ron, looking at her in the mirror.

"Nobody," said Myrtle, picking moodily at a spot on her chin. "He said he'd come back and see me, but then *you* said you'd pop in and visit me too" — she gave Harry a reproachful look — "and I haven't seen you for months and months. I've learned not to expect too much from boys."

"I thought you lived in that girls' bathroom?" said Harry, who had been careful to give the place a wide berth for some years now.

"I do," she said, with a sulky little shrug, "but that doesn't mean I can't *visit* other places. I came and saw you in your bath once, remember?"

"Vividly," said Harry.

"But I thought he liked me," she said plaintively. "Maybe if you two left, he'd come back again. . . . We had lots in common. . . . I'm sure he felt it. . . ."

And she looked hopefully toward the door.

"When you say you had lots in common," said Ron, sounding rather amused now, "d'you mean he lives in an S-bend too?"

"No," said Myrtle defiantly, her voice echoing loudly around the old tiled bathroom. "I mean he's sensitive, people bully him too, and he feels lonely and hasn't got anybody to talk to, and he's not afraid to show his feelings and cry!"

"There's been a boy in here crying?" said Harry curiously. "A young boy?"

"Never you mind!" said Myrtle, her small, leaky eyes fixed on Ron, who was now definitely grinning. "I promised I wouldn't tell anyone, and I'll take his secret to the —"

"— not the grave, surely?" said Ron with a snort. "The sewers, maybe . . ."

Myrtle gave a howl of rage and dived back into the toilet, causing water to slop over the sides and onto the floor. Goading Myrtle seemed to have put fresh heart into Ron.

"You're right," he said, swinging his schoolbag back over his shoulder, "I'll do the practice sessions in Hogsmeade before I decide about taking the test."

And so the following weekend, Ron joined Hermione and the rest of the sixth years who would turn seventeen in time to take the test in a fortnight. Harry felt rather jealous watching them all get ready to go into the village; he missed making trips there, and it was a particularly fine spring day, one of the first clear skies they had seen in a long time. However, he had decided to use the time to attempt another assault on the Room of Requirement.

"You'd do better," said Hermione, when he confided this plan to Ron and her in the entrance hall, "to go straight to Slughorn's office and try and get that memory from him."

"I've been trying!" said Harry crossly, which was perfectly true. He had lagged behind after every Potions lesson that week in an attempt to corner Slughorn, but the Potions master always left the dungeon so fast that Harry had not been able to catch him. Twice, Harry had gone to his office and knocked, but received no reply, though on the second occasion he was sure he had heard the quickly stifled sounds of an old gramophone.

"He doesn't want to talk to me, Hermione! He can tell I've been trying to get him on his own again, and he's not going to let it happen!"

"Well, you've just got to keep at it, haven't you?"

The short queue of people waiting to file past Filch, who was doing his usual prodding act with the Secrecy Sensor, moved forward a few steps and Harry did not answer in case he was overheard by the caretaker. He wished Ron and Hermione both luck, then turned and climbed the marble staircase again, determined, whatever Hermione said, to devote an hour or two to the Room of Requirement.

Once out of sight of the entrance hall, Harry pulled the Marauder's Map and his Invisibility Cloak from his bag. Having concealed himself, he tapped the map, murmured, *"I solemnly swear that I am up to no good,"* and scanned it carefully.

As it was Sunday morning, nearly all the students were inside their various common rooms, the Gryffindors in one tower, the Ravenclaws in another, the Slytherins in the dungeons, and the Hufflepuffs in the basement near the kitchens. Here and there a stray person meandered around the library or up a corridor. . . . There were a few people out in the grounds . . . and there, alone in the seventh-floor corridor, was Gregory Goyle. There was no sign of the Room of Requirement, but Harry was not worried about that; if Goyle was standing guard outside it, the room was open, whether the map was aware of it or not. He therefore sprinted up the stairs, slowing down only when he reached the corner into the corridor, when he began to creep, very slowly, toward the very same little girl, clutching her heavy brass scales, that Hermione had so kindly helped a fortnight before. He waited until he was right behind her before bending very low and whispering, "Hello . . . you're very pretty, aren't you?"

Goyle gave a high-pitched scream of terror, threw the scales up into the air, and sprinted away, vanishing from sight long before the sound of the scales smashing had stopped echoing around the corridor. Laughing, Harry turned to contemplate the blank wall behind which, he was sure, Draco Malfoy was now standing frozen, aware that someone unwelcome was out there, but not daring to make an appearance. It gave Harry a most agreeable feeling of power as he tried to remember what form of words he had not yet tried.

Yet this hopeful mood did not last long. Half an hour later, having tried many more variations of his request to see what Malfoy was up to, the wall was just as doorless as ever. Harry felt frustrated beyond belief; Malfoy might be just feet away from him, and there was still not the tiniest shred of evidence as to what he was doing in there. Losing his patience completely, Harry ran at the wall and kicked it.

"OUCH!"

He thought he might have broken his toe; as he clutched it and hopped on one foot, the Invisibility Cloak slipped off him.

"Harry?"

He spun around, one-legged, and toppled over. There, to his utter astonishment, was Tonks, walking toward him as though she frequently strolled up this corridor.

"What're you doing here?" he said, scrambling to his feet again; why did she always have to find him lying on the floor?

"I came to see Dumbledore," said Tonks.

Harry thought she looked terrible: thinner than usual, her mouse-colored hair lank.

"His office isn't here," said Harry, "it's round the other side of the castle, behind the gargoyle —"

"I know," said Tonks. "He's not there. Apparently he's gone away again."

"Has he?" said Harry, putting his bruised foot gingerly back on the floor. "Hey — you don't know where he goes, I suppose?"

"No," said Tonks.

"What did you want to see him about?"

"Nothing in particular," said Tonks, picking, apparently unconsciously, at the sleeve of her robe. "I just thought he might know what's going on. . . . I've heard rumors . . . people getting hurt . . ."

"Yeah, I know, it's all been in the papers," said Harry. "That little kid trying to kill his —"

"The *Prophet*'s often behind the times," said Tonks, who didn't seem to be listening to him. "You haven't had any letters from anyone in the Order recently?"

"No one from the Order writes to me anymore," said Harry, "not since Sirius —"

He saw that her eyes had filled with tears.

"I'm sorry," he muttered awkwardly. "I mean . . . I miss him, as well. . . ."

"What?" said Tonks blankly, as though she had not heard him. "Well . . . I'll see you around, Harry . . ."

And she turned abruptly and walked back down the corridor, leaving Harry to stare after her. After a minute or so, he pulled the Invisibility Cloak on again and resumed his efforts to get into the Room of Requirement, but his heart was not in it. Finally, a hollow feeling in his stomach and the knowledge that Ron and Hermione would soon be back for lunch made him abandon the attempt and leave the corridor to Malfoy who, hopefully, would be too afraid to leave for some hours to come.

He found Ron and Hermione in the Great Hall, already halfway through an early lunch.

"I did it — well, kind of!" Ron told Harry enthusiastically when he caught sight of him. "I was supposed to be Apparating to outside Madam Puddifoot's Tea Shop and I overshot it a bit, ended up near Scrivenshaft's, but at least I moved!"

"Good one," said Harry. "How'd you do, Hermione?"

"Oh, she was perfect, obviously," said Ron, before Hermione could answer. "Perfect deliberation, divination, and desperation or whatever the hell it is — we all went for a quick drink in the Three Broomsticks after and you should've heard Twycross going on about her — I'll be surprised if he doesn't pop the question soon —"

"And what about you?" asked Hermione, ignoring Ron. "Have you been up at the Room of Requirement all this time?"

"Yep," said Harry. "And guess who I ran into up there? Tonks!"

"Tonks?" repeated Ron and Hermione together, looking surprised.

"Yeah, she said she'd come to visit Dumbledore. . . ."

"If you ask me," said Ron once Harry had finished describing his conversation with Tonks, "she's cracking up a bit. Losing her nerve after what happened at the Ministry."

"It's a bit odd," said Hermione, who for some reason looked very concerned. "She's supposed to be guarding the school, why's she suddenly abandoning her post to come and see Dumbledore when he's not even here?"

"I had a thought," said Harry tentatively. He felt strange about voicing it; this was much more Hermione's territory than his. "You don't think she can have been . . . you know . . . in love with Sirius?"

Hermione stared at him.

"What on earth makes you say that?"

"I dunno," said Harry, shrugging, "but she was nearly crying when I mentioned his name . . . and her Patronus is a big four-legged thing now. . . . I wondered whether it hadn't become . . . you know . . . him."

"It's a thought," said Hermione slowly. "But I still don't know why she'd be bursting into the castle to see Dumbledore, if that's really why she was here. . . ."

"Goes back to what I said, doesn't it?" said Ron, who was now shoveling mashed potato into his mouth. "She's gone a bit funny.

Lost her nerve. Women," he said wisely to Harry, "they're easily upset."

"And yet," said Hermione, coming out of her reverie, "I doubt you'd find a *woman* who sulked for half an hour because Madam Rosmerta didn't laugh at their joke about the hag, the Healer, and the *Mimbulus mimbletonia*."

Ron scowled.

CHAPTER TWENTY-TWO

AFTER THE BURIAL

Patches of bright blue sky were beginning to appear over the castle turrets, but these signs of approaching summer did not lift Harry's mood. He had been thwarted, both in his attempts to find out what Malfoy was doing, and in his efforts to start a conversation with Slughorn that might lead, somehow, to Slughorn handing over the memory he had apparently suppressed for decades.

"For the last time, just forget about Malfoy," Hermione told Harry firmly.

They were sitting with Ron in a sunny corner of the courtyard after lunch. Hermione and Ron were both clutching a Ministry of Magic leaflet — *Common Apparition Mistakes and How to Avoid Them* — for they were taking their tests that very afternoon, but by and large the leaflets had not proved soothing to the nerves.

Ron gave a start and tried to hide behind Hermione as a girl came around the corner.

"It isn't Lavender," said Hermione wearily.

"Oh, good," said Ron, relaxing.

"Harry Potter?" said the girl. "I was asked to give you this."

"Thanks . . ."

Harry's heart sank as he took the small scroll of parchment. Once the girl was out of earshot he said, "Dumbledore said we wouldn't be having any more lessons until I got the memory!"

"Maybe he wants to check on how you're doing?" suggested Hermione, as Harry unrolled the parchment; but rather than finding Dumbledore's long, narrow, slanted writing he saw an untidy sprawl, very difficult to read due to the presence of large blotches on the parchment where the ink had run.

> Dear Harry, Ron, and Hermione,
>
> Aragog died last night. Harry and Ron, you met him, and you know how special he was. Hermione, I know you'd have liked him. It would mean a lot to me if you'd nip down for the burial later this evening. I'm planning on doing it round dusk, that was his favorite time of day. I know you're not supposed to be out that late, but you can use the cloak. Wouldn't ask, but I can't face it alone.
>
> Hagrid

"Look at this," said Harry, handing the note to Hermione.

"Oh, for heaven's sake," she said, scanning it quickly and passing it to Ron, who read it through looking increasingly incredulous.

"He's *mental*!" he said furiously. "That thing told its mates to eat

Harry and me! Told them to help themselves! And now Hagrid expects us to go down there and cry over its horrible hairy body!"

"It's not just that," said Hermione. "He's asking us to leave the castle at night and he knows security's a million times tighter and how much trouble we'd be in if we were caught."

"We've been down to see him by night before," said Harry.

"Yes, but for something like this?" said Hermione. "We've risked a lot to help Hagrid out, but after all — Aragog's dead. If it were a question of saving him —"

"— I'd want to go even less," said Ron firmly. "You didn't meet him, Hermione. Believe me, being dead will have improved him a lot."

Harry took the note back and stared down at all the inky blotches all over it. Tears had clearly fallen thick and fast upon the parchment. . . .

"Harry, you *can't* be thinking of going," said Hermione. "It's such a pointless thing to get detention for."

Harry sighed. "Yeah, I know," he said. "I s'pose Hagrid'll have to bury Aragog without us."

"Yes, he will," said Hermione, looking relieved. "Look, Potions will be almost empty this afternoon, with us all off doing our tests. . . . Try and soften Slughorn up a bit then!"

"Fifty-seventh time lucky, you think?" said Harry bitterly.

"Lucky," said Ron suddenly. "Harry, that's it — get lucky!"

"What d'you mean?"

"Use your lucky potion!"

"Ron, that's — that's it!" said Hermione, sounding stunned. "Of course! Why didn't I think of it?"

Harry stared at them both. "Felix Felicis?" he said. "I dunno . . . I was sort of saving it. . . ."

"What for?" demanded Ron incredulously.

"What on earth is more important than this memory, Harry?" asked Hermione.

Harry did not answer. The thought of that little golden bottle had hovered on the edges of his imagination for some time; vague and unformulated plans that involved Ginny splitting up with Dean, and Ron somehow being happy to see her with a new boyfriend, had been fermenting in the depths of his brain, unacknowledged except during dreams or the twilight time between sleeping and waking. . . .

"Harry? Are you still with us?" asked Hermione.

"Wha — ? Yeah, of course," he said, pulling himself together. "Well . . . okay. If I can't get Slughorn to talk this afternoon, I'll take some Felix and have another go this evening."

"That's decided, then," said Hermione briskly, getting to her feet and performing a graceful pirouette. "Destination . . . determination . . . deliberation . . ." she murmured.

"Oh, stop that," Ron begged her, "I feel sick enough as it is — quick, hide me!"

"It isn't Lavender!" said Hermione impatiently, as another couple of girls appeared in the courtyard and Ron dived behind her.

"Cool," said Ron, peering over Hermione's shoulder to check. "Blimey, they don't look happy, do they?"

"They're the Montgomery sisters and of course they don't look happy, didn't you hear what happened to their little brother?" said Hermione.

"I'm losing track of what's happening to everyone's relatives, to be honest," said Ron.

"Well, their brother was attacked by a werewolf. The rumor is that their mother refused to help the Death Eaters. Anyway, the boy was only five and he died in St. Mungo's, they couldn't save him."

"He died?" repeated Harry, shocked. "But surely werewolves don't kill, they just turn you into one of them?"

"They sometimes kill," said Ron, who looked unusually grave now. "I've heard of it happening when the werewolf gets carried away."

"What was the werewolf's name?" said Harry quickly.

"Well, the rumor is that it was that Fenrir Greyback," said Hermione.

"I knew it — the maniac who likes attacking kids, the one Lupin told me about!" said Harry angrily.

Hermione looked at him bleakly.

"Harry, you've got to get that memory," she said. "It's all about stopping Voldemort, isn't it? These dreadful things that are happening are all down to him. . . ."

The bell rang overhead in the castle and both Hermione and Ron jumped to their feet, looking terrified.

"You'll do fine," Harry told them both, as they headed toward the entrance hall to meet the rest of the people taking their Apparition Test. "Good luck."

"And you too!" said Hermione with a significant look, as Harry headed off to the dungeons.

There were only three of them in Potions that afternoon: Harry, Ernie, and Draco Malfoy.

"All too young to Apparate just yet?" said Slughorn genially. "Not turned seventeen yet?"

They shook their heads.

"Ah well," said Slughorn cheerily, "as we're so few, we'll do something *fun*. I want you all to brew me up something amusing!"

"That sounds good, sir," said Ernie sycophantically, rubbing his hands together. Malfoy, on the other hand, did not crack a smile.

"What do you mean, 'something amusing'?" he said irritably.

"Oh, surprise me," said Slughorn airily.

Malfoy opened his copy of *Advanced Potion-Making* with a sulky expression. It could not have been plainer that he thought this lesson was a waste of time. Undoubtedly, Harry thought, watching him over the top of his own book, Malfoy was begrudging the time he could otherwise be spending in the Room of Requirement.

Was it his imagination, or did Malfoy, like Tonks, look thinner? Certainly he looked paler; his skin still had that grayish tinge, probably because he so rarely saw daylight these days. But there was no air of smugness, excitement, or superiority; none of the swagger that he had had on the Hogwarts Express, when he had boasted openly of the mission he had been given by Voldemort. . . . There could be only one conclusion, in Harry's opinion: The mission, whatever it was, was going badly.

Cheered by this thought, Harry skimmed through his copy of *Advanced Potion-Making* and found a heavily corrected Half-Blood Prince's version of "An Elixir to Induce Euphoria," which seemed not only to meet Slughorn's instructions, but which might (Harry's heart leapt as the thought struck him) put Slughorn into such a good mood that he would be prepared to hand over that memory if Harry could persuade him to taste some. . . .

"Well, now, this looks absolutely wonderful," said Slughorn an hour and a half later, clapping his hands together as he stared down into the sunshine yellow contents of Harry's cauldron. "*Euphoria,* I take it? And what's that I smell? Mmmm . . . you've added just a sprig of peppermint, haven't you? Unorthodox, but what a stroke of inspiration, Harry, of course, that would tend to counterbalance the occasional side effects of excessive singing and nose-tweaking. . . . I really don't know where you get these brain waves, my boy . . . unless —"

Harry pushed the Half-Blood Prince's book deeper into his bag with his foot.

"— it's just your mother's genes coming out in you!"

"Oh . . . yeah, maybe," said Harry, relieved.

Ernie was looking rather grumpy; determined to outshine Harry for once, he had most rashly invented his own potion, which had curdled and formed a kind of purple dumpling at the bottom of his cauldron. Malfoy was already packing up, sour-faced; Slughorn had pronounced his Hiccuping Solution merely "passable."

The bell rang and both Ernie and Malfoy left at once.

"Sir," Harry began, but Slughorn immediately glanced over his shoulder; when he saw that the room was empty but for himself and Harry, he hurried away as fast as he could.

"Professor — Professor, don't you want to taste my po — ?" called Harry desperately.

But Slughorn had gone. Disappointed, Harry emptied the cauldron, packed up his things, left the dungeon, and walked slowly back upstairs to the common room.

Ron and Hermione returned in the late afternoon.

"Harry!" cried Hermione as she climbed through the portrait hole. "Harry, I passed!"

"Well done!" he said. "And Ron?"

"He — he *just* failed," whispered Hermione, as Ron came slouching into the room looking most morose. "It was really unlucky, a tiny thing, the examiner just spotted that he'd left half an eyebrow behind. . . . How did it go with Slughorn?"

"No joy," said Harry, as Ron joined them. "Bad luck, mate, but you'll pass next time — we can take it together."

"Yeah, I s'pose," said Ron grumpily. "But *half an eyebrow*! Like that matters!"

"I know," said Hermione soothingly, "it does seem really harsh. . . ."

They spent most of their dinner roundly abusing the Apparition examiner, and Ron looked fractionally more cheerful by the time they set off back to the common room, now discussing the continuing problem of Slughorn and the memory.

"So, Harry — you going to use the Felix Felicis or what?" Ron demanded.

"Yeah, I s'pose I'd better," said Harry. "I don't reckon I'll need all of it, not twelve hours' worth, it can't take all night. . . . I'll just take a mouthful. Two or three hours should do it."

"It's a great feeling when you take it," said Ron reminiscently. "Like you can't do anything wrong."

"What are you talking about?" said Hermione, laughing. "You've never taken any!"

"Yeah, but I *thought* I had, didn't I?" said Ron, as though explaining the obvious. "Same difference really . . ."

As they had only just seen Slughorn enter the Great Hall and knew that he liked to take time over meals, they lingered for a while in the common room, the plan being that Harry should go to

Slughorn's office once the teacher had had time to get back there. When the sun had sunk to the level of the treetops in the Forbidden Forest, they decided the moment had come, and after checking carefully that Neville, Dean, and Seamus were all in the common room, sneaked up to the boys' dormitory.

Harry took out the rolled-up socks at the bottom of his trunk and extracted the tiny, gleaming bottle.

"Well, here goes," said Harry, and he raised the little bottle and took a carefully measured gulp.

"What does it feel like?" whispered Hermione.

Harry did not answer for a moment. Then, slowly but surely, an exhilarating sense of infinite opportunity stole through him; he felt as though he could have done anything, anything at all . . . and getting the memory from Slughorn seemed suddenly not only possible, but positively easy. . . .

He got to his feet, smiling, brimming with confidence.

"Excellent," he said. "Really excellent. Right . . . I'm going down to Hagrid's."

"What?" said Ron and Hermione together, looking aghast.

"No, Harry — you've got to go and see Slughorn, remember?" said Hermione.

"No," said Harry confidently. "I'm going to Hagrid's, I've got a good feeling about going to Hagrid's."

"You've got a good feeling about burying a giant spider?" asked Ron, looking stunned.

"Yeah," said Harry, pulling his Invisibility Cloak out of his bag. "I feel like it's the place to be tonight, you know what I mean?"

"No," said Ron and Hermione together, both looking positively alarmed now.

"This *is* Felix Felicis, I suppose?" said Hermione anxiously, holding up the bottle to the light. "You haven't got another little bottle full of — I don't know —"

"Essence of Insanity?" suggested Ron, as Harry swung his cloak over his shoulders.

Harry laughed, and Ron and Hermione looked even more alarmed.

"Trust me," he said. "I know what I'm doing . . . or at least" — he strolled confidently to the door — "Felix does."

He pulled the Invisibility Cloak over his head and set off down the stairs, Ron and Hermione hurrying along behind him. At the foot of the stairs, Harry slid through the open door.

"What were you doing up there with *her*?" shrieked Lavender Brown, staring right through Harry at Ron and Hermione emerging together from the boys' dormitories. Harry heard Ron spluttering behind him as he darted across the room away from them.

Getting through the portrait hole was simple; as he approached it, Ginny and Dean came through it, and Harry was able to slip between them. As he did so, he brushed accidentally against Ginny.

"*Don't* push me, please, Dean," she said, sounding annoyed. "You're always doing that, I can get through perfectly well on my own. . . ."

The portrait swung closed behind Harry, but not before he had heard Dean make an angry retort. . . . His feeling of elation increasing, Harry strode off through the castle. He did not have to creep along, for he met nobody on his way, but this did not surprise him in the slightest: This evening, he was the luckiest person at Hogwarts.

Why he knew that going to Hagrid's was the right thing to do, he had no idea. It was as though the potion was illuminating a few steps of the path at a time: He could not see the final destination, he could not see where Slughorn came in, but he knew that he was going the right way to get that memory. When he reached the entrance hall he saw that Filch had forgotten to lock the front door. Beaming, Harry threw it open and breathed in the smell of clean air and grass for a moment before walking down the steps into the dusk.

It was when he reached the bottom step that it occurred to him how very pleasant it would be to pass the vegetable patch on his walk to Hagrid's. It was not strictly on the way, but it seemed clear to Harry that this was a whim on which he should act, so he directed his feet immediately toward the vegetable patch, where he was pleased, but not altogether surprised, to find Professor Slughorn in conversation with Professor Sprout. Harry lurked behind a low stone wall, feeling at peace with the world and listening to their conversation.

"I do thank you for taking the time, Pomona," Slughorn was saying courteously, "most authorities agree that they are at their most efficacious if picked at twilight."

"Oh, I quite agree," said Professor Sprout warmly. "That enough for you?"

"Plenty, plenty," said Slughorn, who, Harry saw, was carrying an armful of leafy plants. "This should allow for a few leaves for each of my third years, and some to spare if anybody over-stews them. . . . Well, good evening to you, and many thanks again!"

Professor Sprout headed off into the gathering darkness in the direction of her greenhouses, and Slughorn directed his steps to the spot where Harry stood, invisible.

Seized with an immediate desire to reveal himself, Harry pulled off the cloak with a flourish.

"Good evening, Professor."

"Merlin's beard, Harry, you made me jump," said Slughorn, stopping dead in his tracks and looking wary. "How did you get out of the castle?"

"I think Filch must've forgotten to lock the doors," said Harry cheerfully, and was delighted to see Slughorn scowl.

"I'll be reporting that man, he's more concerned about litter than proper security if you ask me. . . . But why are you out here, Harry?"

"Well, sir, it's Hagrid," said Harry, who knew that the right thing to do just now was to tell the truth. "He's pretty upset. . . . But you won't tell anyone, Professor? I don't want trouble for him. . . ."

Slughorn's curiosity was evidently aroused. "Well, I can't promise that," he said gruffly. "But I know that Dumbledore trusts Hagrid to the hilt, so I'm sure he can't be up to anything very dreadful. . . ."

"Well, it's this giant spider, he's had it for years. . . . It lived in the forest. . . . It could talk and everything —"

"I heard rumors there were acromantulas in the forest," said Slughorn softly, looking over at the mass of black trees. "It's true, then?"

"Yes," said Harry. "But this one, Aragog, the first one Hagrid ever got, it died last night. He's devastated. He wants company while he buries it and I said I'd go."

"Touching, touching," said Slughorn absentmindedly, his large droopy eyes fixed upon the distant lights of Hagrid's cabin. "But acromantula venom is very valuable . . . If the beast only just died it might not yet have dried out. . . . Of course, I wouldn't want to do anything insensitive if Hagrid is upset . . . but if there was any way to procure some . . . I mean, it's almost impossible to get venom from an acromantula while it's alive. . . ."

Slughorn seemed to be talking more to himself than Harry now.

". . . seems an awful waste not to collect it . . . might get a hundred Galleons a pint. . . . To be frank, my salary is not large. . . ."

And now Harry saw clearly what was to be done.

"Well," he said, with a most convincing hesitancy, "well, if you wanted to come, Professor, Hagrid would probably be really pleased. . . . Give Aragog a better send-off, you know . . ."

"Yes, of course," said Slughorn, his eyes now gleaming with enthusiasm. "I tell you what, Harry, I'll meet you down there with a bottle or two. . . . We'll drink the poor beast's — well — not health — but we'll send it off in style, anyway, once it's buried. And I'll change my tie, this one is a little exuberant for the occasion. . . ."

He bustled back into the castle, and Harry sped off to Hagrid's, delighted with himself.

"Yeh came," croaked Hagrid, when he opened the door and saw Harry emerging from the Invisibility Cloak in front of him.

"Yeah — Ron and Hermione couldn't, though," said Harry. "They're really sorry."

"Don' — don' matter . . . He'd've bin touched yeh're here, though, Harry. . . ."

Hagrid gave a great sob. He had made himself a black armband out of what looked like a rag dipped in boot polish, and his eyes

CHAPTER TWENTY-TWO

were puffy, red, and swollen. Harry patted him consolingly on the elbow, which was the highest point of Hagrid he could easily reach.

"Where are we burying him?" he asked. "The forest?"

"Blimey, no," said Hagrid, wiping his streaming eyes on the bottom of his shirt. "The other spiders won' let me anywhere near their webs now Aragog's gone. Turns out it was on'y on his orders they didn' eat me! Can yeh believe that, Harry?"

The honest answer was "yes"; Harry recalled with painful ease the scene when he and Ron had come face-to-face with the acromantulas: They had been quite clear that Aragog was the only thing that stopped them from eating Hagrid.

"Never bin an area o' the forest I couldn' go before!" said Hagrid, shaking his head. "It wasn' easy, gettin' Aragog's body out o' there, I can tell yeh — they usually eat their dead, see. . . . But I wanted ter give 'im a nice burial . . . a proper send-off . . ."

He broke into sobs again and Harry resumed the patting of his elbow, saying as he did so (for the potion seemed to indicate that it was the right thing to do), "Professor Slughorn met me coming down here, Hagrid."

"Not in trouble, are yeh?" said Hagrid, looking up, alarmed. "Yeh shouldn' be outta the castle in the evenin', I know it, it's my fault —"

"No, no, when he heard what I was doing he said he'd like to come and pay his last respects to Aragog too," said Harry. "He's gone to change into something more suitable, I think . . . and he said he'd bring some bottles so we can drink to Aragog's memory. . . ."

"Did he?" said Hagrid, looking both astonished and touched.

"Tha's — tha's righ' nice of him, that is, an' not turnin' yeh in either. I've never really had a lot ter do with Horace Slughorn before. . . . Comin' ter see old Aragog off, though, eh? Well . . . he'd've liked that, Aragog would. . . ."

Harry thought privately that what Aragog would have liked most about Slughorn was the ample amount of edible flesh he provided, but he merely moved to the rear window of Hagrid's hut, where he saw the rather horrible sight of the enormous dead spider lying on its back outside, its legs curled and tangled.

"Are we going to bury him here, Hagrid, in your garden?"

"Jus' beyond the pumpkin patch, I thought," said Hagrid in a choked voice. "I've already dug the — yeh know — grave. Jus' thought we'd say a few nice things over him — happy memories, yeh know —"

His voice quivered and broke. There was a knock on the door, and he turned to answer it, blowing his nose on his great spotted handkerchief as he did so. Slughorn hurried over the threshold, several bottles in his arms, and wearing a somber black cravat.

"Hagrid," he said, in a deep, grave voice. "So very sorry to hear of your loss."

"Tha's very nice of yeh," said Hagrid. "Thanks a lot. An' thanks fer not givin' Harry detention neither. . . ."

"Wouldn't have dreamed of it," said Slughorn. "Sad night, sad night . . . Where is the poor creature?"

"Out here," said Hagrid in a shaking voice. "Shall we — shall we do it, then?"

The three of them stepped out into the back garden. The moon was glistening palely through the trees now, and its rays mingled with the light spilling from Hagrid's window to illuminate Aragog's body lying on the edge of a massive pit beside a ten-foot-high mound of freshly dug earth.

"Magnificent," said Slughorn, approaching the spider's head, where eight milky eyes stared blankly at the sky and two huge, curved pincers shone, motionless, in the moonlight. Harry thought he heard the tinkle of bottles as Slughorn bent over the pincers, apparently examining the enormous hairy head.

"It's not ev'ryone appreciates how beau'iful they are," said Hagrid to Slughorn's back, tears leaking from the corners of his crinkled eyes. "I didn' know yeh were int'rested in creatures like Aragog, Horace."

"Interested? My dear Hagrid, I revere them," said Slughorn, stepping back from the body. Harry saw the glint of a bottle disappear beneath his cloak, though Hagrid, mopping his eyes once more, noticed nothing. "Now . . . shall we proceed to the burial?"

Hagrid nodded and moved forward. He heaved the gigantic spider into his arms and, with an enormous grunt, rolled it into the dark pit. It hit the bottom with a rather horrible, crunchy thud. Hagrid started to cry again.

"Of course, it's difficult for you, who knew him best," said Slughorn, who like Harry could reach no higher than Hagrid's elbow, but patted it all the same. "Why don't I say a few words?"

He must have got a lot of good quality venom from Aragog, Harry thought, for Slughorn wore a satisfied smirk as he stepped up to the rim of the pit and said, in a slow, impressive voice, "Farewell, Aragog, king of arachnids, whose long and faithful friendship those who knew you won't forget! Though your body will decay, your spirit lingers on in the quiet, web-spun places of your forest home. May your many-eyed descendants ever flourish and your human friends find solace for the loss they have sustained."

"Tha' was . . . tha' was . . . beau'iful!" howled Hagrid, and he collapsed onto the compost heap, crying harder than ever.

"There, there," said Slughorn, waving his wand so that the huge pile of earth rose up and then fell, with a muffled sort of crash, onto the dead spider, forming a smooth mound. "Let's get inside and have a drink. Get on his other side, Harry. . . . That's it. . . . Up you come, Hagrid . . . Well done . . ."

They deposited Hagrid in a chair at the table. Fang, who had been skulking in his basket during the burial, now came padding softly across to them and put his heavy head into Harry's lap as usual. Slughorn uncorked one of the bottles of wine he had brought.

"I have had it *all* tested for poison," he assured Harry, pouring most of the first bottle into one of Hagrid's bucket-sized mugs and handing it to Hagrid. "Had a house-elf taste every bottle after what happened to your poor friend Rupert."

Harry saw, in his mind's eye, the expression on Hermione's face if she ever heard about this abuse of house-elves, and decided never to mention it to her.

"One for Harry . . ." said Slughorn, dividing a second bottle between two mugs, ". . . and one for me. Well" — he raised his mug high — "to Aragog."

"Aragog," said Harry and Hagrid together.

Both Slughorn and Hagrid drank deeply. Harry, however, with the way ahead illuminated for him by Felix Felicis, knew that he must not drink, so he merely pretended to take a gulp and then set the mug back on the table before him.

"I had him from an egg, yeh know," said Hagrid morosely. "Tiny little thing he was when he hatched. 'Bout the size of a Pekingese."

"Sweet," said Slughorn.

"Used ter keep him in a cupboard up at the school until . . . well . . ."

Hagrid's face darkened and Harry knew why: Tom Riddle had contrived to have Hagrid thrown out of school, blamed for opening the Chamber of Secrets. Slughorn, however, did not seem to be listening; he was looking up at the ceiling, from which a number of brass pots hung, and also a long, silky skein of bright white hair.

"That's never unicorn hair, Hagrid?"

"Oh, yeah," said Hagrid indifferently. "Gets pulled out of their tails, they catch it on branches an' stuff in the forest, yeh know . . ."

"But my dear chap, do you know how much that's *worth*?"

"I use it fer bindin' on bandages an' stuff if a creature gets injured," said Hagrid, shrugging. "It's dead useful . . . very strong, see."

Slughorn took another deep draught from his mug, his eyes moving carefully around the cabin now, looking, Harry knew, for more treasures that he might be able to convert into a plentiful supply of oak-matured mead, crystalized pineapple, and velvet smoking jackets. He refilled Hagrid's mug and his own, and questioned him about the creatures that lived in the forest these days and how Hagrid was able to look after them all. Hagrid, becoming expansive under the influence of the drink and Slughorn's flattering interest, stopped mopping his eyes and entered happily into a long explanation of bowtruckle husbandry.

The Felix Felicis gave Harry a little nudge at this point, and he noticed that the supply of drink that Slughorn had brought was running out fast. Harry had not yet managed to bring off the Refilling Charm without saying the incantation aloud, but the idea that he might not be able to do it tonight was laughable: Indeed, Harry grinned to himself as, unnoticed by either Hagrid or Slughorn (now swapping tales of the illegal trade in dragon eggs) he pointed his wand under the table at the emptying bottles and they immediately began to refill.

After an hour or so, Hagrid and Slughorn began making extravagant toasts: to Hogwarts, to Dumbledore, to elf-made wine, and to —

"Harry Potter!" bellowed Hagrid, slopping some of his fourteenth bucket of wine down his chin as he drained it.

"Yes, indeed," cried Slughorn a little thickly, "Parry Otter, the Chosen Boy Who — well — something of that sort," he mumbled, and drained his mug too.

Not long after this, Hagrid became tearful again and pressed the whole unicorn tail upon Slughorn, who pocketed it with cries of, "To friendship! To generosity! To ten Galleons a hair!"

And for a while after that, Hagrid and Slughorn were sitting side by side, arms around each other, singing a slow sad song about a dying wizard called Odo.

"Aaargh, the good die young," muttered Hagrid, slumping low onto the table, a little cross-eyed, while Slughorn continued to warble the refrain. "Me dad was no age ter go . . . nor were yer mum an' dad, Harry . . ."

Great fat tears oozed out of the corners of Hagrid's crinkled eyes again; he grasped Harry's arm and shook it.

"Bes' wiz and witchard o' their age I never knew . . . terrible thing . . . terrible thing . . ."

And Odo the hero, they bore him back home
To the place that he'd known as a lad,

sang Slughorn plaintively.

They laid him to rest with his hat inside out
And his wand snapped in two, which was sad.

". . . terrible," Hagrid grunted, and his great shaggy head rolled sideways onto his arms and he fell asleep, snoring deeply.

"Sorry," said Slughorn with a hiccup. "Can't carry a tune to save my life."

"Hagrid wasn't talking about your singing," said Harry quietly. "He was talking about my mum and dad dying."

"Oh," said Slughorn, repressing a large belch. "Oh dear. Yes, that was — was terrible indeed. Terrible . . . terrible . . ."

He looked quite at a loss for what to say, and resorted to refilling their mugs.

"I don't — don't suppose you remember it, Harry?" he asked awkwardly.

"No — well, I was only one when they died," said Harry, his eyes on the flame of the candle flickering in Hagrid's heavy snores. "But I've found out pretty much what happened since. My dad died first. Did you know that?"

"I — I didn't," said Slughorn in a hushed voice.

"Yeah . . . Voldemort murdered him and then stepped over his body toward my mum," said Harry.

Slughorn gave a great shudder, but he did not seem able to tear his horrified gaze away from Harry's face.

"He told her to get out of the way," said Harry remorselessly. "He told me she needn't have died. He only wanted me. She could have run."

"Oh dear," breathed Slughorn. "She could have . . . she needn't . . . That's awful. . . ."

"It is, isn't it?" said Harry, in a voice barely more than a whisper. "But she didn't move. Dad was already dead, but she didn't want me to go too. She tried to plead with Voldemort . . . but he just laughed. . . ."

"That's enough!" said Slughorn suddenly, raising a shaking hand. "Really, my dear boy, enough . . . I'm an old man . . . I don't need to hear . . . I don't want to hear . . ."

"I forgot," lied Harry, Felix Felicis leading him on. "You liked her, didn't you?"

"Liked her?" said Slughorn, his eyes brimming with tears once more. "I don't imagine anyone who met her wouldn't have liked her. . . . Very brave . . . Very funny . . . It was the most horrible thing. . . ."

"But you won't help her son," said Harry. "She gave me her life, but you won't give me a memory."

Hagrid's rumbling snores filled the cabin. Harry looked steadily into Slughorn's tear-filled eyes. The Potions master seemed unable to look away.

"Don't say that," he whispered. "It isn't a question . . . If it were to help you, of course . . . but no purpose can be served . . ."

"It can," said Harry clearly. "Dumbledore needs information. I need information."

He knew he was safe: Felix was telling him that Slughorn would remember nothing of this in the morning. Looking Slughorn straight in the eye, Harry leaned forward a little.

"I am the Chosen One. I have to kill him. I need that memory."

Slughorn turned paler than ever; his shiny forehead gleamed with sweat.

"You *are* the Chosen One?"

"Of course I am," said Harry calmly.

"But then . . . my dear boy . . . you're asking a great deal . . . you're asking me, in fact, to aid you in your attempt to destroy —"

"You don't want to get rid of the wizard who killed Lily Evans?"

"Harry, Harry, of course I do, but —"

"You're scared he'll find out you helped me?"

Slughorn said nothing; he looked terrified.

"Be brave like my mother, Professor. . . ."

Slughorn raised a pudgy hand and pressed his shaking fingers to his mouth; he looked for a moment like an enormously overgrown baby.

"I am not proud . . ." he whispered through his fingers. "I am ashamed of what — of what that memory shows. . . . I think I may have done great damage that day. . . ."

"You'd cancel out anything you did by giving me the memory," said Harry. "It would be a very brave and noble thing to do."

Hagrid twitched in his sleep and snored on. Slughorn and Harry stared at each other over the guttering candle. There was a long, long silence, but Felix Felicis told Harry not to break it, to wait.

Then, very slowly, Slughorn put his hand in his pocket and pulled out his wand. He put his other hand inside his cloak and took out a small, empty bottle. Still looking into Harry's eyes,

Slughorn touched the tip of his wand to his temple and withdrew it, so that a long, silver thread of memory came away too, clinging to the wand tip. Longer and longer the memory stretched until it broke and swung, silvery bright, from the wand. Slughorn lowered it into the bottle where it coiled, then spread, swirling like gas. He corked the bottle with a trembling hand and then passed it across the table to Harry.

"Thank you very much, Professor."

"You're a good boy," said Professor Slughorn, tears trickling down his fat cheeks into his walrus mustache. "And you've got her eyes. . . . Just don't think too badly of me once you've seen it. . . ."

And he too put his head on his arms, gave a deep sigh, and fell asleep.

HORCRUXES

Harry could feel the Felix Felicis wearing off as he crept back into the castle. The front door had remained unlocked for him, but on the third floor he met Peeves and only narrowly avoided detection by diving sideways through one of his shortcuts. By the time he got up to the portrait of the Fat Lady and pulled off his Invisibility Cloak, he was not surprised to find her in a most unhelpful mood.

"What sort of time do you call this?"

"I'm really sorry — I had to go out for something important —"

"Well, the password changed at midnight, so you'll just have to sleep in the corridor, won't you?"

"You're joking!" said Harry. "Why did it have to change at midnight?"

"That's the way it is," said the Fat Lady. "If you're angry, go and take it up with the headmaster, he's the one who's tightened security."

"Fantastic," said Harry bitterly, looking around at the hard floor. "Really brilliant. Yeah, I would go and take it up with Dumbledore if he was here, because he's the one who wanted me to —"

"He is here," said a voice behind Harry. "Professor Dumbledore returned to the school an hour ago."

Nearly Headless Nick was gliding toward Harry, his head wobbling as usual upon his ruff.

"I had it from the Bloody Baron, who saw him arrive," said Nick. "He appeared, according to the Baron, to be in good spirits, though a little tired, of course."

"Where is he?" said Harry, his heart leaping.

"Oh, groaning and clanking up on the Astronomy Tower, it's a favorite pastime of his —"

"Not the Bloody Baron — Dumbledore!"

"Oh — in his office," said Nick. "I believe, from what the Baron said, that he had business to attend to before turning in —"

"Yeah, he has," said Harry, excitement blazing in his chest at the prospect of telling Dumbledore he had secured the memory. He wheeled about and sprinted off again, ignoring the Fat Lady who was calling after him.

"Come back! All right, I lied! I was annoyed you woke me up! The password's still 'tapeworm'!"

But Harry was already hurtling back along the corridor and within minutes, he was saying "toffee éclairs" to Dumbledore's gargoyle, which leapt aside, permitting Harry entrance onto the spiral staircase.

"Enter," said Dumbledore when Harry knocked. He sounded exhausted.

Harry pushed open the door. There was Dumbledore's office,

looking the same as ever, but with black, star-strewn skies beyond the windows.

"Good gracious, Harry," said Dumbledore in surprise. "To what do I owe this very late pleasure?"

"Sir — I've got it. I've got the memory from Slughorn."

Harry pulled out the tiny glass bottle and showed it to Dumbledore. For a moment or two, the headmaster looked stunned. Then his face split in a wide smile.

"Harry, this is spectacular news! Very well done indeed! I knew you could do it!"

All thought of the lateness of the hour apparently forgotten, he hurried around his desk, took the bottle with Slughorn's memory in his uninjured hand, and strode over to the cabinet where he kept the Pensieve.

"And now," said Dumbledore, placing the stone basin upon his desk and emptying the contents of the bottle into it. "Now, at last, we shall see. Harry, quickly . . ."

Harry bowed obediently over the Pensieve and felt his feet leave the office floor. . . . Once again he fell through darkness and landed in Horace Slughorn's office many years before.

There was the much younger Slughorn, with his thick, shiny, straw-colored hair and his gingery-blond mustache, sitting again in the comfortable winged armchair in his office, his feet resting upon a velvet pouffe, a small glass of wine in one hand, the other rummaging in a box of crystalized pineapple. And there were the half-dozen teenage boys sitting around Slughorn with Tom Riddle in the midst of them, Marvolo's gold-and-black ring gleaming on his finger.

Dumbledore landed beside Harry just as Riddle asked, "Sir, is it true that Professor Merrythought is retiring?"

"Tom, Tom, if I knew I couldn't tell you," said Slughorn, wagging his finger reprovingly at Riddle, though winking at the same time. "I must say, I'd like to know where you get your information, boy, more knowledgeable than half the staff, you are."

Riddle smiled; the other boys laughed and cast him admiring looks.

"What with your uncanny ability to know things you shouldn't, and your careful flattery of the people who matter — thank you for the pineapple, by the way, you're quite right, it is my favorite —"

Several of the boys tittered again.

"— I confidently expect you to rise to Minister of Magic within twenty years. Fifteen, if you keep sending me pineapple, I have *excellent* contacts at the Ministry."

Tom Riddle merely smiled as the others laughed again. Harry noticed that he was by no means the eldest of the group of boys, but that they all seemed to look to him as their leader.

"I don't know that politics would suit me, sir," he said when the laughter had died away. "I don't have the right kind of background, for one thing."

A couple of the boys around him smirked at each other. Harry was sure they were enjoying a private joke, undoubtedly about what they knew, or suspected, regarding their gang leader's famous ancestor.

"Nonsense," said Slughorn briskly, "couldn't be plainer you come from decent Wizarding stock, abilities like yours. No, you'll go far, Tom, I've never been wrong about a student yet."

The small golden clock standing upon Slughorn's desk chimed eleven o'clock behind him and he looked around.

"Good gracious, is it that time already? You'd better get going, boys, or we'll all be in trouble. Lestrange, I want your essay by tomorrow or it's detention. Same goes for you, Avery."

One by one, the boys filed out of the room. Slughorn heaved himself out of his armchair and carried his empty glass over to his desk. A movement behind him made him look around; Riddle was still standing there.

"Look sharp, Tom, you don't want to be caught out of bed out of hours, and you a prefect . . ."

"Sir, I wanted to ask you something."

"Ask away, then, m'boy, ask away. . . ."

"Sir, I wondered what you know about . . . about Horcruxes?"

Slughorn stared at him, his thick fingers absentmindedly caressing the stem of his wine glass.

"Project for Defense Against the Dark Arts, is it?"

But Harry could tell that Slughorn knew perfectly well that this was not schoolwork.

"Not exactly, sir," said Riddle. "I came across the term while reading and I didn't fully understand it."

"No . . . well . . . you'd be hard-pushed to find a book at Hogwarts that'll give you details on Horcruxes, Tom, that's very Dark stuff, very Dark indeed," said Slughorn.

"But you obviously know all about them, sir? I mean, a wizard like you — sorry, I mean, if you can't tell me, obviously — I just knew if anyone could tell me, you could — so I just thought I'd ask —"

It was very well done, thought Harry, the hesitancy, the casual tone, the careful flattery, none of it overdone. He, Harry, had had too much experience of trying to wheedle information out of reluctant people not to recognize a master at work. He could tell that Riddle wanted the information very, very much; perhaps had been working toward this moment for weeks.

"Well," said Slughorn, not looking at Riddle, but fiddling with the ribbon on top of his box of crystalized pineapple, "well, it can't hurt to give you an overview, of course. Just so that you understand the term. A Horcrux is the word used for an object in which a person has concealed part of their soul."

"I don't quite understand how that works, though, sir," said Riddle.

His voice was carefully controlled, but Harry could sense his excitement.

"Well, you split your soul, you see," said Slughorn, "and hide part of it in an object outside the body. Then, even if one's body is attacked or destroyed, one cannot die, for part of the soul remains earthbound and undamaged. But of course, existence in such a form . . ."

Slughorn's face crumpled and Harry found himself remembering words he had heard nearly two years before: *I was ripped from my body, I was less than spirit, less than the meanest ghost . . . but still, I was alive.*

". . . few would want it, Tom, very few. Death would be preferable."

But Riddle's hunger was now apparent; his expression was greedy, he could no longer hide his longing.

"How do you split your soul?"

"Well," said Slughorn uncomfortably, "you must understand

that the soul is supposed to remain intact and whole. Splitting it is an act of violation, it is against nature."

"But how do you do it?"

"By an act of evil — the supreme act of evil. By committing murder. Killing rips the soul apart. The wizard intent upon creating a Horcrux would use the damage to his advantage: He would encase the torn portion —"

"Encase? But how — ?"

"There is a spell, do not ask me, I don't know!" said Slughorn, shaking his head like an old elephant bothered by mosquitoes. "Do I look as though I have tried it — do I look like a killer?"

"No, sir, of course not," said Riddle quickly. "I'm sorry . . . I didn't mean to offend . . ."

"Not at all, not at all, not offended," said Slughorn gruffly. "It's natural to feel some curiosity about these things. . . . Wizards of a certain caliber have always been drawn to that aspect of magic. . . ."

"Yes, sir," said Riddle. "What I don't understand, though — just out of curiosity — I mean, would one Horcrux be much use? Can you only split your soul once? Wouldn't it be better, make you stronger, to have your soul in more pieces, I mean, for instance, isn't seven the most powerfully magical number, wouldn't seven — ?"

"Merlin's beard, Tom!" yelped Slughorn. "Seven! Isn't it bad enough to think of killing one person? And in any case . . . bad enough to divide the soul . . . but to rip it into seven pieces . . ."

Slughorn looked deeply troubled now: He was gazing at Riddle as though he had never seen him plainly before, and Harry could tell that he was regretting entering into the conversation at all.

"Of course," he muttered, "this is all hypothetical, what we're discussing, isn't it? All academic . . ."

"Yes, sir, of course," said Riddle quickly.

"But all the same, Tom . . . keep it quiet, what I've told — that's to say, what we've discussed. People wouldn't like to think we've been chatting about Horcruxes. It's a banned subject at Hogwarts, you know. . . . Dumbledore's particularly fierce about it. . . ."

"I won't say a word, sir," said Riddle, and he left, but not before Harry had glimpsed his face, which was full of that same wild happiness it had worn when he had first found out that he was a wizard, the sort of happiness that did not enhance his handsome features, but made them, somehow, less human. . . .

"Thank you, Harry," said Dumbledore quietly. "Let us go. . . ."

When Harry landed back on the office floor Dumbledore was already sitting down behind his desk. Harry sat too and waited for Dumbledore to speak.

"I have been hoping for this piece of evidence for a very long time," said Dumbledore at last. "It confirms the theory on which I have been working, it tells me that I am right, and also how very far there is still to go. . . ."

Harry suddenly noticed that every single one of the old headmasters and headmistresses in the portraits around the walls was awake and listening in on their conversation. A corpulent, red-nosed wizard had actually taken out an ear trumpet.

"Well, Harry," said Dumbledore, "I am sure you understood the significance of what we just heard. At the same age as you are now, give or take a few months, Tom Riddle was doing all he could to find out how to make himself immortal."

"You think he succeeded then, sir?" asked Harry. "He made a Horcrux? And that's why he didn't die when he attacked me? He had a Horcrux hidden somewhere? A bit of his soul was safe?"

"A bit . . . or more," said Dumbledore. "You heard Voldemort: What he particularly wanted from Horace was an opinion on what would happen to the wizard who created more than one Horcrux, what would happen to the wizard so determined to evade death that he would be prepared to murder many times, rip his soul repeatedly, so as to store it in many, separately concealed Horcruxes. No book would have given him that information. As far as I know — as far, I am sure, as Voldemort knew — no wizard had ever done more than tear his soul in two."

Dumbledore paused for a moment, marshaling his thoughts, and then said, "Four years ago, I received what I considered certain proof that Voldemort had split his soul."

"Where?" asked Harry. "How?"

"You handed it to me, Harry," said Dumbledore. "The diary, Riddle's diary, the one giving instructions on how to reopen the Chamber of Secrets."

"I don't understand, sir," said Harry.

"Well, although I did not see the Riddle who came out of the diary, what you described to me was a phenomenon I had never witnessed. A mere memory starting to act and think for itself? A mere memory, sapping the life out of the girl into whose hands it had fallen? No, something much more sinister had lived inside that book. . . . a fragment of soul, I was almost sure of it. The diary had been a Horcrux. But this raised as many questions as it answered.

"What intrigued and alarmed me most was that that diary had been intended as a weapon as much as a safeguard."

"I still don't understand," said Harry.

"Well, it worked as a Horcrux is supposed to work — in other words, the fragment of soul concealed inside it was kept safe and had undoubtedly played its part in preventing the death of its owner. But there could be no doubt that Riddle really wanted that diary read, wanted the piece of his soul to inhabit or possess somebody else, so that Slytherin's monster would be unleashed again."

"Well, he didn't want his hard work to be wasted," said Harry. "He wanted people to know he was Slytherin's heir, because he couldn't take credit at the time."

"Quite correct," said Dumbledore, nodding. "But don't you see, Harry, that if he intended the diary to be passed to, or planted on, some future Hogwarts student, he was being remarkably blasé about that precious fragment of his soul concealed within it. The point of a Horcrux is, as Professor Slughorn explained, to keep part of the self hidden and safe, not to fling it into somebody else's path and run the risk that they might destroy it — as indeed happened: That particular fragment of soul is no more; you saw to that.

"The careless way in which Voldemort regarded this Horcrux seemed most ominous to me. It suggested that he must have made — or been planning to make — more Horcruxes, so that the loss of his first would not be so detrimental. I did not wish to believe it, but nothing else seemed to make sense.

"Then you told me, two years later, that on the night that Voldemort returned to his body, he made a most illuminating and alarming statement to his Death Eaters. *'I, who have gone further than anybody along the path that leads to immortality.'* That was what you told me he said. *'Further than anybody.'* And I thought I knew what that meant, though the Death Eaters did not. He was referring to his Horcruxes, Horcruxes in the plural, Harry, which I do not believe any other wizard has ever had. Yet it fitted: Lord Voldemort has seemed to grow less human with the passing years, and the transformation he has undergone seemed to me to be only explicable if his soul was mutilated beyond the realms of what we might call 'usual evil' . . ."

"So he's made himself impossible to kill by murdering other people?" said Harry. "Why couldn't he make a Sorcerer's Stone, or steal one, if he was so interested in immortality?"

"Well, we know that he tried to do just that, five years ago," said Dumbledore. "But there are several reasons why, I think, a Sorcerer's Stone would appeal less than Horcruxes to Lord Voldemort.

"While the Elixir of Life does indeed extend life, it must be drunk regularly, for all eternity, if the drinker is to maintain their immortality. Therefore, Voldemort would be entirely dependent on the Elixir, and if it ran out, or was contaminated, or if the Stone was stolen, he would die just like any other man. Voldemort likes to operate alone, remember. I believe that he would have found the thought of being dependent, even on the Elixir, intolerable. Of course he was prepared to drink it if it would take him out of the horrible part-life to which he was condemned after attacking you, but only to regain a body. Thereafter, I am convinced, he intended to continue to rely on his Horcruxes: He would need nothing more, if only he could regain a human form. He was already immortal, you see . . . or as close to immortal as any man can be.

"But now, Harry, armed with this information, the crucial memory you have succeeded in procuring for us, we are closer to the secret of finishing Lord Voldemort than anyone has ever been before. You heard him, Harry: 'Wouldn't it be better, make you stronger, to have your soul in more pieces . . . isn't seven the most powerfully magical number . . .' *Isn't seven the most powerfully magical number.* Yes, I think the idea of a seven-part soul would greatly appeal to Lord Voldemort."

"He made *seven* Horcruxes?" said Harry, horror-struck, while several of the portraits on the walls made similar noises of shock and outrage. "But they could be anywhere in the world — hidden — buried or invisible —"

"I am glad to see you appreciate the magnitude of the problem," said Dumbledore calmly. "But firstly, no, Harry, not seven Hor-cruxes: six. The seventh part of his soul, however maimed, resides inside his regenerated body. That was the part of him that lived a spectral existence for so many years during his exile; without that, he has no self at all. That seventh piece of soul will be the last that anybody wishing to kill Voldemort must attack — the piece that lives in his body."

"But the six Horcruxes, then," said Harry, a little desperately, "how are we supposed to find them?"

"You are forgetting . . . you have already destroyed one of them. And I have destroyed another."

"You have?" said Harry eagerly.

"Yes indeed," said Dumbledore, and he raised his blackened, burned-looking hand. "The ring, Harry. Marvolo's ring. And a ter-rible curse there was upon it too. Had it not been — forgive me the lack of seemly modesty — for my own prodigious skill, and for Professor Snape's timely action when I returned to Hogwarts, des-perately injured, I might not have lived to tell the tale. However, a withered hand does not seem an unreasonable exchange for a sev-enth of Voldemort's soul. The ring is no longer a Horcrux."

"But how did you find it?"

"Well, as you now know, for many years I have made it my business to discover as much as I can about Voldemort's past life. I have traveled widely, visiting those places he once knew. I stumbled across the ring hidden in the ruin of the Gaunts' house. It seems that once Voldemort had succeeded in sealing a piece of his soul inside it, he did not want to wear it anymore. He hid it, protected by many powerful enchantments, in the shack where his ancestors had once lived (Morfin having been carted off to Azkaban, of course), never guessing that I might one day take the trouble to visit the ruin, or that I might be keeping an eye open for traces of magical concealment.

"However, we should not congratulate ourselves too heartily. You destroyed the diary and I the ring, but if we are right in our theory of a seven-part soul, four Horcruxes remain."

"And they could be anything?" said Harry. "They could be old tin cans or, I dunno, empty potion bottles. . . ."

"You are thinking of Portkeys, Harry, which must be ordinary objects, easy to overlook. But would Lord Voldemort use tin cans or old potion bottles to guard his own precious soul? You are forgetting what I have showed you. Lord Voldemort liked to collect trophies, and he preferred objects with a powerful magical history. His pride, his belief in his own superiority, his determination to carve for himself a startling place in magical history; these things suggest to me that Voldemort would have chosen his Horcruxes with some care, favoring objects worthy of the honor."

"The diary wasn't that special."

"The diary, as you have said yourself, was proof that he was the

Heir of Slytherin; I am sure that Voldemort considered it of stupendous importance."

"So, the other Horcruxes?" said Harry. "Do you think you know what they are, sir?"

"I can only guess," said Dumbledore. "For the reasons I have already given, I believe that Lord Voldemort would prefer objects that, in themselves, have a certain grandeur. I have therefore trawled back through Voldemort's past to see if I can find evidence that such artifacts have disappeared around him."

"The locket!" said Harry loudly. "Hufflepuff's cup!"

"Yes," said Dumbledore, smiling, "I would be prepared to bet — perhaps not my other hand — but a couple of fingers, that they became Horcruxes three and four. The remaining two, assuming again that he created a total of six, are more of a problem, but I will hazard a guess that, having secured objects from Hufflepuff and Slytherin, he set out to track down objects owned by Gryffindor or Ravenclaw. Four objects from the four founders would, I am sure, have exerted a powerful pull over Voldemort's imagination. I cannot answer for whether he ever managed to find anything of Ravenclaw's. I am confident, however, that the only known relic of Gryffindor remains safe."

Dumbledore pointed his blackened fingers to the wall behind him, where a ruby-encrusted sword reposed within a glass case.

"Do you think that's why he really wanted to come back to Hogwarts, sir?" said Harry. "To try and find something from one of the other founders?"

"My thoughts precisely," said Dumbledore. "But unfortunately, that does not advance us much further, for he was turned away, or so I believe, without the chance to search the school. I am forced to conclude that he never fulfilled his ambition of collecting four founders' objects. He definitely had two — he may have found three — that is the best we can do for now."

"Even if he got something of Ravenclaw's or of Gryffindor's, that leaves a sixth Horcrux," said Harry, counting on his fingers. "Unless he got both?"

"I don't think so," said Dumbledore. "I think I know what the sixth Horcrux is. I wonder what you will say when I confess that I have been curious for a while about the behavior of the snake, Nagini?"

"The snake?" said Harry, startled. "You can use animals as Horcruxes?"

"Well, it is inadvisable to do so," said Dumbledore, "because to confide a part of your soul to something that can think and move for itself is obviously a very risky business. However, if my calculations are correct, Voldemort was still at least one Horcrux short of his goal of six when he entered your parents' house with the intention of killing you.

"He seems to have reserved the process of making Horcruxes for particularly significant deaths. You would certainly have been that. He believed that in killing you, he was destroying the danger the prophecy had outlined. He believed he was making himself invincible. I am sure that he was intending to make his final Horcrux with your death.

"As we know, he failed. After an interval of some years, however, he used Nagini to kill an old Muggle man, and it might then have occurred to him to turn her into his last Horcrux. She underlines the Slytherin connection, which enhances Lord Voldemort's mystique; I think he is perhaps as fond of her as he can be of anything;

he certainly likes to keep her close, and he seems to have an un-usual amount of control over her, even for a Parselmouth."

"So," said Harry, "the diary's gone, the ring's gone. The cup, the locket, and the snake are still intact, and you think there might be a Horcrux that was once Ravenclaw's or Gryffindor's?"

"An admirably succinct and accurate summary, yes," said Dumbledore, bowing his head.

"So . . . are you still looking for them, sir? Is that where you've been going when you've been leaving the school?"

"Correct," said Dumbledore. "I have been looking for a very long time. I think . . . perhaps . . . I may be close to finding another one. There are hopeful signs."

"And if you do," said Harry quickly, "can I come with you and help get rid of it?"

Dumbledore looked at Harry very intently for a moment before saying, "Yes, I think so."

"I can?" said Harry, thoroughly taken aback.

"Oh yes," said Dumbledore, smiling slightly. "I think you have earned that right."

Harry felt his heart lift. It was very good not to hear words of caution and protection for once. The headmasters and head-mistresses around the walls seemed less impressed by Dumbledore's decision; Harry saw a few of them shaking their heads and Phineas Nigellus actually snorted.

"Does Voldemort know when a Horcrux is destroyed, sir? Can he feel it?" Harry asked, ignoring the portraits.

"A very interesting question, Harry. I believe not. I believe that Voldemort is now so immersed in evil, and these crucial parts of himself have been detached for so long, he does not feel as we do.

Perhaps, at the point of death, he might be aware of his loss . . . but he was not aware, for instance, that the diary had been destroyed until he forced the truth out of Lucius Malfoy. When Voldemort discovered that the diary had been mutilated and robbed of all its powers, I am told that his anger was terrible to behold."

"But I thought he meant Lucius Malfoy to smuggle it into Hogwarts?"

"Yes, he did, years ago, when he was sure he would be able to create more Horcruxes, but still Lucius was supposed to wait for Voldemort's say-so, and he never received it, for Voldemort vanished shortly after giving him the diary.

"No doubt he thought that Lucius would not dare do anything with the Horcrux other than guard it carefully, but he was counting too much upon Lucius's fear of a master who had been gone for years and whom Lucius believed dead. Of course, Lucius did not know what the diary really was. I understand that Voldemort had told him the diary would cause the Chamber of Secrets to reopen because it was cleverly enchanted. Had Lucius known he held a portion of his master's soul in his hands, he would undoubtedly have treated it with more reverence — but instead he went ahead and carried out the old plan for his own ends: By planting the diary upon Arthur Weasley's daughter, he hoped to discredit Arthur and get rid of a highly incriminating magical object in one stroke. Ah, poor Lucius . . . what with Voldemort's fury about the fact that he threw away the Horcrux for his own gain, and the fiasco at the Ministry last year, I would not be surprised if he is not secretly glad to be safe in Azkaban at the moment."

Harry sat in thought for a moment, then asked, "So if all of his Horcruxes are destroyed, Voldemort *could* be killed?"

"Yes, I think so," said Dumbledore. "Without his Horcruxes,

Voldemort will be a mortal man with a maimed and diminished soul. Never forget, though, that while his soul may be damaged beyond repair, his brain and his magical powers remain intact. It will take uncommon skill and power to kill a wizard like Voldemort even without his Horcruxes."

"But I haven't got uncommon skill and power," said Harry, before he could stop himself.

"Yes, you have," said Dumbledore firmly. "You have a power that Voldemort has never had. You can —"

"I know!" said Harry impatiently. "I can love!" It was only with difficulty that he stopped himself adding, "Big deal!"

"Yes, Harry, you can love," said Dumbledore, who looked as though he knew perfectly well what Harry had just refrained from saying. "Which, given everything that has happened to you, is a great and remarkable thing. You are still too young to understand how unusual you are, Harry."

"So, when the prophecy says that I'll have 'power the Dark Lord knows not,' it just means — love?" asked Harry, feeling a little let down.

"Yes — just love," said Dumbledore. "But Harry, never forget that what the prophecy says is only significant because Voldemort made it so. I told you this at the end of last year. Voldemort singled you out as the person who would be most dangerous to him — and in doing so, he *made* you the person who would be most dangerous to him!"

"But it comes to the same —"

"No, it doesn't!" said Dumbledore, sounding impatient now. Pointing at Harry with his black, withered hand, he said, "You are setting too much store by the prophecy!"

"But," spluttered Harry, "but you said the prophecy means —"

"If Voldemort had never heard of the prophecy, would it have been fulfilled? Would it have meant anything? Of course not! Do you think every prophecy in the Hall of Prophecy has been fulfilled?"

"But," said Harry, bewildered, "but last year, you said one of us would have to kill the other —"

"Harry, Harry, only because Voldemort made a grave error, and acted on Professor Trelawney's words! If Voldemort had never murdered your father, would he have imparted in you a furious desire for revenge? Of course not! If he had not forced your mother to die for you, would he have given you a magical protection he could not penetrate? Of course not, Harry! Don't you see? Voldemort himself created his worst enemy, just as tyrants everywhere do! Have you any idea how much tyrants fear the people they oppress? All of them realize that, one day, amongst their many victims, there is sure to be one who rises against them and strikes back! Voldemort is no different! Always he was on the lookout for the one who would challenge him. He heard the prophecy and he leapt into action, with the result that he not only handpicked the man most likely to finish him, he handed him uniquely deadly weapons!"

"But —"

"It is essential that you understand this!" said Dumbledore, standing up and striding about the room, his glittering robes swooshing in his wake; Harry had never seen him so agitated. "By attempting to kill you, Voldemort himself singled out the remarkable person who sits here in front of me, and gave him the tools for the job! It is Voldemort's fault that you were able to see into his thoughts, his ambitions, that you even understand the snakelike language in which he gives orders, and yet, Harry, despite your privileged insight into Voldemort's world (which, incidentally, is a gift any Death Eater would kill to have), you have never been seduced by the Dark Arts, never, even for a second, shown the slightest desire to become one of Voldemort's followers!"

"Of course I haven't!" said Harry indignantly. "He killed my mum and dad!"

"You are protected, in short, by your ability to love!" said Dumbledore loudly. "The only protection that can possibly work against the lure of power like Voldemort's! In spite of all the temptation you have endured, all the suffering, you remain pure of heart, just as pure as you were at the age of eleven, when you stared into a mirror that reflected your heart's desire, and it showed you only the way to thwart Lord Voldemort, and not immortality or riches. Harry, have you any idea how few wizards could have seen what you saw in that mirror? Voldemort should have known then what he was dealing with, but he did not!

"But he knows it now. You have flitted into Lord Voldemort's mind without damage to yourself, but he cannot possess you without enduring mortal agony, as he discovered in the Ministry. I do not think he understands why, Harry, but then, he was in such a hurry to mutilate his own soul, he never paused to understand the incomparable power of a soul that is untarnished and whole."

"But, sir," said Harry, making valiant efforts not to sound argumentative, "it all comes to the same thing, doesn't it? I've got to try and kill him, or —"

"Got to?" said Dumbledore. "Of course you've got to! But not because of the prophecy! Because you, yourself, will never rest until you've tried! We both know it! Imagine, please, just for a moment, that you had never heard that prophecy! How would you feel about Voldemort now? Think!"

Harry watched Dumbledore striding up and down in front of him, and thought. He thought of his mother, his father, and Sirius. He thought of Cedric Diggory. He thought of all the terrible deeds he knew Lord Voldemort had done. A flame seemed to leap inside his chest, searing his throat.

"I'd want him finished," said Harry quietly. "And I'd want to do it."

"Of course you would!" cried Dumbledore. "You see, the prophecy does not mean you *have* to do anything! But the prophecy caused Lord Voldemort to *mark you as his equal*. . . . In other words, you are free to choose your way, quite free to turn your back on the prophecy! But Voldemort continues to set store by the prophecy. He will continue to hunt you . . . which makes it certain, really, that —"

"That one of us is going to end up killing the other," said Harry. "Yes."

But he understood at last what Dumbledore had been trying to tell him. It was, he thought, the difference between being dragged into the arena to face a battle to the death and walking into the arena with your head held high. Some people, perhaps, would say that there was little to choose between the two ways, but Dumbledore knew — *and so do I,* thought Harry, with a rush of fierce pride, *and so did my parents* — that there was all the difference in the world.

SECTUMSEMPRA

Exhausted but delighted with his night's work, Harry told Ron and Hermione everything that had happened during next morning's Charms lesson (having first cast the *Muffliato* spell upon those nearest them). They were both satisfyingly impressed by the way he had wheedled the memory out of Slughorn and positively awed when he told them about Voldemort's Horcruxes and Dumbledore's promise to take Harry along, should he find another one.

"Wow," said Ron, when Harry had finally finished telling them everything; Ron was waving his wand very vaguely in the direction of the ceiling without paying the slightest bit of attention to what he was doing. "Wow. You're actually going to go with Dumbledore . . . and try and destroy . . . wow."

"Ron, you're making it snow," said Hermione patiently, grabbing his wrist and redirecting his wand away from the ceiling from which, sure enough, large white flakes had started to fall. Lavender

Brown, Harry noticed, glared at Hermione from a neighboring table through very red eyes, and Hermione immediately let go of Ron's arm.

"Oh yeah," said Ron, looking down at his shoulders in vague surprise. "Sorry . . . looks like we've all got horrible dandruff now. . . ."

He brushed some of the fake snow off Hermione's shoulder. Lavender burst into tears. Ron looked immensely guilty and turned his back on her.

"We split up," he told Harry out of the corner of his mouth. "Last night. When she saw me coming out of the dormitory with Hermione. Obviously she couldn't see you, so she thought it had just been the two of us."

"Ah," said Harry. "Well — you don't mind it's over, do you?"

"No," Ron admitted. "It was pretty bad while she was yelling, but at least I didn't have to finish it."

"Coward," said Hermione, though she looked amused. "Well, it was a bad night for romance all around. Ginny and Dean split up too, Harry."

Harry thought there was a rather knowing look in her eye as she told him that, but she could not possibly know that his insides were suddenly dancing the conga. Keeping his face as immobile and his voice as indifferent as he could, he asked, "How come?"

"Oh, something really silly . . . She said he was always trying to help her through the portrait hole, like she couldn't climb in herself . . . but they've been a bit rocky for ages."

Harry glanced over at Dean on the other side of the classroom. He certainly looked unhappy.

"Of course, this puts you in a bit of a dilemma, doesn't it?" said Hermione.

"What d'you mean?" said Harry quickly.

"The Quidditch team," said Hermione. "If Ginny and Dean aren't speaking . . ."

"Oh — oh yeah," said Harry.

"Flitwick," said Ron in a warning tone. The tiny little Charms master was bobbing his way toward them, and Hermione was the only one who had managed to turn vinegar into wine; her glass flask was full of deep crimson liquid, whereas the contents of Harry's and Ron's were still murky brown.

"Now, now, boys," squeaked Professor Flitwick reproachfully. "A little less talk, a little more action . . . Let me see you try. . . ."

Together they raised their wands, concentrating with all their might, and pointed them at their flasks. Harry's vinegar turned to ice; Ron's flask exploded.

"Yes . . . for homework," said Professor Flitwick, reemerging from under the table and pulling shards of glass out of the top of his hat, *"practice."*

They had one of their rare joint free periods after Charms and walked back to the common room together. Ron seemed to be positively lighthearted about the end of his relationship with Lavender, and Hermione seemed cheery too, though when asked what she was grinning about she simply said, "It's a nice day." Neither of them seemed to have noticed that a fierce battle was raging inside Harry's brain:

She's Ron's sister.

But she's ditched Dean!

She's still Ron's sister.

I'm his best mate!

That'll make it worse.

If I talked to him first —

He'd hit you.

What if I don't care?

He's your best mate!

Harry barely noticed that they were climbing through the portrait hole into the sunny common room, and only vaguely registered the small group of seventh years clustered together there, until Hermione cried, "Katie! You're back! Are you okay?"

Harry stared: It was indeed Katie Bell, looking completely healthy and surrounded by her jubilant friends.

"I'm really well!" she said happily. "They let me out of St. Mungo's on Monday, I had a couple of days at home with Mum and Dad and then came back here this morning. Leanne was just telling me about McLaggen and the last match, Harry. . . ."

"Yeah," said Harry, "well, now you're back and Ron's fit, we'll have a decent chance of thrashing Ravenclaw, which means we could still be in the running for the Cup. Listen, Katie . . ."

He had to put the question to her at once; his curiosity even drove Ginny temporarily from his brain. He dropped his voice as Katie's friends started gathering up their things; apparently they were late for Transfiguration.

". . . that necklace . . . can you remember who gave it to you now?"

"No," said Katie, shaking her head ruefully. "Everyone's been asking me, but I haven't got a clue. The last thing I remember was walking into the ladies' in the Three Broomsticks."

"You definitely went into the bathroom, then?" said Hermione.

"Well, I know I pushed open the door," said Katie, "so I suppose whoever Imperiused me was standing just behind it. After that, my memory's a blank until about two weeks ago in St. Mungo's. Listen, I'd better go, I wouldn't put it past McGonagall to give me lines even if it is my first day back. . . ."

She caught up her bag and books and hurried after her friends, leaving Harry, Ron, and Hermione to sit down at a window table and ponder what she had told them.

"So it must have been a girl or a woman who gave Katie the necklace," said Hermione, "to be in the ladies' bathroom."

"Or someone who looked like a girl or a woman," said Harry. "Don't forget, there was a cauldron full of Polyjuice Potion at Hogwarts. We know some of it got stolen. . . ."

In his mind's eye, he watched a parade of Crabbes and Goyles prance past, all transformed into girls.

"I think I'm going to take another swig of Felix," said Harry, "and have a go at the Room of Requirement again."

"That would be a complete waste of potion," said Hermione flatly, putting down the copy of *Spellman's Syllabary* she had just taken out of her bag. "Luck can only get you so far, Harry. The situation with Slughorn was different; you always had the ability to persuade him, you just needed to tweak the circumstances a bit. Luck isn't enough to get you through a powerful enchantment, though. Don't go wasting the rest of that potion! You'll need all the luck you can get if Dumbledore takes you along with him . . ." She dropped her voice to a whisper.

"Couldn't we make some more?" Ron asked Harry, ignoring Hermione. "It'd be great to have a stock of it. . . . Have a look in the book . . ."

Harry pulled his copy of *Advanced Potion-Making* out of his bag and looked up Felix Felicis.

"Blimey, it's seriously complicated," he said, running an eye down the list of ingredients. "And it takes six months . . . You've got to let it stew. . . ."

"Typical," said Ron.

Harry was about to put his book away again when he noticed the corner of a page folded down; turning to it, he saw the *Sectumsempra* spell, captioned "For Enemies," that he had marked a few weeks previously. He had still not found out what it did, mainly because he did not want to test it around Hermione, but he was considering trying it out on McLaggen next time he came up behind him unawares.

The only person who was not particularly pleased to see Katie Bell back at school was Dean Thomas, because he would no longer be required to fill her place as Chaser. He took the blow stoically enough when Harry told him, merely grunting and shrugging, but Harry had the distinct feeling as he walked away that Dean and Seamus were muttering mutinously behind his back.

The following fortnight saw the best Quidditch practices Harry had known as Captain. His team was so pleased to be rid of McLaggen, so glad to have Katie back at last, that they were flying extremely well.

Ginny did not seem at all upset about the breakup with Dean; on the contrary, she was the life and soul of the team. Her imitations of Ron anxiously bobbing up and down in front of the goal posts as the Quaffle sped toward him, or of Harry bellowing orders at McLaggen before being knocked out cold, kept them all highly amused. Harry, laughing with the others, was glad to have an innocent reason to look at Ginny; he had received several more Bludger injuries during practice because he had not been keeping his eyes on the Snitch.

The battle still raged inside his head: *Ginny or Ron?* Sometimes he thought that the post-Lavender Ron might not mind too much if he asked Ginny out, but then he remembered Ron's expression when he had seen her kissing Dean, and was sure that Ron would consider it base treachery if Harry so much as held her hand. . . .

Yet Harry could not help himself talking to Ginny, laughing with her, walking back from practice with her; however much his conscience ached, he found himself wondering how best to get her on her own. It would have been ideal if Slughorn had given another of his little parties, for Ron would not be around — but unfortunately, Slughorn seemed to have given them up. Once or twice Harry considered asking for Hermione's help, but he did not think he could stand seeing the smug look on her face; he thought he caught it sometimes when Hermione spotted him staring at Ginny or laughing at her jokes. And to complicate matters, he had the nagging worry that if he didn't do it, somebody else was sure to ask Ginny out soon: He and Ron were at least agreed on the fact that she was too popular for her own good.

All in all, the temptation to take another gulp of Felix Felicis was becoming stronger by the day, for surely this was a case for, as Hermione put it, "tweaking the circumstances"? The balmy days slid gently through May, and Ron seemed to be there at Harry's shoulder every time he saw Ginny. Harry found himself longing for a stroke of luck that would somehow cause Ron to realize that nothing would make him happier than his best friend and his sister falling for each other and to leave them alone together for longer than a few seconds. There seemed no chance of either while the final Quidditch game of the season was looming; Ron wanted to talk tactics with Harry all the time and had little thought for anything else.

Ron was not unique in this respect; interest in the Gryffindor-Ravenclaw game was running extremely high throughout the school, for the match would decide the Championship, which was still wide open. If Gryffindor beat Ravenclaw by a margin of three hundred points (a tall order, and yet Harry had never known his team to fly better) then they would win the Championship. If they won by less than three hundred points, they would come second to Ravenclaw; if they lost by a hundred points they would be third behind Hufflepuff and if they lost by more than a hundred, they would be in fourth place and nobody, Harry thought, would ever, ever let him forget that it had been he who had captained Gryffindor to their first bottom-of-the-table defeat in two centuries.

The run-up to this crucial match had all the usual features: members of rival Houses attempting to intimidate opposing teams in the corridors; unpleasant chants about individual players being rehearsed loudly as they passed; the team members themselves either swaggering around enjoying all the attention or else dashing into bathrooms between classes to throw up. Somehow, the game had become inextricably linked in Harry's mind with success or failure in his plans for Ginny. He could not help feeling that if they won by more than three hundred points, the scenes of euphoria and a nice loud after-match party might be just as good as a hearty swig of Felix Felicis.

In the midst of all his preoccupations, Harry had not forgotten his other ambition: finding out what Malfoy was up to in the

Room of Requirement. He was still checking the Marauder's Map, and as he was unable to locate Malfoy on it, deduced that Malfoy was still spending plenty of time within the room. Although Harry was losing hope that he would ever succeed in getting inside the Room of Requirement, he attempted it whenever he was in the vicinity, but no matter how he reworded his request, the wall remained firmly doorless.

A few days before the match against Ravenclaw, Harry found himself walking down to dinner alone from the common room, Ron having rushed off into a nearby bathroom to throw up yet again, and Hermione having dashed off to see Professor Vector about a mistake she thought she might have made in her last Arithmancy essay. More out of habit than anything, Harry made his usual detour along the seventh-floor corridor, checking the Marauder's Map as he went. For a moment he could not find Malfoy anywhere and assumed he must indeed be inside the Room of Requirement again, but then he saw Malfoy's tiny, labeled dot standing in a boys' bathroom on the floor below, accompanied, not by Crabbe or Goyle, but by Moaning Myrtle.

Harry only stopped staring at this unlikely coupling when he walked right into a suit of armor. The loud crash brought him out of his reverie; hurrying from the scene lest Filch turn up, he dashed down the marble staircase and along the passageway below. Outside the bathroom, he pressed his ear against the door. He could not hear anything. He very quietly pushed the door open.

Draco Malfoy was standing with his back to the door, his hands clutching either side of the sink, his white-blond head bowed.

"Don't," crooned Moaning Myrtle's voice from one of the cubicles. "Don't . . . tell me what's wrong . . . I can help you. . . ."

"No one can help me," said Malfoy. His whole body was shaking. "I can't do it. . . . I can't. . . . It won't work . . . and unless I do it soon . . . he says he'll kill me. . . ."

And Harry realized, with a shock so huge it seemed to root him to the spot, that Malfoy was crying — actually crying — tears streaming down his pale face into the grimy basin. Malfoy gasped and gulped and then, with a great shudder, looked up into the cracked mirror and saw Harry staring at him over his shoulder.

Malfoy wheeled around, drawing his wand. Instinctively, Harry pulled out his own. Malfoy's hex missed Harry by inches, shattering the lamp on the wall beside him; Harry threw himself sideways, thought *Levicorpus!* and flicked his wand, but Malfoy blocked the jinx and raised his wand for another —

"No! No! Stop it!" squealed Moaning Myrtle, her voice echoing loudly around the tiled room. "Stop! STOP!"

There was a loud bang and the bin behind Harry exploded; Harry attempted a Leg-Locker Curse that backfired off the wall behind Malfoy's ear and smashed the cistern beneath Moaning Myrtle, who screamed loudly; water poured everywhere and Harry slipped as Malfoy, his face contorted, cried, *"Cruci —"*

"SECTUMSEMPRA!" bellowed Harry from the floor, waving his wand wildly.

Blood spurted from Malfoy's face and chest as though he had been slashed with an invisible sword. He staggered backward and collapsed onto the waterlogged floor with a great splash, his wand falling from his limp right hand.

"No —" gasped Harry.

Slipping and staggering, Harry got to his feet and plunged

toward Malfoy, whose face was now shining scarlet, his white hands scrabbling at his blood-soaked chest.

"No — I didn't —"

Harry did not know what he was saying; he fell to his knees beside Malfoy, who was shaking uncontrollably in a pool of his own blood. Moaning Myrtle let out a deafening scream: "MURDER! MURDER IN THE BATHROOM! MURDER!"

The door banged open behind Harry and he looked up, terrified: Snape had burst into the room, his face livid. Pushing Harry roughly aside, he knelt over Malfoy, drew his wand, and traced it over the deep wounds Harry's curse had made, muttering an incantation that sounded almost like song. The flow of blood seemed to ease; Snape wiped the residue from Malfoy's face and repeated his spell. Now the wounds seemed to be knitting.

Harry was still watching, horrified by what he had done, barely aware that he too was soaked in blood and water. Moaning Myrtle was still sobbing and wailing overhead. When Snape had performed his countercurse for the third time, he half-lifted Malfoy into a standing position.

"You need the hospital wing. There may be a certain amount of scarring, but if you take dittany immediately we might avoid even that. . . . Come. . . ."

He supported Malfoy across the bathroom, turning at the door to say in a voice of cold fury, "And you, Potter . . . You wait here for me."

It did not occur to Harry for a second to disobey. He stood up slowly, shaking, and looked down at the wet floor. There were bloodstains floating like crimson flowers across its surface. He could not even find it in himself to tell Moaning Myrtle to be quiet, as she continued to wail and sob with increasingly evident enjoyment.

Snape returned ten minutes later. He stepped into the bathroom and closed the door behind him.

"Go," he said to Myrtle, and she swooped back into her toilet at once, leaving a ringing silence behind her.

"I didn't mean it to happen," said Harry at once. His voice echoed in the cold, watery space. "I didn't know what that spell did."

But Snape ignored this. "Apparently I underestimated you, Potter," he said quietly. "Who would have thought you knew such Dark Magic? Who taught you that spell?"

"I — read about it somewhere."

"Where?"

"It was — a library book," Harry invented wildly. "I can't remember what it was call —"

"Liar," said Snape. Harry's throat went dry. He knew what Snape was going to do and he had never been able to prevent it. . . .

The bathroom seemed to shimmer before his eyes; he struggled to block out all thought, but try as he might, the Half-Blood Prince's copy of *Advanced Potion-Making* swam hazily to the forefront of his mind.

And then he was staring at Snape again, in the midst of this wrecked, soaked bathroom. He stared into Snape's black eyes, hoping against hope that Snape had not seen what he feared, but —

"Bring me your schoolbag," said Snape softly, "and all of your schoolbooks. *All* of them. Bring them to me here. Now!"

There was no point arguing. Harry turned at once and splashed out of the bathroom. Once in the corridor, he broke into a run to-ward Gryffindor Tower. Most people were walking the other way; they gaped at him, drenched in water and blood, but he answered none of the questions fired at him as he ran past.

He felt stunned; it was as though a beloved pet had turned sud-denly savage; what had the Prince been thinking to copy such a spell into his book? And what would happen when Snape saw it? Would he tell Slughorn — Harry's stomach churned — how Harry had been achieving such good results in Potions all year? Would he confiscate or destroy the book that had taught Harry so much . . . the book that had become a kind of guide and friend? Harry could not let it happen. . . . He could not . . .

"Where've you — ? Why are you soaking — ? Is that *blood*?"

Ron was standing at the top of the stairs, looking bewildered at the sight of Harry.

"I need your book," Harry panted. "Your Potions book. Quick . . . give it to me . . ."

"But what about the Half-Blood —"

"I'll explain later!"

Ron pulled his copy of *Advanced Potion-Making* out of his bag and handed it over; Harry sprinted off past him and back to the common room. Here, he seized his schoolbag, ignoring the amazed looks of several people who had already finished their dinner, threw himself back out of the portrait hole, and hurtled off along the seventh-floor corridor.

He skidded to a halt beside the tapestry of dancing trolls, closed his eyes, and began to walk.

I need a place to hide my book. . . . I need a place to hide my book. . . . I need a place to hide my book. . . .

Three times he walked up and down in front of the stretch of blank wall. When he opened his eyes, there it was at last: the door to the Room of Requirement. Harry wrenched it open, flung himself inside, and slammed it shut.

He gasped. Despite his haste, his panic, his fear of what awaited him back in the bathroom, he could not help but be overawed by what he was looking at. He was standing in a room the size of a large cathedral, whose high windows were sending shafts of light down upon what looked like a city with towering walls, built of what Harry knew must be objects hidden by generations of Hogwarts inhabitants. There were alleyways and roads bordered by teetering piles of broken and damaged furniture, stowed away, perhaps, to hide the evidence of mishandled magic, or else hidden by castle-proud house-elves. There were thousands and thousands of books, no doubt banned or graffitied or stolen. There were winged catapults and Fanged Frisbees, some still with enough life in them to hover halfheartedly over the mountains of other forbidden items; there were chipped bottles of congealed potions, hats, jewels, cloaks; there were what looked like dragon eggshells, corked bottles whose contents still shimmered evilly, several rusting swords, and a heavy, bloodstained axe.

Harry hurried forward into one of the many alleyways between all this hidden treasure. He turned right past an enormous stuffed troll, ran on a short way, took a left at the broken Vanishing Cabinet in which Montague had got lost the previous year, finally pausing beside a large cupboard that seemed to have had acid thrown at its blistered surface. He opened one of the cupboard's creaking doors: It had already been used as a hiding place for something in a cage that had long since died; its skeleton had five legs. He stuffed the Half-Blood Prince's book behind the cage and slammed the door. He paused for a moment, his heart thumping horribly, gazing around at all the clutter. . . . Would he be able to find this spot again amidst all this junk? Seizing the chipped bust of an ugly old warlock from on top of a nearby crate, he stood it on top of the cupboard where the book was now hidden, perched a dusty old wig and a tarnished tiara on the statue's head to make it more distinctive, then sprinted back through the alleyways of hidden junk as fast as he could go, back to the door, back out onto the corridor, where he slammed the door behind him, and it turned at once back into stone.

Harry ran flat-out toward the bathroom on the floor below, cramming Ron's copy of *Advanced Potion-Making* into his bag as he did so. A minute later, he was back in front of Snape, who held out his hand wordlessly for Harry's schoolbag. Harry handed it over, panting, a searing pain in his chest, and waited.

One by one, Snape extracted Harry's books and examined them. Finally, the only book left was the Potions book, which he looked at very carefully before speaking.

"This is your copy of *Advanced Potion-Making*, is it, Potter?"

"Yes," said Harry, still breathing hard.

"You're quite sure of that, are you, Potter?"

"Yes," said Harry, with a touch more defiance.

"This is the copy of *Advanced Potion-Making* that you purchased from Flourish and Blotts?"

"Yes," said Harry firmly.

"Then why," asked Snape, "does it have the name 'Roonil Waz-lib' written inside the front cover?"

Harry's heart missed a beat. "That's my nickname," he said.

"Your nickname," repeated Snape.

"Yeah . . . that's what my friends call me," said Harry.

"I understand what a nickname is," said Snape. The cold, black eyes were boring once more into Harry's; he tried not to look into them. *Close your mind. . . . Close your mind. . . .* But he had never learned how to do it properly. . . .

"Do you know what I think, Potter?" said Snape, very quietly. "I think that you are a liar and a cheat and that you deserve detention with me every Saturday until the end of term. What do you think, Potter?"

"I — I don't agree, sir," said Harry, still refusing to look into Snape's eyes.

"Well, we shall see how you feel after your detentions," said Snape. "Ten o'clock Saturday morning, Potter. My office."

"But sir . . ." said Harry, looking up desperately. "Quidditch . . . the last match of the . . ."

"Ten o'clock," whispered Snape, with a smile that showed his yellow teeth. "Poor Gryffindor . . . fourth place this year, I fear . . ."

And he left the bathroom without another word, leaving Harry to stare into the cracked mirror, feeling sicker, he was sure, than Ron had ever felt in his life.

"I won't say 'I told you so,'" said Hermione, an hour later in the common room.

"Leave it, Hermione," said Ron angrily.

Harry had never made it to dinner; he had no appetite at all. He had just finished telling Ron, Hermione, and Ginny what had happened, not that there seemed to have been much need. The news had traveled very fast: Apparently Moaning Myrtle had taken it upon herself to pop up in every bathroom in the castle to tell the story; Malfoy had already been visited in the hospital wing by Pansy Parkinson, who had lost no time in vilifying Harry far and wide, and Snape had told the staff precisely what had happened. Harry had already been called out of the common room to endure fifteen highly unpleasant minutes in the company of Professor McGonagall, who had told him he was lucky not to have been expelled and that she supported wholeheartedly Snape's punishment of detention every Saturday until the end of term.

"I told you there was something wrong with that Prince person," Hermione said, evidently unable to stop herself. "And I was right, wasn't I?"

"No, I don't think you were," said Harry stubbornly.

He was having a bad enough time without Hermione lecturing him; the looks on the Gryffindor team's faces when he had told them he would not be able to play on Saturday had been the worst punishment of all. He could feel Ginny's eyes on him now but did not meet them; he did not want to see disappointment or anger there. He had just told her that she would be playing Seeker on Saturday and that Dean would be rejoining the team as Chaser in her place. Perhaps, if they won, Ginny and Dean would make up during the post-match euphoria. . . . The thought went through Harry like an icy knife. . . .

"Harry," said Hermione, "how can you still stick up for that book when that spell —"

"Will you stop harping on about the book!" snapped Harry. "The Prince only copied it out! It's not like he was advising anyone to use it! For all we know, he was making a note of something that had been used against him!"

"I don't believe this," said Hermione. "You're actually defending —"

"I'm not defending what I did!" said Harry quickly. "I wish I hadn't done it, and not just because I've got about a dozen detentions. You know I wouldn't've used a spell like that, not even on Malfoy, but you can't blame the Prince, he hadn't written 'try this out, it's really good' — he was just making notes for himself, wasn't he, not for anyone else. . . ."

"Are you telling me," said Hermione, "that you're going to go back — ?"

"And get the book? Yeah, I am," said Harry forcefully. "Listen, without the Prince I'd never have won the Felix Felicis. I'd never have known how to save Ron from poisoning, I'd never have —"

"— got a reputation for Potions brilliance you don't deserve," said Hermione nastily.

"Give it a rest, Hermione!" said Ginny, and Harry was so amazed, so grateful, he looked up. "By the sound of it, Malfoy was trying to use an Unforgivable Curse, you should be glad Harry had something good up his sleeve!"

"Well, of course I'm glad Harry wasn't cursed!" said Hermione, clearly stung. "But you can't call that Sectumsempra spell good, Ginny, look where it's landed him! And I'd have thought, seeing what this has done to your chances in the match —"

"Oh, don't start acting as though you understand Quidditch," snapped Ginny, "you'll only embarrass yourself."

Harry and Ron stared: Hermione and Ginny, who had always got on together very well, were now sitting with their arms folded, glaring in opposite directions. Ron looked nervously at Harry, then snatched up a book at random and hid behind it. Harry, however, little though he knew he deserved it, felt unbelievably cheerful all of a sudden, even though none of them spoke again for the rest of the evening.

His lightheartedness was short-lived. There were Slytherin taunts to be endured next day, not to mention much anger from fellow Gryffindors, who were most unhappy that their Captain had got himself banned from the final match of the season. By Saturday morning, whatever he might have told Hermione, Harry would have gladly exchanged all the Felix Felicis in the world to be walking down to the Quidditch pitch with Ron, Ginny, and the others. It was almost unbearable to turn away from the mass of students streaming out into the sunshine, all of them wearing rosettes and hats and brandishing banners and scarves, to descend the stone steps into the dungeons and walk until the distant sounds of the crowd were quite obliterated, knowing that he would not be able to hear a word of commentary or a cheer or groan.

"Ah, Potter," said Snape, when Harry had knocked on his door and entered the unpleasantly familiar office that Snape, despite teaching floors above now, had not vacated; it was as dimly lit as ever and the same slimy dead objects were suspended in colored potions all around the walls. Ominously, there were many cob-webbed boxes piled on a table where Harry was clearly supposed to sit; they had an aura of tedious, hard, and pointless work about them.

"Mr. Filch has been looking for someone to clear out these old files," said Snape softly. "They are the records of other Hogwarts wrongdoers and their punishments. Where the ink has grown faint, or the cards have suffered damage from mice, we would like you to copy out the crimes and punishments afresh and, making sure that they are in alphabetical order, replace them in the boxes. You will not use magic."

"Right, Professor," said Harry, with as much contempt as he could put into the last three syllables.

"I thought you could start," said Snape, a malicious smile on his lips, "with boxes one thousand and twelve to one thousand and fifty-six. You will find some familiar names in there, which should add interest to the task. Here, you see . . ."

He pulled out a card from one of the topmost boxes with a flourish and read, "*'James Potter and Sirius Black. Apprehended using an illegal hex upon Bertram Aubrey. Aubrey's head twice normal size. Double detention.'*" Snape sneered. "It must be such a comfort to think that, though they are gone, a record of their great achievements remains. . . ."

Harry felt the familiar boiling sensation in the pit of his stomach. Biting his tongue to prevent himself retaliating, he sat down in front of the boxes and pulled one toward him.

It was, as Harry had anticipated, useless, boring work, punctuated (as Snape had clearly planned) with the regular jolt in the stomach that meant he had just read his father or Sirius's names, usually coupled together in various petty misdeeds, occasionally accompanied by those of Remus Lupin and Peter Pettigrew. And while he copied out all their various offenses and punishments, he wondered what was going on outside, where the match would have just started . . . Ginny playing Seeker against Cho . . .

Harry glanced again and again at the large clock ticking on the wall. It seemed to be moving half as fast as a regular clock; perhaps Snape had bewitched it to go extra slowly? He could not have been here for only half an hour . . . an hour . . . an hour and a half. . . .

Harry's stomach started rumbling when the clock showed half past twelve. Snape, who had not spoken at all since setting Harry his task, finally looked up at ten past one.

"I think that will do," he said coldly. "Mark the place you have reached. You will continue at ten o'clock next Saturday."

"Yes, sir."

Harry stuffed a bent card into the box at random and hurried out of the door before Snape could change his mind, racing back up the stone steps, straining his ears to hear a sound from the pitch, but all was quiet. . . . It was over, then. . . .

He hesitated outside the crowded Great Hall, then ran up the marble staircase; whether Gryffindor had won or lost, the team usually celebrated or commiserated in their own common room.

"Quid agis?" he said tentatively to the Fat Lady, wondering what he would find inside.

Her expression was unreadable as she replied, "You'll see."

And she swung forward.

A roar of celebration erupted from the hole behind her. Harry gaped as people began to scream at the sight of him; several hands pulled him into the room.

"We won!" yelled Ron, bounding into sight and brandishing the silver Cup at Harry. "We won! Four hundred and fifty to a hundred and forty! We won!"

Harry looked around; there was Ginny running toward him; she had a hard, blazing look in her face as she threw her arms around him. And without thinking, without planning it, without worrying about the fact that fifty people were watching, Harry kissed her.

After several long moments — or it might have been half an hour — or possibly several sunlit days — they broke apart. The room had gone very quiet. Then several people wolf-whistled and there was an outbreak of nervous giggling. Harry looked over the top of Ginny's head to see Dean Thomas holding a shattered glass in his hand, and Romilda Vane looking as though she might throw something. Hermione was beaming, but Harry's eyes sought Ron. At last he found him, still clutching the Cup and wearing an expression appropriate to having been clubbed over the head. For a fraction of a second they looked at each other, then Ron gave a tiny jerk of the head that Harry understood to mean, *Well — if you must.*

The creature in his chest roaring in triumph, he grinned down at Ginny and gestured wordlessly out of the portrait hole. A long walk in the grounds seemed indicated, during which — if they had time — they might discuss the match.

THE SEER OVERHEARD

The fact that Harry Potter was going out with Ginny Weasley seemed to interest a great number of people, most of them girls, yet Harry found himself newly and happily impervious to gossip over the next few weeks. After all, it made a very nice change to be talked about because of something that was making him happier than he could remember being for a very long time, rather than because he had been involved in horrific scenes of Dark Magic.

"You'd think people had better things to gossip about," said Ginny, as she sat on the common room floor, leaning against Harry's legs and reading the *Daily Prophet*. "Three dementor attacks in a week, and all Romilda Vane does is ask me if it's true you've got a hippogriff tattooed across your chest."

Ron and Hermione both roared with laughter. Harry ignored them.

"What did you tell her?"

"I told her it's a Hungarian Horntail," said Ginny, turning a page of the newspaper idly. "Much more macho."

"Thanks," said Harry, grinning. "And what did you tell her Ron's got?"

"A Pygmy Puff, but I didn't say where."

Ron scowled as Hermione rolled around laughing.

"Watch it," he said, pointing warningly at Harry and Ginny. "Just because I've given my permission doesn't mean I can't withdraw it —"

"*Your permission,*" scoffed Ginny. "Since when did you give me permission to do anything? Anyway, you said yourself you'd rather it was Harry than Michael or Dean."

"Yeah, I would," said Ron grudgingly. "And just as long as you don't start snogging each other in public —"

"You filthy hypocrite! What about you and Lavender, thrashing around like a pair of eels all over the place?" demanded Ginny.

But Ron's tolerance was not to be tested much as they moved into June, for Harry and Ginny's time together was becoming increasingly restricted. Ginny's O.W.L.s were approaching and she was therefore forced to study for hours into the night. On one such evening, when Ginny had retired to the library, and Harry was sitting beside the window in the common room, supposedly finishing his Herbology homework but in reality reliving a particularly happy hour he had spent down by the lake with Ginny at lunchtime, Hermione dropped into the seat between him and Ron with an unpleasantly purposeful look on her face.

"I want to talk to you, Harry."

"What about?" said Harry suspiciously. Only the previous day,

Hermione had told him off for distracting Ginny when she ought to be working hard for her examinations.

"The so-called Half-Blood Prince."

"Oh, not again," he groaned. "Will you please drop it?"

He had not dared to return to the Room of Requirement to retrieve his book, and his performance in Potions was suffering accordingly (though Slughorn, who approved of Ginny, had jocularly attributed this to Harry being lovesick). But Harry was sure that Snape had not yet given up hope of laying hands on the Prince's book, and was determined to leave it where it was while Snape remained on the lookout.

"I'm not dropping it," said Hermione firmly, "until you've heard me out. Now, I've been trying to find out a bit about who might make a hobby of inventing Dark spells —"

"He didn't make a hobby of it —"

"He, he — who says it's a he?"

"We've been through this," said Harry crossly. "*Prince,* Hermione, *Prince!*"

"Right!" said Hermione, red patches blazing in her cheeks as she pulled a very old piece of newsprint out of her pocket and slammed it down on the table in front of Harry. "Look at that! Look at the picture!"

Harry picked up the crumbling piece of paper and stared at the moving photograph, yellowed with age; Ron leaned over for a look too. The picture showed a skinny girl of around fifteen. She was not pretty; she looked simultaneously cross and sullen, with heavy brows and a long, pallid face. Underneath the photograph was the caption: EILEEN PRINCE, CAPTAIN OF THE HOGWARTS GOBSTONES TEAM.

"So?" said Harry, scanning the short news item to which the picture belonged; it was a rather dull story about interschool competitions.

"Her name was Eileen Prince. *Prince,* Harry."

They looked at each other, and Harry realized what Hermione was trying to say. He burst out laughing.

"No way."

"What?"

"You think *she* was the Half-Blood . . . ? Oh, come on."

"Well, why not? Harry, there aren't any real princes in the Wizarding world! It's either a nickname, a made-up title somebody's given themselves, or it could be their actual name, couldn't it? No, listen! If, say, her father was a wizard whose surname was Prince, and her mother was a Muggle, then that would make her a 'half-blood Prince'!"

"Yeah, very ingenious, Hermione . . ."

"But it would! Maybe she was proud of being half a Prince!"

"Listen, Hermione, I can tell it's not a girl. I can just tell."

"The truth is that you don't think a girl would have been clever enough," said Hermione angrily.

"How can I have hung round with you for five years and not think girls are clever?" said Harry, stung by this. "It's the way he writes, I just know the Prince was a bloke, I can tell. This girl hasn't got anything to do with it. Where did you get this anyway?"

"The library," said Hermione predictably. "There's a whole collection of old *Prophets* up there. Well, I'm going to find out more about Eileen Prince if I can."

"Enjoy yourself," said Harry irritably.

"I will," said Hermione. "And the first place I'll look," she shot at him, as she reached the portrait hole, "is records of old Potions awards!"

Harry scowled after her for a moment, then continued his contemplation of the darkening sky.

"She's just never got over you outperforming her in Potions," said Ron, returning to his copy of *One Thousand Magical Herbs and Fungi*.

"You don't think I'm mad, wanting that book back, do you?"

"'Course not," said Ron robustly. "He was a genius, the Prince. Anyway . . . without his bezoar tip . . ." He drew his finger significantly across his own throat. "I wouldn't be here to discuss it, would I? I mean, I'm not saying that spell you used on Malfoy was great —"

"Nor am I," said Harry quickly.

"But he healed all right, didn't he? Back on his feet in no time."

"Yeah," said Harry; this was perfectly true, although his conscience squirmed slightly all the same. "Thanks to Snape . . ."

"You still got detention with Snape this Saturday?" Ron continued.

"Yeah, and the Saturday after that, and the Saturday after that," sighed Harry. "And he's hinting now that if I don't get all the boxes done by the end of term, we'll carry on next year."

He was finding these detentions particularly irksome because they cut into the already limited time he could have been spending with Ginny. Indeed, he had frequently wondered lately whether Snape did not know this, for he was keeping Harry later and later every time, while making pointed asides about Harry having to miss the good weather and the varied opportunities it offered.

Harry was shaken from these bitter reflections by the appearance at his side of Jimmy Peakes, who was holding out a scroll of parchment.

"Thanks, Jimmy . . . Hey, it's from Dumbledore!" said Harry excitedly, unrolling the parchment and scanning it. "He wants me to go to his office as quick as I can!"

They stared at each other.

"Blimey," whispered Ron. "You don't reckon . . . he hasn't found . . . ?"

"Better go and see, hadn't I?" said Harry, jumping to his feet.

He hurried out of the common room and along the seventh floor as fast as he could, passing nobody but Peeves, who swooped past in the opposite direction, throwing bits of chalk at Harry in a routine sort of way and cackling loudly as he dodged Harry's defensive jinx. Once Peeves had vanished, there was silence in the corridors; with only fifteen minutes left until curfew, most people had already returned to their common rooms.

And then Harry heard a scream and a crash. He stopped in his tracks, listening.

"How — *dare* — you — aaaaargh!"

The noise was coming from a corridor nearby; Harry sprinted toward it, his wand at the ready, hurtled around another corner, and saw Professor Trelawney sprawled upon the floor, her head covered in one of her many shawls, several sherry bottles lying beside her, one broken.

"Professor —"

Harry hurried forward and helped Professor Trelawney to her feet. Some of her glittering beads had become entangled with her glasses. She hiccuped loudly, patted her hair, and pulled herself up on Harry's helping arm.

"What happened, Professor?"

"You may well ask!" she said shrilly. "I was strolling along, brooding upon certain dark portents I happen to have glimpsed . . ."

But Harry was not paying much attention. He had just noticed where they were standing: There on the right was the tapestry of dancing trolls, and on the left, that smoothly impenetrable stretch of stone wall that concealed —

"Professor, were you trying to get into the Room of Requirement?"

". . . omens I have been vouchsafed — what?" She looked suddenly shifty.

"The Room of Requirement," repeated Harry. "Were you trying to get in there?"

"I — well — I didn't know students knew about —"

"Not all of them do," said Harry. "But what happened? You screamed. . . . It sounded as though you were hurt. . . ."

"I — well," said Professor Trelawney, drawing her shawls around her defensively and staring down at him with her vastly magnified eyes. "I wished to — ah — deposit certain — um — personal items in the room. . . ." And she muttered something about "nasty accusations."

"Right," said Harry, glancing down at the sherry bottles. "But you couldn't get in and hide them?"

He found this very odd; the room had opened for him, after all, when he had wanted to hide the Half-Blood Prince's book.

"Oh, I got in all right," said Professor Trelawney, glaring at the wall. "But there was somebody already in there."

"Somebody in — ? Who?" demanded Harry. "Who was in there?"

"I have no idea," said Professor Trelawney, looking slightly taken aback at the urgency in Harry's voice. "I walked into the room and I heard a voice, which has never happened before in all my years of hiding — of using the room, I mean."

"A voice? Saying what?"

"I don't know that it was saying anything," said Professor Trelawney. "It was . . . whooping."

"Whooping?"

"Gleefully," she said, nodding.

Harry stared at her.

"Was it male or female?"

"I would hazard a guess at male," said Professor Trelawney.

"And it sounded happy?"

"Very happy," said Professor Trelawney sniffily.

"As though it was celebrating?"

"Most definitely."

"And then — ?"

"And then I called out 'Who's there?'"

"You couldn't have found out who it was without asking?" Harry asked her, slightly frustrated.

"The Inner Eye," said Professor Trelawney with dignity, straightening her shawls and many strands of glittering beads, "was fixed upon matters well outside the mundane realms of whooping voices."

"Right," said Harry hastily; he had heard about Professor Trelawney's Inner Eye all too often before. "And did the voice say who was there?"

"No, it did not," she said. "Everything went pitch-black and the next thing I knew, I was being hurled headfirst out of the room!"

"And you didn't see that coming?" said Harry, unable to help himself.

"No, I did not, as I say, it was pitch —" She stopped and glared at him suspiciously.

"I think you'd better tell Professor Dumbledore," said Harry. "He ought to know Malfoy's celebrating — I mean, that someone threw you out of the room."

To his surprise, Professor Trelawney drew herself up at this suggestion, looking haughty.

"The headmaster has intimated that he would prefer fewer visits from me," she said coldly. "I am not one to press my company upon those who do not value it. If Dumbledore chooses to ignore the warnings the cards show —" Her bony hand closed suddenly around Harry's wrist. "Again and again, no matter how I lay them out —" And she pulled a card dramatically from underneath her shawls. "— the lightning-struck tower," she whispered. "Calamity. Disaster. Coming nearer all the time . . ."

"Right," said Harry again. "Well . . . I still think you should tell Dumbledore about this voice, and everything going dark and being thrown out of the room. . . ."

"You think so?" Professor Trelawney seemed to consider the matter for a moment, but Harry could tell that she liked the idea of retelling her little adventure.

"I'm going to see him right now," said Harry. "I've got a meeting with him. We could go together."

"Oh, well, in that case," said Professor Trelawney with a smile. She bent down, scooped up her sherry bottles, and dumped them unceremoniously in a large blue-and-white vase standing in a nearby niche.

"I miss having you in my classes, Harry," she said soulfully as they set off together. "You were never much of a Seer . . . but you were a wonderful Object . . ."

Harry did not reply; he had loathed being the Object of Professor Trelawney's continual predictions of doom.

"I am afraid," she went on, "that the nag — I'm sorry, the centaur — knows nothing of cartomancy. I asked him — one Seer to another — had he not, too, sensed the distant vibrations of coming catastrophe? But he seemed to find me almost comical. Yes, comical!"

Her voice rose rather hysterically, and Harry caught a powerful whiff of sherry even though the bottles had been left behind.

"Perhaps the horse has heard people say that I have not inherited my great-great-grandmother's gift. Those rumors have been bandied about by the jealous for years. You know what I say to such people, Harry? Would Dumbledore have let me teach at this great school, put so much trust in me all these years, had I not proved myself to him?"

Harry mumbled something indistinct.

"I well remember my first interview with Dumbledore," went on Professor Trelawney, in throaty tones. "He was deeply impressed, of course, deeply impressed. . . . I was staying at the Hog's Head, which I do not advise, incidentally — bedbugs, dear boy — but funds were low. Dumbledore did me the courtesy of calling upon me in my room. He questioned me. . . . I must confess that, at first, I thought he seemed ill-disposed toward Divination . . . and I remember I was starting to feel a little odd, I had not eaten much that day . . . but then . . ."

And now Harry was paying attention properly for the first time, for he knew what had happened then: Professor Trelawney had made the prophecy that had altered the course of his whole life, the prophecy about him and Voldemort.

". . . but then we were rudely interrupted by Severus Snape!"

"What?"

"Yes, there was a commotion outside the door and it flew open, and there was that rather uncouth barman standing with Snape, who was waffling about having come the wrong way up the stairs, although I'm afraid that I myself rather thought he had been apprehended eavesdropping on my interview with Dumbledore — you see, he himself was seeking a job at the time, and no doubt hoped to pick up tips! Well, after that, you know, Dumbledore seemed much more disposed to give me a job, and I could not help thinking, Harry, that it was because he appreciated the stark contrast between my own unassuming manners and quiet talent, compared to the pushing, thrusting young man who was prepared to listen at keyholes — Harry, dear?"

She looked back over her shoulder, having only just realized that Harry was no longer with her; he had stopped walking and they were now ten feet from each other.

"Harry?" she repeated uncertainly.

Perhaps his face was white to make her look so concerned and frightened. Harry was standing stock-still as waves of shock crashed over him, wave after wave, obliterating everything except the information that had been kept from him for so long. . . .

It was Snape who had overheard the prophecy. It was Snape who had carried the news of the prophecy to Voldemort. Snape and Peter Pettigrew together had sent Voldemort hunting after Lily and James and their son. . . .

Nothing else mattered to Harry just now.

"Harry?" said Professor Trelawney again. "Harry — I thought we were going to see the headmaster together?"

"You stay here," said Harry through numb lips.

"But dear . . . I was going to tell him how I was assaulted in the Room of —"

"You stay here!" Harry repeated angrily.

She looked alarmed as he ran past her, around the corner into Dumbledore's corridor, where the lone gargoyle stood sentry. Harry shouted the password at the gargoyle and ran up the moving spiral staircase three steps at a time. He did not knock upon Dumbledore's door, he hammered; and the calm voice answered, "Enter" after Harry had already flung himself into the room.

Fawkes the phoenix looked around, his bright black eyes gleaming with reflected gold from the sunset beyond the windows. Dumbledore was standing at the window looking out at the grounds, a long, black traveling cloak in his arms.

"Well, Harry, I promised that you could come with me."

For a moment or two, Harry did not understand; the conversation with Trelawney had driven everything else out of his head and his brain seemed to be moving very slowly.

"Come . . . with you . . . ?"

"Only if you wish it, of course."

"If I . . ."

And then Harry remembered why he had been eager to come to Dumbledore's office in the first place. "You've found one? You've found a Horcrux?"

"I believe so."

Rage and resentment fought shock and excitement: For several moments, Harry could not speak.

"It is natural to be afraid," said Dumbledore.

"I'm not scared!" said Harry at once, and it was perfectly true; fear was one emotion he was not feeling at all. "Which Horcrux is it? Where is it?"

"I am not sure which it is — though I think we can rule out the snake — but I believe it to be hidden in a cave on the coast many miles from here, a cave I have been trying to locate for a very long time: the cave in which Tom Riddle once terrorized two children from his orphanage on their annual trip; you remember?"

"Yes," said Harry. "How is it protected?"

"I do not know; I have suspicions that may be entirely wrong." Dumbledore hesitated, then said, "Harry, I promised you that you could come with me, and I stand by that promise, but it would be very wrong of me not to warn you that this will be exceedingly dangerous."

"I'm coming," said Harry, almost before Dumbledore had finished speaking. Boiling with anger at Snape, his desire to do something desperate and risky had increased tenfold in the last few minutes. This seemed to show on Harry's face, for Dumbledore moved away from the window and looked more closely at Harry, a slight crease between his silver eyebrows.

"What has happened to you?"

"Nothing," lied Harry promptly.

"What has upset you?"

"I'm not upset."

"Harry, you were never a good Occlumens —"

The word was the spark that ignited Harry's fury.

"Snape!" he said, very loudly, and Fawkes gave a soft squawk behind them. "Snape's what's happened! He told Voldemort about the prophecy, it was *him*, he listened outside the door, Trelawney told me!"

Dumbledore's expression did not change, but Harry thought his face whitened under the bloody tinge cast by the setting sun. For a long moment, Dumbledore said nothing. "When did you find out about this?" he asked at last.

"Just now!" said Harry, who was refraining from yelling with enormous difficulty. And then, suddenly, he could not stop himself. "AND YOU LET HIM TEACH HERE AND HE TOLD VOLDEMORT TO GO AFTER MY MUM AND DAD!"

Breathing hard as though he was fighting, Harry turned away from Dumbledore, who still had not moved a muscle, and paced up and down the study, rubbing his knuckles in his hand and exercising every last bit of restraint to prevent himself knocking things over. He wanted to rage and storm at Dumbledore, but he also wanted to go with him to try and destroy the Horcrux; he wanted to tell him that he was a foolish old man for trusting Snape, but he was terrified that Dumbledore would not take him along unless he mastered his anger. . . .

"Harry," said Dumbledore quietly. "Please listen to me."

It was as difficult to stop his relentless pacing as to refrain from shouting. Harry paused, biting his lip, and looked into Dumbledore's lined face.

"Professor Snape made a terrible —"

"Don't tell me it was a mistake, sir, he was listening at the door!"

"Please let me finish." Dumbledore waited until Harry had

nodded curtly, then went on. "Professor Snape made a terrible mistake. He was still in Lord Voldemort's employ on the night he heard the first half of Professor Trelawney's prophecy. Naturally, he hastened to tell his master what he had heard, for it concerned his master most deeply. But he did not know — he had no possible way of knowing — which boy Voldemort would hunt from then onward, or that the parents he would destroy in his murderous quest were people that Professor Snape knew, that they were your mother and father —"

Harry let out a yell of mirthless laughter.

"He hated my dad like he hated Sirius! Haven't you noticed, Professor, how the people Snape hates tend to end up dead?"

"You have no idea of the remorse Professor Snape felt when he realized how Lord Voldemort had interpreted the prophecy, Harry. I believe it to be the greatest regret of his life and the reason that he returned —"

"But *he's* a very good Occlumens, isn't he, sir?" said Harry, whose voice was shaking with the effort of keeping it steady. "And isn't Voldemort convinced that Snape's on his side, even now? Professor . . . how can you be *sure* Snape's on our side?"

Dumbledore did not speak for a moment; he looked as though he was trying to make up his mind about something. At last he said, "I am sure. I trust Severus Snape completely."

Harry breathed deeply for a few moments in an effort to steady himself. It did not work.

"Well, I don't!" he said, as loudly as before. "He's up to something with Draco Malfoy right now, right under your nose, and you still —"

"We have discussed this, Harry," said Dumbledore, and now he sounded stern again. "I have told you my views."

"You're leaving the school tonight, and I'll bet you haven't even considered that Snape and Malfoy might decide to —"

"To what?" asked Dumbledore, his eyebrows raised. "What is it that you suspect them of doing, precisely?"

"I . . . they're up to something!" said Harry, and his hands curled into fists as he said it. "Professor Trelawney was just in the Room of Requirement, trying to hide her sherry bottles, and she heard Malfoy whooping, celebrating! He's trying to mend something dangerous in there and if you ask me, he's fixed it at last and you're about to just walk out of school without —"

"Enough," said Dumbledore. He said it quite calmly, and yet Harry fell silent at once; he knew that he had finally crossed some invisible line. "Do you think that I have once left the school unprotected during my absences this year? I have not. Tonight, when I leave, there will again be additional protection in place. Please do not suggest that I do not take the safety of my students seriously, Harry."

"I didn't —" mumbled Harry, a little abashed, but Dumbledore cut across him.

"I do not wish to discuss the matter any further."

Harry bit back his retort, scared that he had gone too far, that he had ruined his chance of accompanying Dumbledore, but Dumbledore went on, "Do you wish to come with me tonight?"

"Yes," said Harry at once.

"Very well, then: Listen." Dumbledore drew himself up to his full height. "I take you with me on one condition: that you obey any command I might give you at once, and without question."

"Of course."

"Be sure to understand me, Harry. I mean that you must follow even such orders as 'run,' 'hide,' or 'go back.' Do I have your word?"

"I — yes, of course."

"If I tell you to hide, you will do so?"

"Yes."

"If I tell you to flee, you will obey?"

"Yes."

"If I tell you to leave me and save yourself, you will do as I tell you?"

"I —"

"Harry?"

They looked at each other for a moment.

"Yes, sir."

"Very good. Then I wish you to go and fetch your Invisibility Cloak and meet me in the entrance hall in five minutes' time."

Dumbledore turned back to look out of the fiery window; the sun was now a ruby red glare along the horizon. Harry walked quickly from the office and down the spiral staircase. His mind was oddly clear all of a sudden. He knew what to do.

Ron and Hermione were sitting together in the common room when he came back. "What does he want?" Hermione said at once. "Harry, are you okay?" she added anxiously.

"I'm fine," said Harry shortly, racing past them. He dashed up the stairs and into his dormitory, where he flung open his trunk and pulled out the Marauder's Map and a pair of balled-up socks. Then he sped back down the stairs and into the common room, skidding to a halt where Ron and Hermione sat, looking stunned.

"I've got to be quick," Harry panted. "Dumbledore thinks I'm getting my Invisibility Cloak. Listen. . . ."

Quickly he told them where he was going and why. He did not pause either for Hermione's gasps of horror or for Ron's hasty questions; they could work out the finer details for themselves later.

"... so you see what this means?" Harry finished at a gallop. "Dumbledore won't be here tonight, so Malfoy's going to have another clear shot at whatever he's up to. *No, listen to me!*" he hissed angrily, as both Ron and Hermione showed every sign of interrupting. "I know it was Malfoy celebrating in the Room of Requirement. Here —" He shoved the Marauder's Map into Hermione's hands. "You've got to watch him and you've got to watch Snape too. Use anyone else who you can rustle up from the D.A., Hermione, those contact Galleons will still work, right? Dumbledore says he's put extra protection in the school, but if Snape's involved, he'll know what Dumbledore's protection is, and how to avoid it — but he won't be expecting you lot to be on the watch, will he?"

"Harry —" began Hermione, her eyes huge with fear.

"I haven't got time to argue," said Harry curtly. "Take this as well —"

He thrust the socks into Ron's hands.

"Thanks," said Ron. "Er — why do I need socks?"

"You need what's wrapped in them, it's the Felix Felicis. Share it between yourselves and Ginny too. Say good-bye to her for me. I'd better go, Dumbledore's waiting —"

"No!" said Hermione, as Ron unwrapped the tiny little bottle of golden potion, looking awestruck. "We don't want it, you take it, who knows what you're going to be facing?"

"I'll be fine, I'll be with Dumbledore," said Harry. "I want to know you lot are okay. . . . Don't look like that, Hermione, I'll see you later. . . ."

And he was off, hurrying back through the portrait hole and toward the entrance hall.

Dumbledore was waiting beside the oaken front doors. He turned as Harry came skidding out onto the topmost stone step, panting hard, a searing stitch in his side.

"I would like you to wear your cloak, please," said Dumbledore, and he waited until Harry had thrown it on before saying, "Very good. Shall we go?"

Dumbledore set off at once down the stone steps, his own traveling cloak barely stirring in the still summer air. Harry hurried alongside him under the Invisibility Cloak, still panting and sweating rather a lot.

"But what will people think when they see you leaving, Professor?" Harry asked, his mind on Malfoy and Snape.

"That I am off into Hogsmeade for a drink," said Dumbledore lightly. "I sometimes offer Rosmerta my custom, or else visit the Hog's Head . . . or I appear to. It is as good a way as any of disguising one's true destination."

They made their way down the drive in the gathering twilight. The air was full of the smells of warm grass, lake water, and wood smoke from Hagrid's cabin. It was difficult to believe that they were heading for anything dangerous or frightening.

"Professor," said Harry quietly, as the gates at the bottom of the drive came into view, "will we be Apparating?"

"Yes," said Dumbledore. "You can Apparate now, I believe?"

"Yes," said Harry, "but I haven't got a license."

He felt it best to be honest; what if he spoiled everything by turning up a hundred miles from where he was supposed to go?

"No matter," said Dumbledore, "I can assist you again."

They turned out of the gates into the twilit, deserted lane to Hogsmeade. Darkness descended fast as they walked, and by the time they reached the High Street night was falling in earnest. Lights twinkled from windows over shops and as they neared the Three Broomsticks they heard raucous shouting.

"— and stay out!" shouted Madam Rosmerta, forcibly ejecting a grubby-looking wizard. "Oh, hello, Albus . . . You're out late . . ."

"Good evening, Rosmerta, good evening . . . forgive me, I'm off to the Hog's Head. . . . No offense, but I feel like a quieter atmosphere tonight. . . ."

A minute later they turned the corner into the side street where the Hog's Head's sign creaked a little, though there was no breeze. In contrast to the Three Broomsticks, the pub appeared to be completely empty.

"It will not be necessary for us to enter," muttered Dumbledore, glancing around. "As long as nobody sees us go . . . now place your hand upon my arm, Harry. There is no need to grip too hard, I am merely guiding you. On the count of three . . . One . . . two . . . three . . ."

Harry turned. At once, there was that horrible sensation that he was being squeezed through a thick rubber tube; he could not draw breath, every part of him was being compressed almost past endurance and then, just when he thought he must suffocate, the invisible bands seemed to burst open, and he was standing in cool darkness, breathing in lungfuls of fresh, salty air.

THE CAVE

Harry could smell salt and hear rushing waves; a light, chilly breeze ruffled his hair as he looked out at moonlit sea and star-strewn sky. He was standing upon a high outcrop of dark rock, water foaming and churning below him. He glanced over his shoulder. A towering cliff stood behind them, a sheer drop, black and faceless. A few large chunks of rock, such as the one upon which Harry and Dumbledore were standing, looked as though they had broken away from the cliff face at some point in the past. It was a bleak, harsh view, the sea and the rock unrelieved by any tree or sweep of grass or sand.

"What do you think?" asked Dumbledore. He might have been asking Harry's opinion on whether it was a good site for a picnic.

"They brought the kids from the orphanage here?" asked Harry, who could not imagine a less cozy spot for a day trip.

"Not here, precisely," said Dumbledore. "There is a village of sorts about halfway along the cliffs behind us. I believe the orphans were taken there for a little sea air and a view of the waves. No, I think it was only ever Tom Riddle and his youthful victims who visited this spot. No Muggle could reach this rock unless they were uncommonly good mountaineers, and boats cannot approach the cliffs, the waters around them are too dangerous. I imagine that Riddle climbed down; magic would have served better than ropes. And he brought two small children with him, probably for the pleasure of terrorizing them. I think the journey alone would have done it, don't you?"

Harry looked up at the cliff again and felt goose bumps.

"But his final destination — and ours — lies a little farther on. Come."

Dumbledore beckoned Harry to the very edge of the rock where a series of jagged niches made footholds leading down to boulders that lay half-submerged in water and closer to the cliff. It was a treacherous descent and Dumbledore, hampered slightly by his withered hand, moved slowly. The lower rocks were slippery with seawater. Harry could feel flecks of cold salt spray hitting his face.

"*Lumos,*" said Dumbledore, as he reached the boulder closest to the cliff face. A thousand flecks of golden light sparkled upon the dark surface of the water a few feet below where he crouched; the black wall of rock beside him was illuminated too.

"You see?" said Dumbledore quietly, holding his wand a little higher. Harry saw a fissure in the cliff into which dark water was swirling.

"You will not object to getting a little wet?"

"No," said Harry.

"Then take off your Invisibility Cloak — there is no need for it now — and let us take the plunge."

And with the sudden agility of a much younger man, Dumbledore slid from the boulder, landed in the sea, and began to swim, with a perfect breaststroke, toward the dark slit in the rock face, his lit wand held in his teeth. Harry pulled off his cloak, stuffed it into his pocket, and followed.

The water was icy; Harry's waterlogged clothes billowed around him and weighed him down. Taking deep breaths that filled his nostrils with the tang of salt and seaweed, he struck out for the shimmering, shrinking light now moving deeper into the cliff.

The fissure soon opened into a dark tunnel that Harry could tell would be filled with water at high tide. The slimy walls were barely three feet apart and glimmered like wet tar in the passing light of Dumbledore's wand. A little way in, the passageway curved to the left, and Harry saw that it extended far into the cliff. He continued to swim in Dumbledore's wake, the tips of his benumbed fingers brushing the rough, wet rock.

Then he saw Dumbledore rising out of the water ahead, his silver hair and dark robes gleaming. When Harry reached the spot he found steps that led into a large cave. He clambered up them, water streaming from his soaking clothes, and emerged, shivering uncontrollably, into the still and freezing air.

Dumbledore was standing in the middle of the cave, his wand held high as he turned slowly on the spot, examining the walls and ceiling.

"Yes, this is the place," said Dumbledore.

"How can you tell?" Harry spoke in a whisper.

"It has known magic," said Dumbledore simply.

Harry could not tell whether the shivers he was experiencing were due to his spine-deep coldness or to the same awareness of enchantments. He watched as Dumbledore continued to revolve on the spot, evidently concentrating on things Harry could not see.

"This is merely the antechamber, the entrance hall," said Dumbledore after a moment or two. "We need to penetrate the inner place. . . . Now it is Lord Voldemort's obstacles that stand in our way, rather than those nature made. . . ."

Dumbledore approached the wall of the cave and caressed it with his blackened fingertips, murmuring words in a strange tongue that Harry did not understand. Twice Dumbledore walked right around the cave, touching as much of the rough rock as he could, occasionally pausing, running his fingers backward and forward over a particular spot, until finally he stopped, his hand pressed flat against the wall.

"Here," he said. "We go on through here. The entrance is concealed."

Harry did not ask how Dumbledore knew. He had never seen a wizard work things out like this, simply by looking and touching; but Harry had long since learned that bangs and smoke were more often the marks of ineptitude than expertise.

Dumbledore stepped back from the cave wall and pointed his wand at the rock. For a moment, an arched outline appeared there, blazing white as though there was a powerful light behind the crack.

"You've d-done it!" said Harry through chattering teeth, but before the words had left his lips the outline had gone, leaving the rock as bare and solid as ever. Dumbledore looked around.

"Harry, I'm so sorry, I forgot," he said; he now pointed his wand at Harry and at once, Harry's clothes were as warm and dry as if they had been hanging in front of a blazing fire.

"Thank you," said Harry gratefully, but Dumbledore had already turned his attention back to the solid cave wall. He did not try any more magic, but simply stood there staring at it intently, as though something extremely interesting was written on it. Harry stayed quite still; he did not want to break Dumbledore's concentration. Then, after two solid minutes, Dumbledore said quietly, "Oh, surely not. So crude."

"What is it, Professor?"

"I rather think," said Dumbledore, putting his uninjured hand inside his robes and drawing out a short silver knife of the kind Harry used to chop potion ingredients, "that we are required to make payment to pass."

"Payment?" said Harry. "You've got to give the door something?"

"Yes," said Dumbledore. "Blood, if I am not much mistaken."

"*Blood?*"

"I said it was crude," said Dumbledore, who sounded disdainful, even disappointed, as though Voldemort had fallen short of the standards Dumbledore expected. "The idea, as I am sure you will have gathered, is that your enemy must weaken him- or herself to enter. Once again, Lord Voldemort fails to grasp that there are much more terrible things than physical injury."

"Yeah, but still, if you can avoid it . . ." said Harry, who had experienced enough pain not to be keen for more.

"Sometimes, however, it is unavoidable," said Dumbledore, shaking back the sleeve of his robes and exposing the forearm of his injured hand.

"Professor!" protested Harry, hurrying forward as Dumbledore raised his knife. "I'll do it, I'm —"

He did not know what he was going to say — younger, fitter?

But Dumbledore merely smiled. There was a flash of silver, and a spurt of scarlet; the rock face was peppered with dark, glistening drops.

"You are very kind, Harry," said Dumbledore, now passing the tip of his wand over the deep cut he had made in his own arm, so that it healed instantly, just as Snape had healed Malfoy's wounds. "But your blood is worth more than mine. Ah, that seems to have done the trick, doesn't it?"

The blazing silver outline of an arch had appeared in the wall once more, and this time it did not fade away: The blood-spattered rock within it simply vanished, leaving an opening into what seemed total darkness.

"After me, I think," said Dumbledore, and he walked through the archway with Harry on his heels, lighting his own wand hastily as he went.

An eerie sight met their eyes: They were standing on the edge of a great black lake, so vast that Harry could not make out the distant banks, in a cavern so high that the ceiling too was out of sight. A misty greenish light shone far away in what looked like the middle of the lake; it was reflected in the completely still water below. The greenish glow and the light from the two wands were the only things that broke the otherwise velvety blackness, though their rays did not penetrate as far as Harry would have expected. The darkness was somehow denser than normal darkness.

"Let us walk," said Dumbledore quietly. "Be very careful not to step into the water. Stay close to me."

He set off around the edge of the lake, and Harry followed close behind him. Their footsteps made echoing, slapping sounds on the narrow rim of rock that surrounded the water. On and on they walked, but the view did not vary: on one side of them, the rough cavern wall, on the other, the boundless expanse of smooth, glassy blackness, in the very middle of which was that mysterious greenish glow. Harry found the place and the silence oppressive, unnerving.

"Professor?" he said finally. "Do you think the Horcrux is here?"

"Oh yes," said Dumbledore. "Yes, I'm sure it is. The question is, how do we get to it?"

"We couldn't . . . we couldn't just try a Summoning Charm?" Harry said, sure that it was a stupid suggestion. But he was much keener than he was prepared to admit on getting out of this place as soon as possible.

"Certainly we could," said Dumbledore, stopping so suddenly that Harry almost walked into him. "Why don't you do it?"

"Me? Oh . . . okay . . ."

Harry had not expected this, but cleared his throat and said loudly, wand aloft, *"Accio Horcrux!"*

With a noise like an explosion, something very large and pale erupted out of the dark water some twenty feet away; before Harry could see what it was, it had vanished again with a crashing splash that made great, deep ripples on the mirrored surface. Harry leapt backward in shock and hit the wall; his heart was still thundering as he turned to Dumbledore.

"What was that?"

"Something, I think, that is ready to respond should we attempt to seize the Horcrux."

Harry looked back at the water. The surface of the lake was once more shining black glass: The ripples had vanished unnaturally fast; Harry's heart, however, was still pounding.

"Did you think that would happen, sir?"

"I thought *something* would happen if we made an obvious attempt to get our hands on the Horcrux. That was a very good idea, Harry; much the simplest way of finding out what we are facing."

"But we don't know what the thing was," said Harry, looking at the sinisterly smooth water.

"What the things *are,* you mean," said Dumbledore. "I doubt very much that there is only one of them. Shall we walk on?"

"Professor?"

"Yes, Harry?"

"Do you think we're going to have to go into the lake?"

"Into it? Only if we are very unfortunate."

"You don't think the Horcrux is at the bottom?"

"Oh no . . . I think the Horcrux is in the *middle.*"

And Dumbledore pointed toward the misty green light in the center of the lake.

"So we're going to have to cross the lake to get to it?"

"Yes, I think so."

Harry did not say anything. His thoughts were all of water monsters, of giant serpents, of demons, kelpies, and sprites. . . .

"Aha," said Dumbledore, and he stopped again; this time, Harry really did walk into him; for a moment he toppled on the edge of the dark water, and Dumbledore's uninjured hand closed tightly around his upper arm, pulling him back. "So sorry, Harry, I should have given warning. Stand back against the wall, please; I think I have found the place."

Harry had no idea what Dumbledore meant; this patch of dark bank was exactly like every other bit as far as he could tell, but Dumbledore seemed to have detected something special about it. This time he was running his hand, not over the rocky wall, but through the thin air, as though expecting to find and grip something invisible.

"Oho," said Dumbledore happily, seconds later. His hand had closed in midair upon something Harry could not see. Dumbledore moved closer to the water; Harry watched nervously as the tips of Dumbledore's buckled shoes found the utmost edge of the rock rim. Keeping his hand clenched in midair, Dumbledore raised his wand with the other and tapped his fist with the point.

Immediately a thick coppery green chain appeared out of thin air, extending from the depths of the water into Dumbledore's clenched hand. Dumbledore tapped the chain, which began to slide through his fist like a snake, coiling itself on the ground with a clinking sound that echoed noisily off the rocky walls, pulling something from the depths of the black water. Harry gasped as the ghostly prow of a tiny boat broke the surface, glowing as green as the chain, and floated, with barely a ripple, toward the place on the bank where Harry and Dumbledore stood.

"How did you know that was there?" Harry asked in astonishment.

"Magic always leaves traces," said Dumbledore, as the boat hit the bank with a gentle bump, "sometimes very distinctive traces. I taught Tom Riddle. I know his style."

"Is . . . is this boat safe?"

"Oh yes, I think so. Voldemort needed to create a means to cross the lake without attracting the wrath of those creatures he had placed within it in case he ever wanted to visit or remove his Horcrux."

"So the things in the water won't do anything to us if we cross in Voldemort's boat?"

"I think we must resign ourselves to the fact that they will, at some point, realize we are not Lord Voldemort. Thus far, however, we have done well. They have allowed us to raise the boat."

"But why have they let us?" asked Harry, who could not shake off the vision of tentacles rising out of the dark water the moment they were out of sight of the bank.

"Voldemort would have been reasonably confident that none but a very great wizard would have been able to find the boat," said Dumbledore. "I think he would have been prepared to risk what was, to his mind, the most unlikely possibility that somebody else would find it, knowing that he had set other obstacles ahead that only he would be able to penetrate. We shall see whether he is right."

Harry looked down into the boat. It really was very small.

"It doesn't look like it was built for two people. Will it hold both of us? Will we be too heavy together?"

Dumbledore chuckled.

"Voldemort will not have cared about the weight, but about the amount of magical power that crossed his lake. I rather think an enchantment will have been placed upon this boat so that only one wizard at a time will be able to sail in it."

"But then — ?"

"I do not think you will count, Harry: You are underage and unqualified. Voldemort would never have expected a sixteen-year-old to reach this place: I think it unlikely that your powers will register compared to mine."

These words did nothing to raise Harry's morale; perhaps Dumbledore knew it, for he added, "Voldemort's mistake, Harry, Voldemort's mistake . . . Age is foolish and forgetful when it underestimates youth. . . . Now, you first this time, and be careful not to touch the water."

Dumbledore stood aside and Harry climbed carefully into the boat. Dumbledore stepped in too, coiling the chain onto the floor. They were crammed in together; Harry could not comfortably sit, but crouched, his knees jutting over the edge of the boat, which began to move at once. There was no sound other than the silken rustle of the boat's prow cleaving the water; it moved without their help, as though an invisible rope was pulling it onward toward the light in the center. Soon they could no longer see the walls of the cavern; they might have been at sea except that there were no waves.

Harry looked down and saw the reflected gold of his wandlight sparkling and glittering on the black water as they passed. The boat was carving deep ripples upon the glassy surface, grooves in the dark mirror. . . .

And then Harry saw it, marble white, floating inches below the surface.

"Professor!" he said, and his startled voice echoed loudly over the silent water.

"Harry?"

"I think I saw a hand in the water — a human hand!"

"Yes, I am sure you did," said Dumbledore calmly.

Harry stared down into the water, looking for the vanished hand, and a sick feeling rose in his throat.

"So that thing that jumped out of the water — ?"

But Harry had his answer before Dumbledore could reply; the wandlight had slid over a fresh patch of water and showed him, this time, a dead man lying faceup inches beneath the surface, his open eyes misted as though with cobwebs, his hair and his robes swirling around him like smoke.

"There are bodies in here!" said Harry, and his voice sounded much higher than usual and most unlike his own.

"Yes," said Dumbledore placidly, "but we do not need to worry about them at the moment."

"At the moment?" Harry repeated, tearing his gaze from the water to look at Dumbledore.

"Not while they are merely drifting peacefully below us," said Dumbledore. "There is nothing to be feared from a body, Harry, any more than there is anything to be feared from the darkness. Lord Voldemort, who of course secretly fears both, disagrees. But once again he reveals his own lack of wisdom. It is the unknown we fear when we look upon death and darkness, nothing more."

Harry said nothing; he did not want to argue, but he found the idea that there were bodies floating around them and beneath them horrible and, what was more, he did not believe that they were not dangerous.

"But one of them jumped," he said, trying to make his voice as level and calm as Dumbledore's. "When I tried to Summon the Horcrux, a body leapt out of the lake."

"Yes," said Dumbledore. "I am sure that once we take the Horcrux, we shall find them less peaceable. However, like many creatures that dwell in cold and darkness, they fear light and warmth, which we shall therefore call to our aid should the need arise. Fire, Harry," Dumbledore added with a smile, in response to Harry's bewildered expression.

"Oh . . . right . . ." said Harry quickly. He turned his head to look at the greenish glow toward which the boat was still inexorably sailing. He could not pretend now that he was not scared. The great black lake, teeming with the dead . . . It seemed hours and hours ago that he had met Professor Trelawney, that he had given Ron and Hermione Felix Felicis. . . . He suddenly wished he had said a better good-bye to them . . . and he hadn't seen Ginny at all. . . .

"Nearly there," said Dumbledore cheerfully.

Sure enough, the greenish light seemed to be growing larger at last, and within minutes, the boat had come to a halt, bumping gently into something that Harry could not see at first, but when he raised his illuminated wand he saw that they had reached a small island of smooth rock in the center of the lake.

"Careful not to touch the water," said Dumbledore again as Harry climbed out of the boat.

The island was no larger than Dumbledore's office, an expanse of flat dark stone on which stood nothing but the source of that greenish light, which looked much brighter when viewed close to. Harry squinted at it; at first, he thought it was a lamp of some kind, but then he saw that the light was coming from a stone basin rather like the Pensieve, which was set on top of a pedestal.

Dumbledore approached the basin and Harry followed. Side by side, they looked down into it. The basin was full of an emerald liquid emitting that phosphorescent glow.

"What is it?" asked Harry quietly.

"I am not sure," said Dumbledore. "Something more worrisome than blood and bodies, however."

Dumbledore pushed back the sleeve of his robe over his blackened hand, and stretched out the tips of his burned fingers toward the surface of the potion.

"Sir, no, don't touch — !"

"I cannot touch," said Dumbledore, smiling faintly. "See? I cannot approach any nearer than this. You try."

Staring, Harry put his hand into the basin and attempted to touch the potion. He met an invisible barrier that prevented him coming within an inch of it. No matter how hard he pushed, his fingers encountered nothing but what seemed to be solid and inflexible air.

"Out of the way, please, Harry," said Dumbledore. He raised his wand and made complicated movements over the surface of the potion, murmuring soundlessly. Nothing happened, except perhaps that the potion glowed a little brighter. Harry remained silent while Dumbledore worked, but after a while Dumbledore withdrew his wand, and Harry felt it was safe to talk again.

"You think the Horcrux is in there, sir?"

"Oh yes." Dumbledore peered more closely into the basin. Harry saw his face reflected, upside down, in the smooth surface of the green potion. "But how to reach it? This potion cannot be penetrated by hand, Vanished, parted, scooped up, or siphoned away, nor can it be Transfigured, Charmed, or otherwise made to change its nature."

Almost absentmindedly, Dumbledore raised his wand again, twirled it once in midair, and then caught the crystal goblet that he had conjured out of nowhere.

"I can only conclude that this potion is supposed to be drunk."

"What?" said Harry. "No!"

"Yes, I think so: Only by drinking it can I empty the basin and see what lies in its depths."

"But what if — what if it kills you?"

"Oh, I doubt that it would work like that," said Dumbledore

easily. "Lord Voldemort would not want to kill the person who reached this island."

Harry couldn't believe it. Was this more of Dumbledore's insane determination to see good in everyone?

"Sir," said Harry, trying to keep his voice reasonable, "sir, this is *Voldemort* we're —"

"I'm sorry, Harry; I should have said, he would not want to *immediately* kill the person who reached this island," Dumbledore corrected himself. "He would want to keep them alive long enough to find out how they managed to penetrate so far through his defenses and, most importantly of all, why they were so intent upon emptying the basin. Do not forget that Lord Voldemort believes that he alone knows about his Horcruxes."

Harry made to speak again, but this time Dumbledore raised his hand for silence, frowning slightly at the emerald liquid, evidently thinking hard.

"Undoubtedly," he said, finally, "this potion must act in a way that will prevent me taking the Horcrux. It might paralyze me, cause me to forget what I am here for, create so much pain I am distracted, or render me incapable in some other way. This being the case, Harry, it will be your job to make sure I keep drinking, even if you have to tip the potion into my protesting mouth. You understand?"

Their eyes met over the basin, each pale face lit with that strange, green light. Harry did not speak. Was this why he had been invited along — so that he could force-feed Dumbledore a potion that might cause him unendurable pain?

"You remember," said Dumbledore, "the condition on which I brought you with me?"

Harry hesitated, looking into the blue eyes that had turned green in the reflected light of the basin.

"But what if — ?"

"You swore, did you not, to follow any command I gave you?"

"Yes, but —"

"I warned you, did I not, that there might be danger?"

"Yes," said Harry, "but —"

"Well, then," said Dumbledore, shaking back his sleeves once more and raising the empty goblet, "you have my orders."

"Why can't I drink the potion instead?" asked Harry desperately.

"Because I am much older, much cleverer, and much less valuable," said Dumbledore. "Once and for all, Harry, do I have your word that you will do all in your power to make me keep drinking?"

"Couldn't — ?"

"Do I have it?"

"But —"

"Your word, Harry."

"I — all right, but —"

Before Harry could make any further protest, Dumbledore lowered the crystal goblet into the potion. For a split second, Harry hoped that he would not be able to touch the potion with the goblet, but the crystal sank into the surface as nothing else had; when the glass was full to the brim, Dumbledore lifted it to his mouth.

"Your good health, Harry."

And he drained the goblet. Harry watched, terrified, his hands gripping the rim of the basin so hard that his fingertips were numb.

"Professor?" he said anxiously, as Dumbledore lowered the empty glass. "How do you feel?"

Dumbledore shook his head, his eyes closed. Harry wondered whether he was in pain. Dumbledore plunged the glass blindly back into the basin, refilled it, and drank once more.

In silence, Dumbledore drank three gobletsful of the potion. Then, halfway through the fourth goblet, he staggered and fell forward against the basin. His eyes were still closed, his breathing heavy.

"Professor Dumbledore?" said Harry, his voice strained. "Can you hear me?"

Dumbledore did not answer. His face was twitching as though he was deeply asleep, but dreaming a horrible dream. His grip on the goblet was slackening; the potion was about to spill from it. Harry reached forward and grasped the crystal cup, holding it steady.

"Professor, can you hear me?" he repeated loudly, his voice echoing around the cavern.

Dumbledore panted and then spoke in a voice Harry did not recognize, for he had never heard Dumbledore frightened like this.

"I don't want . . . Don't make me . . ."

Harry stared into the whitened face he knew so well, at the crooked nose and half-moon spectacles, and did not know what to do.

". . . don't like . . . want to stop . . ." moaned Dumbledore.

"You . . . you can't stop, Professor," said Harry. "You've got to keep drinking, remember? You told me you had to keep drinking. Here . . ."

Hating himself, repulsed by what he was doing, Harry forced the goblet back toward Dumbledore's mouth and tipped it, so that Dumbledore drank the remainder of the potion inside.

"No . . ." he groaned, as Harry lowered the goblet back into the basin and refilled it for him. "I don't want to. . . . I don't want to. . . . Let me go. . . ."

"It's all right, Professor," said Harry, his hand shaking. "It's all right, I'm here —"

"Make it stop, make it stop," moaned Dumbledore.

"Yes . . . yes, this'll make it stop," lied Harry. He tipped the contents of the goblet into Dumbledore's open mouth.

Dumbledore screamed; the noise echoed all around the vast chamber, across the dead black water.

"No, no, no, no, I can't, I can't, don't make me, I don't want to. . . ."

"It's all right, Professor, it's all right!" said Harry loudly, his hands shaking so badly he could hardly scoop up the sixth gobletful of potion; the basin was now half empty. "Nothing's happening to you, you're safe, it isn't real, I swear it isn't real — take this, now, take this. . . ."

And obediently, Dumbledore drank, as though it was an antidote Harry offered him, but upon draining the goblet, he sank to his knees, shaking uncontrollably.

"It's all my fault, all my fault," he sobbed. "Please make it stop, I know I did wrong, oh please make it stop and I'll never, never again . . ."

"This will make it stop, Professor," Harry said, his voice cracking as he tipped the seventh glass of potion into Dumbledore's mouth.

Dumbledore began to cower as though invisible torturers surrounded him; his flailing hand almost knocked the refilled goblet from Harry's trembling hands as he moaned, "Don't hurt them, don't hurt them, please, please, it's my fault, hurt me instead . . ."

"Here, drink this, drink this, you'll be all right," said Harry desperately, and once again Dumbledore obeyed him, opening his mouth even as he kept his eyes tight shut and shook from head to foot.

And now he fell forward, screaming again, hammering his fists upon the ground, while Harry filled the ninth goblet.

"Please, please, please, no . . . not that, not that, I'll do anything . . ."

"Just drink, Professor, just drink . . ."

Dumbledore drank like a child dying of thirst, but when he had finished, he yelled again as though his insides were on fire. "No more, please, no more . . ."

Harry scooped up a tenth gobletful of potion and felt the crystal scrape the bottom of the basin.

"We're nearly there, Professor. Drink this, drink it. . . ."

He supported Dumbledore's shoulders and again, Dumbledore drained the glass; then Harry was on his feet once more, refilling the goblet as Dumbledore began to scream in more anguish than ever, "I want to die! I want to die! Make it stop, make it stop, I want to die!"

"Drink this, Professor. Drink this. . . ."

Dumbledore drank, and no sooner had he finished than he yelled, "KILL ME!"

"This — this one will!" gasped Harry. "Just drink this . . . It'll be over . . . all over!"

Dumbledore gulped at the goblet, drained every last drop, and then, with a great, rattling gasp, rolled over onto his face.

"No!" shouted Harry, who had stood to refill the goblet again; instead he dropped the cup into the basin, flung himself down beside Dumbledore, and heaved him over onto his back; Dumbledore's glasses were askew, his mouth agape, his eyes closed. "No," said Harry, shaking Dumbledore, "no, you're not dead, you said it wasn't poison, wake up, wake up — *Rennervate!*" he cried, his wand pointing at Dumbledore's chest; there was a flash of red light but nothing happened. "*Rennervate* — sir — please —"

Dumbledore's eyelids flickered; Harry's heart leapt.

"Sir, are you — ?"

"Water," croaked Dumbledore.

"Water," panted Harry. "Yes —"

He leapt to his feet and seized the goblet he had dropped in the basin; he barely registered the golden locket lying curled beneath it.

"*Aguamenti!*" he shouted, jabbing the goblet with his wand.

The goblet filled with clear water; Harry dropped to his knees beside Dumbledore, raised his head, and brought the glass to his lips — but it was empty. Dumbledore groaned and began to pant.

"But I had some — wait — *Aguamenti!*" said Harry again, pointing his wand at the goblet. Once more, for a second, clear water gleamed within it, but as he approached Dumbledore's mouth, the water vanished again.

"Sir, I'm trying, I'm trying!" said Harry desperately, but he did not think that Dumbledore could hear him; he had rolled onto his side and was drawing great, rattling breaths that sounded agonizing. "*Aguamenti — Aguamenti — AGUAMENTI!*"

The goblet filled and emptied once more. And now Dumbledore's breathing was fading. His brain whirling in panic, Harry knew, instinctively, the only way left to get water, because Voldemort had planned it so . . .

He flung himself over to the edge of the rock and plunged the goblet into the lake, bringing it up full to the brim of icy water that did not vanish.

"Sir — here!" Harry yelled, and lunging forward, he tipped the water clumsily over Dumbledore's face.

It was the best he could do, for the icy feeling on his arm not holding the cup was not the lingering chill of the water. A slimy white hand had gripped his wrist, and the creature to whom it belonged was pulling him, slowly, backward across the rock. The surface of the lake was no longer mirror-smooth; it was churning, and everywhere Harry looked, white heads and hands were emerging from the dark water, men and women and children with sunken, sightless eyes were moving toward the rock: an army of the dead rising from the black water.

"Petrificus Totalus!" yelled Harry, struggling to cling to the smooth, soaked surface of the island as he pointed his wand at the Inferius that had his arm: It released him, falling backward into the water with a splash; he scrambled to his feet, but many more Inferi were already climbing onto the rock, their bony hands clawing at its slippery surface, their blank, frosted eyes upon him, trailing waterlogged rags, sunken faces leering.

"Petrificus Totalus!" Harry bellowed again, backing away as he swiped his wand through the air; six or seven of them crumpled, but more were coming toward him. "Impedimenta! Incarcerous!"

A few of them stumbled, one or two of them bound in ropes, but those climbing onto the rock behind them merely stepped over or on the fallen bodies. Still slashing at the air with his wand, Harry yelled, "Sectumsempra! SECTUMSEMPRA!"

But though gashes appeared in their sodden rags and their icy skin, they had no blood to spill: They walked on, unfeeling, their shrunken hands outstretched toward him, and as he backed away still farther, he felt arms enclose him from behind, thin, fleshless arms cold as death, and his feet left the ground as they lifted him and began to carry him, slowly and surely, back to the water, and he knew there would be no release, that he would be drowned, and become one more dead guardian of a fragment of Voldemort's shattered soul. . . .

But then, through the darkness, fire erupted: crimson and gold, a ring of fire that surrounded the rock so that the Inferi holding Harry so tightly stumbled and faltered; they did not dare pass through the flames to get to the water. They dropped Harry; he hit the ground, slipped on the rock, and fell, grazing his arms, but scrambled back up, raising his wand and staring around.

Dumbledore was on his feet again, pale as any of the surrounding Inferi, but taller than any too, the fire dancing in his eyes; his wand was raised like a torch and from its tip emanated the flames, like a vast lasso, encircling them all with warmth.

The Inferi bumped into each other, attempting, blindly, to escape the fire in which they were enclosed. . . .

Dumbledore scooped the locket from the bottom of the stone basin and stowed it inside his robes. Wordlessly, he gestured to Harry to come to his side. Distracted by the flames, the Inferi seemed unaware that their quarry was leaving as Dumbledore led Harry back to the boat, the ring of fire moving with them, around them, the bewildered Inferi accompanying them to the water's edge, where they slipped gratefully back into their dark waters.

Harry, who was shaking all over, thought for a moment that Dumbledore might not be able to climb into the boat; he staggered a little as he attempted it; all his efforts seemed to be going into maintaining the ring of protective flame around them. Harry seized him and helped him back to his seat. Once they were both safely jammed inside again, the boat began to move back across the black water, away from the rock, still encircled by that ring of fire, and it seemed that the Inferi swarming below them did not dare resurface.

"Sir," panted Harry, "sir, I forgot — about fire — they were coming at me and I panicked —"

"Quite understandable," murmured Dumbledore. Harry was alarmed to hear how faint his voice was.

They reached the bank with a little bump and Harry leapt out, then turned quickly to help Dumbledore. The moment that Dumbledore reached the bank he let his wand hand fall; the ring of fire vanished, but the Inferi did not emerge again from the water. The little boat sank into the water once more; clanking and tinkling, its chain slithered back into the lake too. Dumbledore gave a great sigh and leaned against the cavern wall.

"I am weak. . . ." he said.

"Don't worry, sir," said Harry at once, anxious about Dumbledore's extreme pallor and by his air of exhaustion. "Don't worry, I'll get us back. . . . Lean on me, sir. . . ."

And pulling Dumbledore's uninjured arm around his shoulders, Harry guided his headmaster back around the lake, bearing most of his weight.

"The protection was . . . after all . . . well-designed," said Dumbledore faintly. "One alone could not have done it. . . . You did well, very well, Harry. . . ."

"Don't talk now," said Harry, fearing how slurred Dumbledore's voice had become, how much his feet dragged. "Save your energy, sir. . . . We'll soon be out of here. . . ."

"The archway will have sealed again. . . . My knife . . ."

"There's no need, I got cut on the rock," said Harry firmly. "Just tell me where. . . ."

"Here . . ."

Harry wiped his grazed forearm upon the stone: Having received its tribute of blood, the archway reopened instantly. They crossed the outer cave, and Harry helped Dumbledore back into the icy seawater that filled the crevice in the cliff.

"It's going to be all right, sir," Harry said over and over again, more worried by Dumbledore's silence than he had been by his weakened voice. "We're nearly there. . . . I can Apparate us both back. . . . Don't worry. . . ."

"I am not worried, Harry," said Dumbledore, his voice a little stronger despite the freezing water. "I am with you."

THE LIGHTNING-
STRUCK TOWER

Once back under the starry sky, Harry heaved Dumbledore onto the top of the nearest boulder and then to his feet. Sodden and shivering, Dumbledore's weight still upon him, Harry concentrated harder than he had ever done upon his destination: Hogsmeade. Closing his eyes, gripping Dumbledore's arm as tightly as he could, he stepped forward into that feeling of horrible compression.

He knew it had worked before he opened his eyes: The smell of salt, the sea breeze had gone. He and Dumbledore were shivering and dripping in the middle of the dark High Street in Hogsmeade. For one horrible moment Harry's imagination showed him more Inferi creeping toward him around the sides of shops, but he blinked and saw that nothing was stirring; all was still, the darkness complete but for a few streetlamps and lit upper windows.

"We did it, Professor!" Harry whispered with difficulty; he

suddenly realized that he had a searing stitch in his chest. "We did it! We got the Horcrux!"

Dumbledore staggered against him. For a moment, Harry thought that his inexpert Apparition had thrown Dumbledore off balance; then he saw his face, paler and damper than ever in the distant light of a streetlamp.

"Sir, are you all right?"

"I've been better," said Dumbledore weakly, though the corners of his mouth twitched. "That potion . . . was no health drink. . . ."

And to Harry's horror, Dumbledore sank onto the ground.

"Sir — it's okay, sir, you're going to be all right, don't worry —"

He looked around desperately for help, but there was nobody to be seen and all he could think was that he must somehow get Dumbledore quickly to the hospital wing.

"We need to get you up to the school, sir. . . . Madam Pomfrey . . ."

"No," said Dumbledore. "It is . . . Professor Snape whom I need. . . . But I do not think . . . I can walk very far just yet. . . ."

"Right — sir, listen — I'm going to knock on a door, find a place you can stay — then I can run and get Madam —"

"Severus," said Dumbledore clearly. "I need Severus. . . ."

"All right then, Snape — but I'm going to have to leave you for a moment so I can —"

Before Harry could make a move, however, he heard running footsteps. His heart leapt: Somebody had seen, somebody knew they needed help — and looking around he saw Madam Rosmerta scurrying down the dark street toward them on high-heeled, fluffy slippers, wearing a silk dressing gown embroidered with dragons.

"I saw you Apparate as I was pulling my bedroom curtains!

Thank goodness, thank goodness, I couldn't think what to — but what's wrong with Albus?"

She came to a halt, panting, and stared down, wide-eyed, at Dumbledore.

"He's hurt," said Harry. "Madam Rosmerta, can he come into the Three Broomsticks while I go up to the school and get help for him?"

"You can't go up there alone! Don't you realize — haven't you seen — ?"

"If you help me support him," said Harry, not listening to her, "I think we can get him inside —"

"What has happened?" asked Dumbledore. "Rosmerta, what's wrong?"

"The — the Dark Mark, Albus."

And she pointed into the sky, in the direction of Hogwarts. Dread flooded Harry at the sound of the words. . . . He turned and looked.

There it was, hanging in the sky above the school: the blazing green skull with a serpent tongue, the mark Death Eaters left behind whenever they had entered a building . . . wherever they had murdered. . . .

"When did it appear?" asked Dumbledore, and his hand clenched painfully upon Harry's shoulder as he struggled to his feet.

"Must have been minutes ago, it wasn't there when I put the cat out, but when I got upstairs —"

"We need to return to the castle at once," said Dumbledore. "Rosmerta" — and though he staggered a little, he seemed wholly in command of the situation — "we need transport — brooms —"

"I've got a couple behind the bar," she said, looking very frightened. "Shall I run and fetch — ?"

"No, Harry can do it."

Harry raised his wand at once.

"Accio Rosmerta's Brooms!"

A second later they heard a loud bang as the front door of the pub burst open; two brooms had shot out into the street and were racing each other to Harry's side, where they stopped dead, quivering slightly at waist height.

"Rosmerta, please send a message to the Ministry," said Dumbledore, as he mounted the broom nearest him. "It might be that nobody within Hogwarts has yet realized anything is wrong. . . . Harry, put on your Invisibility Cloak."

Harry pulled his Cloak out of his pocket and threw it over himself before mounting his broom: Madam Rosmerta was already tottering back toward her pub as Harry and Dumbledore kicked off from the ground and rose up into the air. As they sped toward the castle, Harry glanced sideways at Dumbledore, ready to grab him should he fall, but the sight of the Dark Mark seemed to have acted upon Dumbledore like a stimulant: He was bent low over his broom, his eyes fixed upon the Mark, his long silver hair and beard flying behind him on the night air. And Harry too looked ahead at the skull, and fear swelled inside him like a venomous bubble, compressing his lungs, driving all other discomfort from his mind. . . .

How long had they been away? Had Ron, Hermione, and Ginny's luck run out by now? Was it one of them who had caused the Mark to be set over the school, or was it Neville, or Luna, or some other member of the D.A.? And if it was . . . he was the one who had told them to patrol the corridors, he had asked them to leave the safety of their beds. . . . Would he be responsible, again, for the death of a friend?

As they flew over the dark, twisting lane down which they had walked earlier, Harry heard, over the whistling of the night air in his ears, Dumbledore muttering in some strange language again. He thought he understood why as he felt his broom shudder when they flew over the boundary wall into the grounds: Dumbledore was undoing the enchantments he himself had set around the castle so they could enter at speed. The Dark Mark was glittering directly above the Astronomy Tower, the highest of the castle. Did that mean the death had occurred there?

Dumbledore had already crossed the crenellated ramparts and was dismounting; Harry landed next to him seconds later and looked around.

The ramparts were deserted. The door to the spiral staircase that led back into the castle was closed. There was no sign of a struggle, of a fight to the death, of a body.

"What does it mean?" Harry asked Dumbledore, looking up at the green skull with its serpent's tongue glinting evilly above them. "Is it the real Mark? Has someone definitely been — Professor?"

In the dim green glow from the Mark, Harry saw Dumbledore clutching at his chest with his blackened hand.

"Go and wake Severus," said Dumbledore faintly but clearly. "Tell him what has happened and bring him to me. Do nothing else, speak to nobody else, and do not remove your cloak. I shall wait here."

"But —"

"You swore to obey me, Harry — go!"

Harry hurried over to the door leading to the spiral staircase, but his hand had only just closed upon the iron ring of the door when he heard running footsteps on the other side. He looked around at Dumbledore, who gestured him to retreat. Harry backed away, drawing his wand as he did so.

The door burst open and somebody erupted through it and shouted, *"Expelliarmus!"*

Harry's body became instantly rigid and immobile, and he felt himself fall back against the tower wall, propped like an unsteady statue, unable to move or speak. He could not understand how it had happened — *Expelliarmus* was not a Freezing Charm —

Then, by the light of the Mark, he saw Dumbledore's wand flying in an arc over the edge of the ramparts and understood. . . . Dumbledore had wordlessly immobilized Harry, and the second he had taken to perform the spell had cost him the chance of defending himself.

Standing against the ramparts, very white in the face, Dumbledore still showed no sign of panic or distress. He merely looked across at his disarmer and said, "Good evening, Draco."

Malfoy stepped forward, glancing around quickly to check that he and Dumbledore were alone. His eyes fell upon the second broom.

"Who else is here?"

"A question I might ask you. Or are you acting alone?"

Harry saw Malfoy's pale eyes shift back to Dumbledore in the greenish glare of the Mark.

"No," he said. "I've got backup. There are Death Eaters here in your school tonight."

"Well, well," said Dumbledore, as though Malfoy was showing

him an ambitious homework project. "Very good indeed. You found a way to let them in, did you?"

"Yeah," said Malfoy, who was panting. "Right under your nose and you never realized!"

"Ingenious," said Dumbledore. "Yet . . . forgive me . . . where are they now? You seem unsupported."

"They met some of your guards. They're having a fight down below. They won't be long. . . . I came on ahead. I — I've got a job to do."

"Well, then, you must get on and do it, my dear boy," said Dumbledore softly.

There was silence. Harry stood imprisoned within his own invisible, paralyzed body, staring at the two of them, his ears straining to hear sounds of the Death Eaters' distant fight, and in front of him, Draco Malfoy did nothing but stare at Albus Dumbledore, who, incredibly, smiled.

"Draco, Draco, you are not a killer."

"How do you know?" said Malfoy at once.

He seemed to realize how childish the words had sounded; Harry saw him flush in the Mark's greenish light.

"You don't know what I'm capable of," said Malfoy more forcefully. "You don't know what I've done!"

"Oh yes, I do," said Dumbledore mildly. "You almost killed Katie Bell and Ronald Weasley. You have been trying, with increasing desperation, to kill me all year. Forgive me, Draco, but they have been feeble attempts. . . . So feeble, to be honest, that I wonder whether your heart has been really in it."

"It has been in it!" said Malfoy vehemently. "I've been working on it all year, and tonight —"

Somewhere in the depths of the castle below Harry heard a muffled yell. Malfoy stiffened and glanced over his shoulder.

"Somebody is putting up a good fight," said Dumbledore conversationally. "But you were saying . . . yes, you have managed to introduce Death Eaters into my school, which, I admit, I thought impossible. . . . How did you do it?"

But Malfoy said nothing: He was still listening to whatever was happening below and seemed almost as paralyzed as Harry was.

"Perhaps you ought to get on with the job alone," suggested Dumbledore. "What if your backup has been thwarted by my guard? As you have perhaps realized, there are members of the Order of the Phoenix here tonight too. And after all, you don't really need help. . . . I have no wand at the moment. . . . I cannot defend myself."

Malfoy merely stared at him.

"I see," said Dumbledore kindly, when Malfoy neither moved nor spoke. "You are afraid to act until they join you."

"I'm not afraid!" snarled Malfoy, though he still made no move to hurt Dumbledore. "It's you who should be scared!"

"But why? I don't think you will kill me, Draco. Killing is not nearly as easy as the innocent believe. . . . So tell me, while we wait for your friends . . . how did you smuggle them in here? It seems to have taken you a long time to work out how to do it."

Malfoy looked as though he was fighting down the urge to shout, or to vomit. He gulped and took several deep breaths, glaring at Dumbledore, his wand pointing directly at the latter's heart. Then, as though he could not help himself, he said, "I had to mend that broken Vanishing Cabinet that no one's used for years. The one Montague got lost in last year."

"Aaaah." Dumbledore's sigh was half a groan. He closed his eyes for a moment. "That was clever. . . . There is a pair, I take it?"

"In Borgin and Burkes," said Malfoy, "and they make a kind of passage between them. Montague told me that when he was stuck in the Hogwarts one, he was trapped in limbo but sometimes he could hear what was going on at school, and sometimes what was going on in the shop, as if the cabinet was traveling between them, but he couldn't make anyone hear him. . . . In the end, he managed to Apparate out, even though he'd never passed his test. He nearly died doing it. Everyone thought it was a really good story, but I was the only one who realized what it meant — even Borgin didn't know — I was the one who realized there could be a way into Hogwarts through the cabinets if I fixed the broken one."

"Very good," murmured Dumbledore. "So the Death Eaters were able to pass from Borgin and Burkes into the school to help you. . . . A clever plan, a very clever plan . . . and, as you say, right under my nose."

"Yeah," said Malfoy, who bizarrely seemed to draw courage and comfort from Dumbledore's praise. "Yeah, it was!"

"But there were times," Dumbledore went on, "weren't there, when you were not sure you would succeed in mending the cabinet? And you resorted to crude and badly judged measures such as sending me a cursed necklace that was bound to reach the wrong hands . . . poisoning mead there was only the slightest chance I might drink. . . ."

"Yeah, well, you still didn't realize who was behind that stuff, did you?" sneered Malfoy, as Dumbledore slid a little down the ramparts, the strength in his legs apparently fading, and Harry struggled fruitlessly, mutely, against the enchantment binding him.

"As a matter of fact, I did," said Dumbledore. "I was sure it was you."

"Why didn't you stop me, then?" Malfoy demanded.

"I tried, Draco. Professor Snape has been keeping watch over you on my orders —"

"He hasn't been doing *your* orders, he promised my mother —"

"Of course that is what he would tell you, Draco, but —"

"He's a double agent, you stupid old man, he isn't working for you, you just think he is!"

"We must agree to differ on that, Draco. It so happens that I trust Professor Snape —"

"Well, you're losing your grip, then!" sneered Malfoy. "He's been offering me plenty of help — wanting all the glory for himself — wanting a bit of the action — 'What are you doing?' 'Did you do the necklace, that was stupid, it could have blown everything —' But I haven't told him what I've been doing in the Room of Requirement, he's going to wake up tomorrow and it'll all be over and he won't be the Dark Lord's favorite anymore, he'll be nothing compared to me, nothing!"

"Very gratifying," said Dumbledore mildly. "We all like appreciation for our own hard work, of course. But you must have had an accomplice, all the same . . . someone in Hogsmeade, someone who was able to slip Katie the — the — aaaah . . ."

Dumbledore closed his eyes again and nodded, as though he was about to fall asleep. ". . . of course . . . Rosmerta. How long has she been under the Imperius Curse?"

"Got there at last, have you?" Malfoy taunted.

There was another yell from below, rather louder than the last.

Malfoy looked nervously over his shoulder again, then back at Dumbledore, who went on: "So poor Rosmerta was forced to lurk in her own bathroom and pass that necklace to any Hogwarts student who entered the room unaccompanied? And the poisoned mead . . . well, naturally, Rosmerta was able to poison it for you before she sent the bottle to Slughorn, believing that it was to be my Christmas present. . . . Yes, very neat . . . very neat . . . Poor Mr. Filch would not, of course, think to check a bottle of Rosmerta's. Tell me, how have you been communicating with Rosmerta? I thought we had all methods of communication in and out of the school monitored."

"Enchanted coins," said Malfoy, as though he was compelled to keep talking, though his wand hand was shaking badly. "I had one and she had the other and I could send her messages —"

"Isn't that the secret method of communication the group that called themselves Dumbledore's Army used last year?" asked Dumbledore. His voice was light and conversational, but Harry saw him slip an inch lower down the wall as he said it.

"Yeah, I got the idea from them," said Malfoy, with a twisted smile. "I got the idea of poisoning the mead from the Mudblood Granger as well, I heard her talking in the library about Filch not recognizing potions."

"Please do not use that offensive word in front of me," said Dumbledore.

Malfoy gave a harsh laugh. "You care about me saying 'Mudblood' when I'm about to kill you?"

"Yes, I do," said Dumbledore, and Harry saw his feet slide a little on the floor as he struggled to remain upright. "But as for being about to kill me, Draco, you have had several long minutes now, we are quite alone, I am more defenseless than you can have dreamed of finding me, and still you have not acted. . . ."

Malfoy's mouth contorted involuntarily, as though he had tasted something very bitter.

"Now, about tonight," Dumbledore went on, "I am a little puzzled about how it happened. . . . You knew that I had left the school? But of course," he answered his own question, "Rosmerta saw me leaving, she tipped you off using your ingenious coins, I'm sure."

"That's right," said Malfoy. "But she said you were just going for a drink, you'd be back. . . ."

"Well, I certainly did have a drink . . . and I came back . . . after a fashion," mumbled Dumbledore. "So you decided to spring a trap for me?"

"We decided to put the Dark Mark over the tower and get you to hurry up here, to see who'd been killed," said Malfoy. "And it worked!"

"Well . . . yes and no . . ." said Dumbledore. "But am I to take it, then, that nobody has been murdered?"

"Someone's dead," said Malfoy, and his voice seemed to go up an octave as he said it. "One of your people . . . I don't know who, it was dark. . . . I stepped over the body. . . . I was supposed to be waiting up here when you got back, only your Phoenix lot got in the way. . . ."

"Yes, they do that," said Dumbledore.

There was a bang and shouts from below, louder than ever; it sounded as though people were fighting on the actual spiral staircase that led to where Dumbledore, Malfoy, and Harry stood, and

Harry's heart thundered unheard in his invisible chest. . . . Someone was dead. . . . Malfoy had stepped over the body . . . but who was it?

"There is little time, one way or another," said Dumbledore. "So let us discuss your options, Draco."

"*My* options!" said Malfoy loudly. "I'm standing here with a wand — I'm about to kill you —"

"My dear boy, let us have no more pretense about that. If you were going to kill me, you would have done it when you first disarmed me, you would not have stopped for this pleasant chat about ways and means."

"I haven't got any options!" said Malfoy, and he was suddenly white as Dumbledore. "I've got to do it! He'll kill me! He'll kill my whole family!"

"I appreciate the difficulty of your position," said Dumbledore. "Why else do you think I have not confronted you before now? Because I knew that you would have been murdered if Lord Voldemort realized that I suspected you."

Malfoy winced at the sound of the name.

"I did not dare speak to you of the mission with which I knew you had been entrusted, in case he used Legilimency against you," continued Dumbledore. "But now at last we can speak plainly to each other. . . . No harm has been done, you have hurt nobody, though you are very lucky that your unintentional victims survived. . . . I can help you, Draco."

"No, you can't," said Malfoy, his wand hand shaking very badly indeed. "Nobody can. He told me to do it or he'll kill me. I've got no choice."

"Come over to the right side, Draco, and we can hide you more completely than you can possibly imagine. What is more, I can send members of the Order to your mother tonight to hide her likewise. Your father is safe at the moment in Azkaban. . . . When the time comes, we can protect him too. . . . Come over to the right side, Draco . . . you are not a killer. . . ."

Malfoy stared at Dumbledore.

"But I got this far, didn't I?" he said slowly. "They thought I'd die in the attempt, but I'm here . . . and you're in my power. . . . I'm the one with the wand. . . . You're at my mercy. . . ."

"No, Draco," said Dumbledore quietly. "It is my mercy, and not yours, that matters now."

Malfoy did not speak. His mouth was open, his wand hand still trembling. Harry thought he saw it drop by a fraction —

But suddenly footsteps were thundering up the stairs, and a second later Malfoy was buffeted out of the way as four people in black robes burst through the door onto the ramparts. Still paralyzed, his eyes staring unblinkingly, Harry gazed in terror upon four strangers: It seemed the Death Eaters had won the fight below.

A lumpy-looking man with an odd lopsided leer gave a wheezy giggle.

"Dumbledore cornered!" he said, and he turned to a stocky little woman who looked as though she could be his sister and who was grinning eagerly. "Dumbledore wandless, Dumbledore alone! Well done, Draco, well done!"

"Good evening, Amycus," said Dumbledore calmly, as though welcoming the man to a tea party. "And you've brought Alecto too. . . . Charming . . ."

The woman gave an angry little titter. "Think your little jokes'll help you on your deathbed then?" she jeered.

"Jokes? No, no, these are manners," replied Dumbledore.

"Do it," said the stranger standing nearest to Harry, a big, rangy man with matted gray hair and whiskers, whose black Death Eater's robes looked uncomfortably tight. He had a voice like none that Harry had ever heard: a rasping bark of a voice. Harry could smell a powerful mixture of dirt, sweat, and, unmistakably, blood coming from him. His filthy hands had long yellowish nails.

"Is that you, Fenrir?" asked Dumbledore.

"That's right," rasped the other. "Pleased to see me, Dumbledore?"

"No, I cannot say that I am."

Greyback grinned, showing pointed teeth. Blood trickled down his chin and he licked his lips slowly, obscenely.

"But you know how much I like kids, Dumbledore."

"Am I to take it that you are attacking even without the full moon now? This is most unusual. . . . You have developed a taste for human flesh that cannot be satisfied once a month?"

"That's right," said Fenrir Greyback. "Shocks you that, does it, Dumbledore? Frightens you?"

"Well, I cannot pretend it does not disgust me a little," said Dumbledore. "And, yes, I am a little shocked that Draco here invited you, of all people, into the school where his friends live. . . ."

"I didn't," breathed Malfoy. He was not looking at Fenrir; he did not seem to want to even glance at him. "I didn't know he was going to come —"

"I wouldn't want to miss a trip to Hogwarts, Dumbledore," rasped Greyback. "Not when there are throats to be ripped out . . . Delicious, delicious . . ."

And he raised a yellow fingernail and picked at his front teeth, leering at Dumbledore. "I could do you for afters, Dumbledore."

"No," said the fourth Death Eater sharply. He had a heavy, brutal-looking face. "We've got orders. Draco's got to do it. Now, Draco, and quickly."

Malfoy was showing less resolution than ever. He looked terrified as he stared into Dumbledore's face, which was even paler, and rather lower than usual, as he had slid so far down the rampart wall.

"He's not long for this world anyway, if you ask me!" said the lopsided man, to the accompaniment of his sister's wheezing giggles. "Look at him — what's happened to you, then, Dumby?"

"Oh, weaker resistance, slower reflexes, Amycus," said Dumbledore. "Old age, in short . . . One day, perhaps, it will happen to you . . . if you are lucky. . . ."

"What's that mean, then, what's that mean?" yelled the Death Eater, suddenly violent. "Always the same, weren't yeh, Dumby, talking and doing nothing, nothing. I don't even know why the Dark Lord's bothering to kill yer! Come on, Draco, do it!"

But at that moment there were renewed sounds of scuffling from below and a voice shouted, *"They've blocked the stairs — Reducto! REDUCTO!"*

Harry's heart leapt: So these four had not eliminated all opposition, but merely broken through the fight to the top of the tower, and, by the sound of it, created a barrier behind them —

"Now, Draco, quickly!" said the brutal-faced man angrily.

But Malfoy's hand was shaking so badly that he could barely aim.

"I'll do it," snarled Fenrir, moving toward Dumbledore with his hands outstretched, his teeth bared.

"I said no!" shouted the brutal-faced man; there was a flash of light and the werewolf was blasted out of the way; he hit the ramparts and staggered, looking furious. Harry's heart was hammering so hard it seemed impossible that nobody could hear him standing there, imprisoned by Dumbledore's spell — if he could only move, he could aim a curse from under the cloak —

"Draco, do it or stand aside so one of us —" screeched the woman, but at that precise moment, the door to the ramparts burst open once more and there stood Snape, his wand clutched in his hand as his black eyes swept the scene, from Dumbledore slumped against the wall, to the four Death Eaters, including the enraged werewolf, and Malfoy.

"We've got a problem, Snape," said the lumpy Amycus, whose eyes and wand were fixed alike upon Dumbledore, "the boy doesn't seem able —"

But somebody else had spoken Snape's name, quite softly.

"Severus . . ."

The sound frightened Harry beyond anything he had experienced all evening. For the first time, Dumbledore was pleading.

Snape said nothing, but walked forward and pushed Malfoy roughly out of the way. The three Death Eaters fell back without a word. Even the werewolf seemed cowed.

Snape gazed for a moment at Dumbledore, and there was revulsion and hatred etched in the harsh lines of his face.

"Severus . . . please . . ."

Snape raised his wand and pointed it directly at Dumbledore.

"Avada Kedavra!"

A jet of green light shot from the end of Snape's wand and hit

Dumbledore squarely in the chest. Harry's scream of horror never left him; silent and unmoving, he was forced to watch as Dumbledore was blasted into the air. For a split second, he seemed to hang suspended beneath the shining skull, and then he fell slowly backward, like a great rag doll, over the battlements and out of sight.

FLIGHT OF
THE PRINCE

*H*arry felt as though he too were hurtling through space; *it had not happened. . . . It could not have happened. . . .*

"Out of here, quickly," said Snape.

He seized Malfoy by the scruff of the neck and forced him through the door ahead of the rest; Greyback and the squat brother and sister followed, the latter both panting excitedly. As they vanished through the door, Harry realized he could move again. What was now holding him paralyzed against the wall was not magic, but horror and shock. He threw the Invisibility Cloak aside as the brutal-faced Death Eater, last to leave the tower top, was disappearing through the door.

"Petrificus Totalus!"

The Death Eater buckled as though hit in the back with something solid and fell to the ground, rigid as a waxwork, but he had barely hit the floor when Harry was clambering over him and running down the darkened staircase.

Terror tore at Harry's heart. . . . He had to get to Dumbledore and he had to catch Snape. . . . Somehow the two things were linked. . . . He could reverse what had happened if he had them both together. . . . Dumbledore could not have died. . . .

He leapt the last ten steps of the spiral staircase and stopped where he landed, his wand raised: The dimly lit corridor was full of dust; half the ceiling seemed to have fallen in; and a battle was raging before him, but even as he attempted to make out who was fighting whom, he heard the hated voice shout, *"It's over, time to go!"* and saw Snape disappearing around the corner at the far end of the corridor; he and Malfoy seemed to have forced their way through the fight unscathed. As Harry plunged after them, one of the fighters detached themselves from the fray and flew at him: It was the werewolf, Fenrir. He was on top of Harry before Harry could raise his wand: Harry fell backward, with filthy matted hair in his face, the stench of sweat and blood filling his nose and mouth, hot greedy breath at his throat —

"Petrificus Totalus!"

Harry felt Fenrir collapse against him; with a stupendous effort he pushed the werewolf off and onto the floor as a jet of green light came flying toward him; he ducked and ran, headfirst, into the fight. His feet met something squashy and slippery on the floor and he stumbled: There were two bodies lying there, lying facedown in a pool of blood, but there was no time to investigate. Harry now saw red hair flying like flames in front of him: Ginny was locked in combat with the lumpy Death Eater, Amycus, who was throwing hex after hex at her while she dodged them: Amycus was giggling, enjoying the sport: *"Crucio — Crucio —* you can't dance forever, pretty —"

"Impedimenta!" yelled Harry.

His jinx hit Amycus in the chest: He gave a piglike squeal of pain, was lifted off his feet and slammed into the opposite wall, slid down it, and fell out of sight behind Ron, Professor McGonagall, and Lupin, each of whom was battling a separate Death Eater. Beyond them, Harry saw Tonks fighting an enormous blond wizard who was sending curses flying in all directions, so that they ricocheted off the walls around them, cracking stone, shattering the nearest window —

"Harry, where did you come from?" Ginny cried, but there was no time to answer her. He put his head down and sprinted forward, narrowly avoiding a blast that erupted over his head, showering them all in bits of wall. Snape must not escape, he must catch up with Snape —

"Take *that*!" shouted Professor McGonagall, and Harry glimpsed the female Death Eater, Alecto, sprinting away down the corridor with her arms over her head, her brother right behind her. He launched himself after them but his foot caught on something, and next moment he was lying across someone's legs. Looking around, he saw Neville's pale, round face flat against the floor.

"Neville, are you — ?"

"M'all right," muttered Neville, who was clutching his stomach, "Harry . . . Snape 'n' Malfoy . . . ran past . . ."

"I know, I'm on it!" said Harry, aiming a hex from the floor at the enormous blond Death Eater who was causing most of the chaos. The man gave a howl of pain as the spell hit him in the face: He wheeled around, staggered, and then pounded away after the brother and sister. Harry scrambled up from the floor and began to sprint along the corridor, ignoring the bangs issuing from behind him, the yells of the others to come back, and the mute call of the figures on the ground whose fate he did not yet know. . . .

He skidded around the corner, his trainers slippery with blood; Snape had an immense head start. Was it possible that he had already entered the cabinet in the Room of Requirement, or had the Order made steps to secure it, to prevent the Death Eaters retreating that way? He could hear nothing but his own pounding feet, his own hammering heart as he sprinted along the next empty corridor, but then spotted a bloody footprint that showed at least one of the fleeing Death Eaters was heading toward the front doors — perhaps the Room of Requirement was indeed blocked —

He skidded around another corner and a curse flew past him; he dived behind a suit of armor that exploded. He saw the brother and sister running down the marble staircase ahead and aimed jinxes at them, but merely hit several bewigged witches in a portrait on the landing, who ran screeching into neighboring paintings. As he leapt the wreckage of armor, Harry heard more shouts and screams; other people within the castle seemed to have awoken. . . .

He pelted toward a shortcut, hoping to overtake the brother and sister and close in on Snape and Malfoy, who must surely have reached the grounds by now. Remembering to leap the vanishing step halfway down the concealed staircase, he burst through a tapestry at the bottom and out into a corridor where a number of bewildered and pajama-clad Hufflepuffs stood.

"Harry! We heard a noise, and someone said something about the Dark Mark —" began Ernie Macmillan.

"Out of the way!" yelled Harry, knocking two boys aside as he sprinted toward the landing and down the remainder of the marble staircase. The oak front doors had been blasted open, there were smears of blood on the flagstones, and several terrified students stood huddled against the walls, one or two still cowering with their arms over their faces. The giant Gryffindor hourglass had been hit by a curse, and the rubies within were still falling, with a loud rattle, onto the flagstones below.

Harry flew across the entrance hall and out into the dark grounds: He could just make out three figures racing across the lawn, heading for the gates beyond which they could Disapparate — by the looks of them, the huge blond Death Eater and, some way ahead of him, Snape and Malfoy . . .

The cold night air ripped at Harry's lungs as he tore after them; he saw a flash of light in the distance that momentarily silhouetted his quarry. He did not know what it was but continued to run, not yet near enough to get a good aim with a curse —

Another flash, shouts, retaliatory jets of light, and Harry understood: Hagrid had emerged from his cabin and was trying to stop the Death Eaters escaping, and though every breath seemed to shred his lungs and the stitch in his chest was like fire, Harry sped up as an unbidden voice in his head said: *not Hagrid . . . not Hagrid too . . .*

Something caught Harry hard in the small of the back and he fell forward, his face smacking the ground, blood pouring out of both nostrils: He knew, even as he rolled over, his wand ready, that the brother and sister he had overtaken using his shortcut were closing in behind him. . . .

"Impedimenta!" he yelled as he rolled over again, crouching close to the dark ground, and miraculously his jinx hit one of them, who stumbled and fell, tripping up the other; Harry leapt to his feet and sprinted on after Snape.

And now he saw the vast outline of Hagrid, illuminated by the light of the crescent moon revealed suddenly behind clouds; the blond Death Eater was aiming curse after curse at the gamekeeper; but Hagrid's immense strength and the toughened skin he had inherited from his giantess mother seemed to be protecting him. Snape and Malfoy, however, were still running; they would soon be beyond the gates, able to Disapparate —

Harry tore past Hagrid and his opponent, took aim at Snape's back, and yelled, *"Stupefy!"*

He missed; the jet of red light soared past Snape's head; Snape shouted, *"Run, Draco!"* and turned. Twenty yards apart, he and Harry looked at each other before raising their wands simultaneously.

"Cruc —"

But Snape parried the curse, knocking Harry backward off his feet before he could complete it; Harry rolled over and scrambled back up again as the huge Death Eater behind him yelled, *"Incendio!"* Harry heard an explosive bang and a dancing orange light spilled over all of them: Hagrid's house was on fire.

"Fang's in there, yer evil — !" Hagrid bellowed.

"Cruc —" yelled Harry for the second time, aiming for the figure ahead illuminated in the dancing firelight, but Snape blocked the spell again. Harry could see him sneering.

"No Unforgivable Curses from you, Potter!" he shouted over the rushing of the flames, Hagrid's yells, and the wild yelping of the trapped Fang. "You haven't got the nerve or the ability —"

"Incarc —" Harry roared, but Snape deflected the spell with an almost lazy flick of his arm.

"Fight back!" Harry screamed at him. "Fight back, you cowardly —"

"Coward, did you call me, Potter?" shouted Snape. "Your father would never attack me unless it was four on one, what would you call him, I wonder?"

"*Stupe* —"

"Blocked again and again and again until you learn to keep your mouth shut and your mind closed, Potter!" sneered Snape, deflecting the curse once more. "Now *come*!" he shouted at the huge Death Eater behind Harry. "It is time to be gone, before the Ministry turns up —"

"*Impedi* —"

But before he could finish this jinx, excruciating pain hit Harry; he keeled over in the grass. Someone was screaming, he would surely die of this agony, Snape was going to torture him to death or madness —

"No!" roared Snape's voice and the pain stopped as suddenly as it had started; Harry lay curled on the dark grass, clutching his wand and panting; somewhere overhead Snape was shouting, "Have you forgotten our orders? Potter belongs to the Dark Lord — we are to leave him! Go! Go!"

And Harry felt the ground shudder under his face as the brother and sister and the enormous Death Eater obeyed, running toward the gates. Harry uttered an inarticulate yell of rage: In that instant, he cared not whether he lived or died. Pushing himself to his feet again, he staggered blindly toward Snape, the man he now hated as much as he hated Voldemort himself —

"*Sectum* — !"

Snape flicked his wand and the curse was repelled yet again; but Harry was mere feet away now and he could see Snape's face clearly at last: He was no longer sneering or jeering; the blazing flames showed a face full of rage. Mustering all his powers of concentration, Harry thought, *Levi —*

"No, Potter!" screamed Snape. There was a loud BANG and Harry was soaring backward, hitting the ground hard again, and this time his wand flew out of his hand. He could hear Hagrid yelling and Fang howling as Snape closed in and looked down on him where he lay, wandless and defenseless as Dumbledore had been. Snape's pale face, illuminated by the flaming cabin, was suffused with hatred just as it had been before he had cursed Dumbledore.

"You dare use my own spells against me, Potter? It was I who invented them — I, the Half-Blood Prince! And you'd turn my inventions on me, like your filthy father, would you? I don't think so . . . *no!*"

Harry had dived for his wand; Snape shot a hex at it and it flew feet away into the darkness and out of sight.

"Kill me then," panted Harry, who felt no fear at all, but only rage and contempt. "Kill me like you killed him, you coward —"

"DON'T —" screamed Snape, and his face was suddenly demented, inhuman, as though he was in as much pain as the yelping, howling dog stuck in the burning house behind them — "CALL ME COWARD!"

And he slashed at the air: Harry felt a white-hot, whiplike something hit him across the face and was slammed backward into the ground. Spots of light burst in front of his eyes and for a moment all the breath seemed to have gone from his body, then he heard a rush of wings above him and something enormous obscured the stars. Buckbeak had flown at Snape, who staggered backward as the razor-sharp claws slashed at him. As Harry raised himself into a sitting position, his head still swimming from its last contact with the ground, he saw Snape running as hard as he could, the enormous beast flapping behind him and screeching as Harry had never heard him screech —

Harry struggled to his feet, looking around groggily for his wand, hoping to give chase again, but even as his fingers fumbled in the grass, discarding twigs, he knew it would be too late, and sure enough, by the time he had located his wand, he turned only to see the hippogriff circling the gates. Snape had managed to Disapparate just beyond the school's boundaries.

"Hagrid," muttered Harry, still dazed, looking around. "HAGRID?"

He stumbled toward the burning house as an enormous figure emerged from out of the flames carrying Fang on his back. With a cry of thankfulness, Harry sank to his knees; he was shaking in every limb, his body ached all over, and his breath came in painful stabs.

"Yeh all righ', Harry? Yeh all righ'? Speak ter me, Harry. . . ."

Hagrid's huge, hairy face was swimming above Harry, blocking out the stars. Harry could smell burnt wood and dog hair; he put out a hand and felt Fang's reassuringly warm and alive body quivering beside him.

"I'm all right," panted Harry. "Are you?"

"'Course I am . . . take more'n that ter finish me."

Hagrid put his hands under Harry's arms and raised him up with such force that Harry's feet momentarily left the ground before Hagrid set him upright again. He could see blood trickling down Hagrid's cheek from a deep cut under one eye, which was swelling rapidly.

"We should put out your house," said Harry, "the charm's 'Aguamenti' . . ."

"Knew it was summat like that," mumbled Hagrid, and he raised a smoldering pink, flowery umbrella and said, *"Aguamenti!"*

A jet of water flew out of the umbrella tip. Harry raised his wand arm, which felt like lead, and murmured *"Aguamenti"* too: Together, he and Hagrid poured water on the house until the last flame was extinguished.

"S'not too bad," said Hagrid hopefully a few minutes later, looking at the smoking wreck. "Nothin' Dumbledore won' be able to put righ' . . ."

Harry felt a searing pain in his stomach at the sound of the name. In the silence and the stillness, horror rose inside him.

"Hagrid . . ."

"I was bindin' up a couple o' bowtruckle legs when I heard 'em comin'," said Hagrid sadly, still staring at his wrecked cabin. "They'll've bin burnt ter twigs, poor little things. . . ."

"Hagrid . . ."

"But what happened, Harry? I jus' saw them Death Eaters runnin' down from the castle, but what the ruddy hell was Snape doin' with 'em? Where's he gone — was he chasin' them?"

"He . . ." Harry cleared his throat; it was dry from panic and the smoke. "Hagrid, he killed . . ."

"Killed?" said Hagrid loudly, staring down at Harry. "Snape killed? What're yeh on abou', Harry?"

"Dumbledore," said Harry. "Snape killed . . . Dumbledore."

Hagrid simply looked at him, the little of his face that could be seen completely blank, uncomprehending.

"Dumbledore wha', Harry?"

"He's dead. Snape killed him. . . ."

"Don' say that," said Hagrid roughly. "Snape kill Dumbledore — don' be stupid, Harry. Wha's made yeh say tha'?"

"I saw it happen."

"Yeh couldn' have."

"I saw it, Hagrid."

Hagrid shook his head; his expression was disbelieving but sympathetic, and Harry knew that Hagrid thought he had sustained a blow to the head, that he was confused, perhaps by the aftereffects of a jinx. . . .

"What musta happened was, Dumbledore musta told Snape ter go with them Death Eaters," Hagrid said confidently. "I suppose he's gotta keep his cover. Look, let's get yeh back up ter the school. Come on, Harry. . . ."

Harry did not attempt to argue or explain. He was still shaking uncontrollably. Hagrid would find out soon enough, too soon. . . . As they directed their steps back toward the castle, Harry saw that many of its windows were lit now. He could imagine, clearly, the scenes inside as people moved from room to room, telling each other that Death Eaters had got in, that the Mark was shining over Hogwarts, that somebody must have been killed. . . .

The oak front doors stood open ahead of them, light flooding out onto the drive and the lawn. Slowly, uncertainly, dressing-gowned people were creeping down the steps, looking around nervously for some sign of the Death Eaters who had fled into the night. Harry's eyes, however, were fixed upon the ground at the foot of the tallest tower. He imagined that he could see a black, huddled mass lying in the grass there, though he was really too far away to see anything of the sort. Even as he stared wordlessly at the place where he thought

Dumbledore's body must lie, however, he saw people beginning to move toward it.

"What're they all lookin' at?" said Hagrid, as he and Harry approached the castle front, Fang keeping as close as he could to their ankles. "Wha's tha', lyin' on the grass?" Hagrid added sharply, heading now toward the foot of the Astronomy Tower, where a small crowd was congregating. "See it, Harry? Righ' at the foot o' the tower? Under where the Mark . . . Blimey . . . yeh don' think someone got thrown — ?"

Hagrid fell silent, the thought apparently too horrible to express aloud. Harry walked alongside him, feeling the aches and pains in his face and his legs where the various hexes of the last half hour had hit him, though in an oddly detached way, as though somebody near him was suffering them. What was real and inescapable was the awful pressing feeling in his chest. . . .

He and Hagrid moved, dreamlike, through the murmuring crowd to the very front, where the dumbstruck students and teachers had left a gap.

Harry heard Hagrid's moan of pain and shock, but he did not stop; he walked slowly forward until he reached the place where Dumbledore lay and crouched down beside him. He had known there was no hope from the moment that the full Body-Bind Curse Dumbledore had placed upon him lifted, known that it could have happened only because its caster was dead, but there was still no preparation for seeing him here, spread-eagled, broken: the greatest wizard Harry had ever, or would ever, meet.

Dumbledore's eyes were closed; but for the strange angle of his arms and legs, he might have been sleeping. Harry reached out, straightened the half-moon spectacles upon the crooked nose, and wiped a trickle of blood from the mouth with his own sleeve. Then he gazed down at the wise old face and tried to absorb the enormous and incomprehensible truth: that never again would Dumbledore speak to him, never again could he help. . . .

The crowd murmured behind Harry. After what seemed like a long time, he became aware that he was kneeling upon something hard and looked down.

The locket they had managed to steal so many hours before had fallen out of Dumbledore's pocket. It had opened, perhaps due to the force with which it hit the ground. And although he could not feel more shock or horror or sadness than he felt already, Harry knew, as he picked it up, that there was something wrong. . . .

He turned the locket over in his hands. This was neither as large as the locket he remembered seeing in the Pensieve, nor were there any markings upon it, no sign of the ornate *S* that was supposed to be Slytherin's mark. Moreover, there was nothing inside but for a scrap of folded parchment wedged tightly into the place where a portrait should have been.

Automatically, without really thinking about what he was doing, Harry pulled out the fragment of parchment, opened it, and read by the light of the many wands that had now been lit behind him:

To the Dark Lord

I know I will be dead long before you read this
but I want you to know that it was I who discovered your secret.
I have stolen the real Horcrux and intend to destroy it as soon as I can.
I face death in the hope that when you meet your match,
you will be mortal once more.

R.A.B.

Harry neither knew nor cared what the message meant. Only one thing mattered: This was not a Horcrux. Dumbledore had weakened himself by drinking that terrible potion for nothing. Harry crumpled the parchment in his hand, and his eyes burned with tears as behind him Fang began to howl.

THE PHOENIX LAMENT

C'mere, Harry . . ."

"No."

"Yeh can' stay here, Harry. . . . Come on, now. . . ."

"No."

He did not want to leave Dumbledore's side, he did not want to move anywhere. Hagrid's hand on his shoulder was trembling. Then another voice said, "Harry, come on."

A much smaller and warmer hand had enclosed his and was pulling him upward. He obeyed its pressure without really thinking about it. Only as he walked blindly back through the crowd did he realize, from a trace of flowery scent on the air, that it was Ginny who was leading him back into the castle. Incomprehensible voices battered him, sobs and shouts and wails stabbed the night, but Harry and Ginny walked on, back up the steps into the entrance hall. Faces swam on the edges of Harry's vision, people were peering at him, whispering, wondering, and Gryffindor rubies glistened on the floor like drops of blood as they made their way toward the marble staircase.

"We're going to the hospital wing," said Ginny.

"I'm not hurt," said Harry.

"It's McGonagall's orders," said Ginny. "Everyone's up there, Ron and Hermione and Lupin and everyone —"

Fear stirred in Harry's chest again: He had forgotten the inert figures he had left behind.

"Ginny, who else is dead?"

"Don't worry, none of us."

"But the Dark Mark — Malfoy said he stepped over a body —"

"He stepped over Bill, but it's all right, he's alive."

There was something in her voice, however, that Harry knew boded ill.

"Are you sure?"

"Of course I'm sure . . . he's a — a bit of a mess, that's all. Greyback attacked him. Madam Pomfrey says he won't — won't look the same anymore. . . ."

Ginny's voice trembled a little.

"We don't really know what the aftereffects will be — I mean, Greyback being a werewolf, but not transformed at the time."

"But the others . . . There were other bodies on the ground. . . ."

"Neville and Professor Flitwick are both hurt, but Madam Pomfrey says they'll be all right. And a Death Eater's dead, he got hit by a Killing Curse that huge blond one was firing off everywhere — Harry, if we hadn't had your Felix potion, I think we'd all have been killed, but everything seemed to just miss us —"

They had reached the hospital wing. Pushing open the doors, Harry saw Neville lying, apparently asleep, in a bed near the door. Ron, Hermione, Luna, Tonks, and Lupin were gathered around another bed near the far end of the ward. At the sound of the doors opening, they all looked up. Hermione ran to Harry and hugged him; Lupin moved forward too, looking anxious.

"Are you all right, Harry?"

"I'm fine. . . . How's Bill?"

Nobody answered. Harry looked over Hermione's shoulder and saw an unrecognizable face lying on Bill's pillow, so badly slashed and ripped that he looked grotesque. Madam Pomfrey was dabbing at his wounds with some harsh-smelling green ointment. Harry remembered how Snape had mended Malfoy's *Sectumsempra* wounds so easily with his wand.

"Can't you fix them with a charm or something?" he asked the matron.

"No charm will work on these," said Madam Pomfrey. "I've tried everything I know, but there is no cure for werewolf bites."

"But he wasn't bitten at the full moon," said Ron, who was gazing down into his brother's face as though he could somehow force him to mend just by staring. "Greyback hadn't transformed, so surely Bill won't be a — a real — ?"

He looked uncertainly at Lupin.

"No, I don't think that Bill will be a true werewolf," said Lupin, "but that does not mean that there won't be some contamination. Those are cursed wounds. They are unlikely ever to heal fully, and — and Bill might have some wolfish characteristics from now on."

"Dumbledore might know something that'd work, though," Ron said. "Where is he? Bill fought those maniacs on Dumbledore's orders, Dumbledore owes him, he can't leave him in this state —"

"Ron — Dumbledore's dead," said Ginny.

"No!" Lupin looked wildly from Ginny to Harry, as though hoping the latter might contradict her, but when Harry did not, Lupin collapsed into a chair beside Bill's bed, his hands over his face. Harry had never seen Lupin lose control before; he felt as though he was intruding upon something private, indecent. He turned away and caught Ron's eye instead, exchanging in silence a look that confirmed what Ginny had said.

"How did he die?" whispered Tonks. "How did it happen?"

"Snape killed him," said Harry. "I was there, I saw it. We arrived back on the Astronomy Tower because that's where the Mark was. . . . Dumbledore was ill, he was weak, but I think he realized it was a trap when we heard footsteps running up the stairs. He immobilized me, I couldn't do anything, I was under the Invisibility Cloak — and then Malfoy came through the door and disarmed him —"

Hermione clapped her hands to her mouth and Ron groaned. Luna's mouth trembled.

"— more Death Eaters arrived — and then Snape — and Snape did it. The *Avada Kedavra*." Harry couldn't go on.

Madam Pomfrey burst into tears. Nobody paid her any attention except Ginny, who whispered, "Shh! Listen!"

Gulping, Madam Pomfrey pressed her fingers to her mouth, her eyes wide. Somewhere out in the darkness, a phoenix was singing in a way Harry had never heard before: a stricken lament of terrible beauty. And Harry felt, as he had felt about phoenix song before, that the music was inside him, not without: It was his own grief turned magically to song that echoed across the grounds and through the castle windows.

How long they all stood there, listening, he did not know, nor why it seemed to ease their pain a little to listen to the sound of their mourning, but it felt like a long time later that the hospital door opened again and Professor McGonagall entered the ward. Like all the rest, she bore marks of the recent battle: There were grazes on her face and her robes were ripped.

"Molly and Arthur are on their way," she said, and the spell of the music was broken: Everyone roused themselves as though coming out of trances, turning again to look at Bill, or else to rub their own eyes, shake their heads. "Harry, what happened? According to Hagrid you were with Professor Dumbledore when he — when it happened. He says Professor Snape was involved in some —"

"Snape killed Dumbledore," said Harry.

She stared at him for a moment, then swayed alarmingly; Madam Pomfrey, who seemed to have pulled herself together, ran forward, conjuring a chair from thin air, which she pushed under McGonagall.

"Snape," repeated McGonagall faintly, falling into the chair. "We all wondered . . . but he trusted . . . always . . . *Snape* . . . I can't believe it. . . ."

"Snape was a highly accomplished Occlumens," said Lupin, his voice uncharacteristically harsh. "We always knew that."

"But Dumbledore swore he was on our side!" whispered Tonks. "I always thought Dumbledore must know something about Snape that we didn't. . . ."

"He always hinted that he had an ironclad reason for trusting Snape," muttered Professor McGonagall, now dabbing at the corners of her leaking eyes with a tartan-edged handkerchief. "I mean . . . with Snape's history . . . of course people were bound to wonder . . . but Dumbledore told me explicitly that Snape's repentance was absolutely genuine. . . . Wouldn't hear a word against him!"

"I'd love to know what Snape told him to convince him," said Tonks.

"I know," said Harry, and they all turned to look at him. "Snape passed Voldemort the information that made Voldemort hunt down my mum and dad. Then Snape told Dumbledore he hadn't realized what he was doing, he was really sorry he'd done it, sorry that they were dead."

They all stared at him.

"And Dumbledore believed that?" said Lupin incredulously. "Dumbledore believed Snape was sorry James was dead? Snape *hated* James. . . ."

"And he didn't think my mother was worth a damn either," said Harry, "because she was Muggle-born. . . . 'Mudblood,' he called her. . . ."

Nobody asked how Harry knew this. All of them seemed to be lost in horrified shock, trying to digest the monstrous truth of what had happened.

"This is all my fault," said Professor McGonagall suddenly. She looked disoriented, twisting her wet handkerchief in her hands. "My fault. I sent Filius to fetch Snape tonight, I actually sent for him to come and help us! If I hadn't alerted Snape to what was going on, he might never have joined forces with the Death Eaters. I don't think he knew they were there before Filius told him, I don't think he knew they were coming."

"It isn't your fault, Minerva," said Lupin firmly. "We all wanted more help, we were glad to think Snape was on his way. . . ."

"So when he arrived at the fight, he joined in on the Death Eaters' side?" asked Harry, who wanted every detail of Snape's duplicity and infamy, feverishly collecting more reasons to hate him, to swear vengeance.

"I don't know exactly how it happened," said Professor McGonagall distractedly. "It's all so confusing. . . . Dumbledore had told us that he would be leaving the school for a few hours and that we were to patrol the corridors just in case . . . Remus, Bill, and Nymphadora were to join us . . . and so we patrolled. All seemed quiet. Every secret passageway out of the school was covered. We knew nobody could fly in. There were powerful enchantments on every entrance into the castle. I still don't know how the Death Eaters can possibly have entered. . . ."

"I do," said Harry, and he explained, briefly, about the pair of Vanishing Cabinets and the magical pathway they formed. "So they got in through the Room of Requirement."

Almost against his will he glanced from Ron to Hermione, both of whom looked devastated.

"I messed up, Harry," said Ron bleakly. "We did like you told us: We checked the Marauder's Map and we couldn't see Malfoy on it, so we thought he must be in the Room of Requirement, so me, Ginny, and Neville went to keep watch on it . . . but Malfoy got past us."

"He came out of the room about an hour after we started

keeping watch," said Ginny. "He was on his own, clutching that awful shriveled arm —"

"His Hand of Glory," said Ron. "Gives light only to the holder, remember?"

"Anyway," Ginny went on, "he must have been checking whether the coast was clear to let the Death Eaters out, because the moment he saw us he threw something into the air and it all went pitch-black —"

"— Peruvian Instant Darkness Powder," said Ron bitterly. "Fred and George's. I'm going to be having a word with them about who they let buy their products."

"We tried everything, Lumos, Incendio," said Ginny. "Nothing would penetrate the darkness; all we could do was grope our way out of the corridor again, and meanwhile we could hear people rushing past us. Obviously Malfoy could see because of that hand thing and was guiding them, but we didn't dare use any curses or anything in case we hit each other, and by the time we'd reached a corridor that was light, they'd gone."

"Luckily," said Lupin hoarsely, "Ron, Ginny, and Neville ran into us almost immediately and told us what had happened. We found the Death Eaters minutes later, heading in the direction of the Astronomy Tower. Malfoy obviously hadn't expected more people to be on the watch; he seemed to have exhausted his supply of Darkness Powder, at any rate. A fight broke out, they scattered and we gave chase. One of them, Gibbon, broke away and headed up the tower stairs —"

"To set off the Mark?" asked Harry.

"He must have done, yes, they must have arranged that before they left the Room of Requirement," said Lupin. "But I don't think

Gibbon liked the idea of waiting up there alone for Dumbledore, because he came running back downstairs to rejoin the fight and was hit by a Killing Curse that just missed me."

"So if Ron was watching the Room of Requirement with Ginny and Neville," said Harry, turning to Hermione, "were you — ?"

"Outside Snape's office, yes," whispered Hermione, her eyes sparkling with tears, "with Luna. We hung around for ages outside it and nothing happened. . . . We didn't know what was going on upstairs, Ron had taken the map. . . . It was nearly midnight when Professor Flitwick came sprinting down into the dungeons. He was shouting about Death Eaters in the castle, I don't think he really registered that Luna and I were there at all, he just burst his way into Snape's office and we heard him saying that Snape had to go back with him and help and then we heard a loud thump and Snape came hurtling out of his room and he saw us and — and —"

"What?" Harry urged her.

"I was so stupid, Harry!" said Hermione in a high-pitched whisper. "He said Professor Flitwick had collapsed and that we should go and take care of him while he — while he went to help fight the Death Eaters —" She covered her face in shame and continued to talk into her fingers, so that her voice was muffled. "We went into his office to see if we could help Professor Flitwick and found him unconscious on the floor . . . and oh, it's so obvious now, Snape must have Stupefied Flitwick, but we didn't realize, Harry, we didn't realize, we just let Snape go!"

"It's not your fault," said Lupin firmly. "Hermione, had you not obeyed Snape and got out of the way, he probably would have killed you and Luna."

"So then he came upstairs," said Harry, who was watching Snape running up the marble staircase in his mind's eye, his black robes billowing behind him as ever, pulling his wand from under his cloak as he ascended, "and he found the place where you were all fighting. . . ."

"We were in trouble, we were losing," said Tonks in a low voice. "Gibbon was down, but the rest of the Death Eaters seemed ready to fight to the death. Neville had been hurt, Bill had been savaged by Greyback . . . It was all dark . . . curses flying everywhere . . . The Malfoy boy had vanished, he must have slipped past, up the stairs . . . then more of them ran after him, but one of them blocked the stair behind them with some kind of curse. . . . Neville ran at it and got thrown up into the air —"

"None of us could break through," said Ron, "and that massive Death Eater was still firing off jinxes all over the place, they were bouncing off the walls and barely missing us. . . ."

"And then Snape was there," said Tonks, "and then he wasn't —"

"I saw him running toward us, but that huge Death Eater's jinx just missed me right afterward and I ducked and lost track of things," said Ginny.

"I saw him run straight through the cursed barrier as though it wasn't there," said Lupin. "I tried to follow him, but was thrown back just like Neville. . . ."

"He must have known a spell we didn't," whispered McGonagall. "After all — he was the Defense Against the Dark Arts teacher. . . . I just assumed that he was in a hurry to chase after the Death Eaters who'd escaped up to the tower. . . ."

"He was," said Harry savagely, "but to help them, not to stop them . . . and I'll bet you had to have a Dark Mark to get through that barrier — so what happened when he came back down?"

"Well, the big Death Eater had just fired off a hex that caused half the ceiling to fall in, and also broke the curse blocking the stairs," said Lupin. "We all ran forward — those of us who were still standing anyway — and then Snape and the boy emerged out of the dust — obviously, none of us attacked them —"

"We just let them pass," said Tonks in a hollow voice. "We thought they were being chased by the Death Eaters — and next thing, the other Death Eaters and Greyback were back and we were fighting again — I thought I heard Snape shout something, but I don't know what —"

"He shouted, 'It's over,'" said Harry. "He'd done what he'd meant to do."

They all fell silent. Fawkes's lament was still echoing over the dark grounds outside. As the music reverberated upon the air, unbidden, unwelcome thoughts slunk into Harry's mind. . . . Had they taken Dumbledore's body from the foot of the tower yet? What would happen to it next? Where would it rest? He clenched his fists tightly in his pockets. He could feel the small cold lump of the fake Horcrux against the knuckles of his right hand.

The doors of the hospital wing burst open, making them all jump: Mr. and Mrs. Weasley were striding up the ward, Fleur just behind them, her beautiful face terrified.

"Molly — Arthur —" said Professor McGonagall, jumping up and hurrying to greet them. "I am so sorry —"

"Bill," whispered Mrs. Weasley, darting past Professor McGonagall as she caught sight of Bill's mangled face. "Oh, *Bill*!"

Lupin and Tonks had got up hastily and retreated so that Mr. and Mrs. Weasley could get nearer to the bed. Mrs. Weasley bent over her son and pressed her lips to his bloody forehead.

"You said Greyback attacked him?" Mr. Weasley asked Professor McGonagall distractedly. "But he hadn't transformed? So what does that mean? What will happen to Bill?"

"We don't yet know," said Professor McGonagall, looking helplessly at Lupin.

"There will probably be some contamination, Arthur," said Lupin. "It is an odd case, possibly unique. . . . We don't know what his behavior might be like when he awakens. . . ."

Mrs. Weasley took the nasty-smelling ointment from Madam Pomfrey and began dabbing at Bill's wounds.

"And Dumbledore . . ." said Mr. Weasley. "Minerva, is it true . . . Is he really . . . ?"

As Professor McGonagall nodded, Harry felt Ginny move beside him and looked at her. Her slightly narrowed eyes were fixed upon Fleur, who was gazing down at Bill with a frozen expression on her face.

"Dumbledore gone," whispered Mr. Weasley, but Mrs. Weasley had eyes only for her eldest son; she began to sob, tears falling onto Bill's mutilated face.

"Of course, it doesn't matter how he looks. . . . It's not r-really important . . . but he was a very handsome little b-boy . . . always very handsome . . . and he was g-going to be married!"

"And what do you mean by zat?" said Fleur suddenly and loudly. "What do you mean, ''e was *going* to be married?'"

Mrs. Weasley raised her tear-stained face, looking startled. "Well — only that —"

"You theenk Bill will not wish to marry me anymore?" demanded Fleur. "You theenk, because of these bites, he will not love me?"

"No, that's not what I —"

"Because 'e will!" said Fleur, drawing herself up to her full height and throwing back her long mane of silver hair. "It would take more zan a werewolf to stop Bill loving me!"

"Well, yes, I'm sure," said Mrs. Weasley, "but I thought perhaps — given how — how he —"

"You thought I would not weesh to marry him? Or per'aps, you hoped?" said Fleur, her nostrils flaring. "What do I care how he looks? I am good-looking enough for both of us, I theenk! All these scars show is zat my husband is brave! And I shall do zat!" she added fiercely, pushing Mrs. Weasley aside and snatching the ointment from her.

Mrs. Weasley fell back against her husband and watched Fleur mopping up Bill's wounds with a most curious expression upon her face. Nobody said anything; Harry did not dare move. Like everybody else, he was waiting for the explosion.

"Our Great-Auntie Muriel," said Mrs. Weasley after a long pause, "has a very beautiful tiara — goblin-made — which I am sure I could persuade her to lend you for the wedding. She is very fond of Bill, you know, and it would look lovely with your hair."

"Thank you," said Fleur stiffly. "I am sure zat will be lovely."

And then, Harry did not quite see how it happened, both women were crying and hugging each other. Completely bewildered, wondering whether the world had gone mad, he turned around: Ron looked as stunned as he felt and Ginny and Hermione were exchanging startled looks.

"You see!" said a strained voice. Tonks was glaring at Lupin. "She still wants to marry him, even though he's been bitten! She doesn't care!"

"It's different," said Lupin, barely moving his lips and looking suddenly tense. "Bill will not be a full werewolf. The cases are completely —"

"But I don't care either, I don't care!" said Tonks, seizing the front of Lupin's robes and shaking them. "I've told you a million times. . . ."

And the meaning of Tonks's Patronus and her mouse-colored hair, and the reason she had come running to find Dumbledore when she had heard a rumor someone had been attacked by Greyback, all suddenly became clear to Harry; it had not been Sirius that Tonks had fallen in love with after all.

"And I've told *you* a million times," said Lupin, refusing to meet her eyes, staring at the floor, "that I am too old for you, too poor . . . too dangerous. . . ."

"I've said all along you're taking a ridiculous line on this, Remus," said Mrs. Weasley over Fleur's shoulder as she patted her on the back.

"I am not being ridiculous," said Lupin steadily. "Tonks deserves somebody young and whole."

"But she wants you," said Mr. Weasley, with a small smile. "And after all, Remus, young and whole men do not necessarily remain so."

He gestured sadly at his son, lying between them.

"This is . . . not the moment to discuss it," said Lupin, avoiding everybody's eyes as he looked around distractedly. "Dumbledore is dead. . . ."

"Dumbledore would have been happier than anybody to think that there was a little more love in the world," said Professor McGonagall curtly, just as the hospital doors opened again and Hagrid walked in.

The little of his face that was not obscured by hair or beard was soaking and swollen; he was shaking with tears, a vast, spotted handkerchief in his hand.

"I've . . . I've done it, Professor," he choked. "M-moved him. Professor Sprout's got the kids back in bed. Professor Flitwick's lyin' down, but he says he'll be all righ' in a jiffy, an' Professor Slughorn says the Ministry's bin informed."

"Thank you, Hagrid," said Professor McGonagall, standing up at once and turning to look at the group around Bill's bed. "I shall have to see the Ministry when they get here. Hagrid, please tell the Heads of Houses — Slughorn can represent Slytherin — that I want to see them in my office forthwith. I would like you to join us too."

As Hagrid nodded, turned, and shuffled out of the room again, she looked down at Harry. "Before I meet them I would like a quick word with you, Harry. If you'll come with me. . . ."

Harry stood up, murmured "See you in a bit" to Ron, Hermione, and Ginny, and followed Professor McGonagall back down the ward. The corridors outside were deserted and the only sound was the distant phoenix song. It was several minutes before Harry became aware that they were not heading for Professor McGonagall's office, but for Dumbledore's, and another few seconds before he realized that of course, she had been deputy headmistress. . . . Apparently she was now headmistress . . . so the room behind the gargoyle was now hers.

In silence they ascended the moving spiral staircase and entered the circular office. He did not know what he had expected: that the room would be draped in black, perhaps, or even that Dumbledore's body might be lying there. In fact, it looked almost exactly as it had done when he and Dumbledore had left it mere hours previously: the silver instruments whirring and puffing on their spindle-legged tables, Gryffindor's sword in its glass case gleaming in the moonlight, the Sorting Hat on a shelf behind the desk. But Fawkes's perch stood empty, he was still crying his lament to the grounds. And a new portrait had joined the ranks of the dead headmasters and headmistresses of Hogwarts: Dumbledore was slumbering in a golden frame over the desk, his half-moon spectacles perched upon his crooked nose, looking peaceful and untroubled.

After glancing once at this portrait, Professor McGonagall made an odd movement as though steeling herself, then rounded the desk to look at Harry, her face taut and lined.

"Harry," she said, "I would like to know what you and Professor Dumbledore were doing this evening when you left the school."

"I can't tell you that, Professor," said Harry. He had expected the question and had his answer ready. It had been here, in this very room, that Dumbledore had told him that he was to confide the contents of their lessons to nobody but Ron and Hermione.

"Harry, it might be important," said Professor McGonagall.

"It is," said Harry, "very, but he didn't want me to tell anyone."

Professor McGonagall glared at him. "Potter" — Harry registered the renewed use of his surname — "in the light of Professor Dumbledore's death, I think you must see that the situation has changed somewhat —"

"I don't think so," said Harry, shrugging. "Professor Dumbledore never told me to stop following his orders if he died."

"But —"

"There's one thing you should know before the Ministry gets

here, though. Madam Rosmerta's under the Imperius Curse, she was helping Malfoy and the Death Eaters, that's how the necklace and the poisoned mead —"

"Rosmerta?" said Professor McGonagall incredulously, but before she could go on, there was a knock on the door behind them and Professors Sprout, Flitwick, and Slughorn traipsed into the room, followed by Hagrid, who was still weeping copiously, his huge frame trembling with grief.

"Snape!" ejaculated Slughorn, who looked the most shaken, pale and sweating. "Snape! I taught him! I thought I knew him!"

But before any of them could respond to this, a sharp voice spoke from high on the wall: A sallow-faced wizard with a short black fringe had just walked back into his empty canvas.

"Minerva, the Minister will be here within seconds, he has just Disapparated from the Ministry."

"Thank you, Everard," said Professor McGonagall, and she turned quickly to her teachers.

"I want to talk about what happens to Hogwarts before he gets here," she said quickly. "Personally, I am not convinced that the school should reopen next year. The death of the headmaster at the hands of one of our colleagues is a terrible stain upon Hogwarts's history. It is horrible."

"I am sure Dumbledore would have wanted the school to remain open," said Professor Sprout. "I feel that if a single pupil wants to come, then the school ought to remain open for that pupil."

"But will we have a single pupil after this?" said Slughorn, now dabbing his sweating brow with a silken handkerchief. "Parents will want to keep their children at home and I can't say I blame them. Personally, I don't think we're in more danger at Hogwarts than we are anywhere else, but you can't expect mothers to think like that. They'll want to keep their families together, it's only natural."

"I agree," said Professor McGonagall. "And in any case, it is not true to say that Dumbledore never envisaged a situation in which Hogwarts might close. When the Chamber of Secrets reopened he considered the closure of the school — and I must say that Professor Dumbledore's murder is more disturbing to me than the idea of Slytherin's monster living undetected in the bowels of the castle. . . ."

"We must consult the governors," said Professor Flitwick in his squeaky little voice; he had a large bruise on his forehead but seemed otherwise unscathed by his collapse in Snape's office. "We must follow the established procedures. A decision should not be made hastily."

"Hagrid, you haven't said anything," said Professor McGonagall. "What are your views, ought Hogwarts to remain open?"

Hagrid, who had been weeping silently into his large, spotted handkerchief throughout this conversation, now raised puffy red eyes and croaked, "I dunno, Professor . . . that's fer the Heads of House an' the headmistress ter decide . . ."

"Professor Dumbledore always valued your views," said Professor McGonagall kindly, "and so do I."

"Well, I'm stayin'," said Hagrid, fat tears still leaking out of the corners of his eyes and trickling down into his tangled beard. "It's me home, it's bin me home since I was thirteen. An' if there's kids who wan' me ter teach 'em, I'll do it. But . . . I dunno . . .

Hogwarts without Dumbledore . . ." He gulped and disappeared behind his handkerchief once more, and there was silence.

"Very well," said Professor McGonagall, glancing out of the window at the grounds, checking to see whether the Minister was yet approaching, "then I must agree with Filius that the right thing to do is to consult the governors, who will make the final decision.

"Now, as to getting students home . . . there is an argument for doing it sooner rather than later. We could arrange for the Hogwarts Express to come tomorrow if necessary —"

"What about Dumbledore's funeral?" said Harry, speaking at last.

"Well . . ." said Professor McGonagall, losing a little of her briskness as her voice shook. "I — I know that it was Dumbledore's wish to be laid to rest here, at Hogwarts —"

"Then that's what'll happen, isn't it?" said Harry fiercely.

"If the Ministry thinks it appropriate," said Professor McGonagall. "No other headmaster or headmistress has ever been —"

"No other headmaster or headmistress ever gave more to this school," growled Hagrid.

"Hogwarts should be Dumbledore's final resting place," said Professor Flitwick.

"Absolutely," said Professor Sprout.

"And in that case," said Harry, "you shouldn't send the students home until the funeral's over. They'll want to say —"

The last word caught in his throat, but Professor Sprout completed the sentence for him.

"Good-bye."

"Well said," squeaked Professor Flitwick. "Well said indeed! Our students should pay tribute, it is fitting. We can arrange transport home afterward."

"Seconded," barked Professor Sprout.

"I suppose . . . yes . . ." said Slughorn in a rather agitated voice, while Hagrid let out a strangled sob of assent.

"He's coming," said Professor McGonagall suddenly, gazing down into the grounds. "The Minister . . . and by the looks of it, he's brought a delegation . . ."

"Can I leave, Professor?" said Harry at once.

He had no desire at all to see, or be interrogated by, Rufus Scrimgeour tonight.

"You may," said Professor McGonagall. "And quickly."

She strode toward the door and held it open for him. He sped down the spiral staircase and off along the deserted corridor; he had left his Invisibility Cloak at the top of the Astronomy Tower, but it did not matter; there was nobody in the corridors to see him pass, not even Filch, Mrs. Norris, or Peeves. He did not meet another soul until he turned into the passage leading to the Gryffindor common room.

"Is it true?" whispered the Fat Lady as he approached her. "It is really true? Dumbledore — dead?"

"Yes," said Harry.

She let out a wail and, without waiting for the password, swung forward to admit him.

As Harry had suspected it would be, the common room was jam-packed. The room fell silent as he climbed through the portrait hole. He saw Dean and Seamus sitting in a group nearby: This meant that the dormitory must be empty, or nearly so. Without speaking to anybody, without making eye contact at all, Harry walked straight across the room and through the door to the boys' dormitories.

As he had hoped, Ron was waiting for him, still fully dressed, sitting on his bed. Harry sat down on his own four-poster and for a moment, they simply stared at each other.

"They're talking about closing the school," said Harry.

"Lupin said they would," said Ron.

There was a pause.

"So?" said Ron in a very low voice, as though he thought the furniture might be listening in. "Did you find one? Did you get it? A — a Horcrux?"

Harry shook his head. All that had taken place around that black lake seemed like an old nightmare now; had it really happened, and only hours ago?

"You didn't get it?" said Ron, looking crestfallen. "It wasn't there?"

"No," said Harry. "Someone had already taken it and left a fake in its place."

"Already *taken* — ?"

Wordlessly, Harry pulled the fake locket from his pocket, opened it, and passed it to Ron. The full story could wait. . . . It did not matter tonight . . . nothing mattered except the end, the end of their pointless adventure, the end of Dumbledore's life. . . .

"R.A.B.," whispered Ron, "but who was that?"

"Dunno," said Harry, lying back on his bed fully clothed and staring blankly upwards. He felt no curiosity at all about R.A.B.: He doubted that he would ever feel curious again. As he lay there, he became aware suddenly that the grounds were silent. Fawkes had stopped singing.

And he knew, without knowing how he knew it, that the phoenix had gone, had left Hogwarts for good, just as Dumbledore had left the school, had left the world . . . had left Harry.

CHAPTER THIRTY

THE WHITE TOMB

All lessons were suspended, all examinations postponed. Some students were hurried away from Hogwarts by their parents over the next couple of days — the Patil twins were gone before breakfast on the morning following Dumbledore's death, and Zacharias Smith was escorted from the castle by his haughty-looking father. Seamus Finnigan, on the other hand, refused point-blank to accompany his mother home; they had a shouting match in the entrance hall that was resolved when she agreed that he could remain behind for the funeral. She had difficulty in finding a bed in Hogsmeade, Seamus told Harry and Ron, for wizards and witches were pouring into the village, preparing to pay their last respects to Dumbledore.

Some excitement was caused among the younger students, who had never seen it before, when a powder-blue carriage the size of a house, pulled by a dozen giant winged palominos, came soaring out of the sky in the late afternoon before the funeral and landed on the edge of the forest. Harry watched from a window as a gigantic and handsome olive-skinned, black-haired woman descended the carriage steps and threw herself into the waiting Hagrid's arms. Meanwhile a delegation of Ministry officials, including the Minister of Magic himself, was being accommodated within the castle. Harry was diligently avoiding contact with any of them; he was sure that, sooner or later, he would be asked again to account for Dumbledore's last excursion from Hogwarts.

Harry, Ron, Hermione, and Ginny were spending all of their time together. The beautiful weather seemed to mock them; Harry could imagine how it would have been if Dumbledore had not died, and they had had this time together at the very end of the year, Ginny's examinations finished, the pressure of homework lifted . . . and hour by hour, he put off saying the thing that he knew he must say, doing what he knew was right to do, because it was too hard to forgo his best source of comfort.

They visited the hospital wing twice a day: Neville had been discharged, but Bill remained under Madam Pomfrey's care. His scars were as bad as ever — in truth, he now bore a distinct resemblance to Mad-Eye Moody, though thankfully with both eyes and legs — but in personality he seemed just the same as ever. All that appeared to have changed was that he now had a great liking for very rare steaks.

". . . so eet ees lucky 'e is marrying me," said Fleur happily, plumping up Bill's pillows, "because ze British overcook their meat, I 'ave always said this."

"I suppose I'm just going to have to accept that he really is going to marry her," sighed Ginny later that evening, as she, Harry, Ron, and Hermione sat beside the open window of the Gryffindor common room, looking out over the twilit grounds.

"She's not that bad," said Harry. "Ugly, though," he added hastily, as Ginny raised her eyebrows, and she let out a reluctant giggle.

"Well, I suppose if Mum can stand it, I can."

"Anyone else we know died?" Ron asked Hermione, who was perusing the *Evening Prophet*.

Hermione winced at the forced toughness in his voice. "No," she said reprovingly, folding up the newspaper. "They're still looking for Snape but no sign . . ."

"Of course there isn't," said Harry, who became angry every time this subject cropped up. "They won't find Snape till they find Voldemort, and seeing as they've never managed to do that in all this time . . ."

"I'm going to go to bed," yawned Ginny. "I haven't been sleeping that well since . . . well . . . I could do with some sleep."

She kissed Harry (Ron looked away pointedly), waved at the other two, and departed for the girls' dormitories. The moment the door had closed behind her, Hermione leaned forward toward Harry with a most Hermione-ish look on her face.

"Harry, I found something out this morning, in the library."

"R.A.B.?" said Harry, sitting up straight.

He did not feel the way he had so often felt before, excited, curious, burning to get to the bottom of a mystery; he simply knew that the task of discovering the truth about the real Horcrux had to be completed before he could move a little farther along the dark and winding path stretching ahead of him, the path that he and

Dumbledore had set out upon together, and which he now knew he would have to journey alone. There might still be as many as four Horcruxes out there somewhere, and each would need to be found and eliminated before there was even a possibility that Voldemort could be killed. He kept reciting their names to himself, as though by listing them he could bring them within reach: *the locket . . . the cup . . . the snake . . . something of Gryffindor's or Ravenclaw's . . . the locket . . . the cup . . . the snake . . . something of Gryffindor's or Ravenclaw's . . .*

This mantra seemed to pulse through Harry's mind as he fell asleep at night, and his dreams were thick with cups, lockets, and mysterious objects that he could not quite reach, though Dumbledore helpfully offered Harry a rope ladder that turned to snakes the moment he began to climb. . . .

He had shown Hermione the note inside the locket the morning after Dumbledore's death, and although she had not immediately recognized the initials as belonging to some obscure wizard about whom she had been reading, she had since been rushing off to the library a little more often than was strictly necessary for somebody who had no homework to do.

"No," she said sadly, "I've been trying, Harry, but I haven't found anything. . . . There are a couple of reasonably well-known wizards with those initials — Rosalind Antigone Bungs . . . Rupert 'Axebanger' Brookstanton . . . but they don't seem to fit at all. Judging by that note, the person who stole the Horcrux knew Voldemort, and I can't find a shred of evidence that Bungs or Axebanger ever had anything to do with him. . . . No, actually, it's about . . . well, Snape."

She looked nervous even saying the name again.

"What about him?" asked Harry heavily, slumping back in his chair.

"Well, it's just that I was sort of right about the Half-Blood Prince business," she said tentatively.

"D'you have to rub it in, Hermione? How d'you think I feel about that now?"

"No — no — Harry, I didn't mean that!" she said hastily, looking around to check that they were not being overheard. "It's just that I was right about Eileen Prince once owning the book. You see . . . she was Snape's mother!"

"I thought she wasn't much of a looker," said Ron. Hermione ignored him.

"I was going through the rest of the old *Prophets* and there was a tiny announcement about Eileen Prince marrying a man called Tobias Snape, and then later an announcement saying that she'd given birth to a —"

"— murderer," spat Harry.

"Well . . . yes," said Hermione. "So . . . I was sort of right. Snape must have been proud of being 'half a Prince,' you see? Tobias Snape was a Muggle from what it said in the *Prophet*."

"Yeah, that fits," said Harry. "He'd play up the pure-blood side so he could get in with Lucius Malfoy and the rest of them. . . . He's just like Voldemort. Pure-blood mother, Muggle father . . . ashamed of his parentage, trying to make himself feared using the Dark Arts, gave himself an impressive new name — *Lord* Voldemort — the Half-Blood *Prince* — how could Dumbledore have missed — ?"

He broke off, looking out the window. He could not stop himself dwelling upon Dumbledore's inexcusable trust in Snape . . .

but as Hermione had just inadvertently reminded him, he, Harry, had been taken in just the same. . . . In spite of the increasing nastiness of those scribbled spells, he had refused to believe ill of the boy who had been so clever, who had helped him so much. . . .

Helped him . . . it was an almost unendurable thought now.

"I still don't get why he didn't turn you in for using that book," said Ron. "He must've known where you were getting it all from."

"He knew," said Harry bitterly. "He knew when I used Sectumsempra. He didn't really need Legilimency. . . . He might even have known before then, with Slughorn talking about how brilliant I was at Potions. . . . Shouldn't have left his old book in the bottom of that cupboard, should he?"

"But why didn't he turn you in?"

"I don't think he wanted to associate himself with that book," said Hermione. "I don't think Dumbledore would have liked it very much if he'd known. And even if Snape pretended it hadn't been his, Slughorn would have recognized his writing at once. Anyway, the book was left in Snape's old classroom, and I'll bet Dumbledore knew his mother was called 'Prince.'"

"I should've shown the book to Dumbledore," said Harry. "All that time he was showing me how Voldemort was evil even when he was at school, and I had proof Snape was too —"

"'Evil' is a strong word," said Hermione quietly.

"You were the one who kept telling me the book was dangerous!"

"I'm trying to say, Harry, that you're putting too much blame on yourself. I thought the Prince seemed to have a nasty sense of humor, but I would never have guessed he was a potential killer. . . ."

"None of us could've guessed Snape would . . . you know," said Ron.

Silence fell between them, each of them lost in their own thoughts, but Harry was sure that they, like him, were thinking about the following morning, when Dumbledore's body would be laid to rest. He had never attended a funeral before; there had been no body to bury when Sirius had died. He did not know what to expect and was a little worried about what he might see, about how he would feel. He wondered whether Dumbledore's death would be more real to him once it was over. Though he had moments when the horrible fact of it threatened to overwhelm him, there were blank stretches of numbness where, despite the fact that nobody was talking about anything else in the whole castle, he still found it difficult to believe that Dumbledore had really gone. Admittedly he had not, as he had with Sirius, looked desperately for some kind of loophole, some way that Dumbledore would come back. . . . He felt in his pocket for the cold chain of the fake Horcrux, which he now carried with him everywhere, not as a talisman, but as a reminder of what it had cost and what remained still to do.

Harry rose early to pack the next day; the Hogwarts Express would be leaving an hour after the funeral. Downstairs, he found the mood in the Great Hall subdued. Everybody was wearing their dress robes and no one seemed very hungry. Professor McGonagall had left the thronelike chair in the middle of the staff table empty. Hagrid's chair was deserted too; Harry thought that perhaps he had not been able to face breakfast, but Snape's place had been unceremoniously filled by Rufus Scrimgeour. Harry avoided his yellowish eyes as they scanned the Hall; Harry had the uncomfortable feeling that Scrimgeour was looking for him. Among Scrimgeour's entourage Harry spotted the red hair and horn-rimmed glasses of Percy Weasley. Ron gave no sign that he was aware of Percy, apart from stabbing pieces of kipper with unwonted venom.

Over at the Slytherin table Crabbe and Goyle were muttering together. Hulking boys though they were, they looked oddly lonely without the tall, pale figure of Malfoy between them, bossing them around. Harry had not spared Malfoy much thought. His animosity was all for Snape, but he had not forgotten the fear in Malfoy's voice on that tower top, nor the fact that he had lowered his wand before the other Death Eaters arrived. Harry did not believe that Malfoy would have killed Dumbledore. He despised Malfoy still for his infatuation with the Dark Arts, but now the tiniest drop of pity mingled with his dislike. Where, Harry wondered, was Malfoy now, and what was Voldemort making him do under threat of killing him and his parents?

Harry's thoughts were interrupted by a nudge in the ribs from Ginny. Professor McGonagall had risen to her feet, and the mournful hum in the Hall died away at once.

"It is nearly time," she said. "Please follow your Heads of Houses out into the grounds. Gryffindors, after me."

They filed out from behind their benches in near silence. Harry glimpsed Slughorn at the head of the Slytherin column, wearing magnificent, long, emerald green robes embroidered with silver. He had never seen Professor Sprout, Head of the Hufflepuffs, looking so clean; there was not a single patch on her hat, and when they reached the entrance hall, they found Madam Pince standing beside Filch, she in a thick black veil that fell to her knees, he in an ancient black suit and tie reeking of mothballs.

They were heading, as Harry saw when he stepped out onto the stone steps from the front doors, toward the lake. The warmth of the sun caressed his face as they followed Professor McGonagall in silence to the place where hundreds of chairs had been set out in rows. An aisle ran down the center of them: There was a marble table standing at the front, all chairs facing it. It was the most beautiful summer's day.

An extraordinary assortment of people had already settled into half of the chairs; shabby and smart, old and young. Most Harry did not recognize, but a few he did, including members of the Order of the Phoenix: Kingsley Shacklebolt; Mad-Eye Moody; Tonks, her hair miraculously returned to vividest pink; Remus Lupin, with whom she seemed to be holding hands; Mr. and Mrs. Weasley; Bill supported by Fleur and followed by Fred and George, who were wearing jackets of black dragon skin. Then there was Madame Maxime, who took up two and a half chairs on her own; Tom, the landlord of the Leaky Cauldron in London; Arabella Figg, Harry's Squib neighbor; the hairy bass player from the Wizarding group the Weird Sisters; Ernie Prang, driver of the Knight Bus; Madam Malkin, of the robe shop in Diagon Alley; and some people whom Harry merely knew by sight, such as the barman of the Hog's Head and the witch who pushed the trolley on the Hogwarts Express. The castle ghosts were there too, barely visible in the bright sunlight, discernible only when they moved, shimmering insubstantially on the gleaming air.

Harry, Ron, Hermione, and Ginny filed into seats at the end of a row beside the lake. People were whispering to each other; it sounded like a breeze in the grass, but the birdsong was louder by far. The crowd continued to swell; with a great rush of affection for both of them, Harry saw Neville being helped into a seat by Luna. Neville and Luna alone of the D.A. had responded to Hermione's summons the night that Dumbledore had died, and Harry knew why: They were the ones who had missed the D.A. most . . . probably the ones who had checked their coins regularly in the hope that there would be another meeting.

Cornelius Fudge walked past toward the front rows, his expression miserable, twirling his green bowler hat as usual; Harry next recognized Rita Skeeter, who, he was infuriated to see, had a notebook clutched in her red-taloned hand, and then, with a worse jolt of fury, Dolores Umbridge, an unconvincing expression of grief upon her toadlike face, a black velvet bow set atop her iron-colored curls. At the sight of the centaur Firenze, who was standing like a sentinel near the water's edge, she gave a start and scurried hastily into a seat a good distance away.

The staff was seated at last. Harry could see Scrimgeour looking grave and dignified in the front row with Professor McGonagall. He wondered whether Scrimgeour or any of these important people were really sorry that Dumbledore was dead. But then he heard music, strange, otherworldly music, and he forgot his dislike of the Ministry in looking around for the source of it. He was not the only one: Many heads were turning, searching, a little alarmed.

"In there," whispered Ginny in Harry's ear.

And he saw them in the clear green sunlit water, inches below the surface, reminding him horribly of the Inferi: a chorus of merpeople singing in a strange language he did not understand, their pallid faces rippling, their purplish hair flowing all around them. The music made the hair on Harry's neck stand up, and yet it was not unpleasant. It spoke very clearly of loss and of despair. As he looked down into the wild faces of the singers, he had the feeling that they, at least, were sorry for Dumbledore's passing. Then Ginny nudged him again and he looked around.

Hagrid was walking slowly up the aisle between the chairs. He was crying quite silently, his face gleaming with tears, and in his arms, wrapped in purple velvet spangled with golden stars, was what Harry knew to be Dumbledore's body. A sharp pain rose in Harry's throat at this sight: For a moment, the strange music and the knowledge that Dumbledore's body was so close seemed to take all warmth from the day. Ron looked white and shocked. Tears were falling thick and fast into both Ginny's and Hermione's laps.

They could not see clearly what was happening at the front. Hagrid seemed to have placed the body carefully upon the table. Now he retreated down the aisle, blowing his nose with loud trumpeting noises that drew scandalized looks from some, including, Harry saw, Dolores Umbridge . . . but Harry knew that Dumbledore would not have cared. He tried to make a friendly gesture to Hagrid as he passed, but Hagrid's eyes were so swollen it was a wonder he could see where he was going. Harry glanced at the back row to which Hagrid was heading and realized what was guiding him, for there, dressed in a jacket and trousers each the size of a small marquee, was the giant Grawp, his great ugly boulderlike head bowed, docile, almost human. Hagrid sat down next to his half-brother, and Grawp patted Hagrid hard on the head, so that his chair legs sank into the ground. Harry had a wonderful momentary urge to laugh. But then the music stopped, and he turned to face the front again.

A little tufty-haired man in plain black robes had got to his feet and stood now in front of Dumbledore's body. Harry could not hear what he was saying. Odd words floated back to them over the hundreds of heads. "Nobility of spirit" . . . "intellectual contribution" . . . "greatness of heart". . . It did not mean very much. It had little to do with Dumbledore as Harry had known him. He suddenly remembered Dumbledore's idea of a few words, "nitwit," "oddment," "blubber," and "tweak," and again had to suppress a grin. . . . What was the matter with him?

There was a soft splashing noise to his left and he saw that the merpeople had broken the surface to listen too. He remembered Dumbledore crouching at the water's edge two years ago, very close to where Harry now sat, and conversing in Mermish with the Merchieftainess. Harry wondered where Dumbledore had learned Mermish. There was so much he had never asked him, so much he should have said. . . .

And then, without warning, it swept over him, the dreadful truth, more completely and undeniably than it had until now. Dumbledore was dead, gone. . . . He clutched the cold locket in his hand so tightly that it hurt, but he could not prevent hot tears spilling from his eyes: He looked away from Ginny and the others and stared out over the lake, toward the forest, as the little man in black droned on. . . . There was movement among the trees. The centaurs had come to pay their respects too. They did not move into the open but Harry saw them standing quite still, half hidden in shadow, watching the wizards, their bows hanging at their sides. And Harry remembered his first nightmarish trip into the forest, the first time he had ever encountered the thing that was then Voldemort, and how he had faced him, and how he and Dumbledore had discussed fighting a losing battle not long thereafter. It was important, Dumbledore said, to fight, and fight again, and keep fighting, for only then could evil be kept at bay, though never quite eradicated. . . .

And Harry saw very clearly as he sat there under the hot sun how people who cared about him had stood in front of him one by one, his mother, his father, his godfather, and finally Dumbledore, all determined to protect him; but now that was over. He could not let anybody else stand between him and Voldemort; he must abandon forever the illusion he ought to have lost at the age of one, that the shelter of a parent's arms meant that nothing could hurt him. There was no waking from his nightmare, no comforting whisper in the dark that he was safe really, that it was all in his imagination; the last and greatest of his protectors had died, and he was more alone than he had ever been before.

The little man in black had stopped speaking at last and resumed his seat. Harry waited for somebody else to get to their feet; he expected speeches, probably from the Minister, but nobody moved.

Then several people screamed. Bright, white flames had erupted around Dumbledore's body and the table upon which it lay: Higher and higher they rose, obscuring the body. White smoke spiraled into the air and made strange shapes: Harry thought, for one heart-stopping moment, that he saw a phoenix fly joyfully into the blue, but next second the fire had vanished. In its place was a white marble tomb, encasing Dumbledore's body and the table on which he had rested.

There were a few more cries of shock as a shower of arrows soared through the air, but they fell far short of the crowd. It was,

Harry knew, the centaurs' tribute: He saw them turn tail and disappear back into the cool trees. Likewise, the merpeople sank
slowly back into the green water and were lost from view.

Harry looked at Ginny, Ron, and Hermione: Ron's face was
screwed up as though the sunlight were blinding him. Hermione's
face was glazed with tears, but Ginny was no longer crying. She
met Harry's gaze with the same hard, blazing look that he had seen
when she had hugged him after winning the Quidditch Cup in his
absence, and he knew that at that moment they understood each
other perfectly, and that when he told her what he was going to do
now, she would not say, "Be careful," or "Don't do it," but accept
his decision, because she would not have expected anything less of
him. And so he steeled himself to say what he had known he must
say ever since Dumbledore had died.

"Ginny, listen . . ." he said very quietly, as the buzz of conversation grew louder around them and people began to get to their feet,
"I can't be involved with you anymore. We've got to stop seeing
each other. We can't be together."

She said, with an oddly twisted smile, "It's for some stupid, noble reason, isn't it?"

"It's been like . . . like something out of someone else's life, these
last few weeks with you," said Harry. "But I can't . . . we can't . . .
I've got things to do alone now."

She did not cry, she simply looked at him.

"Voldemort uses people his enemies are close to. He's already
used you as bait once, and that was just because you're my best
friend's sister. Think how much danger you'll be in if we keep this
up. He'll know, he'll find out. He'll try and get to me through you."

"What if I don't care?" said Ginny fiercely.

· "I care," said Harry. "How do you think I'd feel if this was your funeral . . . and it was my fault. . . ."

She looked away from him, over the lake.

"I never really gave up on you," she said. "Not really. I always hoped. . . . Hermione told me to get on with life, maybe go out with some other people, relax a bit around you, because I never used to be able to talk if you were in the room, remember? And she thought you might take a bit more notice if I was a bit more — myself."

"Smart girl, that Hermione," said Harry, trying to smile. "I just wish I'd asked you sooner. We could've had ages . . . months . . . years maybe. . . ."

"But you've been too busy saving the Wizarding world," said Ginny, half laughing. "Well . . . I can't say I'm surprised. I knew this would happen in the end. I knew you wouldn't be happy unless you were hunting Voldemort. Maybe that's why I like you so much."

Harry could not bear to hear these things, nor did he think his resolution would hold if he remained sitting beside her. Ron, he saw, was now holding Hermione and stroking her hair while she sobbed into his shoulder, tears dripping from the end of his own long nose. With a miserable gesture, Harry got up, turned his back on Ginny and on Dumbledore's tomb, and walked away around the lake. Moving felt much more bearable than sitting still, just as setting out as soon as possible to track down the Horcruxes and kill Voldemort would feel better than waiting to do it. . . .

"Harry!"

He turned. Rufus Scrimgeour was limping rapidly toward him around the bank, leaning on his walking stick.

"I've been hoping to have a word . . . do you mind if I walk a little way with you?"

"No," said Harry indifferently, and set off again.

"Harry, this was a dreadful tragedy," said Scrimgeour quietly. "I cannot tell you how appalled I was to hear of it. Dumbledore was a very great wizard. We had our disagreements, as you know, but no one knows better than I —"

"What do you want?" asked Harry flatly.

Scrimgeour looked annoyed, but as before, hastily modified his expression to one of sorrowful understanding.

"You are, of course, devastated," he said. "I know that you were very close to Dumbledore. I think you may have been his favorite pupil ever. The bond between the two of you —"

"What do you want?" Harry repeated, coming to a halt.

Scrimgeour stopped too, leaned on his stick, and stared at Harry, his expression shrewd now.

"The word is that you were with him when he left the school the night that he died."

"Whose word?" said Harry.

"Somebody Stupefied a Death Eater on top of the tower after Dumbledore died. There were also two broomsticks up there. The Ministry can add two and two, Harry."

"Glad to hear it," said Harry. "Well, where I went with Dumbledore and what we did is my business. He didn't want people to know."

"Such loyalty is admirable, of course," said Scrimgeour, who seemed to be restraining his irritation with difficulty, "but Dumbledore is gone, Harry. He's gone."

"He will only be gone from the school when none here are loyal to him," said Harry, smiling in spite of himself.

"My dear boy . . . even Dumbledore cannot return from the —"

"I am not saying he can. You wouldn't understand. But I've got nothing to tell you."

Scrimgeour hesitated, then said, in what was evidently supposed to be a tone of delicacy, "The Ministry can offer you all sorts of protection, you know, Harry. I would be delighted to place a couple of my Aurors at your service —"

Harry laughed. "Voldemort wants to kill me himself, and Aurors won't stop him. So thanks for the offer, but no thanks."

"So," said Scrimgeour, his voice cold now, "the request I made of you at Christmas —"

"What request? Oh yeah . . . the one where I tell the world what a great job you're doing in exchange for —"

"— for raising everyone's morale!" snapped Scrimgeour.

Harry considered him for a moment.

"Released Stan Shunpike yet?"

Scrimgeour turned a nasty purple color highly reminiscent of Uncle Vernon.

"I see you are —"

"Dumbledore's man through and through," said Harry. "That's right."

Scrimgeour glared at him for another moment, then turned and limped away without another word. Harry could see Percy and the rest of the Ministry delegation waiting for him, casting nervous glances at the sobbing Hagrid and Grawp, who were still in their seats. Ron and Hermione were hurrying toward Harry, passing

Scrimgeour going in the opposite direction. Harry turned and walked slowly on, waiting for them to catch up, which they finally did in the shade of a beech tree under which they had sat in happier times.

"What did Scrimgeour want?" Hermione whispered.

"Same as he wanted at Christmas," shrugged Harry. "Wanted me to give him inside information on Dumbledore and be the Ministry's new poster boy."

Ron seemed to struggle with himself for a moment, then he said loudly to Hermione, "Look, let me go back and hit Percy!"

"No," she said firmly, grabbing his arm.

"It'll make me feel better!"

Harry laughed. Even Hermione grinned a little, though her smile faded as she looked up at the castle.

"I can't bear the idea that we might never come back," she said softly. "How can Hogwarts close?"

"Maybe it won't," said Ron. "We're not in any more danger here than we are at home, are we? Everywhere's the same now. I'd even say Hogwarts is safer, there are more wizards inside to defend the place. What d'you reckon, Harry?"

"I'm not coming back even if it does reopen," said Harry.

Ron gaped at him, but Hermione said sadly, "I knew you were going to say that. But then what will you do?"

"I'm going back to the Dursleys' once more, because Dumbledore wanted me to," said Harry. "But it'll be a short visit, and then I'll be gone for good."

"But where will you go if you don't come back to school?"

"I thought I might go back to Godric's Hollow," Harry muttered. He had had the idea in his head ever since the night of

Dumbledore's death. "For me, it started there, all of it. I've just got a feeling I need to go there. And I can visit my parents' graves, I'd like that."

"And then what?" said Ron.

"Then I've got to track down the rest of the Horcruxes, haven't I?" said Harry, his eyes upon Dumbledore's white tomb, reflected in the water on the other side of the lake. "That's what he wanted me to do, that's why he told me all about them. If Dumbledore was right — and I'm sure he was — there are still four of them out there. I've got to find them and destroy them, and then I've got to go after the seventh bit of Voldemort's soul, the bit that's still in his body, and I'm the one who's going to kill him. And if I meet Severus Snape along the way," he added, "so much the better for me, so much the worse for him."

There was a long silence. The crowd had almost dispersed now, the stragglers giving the monumental figure of Grawp a wide berth as he cuddled Hagrid, whose howls of grief were still echoing across the water.

"We'll be there, Harry," said Ron.

"What?"

"At your aunt and uncle's house," said Ron. "And then we'll go with you wherever you're going."

"No —" said Harry quickly; he had not counted on this, he had meant them to understand that he was undertaking this most dangerous journey alone.

"You said to us once before," said Hermione quietly, "that there was time to turn back if we wanted to. We've had time, haven't we?"

"We're with you whatever happens," said Ron. "But mate, you're going to have to come round my mum and dad's house before we do anything else, even Godric's Hollow."

"Why?"

"Bill and Fleur's wedding, remember?"

Harry looked at him, startled; the idea that anything as normal as a wedding could still exist seemed incredible and yet wonderful.

"Yeah, we shouldn't miss that," he said finally.

His hand closed automatically around the fake Horcrux, but in spite of everything, in spite of the dark and twisting path he saw stretching ahead for himself, in spite of the final meeting with Voldemort he knew must come, whether in a month, in a year, or in ten, he felt his heart lift at the thought that there was still one last golden day of peace left to enjoy with Ron and Hermione.